Hoffman / Cred Land

Also by MEL KEEGAN

In GMP and Millivres:
ICE, WIND AND FIRE
DEATH'S HEAD (abridged)
EQUINOX
FORTUNES OF WAR
STORM TIDE
WHITE ROSE OF NIGHT
AN EAST WIND BLOWING
AQUAMARINE

In DreamCraft:
HELLGATE: The Rabelais Alliance
HELLGATE: Deep Sky
THE DECEIVERS
NOCTURNE
THE SWORDSMAN (due 2004)

NARC Series:
DEATH'S HEAD (Complete & Unabridged)
EQUINOX (reprint)
SCORPIO (due 2004)

NARC #1
DEATHS HEAD

MEL KEEGAN

chees —

Mel Keegan

DreamCraft Multimedia, Australia

in memory of
Richard Dipple,
who was the start of everything

CHAPTER ONE

One of the big rimrunners was on prelaunch procedures. The acrid stink of the freighter's exhaust, the din of its engines, rolled about the docking bays. As the drive began to run up to peak thrust the noise reached a painful crescendo. In the thick darkness behind the trashpack, Kevin Jarrat pushed his knuckles into his ears and waited for the punishing shockwave of launch, but after almost a minute on test the engines shut back to just above idling.

The alley was lit only by reflected light, a confusion of red and green, reaching weakly about the curvature of Dock Row. Smog from the lifter's exhaust thickened the air to chemical soup. It was hard to see, difficult to breathe, and the acid smog made a man's lungs burn. Jarrat took his hands from his ears as the rimrunner's engines shut back and slid the Colt AP-60 out of the holster he wore concealed beneath his jacket.

The weapon had warmed in contact with his body. Its familiar, even reassuring weight filled his right fist while his belly churned with what he would always think of as 'stage fright.' No matter how often he found himself in situations like this, it was the same. Training, simulation and hard, real-world experience honed the skills, sharpened the reflexes, but the inescapable fact was, he could die in this alley between the docking bays. His life expectancy might be measured in minutes.

He swallowed hard on a dry throat and pulled back the charger that ran along the top of the black steel barrel. Primed, the Colt would fire ten hollow-nosed, teflon-coated rounds per second. Those rounds could pierce two centimeters of steel plate at a hundred meters range. At the kind of range in this alley on Dock Row they would fragment an unarmored civilian vehicle. The knowledge made Jarrat's heart beat a little easier.

Behind the trashpack, he stood with both shoulders pressed against the brickwork. At his left was a smaller man who clutched a big handgun in both fists. Roon leaned flat against the plastex side of the dumpster and, as Jarrat watched, he moved out to peer up the alley into the murk. He ducked back again fast.

"You see them, Roon?" Jarrat hissed. His voice just rose above the muted roar of the rimrunner's idling engines.

"Can't see nothing," Roon yelled over the noise, and hunched over to cough on the smog. "Too goddamned dark, isn't it?

"There's no shoot hole up there," Jarrat mused. "Nowhere to hide." He knew the warren of city bottom around the spaceport well after eight weeks of living and working on the streets of Chell.

"But some stupid bugger's left a Skyvan parked at the end. The shooters have to be tucked in behind." Roon gave Jarrat's dim form one glance. "Why don't you use that cannon of yours and burn it?"

"Why don't I? Suits me fine." Jarrat took a shallow breath of the toxic, soupy air. He wanted only to get the job done and get out. Throwing his life away in an alley off Dock Row would be the ultimate waste in what had long been a precarious existence. He took the big weapon in a vice-like grip, only his trigger finger loose. The Colt kicked like a young hustler when it was locked on full-auto. Spent gasses were exhausted through a port in the bottom of the single chamber, propelling the weapon upward. It could be a task to hold on target, and it was not a novice's gun.

He sucked in a breath of the stinking draft from the docking bays and brought the Colt up to chest height before he stepped out from the cover of the trashpack. The trigger depressed just a fraction of a centimeter under his finger and the gun bucked in his hands as if it were alive. He held it level with the ease of long use while every nerve along his spine crawled. Its bright muzzle flash made an inviting target of him in the near-darkness, and his quarry was armed, though with what, Jarrat did not yet know.

At the other end of the alley, fifty meters from the bulk of the dumpster, was a blue Skyvan, the kind of underpowered, overrated civvy joy-toy purchased by well-lubricated suburban families. It had a sensor pod inside the blunt nose, a ride capsule, transparent gullwings, four rear mounted engines in racks of two, and solid undergear struts which would pull up when the repulsion kicked in. He hoped the owner was well insured.

He knew exactly where to shoot to burn it. The Colt punched forty rounds into it, dead on target, and the whole electrical system shorted out in a miniature firestorm. Magnesium-bright flares spattered about, the gullwings turned to putty and collapsed into the ride capsule, and black smoke billowed upward in a poisonous greasy pall.

Then Jarrat waited, eyes screwed shut against the sudden glare. The two men had run this way, they had no way out and they could not have got into the 'van. No one in his right mind left expensive vehicles unlocked on the street in city bottom. "Where the hell are they?" Jarrat muttered, hoarse under the continuing din of engine noise from the launch bay. He had begun to wonder if stray rounds had dropped his quarry when a rattling volley of return fire leapt out of the smoke at him.

Shots smacked into the trashpack. A surge of raw adrenaline began to pound through Jarrat's head, and he heard Roon yelp sharply. In his peripheral vision he saw the smaller man sag back against the wall and slide down, clutching his left arm and wailing every profanity he could remember. If the shells had gone through the tough plastex hopper, they were almost certainly armor-piercers. Taking cover was pointless.

Jarrat knuckled his smarting eyes and swore. The Colt had a hundred rounds left in the magazine. The red LED counter had not yet begun to blink a 'low ammo' warning, and when it did, he had a pocketful of reloads. He held down the trigger to snap off twenty with the machine pistol aimed loosely into the smoke. He did not see the man go down but heard a stifled cry, the muffled sound of a body falling, a curse. Then silence. Which one was it — the shooter or the money man Jarrat had been sent here to find?

He cleared his throat of its furring of smog and played a hunch. "Vazell!" It was a safe bet the shooter would have been in the open, trying for a kill shot, while Deek Vazell would have been on his hands and knees behind what was left of the 'van. Was Vazell armed also? The man was ruthless, feared and grudgingly respected in the city bottoms of two continents. Jarrat had learned his name even before he came groundside on this godforsaken colony world, and his belly clenched like a fist. "Vazell, get out here! I swear, I'll rip the rest of this mag and scrape you off the walls

6

later!" Intimidation was a weapon in itself.

Again, silence, and then Jarrat heard scuffling sounds. The wreck was burning fiercely enough to light the alley. Weird, grotesque shadows danced on the walls, half-seen through the murk. The image was confusing but he could make out the figure staggering toward him through the smoke. It could only be Vazell — stout, as broad as he was tall, with a spraddle-legged gait. There was no mistaking the blocky figure though he wore a smog mask, the molded transparent facescreen and respirator many people were wearing since the air around the spaceport had turned into toxic soup.

Mask or no, Vazell coughed violently as he shuffled forward, and he held his hands well clear of his sides. He was armed, but the weapon, an Edson automatic, hung loosely in a useless right hand. Blood gushed from a wound at the juncture of arm and shoulder: an artery had been nicked. Not even Deek Vazell, who had earned the reputation of a trickster as well as a killer without conscience, could fake that. Jarrat's heart slowed again. He paced down the alley toward the fat man, and with his left hand lifted the mask from Vazell's flaccid face. A pudgy left hand covered Vazell's nose and mouth and swabbed at his streaming eyes.

"Don't shoot, man, all right?" he wheezed. "What use am I going to be to you dead?"

"Ask Hal Mavvik," Jarrat said acidly. "He sent me to get his money."

"His what? I don't have it on me, for chrissakes," Vazell panted.

"Surprising." Jarrat lifted the Colt. Mavvik's orders were specific: bring the money or frag Vazell ... burn one of city bottom's notorious celebrities, win powerful points where they mattered. Jarrat was merely weary of the whole charade and longed to leave it behind.

As the hot barrel touched his temple Vazell came to life. "I can get it," he rasped. "You think I carry it on me? What kind of shit-for-brains do you take me for? But I can take you to it." His voice was weakening.

"Where?" Jarrat demanded. "Let's have it, right now, Deek. All I want is to get the man's cash and get the hell out of this muck you people call air, so don't push your luck. Where is it?"

"I'll take you to it."

"You'll tell me where it is." Jarrat shifted the gun ominously. His lungs were burning, his head swam in the outfall of fumes both from the wreck and the freighter which continued to roar in a bay, too close on Dock Row.

Vazell gulped and waved his hands animatedly. "There's a warehouse over on Windrigger — Jeez, you're an asshole, Jarrat — the warehouse where they stored the old mass driver in bits, you know the one?" At Jarrat's nod he went on, "The basement under the warehouse. We got a safe-house there. Midge and the others are sitting on the whole stash, every-thing Mavvik's expecting. They've got your shitty money."

Jarrat lifted the gun away. "If you've lied to me, Deek, I'll be back and fry you alive, and that's a promise." *Or Mavvik will fry my balls, and better his than mine*, Jarrat thought ruefully as he stepped back from the fat little money man who had scored more lethal hits than many a contract shooter.

"S' the truth," Vazell protested weakly, glaring up at Jarrat out of wide, glassy eyes. "Would I lie to you, when I'm standing here with my fuckin' *life* leaking out of me? Christ! You gonna help me now, or what?"

7

Turning back toward the trashpack, Jarrat saw Roon sitting on the concrete, moaning inarticulately. He had walked a half-dozen steps when he felt the sudden stab of pain in his left shoulder. It raced through his nervous system like an electric shock and cold sweat broke from every pore as his vision blurred for an instant. He sucked in a breath as dread rushed through him in the wake of the pain — it could only be a quilldart.

They were stealth weapons, devious, with no iota of the city bottom warrior's perverse sense of honor: they were for murder, and most often poisoned or drugged. He should have expected it of Vazell. Jarrat knew all this and froze, feeling for his extremities, blinking hard as his senses first spun in shock and then stabilized into surreal, icy calm. Automatics kicked in, the instincts of a decade of training, simulations and experience.

Nothing. So Vazell kept a pocketful of darts, and tipped them with drug or poison when he needed them. But he could not do it one-handed, and this one was 'bare,' flung out of desperation, spite or fury. It had been aimed for the back of his neck, Jarrat knew. Maimed as he was, prone in the half-dark, Vazell was no more than a hand's span off-target.

Seconds passed and Jarrat's head was still clear. He was in complete command of his senses when he spun back toward Vazell, for the moment ignoring the little barbed blade which had embedded in his muscles.

The dart was surely intended to kill. Lodged in Jarrat's neck at the base of his skull, it would have. Vazell's eyes were bulging, insectoidal in the nasty, pasty face. The obese jowls quivered now in genuine terror. Jarrat raised the Colt again. Pain spurred him to anger, and for a moment he aimed squarely into the man's belly. Only then did he begin to think, and he twitched the Colt aside, aimed just as precisely but for a different target.

The single round took the flesh right off Vazell's upper arm, spun him about and flung him to the ground. Blood fanned about, black on the stained concrete, but he was not dead. Jarrat spared the twitching body one glance before he returned to Roon.

"D'ye kill the bastard?" Roon grunted.

"Blew him the hell out of there," Jarrat lied through gritted teeth. His shoulder was alight, now the tide of anger had calmed and he was feeling once more. Fury was the best painkiller he knew, but it did not last.

"Oh, Mavvik is going to just love this. What about his money?"

"Vazell told me where the stash is." Jarrat had pushed the hot Colt back into its holster. He gave his right hand to Roon, who still sat on the ground with his back against the dumpster. "Get up on your feet, damnit! You think I'm going to carry you?"

"Ah — careful." Roon hoisted himself up, stood swaying and rubbing his sweating face. "You believe 'im? Vazell could have fed you a whole bunch of horseshit, we'd never know the difference till we got there and saw a big empty place where the money ought to be." He gave Jarrat a leer of delight. "Jarrat, you've got this one coming. Mavvik is going to have you. He's gonna eat your liver, pretty boy." He spoke as if he had waited almost two months in the hopes of watching.

"Mavvik won't screw with me," Jarrat muttered. He worked the shoulder around carefully, and wished he had not. "He isn't stupid."

"But what about the warehouse where they keep the old 'driver? We better fix this mess, Jarrat, before word gets back to Midge and the buggers that Vazell and his shooter are dogmeat."

Jarrat's senses had begun to wander, whether with the dart or the chemical stew he was breathing. "So why don't you shove off back to the car, Roon, get on your little radio and call it in? I'll dump the bodies in the trashpack and meet you out there. Move, damnit!"

Roon hurried away. As they separated he glanced back at Jarrat and swore. "You do know there's a quilldart in your shoulder, don't you?"

"I know," Jarrat grunted. "It wasn't poisoned. The bastard was aiming for the back of my neck, top of the spine. It must've hit a rib — these useless little things are good for nothing. Get out of here, Roon."

As the other man left the alley Jarrat allowed himself to relax a little. He reached gingerly for the dart, found its flighted butt and pulled experimentally. Pain seared through him at once but the blade did not move. He pulled harder, against the barbs, and it shifted a fraction. Blood gushed warmly down the inside of his shirt and he gasped as the dizziness swamped him. It was better to leave the dart where it was, until it could be cut out. He did not want to lose any more blood than he must.

He glanced over his shoulder to make sure Roon was gone. The alley was empty but for himself, Vazell and the smoke-belching wreck. Fire Control would be here as soon as the spaceport's sensors could tell the Skyvan fire from the heavy, toxic outfall of the rimrunner, which was still idling in the docking bay not a hundred meters away. Engine trouble was keeping the freighter on the ground, Jarrat guessed, and the pilot had already contravened a dozen pollution-control regulations.

With a curse, he went to one knee beside the fat man and peered into his face. Against the odds, Vazell was awake, clinging to consciousness with surprising tenacity, and Jarrat made an expression of distaste as he doubled his fist. Its knuckles smacked into the thickly-padded jaw and Vazell was out cold. The jolt of the blow rushed painfully through Jarrat, and he whooped for air. As he came to his feet he drew his sleeve across his face. Sweat stung his eyes and his lungs spasmed in the smoke.

With his good hand he reached into his inside pocket to bring out a small but extremely powerful microtransmitter. It was housed in the case of a gold cigarette lighter, but when Jarrat flipped up the top and extended the aerial wire it became a highband transceiver of great range.

"Raven 9.4 to Raven Leader," he said tersely. Static answered him, cutting, rhythmic blasts of white noise from the nearby spaceport radars. "Raven 9.4 to Raven Leader. Stoney, where the hell are you!"

As he spoke the name, Jerry Stone's voice came on the air. Powerful transmission gear on the ship cut through the background interference from the 'port's tracking arrays. "Jesus Christ, Kevin, it's been more than forty hours since you called in. Where the hell have you been?"

The sound of his friend's voice was like balm on Jarrat's raw nerves and he smiled tiredly. "Been busy. I couldn't get out of the palace, and I've got enough brains left not to try calling from inside!"

"Where are you now?" Stone's old-world London accent thickened, betraying concern. His voice was baritone, rich, even over a tiny speaker.

"I'm on Dock Row, in the alley between Bays 4 and 5," Jarrat told him. "Mavvik sent me to lean on Deek Vazell. They think I've killed him but he'll survive and he's all yours. I've told them I'll get rid of the body — just wait till I get out of here and send a squad to retrieve him. You should be able to patch him up and pump him for what he knows."

"Bay 4 and Bay 5," Stone repeated. His next words were directed not at his partner but at the intercom, and the crew on the standby gunship.

"Blue Raven 6, Blue Raven 7, get your gear on, launch in five." Then he returned to Jarrat. "Time you got out of there, Kev. If you can get to the extraction point the Blue Ravens can pull you out in twenty minutes."

The offer of safety was powerfully seductive. He could be back on the carrier in an hour, filing the report and trying to forget the ridiculous jeopardy he had lived with for over seven weeks. Back on the carrier: Irish coffee, late-night paperwork, tall stories, the sound of Stoney's husky laughter. But a bug was still gnawing at him, and on a shrewd hunch Jarrat set aside his more personal desires and said, "Not yet — not that I'm staying for the fun of it, mind you. There's a man I want. The mule. If I stick around a couple more days he's going to be here in Chell —"

"And you could be in a hole in the ground!" Stone snapped.

Jarrat smiled at the sharp edge in his partner's voice. Stone always snarled when he was worried. Jarrat had known him long enough to read him like a book. "Relax, Stoney. Mavvik won't screw with me, I'm costing him way too much." He spoke glibly, but in fact Stone was right, and Jarrat knew it. The job was getting dangerous. Not that any aspect of this assignment had ever been safe. "When you pay a fortune to buy yourself a king shooter," he added tersely, "you tend to respect the kid."

"But you just killed the Chell money man," Stone argued.

"Self-defense, Stoney," Jarrat told him, not quite offhandly. "I've got the quilldart in my back to prove it."

Stone was silent for a moment and then came back quickly. Jarrat heard a half-smothered curse, and then, "Drugged? Poisoned?"

"No," Jarrat said quickly, "just as they come ... and if he'd been dead on-target I'd still be flat on my face. Luckily, his aim was wide."

"That's it," Stone barked, "I'm pulling you out. Enough's enough. The Ravens can pick you up out of the alley, bugger the extraction point."

"I want the mule!" Jarrat repeated, louder. "I'm okay, Stoney, really. You do your job, leave me to do mine."

Anger sharpened Stone's voice. "It's your neck, I suppose, if you want to go out and get it busted ... Blue Raven units report standing by to launch, Kevin. Get the hell out of there while you can."

"I will," Jarrat told him. "Oh, Stoney, there's something you can do for me." He gave Vazell's limp, beached-whale body a glare. "When you get this bastard aboard, shoot him with something, I don't particularly care what. He said there's a safehouse under the old mass driver on Windrigger. Find out if he lied. It could be my hide if he's telling me stories."

"Will do," Stone said resignedly. His voice was sharp, with a ragged edge. "For Christ's sake look out for yourself, Kevin. Raven Leader out."

"I'll do that," Jarrat said to the dead transceiver before he folded it on itself, slipped it back into his inside pocket and stooped to pick up Vazell's discarded smog mask. He could imagine the expression on Stone's handsome face at this moment. Exasperated, annoyed, concerned, that wide mouth compressed, the dark blue eyes glittering. "Soon, Stoney," Jarrat muttered as he tightened the straps of the smog mask, clasped its molded plastic shape firmly over his face and walked deliberately into the greasy, poisonous smoke that still billowed out of the blazing wreck.

The heat was fierce enough to parch his eyeballs through the mask. It was like walking into a blast furnace, and he was working blind. He found the body in moments, and he knew the face, half of which had survived intact. So this was Vazell's shooter. Just a cheap cityside assassin who went

10

by the name of Kenichi. Otherwise, the Colt had mauled the body badly. Blood and entrails made an aromatic sludge underfoot and he bent over the mess to go through its pockets in search of the shooter's ID.

He had no real need to dump the remains into the trashpack, but the ID would tell Chell Tactical too much. He would score no points by giving them gifts of information at this stage, and Tactical involvement could make his position dangerous. The ultimate irony would be to find himself in a standup fight with Tac, and be a statistic of 'friendly fire.'

Jarrat palmed the greasy card and walked out of the smoke. Halfway up the alley, he tore off the smog mask and paused briefly to check Vazell. The man was still out cold and the men from Blue Raven unit would arrive in minutes. *To collect the garbage,* he thought acidly. Stoney would turn the toad inside out, as he had pumped seven others for every shred of information they had during the two months the NARC carrier *Athena* had ridden in geosynchronous orbit, high over this troubled city. But one berry was not yet plucked, and Jarrat was determined to have it.

The mule. He did not yet know the man's name, but he would be in the city of Chell in two, three days No one in the palace had any reason to be suspicious of Jarrat. The only minor problem was Vazell's 'death' and even Hal Mavvik himself would be slow to argue with the killing when his king shooter came home with a quilldart in his back. It would cost Mavvik more to replace Jarrat than he would lose if Vazell's steer did turn out to be the bullshit Roon speculated. But Stone would get the truth before long. Jarrat was as yet unconcerned.

He paced stiffly back to the car, which lay parked under the fluoros outside the office that processed data for Bays 4 and 5. One of the fluoros was faulty, fluttering hysterically. Roon sat in the car, watching its antics. The vehicle belonged to Mavvik's private garage. It was big, powerful, blue but looking purple under the lights. The aeroshell was backswept, graceful, its gullwings locked in the 'up' position as Roon waited for the boss's shooter to return. In the tail were two small jet engines, and Jarrat knew they were rated at just a little over four hundred horses each. It rode on a repulsion field, anchored to the spot by brake tractors.

The car rocked on the repulsion cushion as Jarrat fell into the left-hand seat. Roon was driving. He clutched painfully at his left arm, but with the dart in him Jarrat could not lean squarely into the seat to drive. Roon wrinkled his nose as the gullwings whined down and locked.

"You stink, Jarrat. What you been wading in?"

"Vazell's guts, and his shooter's," Jarrat growled. "Move it, will you? This dart's giving me hell."

"Not half as much hell as Mavvik's going to give you." Roon grinned and with an angry thrust, jammed the key into the ignition.

The jets exploded into life with a raucous howl before Roon put the shift into reverse. The car took off like a missile, screaming up the access road and into the twelve-laner, the Chell Spaceport Clearway. Jarrat gritted his teeth as the pressure of the seat tried to push the quilldart into him. He twisted in the harness to ease it and looked up the road. Ahead, the city glittered, a carnival in the night. Darkness and neon masked squalor and poverty. Any city looked beautiful at night.

It was too bad, he thought, that the sun had to come up and show the truth. Chell was old, raddled, about a century past its prime, clawing to hang onto its youth and vitality like an old woman painting over her sags and bags and calling the deception regeneration. On the surface the city was bright. The paint was new, the weeds poisoned off, the glass polished.

But beneath the brash veneer Chell was no different from many other cities in the colonies which straggled back from the frontier to the old world. She was diseased, rancid — and happy. Chell was happy to the point of mania. Waves of ecstasy rolled over her like breakers on a beach. In the dead of night one could physically feel it, wafting up out of both the poor quarters of city bottom and the rich men's mansions which perched above the smogline. The phenomenon was quite common. Happiness was for sale. Joy retailed for forty credits a pop, it was not even expensive.

They called it *Angel.*

Searchlights speared down out of the sky like quadruple laser lances and heavy lifters pounded into the concrete. Sirens wailed across the docking bays, sending civilians scurrying for cover. Those with helmets stood with lowered visors to watch the gunship drop in over Dock Row. The hull was almost invisible in the glare and massive repulsion motors kicked up a hurricane of dust and debris, shrouding the heavy lifter.

Hatches in the belly of the craft slammed open. Those who watched from below could not quite make out the drop bay. It seemed to them that two figures jumped right out of the lights, riding down in the wash of the floodlights like locusts, an impression reinforced by the exoskeletal design of their armor.

They were suits of riot armor and literally indestructible. The surface of the kevlex-titanium was featureless, black, mirror-glossy. The helmet was full-visor, sealed. Umbilici sprouted like twin tusks from the chin contour. Twin whip antennae arced up from the back-mounted powerpacks. Across the front of the helmet was the legend, NARC-*Athena*, and above the letters, the decal of a raven in blue and the operative number.

These were Blue Raven 6 and Blue Raven 7.

Deek Vazell had woken moments before. Blinded by the dust, deafened by the noise, he lay on his back, gasping on the alley floor where Jarrat had dropped him, and saw the locust shapes of the NARC troopers jump. They could see him before they cleared the hatch. As he watched they feathered down to land on either side of him. Vazell's mouth dried out to parchment. He struggled to get up but his left arm was useless, dead weight, and his head swam dizzily. He felt like a stranded porpoise.

The locust-like forms stooped toward him. Steel hands closed about his arms and legs. He screamed, half in pain, half in fright, as they lifted him without effort. Then their repulsion began to bluster. He felt the kick in the back of upward acceleration, and they rose fast into the halo of light. At the last moment Vazell made out the shape of the gunship, before blue-white light swallowed him whole.

The watching civilians began to breathe again as engines ran up and floodlights doused. It was over. NARC was gone and they were alive, at liberty and uninjured. Just as frequently, the appearance of a NARC gunship meant the dopers were at war again, fighting it out in the street for their 'Angel rights'. Vigilantes fought back and blood was let. Trapped in the crossfire, Tactical called for NARC, and the battle was on.

The hatch slammed shut. Vazell's vision was distorted by the green blotches of corneal afterimages. As he began to see again he focused on the men who hurried toward him with a gurney. Two orderlies and a medical officer. All wore white, with NARC emblems on the shoulders and unit badges on the collars. One read 'Raven'. Another read *Athena*.

And with a blinding flash of realization Deek Vazell knew where he was. He also knew it was too late to panic but still fear tightened under his heart and his pulse hammered. He felt the gurney roll in under him as he was held suspended by the two riot-armored troopers. He yelped again at the sharp jab of a needle low in his neck, and his vision cut out once more.

Twenty minutes later the Blue Raven medics rolled Vazell into the carrier's Infirmary, two decks above the docking bay in the *Athena*'s belly. The gunship had touched down minutes before, and Captain Jerry Stone stood at the workstation just inside the Infirmary, appending his authorization to the pickup order.

Blue Raven 6 had followed the gurney up. He had removed his helmet, tucked it under his arm, and watched the Captain authorize the minor action. One big hand, gloved in a mesh of kevlex-titanium, ran over his smooth-shaven head. His name was stenciled in white on the black breastplate: Sgt. G. Cronin. He was taller than Stone by half a head and much, much heavier, but this was regulation. Stone was an officer with a NARC license; Gil Cronin served with the descant force. Both were soldiers in a paramilitary that functioned autonomously with government sanction.

Stone was tall enough. His hair was black and worn short, his eyes were smoldering blue and he was built like an athlete, with long limbs and broad shoulders. NARC demanded a high level of athletic proficiency from its officers. The physicals came up six monthly, three days of exhaustive testing designed to weed the active from the passengers. Stone was two years past his thirtieth birthday but looked younger. He wore plain clothes, the privilege of rank, a cream shirt and blue slacks tucked into the uniform boots which were common issue to Tactical on a dozen colony worlds.

His eyes followed the gurney as the medics wheeled Vazell into the OR. So this was the Chell money man. NARC knew him well by reputation, but it was the first time Stone had physically set eyes on him. Vazell was a grotesque parody of a human being, whose ugly exterior concealed a pitiless, dangerous personality. The impression was about to become more pronounced when the medics were done. Vazell would lose the arm. Jarrat had aimed just a finger's span too far left ...

Jarrat had a quilldart in him. Anger tightened Stone's face. He had lean, strong features, good bones, and many would have called him handsome. But now his wide mouth had tugged into an expression of distaste and exasperation. Kevin Jarrat was notoriously stubborn. He was also the best. Stone had never worked with another field agent who could claim Jarrat's repertoire of skills — or his luck. And the decision to come out of deep cover was his to make, leaving Stone resigned, annoyed. *Frustrated*, he added, mocking himself a little.

Gil Cronin had seen the press of his mouth and raised a curious brow at him. "That's a mean looking bastard we just brought up. What do we want him for?"

Stone stirred, coming awake as he was jolted from the reverie. "He's the money man. The distributor, if you like. The money goes home to Mavvik, but Mavvik doesn't get involved with the boot-end of the business — the street. He has money men everywhere, hundreds, maybe thousands of them in towns like Foster and Pentecost. Vazell is just one, and in any case the dealers are the least of our worries. We want the investor."

"Hal Mawik himself," Cronin said dryly. He cast a sidelong glance at Stone. "Cap Jarrat's been in there a hulluva long time."

"You're not wrong," Stone agreed. In fact, Jarrat had been buried in the assignment for two and three times as long as was normal. The longer an assignment ran, the more hazard multiplied, like fungus. Past a certain point, the only thing that made any sense was to get out with a whole skin and what data you had. And a week ago Stone would have said Jarrat was way past that point. He took a deep breath and turned toward Cronin, who towered beside him, massive in the mirror-polished armor. "The toad you just picked up put a dart in Kevin."

"A quilldart? Shit," Cronin breathed. "That's getting close."

"Too close," Stone agreed. You drew the graveyard shift, Gil?"

Cronin nodded. "Ain't that the truth."

"Yeah, well stay on your rocking horse. I reckon Jarrat might have his hands full with the boss. If the water gets too hot he'll yell to come out."

"If," Cronin added darkly, "he's in any position to yell."

"Are you kidding?" Stone demanded, constructing a flint-hard façade of bravado. "Him? He's got the luck of the devil, he always did have. He'll be back in the palace, three-parts stoned, hip-deep in some luscious number on Mawik's private payroll. You know Kevin Jarrat."

The sergeant who commanded the Blue Raven descant unit grinned widely. "I ought to know him. After two years of bumming around with you two loons ...? Damned officers, they always get all the perks."

"So try out for officer selection," Stone suggested glibly.

"Don't have the qualifications," Cronin said with a resigned shrug of his enormous, armored shoulders.

"And I didn't grow big enough to get into a descant unit," Stone retorted. "You want a coffee and a smoke, Gil?"

Cronin stirred, passing the helmet from hand to hand. "Rain check, Cap. Indian Joe's got next week's pay off me in IOUs and I want it back before the cards cool off." He gave the younger, smaller man, who was by far his superior officer, a vague salute and ambled away toward the elevator which would return him to the Blue Ravens' ready room.

Alone, Stone paced to the wide observation window and glared moodily into the brightly-lit cavern of the OR. Surgeon Captain Reardon was already working on Vazell, flanked by the usual team of three. He was a neurosurgeon, and a good one, but he was also a *combat* surgeon with experience on several warships, Army carriers, before he transferred over to NARC. Stone valued him more in this area. He watched with grim curiosity as the surgical team took Vazell's ruined arm off at the shoulder.

The bastard had put a quilldart into Jarrat, and Stone could find no pity for the man. Bravado aside, Kevin was more likely to be hip-deep in *trouble* than one of Mawik's expensive hustlers, and Stone was on edge. Jarrat's survival might depend on how honest Vazell had been under duress, bargaining for his life with the only thing he had left — information. If he had been scared enough he might have babbled the truth before his mind was working fast enough for him to fabricate a story. Certainly, Jarrat had forged a hell of a reputation for himself, and the testimony of a king shooter would not be dismissed lightly, even by Hal Mawik.

Stone lit a cigarette, dragged deeply and waited for his nerves to settle. The scent of kipgrass and jasmine clouded him and he frowned at the red-hot tip of the cigarette. All he wanted was Kevin out of there, safe, right now. But Jarrat was a wayward, stubborn character. Stone watched Reardon's crew close up without really seeing them work. Jarrat had the luck of the devil. But those who lived long enough swore Hal Mavvik *was* the devil. Stone took a last drag on the cigarette and stubbed it out.

If Mavvik was the devil, Jarrat was a NARC, which city bottom lore swore was the next best thing. Stone gave a grim smile to his faintly-seen reflection in the observation window, pondering the perversity of his luck.

Two long years, he thought, and the hunger to have Jarrat was keener than ever. Forbidden fruit always looked sweetest, and it was always just out of reach, taunting, tormenting. Not that Jarrat knew he was taunting, Stone allowed. Kevin never flaunted himself. Nor had he ever given Stone any reason to think the powerful attraction was mutual. Emotions as old as time, primal, irresistible, jolted through Stone like a static shock whenever Jarrat was near. Often, it was all he could do to keep the mask in place, keep the truth to himself and hold his personal demons on the short leash.

In many ways it was easier when the deep cover assignments separated them. Days would pass without any contact with Jarrat. The wanting would settle back to an old, familiar ache. Sometimes he told himself he was getting over it, until the small voice in the back of his mind whispered how futile it was for a man to lie to himself.

By shiptime it was late when he finished his duty shift and returned to his quarters. The day's business remained on hold, the evening's data waited to be processed. He drank coffee as he ran the file quickly. With his authorization and approval it would be boosted on, back to Sector Central, a week away on Darwin's World, where old men and computers would dissect, digest and grant belated approbation. Or not. Responsibility weighed heavily on Stone's shoulders and he was never unaware of it.

Four people had died in the Angel riot in Hague Plaza, in north Chell. The Corunna sector was uptown, unaccustomed to streetwar. The dopers had come in with a new bill, little more than a pastiche of legal jargonese. The bottom line was another crusade to decriminalize the manufacture, retail and possession of Angel. Then the vigilantes had come in to join them and the shouting began. Those who had lost children, siblings, lovers, to the drug marched out to protest the arguments of dopeheads who wanted to legalize poison for public consumption, and rationalized their approval of suicide and murder with old, worn-out arguments about freedom of choice. All too often the victims of Angel were given no choice. One mistake was all it took. Or one act of wanton revenge, to spite a rival.

The full-scale riot began with shouting and bricks but someone had come armed. Phosphor grenades burst among the trooper squads from Tactical, and the fight erupted with a vengeance. Tac got between the combatants but the civilians on both sides were better armed. Several casualties and two of the dead wore Tac fatigues. NARC had been on standby for twenty minutes when Colonel Stacy called for the Ravens to deploy.

Dealers, pimps and lawyers on one side, and grieving survivors on the other, broke up into a frenzied shambles as the Red Raven gunship appeared out of the dense tropical overcast which blanketed the equatorial spaceport city. Sirens wailed, the Ravens jumped, and the newsvid cameras were rolling as the spectacle unfolded in Corunna's picturesque Hague Plaza. The mirror-black locusts looked odd among ornamental fountains, but ten minutes later the vicious 'packriot' was over. The brief action left four dead, twenty injured.

Angel was an industry. It was a madness, Stone thought as he reviewed the data. The swift, 'surgical intervention' might have saved a hundred lives. Angel would kill twice as many in a single night, perhaps not all in Chell, but across this colony. Between the frontier and the 'old world' — Stone's home, Earth itself — hundreds perished every night, while the syndicate lawyers who framed each new decriminalization bill would assault NARC in the press again. It was the same after every action, but their shots were cheap, impotent. Both Tactical and NARC shrugged them off.

Satisfied, tired yet still restless, Stone approved the day's records and closed the file.

CHAPTER TWO

The first brandy had burned the nerve endings out of his gullet; the second was smoother. Jarrat swallowed hard on it as the needle knitted quickly to and fro along the wound where the quilldart had been. Bradley was almost finished. It had slipped out at a touch of a scalpel so sharp he had barely felt the nick. Bradley was a decent cutter, even if he did work for Mavvik. Jarrat lifted his head to look across the softly-lit lounge.

Roon sat on one end of the plush leather sofa, a white bandage about his left arm. He was doped, glassy eyed, watchful. And the man himself stood silently at the other end of the couch, his eyes on the dart that had been sliced out of Jarrat's back moments before. Hal Mavvik was a man of sixty. He was badger gray but not bald, lined but not seamed, and the scarlet robe he wore concealed a body that was still taut, despite his excesses.

His weaknesses were alcohol, food and women, apparently in no specific order. The palace, high on the slopes of Monte San Angelo — with the city lights of Chell like a sparkling carpet unrolled below — was full of all three. He had been with one of his women when Roon paged him over the house intercom. The sour look on Hal Mavvik's face had as much to do with the interruption of his private entertainment as with the death of the money man and the possible loss of his cash. He transferred a bleak, hard-eyed gaze to Jarrat as Bradley put the snips through the loose ends of the sutures and pressed an adhesive bandage into place over them.

"All right. You can tell me now."

Roon looked up petulantly. "But I already —"

"Shut it, Rooney. I want to hear it from the shooter." Mavvik's voice was deceptively soft, like a thin veneer of tissue over razor blades.

The man spoke with one of the American accents. Jarrat, who had never visited Earth, was not sure which. Moving the shoulder experimentally, he got to his feet. "It's like Roon told you. Vazell had a contract shooter of his own. You know the name of Freddie Kenichi?"

"I know it." Mavvik's eyes narrowed. "He's scum. Trash."

"He's dead trash now," Jarrat added in a rasp as the feeling began to return to the shoulder Bradley had numbed. "Vazell and Kenichi were there early. They must have seen Roon and me park outside the Bay office and ran into the alley, trapped themselves. It's easy to do ... some alleys go

16

right through, some dead-end. Even the rats don't know them all."

"You killed Freddie Kenichi and scared the shit out of the fat man," Mavvik said slowly. "So Vazell put a dart in you. He hadn't primed it. If he had, you'd be dead as Kenichi."

"Just lucky." With a grimace, Jarrat worked the shoulder around. "Luck's a big part of this game. The day it runs out, you either quit or they bury you. Vazell knew the truth of that as well as you do. Tonight? I had the luck. And I blew him away." Jarrat lifted his chin. "When somebody tries to kill me, you want me to blow him kisses?"

Mavvik's mouth drew tight. "You could have dropped him, kept him alive and brought him back here."

"With the Colt? In the dark? What am I, a bloody magician?"

"The wreck was burning," Mavvik said angrily. "You could see."

"Maybe I didn't want to," Jarrat said flatly. Was this what Mavvik wanted to hear? He looked the boss squarely in the eye. "He put a dart in me. Maybe I wanted to frag him."

For a time they looked intently at one another, and Jarrat knew Hal Mavvik would buy that line. He would buy it because in the same situation he would have done the same thing himself. Vengeance, quick, efficient, deadly. At last the badger-gray head nodded deeply. "All right. Vazell had it coming. Death's Head can do without privateers. But I want the money, Jarrat, one way or the other. If the boys come up empty at the warehouse on Windrigger, you get on your bike, you find Vazell's people and you kick ass until you get it. *All* of it. You hear me?"

"I hear you," Jarrat said levelly, folding his arms on his bare chest. "And when they start to kick back?"

"Do what you're paid to do," Mavvik said in a mocking tone. "Grease the kickers till the rest of them quit. And speaking of kickers," he added, giving Roon a hard look, "the next time you have news that just can't wait, you give it to Grenville or Porter, not me." He smoothed the folds of the red silk robe, pulled hastily about him as he rolled out of bed.

On the table beside Bradley's case was the R/T. A hiss of static white noise issued from it as the channel was left open. They were waiting for Grenville's call. He had taken a quartet of the palace guard half an hour before, as Jarrat and Roon made it back. They should already be at the warehouse, Jarrat judged. The call would not be long in coming. Mavvik watched him closely. He pretended not to notice the scrutiny but he was aware he was being appraised, measured up, again.

He was tall, not as tall as Stone but above average height, with the athletic built typical of the NARC field agent. Without his shirt, the breadth of his shoulders was more obvious. His long legs were clad in tight black denim. His eyes were slate gray, wide and expressive, given to laughter. His hair was a mix of sun blond and brown, wayward and worn long. Kevin Jarrat was thirty-one and took pride in the fact that, if he had to, he could still pass for a kid. Sometimes the job required it.

But Jarrat was not a kid. The boyish good looks were a tool, and occasionally a weapon. He could fool, dupe his way around men and women alike. For two months he had lived in the palace here on Monte San Angelo, playing the part of a king shooter, and they believed implicitly in him. He knew how to harden his face until the boyishness became wicked and even his smile resembled that of a snake.

The pretense took skill and energy. Almost eight weeks of it had drain-

17

ed him until he was weary. When Stoney offered him extraction by the Blue Raven unit every bone in his body said *get out, go!* But he and Stone still needed the final pickup, the mule, or they would forfeit the very data they needed to close down once and for all not only Mavvik's operation on this continent, but the whole Angel trade on the colony world of Rethan. The mule ran for the *manufacturer*, and was their link back to the source.

The R/T gave a blast of static before Grenville's voice bawled, thinned by the little speaker, "Charlie to Home Base. It's here, Hal. You can take the bamboo out of sonny boy's fingernails. He must've put the fear of God into Vazell. The stupid sonofabitch told the truth."

Mavvik picked up the small, black shape of the R/T. "They gave you a fight there, Charlie?"

"Not after we put away the first two," Grenville snickered. "There's an old sod down here who wants to be the money man now. You want to check him out for the job?"

"Later," Mavvik said tersely. "Come on back, Charlie, he'll keep. Home Base out." He tossed the R/T back onto the table with a plastic clatter. "Seems you're off the hook, Jarrat. In fact, I come up owing you one. The truth is, that bastard Vazell's been a thorn in my ass for a year. If you hadn't *itemized* him tonight, rather sooner than later I would have."

"So pay me a nice, fat bonus," Jarrat said brashly.

The older man glared thoughtfully at him. "Death's Head can always use a king shooter, and I like initiative. You're good, I don't deny it. But I'm warning you, kid, and remember this: there's a difference between a shooter who can do as he's told and a trigger-happy bastard who can't or won't take an order. One I can use, the other's going to end up dogmeat sooner or later. You follow me?"

Jarrat smiled that snake smile. "I hear you."

"Which means what?" Mavvik demanded hoarsely. Anger tightened his voice. "You just do as you're told, boy. The day you fuck up a job is the day you get pinned to the wall. Death's Head isn't a bunch of chicken-brained individuals. If it was, NARC would have had us in a hole years ago. You follow orders, you're in for the run. Make a monkey out of me once, just once, and you go out through the door in a box. You follow me now?"

Jarrat made a patently mock obeisance.

"Fine," Mavvik rumbled. "Then I have some interrupted business to attend to. Good night to you all."

With that he left. The lounge was silent in his wake. Bradley repacked his bag and was on the point of leaving when Roon chuckled. "You're a lucky boy, Jarrat. I thought he was going to chew out your liver."

"Like he said," Jarrat said tiredly, "shut it, Roon. I've had enough out of you for one day ... thanks for the job, Brad. It feels as good as new."

The medic smiled. He was a young man no older than Jarrat himself, very blond with a ruddy complexion and a sunburned, peeling nose. "Not yet, but it will be. I can yank the sutures for you in the morning when you come in for a proper laser job."

"Thanks, I'll do that." Jarrat tried the shoulder and found it hot, stiff. "I heal fast in any case. 'Night, Brad."

Collecting the Colt and its harness from the back of a chair, he left the lounge by the door leading westward into the enormous house which was rightly called a palace. It stood in private parklands on the shoulder of the mountain, comfortably high above the city and the noisy, toxic spaceport.

The city lights were blurred, diffused by the smog layer. Swathes of them were obliterated by denser palls. The Rethan colony was more than a century and a half old now, and since heavy industry was its whole reason for being, like virtually every colony, it rushed past its prime and got dirty and crowded fast. Poverty and desperation bred like rats in city bottom, and Angel abuse flourished in that soil.

On his way back to his apartment Jarrat paused to look down from a terrace window onto the smog-shrouded plain stretching away toward the spaceport on the horizon. At this altitude the air was fresh. The palace was senselessly opulent, making a mockery of good taste. At first it had been a novelty to live among the unbelievably rich but the company soon became tiresome. To Jarrat it was a job like any other, with its own inherent perils.

And its perks. The lights were on in his apartment. As he had expected, Lee had stayed up for him. He closed the door quietly, placed the Colt on a chair and glanced once about the boudoir. It was decorated in pale green but the curtains and bedspread were pale blue. The open windows admitted the cool, shifting night wind, a luxury which was unknown down in the city, under a smog blanket through which stars seldom showed.

Lee sprawled on top of the quilted bedspread, a lithe, coffee-brown figure wearing one of Jarrat's own shirts. It looked better on the boy than on himself, Jarrat thought. Lee's hair, black as jet, spilled over both his shoulders and hung to his waist. The legs were pure perfection. The shirt had hitched up and beneath it the curves of buttocks were round and alluring. He had been reading but tossed the tape aside as Jarrat appeared.

"Kevin, thank God — I thought something must have gone wrong," he began as he rolled off the enormous bed.

"Something did," Jarrat told him wryly, opening his arms. "*Something* almost always does. Come here."

The boy stepped into his embrace. Jarrat smelt cedar and musk, some expensive scent that seemed to cling about him, morning and night.

"Fixed?" Lee asked. He sank sharp teeth into Jarrat's shoulder.

"Fixed," he said emphatically. The kid lifted his head, searching for Jarrat's lips. He was nearly as tall as the man he knew as a top contract shooter. They could kiss without Jarrat stooping. Lee's mouth was hot, his tongue demanding, and the kiss was hard. One leg slid in between Jarrat's, the knee lifting to rub into his crotch, drawing an insistent caress across the black denim.

Jarrat broke free of his lips and gave the boy an amused look. "You know how to get your own way, don't you?" Then again, Lee had been well taught. He came from an uptown den. Mavvik had hired a bevy of such beautiful creatures for a party; one or two had been kept on. Lee tossed his hair back over both shoulders and smiled wickedly. He was breathtaking at eighteen years old. Jarrat caught his raven-maned head in both hands and had his mouth again. "What were you reading? Or do you get the hots just looking at me?"

Lee chuckled. "I get the hots just *thinking* about you, sugar. You're like a breath of fresh air in this place, it's why they hate you. You're the king and they're jealous to death. Roon, and Grenville and Porter. I thought I'd die of boredom before you got here." Lee filled his crotch with a sinewy bare knee again. "King shooter. In more ways than one, right?"

"And I suppose you kiss and tell," Jarrat said as his fingers slipped the shirt's buttons undone. The garment was loose about the boy.

19

"I don't have to," Lee laughed. "I just look shagged to death all day and they can dream up whatever they like. Christ knows what they think you do to me, but — oh, they hate you." He shrugged out of the shirt and arched his back to thrust ringed nipples into Jarrat's palms. Jarrat rubbed them gently. "Been waiting for you for ages. I thought you'd never come."

"I wouldn't say *never*," Jarrat said dryly. He looked down at the supple young body and resisted the impulse to do just that as Lee wriggled deliciously to rub those ringed nipples on his open palms. The kid wore a thin gold cockring to make the most of nature's endowments. He was not as heavily hung as he would have wished, but Jarrat was more than satisfied. "You're not going to give me a sporting chance, are you?" he asked, tweaking both Lee's beautiful gold nipple ornaments.

"Not this time," Lee affirmed breathlessly. "Maybe later." He hooked his fingers into Jarrat's belt, pulled him toward the vast bed and plunked down on the quilt to watch him pull off his boots. As he sat on the side of the mattress to do so, Lee saw the adhesive dressing on his shoulder. His tone of teasing, seductive banter changed abruptly to one of genuine concern. "Hey, sugar, what have you done to yourself now?"

"Nothing that won't mend," Jarrat said evasively. "I've had worse."

Lee's fingers knotted into the wayward brown hair to draw Jarrat down onto the bed. As he was straddled, Jarrat began to wish the denim was not so fashionably tight. Lee had the kind of body artists dreamed about, here and there highlighted with jewelry. The lamplight gleamed on the gold at ears, wrists, breast and groin, chains, rings, bangles. He was of hybrid stock, a little African, a little Asian, a little native American — even Lee was not sure. Many young people out in the colonies had begun to forget that their history had begun on Earth, a world they had never visited and perhaps never would.

Time would be the great leveler, Jarrat guessed as he gazed up at Lee with bemused eyes, but for now the 'Companion' was nothing less than incredible. He was still little more than a boy and had been a professional boudoir *artiste* for six years.

With a rasping *churr* of unmeshing metal some of the denim's pressure released. Jarrat raised both knees, rolled him off and undressed quickly. Lee wound arms and legs tightly about him. It was like wrestling a python, and they both loved it. Then Lee knelt up and spread and Jarrat saw the moist glistening of lube on his skin. He slid into the hot depths of the boy's body and paused to regain some measure of control. His balls had their own ideas.

His hands cradled narrow hips as Lee wrenched back to impale himself with a wild little cry of pagan delight and began to heave. For the thousandth time Jarrat wondered fleetingly, foolishly, if Stoney would make that little cry of delight for some lucky lover. It was a ridiculous question. Stupid to even think it, or to imagine the way Stone's face would crease with self-absorption, how his hands would first feather caresses and then grasp, take what he wanted and needed.

Jarrat savored the speculation for just a moment and then deliberately put it from him to concentrate on Lee. Stone was far, far off-limits. And Stoney had better sense than to violate the most basic regulation in the NARC rule book. Officers did not become emotionally involved. Never. There was the start and end of it, for reasons too good to be argued. Jarrat had agreed with them when he transferred over from the Army and signed the NARC contract. He still agreed with them. And Stoney's face still haunted him when he made love, no matter with whom, or where, or how. Two years was a long time to want, with no real hope of having.

Meanwhile Lee was wild, fighting for every second he could make it last. Jarrat punished his quivering muscles as if he were engaged in some ritual bloodsport where the prey was orgasm, slippery, elusive, sadly brief.

It was only later, when the room had righted and he had drifted back to awareness, that he realized his muscles were like rubber and the wound in his back was on fire. The local had worn off and the sutures could have been made of barbed wire. Climbing off Lee as he sprawled in satiated contentment, Jarrat flopped belly-down, buried his face in the pillows and groaned. He felt the flutter of soft hands on his back, felt the brush of Lee's luxurious hair and the tickle of kisses, but did not move. "Go away and let me die in peace."

"Sugar?" Lee's lips feathered his back. "You hurting, Kevin?"

"Yes. Don't worry about it." Jarrat forced his leaden limbs to move, rolled over and took Lee against him. "You were great, kiddo. You're too good to be working in this place."

"The money's right," Lee said shrewdly. He stroked through the pale gold hair dusting Jarrat's hard chest. "Mind you, when you leave all you'd have to do is give me a nod and I'd go with you."

"I couldn't afford you," Jarrat told him honestly. "Even I don't get paid that much." He reached for the supple young buttocks and kneaded them. "And don't say you'd pauper yourself and share my bed for the joy of it, because I don't believe you."

The cascade of raven hair tossed as Lee laughed and took Jarrat's hand to his chest, rubbing it there. The gold cockring kept him half-hard and he was humping slowly at Jarrat's hip. "Still, I'll miss you."

"Go to sleep. It's late," Jarrat said bluffly, tweaking one of the matching ornaments to make the boy arch with sensuous pleasure.

Lee snatched up the quilt and rolled them in it. Jarrat would have been pleased to subside into sleep, but his mind returned willfully to Stone. In two years of serving together they had actually spent only a little more than six months in each other's company. The way a NARC partnership operated, more often than not one officer was on the ship, the other was in deep cover, and frequently weeks would go by while the only contact between them was radio. It was close to two months since he had seen Stone's face.

Absence made the heart grow fonder. Jarrat mocked himself as his mind defied sleep and returned to work. Stone would have Vazell on the rack soon, and in two days, three, the mule would be in Chell. One more pickup and the job would be finished, he would be out of here. Life would be less exhausting without Lee, but no good thing lasted forever. He would return to the bittersweet pleasure of sharing duty with Stone, keeping up a pretense for the other man's benefit, until the next job began and it was Stoney's turn to do the ground work, buried in another deep cover assignment while Jarrat monitored the ship and kept up the telemetry transmissions to Sector Central, the NARC facility on Darwin's World.

He smiled, holding Lee against him. When Mavvik was in custody and the whole Death's Head infrastructure came apart at the seams, the kid would be out of a job. But Lee would prosper. He knew half the merchant princes in the palaces above the smogline. He would be in some other rich

21

man's bed before the week was out, pampered and fawned on. Jarrat would miss him, miss the easy, comfortable loving of male and male.

But when Death's Head was gone, when Hal Mavvik was in a deep, unmarked hole in the ground, the trade in Angel would come to a jolting dead stop on this world.

And that was what NARC was about.

CHAPTER THREE

The targets stood a hundred meters away at the other end of the gun range. Jarrat regarded them indifferently, more intent on the gunsights than on them. The old HK .60 caliber was still shooting high and left. He thumbed the adjuster a fraction over, took the automatic in both hands and sighted on the center target again. The handgun had a lot of kick though it was more than a century old. It had been in Mavvik's armory for years, corroding, replaced by newer weapons, laser sighted snipers' tools, and machine pistols like the Colt that was his own usual weapon.

Old and unusual handguns were Jarrat's only real weakness. He had taken the HK from its tomb a week before. Its renovation was absorbing. It was clean and cycling smoothing now, but ammunition for it was hard to come by since it used bullets which had to be primed with a cartridge apiece, archaic technology. The rounds he was shooting on the gun range had been custom made by an associate of Mavvik's, the gunsmith who serviced the Death's Head arsenal. The man was an artist. And he was going down with Mavvik when the time came, Jarrat would see to it.

Nine rounds, heavy caliber, were loaded into the magazine in the butt. It was a weighty piece and he could feel the drag on his forearms and elbows as he ripped off the whole clip.

The HK roared with a louder voice than the Colt. The noise slammed back off the white concrete walls, reverberating as Jarrat removed the empty magazine and reloaded with another. He thumbed the adjuster again and repeated the whole procedure. The gun was still shooting left. He burned off a third clip, made further minor adjustments and reloaded. This time six of the nine rounds punched into the target dead center and he was satisfied. He pulled the concussion pads from his ears and changed clips once more. His pockets were full of reloads. By habit he always carried plenty of spares.

Nine more rounds hammered in on target, pushing the bullseye right out of the steel plate and his ears rang with the unblanketed noise. As the shots echoed into silence they were seconded by applause, a few claps that announced Mavvik's presence. Jarrat turned toward the sound. He had not been aware he was observed. "Thank Christ you're on our team," Mavvik said with a grin displaying his perfect dental replicas. He held out one hand for the gun and Jarrat passed it over. Grasping it in both fists, Mavvik aimed it levelly between the king shooter's eyes.

"It's loaded," Jarrat said quietly. His spine prickled although he knew Mavvik would never trigger the gun. Looking into the barrel of a weapon was not an experience a man enjoyed.

"Is that a fact?" Mavvik's grin widened. "Don't fret. You're too valuable to Death's Head. I wouldn't burn a hair on your head." He turned away, sighted on the left hand target and emptied the magazine into it. Jarrat's narrowed eyes shifted focus. He was not surprised to see the rounds had found their mark as accurately as his own. Mavvik nodded his appreciation. "Nice weapon."

"More interplay between the shooter and his gun," Jarrat agreed. "These days the guns do all the hard stuff. It's almost impossible to miss." He grinned brashly at his employer. "There's going to come a day when I'm out of a job. A kid like Lee could do the honors with a cannon in his fist that's more computer than gun." Which also meant NARC would be up against such weapons in the hands of the dopers and vigilantes who were rapidly outclassing Tactical. The thought sickened Jarrat.

"Speaking of work," Mavvik mused, "you're on." He threw a keyring at the younger man and Jarrat plucked it deftly out of the air. "Take the Rand. It's bulletproof."

"Take it where — and who's shooting at me?" Jarrat was already moving. His insides had tightened at once. This had to be it. Showtime.

"Our guest is coming in on the next shuttle," Mavvik told him. "All you have to do is pick him up, deliver him and his baggage, to Armand's."

The mule. "How will I know him?" Jarrat asked. "There'll be a hundred or more passengers getting off that skybus."

In answer Mavvik lifted a photograph from his billfold and passed it into Jarrat's waiting fingers. "His name is Dressler. They're waiting for him at Armand's already. Get your ass into gear, Jarrat, get out of here."

Jarrat left the gun range without a word. He looked once at the picture before slipping it into his hip pocket. It was a candid holosnap of a nondescript little man who was instantly forgettable, a face to be overlooked in any crowd. In fact, *this* face was burned into Jarrat's mind.

He jogged back through the palace's cool, air-conditioned passages to his apartment to collect the Colt and a jacket. Lee was there, in his familiar state of undress. His brown skin shone and steam still billowed out of the bathroom. A pang of regret caught Jarrat in the chest. This was goodbye, but Lee was not to know it.

They had made love in the morning, waking late, breakfasting in the enormous bed and wrestling there until it was a confusion of tangled black silk sheets. Lee had given him everything, much more than would have been required, or even asked, of a professional Companion. Lee gave because he wanted to give. He was an uptown hustler, but what he had shared with Jarrat for two months was something very special.

"Hey, kiddo, come here," Jarrat growled from the door as he picked up the Colt. Lee came to him with that hippy walk and pressed against his clothes. Jarrat just held him, stroked his back for a moment and wished there was some way to thank him, say goodbye. Lee was dewy-damp and sweet smelling. The long, black hair seduced Jarrat's fingers for the thousandth time and he lifted the boy's chin to kiss his mouth.

"Kevin?" Lee asked a full minute later. "What did I do to deserve all this? You want to jump back into bed?"

"I haven't time," Jarrat told him with genuine regret. "Not that I wouldn't if I could! You're beautiful, kiddo, and like I told you once before, you deserve better than this place. Why don't you go and sweet talk one of those good old boys who drool over you when Mavvik throws a party? Get yourself a loving sugar daddy."

"You mean the ones who dribble while I dance?" Lee made a face.

"The money would be good and you wouldn't be serving vermin!" Jarrat tweaked both the gold nipple rings in admonition.

"You're not vermin," Lee said in sultry tones.

And I'm probably not coming back. Jarrat sighed soundlessly. "Suit yourself, beautiful." He patted the voluptuous buttocks and let Lee slip out of his arms for the last time. "Whatever happens, you look after yourself."

Lee frowned. "Why are you talking like this? Somebody gunning for you, Kevin? You make it sound like the end of life as we know it!"

He would know the truth soon enough. Jarrat only smiled and gave him a wink before he pulled on the Colt's shoulder harness. A swift pain in his back made him grimace, but the wound was only a slight annoyance now. The laser weld was perfect, it would heal without leaving even a trace of a scar. Bradley was very good. Kip Reardon would check it out when he returned to the ship, but the work would not need to be redone. He would be back aboard so soon. Stoney would want to see the wound, would make a mountain out of a molehill as usual. And Jarrat would enjoy the fussing, bask in the concern, take what he could get. A man's friendship was worth a dozen brief, empty affairs that left the heart hungry, needing.

He pulled on a light jacket to conceal the weapon and touched Lee's smooth cheek in farewell. It was still baking with early evening heat outside, but a glimpse of the Colt would be enough to frighten the public and infuriate Tactical. If it was seen, it was enough to get him arrested, and since he was not carrying NARC ID it would take hours for him to clear himself, screwing up the job in the process.

Reluctant, resigned, he left Lee and jogged down the twisting stairway, out through the back vestibule and into the gardens. He had forgotten how many times he had made friends, found lovers, in deep cover assignments, and in the end walked away. In the end, the only constant was Stone, but he was going to miss Lee. The kid deserved better.

The sun was low on the horizon, blazing in the early evening. The sprinkler system cascaded water in great arcs across the lawns, and rainbows danced in the spray. Chell stood squarely on the equator. Spaceports were always situated on or near the equator so launching ships could get the maximum possible kick off the planet's rotation.

The Rethan colony had grown fast over two hundred years since the arrival of the first fleet, the terraformers who took a promising world and beat it into shape for human habitation. Now, the city of Chell — originally named after the explorer Herman Schell, and long mispronounced, misspelled — had grown old and was in a process of decay. Only its neon and plate glass maintained the pretense of vigor. The truth, Jarrat thought bleakly, was down there in city bottom, where beauty and squalor lived cheek by jowl and the 'angelpack' ran wild from sunset to sunup.

Squealing echoed up from the pool as he headed for the garages. Mavvik was entertaining a squadron of women who all fitted more or less into the same genetic pattern. Young, big-breasted, long-legged, clad in what passed for swimwear if you stretched a point. A few scraps of knitted string and a lot of body oil. Roon was getting the *de luxe* treatment from a statuesque blonde, on a banana lounge on the other side of a concrete plantstand. No one seemed to notice. Jarrat spared the tableau a disinterested look and slipped into the dim, cool garage.

The limousines and speed cars stood in orderly ranks, seventeen of them, some on wheels, some on repulsion. The Rand rode repulsion. The body was heavily armored, weighing as much as a small truck. The Colt would still punch through it, but only just, and most man-portable weapons were impotent, useless against it. The lexan gullwings were bulletproof, the jets in the tail sheathed in armor. The hotcore generator driving it, exploding air itself through the jets with a heat of nuclear intensity, was encased in a capsule that could survive the ultimate crash, hard-landing from orbit.

Jarrat sent the gullwings up with the infrabeam key and sank into the deep padding behind the wheel. The jets ran up with a banshee howl. Bigger jets than those of the Chev he and Roon had been in at the spaceport when Vazell was picked up. He was sitting on two thousand horsepower. It was an almost sexual thrill to open the throttle. The erotic sensation did not diminish as he swung the Rand out through the gates and gunned the jets to send it hurtling down the bitumen that wound around the mountain.

As he raced on down he ran into the smog and flicked on the driving lights. Traffic was heavy — it was always heavy. Thirty million people lived in the Chell region. Their industry had long ago darkened the sky. The spaceport existed to handle trade and its smog completed the layer of pollution, shutting out the sun, shutting in the heat. Greenhouse. The warrens of city bottom were always sweltering.

A rimrunner was going out as he rounded the last long, sweeping curve down off the mountain. He could not see its hull for the dense overcast but the tail was sun-bright, like a distress flare in the sky as night fell. Twilight on the equator was short. Jarrat glanced at his watch as he ran into the crush of the traffic and of necessity cut speed. Soon he was braking to queue at the junction with the Clearway. He took the opportunity to lift the gold cigarette lighter from his inside pocket, and in a moment unfolded it into the microtransmitter.

"Raven 9.4 to Raven Leader. Raven 9.4 to Raven Leader. Come on, Stoney, where are you?"

Stone's voice answered a second later. "Right here, old son. What's the big hurry?"

"No hurry. Not yet," Jarrat told him. "But stand by. The mule's coming in on the next domestic shorthaul. His name is Dressler." He spelled it out letter by letter for the computer. "Run an ident on him and get back to me, will you? Soon as you can. I don't have too much time."

"Running it now," Stone reported. "Where are you?"

"On the road into Chell," Jarrat said dryly. "We got lucky for once. The bastards actually sent me to pick him up and take him and the garbage to the lab. Suits us just fine, doesn't it? I'll grab him and head for the extraction point. Keep a trace on me, pick me up. Mavvik won't know to panic till it's all over." He paused to swing around a laden vehicle. "Get me a gunship, Stoney. I'll be there as soon as I can."

"Will do. I have two gunships already on standby, Kevin. Watch yourself. We've got Red Ravens in the suiting room. Have you caught a vidnews show lately? There's a riot brewing. Tactical yelled for NARC half an hour ago, the Red Ravens expect to deploy any time."

"Thanks for the forecast," Jarrat said as he negotiated a snarl of slow traffic. "Where's the fighting? Down by the bays?"

"And a bit further out," Stone told him. "Mind how you go."

"I will! But this one ought to be a walkover. Keep your ears on, Stoney. Talk to you later. 9.4 out."

The Rand butted through the slower traffic like a tank and with time to spare Jarrat slid it in to park on the fourth level of the towering Skypark. The armored limousine barely fit into the angled commercial slot designed for a light truck. Inevitably it drew attention among the cheap little civilian cars. Jarrat locked it up, turned on the alarms and headed for the elevator.

He shouldered in with a crowd of kids in garish costume, bound for a party in some downmarket danceshop. The street was hot, windy, congested with the queues waiting to be admitted to the bunker that housed an old fleapit holotheatre. A hot wind howled in off the desert to the south of Chell, ripping into the smog. The humidity would be high for hours, until the southerly worked its charm in the small hours of the morning, when a few stars would begin to show and the air would be almost breathable so long as the desert wind kept up.

Dodging cars and gyrobikes, Jarrat turned right out of the Skypark's ground level rampway. The domestic shuttles came in to the passenger terminal beyond Bay 10, big, ungainly craft, belly-flopping onto the battered concrete and disgorging their cargo, human and material, before heaving themselves skyward again.

According to the display screens glaring out of the façade of the terminal building, the next domestic shorthaul was due to put down. Jarrat pushed in with the crowd shouldering through the sliding glass doors. He knew the terminal well. The bar was away to his left, already full and noisy. He could have used a beer but the vending machines sold only softies and he had no time to stand in line for service. He pushed a quarter credit coin into the slot and keyed for fruit juice.

The public address bawled a ceaseless stream of data in four assorted languages. When he heard English he pricked up his ears. "Shuttle 616 from Avey is on final approach. Tactical, stand by. Decontamination, stand by. All passengers for Shuttle 616 to Paris, Wellington and Salt Lake, gather at Gate 4."

Under cover of the noise and general confusion Jarrat brought out the little R/T. "Raven 9.4 to Raven Leader." No more than a whisper.

"Right here, Kevin," Stone's voice murmured close by his ear.

"Our man's on Shuttle 616. I'll hook Dressler as soon as Tactical get through with him. He'll have the garbage with him. Jesus, this'd be a fine time for Tac to get efficient."

"Like, they could bust him before we can get to him?" Stone said. "Great. If it even *looks* like they're going to do that, yell, and we'll wire an emergency pickup requisition, fast. And Kevin, Red Raven just jumped, five minutes ago." His voice was taut. "Watch yourself, the dope pack is howling mad down there. Raven Leader out."

Jarrat pocketed the R/T, crushed the paper cup and lobbed it into the compactor beside the vending machine. Neon directions led him to the passenger processing area. From there, standing not far from the Tactical Response men and the Decontamination squad, he watched 616 flounder in out of the smog.

Lights blazed from its belly. Red running lights winked at him, but the armorglass held out most of the storm of engine noise. The floor under his feet reverberated with the terrible concussion as the lift motors screamed up to peak just before 616 bottomed out. Vast pylons took its weight and hydraulic shockers flattened as the shuttle settled.

The Decontamination crew moved first. They hosed down the hull and interior while the cargo of baggage was unloaded from the belly pods that gave these shuttles the look of pregnant boobies. Jarrat waited impatiently. Now the end was in sight he was eager to have it finished.

Tactical went out next to run over the baggage with the whole spectrum of detectors, and Jarrat held his breath. Dressler's merchandise was there somewhere, uncut Angel, enough to keep Chell deliriously happy for another month. If Tac found it there would be a sky-wide mesh of red tape to be hacked through.

But no, Dressler was too careful, too clever. The Tactical squad went over the whole mountain of baggage and turned back to the terminal. The precious, lethal cargo must have been carefully scanner shielded. Jarrat began to breathe again.

He took station by the baggage chute, scanning for the face he would recognize from Mavvik's wallet photo. Forty strangers went by before he picked out the man, and his mouth tightened into an unamused line. Dressler was not alone. A big, burly man accompanied him, a bodyguard if Jarrat had ever seen one. The goliath could not have been armed or he would have tripped every alarm in the terminal on his way in through the Gate. But with his physical stature a cannon seemed superfluous. Traveling with the man was a risk Jarrat was surprised Dressler would run. If Tactical were on their toes, the 'minder' would have aroused their suspicions in a moment. But Chell Tactical appeared to have grown lax, and Dressler seemed to know it.

Stepping forward, Jarrat pinned on a smile. "Mr. Dressler? My name is Jarrat. Mr. Mavvik sent me to meet you."

The mule was of middle height, balding fast and already silvered out. He turned his bloodhound eyes on Jarrat with a rude scrutiny. A pace behind him, the minder was appropriating a robotrolley and loading cases onto it. Jarrat counted six big trunks. If they were packed with Angel, it would be enough to kill a regiment. The carryon slung over Dressler's shoulder would be the real luggage.

When he spoke, the mule sounded slightly drunk. "You're Mavvik's new king shooter? Fuck me through till Friday — you people get younger all the time. He'll be hiring schoolboys next." He thrust out his hand. "Call me Leo. The gorilla is Earl Barnaby. Don't let the muscles fool you. He can read and write. Almost."

If Dressler had not been carrying the drug that had become the single greatest cause of death in any given age bracket on any world throughout the colonies, Jarrat might have liked him. He had a crumpled face, like an old paper bag. He dressed like a door-to-door shoe salesman, and he *was* slightly drunk. But he exuded a sense of humor that was attractive. Mavvik's mountainside palace was a dour place, a mausoleum where humor was in poor supply and the only friendly face belonged to Lee. Jarrat had scarcely laughed in months and had learned to appreciate a little humor.

"I'm supposed to take you directly to Armand's," he said briskly, turning away in the direction of the exit doors. "If you want to wait on the cab rank I'll go and fetch the car down."

As Dressler and his muscle seated themselves under the awnings by the taxi stand Jarrat jogged back to Dock Row. He stopped in a shadowed recess and brought out the microtransmitter. Stone answered at once and he said, "Stoney, we've got a problem. Dressler's got an ape with him, brass knuckles and all."

"Wonderful," Stone breathed. "You want to yell for Tac?"

Jarrat considered the question soberly. "No," he said at last. "If they bolt we could end up with a fistful of air — Mavvik will just vanish."

"You can't nab them both! Can you?" Stone sounded doubtful.

"I can put a bullet in the bodyguard," Jarrat mused. "They've come in loaded, Stoney, and they walked right by Tactical. There's enough Angel in his bags to keep this city flying for a month or more."

"Hence the bodyguard," Stone said dryly. "Though they're taking a risk with him. He'll attract attention."

"Tactical didn't seem to notice the gorilla either," Jarrat retorted. "I think your old mob are going soft, mate."

"Maybe," Stone allowed. "I'll try and get you backup from Red Raven, but the packwar's like a battlefield. No promises, Kevin. Look, put a bullet in the ape, first chance you get. We'll sort them out later. Where are you?"

"Right across from the Skypark. The street's not too busy now. The shows must have started."

"It'll be packwar soon," Stone warned. "Red boys are down by Bay 8. You've got a riot heading your way, Kev. You'll have to get out of there fast. What are you driving? I'll tell them to keep a lookout."

"The Rand Solstice," Jarrat told him. "I'll get out of their way if I can. Tell them to keep a bloody eye open for who they're shooting, will you!"

Then he was running, dodging foot traffic and rumbling gyrobikes. He rode the elevator up to the fourth level and was in the Rand moments later. The jets whined up and he jumped the clutch out fast, reversed out of the space and tailed slow vehicles down to the exit ramp.

It was not going to be the walkover he had hoped, and he swore fluently as he threaded into the port traffic, headed for the cab rank. Dressler had not hesitated to run the risk of traveling with an instantly recognizable bodyguard. Chell Tactical were getting slow, sloppy. In this city, Death's Head had begun to win.

Armand's was a restaurant five kilometers on the north side of the Clearway. It stood in a down-at-heel industrial district, frequented by portside trash, the usual urban wildlife. Somewhere along the road, Earl Barnaby must come to grief, or Jarrat would be reporting mission accomplished to Mavvik and heading for the extraction point with nothing.

The bulk of the Colt pressed hard against his ribs, not letting him relax for a second. His nerves were strung tight as piano wires when he double parked on the rank and opened the cargo locker, which was in front of the ride capsule. He watched Barnaby move as he transferred the cases from the robotrolley. He had the graceless gait of the professional prizefighter, and the stature of one. Leo Dressler lifted himself into the back. The minder dismissed the trolley and, as the machine trundled back to its business, got into the front.

Jarrat brought down the gullwings and forced a smiled. "Next stop, Armand's. They're waiting for you, Leo, so Mavvik told me."

"They?" Dressler echoed. "Grenville and Porter?"

"Probably." Jarrat flicked a glance at the mirror. The courier was framed in it.

"Grenville and Porter. Two assholes without half a brain between the pair of them. Passengers."

"Mavvik doesn't think so." Jarrat took a pensive glance at Barnaby. His face was set into bored lines, side-lit by the garish neon of the signs flanking the road.

"Then Mavvik wants his own brains dry-cleaned. Porter's a dissipated little crock of debauchery —"

"You know him," Jarrat observed with a thin smile.

"Oh, I know him," Dressler rambled, garrulous with the alcohol he had drunk on the flight. "And Grenville. Now there's a pretty boy, isn't he? Not like you, you understand. You're pretty as a picture, I'll grant, but you've got balls to back it up. Now, Grenville — I'm not so sure."

Neither, in all honesty, was Jarrat. His impression of Charlie Grenville was of a weakling who survived by toadying to his betters. He sucked up even to Brett Rooney — 'Roon to my friends' — but if he was assigned to wreak Death's Head's wrath upon an enemy of Mavvik's, he was vicious.

But at the moment Jarrat had no time for Dressler's inebriated gossip. They had run out of Dock Row and across the Clearway junction. Bay 8 lay on their right, and as Jarrat fell in behind a commercial vehicle he saw a flare arc up over the rooftops. The Red Ravens would never quell the Angel riot before the bloodletting began. If he sped into the middle of it he could be cut to scrap before the unit from the *Athena* guessed who they were looking at. Or he could be caught up in the 'packriot,' the street war, and the Rand might easily be blazing shrapnel before he could get under cover of Red Raven's guns.

"What the hell is that?" Barnaby demanded, eyes fixed on the flare.

"That," Jarrat told him dryly, "is NARC. Looks like another dreamhead riot's got away from Tac. They push the panic button and suddenly the heavy brigade's groundside among the docking bays. Hold on."

He swung left into a side road. The car nosed up a street that was deserted and poorly lit. Blind shop frontages lined either curb, and both business people and patrons had bugged out when they heard the NARC sirens, too close. The packriot was just a few streets away and could be on this street in minutes. It would do. Jarrat braked down quickly. Before the Rand had rocked to a vibrating halt he had the Colt in his right hand and the barrel was aimed tightly on Barnaby's face.

"What the Christ are you *doing?*" Dressler squealed in the back.

"Shut up," Jarrat snapped, "and sit still." Barnaby was old enough to be his father. His eyes were sunk deeply into hollows and pouches but the meager lighting somehow struck a glimmer from them. He was not watching the Colt; he was watching Jarrat. "Now, I can put a bullet in you right now, or you can do as you're told," Jarrat offered. "And at this range one round is going blow a hole through you the size of a bucket. Think about it. What's it going to be?"

Barnaby was a man of few words but boundless respect for the gun. "Fuck yourself," he said shortly, and did not move a muscle.

"You're asking to die?" The Colt shifted minutely in Jarrat's grip. For a tenth of a second it seemed he would fire. In the back, Dressler got out the first syllable of his favorite obscenity. In the front Barnaby lunged.

Fists the size of boiled hams, the consistency of concrete, closed about both the Colt and Jarrat's wrists and wrenched the weapon upward. It discharged as if it had a will of its own. A dozen shots ripped through the roof of the Rand, carved the gullwings away. Magnesium-bright sparks showered onto the upholstery and Dressler screamed. The air reeked of the gun's toxic exhaust and scorched lexan.

Jarrat caught his breath in a gasp of agony as he felt a bone in his right wrist snap. He held onto the Colt with his left hand. He knew he was fighting for his life now — offering Barnaby any chance to get out of this scene alive had been a bad mistake. Jarrat squirmed about further, cramped by the steering column, and his right boot lashed upward to bury itself below Barnaby's abdomen. The blow drew a grunt of acknowledgment but the grip on his tortured wrists did not slacken. Jarrat's boot lashed out again with desperate force. It found Barnaby's right kneecap, and another blow found the big man's balls.

At last the pressure on his wrists released. With a sob of relief Jarrat tore himself loose. It was almost impossible to use the Colt one handed, and left handed at that. But at this range he could hardly miss. Four rounds scythed clean through Earl Barnaby. Blood spattered everywhere, black in the thick semi-darkness. Dressler screamed again, more out of hysteria than fright. Then Jarrat was out of the car. He held the gun on the courier, his right hand clutched against his chest.

"Out! Out of the car, right now!"

"You're finished, sugar boy," Dressler told him, but he did as he was instructed. "That cannon of yours is going to draw Death's Head shooters faster than dead meat draws flies."

It was true. The shots had hammered through the night like peals of thunder. The sky was quiet, no engine noise from the 'port, and the din of the riot by Bay 8 was too far away to effectively mask it. The packwar had begun to surge in another direction. It would soon be laying waste to the Stevenage sector, if Jarrat was any judge, leaving a few ragged, bloody-nosed Tactical squads in its wake to clean up the chaos. And if Armand's was half a kilometer up ahead, it could be no further.

Pain fogged Jarrat's mind dangerously. His thoughts were beginning to wander, fever-hot and confused, as his belly turned over. The car was a welter of blood and ooze and he could barely handle the Rand with his wrist out. Still, he had to get out of there. Every instinct told him to *run!* "Stow your crap, Dressler, and get moving," he barked at the mule, who was casting about for any avenue of escape. "That way, the alley. Move!"

The alley cut back up toward Dock Row, level with Bay 8. Desperately sucking air to the bottom of his lungs, Jarrat remembered Stone's warnings about the riot. He strained his ears as he ran, waiting to hear the sounds of it. A long way ahead he heard a mob in full cry. The small war was in high gear, and surely the Red Raven descant unit was on the ground, twenty-five armored troopers from the carrier. Help. If they recognized him on sight in the dead of night.

If they did not, all they would see would be a man with a gun, and he would be lucky if he only collected the full charge from a snapper, rather than running headlong into a brace of rotary cannons.

Riot control weapons were not pleasant but they were, of necessity, effective. The snapper was basically just a four-meter length of uninsulated steel flexicable connected to the suit's powerpack. It delivered the kind of high-amp charge that plunged a man into immediate unconsciousness, and often it cut like a blade, whatever it touched. Jarrat had seen men tempt fate, frenzied in some doped rage. Sometimes NARC had no option but to fight. It was one of the reasons the same dopehead mob that gathered to fight Tactical troops took to its heels and ran when it heard a NARC gunship and watched the descant force deploy ... and Jarrat had no desire to run, unexpected, into the teeth of the Red Ravens.

Panting heavily, he ushered Dressler into a nook between brick walls and somehow transferred the Colt into his right hand. His head spun, the hand was paralyzed, he had no chance of actually using the gun, but Dressler did not know that. He regarded the weapon unblinkingly, terror etched into his features. With his left hand Jarrat fought determinedly to bring out the little R/T and activate it.

"Raven 9.4 to Raven Leader."

There was no response. For a terrible moment he was sure the transmitter had been damaged in the struggle with Barnaby, then he saw the truth — the tiny whip aerial had not extended fully in his clumsy fingers. As he fumbled with it Dressler found his voice.

"Where the fuck do you come from?"

Jarrat spared him one feverish glance. "NARC."

"Narcotics And Riot Control are running us?" Dressler swallowed hard. "Jesus Christ, I'm dead." He huddled abjectly against the brickwork.

"Raven 9.4 to Raven Leader," Jarrat repeated, louder.

This time Stone was on the air at once. "Kevin, you sound —"

"I'm hurt," Jarrat affirmed tersely. "Can you get any Red boys out of the riot? I've got the mule but I need backup, fast."

"I don't know," Stone muttered. "They're tied up — forget Red. Blue Ravens can launch in five minutes."

"I haven't got five minutes!" Jarrat snapped. His head swam and his nerves spasmed savagely. The weight of the Colt on his right wrist was sickening. "I blew it, Stoney, like a rank bloody amateur. I let him jump me. I —" He broke off and his blood turned to ice water as he heard the echoing patter of approaching footfalls. Boots, pounding fast up the alley, from the direction of Armand's.

"Kevin!" Stone barked at him from the tiny speaker in his hand. "Kevin, what's happening?"

"They're right behind me." Jarrat swallowed. "Jesus God, they're right behind me."

Stone's voice came back like a whipcrack. "Who? Who's behind you? Kevin!"

"It's probably shooters from Armand's," Jarrat wheezed.

"Run!" Stone was shouting. "Dump the mule, we'll pick him up later, we know who he is now. Get the hell out of there!"

Jarrat was pleased to comply.

CHAPTER FOUR

The barrel of the Colt machine pistol impacted sharply with the back of Leo Dressler's skull. He went down in a heap and Jarrat peered groggily at the awkward sprawl of limbs. He did not dare trigger off a round now, and he dared not leave the courier behind like a signpost, pointing the way he had gone. The pounding footsteps were too close, up on the main thoroughfare, and this was the only alleyway near the Rand.

He heard their voices rise in consternation as they discovered the car. Someone was throwing up as he saw the reeking mess that had once been Earl Barnaby. Jarrat himself was spattered with the dead man's blood, but he had barely noticed it.

Before Dressler had hit the ground he was running. He transferred the Colt into his left hand and somehow fastened his numb right fingers about the R/T. He could not feel the metal case but he could hear the white noise of static over the open channel. Every sweep of the powerful spaceport radars produced a wave of hissing interference. He found encouragement and comfort in the sound. Stone was monitoring him.

The comfort was an illusion. Jarrat was alone. He took off down the alley, teeth clenched as every step jolted through him. He knew he was shocky and shook his head to rid it of its fog. Other alleys crisscrossed this one but he stayed out of them as long as he could. It would be too easy for him to get lost in the warren.

He had begun to think he had left them behind when the brilliance of flashbeams lanced out of the darkness behind him. His heart hammered painfully at his ribs and he leapt toward the cover of an adjoining alley a fraction of a second before a dozen big-caliber rounds went by so close to his cheek that he felt the cool disturbance in the air. They would be on laser target acquisition, he knew. He recognized the braying voice of the Steyr pistol. It was not fully automatic but it would cycle .44 rounds as fast as the trigger could be tripped.

The Colt that had been his salvation so many times in the past fought him now. He closed both hands on it, teeth clenched on the moan of pain forming in his throat. He flattened out against the coarse plasterwork of the wall with the gun chest-high. He would have a split second to shoot.

He spun out of the alley and touched the feather trigger with his left index finger. The gun pulled up hard on the pressure of its exhausting waste gasses. He rested the weight of his useless right hand on it to hold it down and get off forty rounds that ripped about the alley. Blindfire — he could not pick up a target visually.

A voice screamed. He had hit at least one, but now his right hand was entirely useless, it would go no further. A wave of nausea seethed up and his senses dimmed. He shook his head drunkenly and pounded on. His body reacted like a machine to the training it had absorbed, years before. The Colt had almost eighty rounds left but he would be shooting wild with one hand. Targets would be elusive.

"Kevin! Kevin!" Stone's voice shouted from the R/T. "Blue Raven gunship has just launched. We're not reading your carrier signal. If they're going to locate on your broadcast you're going to have to talk. Kevin!" His voice was taut with anxiety. "The 'port radars are blanketing you out!"

Jarrat lifted the R/T to his lips. "I took one of them," he sobbed. "There's four or five more behind. I've got plenty of ammo if I can just figure out how to use it."

"Stoppage?" Stone asked. "The Colt's jammed?"

"No, the gun's fine. It's my frigging wrist that's broken. My right wrist." Jarrat whooped for air. "The bugger who came in with Dressler broke it. I let him jump me."

Only some sixth sense made him look up.

The tiny red spot of the laser target acquisition beam was projected on the wall in front of him, dancing around as the Death's Head man waved the Steyr pistol about, trying to line up on target. Jarrat dove aside, came up against the wall and snatched the Colt around. The only way he could hold it down as it bucked like a live thing in his hands was to snap off no more than two or three rounds at a time. Since it cycled ten per second this was not easy.

He got off twenty but heard no answering cries. He had made them duck into cover, he knew: no return shots chewed into the plasterwork about him and the laser spot was gone. While he had the chance to make distance Jarrat got up and ran. The alley was dark as the pit. Refuse lay scattered like booby traps before him. It would only be luck if he could stay on his feet.

The Steyr .44 hammered another volley at him. The rounds did not miss by much and he slid around the next corner to get out of the line of fire. Instinct told him to run and keep running but he holed up behind a trash barrel, panted for air and waited. He heard their footfalls and brought up the Colt. Short bursts snapped off and he dragged the gun down into line each time its exhaust gasses shoved it up against his good hand.

This time he saw another of them go down. He caught a glimpse of snow-blond hair as the man sprawled on his face. It was Wes Porter, and he was missing a good deal of his midsection. Three remained, diving for what cover they could find. Jarrat forced his feet to work and pounded on. His legs felt as if they were made of molten plastic. His head buzzed and his vision swam as his body tried to faint. Sheer willpower overrode it. The Colt still had forty rounds in the magazine, he had a chance.

"Kevin!" Stone's voice called urgently. "Kevin, will you talk? We can't find your signal. The spaceport radars are cutting you right out."

Jarrat lifted the R/T in a right hand that seemed to be in a vice. "I can talk or I can run, which do you want? Where the hell is Blue Raven?"

"On reentry procedures," Stone shouted. "Kevin, for chrissakes try!"

The sound of his partner's voice spurred Jarrat to effort. His legs pumped on mechanically and he held the R/T to his lips.

"Don't know where I am. Somewhere out by Bay 9 or 10, I think. I was about half a klick from Armand's when I took the ape ... Jesus, Stoney, I'm lost. Stoney, are you getting this?"

"Every word." Tension snapped Stone's voice. "Hold on, Kevin. Blue Raven have got this on audio, they're locating on you. Just keep talking."

The fog was thickening about Jarrat's frayed senses. He knew as well as Stone knew, it was only a matter of time before he started making mistakes. The first was probably long overdue. A fallen trash barrel loomed up like a landmine, he did not even see it in the gloom. Jarrat caught one foot on it and went down hard. The Colt skittered away from him, out of reach. Only the paralysis of his right fingers held the R/T in his palm. He could not even tell it was there.

The faint rolled over him. Nausea swamped him and for a moment he was out cold. The animal survival instinct roused him to half-consciousness. He came to with a grunt, fighting for fragmentary orientation. It all came back with sickening clarity and he pushed his knees under him, took his weight on his left palm. The Colt was too far away, taunting him.

He scrambled after it, numbed fingers almost touching the hot barrel shroud when an expensive imported leather boot kicked it away. He wrenched up his head, peered at the man above him, but he had seen nothing when the same boot impacted with his middle, lifted him and tossed him over onto his back.

A hand-light glared full in his face and he lifted his left arm to protect his shriveling irises. Dimly he heard and recognized the voice of Charlie

Grenville. "Shit — it's Jarrat! Bloody Jarrat! I told Hal there was something wrong with this hoon. What is he, Tactical?"

The voice that answered belonged to a driver Jarrat knew as Giorgio. "No way, man. Not after he's been in the palace for so long. Tac don't screw around like this, they haven't the talent. Look at him. He's a NARC, you can fuckin' bet on it."

"NARC?" Grenville echoed in the high, wheedling voice. It had grated Jarrat's nerves for two months. He bent, clutched a handful of Jarrat's hair and lifted him. "Are you? Narcotics And Riot Control? You're dead, sweet thing. Mavvik'll cut out your heart and shove it up your ass." He released Jarrat's hair, watched him smack into the concrete and doubled his fist.

Jarrat saw the blow coming and closed his eyes. It exploded against the side of his skull and he hovered on the edge on unconsciousness again, following their conversation blindly.

Grenville had his R/T on him. "Charlie to Home Base. Give me Hal and make it quick."

A long pause followed. Jarrat moved slightly, trying to unpin his right arm, which was caught beneath his weight and protesting. Movement earned him a curse and a kick, and he rode it on his hip, rolled over by it. He was just an observer now. He was dead meat, they had promised, and with the big spaceport radars blanketing his broadcast Blue Raven would never locate on him. He would be lucky if they made it clean.

"Home Base," Mavvik's voice answered at last, distorted by the speaker and the interference. "I told you not to bother me unless the bottom dropped right out, Charlie. This had better be damned good."

"It is," Grenville said. "And the bottom *has* busted loose, Hal. It's your boy Jarrat. He's a chickenshit NARC runner. He's blown Barnaby away, Dressler's squealing with a busted head and the Rand's only fit for burning. You get all that?"

Silence followed for a moment, then Mavvik was back on the air. "Jarrat's a NARC? You're sure?"

"He has to be," Grenville shouted, "it's the only thing makes sense. Tac don't fuck with us. They take us on, we put them in the ground, so they don't even see us, not in years. Jarrat has to be NARC, and this is where it hits the fan, Hal. He'll have been sending home telemetry since the day he signed on. You better get Death's Head in gear, or our asses are going to be stuffed and mounted on some office wall!"

"What about the Angel?" Mavvik barked. "NARC got the Angel?"

"No, we found the car, we found Dressler, we've got the stuff. You're going to blow a seal when you see the Rand. Barnaby's plastered all over it. Jarrat must have pumped a half-dozen into him, point-bloody-blank. And Paul and Sam are dead too, blown away."

"That," Mavvik said quietly, "is the way the horseshit splashes ... forget the car. Leave it where it is. Bring the Angel, bring Dressler and get back here. Fast, Charlie. If NARC wants a war, they can have one they won't forget this side of New Year."

"Copy that," Grenville responded. He peered down at Jarrat's shuddering body. "What do you want done with the pretty boy shooter?"

Mavvik answered without hesitation. "Grease him, any way you want. Let NARC know we mean business, right here, right now. But make it quick, Charlie. You got a packriot headed your way. When the party starts, you won't want to stick your head out the window."

34

As the R/T shut down Grenville pocketed it. He went to one knee and slapped Jarrat's cheeks to rouse him. "You hear that, sugar boy? You hear what the man said? Any way as takes my fancy. Let your mob have the message, loud and clear. *You're* the message, Jarrat, and this is one chore I'm gonna enjoy."

The part of Jarrat's mind that was still functioning prayed for a bullet in the back of the skull, but he did not honestly expect it. He curled up defensively, knees pushed into his middle as blows began to fall and his clothes were ripped away. His body was broken and violated, nothing worked properly, and when the darkness rushed over his head he never expected to see the light again.

The *Athena*'s massive aerials were ranged on Chell's spaceport sector and the gain was cranked to maximum, but the voices were still indistinct, mushy against an impenetrable wall of harsh white noise from the 'port's civilian airsearch network. Incoming radio was routed to the computer for enhancement before being played back, and a specialist tech wrestled with the equipment. Stone knew what he was hearing was on an unavoidable two minute delay, and his heart beat heavily at his ribs.

The voices were being picked up by the powerful condenser mic on Jarrat's R/T, but Kevin himself was not sending anymore. The radio relayed the whole discourse in distorted form, but the spaceport radars were so pervasive, it was impossible to get an accurate locational fix. Stone's mouth was dry as dust. He touched a key on the headset he had pulled on when Kevin called home, and switched up to the encrypted ship-to-ship channel. "Raven Leader to Blue Raven 6."

"Blue Raven 6," Gil Cronin answered at once from the gunship, far below the carrier.

"How long till insertion?"

"We're two hundred K's downrange at ten thousand," the leader of the Blue Raven descant unit told him. "We can see the 'port but I gotta warn you, Jarrat isn't broadcasting. We can't get a squeak out of him."

"We've got his final transmission," Stone said quietly. "A rough triangulation. Standby for datafeed."

When the data came up on the blue-screen com-relay terminal in the darkened jump bay of the gunship, Cronin hissed through his teeth. He passed a hand before his eyes and glared at the dynamic display framed in the CRT. "Jesus Christ, it's an area the size of five football fields, Cap, and the whole shitty place is like an anthill!"

"So get on your bike, earn your money for a change," Stone snapped.

Cronin did not take his abruptness personally. In Stone's place he would have reacted as sharply. Jarrat and Stone had been like a busking double act for two years. Neither man had any family to speak of, and long ago they had adopted one another. In this line it work, any kind of close friendship was probably a mistake. One partner became the Achilles' heel of the other, his vulnerability, his weakness. The cause of pain. Cronin knew Jerry Stone was in love. He and Stone had known each other too long — rising through the ranks in two different branches of the same service — for him to be blind to it, even if Kevin Jarrat had never seen the truth. Never been allowed to see it. But Stoney's involvement was set dead against NARC regulations; it was never mentioned, but it was there.

If Jarrat was dead, it was going to put Stone down as surely as a bullet. Any active NARC field agent lived with the terrible knowledge that any day it could happen, yet every operative in the service clung to the illusion of immortality young people carried with them. The knowledge it could happen ... the blind certainty it never would.

Silent, intent on the glowing instrument surfaces, Cronin watched the ranging data come up on the jump bay's comm-relay terminal. Four kilometers out the broad hatch in the deck of the jump bay opened and the gunship's floodlights and spinners came on. They were running at two hundred meters now. Cronin watched for 00/00, the 'on target' reading, to display. Two klicks out, as the Blue Raven gunship entered the jump zone, the twenty-five men of the descant unit gathered by the open hatch.

Twenty-five glossy black locusts. Riot armor was impervious to furnace temperatures, radiotoxicity and acid, and was tough enough to defy almost any man-portable weapons system. Sealed and on internal power and life support, the armor was operational in vacuum and underwater. The suits weighed two hundred kilos, and if not for the repulsion a man could not even stand up in one, let alone work.

The jump light flashed red, garish crimson, casting weird shadows in the darkened bay. Cronin was the first out through the belly hatch. The repulsion came up automatically as the suit's sensors detected a freefall environment, and Cronin and the men of Blue Raven feathered down through the last hundred meters. The suits were armed. On the right forearm was a rotary cannon cycling fifty 9mm armor-piercing incendiaries per second, triggered by an eyeblink mechanism, leaving the hands free. On the left forearm was a stun cannon, a magnetic field projector that could blanket an area of a hundred square meters, numbing the brains of anyone without a helmet. To the left thigh contour was clipped the coiled snapper.

They were the most potent, feared and respected force on the street, on any world across the colonies. A department answerable to a government so many parsecs away that NARC officers operated on their own initiative. But Stone's mouth was still dry as ancient dust.

He stood in the dimly-illuminated operations room aboard the carrier, eyes moving between a number of comm-relay terminals, watching the same data the Ravens monitored in their helmet displays. Via the headset, he was listening to the signals passing between the Blue Ravens. It was very close to actually being on the gunship or in the field with them.

But Stone's nerves crawled unpleasantly. All he could hear, over and over, was the voice he had come in an instant to hate.

You hear that, sugar-boy? ... any way as take my fancy ... this is one chore I'm gonna enjoy.

Those words had come in eight minutes ago, over Jarrat's still-open R/T. He was transmitting, even though he had gone down, and a terrible, gnawing certainty knotted up under Stone's heart. This time Jarrat would die. Time and again they had stretched their luck past breaking-point. Always, some soldier's god had intervened, snatched them back. But not this time. Stone had heard the muffled sounds of blows landing. How long did it take to beat a man to death? Not long.

Stone's mind had gone beyond that. Jarrat might die, yet still be repairable. Salvageable. If Surgeon Captain Kip Reardon could get hold of him, broken bones and ruptured organs could be fixed or replaced. Surgical hightech. A shred of hope held on in Stone's mind though he was sure Kevin was poised right on the edge this time.

No kind of medical science under this sun or any other could repair him if they had picked up the Colt and cut him to shreds with it. But Stone had heard no braying of the machine pistol that had been Jarrat's signature as long as Stoney had known him. Just the dull, muffled, terrible impacts of blows, beating the life out of him.

Stone reached over to touch a switch. "Infirmary."

"Reardon," the surgeon answer at once.

"You set up, Kip?" Stone asked as the CRT before him reported the Blue Ravens in the air.

"OR is standing by, ready to go ... and I've primed a cryotank," Reardon reported. "I've got my eye on the time, Stoney. There isn't much." He spoke softly, as if —

As if he knows, Stone thought. As if Kip Reardon knew somehow that some acid mix of love and lust, hunger and dread, had been eating the insides out of Jerry Stone for far too long. Smothering a blistering curse, he closed his eyes and waited.

Evelyn Lang had both arms filled with parcels and was trying to juggle them into one hand to get at her hip pocket. The keys to the Skyvan were in it. Behind her, Simon was equally laden but her brother was underage, had no license, no keys. The Marshall Skyvan was parked a few meters from the mouth of the alley. She had left it there, partially concealed, two hours before. It was not safe to park an expensive vehicle unattended in the open in this district. Either it would vanish or mysteriously become a vandalized wreck. She balanced the parcels precariously and had the keys in her right hand when the top one rolled off. It was light and fell with the telling sound of breakages. "Shit!" She muttered angrily. "That's supper done for." The parcel was filled with fragile confectionery.

"They'll go down the same way." Simon shrugged. "And anyway, we can pick up some more when we get to Outbound, can't we?"

"I suppose." Evelyn shifted the keys into her left palm and went after the fallen parcel. "But Outbound is eight hours away. If this lot's ruined we're going to be godawful hungry before ..."

His sister broke off. Simon peered into the darkness. "What's wrong?"

"There's a body on the ground here."

"A dead one?" Simon hurried forward. "I never saw a real deader."

"How would I know?" Evelyn stooped, put the parcels down carefully and gave the keys to her brother. "Open the 'van, put the stuff away. I'd better look at him." She reached down toward the still, naked form but a moment later snatched her hand away. "Christ, there's blood everywhere. He's been done over."

"Dead?" Simon called as he sent the 'van's gullwings up.

Evelyn swallowed, teeth clenched. She reached out again to find the man's throat and press her fingers into the hollow between the collarbones. "God almighty. There's a pulse. Simon, there's a pulse! It's weak but it's there. He's alive."

Simon returned to collect his sister's parcels. "You want to call Tactical? They can send a meat wagon and have him in hospital in ten."

"Maybe," she mused. "But if the loons who did this catch up with him they'll finish the job there. He's left for dead ... Death's Head. Shit, how I hate Death's Head."

"They did this?" Simon murmured. "Yeah, who else would it be, 'round here? I know." He paused. "But he'll die if he doesn't get help."

Although Simon did not sound as if he cared if the stranger lived or died, he was right. The man at Evelyn's feet was young, and his life expectancy was going to be brief, if she walked away from him. Simon would have walked away. Evelyn Lang got to her feet and sifted through her memory. "We're ten hours from home." She was thinking aloud. "What about the clinic in Paddington? That's a half-hour flight. I'd rather take him there than just abandon him to Chell General, and we're just too far out to even think about making the trip home. He'd turn up his toes before we were halfway there."

"He's a total stranger," Simon protested. "Call Tac for a meat wagon and let's get going. I'm suffocating in this smog."

Evelyn almost hit him. She remembered at the last moment, Simon was too young to remember. Ten years ago he would have been just six years old. And Stevie was sixteen. Beautiful Stevie, who came to Chell to go to college and ended up bumming the streets of city bottom. Looking for work that wasn't there to be found, relying on friends who suckered him into bad company, a lover who dumped him ... finding joy in a nose full of Angel. Finding death in an alley very like this one, with his ass raped bloody, his head beaten in, and both hands taken off at the wrists so their palm prints could not be used to ID him.

Grief and revulsion and desperate rage were still a physical sickness in Evelyn's gut, but it was so long in the past, it might as well never have happened at all. "Stevie," she murmured, seeing the long-dead face as it had been in life. "You've got a short memory, haven't you, Simon?"

"But that was Stevie, not this guy," Simon argued. "What's it matter?"

Now Evelyn did hit him. The backhand shocked him and he stumbled away. "If anyone had helped Stevie he might have lived!" She snarled, watching Simon recoil in surprise. "But the world's full of bastards — and you're one of them! It's people like you who let Death's Head have their way. Too gutless to speak out, too couldn't-care-less to lift your bloody little finger when you see a guy who's so far gone, he can't even beg for your help. Now, get out of my way, boy!"

Seething silently with fury, he stood aside to watch. It would be useless to argue with Evelyn and, furious or not, he knew she was right. She spoke from the vantage point of the kind of experience Simon had yet to gather. The body stank of blood, but Evelyn ignored it. She had seen so much blood in the bitter corporate war on Sheal, she ceased to shrink away from it, though it turned Simon's stomach. He hurried away to flick on the Sky-van's floodlights.

As the floods came on, brilliant blue-white in the smog-dim alley, Evelyn swore beneath her breath. She had half-straightened the man's limbs, dredging her memory for details that were growing hazy with the years. Medevac duty. Young, broken bodies. The reek of wounds. In the lights his blood looked like thick, black paint, and there seemed to be an ocean of it. His face was smeared, his nose and mouth caked, his eyes swollen shut. It was dangerous to move him — it could kill him, she knew. But this young man was out of options.

He had two chances to die and a slim one to live. She bent, locked her hands under his shoulders and leaned into the task of dragging him toward the 'van. Simon stood watching mutely until she barked at him. He had heard that tone before, but not in years, not since she had come back from Sheal as a three striper with a voice that could cut steel.

"Get over here and help me, you useless little bugger!"

The body was heavier than it looked, but he was still breathing when they had manhandled him into the back of the 'van. Evelyn ran the straps up tight about him and absently wiped her hands on the seat of her green coveralls, too late remembering her palms were slick with his blood.

Simon was trying to wipe his hands off on a paper sack. "I feel sick," he muttered.

"Then get your puking done before we take off," she told him acidly. "Throw up in the 'van, and you can get out and fuckin' walk. And either make it quick, Simon, or wait here and catch the skybus down to Paddington in the morning." Her sharp words got Simon moving. He was in the 'van before her, teeth clenched, lips mashed together, either in nausea or anger, or both. Evelyn could not have cared less.

A moment later she was bringing down the gullwings and the big lift motors ran quickly up to peak thrust. Evelyn ran through the briefest preflight checklist, then picked up the undergear and gave the throttles a nudge. "This one is for Stevie," she said softly, and gunned the Skyvan hard into the southeast. As it rose into the dense smog layer even its running lights were lost in the red-gold backwash from the spaceport lights.

CHAPTER FIVE

Twenty minutes after Jarrat's final transmission, Stone was locking down the neck seal of the suit of riot armor that carried his name and rank. The waiting was a kind of torment he would not have inflicted on an enemy. Perhaps he was wasting his time, going groundside, but *doing* was better than standing in the ops room and watching.

As he locked down the helmet and activated the life support systems he looked sourly at the suit which stood beside his own in the officers' ready room. On the glossy black breastplate was a name. Capt. K.J. Jarrat. His heart gave a painful squeeze and he turned away. Repulsion normalized the weight of the suit, but in terms of proper mass under one gravity he and it together weighed almost three hundred kilos. He walked easily aft to the hangars. Two of the gunships, Red and Blue, were out. Green and Gold were still on the ramps.

He bypassed them, headed for the shuttle. It was a streamlined space-to-surface plane with variable geometry wings and canards, twin vertical flow separators and an aerodynamic hull configuration that allowed it to function as well in the dense atmospheric environment as in vacuum.

The canopy was up and the engines still shimmered with heat after their routine preflight testfiring. Stone climbed the boarding platform and let himself down into the cockpit's forward acceleration couch. The plane seated two and was intended as a firezone observation and field command craft. He brought down the canopy as sirens began to wail across the hangar deck. Service crews ran for cover as the blue spinners came on.

When the personnel cleared the launch bays, vast cycling machines pumped the compartment to a few percent pressure and the hatch growled open in the belly of the *Athena*. Stone brought up the repulsion, folded the landing gear and advanced the twin throttles by one notch. The shuttle nosed forward and dropped gently out into space. He spared the carrier one glance before turning his plane's sharp nose toward the velvet sphere below, the planet's equatorial night. Chell was down there. Chell, and Death's Head, and Jarrat. Or what was left of him.

Twenty minutes was a long time. But a man was not medically, clinically dead till five minutes after his heart quit. Jarrat was full of life, Stone thought. He must hang on. Two years ago, Stone had been the carrier's Executive Officer, and in charge of the ops room while the NARC Captains, Robson and Standish, were blown away. Their deaths, in the shelling of a Tactical field station, began an Angel syndicate war that laid waste to two cities. As young as Stone was, his was the head bearing the laurels. With Robson and Standish gone, he assumed the rank of acting captain. In the debriefing, the dissection of the action at Central, four months later, the old men and their computers decided to promote rather than censure.

Stone kept the rank of captain, and kept also the carrier that had been his home and base ship for two years already. But a NARC carrier ran with *two* command rank officers, since only one was aboard the majority of the time. On every functional level, of necessity there were two captains, and Standish's replacement was soon rostered over from the *Avenger*.

His name was Jarrat, Kevin J., and the rank of captain was as new to him as to Stone. He won his spurs in an action against an Angel syndicate calling itself Black Unicorn. A NARC gunship was salvaged with most of its crew intact, and a city was *not* obliterated by the detonation of that gunship's powerplant. All this was to Jarrat's credit, and NARC was never slow to rewarded initiative.

But Stone had realized, the moment he read the assignment and even before Kevin came aboard, he and Jarrat were in a make-or-break scenario. Some committee on Darwin's World had thrown the new boys into the melting pot. If they won through they would be rewarded; if they botched the job they would be busted, perhaps right out of the department.

The file on Jarrat, Kevin J., made fascinating reading. Stone had been interested to meet the man with whom he would work, and initially a working relationship was all he had desired, though the file images hinted at a face, a physique, that could not fail to arouse fascination of a much different kind. As a directive, NARC discouraged close friendships between agents. The mortality rate was high, the grief too costly. A good professional footing rated better marks than friendship. Stone had always agreed. Where a billion-credit operation was at stake, personal relationships got in the way. In the end the individual had to suffer, when the job must be given priority.

And then Jarrat transferred aboard and Stone knew in an instant, he was done for. First came the lust, consuming, like an acid bath. Jarrat was everything Stone had dreamed about in the empty drought years since he had left Tactical: long-legged, slim-hipped, with a sultry face that was still boyish, beautifully so, and the whippy physique of an acrobat or a dancer. Academy friendships, sexy and satisfying, taunted Stone across the years as he watched Jarrat walk out of the shuttle hangar, and from that first moment, wanted him.

But Jarrat had better sense than to break the rules. He had been into half the crewgirls who batted their eyelashes at him in the first month aboard, in a series of comradely, no-strings affairs, and Stone knew when to keep his silence. Getting involved was dangerous and few NARC people would allow it to happen. Relationships were kept fleeting, unimportant. The kind of affairs Jarrat was offered, and accepted, after coming aboard. For Stone, those weeks were a painful epiphany. The lust which began at first-sight mellowed as they worked together. Lust morphed into love, and Stone was keenly aware of his predicament.

If he was in love, it was his own hard luck, and he knew it. With ferocious dedication, he turned his attention back to his work and the same no-strings relationships that seemed to amuse Jarrat. The work separated them for weeks, sometimes months at a time. Soon the lust became easier to manage and when they were together Stone reveled in Jarrat's company instead. Friendship was its own reward. The frustrations bedeviling him were worked out with cooperative crewmates aboard and sundry affairs when he was in deep cover. If he had his deep, dark fantasies, neither Jarrat nor NARC itself needed to know about them.

The spaceport radar picked him up five hundred kilometers out and Stone identified himself tersely. "Raven Leader, Narcotics And Riot Control, on a heading for Chell. I am an armed observational space-to-surface intercept vehicle."

They piped nav data, clearances and codes to his onboard deck and Stone rode out the bucking reentry impatiently. The shuttle dropped like a brick through the planet's dense atmosphere. The gull-gray hull heated to a blooming cherry red and the wings were incandescent. The plane was still hot when he brought it down Blue Raven's location beam. The gunship itself did not land, it was too big to set down in any city environment. It hung in the air at two hundred meters, covering the ground with sensors and weapons pods, flooding the streets below with blue-white searchlights.

The shuttle was smaller, much more maneuverable. Stone cut speed as he took the datafeed from Blue Raven unit. "There's a car with a very dead body in it, and a lot of 9.4's ammunition," Gil Cronin was saying over his headset. "Looks like he took off on foot — personally I'd have stayed with the car. It's a Rand, built like the proverbial brick shithouse, bulletproof, for executives with armies of enemies."

"And if your wrist was broken?" Stone muttered.

"Then I might consider alternatives," Cronin admitted. "Besides, the car's like a goddamned slaughterhouse. Blood and guts everywhere. Right now, Cap, we're covering the alleys and buildings on both sides of the road, room by room, yard by yard. Christ knows where he's disappeared to. This place is like a maze. You could go out for a packet of smokes and find your way home five years later."

The carrier's shuttle touched down like a fifty-tonne feather. Stone sent up the canopy and hauled himself out as he called for two Blue Ravens to take station, flanking the aircraft. The only place large enough to land it was in the middle of the street down which Kevin had driven. The bulletproof limousine stood a hundred meters away, just up ahead, in the glare of the gunship's lights. Beyond it Stone glimpsed the spinning red lights of the Tac roadblock which closed off the whole thoroughfare.

He walked lightly in the riot armor. He had adjusted his apparent mass

41

to just fifty kilos and his body felt as if it weighed nothing. The car was parked at the left curb, what remained of the gullwings lifted. He peered in to survey Jarrat's handiwork indifferently. The bodyguard had been torn apart. Some of him seemed to be missing altogether. Earl Barnaby's eyes bulged out of their sockets in an expression of astonishment.

"Don't know what you're so damned surprised about," Stone muttered to the corpse. "You screw about with a king shooter, and what the hell else do you expect?" He turned his back on the mess as Cronin hailed him urgently.

"Cap Stone, the boys are finding .60 caliber ammo in a wall over yonder." Cronin's tone was sharp. "Cap Jarrat might have left us a paper trail after all. Sixty-cal's not so common on the street."

Hurrying in Cronin's wake, Stone checked the time. The LED chrono in his helmet, a hand's breadth from his nose, registered forty minutes elapsed since Jarrat had last said a word. Time was against him. If the body were clinically 'dead,' brain-dead, not even Kip Reardon would be able to breathe life back into it. Reardon was a microsurgeon not a magician, and once the brain had begun to accumulate damage due to the failure of oxygenated blood supply, it was over. A steel hand seemed to clutch Stone's insides.

They were digging Jarrat's rounds out of the wall. Stone pried one out, shoved one armored forefinger straight into the crumbling ceramic and levered out the mangled bullet. Which way now? He turned up his helmet lights, more candlepower than he would ever need. An eye-destroying brilliance flooded the shadows of the alleyway. Which way would Kevin go? He was down to instinct.

Think like a man who's fighting for his life, Stone thought. It was not difficult to project himself into Jarrat's place. His partner's voice haunted him. Kevin had been feverish, barely capable of coherent thought, his body shocky with the broken bone. Fear would have been his companion, riding his shoulders, gibbering at him, forcing him on with the one imperative: *get the hell out of here!* Heart in his mouth, Stone played a hunch and held to the main alley for three hundred meters. Then he began to search for damage inflicted by the Colt.

There it was. Bricking had been chewed away by multiple hits, Jarrat had fired out of an alley which branched off to the right. Stone turned into it, calling Cronin. "More signs up this way. All Blue Ravens, come to me." Now Stone began to pick up his pace. Repulsion cut his weight back to forty kilos and he feathered the ground, covering distance like a sprinter. His eyes flicked repeatedly to the chrono that was blinking Jarrat's chances away, second by second. "Raven Leader to Blue Raven gunship."

"Reading you, Cap." It was the comm operator.

"Tell your Infirmary to set up cryotank," Stone barked. "There won't be much time." A cryogen capsule would in an instant drop Jarrat's body temperature to that of liquid nitrogen and hold him suspended there until he could be returned to Reardon's OR on the carrier. Reardon had full cryogenic facilities on board, and if the damage Jarrat had suffered exceeded his capabilities, requiring the services of a major 'crash shop,' Jarrat would be transferred to a long-duration tank and shipped back to Sector Central, on Darwin's World.

The helmet lights stabbed into one further alley and Stone pulled up short. He saw blood on the ground, looking blackish-purple, a lot of it and a few rags, the remains of torn clothing. But he saw no body. He moved forward until he stood almost on top of the drying smear and cast about for further signs, but he found none. His heart sank like a rock. They must have trashed the body. If it had gone into a compactor, by now not even bone would be left to testify that Kevin Jarrat had ever been alive at all.

He stood rooted to the spot, thinking vaguely that the blood and rags at his feet might easily be the last trace of anything to do with Kevin he would ever see. It was some moments before the motion sensors chirped a quiet alarm, informing him of a trace of activity in a gateway twenty meters up ahead. He panned the helmet light toward it.

A man lay there, tattered, clad in baggy coveralls. He looked old, but you could never tell on sight. A year on Angel and a youth looked decrepit. How long had he been there? Had he been there when it happened? Had he watched? Stone strode forward. The man covered his eyes against the blinding sweep of the lights. Remembering them, Stone cut back the power and keyed in the public address.

"You are in no danger," he told the man, enunciating clearly. If the Angelhead was high, he would have a hard time distinguishing words from sound. "Were you a witness?" Owlish eyes blinked stupidly up at him. "A man was beaten here not long ago. Were you a witness!" The old head wagged at him, indicating yes, and Stone pressed on. "What did you see?"

He was stoned but not flying. Coming down off the high. He could speak with some coherence and Stone hung on every syllable. "Young fella come runnin', tripped over the barrel there. I reckon he had a cannon. Gun. They come after him — had a radio. Didn't hear nothing of what they said, but they kicked shit out of him, I thought he were dead 'fore the woman showed."

Stone swallowed hard and leveled his voice. His heart pounded like a trip-hammer. The hardsuit's telemetry would report it. Let Central make of it what they would. "You *thought* he was dead? What woman? What did you see? Come on, man!"

"The woman with the 'van. The Skyvan, it were parked over there." The old man blinked stupidly, pointing at a blind wall to his left. "She damn-near fell over him. Took him along, in the 'van. I heard her sayin' he were alive, there were a pulse. I dunno nothing 'bout that stuff. But she said he weren't dead. They put him in the 'van, didn't they?"

He was babbling because he was frightened, Stone knew, and he softened his tone. "They? You said only a woman."

"She — she had a kid with her. Not a child, a kid. They dragged the body into the 'van, got in and shoved off." The old face twisted. "I hasn't done nothin'. Leave us alone."

Cold sweat prickled about Stone's ribs. He turned on the helmet recorders. "I'll leave you as soon as I can. Give me a description of the 'van and the woman."

The old man, or young-old, or Angel-old, it was impossible to tell, blinked vacantly. "It were yeller, with red scallops on the nose. Flame things or somethin'."

"What about the registration, the make?"

"Marshall," he stammered. "The reggo were N7-somethin', I didn't see no more. Please, leave us alone!"

"And the woman? Description!" Stone pressed.

"Tall. Big, strong, blonde. It were dark. The 'van were there when I came into the gateway. Leave us alone, I hasn't done nothin'!"

Stone turned off the recorder. "Go back to sleep, old man. Enjoy your dreams." Angel dreams, one day merging into Angeldeath. He left the alley without looking back and headed for the shuttle at a steady jog. "Raven Leader to Blue Raven gunship, stand down your Infirmary."

"Will do," the comm operator said after a moment's pause. "Cap Stone, you, uh, you found Cap Jarrat?" He spoke softly, obviously assuming it was Jarrat's dead body that had been found.

"No," Stone told him as he joined Gil Cronin by the shuttle. "Not yet." Cronin was piecing together what oddments of data they had. A few mangled bullets, some .44, some Colt .60. Sensor readings of blood traces, some Jarrat's, some not. A few torn scraps of clothing, Jarrat's. It was all too little and Stone dismissed the forensic work. He lifted himself back into the aircraft as Cronin watched.

"You in a hurry to leave, Cap?"

"Not to leave," Stone muttered. "I want data, more than the suit can handle ... NARC Raven Leader to Chell Spaceport Central, please respond on priority channel 88."

The response was a few seconds in coming, probably due to sheer consternation. Channel 88 was the military distress frequency. At last a woman's voice replied, "Raven Leader, what is your emergency?"

"Give me Air Traffic Registration, fast," Stone requested tersely.

A pause, then, "Raven Leader, this is not a military emergency situation. You are using this frequency illegally. Please switch down to one of the open channels immediately."

"Not on your life, lady," Stone snapped. "Priority override command, code 707. This is a NARC emergency, please comply with instructions." A brief pause followed. They were clearing the override through the computer. Stone's gloved fingers drummed on the arm of the acceleration couch.

"Your code is affirmed," she said at last. "Proceed."

"Data retrieval request. Transmit a comprehensive of all Skyvans with civil list code prefixed 'N7', manufactured by Marshall, color yellow. Send it on 88, then give me Tracking, and hurry, love. I need this yesterday."

The shuttle's onboard deck had a massive capacity, and needed it. Stone groaned softly and swore as the data came in as a five second cascade. There were thousands. Yellow was the factory's production color; Marshall had operated a plant not far from Chell for a decade, and 'N7' was the prefix code designating one whole year of manufacture. The comprehensive also included the owner details. Stone could collate, looking for a vehicle owned by a blonde woman, but it would be a wild gamble. Too wild. He needed much more to go on.

"That's the lot, Raven Leader," the controller at Chell Field told him. "What else?"

"Tracking," Stone said. "Give me a comprehensive of all civilian Skyvans tracked ex-Chell in the last hour."

"Coming up," she responded, and the data sped through his deck, columns of numbers flickering across the blue comm-relay terminal.

The results of the file search were less daunting. Only twelve had departed, tracked out of the city's airspace via the domestic network, which covered an area with a three thousand kilometer radius about the spaceport. Nine of the 'vans had landed again within that area. Now the hard work began, and Stone knew it would be a ballbreaker. "Thanks, Chell

Field," he muttered. "Shut down."

To better operate the deck's delicate keypad he broke the wrist seals and drew off the armored gloves, broke the neck seal and lifted off the helmet. He took his first breath of the chemical soup that passed for air here, and coughed as his lungs rebelled. How Jarrat had worked in this muck was beyond him. He thumbed the switch that brought down the canopy and locked it, and transferred to internal air.

His fingers pattered quickly over the keys, running collation after collation. Destination of tracked Skyvans against the owner details of vehicles registered in those centers ... Skyvans owned or operated by women in the cities where the 'vans had put down. The data was sketchy and untrustworthy. He was taking a long-shot, and he knew it. The tracked 'vans could have belonged to people on course for their favorite boozer or cathouse, and who would push on for home in the morning.

Only one fact remained: one of the dozen 'vans had Kevin Jarrat aboard. The odds were that it had landed again, not three thousand kilometers away. When it took off again it would be tracked onward by regional, urban flight directors. It was a trail that could be followed.

And if the 'van were one of those that had not landed, and which had flown off the network into the outcountry? Stone did not like to think about it. It gave the 'van a long head start into the jumble of civilian traffic. The only way out of the maze was to investigate three thousand Marshall Skyvans whose registration began with the prefix 'N7.' An impossible task. If the 'van had flown out of the Chell air tracking network and into the civilian muddle of the 'outdistricts,' Kevin was on his own. *Really* on his own. If he had been snatched by a Death's Head runner, God help him. Stone scanned the listed destinations of the nine 'vans that had landed.

Paris, Hallelujah, Easy Street, Avey, Hobart, Sugarloaf, Paddington, Salt Lake, and Petergate. The only practical course was to check out each one individually, cross-reference with the regional flight directors, match tracking data with registrations ... and hope.

He touched the headset tuner. "Blue Ravens, return to the gunship, pull out ... Raven Leader to *Athena*. Raven Leader to —"

"Carrier," said the radio, with Mischa Petrov's thick Russian voice. He was a NARC lieutenant, four years Stone's junior, ambitious, determined, efficient. "What's doing, Stoney? Is Jarrat there or isn't he?"

"No," Stone told him, "but I got a few steers, we might find him."

"But he's dead," Petrov protested.

"He's not," Stone snapped. "I want a half-dozen support troops from Green Raven down here. Armed, but forget the armor, it's not aggro, just legwork. Call Chell Tactical, requisition transport — the flying variety. We've got a lot of ground to cover. Stand by for datafeed." He made the transmission of everything he had as he brought the shuttle's flight systems alive. "You got that, Mischa?"

"I got it," Petrov returned. "It looks like a damn wild goose chase."

"And if it was you out there with your nuts in a grinder, I suppose you'd recommend I ditch you and send home for a replacement?" Stone snarled. "Jarrat's my partner, it's my wild goose chase — privilege of rank, if you like. Move your ass, Mischa."

"Or get it kicked?" Petrov chuckled. "All right, *Captain,* I hear you talking. *Athena* out."

Stone keyed the headset back to the personal band as the sun-bright wash of the gunship's floods lit up the night. The ship was low, not much above the rooftops as it came in for the extraction. Big, heavy, slab shaped, quilled like a porcupine with its cannons and sensor probes, haloed by its floods and riding a storm of repulsion. He would have to wait until it pulled out before lifting off, or the downwash of the heavy lift engines would toss the shuttle about like a toy. He watched it loom over the rooftops across from the Rand limousine. "Blue Raven 6."

"Right here, Cap," Cronin answered, "above you at fifty meters and going up. Soon as your flank guards extract we'll be out of your way."

"Copy that." Stone looked left and right to watch the mirror-black locust shapes of the riot troops feather upward on their suit repulsion.

They rose into the corona of the gunship's lights and were gone. The ship itself lifted straight up before angling its blunt nose for orbit. As the hurricane of gravity-resist diminished Stone ran up his own jets and folded the landing gear. The fifty-tonne feather bobbed up and he jinked the nose skyward. His instruments registered the radar observation from Chell Field. They were tracking him as they tracked the Skyvans, the domestic cargo haulers, the clippers, anything and everything that moved through their space. Stone glanced at the CRT to review the flight data.

Where did he begin? Stick a pin in the list and start from there. For no particular reason he turned the shuttle's nose for Hobart.

"Where the hell are you, Kevin?" he whispered, under the range of the audio pickup. "You've really done it this time." Jarrat's service record, Army and NARC alike read like a novel. He had a history of 'pushing the outside of the envelope' to see where it would break. Where Stone himself was inclined to stand off, calculate, play the odds as if NARC's business were one vast poker tournament, Jarrat plunged in, willing to take risks to get results. And he did get results, for which NARC loved him ... almost as much as Stone had come to love him, albeit for vastly different reasons. Kevin Jarrat was one of a kind. He had run the wild side since he was no more than a child, and a lot of the tear-away kid who had somehow survived his youth on Sheckley was still inside him.

Stone had heard all his stories, told over beers in off-duty hours. Sheckley was a halfway station, servicing the rimrunners. It had always been rough, but it was rotting with Angel by the time Kevin was ten or twelve years old. Stone often wondered how Jarrat, growing up in a hospice, had not simply run with the Angelpack and become a statistic before he was twenty. Kevin possessed the physical beauty that unlocked city bottom's doors. The sweet, rank world of the Angelhead was never far away.

But Jarrat had survived. Stone's heart went out to the kid who had never known his parents, who buried his friends and lovers while he himself was still little more than a child, and as soon as he was old enough, signed an Army enlistment form. It was his one-way ticket out of the dangerous, ugly rat-circus of Sheckley.

Courage was at the core of the man Kevin Jarrat *was*. Stone had lusted for him on sight, respected him later, as he worked alongside him, and before long loved Jarrat for himself. Kevin was complex, a bundle of contradictions with a hot, quick temper, a ferocious intellect, a wide stubborn streak and a capacity for compassion which could still surprise Stone.

The irony struck Stone keenly: every element about Jarrat which had soon made Stoney come to love him had also driven Kevin into more tight corners than either of them cared to remember. It was only ever a matter of time before Kevin did not make it out alive. Rueful, reluctant, Stone admitted to himself, he had been waiting for this day — never quite expecting it, yet always allowing for its possibility.

Hazard went with the territory. NARC suffered higher field casualties than Starfleet, the Army or Tactical. Its operatives accepted the odds when they took the job, because NARC was very close to a vocation. Stone had always assumed he would accept the inevitable, when at last he lost Jarrat, with stiff, professional resignation and dignity. Now it was happening, and he realized how absurd the assumption had been.

As the shuttle tipped a wing and climbed in a steep arc, beginning a ballistic fast-track toward Hobart, he lit the afterburners to hurry the pace.

CHAPTER SiX

The clinic had parking space on the roof. Evelyn Lang had set the yellow Marshall Skyvan down there half an hour before and now she stood with the medic she had known since the war, looking at the mangled body on the gurney. It was feeding him slowly into the cavity of a PET scanner. He was on oxygen and they were running his heart mechanically. He was not about to die, but unassisted he was unable to live. The bitter irony of technology gnawed at her. On the one hand it killed, on the other it preserved life that would otherwise be forfeit.

Simon had wandered away in search of food and amusement but Evelyn was too preoccupied with the stranger to eat. She hung on every word the medic would say. His name was enameled on the tag clipped to his collar: Jeff Bolt. She knew him as Medic Sergeant Bolt, a good friend and a thorough professional. Bolt was forty now, balding, clad in a pale blue surgical smock, faded denims and red carpet slippers. He looked more like a post-grad obstetrics student than a crack combat medic, but she had seen him prove his worth a hundred times in the field. The war on Sheal was long, bloody. No one who fought there, for either of the two vast combatant engineering corporations, would ever escape the bitter memories.

But Bolt was shaking his head as he read off the PET scanner's data. "You're going to have to take this baby to a specialist," he said doubtfully. "I'm just a cut-and-stick wallah. This poor bastard needs the real thing. A nerve-knitter. Jesus Christ, look at the readouts."

She craned her neck to see the screen. "Gibberish to me, sweetie. It needs subtitles."

He touched a toggle on the side control panel. The gurney rolled back through the tube of the scanner and began a second pass. This time Bolt interpreted what he saw. "Well, he's got six — no, seven busted ribs for starters. The spleen is ruptured and he's bleeding into his gut from punctures here, here —" pointing at the graphic "— and the rectum."

"The rectum?" Evelyn shot a glance at the medic's sour profile. "You mean he was raped?"

"That's putting it mildly, lovie. Fisted, I should say, enthusiastically. Never mind, I can mend all that, quit your worrying. He's a toughie, is this one. I keep wondering how come he isn't just plain dead. See here? The pelvis is broken, he's got a disc out here, and the hip's disjointed ... shit,

47

look at his knee. The kneecap's gone. Femur's busted in three places. Who the hell did this?"

"I'll give you three guesses," she said darkly.

The body rolled through until the man's chest and head were in the tube of the scanner. Bolt swore beneath his breath. "The skull is fractured here, and there too ... hello, he's bleeding into his brain. And the lung, what else is new? He's lost so much blood you'd swear a vampire'd sucked him dry. His brain must be black and blue. Bloody great edema, see?"

The streams of data were no more than meaningless numbers to Evelyn. She said nothing, watched the machine swallow the man and scan him again. The old Positron Emission Tomography device was older than she was, and rattling like a coffee grinder, but Bolt swore it was regularly serviced by certified techs from Intelscan itself, and in good order.

"He's lucky the gray matter hasn't hemorrhaged too badly," Bolt mused. "It's bad enough but the brain could have been sloshing in buckets of the red stuff. He's got clotting around the frontal lobes, though. That's going to be a big, big problem. Damnit, Eve, I'm not a microsurgeon."

She met his eyes levelly. "Just do what you can for him."

Bolt sighed. "Shit, lady, I knew you'd say that." He returned to the machine and shook his head over the readouts. "Broken jaw, broken nose. Most of his teeth are busted. Christ, the left retina's detached." He rolled the gurney back out of the machine and turned off the scanner before giving her a cynical look. "They got in one pretty good kick where it hurts most, but he's a lucky pup —"

"Lucky?" Evelyn demanded angrily.

"Yeah, damned lucky," Bolt agreed. "His balls are bruised but nothing's ruptured, or his whole perspective on life could have changed. Who the hell did this, anyway? Stop dropping hints for chrissakes."

She shrugged. "Death's Head, must've been. It's a safe bet he got up and sassed them. You just don't do that in this world, Jeff. If you do, this happens to you." She folded her arms and looked at the man on the gurney. "I didn't want to take him to Chell General, so I brought him here."

"You'd have done better if you'd taken him into the big crash shop in the city," Bolt said carefully. "Some of this work, I'm just not capable of. But I see your point. Death's Head have eyes and ears everywhere, it'd be easy for them to just go in and finish the job right there on the ward."

"Yes." Evelyn bit her lip and studied her old friend's face. "What can you do for him?"

Bolt stirred and rubbed the back of his neck. "Not as much as he needs. I can sort out the spleen, weld tissue, dispel the old blood. Laser work, nothing complicated, no cutting involved, so he won't get any more traumatized than he already is. I can weld his bones back together and seal off the lung."

It was standard battlefield patch-up work, performed on the sidelines of a skirmish, often as not in the back of whatever vehicle was on hand. Evelyn remembered a Medevac skimmer crash she had not walked away from. Combat medics pulled her out of the ruins of her aircraft moments before the engines detonated. Both her legs were shattered. The bones were welded at the aid station, a prefab hooch in a ditch. Twenty-four hours later she walked out and returned to duty. Bolt had done the work.

"I'll yank his teeth while I'm at it, and seal up the lacerations around his lips," the medic was saying thoughtfully. "The teeth'll have to go, nothing's salvageable. You'd swear someone crammed a boot into his mouth."

"Jesus." She closed her eyes and he saw her shudder.

"Hey, Evie." He touched her shoulder. "I'll give him the best I've got here, decent hospital plates. Take him to a good dental mechanic in Eldorado, get some proper work done ... if it's worth it. I mean, you know his brain is busted up, don't you? A real microsurgeon might be able to take a crack at it, but I'm just not in that league, kiddo." He paused, rubbed his chin. "I can drain these bruises, he can do without thrombosis. Get the blood out of his brain, try and see how much damage has been done. I'll do that now, and get after the spleen, fix the lung and bones and such. But his left knee doesn't even *exist* anymore, and the brain and the detached retina are out of my class. This is a clinic, not a cityside crash shop. I fix herpes, deliver babies and supply prophies to the prudent. I just don't get this kind of work. Christ, the last neuro job I saw was a kid from up the street, and I sent him to Chell General to get his foot stapled back on after the stupid sod of a father ran over it with a weeder."

"Do what you can," Evelyn murmured. "Look, fix him up so I can get him as far as Ballyntyre. There are some good cutters in Eldorado. Microsurgeons. I've read about them."

"That's going to cost real money, lady," Bolt said darkly. "This kid is *busted*. Understand what you're getting for your investment. Those cutters in Eldorado could take a crack at him, make a bigger mess of his head than it already is, and cheerfully hand you a six-figure bill."

She gave him a hard look and he nodded. "I know a cutter over there who owes me a few favors," Evelyn said very quietly and very reluctantly.

"So do I," Bolt said acidly, looking at the woman's angular, striking profile. "You're talking about Harry Del, aren't you?"

"You know him?" She was not surprised. Del had a reputation. Perhaps the wrong reputation.

Bolt obviously thought so. "I know him by rep, not personally. The man's not a cutter. Is he?" Bolt pressed.

"Yeah, as a matter of fact he is. He's a damned good cutter." She spoke defensively, aggressively.

Bolt held up his hands as if an gunpoint. "Have it your way, Evie. But I do know the man's a *healer*. Oh, he'll cut and patch the same as the rest of us, sure. But if you give him half a chance he'll get in there and pull stunts I've only heard about. He's a frigging *deviant*. I don't like them. They work on instinct, like playing a hunch. They can't even properly describe what they do — damnit, they don't *know* how they do what they do! But they're happy to get inside a person's body, into the *brain*, and meddle in there." Bolt shook his head. "You know me, kiddo. I'm as easygoing as the next guy, but as a point of professional ethics I won't work with them. It's just not my scene, and I'd take a lot of convincing otherwise."

And Bolt was not alone in his feelings. Evelyn had never been sure what she felt herself. She had known Harry Del for many years, called him a friend, and done him a lot of favors that could be called in when the time was right. But what Del did in the course of his work was beyond anything medical technology understood, and Bolt was right. Even Harry could barely begin to explain or describe his artistry.

"What works is what works," she said softly. "People like Harry do heal people."

"They're parasites." Bolt made a sour face and looked away. "Devos, the whole bunch of them."

She leaned on the PET machine's hooded viewscreen. "I'm not so sure. I watched him fix a woman the rest had given up for dead. She was a bad-tempered, sour old bitch with a big mouth, and when she got hit by a speedy car, who the hell cared? Half her head was punched in, the brains were leaking out of her. Del welded her skull back together, knitted up the nerves he could get at with a probe, and she was a vegetable. She sat in a chair and peed into a bottle taped to her leg for a month. If she'd been a dog they'd have shot her. Harry did whatever it is he does. I admit, no one seems to know what it is — and even he isn't fully sure. But that old woman is *still* a bad tempered bitch with a big mouth. She's alive."

Bolt forewent any comment and at last Evelyn asked, "What about this kid, though? He isn't going to be like her, is he?"

"I don't know. Let me get the blood out of his skull, drain the edema, dispel the bruising. We might get lucky." But Jeff sounded much less than optimistic. When the woman did not respond for some moments he took her arm. "Evie, you have to think this through right now. He's your responsibility, not mine. He's in a mess. Understand that. Borderline case."

She knew what he was saying. If Bolt operated to mend what he could, put the pieces back together, she would be responsible for a complete stranger with probable brain damage. The alternative was to turn off the life support machines right now, strop dragging out the drama, and let him slip away peacefully. "You'd let him die, would you?"

"I didn't say that," Bolt said carefully.

"Harry Del might not be the best option in the world, but he's the only one this kid's going to get," Evelyn said without inflection.

"Evie, the man is a deviate, he's got the bloody T/87 mutant gene!"

"I know. It makes him a *healer*," she retorted. "What, Jeff, fancy-dancing around that hypocritical oath of yours? That's not the guy I use to know who said, 'Hey man, whatever works, right?'"

Exasperated, he gave her a push. "Shove off. I owe you a favor or three myself. If you want to call them in on his account, that's your business. I'll do the work, the best way I know how. Pump some blood into him, fix everything I can fix. Jesus, get in there and seal off the intestine — you know he's poisoning himself while we stand here and chat! I'll even lend you a life support unit, in case he hits trouble on the way east, if you promise — on pain of hump! — you'll bring it back the next time you're out this way. If my boss finds me short one I'll be strung up by the balls."

"On pain of hump?" She echoed, and chuckled. "I never knew you fancied me, Medic Sergeant."

"You bloody well never bothered to find out," Bolt muttered, flustered and coloring. He gave the battered body a frown. "So who is he, anyway?"

She shrugged. "Just another Death's Head victim."

"There's no Angel in his bloodstream."

"Thank Christ." She touched Bolt's shoulder briefly. "Look, do your stuff, Jeff, and thanks. After this I'll owe you one, I reckon."

He lifted one eyebrow at her. "Repayable in horizontal heaven. If ever you're in the mood, *Sergeant,* I've got a year or two going spare."

Evelyn ran her fingers through her long blonde hair. "I'll keep it in mind. Jeff. Give me a yell when you get out of the OR, will you?"

"Sure." Bolt nodded. "But don't hold your breath. This'll take at least six hours. The damage is massive. It's one hell of an investment to make for a guy whose name you don't even know."

"So Simon keeps telling me," Evelyn sighed. "Call it one for Stevie. I just couldn't walk past this one. You know what I'm trying to say? Do it for Stevie if not for me."

Bolt looked levelly at her, seeing sincerity in her blue eyes. He smiled faintly. "Maybe I'll do it for the both of you," he said quietly, and turned away toward the waiting OR.

Sirens whooped into the offloading bay three floors below. Evelyn came awake with a start and peered at the chrono on the wall. It was two in the morning and she was cramped, stiff from sleeping in the chair. Simon had stretched out and was asleep on the couch, but otherwise the waiting room was deserted. She sat up, rubbed her back and yawned. Surely Bolt must be finished by now.

She got her feet under her and wandered stiffly in search of him. The night nurse on the desk was dozing over a cup of coffee. He had his feet up on another chair and a magazine open in his lap. She saw the centerfold, two brown-skinned boys with wrist-thick cocks, tied in a knot of oiled limbs and sucking for all they were worth. Evelyn whistled at the picture and the nurse looked up, startled. He turned the magazine to give her the full view and she shook her head over the models. They were enough to make a grown woman weep. Or a grown man. The nurse was drooling.

"Is Jeff out of the OR yet?"

"He got through just a few minutes ago." The young man yawned. "I had a message from him ... Jeez, look at the time."

"Right." Evelyn leafed through the magazine. "So where is he?"

Beautiful male bodies appeared in every possible contortion, in lace, in leather, in silk and oil. The fuck scenes were breathtaking.

"Why don't you treat yourself to a peek at page 80, and I'll give him a buzz," the nurse offered dryly.

"Thank you kindly," she said mock-sweetly, and turned to the page he suggested as he reached over and thumbed Jeff's beeper. Two young Adonises on velvet cushions, cocks crossed like swords as they kissed ravenously. "Bee-autiful," she admitted, and handed back the magazine.

"Jeff's in ICU," the nurse told her. "You want to see the patient?"

"If he's finished. Look, go back to sleep. I know my way around."

He gave her a withering look. "Please yourself."

Evelyn circuited the desk, turned right into a half-lit side passage and walked by the trauma wards and third floor surgery. The ICU bay was on the right, brightly lit behind swing doors. Through the observation window she could see Bolt. He stood at a water cooler with one hand on the back of his neck and a glass of dissolving ketophen in the other.

She pushed through the swinging doors. He turned toward the sound of footfalls as she approached. "Tough job?"

"Tough, she calls it," Bolt grumbled. "You don't owe me *one* for this, sweet thing, you owe me a half-dozen. You just wait till I call 'em in! I have a skull-cracker the size of this building. But I did the best I could." He swallowed the painkillers and coughed, waving at one of the three occupied beds in the small ward. "There's your boy. What's left of him."

He lay so still, she would not have known the difference if he had been dead. Even his breathing was so shallow as to be unnoticeable. His jaw had been shaved boyishly smooth, part of the medical team's prep work. An IV needle was taped into his left wrist, sensor leads connected him to the ECG monitor and oxygen tubes were in his nostrils. Evelyn moved quietly to the bed and frowned down at him. The massive bruises about his eyes, nose and mouth were gone now, only the palest discoloration remaining. His nose was mended, welded whole and set straight, and Bolt had fitted hospital dental plates after pulling the ruined teeth, so his lips were filled out and looked normal.

A temporary cast was on his left knee and a small white pad was taped over his left eye, immobilizing it to prevent further damage. Evelyn murmured in surprise as she looked down at him. He was beautiful. His skin was honey colored, his chest almost smooth with well defined muscles and a few scars. "He's been shot a couple times," she noticed.

"Jealous lovers, perhaps," Bolt muttered. "Wait till the eye's fixed. Those eyes are gray. Not blue, not green. Silver-gray. Romantic, no?"

She glanced sidelong at him. "Why, Sergeant Bolt, you're jealous."

"Jealous? Me?" Bolt demanded fatuously. "Aside from his rippling muscles, his auburn locks, his beachbum tan and a dick to die for, I can't imagine what a body'd see in him." As Evelyn laughed quietly he rubbed his aching temples. "Seriously, though, his brain is all chewed up. It's a mess in there. A real mess."

Evelyn sobered. "Is he comatose? He's not brain dead?"

"Oh, no, no, he'll wake as soon as the electrosleep wears off. By morning he should be back in the land of the living. But we can't be sure, yet, how bad the damage is. I scanned his brain several times while I was working. His motor and speech centers are intact, so he'll walk, talk, control his bladder. But the rest of it ... damage to the frontal lobes and the neural wiring between the hemispheres. I don't know, love. The truth is, there's a lot about the human brain we still don't understand. I don't know that any of the cutters in Chell or Eldorado will be able to do much for him, but by all means ask. All I know is, it'll take a smarter arse than me."

"Harry Del," Evelyn whispered.

"Harry Del. Shit." Bolt hissed through his teeth. "You haven't the *right* to let a pervo-devo loose inside another person's skull. My God, Eve, healers like Del are one jump up from basic beads and rattles. I'd as soon let a medicine man have a go at me! Okay, you don't give the proverbial flying fuck, I know. It's your business. But maybe *he* won't thank you for letting a tribal witchdoctor loose inside his head. Have you thought about that? He's going to wake up after the circus tricks are over and ask what happened. And when you tell him you let a devo get into his skull, well, he might just spit right in your eye, if he doesn't give you a black one first."

"Maybe," she admitted. "But he'd have to be alive and awake and aware to do that." She looked down at the patient. "You find any ID tattoos on him? Unit badges, something military, maybe Starfleet?"

But Bolt shook his head. "Nope, nothing at all. Was there anything near the body when you found him?"

"Just his clothes, ripped to rags. They just tore them off him and threw them away ... speaking of which, how's his butt, Jeff?"

"Mended." Bolt winked at her. "He'll never be quite the shrinking virgin again — if he ever was — but he'll do, there's no harm done."

"Thanks." She smiled at him warmly. "So what do I call him? John

Citizen? What's on the paperwork?"

"John Citizen #34," Bold amended. "We files 'em like we sees 'em. I ought to give you a copy of his sheet, I suppose, so the cutter you take him to won't be working in the dark." He would not use Harry Del's name. Evelyn sighed. "Right now he's stable but don't wait too long or the eye will worsen. He might lose the sight and transplants come very, very expensive." Bolt stirred. "I reckon he'll be okay so long as he's kept quiet. There's no drugs in him, I did the whole thing under electrosleep. His bones are stronger at the welds than they were before. The organ damage patched up nicely, no problem. Spleen, lung, intestine, all ship-shape — standard combat surgery, I've been doing it for fifteen years. All by laser probe, no incisions, so he'll be on his feet as soon as the work settles in. What more can I tell you?"

"You want to keep him in ICU till he wakes?" Evelyn asked shrewdly.

"I want to try to assess how bad the brain damage really is." Then Bolt mocked himself with a wry chuckle. "What the hell am I doing this for? You're going to take him out of here and I won't see him again! And even if I did assess the damage, there's sweet bugger-all I can do about it."

"You're the same Jeff Bolt I knew years ago," Evelyn said huskily. "Dedicated. Thorough."

"Also stupid, and maybe crazy," he added, and kissed her forehead. "And dead tired. I'm going to crash for a few hours. One of the nurses will keep an eye on him and page you when he wakes."

Evelyn watched her old friend walk tiredly to an unoccupied bed in the corner of the adjacent trauma ward and sprawl face-down on it. In moments he was snoring quietly. She smiled at him and returned her attention to John Citizen. Would a nerve-knitter be able to make sense of his brain? Come to that, would Harry Del? Bolt and most other orthodox medics were scornful of the healer's strange, unresearched, unlicensed practices. How often had she heard Harry referred to as 'Del the deviate?' And Evelyn was mindful of Jeff's warnings about the high cost of neuro work in one of the uptown hospitals in Eldorado or any big city.

If the work was successful and John was mended, the pricetag would have been earned. But they served their bills just as quickly for failures. Exasperated, anxious, Evelyn settled to wait. First, the patient had to wake.

Dawn had flushed rosily cross the sky before the deep electrosleep began to wear off. Evelyn had dozed most of the time on a diagnostic bed in the surgery and heard Bolt's name over the quiet public address. He had just roused when the call went through, and was sitting on the side of a bed in the trauma ward, knuckling eyes which were still bloodshot, testimony to his night's work.

A nurse leaned into the deserted ward. "Dr. Bolt? Your crash job is waking. You'll want to be there."

The cardio-monitor displayed a steady beat of forty a minute, and Bolt checked the computer. The patient's heart was completely stable and had been for hours. He disconnected the ECG leads while Evelyn watched, and slipped the IV needle out of John Citizen's wrist.

"He's not doped but he's going to be shocky, remember," Bolt warned as he played a little mediscanner to and fro over the work he had done. "Do I do good work, or do I? Look at this. The welds have started to settle already. Most of it wasn't a problem, just the old jigsaw puzzle. I'd forgotten how good I used to be at this! And I caught the intestine before peritonitis could get started. The lung perforations were a fiddle, but it looks like we're home free." He turned off the scanner and holstered it securely in the right hip-pocket of his jeans. "Heart is fifty, pulse is strong, BP is only a little low, nothing he'd notice. Physically he's doing good."

Physically? Evelyn held her tongue and came to the bedside. "The nurse said he's stirring."

"Increased alpha wave activity. She must have been scanning," Bolt murmured. "Ah. Here he comes. Speak quietly, Evie, and don't make any quick moves. I'm going to scan his brain but I don't want him to notice what I'm doing. Get his attention if you can, and hold it."

"How?" Evelyn whispered, but Bolt was too busy to answer. He had moved to the head of the bed, with its array of equipment, and had the scanner probe in his left hand, out of the patient's line of sight. A little red light winked on as he activated it, and he held it just a few centimeters from the young victim's hair. Even then the unbandaged eye was opening to a slit showing a dilated pupil.

Evelyn tried to smile at him. "Hello." She spoke little above a whisper. He blinked and swallowed. His hands twitched on the white sheet. She moved closer. "I don't know what to call you. How do you feel? I expect you're aching a lot. You're a lucky kid, you know." The beautiful mouth opened and she saw perfect, white dental plates, the best Bolt could get. Not as natural as designer-work but very serviceable, very bright. Was he trying to speak? His gullet twitched repeatedly.

"Are you thirsty? Would you like a drink? I don't know if you can sit up yet." She looked up at Bolt, who touched a switch on the keypad which cranked up the top of the bed, raising the patient almost to a sitting position. Bolt's face was set into grim lines. His attention was on the scanner, so Evelyn went to the nearby watercooler for a small paper cup. She held it to the young man's lips and he drank thirstily. A little dribbled on his chin and she sopped it up with a corner of the sheet. "There. Better? Can you speak now?"

His brow creased and one hand lifted, feeling for the bandage over his eye. Evelyn caught his wrist before he could touch and perhaps dislodge the dressing. "It's all right. You've been badly hurt but you'll be fine. What's your name?" She looked up at Bolt, who was still intent on the scanner. "Are you aching? I should think they've got some pills around here somewhere. What shall I call you?"

His mouth opened again. He took a deep breath and his good eye blinked at the room. He was becoming aware of his surroundings now, and Evelyn held his hand tightly. Surprisingly, his fingers grasped onto hers strongly, and would not let go. She said no more but waited for him to find his bearings. Above and behind him, Bolt was still taking readings.

A soft moan was his first sound, and when he spoke she had to strain to hear. "Don't 'stand," he whispered. "Where's this? What's happening?" His voice was faint, the words indistinct.

"You were injured," she repeated. "Have you forgotten?"

"Was I?" He blinked at her and yawned, which seemed to hurt his jaw and neck. "Hurts." His voice was breathy, his words indistinct.

"I'm not surprised," Evelyn said softly. "You could probably use a shot.

What's your name, beautiful?"

Again his brow creased. "Don't you know?"

"No. I just found you in the street, thoroughly banged up. You don't remember your name?"

He yawned again, more deeply. "Forgot. Who're you, then? Why does my knee hurt so bad?" The speech was slurred, guileless, soft. The gray eye looking up at Evelyn was filled with thoughtless trust.

With a blinding flash of intuition she knew what the computer probe had been trying to diagnose and affirm for minutes. She caught her breath and looked up at Bolt. He had just turned off the scanner and nodded mutely. Evelyn's heart twisted with pain. She forced a smile as she looked down at the young man. "Your knee is still damaged. We'll fix it, John, don't you worry." She touched his face and wriggled her hand free of his. "You rest. I'll see if I can get you something for the aches and pains."

Bolt beckoned her into the little exam cubicle off to one side of the ward and spoke in a regretful undertone. "I warned you."

Her eyes were misted. "He's a child, isn't he?" The medic nodded. "A beautiful, crippled child. Oh, God."

"I ... did what I could to warn you," Bolt sighed.

"I know you did! And you'd have turned off the machines and let him die last night, would you?"

"That's a tough question," Bolt admitted. "But what's to become of him, Eve. Where does he go from here?"

"I don't know." She raked her fingers through her hair, tousling it. "He doesn't seem to know who he is or where he comes from. In any case, if we sent him back to Chell, Death's Head would only finish what they started. So you're right, I suppose he's my responsibility."

"Yes." Bolt looked across the ward at the man he had put back together. "I'm sorry, really. There was no more I could do. He was just too busted up. The eye and the knee are out of my league, which probably means you'll ask Del to do the cutting work, since he owes you one, same as I did. Note my use of the past tense." She nodded, lost in thought as she studied the young man. Bolt touched her shoulder. "Don't let that deviate loose in his head." But Evelyn did not even acknowledge that she had heard and Bolt sighed again. "Well, go your own way, like you always do. But remember, he's as likely to paralyze you as thank you."

"I know, I know." Evelyn rubbed her face hard. "Give him a shot. He's hurting. Will you have breakfast with me? You must be off-shift by now."

"Hours ago," Bolt yawned. "You'll be wanting to shove off home soon, I expect."

Evelyn looked at the time. "I'm so long overdue they'll be calling Tac and listing me as a missing person! I've got to get moving soon. Is he well enough to travel?"

"So long as you keep him immobile. His big trouble is the knee. I couldn't do much but splint it. If it doesn't get attention he's going to have a granddaddy of a limp, for life. That at least I suppose I'd trust Del to mend. Look, you and Simon go up to the cafeteria, I'll pump some good, old-fashioned tetraphine into John Citizen, and meet you there after I've got your life support unit organized. I don't think he'll need it, but better safe than sorry."

She stood in the ward's open doorway to watch a nurse administer the shot. John's head rolled back onto the pillows as the fierce aches began to ease, and Evelyn returned to the waiting room, wondering how she was going to explain affairs to Simon. Her brother was a stubborn, insensitive little sod. He was still asleep on the couch and she shook his shoulder to rouse him. "Rise and shine, junior. We'll have breakfast here and then get moving. I'll drop you at home and then I've got a call or two to make. Got to look in and see Harry."

"About the guy we picked up?" Simon sat up, yawned and rubbed the sleep out of his eyes. "Bolt didn't fix him, then?"

"There's still some work to be done," Evelyn said evasively. Thankfully, Simon did not question this, and followed her to the elevator.

The clinic's cafeteria was one floor below the vehicle park on the roof, with a view out across 'Paddy,' a quiet backwater far removed from the hustle and smog of Chell. The sky here was blue, the hills burned brown by the equatorial sun. Evelyn ordered coffee and croissants and settled to wait for Bolt. Simon ate steadily but Evelyn was not hungry. She was haunted by the young stranger. Intellectually handicapped. A child, Bolt said. Beautiful, crippled. Helpless. Her responsibility. One for Stevie? She swallowed her coffee without tasting it as Bolt appeared from the elevator.

"I've got you the life support unit but he's not going to need it, his latest readings are excellent. Everything is settling down. Here." He handed over a folded paper, which Evelyn pocketed. "His sheet, comprehensive notes for ... for *Doctor* Del to work from." He slid in at the table and helped himself to croissants and apricot chutney. "Why don't you call me when you've decided what to do with him?" Evelyn frowned at him. "That is," Bolt added, "there are institutions to take care of people like him."

"People like him?" Simon muffled through a mouth full of food. "What's that mean?"

"Brain damaged," Evelyn said quietly.

Simon's cup clattered onto the table. He swallowed the food unchewed. "Brain damaged? You mean he's a vegetable? After all that, after we spent all night here, he's a friggin' cabbage?"

"No, he's not a cabbage." Bolt cuffed the boy's head none too playfully. "But he sustained some crash damage that might not be repairable. It happens to a lot of people, folks who make a habit of writing off their transportation. Think about it, Eve. There's a sanitorium in the hills south of here. I can pull strings, get you a referral. I know some people."

She closed her eyes and nodded. "I'm going to come up owing you the shirt off my back, aren't I?"

"And what's under it." Bolt winked lewdly at her. "Look, get John in the 'van and get going before the shot wears off. I'll give you some pills he can pop that'll get him to Ballyntyre, then he's in Del's tender care." The last was said dubiously and Bolt shrugged. "I don't even want to know what Del does with him, all right? I'll just get mad as hell. Again."

"I won't say a word," Evelyn said softly, soberly. She took both the medic's skilled hands with a nostalgic smile. "It's been a lot like old times."

"You mean, you fly 'em in, I patch 'em up? Don't remind me! I still get nightmares." Jeff Bolt shuddered animatedly. "I'll get the gear organized and call up a gurney team for you. You're parked on the roof?"

Ten minutes later the yellow Marshall Skyvan was open and two beefy orderlies in green clinic coveralls manhandled the gurney in through the rear hatch over the engines. John was too drowsy on tetraphine to know what was happening. He woke for only a moment as Evelyn ran up the straps and bucked him down tight for the ride. He smiled at her, the ready, guileless smile of a child who trusted implicitly. Evelyn bit her lip until she tasted blood, forced a smile to reassure, but he was already asleep again.

The life support unit was a box the size of a suitcase, bleeding leads and tubes. Bolt had stuffed it into a large plastex bag and she wedged it under the strapped-down gurney before slamming and locking the hatch. Bolt was standing in the plate glass foyer which opened into the blustery vehicle park. She sketched him a salute. "I'll see you when I see you, Jeff!"

"And bring the machine back, or the buggers'll make me pay for it!" Bolt called as he waved.

The gullwings locked down and Evelyn fired up the flight systems. The navigation deck came on and she punched in destination coordinates and speed. As soon as the 'van was airborne she could recline the seat and sleep most of the way to Outbound, which was more than eight hours away. Ballyntyre lay two hours beyond, on across the ocean.

The engines pushed the Skyvan up off the roof and Evelyn keyed in the automatics. After the restless, uncomfortable night she was tired to the bone. In the back, John was sound asleep on the shot, but still Evelyn was disturbed. The knowledge that the beautiful stranger was a retard ate at her. Her mind went back again and again to Stevie. Sixteen years old, stone-cold dead and looking forty, the legacy of Angel. By comparison with Stevie Lang, John was still lucky. He was brain damaged but he was alive and would soon be well. Intellectual handicap was not uncommon. And unlike Stevie, John had never taken Angel.

If he had, he would have been an addict on his way to premature old age and joyous death. There was no way back from the first encounter with Angel. After that it was downhill all the way, while Death's Head and syndicates like it grew rich and fat. Armies of John Citizens and Steven Langs were swept up every day by icehouses in Chell and every other city across this planet, and every other colony world, right back to Earth itself.

CHAPTER SEVEN

The *Athena's* shuttle stood in the full blaze of the equatorial sun, parked among the private luxury craft belonging to businessmen and the unspeakably rich. Stone had stopped even wondering where the uptown barons got the money. They had the magic touch and he had not, it was as simple as that. But the shuttle made the civilian craft look cheap and tacky, and it was *his*. He found an intense gratification in the thought.

He stood in the programmer's office in the Air Traffic Control building on the airfield outside Easy Street. From the vantage point of five levels he had an uninterrupted view of the launch and landing facilities. Not much was moving. The air outside the armorglass shimmered with heat. Haze made the middle distance into a mirage lake of water as blue as the sky.

Stone cracked a third can of beer and perched on the edge of the programmer's desk. Behind it sat a woman with hair the color of warm yellow sandstone, green eyes and a painted, smiling mouth. He looked down to watch her fingers work the keyboard. She wore a blouse and side-split skirt and he could see through the fabric of both. She was naked beneath.

He found the woman disturbing, and not because she stirred him to lust. On another day his flattered ego might have inspired a response. Today his attention ran as far as Jarrat. There were, he admitted to himself, many similar days lately. He watched the programmer arch self-consciously to thrust ruby-tipped breasts against the sheer blouse. It was all deliberate and he sighed. He could never prevent himself from comparing such self-conscious deliberation with Kevin's easy, artless charm. The woman seemed to be waiting to be propositioned. On another occasion he might have cynically surrendered to whim, but not now. He was too preoccupied and the wanton provocation merely annoyed. Jarrat was gone, and the thought consumed him.

The programmer's name was Candice Kwan, but she did not look at all Asian. Bloodlines were too mixed up to tell anymore, on colony worlds where several generations had now passed since the immigrant sleeper ships arrived. Stone himself was a mix, as most Londoners were. Kevin had been born offworld and since he had no family, no real idea of his parentage, he could only guess at his pedigree. Stone saw a lot the Celt in him, a touch of the Norse or Slav, and perhaps ten generations ago, some Asian addition to his bloodline, which gave his eyes their almond shape.

Intent on Jarrat, Stone had not been aware of the woman in minutes. He returned to the present as she sat back in the molded plastic chair and read off the data coming up on the screen. He drained the beer and lobbed the can into the waste bin. "How much longer?"

"Not long." She gave him a reproachful look. The chair squealed beneath her as she shifted about, legs spreading with that studied deliberation. "It's collating now, data from as far away as South Atlantis. All we have to do is wait. It could take ten minutes, could take fifteen. Why don't you take a seat? Tell me your life story."

"I've lived longer than that." Stone smiled.

"So think of something else to do," she said silkily, suggestively.

He returned the reproachful look. "In ten minutes?"

"Could take fifteen."

He managed a chuckle. "I'll bet you double park outside the bordello."

She batted her eyelashes at him. "Why sir, you say the quaintest things. Are all you NARC men so pure at heart?"

Stone blinked at the remark. "I haven't time to go into the question, darling ... are you kinky for a bit of NARC in general, or is it me?"

The woman shrugged. "You're the first I ever saw close up without the riot armor. I'm amazed. You're human after all." She put her hand on his thigh. "You sure you don't fancy a quick one?"

Abruptly, Stone felt an upsurgence of annoyance. He took her hand, pinned on a smile and got up from his perch on the corner of the desk. "Ten minutes is *too* quick, ma'am. Maybe some other time."

Shrugging again, she returned to the screen. "Here's your data anyway. Why do these systems take half an hour when you're in a hurry and five minutes when you're trying to make a killing?"

Stone walked about the desk to look over her shoulder at the blue screen of the monitor. On it was a collation: four yellow Marshall 'vans with the registration prefix 'N7' belonged in Easy Street, in the area into which the ATC had tracked one on its landing approach. The time factor sorted the wheat from the chaff. Only one had come home at exactly the right time. It was registered to a man. "Ben Hammond," he read. "Came

home from a jaunt to Chell last night, in a 'van, reggo N74485Z." He read
down the list of data. The other 'vans in Hammond's area were not
tracked ex-Easy Street at all the previous day, so he had to be the one.
"Give me a hardcopy, will you?"

"For you, anything," Candice purred sweetly. "Do you like lasagna?"

The question made him blink. "Yeah. Why?"

"And red roses? And dancing? If you're a Capricorn I'm in love."

"I'm a Scorpio," Stone said brashly with a grin. "Nasty, obnoxious and
obsessed with sex."

"I'm still in love," she decided as the printer spat out a few sheets.
"There you are, Captain, sir. Have fun. When are you coming back this
way? You bring the roses, I'll bring the lasagna, and you can sweep me off
my feet, unless you prefer being swept off yours."

Pocketing the copies, Stone gave her a rueful look. "Thanks for your
help, darling."

"It's been a pleasure," Candice said as he turned toward the door.
"Why are the good looking ones always on the run?"

He left the office and took the elevator down to ground level. Behind
the offices and lounges, at the rear of the building, were the garages. He
had asked for a ground car and the Flight Director, Ern Bateman, had
graciously offered his own. Stone had the keys in his pocket. The car was
a new Mercedes Samurai, a sports roadster, plush and very, very expensive. It stood just inside the garage's shade with the engine casings off.

The heat was like a physical blow and the glare from outside blinded
him. He took the pilot's glasses from his pocket and perched them on his
nose as he came to rest beside the mechanic who was still working on the
Samurai. "We got a problem with this thing?"

The mechanic was a lanky youth in dark blue coveralls. A freckled face
looked up at Stone. "Nothing that can't be fixed, chief. The coupling to
the generator's up the spout. It's a pig of a job to fix it proper, so I'm just
tying it down so it'll last till you get it back. If you don't thrash it, it'll do."
He looked up over the scarlet curvature of the hatch. "You're the NARC,
aren't you?" Stone nodded. "You here to bust someone?"

"Just looking for information."

"Shit. I was hoping to see a show."

"Not this time. Sorry," Stone said dryly. "How long are you going to
be with the Samurai? Is there another car I could take?"

"Search me, chief." The youth shrugged indifferently. "I only work
here. And between you and me it's a cruddy job."

"So quit," Stone suggested in acid tones.

The youth gave him a shrewd, speculative look. "I might. What's a guy
have to do to get into NARC?"

Stone folded his arms on his blue-shirted chest. "Either you qualify in
an academic institution or you learn a trade. Computers, programming,
navigation, weapons systems, vacuum welding, nursing, pastry cook, whatever. Take your choice. Then you take your papers and use them to get
into Tactical, the Army or Starfleet. Or Intelligence, if you're a masochist.
From there you get a transfer if your work grades are up to scratch, and if
your application is approved you either get into the NARC Academy for
training as an officer —"

"Which is you?"

"You noticed. Or you could end up as a trooper, maybe in a descant unit, if you're big enough." Stone smiled thinly. "You're not. So, having a trade, you'd go from Tac or whatever to NARC and end up wielding a spanner in a launch bay, unless you junk it, go back to school and specialize in something else with brighter prospects."

The youth blinked at him. "No shit?"

"None whatsoever." Stone thrust his hands into his hip pockets. "And if you don't measure up, NARC can't and won't carry passengers. You'll rotate right back, end up as an Army or Tac mechanic. Fancy a try?"

"No," the youth muttered, "I bloody don't."

"Fancy fixing this car, then?" Stone asked with mock pleasantness. He glanced at the time. It was 15:30, shiptime. Jarrat had disappeared off the face of the planet more than twenty hours before. Already it felt like a lifetime to Stone. Longer.

In answer, the boy slammed the hatches down over the engines of the scarlet jet roadster. "It'll do. Thrash it and it'll come apart, mind you."

"Thanks. I'll remember that." Stone slid in under the wheel, levered the seat a few notches back to accommodate his long legs and twisted the key in the ignition. The electrical system came alive and the jets fired up willingly. The teardrop canopy locked into place and he shunted into reverse, backed the Samurai out of the shade of the garage and arced about the carpark toward the gate in the south boundary fence.

A man called Ben Hammond lived in a southern suburb. With any luck he would be home. He was listed as unemployed. With a little more luck he would have a tall, blonde wife who had scraped an injured man off the ground in an alleyway in Chell over twenty hours before.

John was awake but groggy. He had slept most of the way, woken for a drink and a chocolate bar at Outbound, swallowed three of Jeff Bolt's prescription painkillers, and slept again. Evelyn had let the 'van do most of the flying, and as they came up on the coastline of South Atlantis she began to listen for John to stir again. Blankets rustled as he moved and she twisted about in her seat to look back at him. In the seat beside her Simon was reading a magazine and took no interest in the survivor. Evelyn smiled as she looked down into John's face. Shadowed with beard stubble, tousled, dopy with drugs, he was still beautiful, and disturbingly vulnerable.

"Hello, John. You feeling any better?" She spoke slowly and distinctly, even then wondering how much he could understand.

"I'm hungry," he said, as if the feeling puzzled him. He lifted a hand to the bandage on his eye. "I can't see proper."

"Leave the bandage alone, sugar." She reached over to catch his hand, and smiled at him as his fingers held tightly to hers. "We'll get that eye fixed. We're headed there right now. There's a man I know."

"Hurts a bit," John said thoughtfully. His brow creased deeply. "Did I fall down or something?"

"Something like that," Evelyn said evasively. "Do you want some more pills? You still aching?"

But he shook his head and yawned. "I feel sort of funny all over. But better."

"Half your bones have been welded back together," she told him. "It takes a little while before it all settles down. So long as you're not in pain."

"Just aches now." John stretched his shoulders. He smiled sleepily, displaying Jeff Bolt's too-white hospital plates. "You're real pretty."

Surprised, delighted, Evelyn chuckled. "So are you. You're very beautiful, John."

"Am I?" His good eye widened, dark with dilation, and then his frown was back. "I don't know what I look like. Have I ever seen myself?"

"Of course you have, but you've forgotten," Evelyn said soothingly. "You rest. We're almost there. You'll be as good as new soon, I promise."

If only it were the truth. As John settled down to rest she turned back to look out at the mountains before the 'van, and Simon closed the magazine. He spoke in low tones, not that the survivor was listening. "The man's a moron. A fifth grade reject."

Anger tightened Evelyn's features. "The man is brain-busted, Simon. What do you want, miracles?"

He slammed the magazine down into the foot well. "And what the fuck are you going to do with him, Eve? Going to take him home with us, prop the door open with him, warm the bed up with him on cold nights?"

"You're a bastard, Simon," she observed bleakly. "He's my responsibility. I made the decisions, I'll pay the price."

"You sure did, and you sure will," Simon muttered. He nodded at the navdeck that was guiding the 'van into the labyrinth of the mountains. "We're making a beeline for Del's place." She glared at him. "You going to let the witchdoctor take a shot at it?"

"His knee and eye have to be looked at," Evelyn said acidly. "The rest of it ... I don't know. I don't know how much I have the right to sanction."

Simon's mouth thinned. "I'll tell you this, Eve. If you let a devo get into *my* skull, when I came to and found out, I'd be after you with a meat cleaver." He nodded at the dozing man in the back. "He'll do the same. For godsake leave well alone."

He had a point, Evelyn admitted. Many people distrusted Harry Del's *kind*. It amounted to a prejudice which could be violent and cruel. Scientists wanted to study them, the medical profession branded them as genetic deviants, a mutation taking place on Rethan in the early days after the terraformers finished. The colonists came in and the human genestrand was soon twisted, warped, by a local factor which had been overlooked. Result, Harry's *kind*. Some outdistricts had forcibly ejected them, because they were feared, misunderstood. Harry had his own horror stories to tell.

"I'll put you off at Gresham's," she offered. "You can get a ride from there." Simon would not appreciate a stopover at Harry's. He was one of those who feared and hated what was not understood. One day, Evelyn hoped, he would grow up.

The Skyvan dropped down into the graveled lot beside Gresham's timber mill and Simon hopped out. He would be home in an hour or two. A transport was on the approach road even then. He waved once and jogged away toward the vehicle. Evelyn brought down the gullwing and nudged up the throttles.

In the back John stirred, woken by the slight jolt of landing. "Are we there?" He sounded sleepy, confused.

"Not yet, sugar. Hold tight, just a little while now." She took the 'van straight up and jinked the nose around into the north. "You hungry? We'll get something to eat, soon as Harry's taken a look at you."

"More doctors?" John's voice rose. "They stuck needles in me. Hurt."

"I suppose it did." Evelyn sighed. "But you have to have your knee mended or you'll limp forever." He seemed to understand. She glanced back at him and felt the familiar wrench. Simon would say it was all for nothing. What use was it if he would be a fifth grade reject for the rest of his life? She sighed, exasperated, tired out by fretting. One thing at a time. The autofly gave a chirp as it came up on the landing coordinates and she took over the controls.

Harry Del's place was a white plantation house cocooned by lush rainforests that had to be cut back by dozers twice a year. She gazed down at the property from two hundred meters, braked to hover and hailed him on his frequency. "Harry? Come on, Harry! It's urgent, man!"

But a woman's voice answered. Evelyn recognized the throaty sound of Tansy, Harry's wife. She was thirty years younger than her husband, the fifth generation of her family to be born on this world. "Eve, is that you?"

"Sure is. Is Harry there?"

"Don't know where he is. Mucking about with the fungus, I should think," Tansy Del guessed.

"Fungus?" Evelyn echoed curiously.

"Euphorics. Mushrooms, absolutely inedible, but medicinal magic," Tansy explained. "You know Harry's pet project. He's still looking for a natural remedy to wean kids off Angel. One day he might find something. It's his dream. What's the rush, Eve?"

The 'van was settling slowly toward the pebbled courtyard at the rear of the house. Three of Harry's children stood with shaded eyes to watch it drop gently out of the sky. He had nine of them. Two were his own, one by Tansy, one by his first wife. The others were adopted and came in all colors and sizes. "I've got a patient aboard," Evelyn said. "He's stable, but he needs a cutter. Actually, he maybe needs more than a cutter, but —"

"But you've got better sense than to mess around with things you don't understand, don't want to understand," Tansy finished. "Smart lady. What's his problem?"

"Busted kneecap, detached retina, dental work. Right up your alley. He's..." She hesitated. "He's brain damaged too. I just got back from Chell, found him in the street, beaten to jelly."

The pebbles scattered away under the blustering repulsion. As the dust settled Evelyn shut down the engines and flight systems and lifted the gullwings. "There, John, we're here. You all right, sugar?" He yawned and nodded, but he was trying to rub the bandaged eye again. It was bothering him more as he began to use his good eye properly.

Tansy appeared from the house as Evelyn stepped down out of the van and unlocked the rear hatch. The engines were hot and aromatic but rapidly cooling as liquid nitrogen was pumped about them. "Hello. Tan, you're looking good," Evelyn said honestly by way of greeting. The other woman was shorter, plumper, with a ruddy complexion under a deep suntan. She dressed in the island manner, in a green kaftan and bare feet, glossy brown hair coiled up on her head. "Give me a hand to get him out."

As the back hatch opened Tansy came to peer at John Citizen's stubbled, confused face. "Oh, we're awake, are we? Okay, sweets, hang on. Grab the other end, Eve." Together, they lifted out the gurney and manhandled it onto its wheels. It rattled precariously over the pebbles toward the house's open door.

"I've got his sheet from the clinic in Paddington," Evelyn offered as they entered the cool interior. "The work was well done, but the medic couldn't do the knee. You reckon Harry can fix it? The kneecap's gone."

Tansy was intent on the patient. "I'll make something to fit in the lab, no worries. Those are hospital plates, are they?" She winked down into John's drowsy face. "Then he'll want proper teeth."

"'fraid so," Evelyn affirmed. She dropped her voice. "The bastards who did him over must've crammed a kick into his mouth. There wasn't much left, so an old friend of mine from the war yanked them and did the best he could on short notice."

"Nice work," Tansy approved as they rolled the gurney into a little infirmary and parked it. "Hardly a mark to show for it. Some of these ex-Army medics are jewels. Now, let's have a look." She unfolded the treatment sheet from the clinic and leaned against a bench to read through it.

This was Harry Del's place of business as well as his home. The west end of the building had been converted into an infirmary with two wards, an OR and several labs. Tansy was a prosthetic design engineer. She would make John Citizen a new knee, stronger and more durable than the old. Evelyn knew her work. The teeth would be beautiful. She was wearing a set of Tansy's teeth herself.

John was still, silent, watchful. As Tansy moved around to his side and took his hand he asked quietly, "You going to fix my leg? It hurts a lot."

"Absolutely I'm going to fix your knee," Tansy assured him. She had read Bolt's paper. She knew the condition of his brain and spoke slowly, clearly. "And your eye, and even your teeth."

"My mouth feels funny," John whispered. "I had an accident. Didn't I, Evie?"

"You did," Evelyn lied. "Will you let Tansy examine you?"

He nodded cautiously, but as soon as she set hands on him began to flinch. Smoothly professional, Tansy took her hands away and smiled. "No problem. I'll just set this up, then we'll get you a drink." In fact she was swiveling the electrosleep machine into position about John's head. He did not know what it was, but in moments after it began to hum he was unconscious. Tansy sighed over him. "The poor kid. Look, Eve, I'm going to find Harry. I'm an engineer, not a doctor. I can take my measurements later, but I think he ought to have some attention first."

As Tansy departed in search of her husband Evelyn sat down on the window seat to watch John's chest rise and fall regularly, thoughtlessly. She heard Tansy calling Harry's name in the glasshouses at the side of the long verandah, and then footsteps rang in the passageway outside.

She greeted the healer with a smile. Harry Del was sixty but looked fifteen years younger: genetics and endocrinology were his pet hobbies. His hair was still black, he was lean and hard, and the collagen supporting his face had not yet begun to dwindle. He was darkly tanned, with green eyes and one of the outdistrict accents. He was born in this very house, not far from Ballyntyre, where Evelyn was born. "Eve!" he said in a pleasant baritone. "Why don't you ever come here for fun? It's always work."

She shrugged. "Busy, busy. I've got a living to make, Harry!" She took his hand. "But this time I need your help. Or, more specifically *he* needs your help."

As Del came to examine John Citizen she spoke quietly, telling him everything she knew. Harry uncovered the patient and went over him with scanners and bare hands from head to foot. He checked every bone, joint, gland, organ. Evelyn watched him work, appreciating his utter profession-alism. Yet this man was a deviant, a *healer*. People like him had been stoned, shot dead, run out of towns for what they did without knowing how they did it. They had been vivisected, incarcerated. Abused by science and the public alike. Evelyn bit her lip as Tansy read aloud the report Jeff Bolt had sent. At the estimation of the extent of the brain damage Harry looked up sharply but said nothing as yet.

"He's actually in pretty good shape," he said when he turned off the scanners at last and covered the patient. "I mean, considering what he's been through. Your friend Bolt does very good work. He's mended the jaw and nose so perfectly, you won't be able to tell they were ever broken as soon as this slight discoloration fades. Say, a day or two." He looked up at his wife. "These are hospital plates, Tan. You want to do a fitting for per-manent teeth now? It'll be the longest job, that and the knee. The eye is very straightforward. His sight won't be affected, I promise you, Eve."

"Thank Christ," Evelyn breathed. "I thought it might be bad enough to go for a tranny, and even if I could afford to pay for it — which I can't — you'd never get the color to match, would you?"

"Gray is fairly rare," Del mused. "Few transplant banks store much by color, you understand. All they worry about is restoring vision!" He held a whirring probe to the patient's skull. "Why is he on electrosleep?"

Tansy stepped forward. "He started to get skittish when I tried to touch him. He still has some pain, and you saw the treatment sheet. He's in limbo, busted back to square one, Harry. Kids frighten easily. This one's a sweetie." She looked down into the stubbled, sleeping face. "How bad is it?" He showed her the scanner screen and she puffed out her cheeks.

"That bad," Harry agreed. "Anyway, one job at a time. You get your work done, or you'll be in the lab till tomorrow." She opened a case of del-icate measuring instruments in preparation for the dental design work, and Harry stepped back to allow her to take John's head in both hands. She parted his lips, wedged his mouth with a spreader and removed the hos-pital plates with surgical forceps. Evelyn looked away. "You didn't know him before, did you? Did you see his original teeth, the color?"

"No. He was a greasy heap when I found him," Evelyn said ruefully. "I can't help you there."

"Well, we'll give him a nice, white smile. Not too big, though. The root spacing says they were straight and quite regular. Hm. This is going to be interesting."

From the teeth, Tansy Del moved on to the knee. The temporary cast came off and Harry peeled away Jeff Bolt's dressing. Evelyn looked once at the gaping red mess and swore beneath her breath.

"The ligaments have gone," Del observed. "Cartilages, tendons, the lot. But the muscle is still there and I can regenerate the neural tissue. Measure him for new ligaments, Tan, and take a scan of the good knee. You'll need a pattern to set the machine up."

The woman grunted, preoccupied with her work. "You do your job, smart-arse, let me do mine!"

While they debated over the patient Evelyn stood in the background. On a computer screen appeared graphics of the materials that would soon take shape, spun out of biosynthetic compounds. Teeth, ligaments, cartil-age. All would be stronger than the man's natural tissues. Only when the probes and scans were complete did Evelyn speak again. Exasperation sharpened her voice. "But what about his head, Harry? What's the point of busting your buns to make him beautiful if all he's ever going to be is, well, Simon said a moron."

Del sighed. "Simon's young. A hard, unforgiving judge." He pulled up a chair and sat down. "Bolt's readings are accurate. The damage to his brain has robbed John of the processes of logic, analysis and foresight. Hemorrhage in the frontal lobes, and so on. But that's not all, Eve. His memory is gone, as you know. He simply can't remember things, what objects are and do, what things mean, complex words and functions. It's as if he's never seen and heard the things you and I take for granted."

She struggled to follow him. "You mean, given the chance he might be able to relearn a lot? Learn how to be an ordinary person?"

"Given even half the chance," Harry affirmed. "He's a blank slate, Eve. Who ever said there's anything wrong with being a kid? Like a kid, he should be able to learn many things. He's young, he'll soon be fit and strong. Intellectual handicap is not the end of the world."

"But he's a retard," Evelyn whispered. "Literally a child."

Again, Harry sighed. "Most of us remember childhood as the best part of our lives, before the pain and hardship set in. I do believe he has the capacity to learn, though as things stand, he'll never be what you or I would call bright. Of course he'll need someone to take responsibility for him. Take care of him. Is this what's troubling you?"

A sudden flicker of guilt flushed her cheeks. "I can't take him home with me, Harry. I'll end up knocking Simon's head off. Jeff told me about an institution, a sanitorium outside Paddy, for people like him."

"Expensive, to keep him there," Harry said dubiously.

"I know." Evelyn rubbed her face. "I'm starting to think I might have made a mistake, Harry."

"How can saving a man's life be a mistake?" Tansy demanded.

"But what can I do for him? Christ," Evelyn muttered, "I never thought it would come to this." She paced between the examination bench and the window. "Simon wanted to call Chell Tactical for a meat wagon. He'd have been in Chell General right now if I had."

Harry followed her to the window and took her arms in both hands. His fingers dug into the muscle, hurting, making her focus. "Is that what you want? To turn him over into the hands of an institution?"

"A sanitorium for people like him, so Jeff said," Evelyn protested.

"He told you half a story," Harry said bitterly. Evelyn looked up, waiting. "Did he say how the inmates of these 'sanitoriums' earn their keep?"

"Earn their keep? What are you talking about?" Her skin crawled.

Harry released her arms. "They use them as lab rats, Eve. Test drugs on them, new synthetic compounds, and the batch-testing of new production runs of established commercial drugs. Animal testing ended centuries ago, when we realized animals and humans just don't react to chemical compounds in the same way. Testing on rats and rabbits doesn't give you much idea of what'll happen when a human ingests the drug. Thalidomide, Hexaacain, Quasimesonin." Names to conjure shivers of horror spanning centuries. "So they use dummies — the fifth grade rejects whose families can't afford to pay for their care and can't or won't keep them at home."

"Can't," Evelyn whispered. "Simon would make his life hell."

"Then knock his bloody block off!" Tansy said sharply. "The little shit has it coming!" She met Evelyn's eyes angrily, and Evelyn knew what she was talking about. Simon had been badmouthing Harry and other healers since the Eldorado Coroner blamed one such physician for the death of a boy. The kid was an Angel addict. The healer had been trying to purge him of the drug. When the youth died with a massive cerebral hemorrhage the healer could have been charged with murder. Only the fact the boy was using Angel made criminal charges void. But the damage was done, and the physician had to get out, fast, to outrun the predictable death threats.

Evelyn closed her eyes. "I've painted myself into a corner, haven't I?"

"Yes," Tansy said ruefully. "I think you have. Still, he'll be staying here for a little while. Let's see how things work out." She frowned then, looking up at her husband. "Harry's not just a cutter, you know."

But Harry shook his head at once. "It can't be my decision to do the work, Tan. And I don't think John Citizen could even begin to understand what it involves."

"So I'm in the damned responsibility seat again," Evelyn said tartly. "Jeff seemed to think I haven't the right to inflict you and your witchdoctor techniques on another human being."

"And you believe him," Tansy observed.

"I don't know," Evelyn admitted. "I'll have to think it through, and right now I'm tired, uptight. Confused." She rubbed her eyes. "Hell, if it works, it works, what else is there? People don't like what you do, but —"

"They call us deviants," Harry said quietly. "Genetic deviants, as if we have two heads, or turn into wolves every time the moon is full." He forced a smile. "This is why I came back here to work after I qualified in their orthodox quackery. I got sick and tired of being called a queer, ridiculed as a pervo-devo, and impeached. I got mauled once too often, and in public, because I carry the T/87 gene. Damn, there's more to life than city smut! As this youngster might find out." He folded his arms and studied the patient shrewdly. "I'd say, physically he's in his middle or late twenties. Fit as God only knows what, which is the only reason they didn't kill him outright. He's got some old bullet wounds. Now, was he shot *by* Tac for bending the law? Or is he *from* Tac himself?"

"I wish I knew," Evelyn admitted. "How long is this going to take?"

The healer pulled at his chin, going through the procedures mentally. "Well, a couple of hours on the eye, same on the knee. And then put the teeth right. Finish up tomorrow evening, I expect. By then Bolt's work will have thoroughly settled in and he'll be feeling much better. Then, we might have a look at the damage to his brain." As Evelyn opened her mouth to protest he added quickly, "With a laser probe. I don't go where I'm not invited. You know me better." He winked at her. "I'll play it by ear."

"So long as you know the tune," Evelyn said with a tired smile. "You want me to stick around or shall I come back tomorrow?"

"Go home," Harry told her. "I'll call when I'm through. This'd cost an arm and a leg if I didn't owe you a few big ones from *way* back when."

"So bill me," Evelyn said brashly.

But Del only smiled. "On the house, love. It's a nice thing you're doing. Cheat Death's Head out of one more. I only wish we could cheat them every time." Then he gave her a push. "I'd better get busy. Why don't you head for home?"

"Why don't I?" She agreed. "I'll see you both tomorrow."

The OR was sealed, decontaminating as she left the plantation house. The deep peace and quiet were beguiling. A water clock dripped in the courtyard where peacocks strutted, displayed, and she heard the sound of love being made in the summerhouse. It was Harry's eldest son, Alex, and one of the students who studied pharmaceutical plant biology here between semesters at the Wing-Parry Institute in the islands. The two boys were moaning among the potted orchids. She saw the rhythmic humping of slender hips as they fucked and was envious of their pleasure as she strolled out to the yard where the 'van stood waiting.

CHAPTER EiGHT

"Raven leader to Raven 7.1," Mischa Petrov's voice said in Stone's ears. Since Stone was off the carrier, Petrov had assumed the mantel of Raven Leader.

The shuttle was looping high over the hills, back in the direction of Chell. Stone's next destination was Paddington. "Raven 7.1," he responded. He closed the twin throttles, shut back to slow cruising, six thousand kilometers per hour, and watched the canards sweep automatically to check turbulence about the nose.

"When are you coming home, Stoney?" Petrov demanded from the carrier's ops room. "You've been shunting around down there for a day and a half for chrissakes."

Stone knew there was more to it than the Russian's aggravation at being left in charge while the pot came to the boil. What he meant was, 'Jarrat's dead, stop making a three-ring circus out of it.' "I'm nearly out of options," he admitted. "Green Raven piped their data from Sugarloaf, Paris and out that way. They came up with zilch —"

"As have you," Petrov added.

"So I'll just see the job out," Stone said tiredly. "Paddington and Clune are the last two possibilities we've got. What's eating you, Mischa?"

The Russian's exasperated exhalation carried over the air. "Tac reports rumblings in the Chell underground. There isn't a shooter loose on the street anymore. A flock of their runners and informants have come up dead, others have *vanished* out of the city. What's that sound like to you?"

"Like Death's Head getting its butt in gear, and some smart shooters had an argument with Mavvik," Stone growled. He looked up into the burnished nitrogen blue of the sky. He was cruising a thousand meters above cloud level. "Have Tactical asked for NARC involvement?"

"Ten minutes ago," Petrov said tartly. "I've got Red and Gold units on standby, but there's more ... stand by for a datafeed. Read this and weep."

Stone watched the comm-relay terminal at his elbow with a frown. It was a report from Tac Command, detailing a robbery during the night. Normally NARC would have nothing to do with theft, but the nature of the goods stolen automatically involved them. Military weapons, heavy cannons, a charged particle projector, armor and grenades, rocket launchers. Stone whistled through his teeth at the list framed in the CRT. "My God. What is this, espionage or another bloody intercorporate shooting match?"

"Search me," Petrov said cynically. "But I'll tell you what scares shit out of me, Stoney. We could be looking down the barrels of that lot soon if the corporate security forces let the stuff hit the civvy marketplace. It's the

Vincent Morello Aerospace plant outside Paris. You better get over there, PDQ. You're the closest senior ranker, and you're already in the air."

"Will do." Stone read off the coordinates and updated the navdeck. "I can be there in fifteen. Buzz them, let them know I'm on my way in. Tell them to get their shit together, I have no time to hang around listening to a lot of moaning while they inventory what they lost! And meanwhile, give me everything you have on file on Morello."

Vincent Morello Aerospace was a hightech developer working mainly in the fields of military and industrial hardware. Like any of the megacompanies, it maintained its own security force, a private army answerable to a corporate high command. Stone disliked such forces intensely. Even under normal circumstances they took liberties with the public and made Tactical's job difficult. When they went to war with some rival corporate monster, the carnage was horrifying. The war on Sheal was only the most recent conflict. Others had raged for months, years, and tens of thousands died in them, mercenaries, civilians and servicemen alike.

The plant outside Paris was a concrete wasteland occupying a square kilometer. Around the gates were manicured lawns, a forecourt, a chrome-and-plate-glass office tower. The factories, storage bunkers, and the weapons testing fields stretched out behind the public facilities. From the air Stone saw no signs of damage to any building or fence.

He adjusted his headset and called, "NARC Raven 7.1 to Vincent Morello. Request landing instructions."

They had reserved him space in the executive carpark. The shuttle set down, its wings inswept, its blistering engines angled away from the Rands, Chevrolets and Mercedes, so as not to strip the paint off the million-credit limousines. Stone lifted off his helmet and sent up the canopy.

Parrots chattered in the trees flanking the carpark and the air smelt dusty. He ran his fingers through hair which had been flattened, dampened by the helmet, and adjusted to the feel of ground beneath his feet as he waited for the little runabout buggy to come out from the office. A uniformed sergeant, armed and grim-faced, brought it right into the shade of the shuttle, waited for him to climb aboard, and returned to the building in an arc about the executive vehicles.

Chilled air and the smell of carpet cleaners greeted him as he stepped through the glass doors. The name of Vincent Morello was up on the wall in red and gold, and the large-scale model of the new VM-104 Corsair space-to-surface interceptor, recently contracted, commanded the attention. Stone looked over its sleek, deadly lines speculatively. NARC would be flying the aircraft in a few months. He and Jarrat would spend a few weeks back at Sector Central on Darwin's World, getting up close and intimate with the Starfleet training squadron who were already flying it. The 104 was a generation younger than the shuttle, lighter, faster, with sharper fangs. Stone knew he was going to enjoy it, as would Jarrat

If Jarrat's alive. Stone's innards churned painfully and he put the bleak thought from him as a man stepped forward. Harassed, angry, flustered, he thrust out his hand in greeting, and Stone took it briefly. He was flabby and enduring the throes of middle age. Typical executive material, on pace for the first of several heart attacks. Stone found a thin smile as the man introduced himself with a tug at the security-coded name tag clipped to the pocket of his pale green jacket.

"I'm Gene McEwan, the Assistant Manager." He smoothed short black hair around his receding forehead.

"Captain Stone, NARC-*Athena.*" Stone looked about the plush foyer, with its royal blue carpets and flickering monitors, its wide reception desk and frazzled secretaries. An older man was haranguing the girls, as if they were in some way responsible for last night's break-in. "Tac supplied an inventory of the stolen *merchandise.* I assume it was accurate."

"As accurate as we can be at this moment," McEwan told him. "We're still inventorying. Have you any idea the size of this facility, Captain?"

"I saw it from the air, on my way in. Actually, how they breached your security interests me more than what they took. There's already enough weapons on the street to make for a real shooting war."

"Military hardware, loose on the street?" McEwan demanded.

"No, I'll grant you, most of the cannons in civvy hands are sporting and special-design items. The Syndicates have the good stuff. I read the list you supplied to Tactical. Is one of your competitors goading for a war?" He lifted one brow at McEwan. "Whom do you suspect?"

But McEwan could only shrug his round shoulders. "I don't know, Captain, I really don't. If it'd been a theft of software, blueprints, I'd have said probably ZephyrTech, and our own security forces would have taken measures by now. But this? This is just robbery. None of our rivals would steal hardware."

"Not to examine it, duplicate the technology?" Stone prompted. "Industrial espionage?"

"Well, espionage is all very well," McEwan admitted, "if we're talking about something new and revolutionary. But we're not." He brandished a hardcopy of the list Stone had read off the screen. "None of the materials stolen last night is under a year old and all have been in use by Starfleet, Tac, also NARC, for at least as long. If ZephyrTech wanted to examine and copy, all they'd have to do is borrow an item, or just go out and buy one. No, no, Captain, this is underground. It must be."

They walked together, out through the rear of the office, down a long airconditioned passage and out through the rear exit. The sun glared down over the wasteland of concrete and bunkers. Stone slipped the pilot's glasses back onto his nose. He was uncomfortably aware of a chilling sense of foreboding. "So it's underground. What's your security setup?"

McEwan pointed out the boundaries, the sensor towers and the barracks buildings. "High-voltage fences, every detector you can think of, all wired to the grunts' quarters. Break one beam, show up on one camera, cut the fence, and a hundred-fifty ex-Army mercenaries are 'round your neck like a dog collar."

"So they obviously didn't get in that way," Stone concluded. "You can't land inside the wire without breaking a beam, tripping the scanners, and you can't just drive through the fence. What's on the computer?"

"Shit," McEwan muttered brokenly. "*Shit* is on the computer That fucking machine never registered so much as a rabbit on the firing range last night! It cost five million, it's supposed to be the most sensitive bio-cyber AI mechanism ever devised, and this is what we get. Zilch."

"That's a little odd, isn't it?" Stone asked as he and the Assistant Manager stepped back into the building's coolness. "It registered nothing at all? You sure it was functional?"

"Its clock was running," McEwan said disgustedly.

"Then has its memory been tampered with?" Stone suggested.

The flabby little man halted in midstride. "Impossible. You need access to house security codes. Just what are you implying, Captain Stone? That this was an inside job?"

Stone took a deep breath. "Or perhaps someone sold the codes for cash or favors. It does happen, McEwan. The human element is the weakness of any system. Or failing that, your codes were simply stolen."

"They're changed every twelve hours at random, for new codes generated by the same goddamned computer that screwed us last night. There was nothing to steal," McEwan said coldly.

"Which means, whoever stole the code took it and used it inside your deadline," Stone said, just as icily. "I'd say your five-million-credit biocyber AI was hacked, McEwan. You're on the network?"

"Well, of course we're on the network! But we're protected," McEwan protested. "We use the same firewall as protects Starfleet's mainframes."

"And apparently it has a flaw." Stone led the way back to the offices. "Any number of individuals could hack you for the hell of it. Students, an employee you fired last week. Or terrorists." *Death's Head*. He groaned soundlessly. "I'd take the machine offline, if I were you. Dig into the security subsystems, see if whoever hacked you left a virus behind for laughs, or if they've screwed you elsewhere. The very least they did is access your codes, turn off your security system, then blank the memory on the way out so you don't even know they were there."

The man's face was three shades of green. "Oh, my God."

"Well, that's business," Stone said cynically. "From your perspective at least. From ours ... I don't know whether you realize this, McEwan, but my men will probably be staring your weapons in the barrel very soon. I think I might know who's responsible for this."

McEwan pounced. "Tell me. Give me a name, Stone, and I'll fillet them, bone from bone. I've got the sanction and the troops to do it with."

For just a moment Stone soberly considered handing Death's Head to Vincent Morello Aerospace on a plate. It would be so easy to do it. Kevin's revenge would be explosive, vast. Satisfying. But at last Stone shook his head with terse reluctance. One word from him now, and the result would be an all-out war, a bloodbath on the streets of Chell. The civilian casualty rates would be sky-high, and no matter what Jarrat had suffered, the ordinary people of Chell should not have to pay for it.

"Classified, McEwan, as well you know. I've no intention of letting you touch off a streetwar. You want to turn this continent into another Sheal, a million hectares of smoldering rubble and air that'll strip bare flesh right off the bone?" He shook his head. "I won't have it on my conscience. I like to sleep nights." He returned the shades to his nose and turned away toward the smoked-glass doors. "When you finish your inventory, send it to Tac and tell them I want a copy. If there are any more developments, let me know. There's nothing I can do for you here, unless you want a NARC biocyber specialist to come and take your AI apart."

"We have four of those on the payroll," McEwan said sourly. "Maybe they'll start earning their pay one of these days. Jesus Christ, it's got to the point where you don't dare fire a shit-faced freeloader for fear he'll hack the guts out of your mainframe for the underground to get back at you!"

It was painfully true, and Stone lifted one brow at the man. "Chase that chain of logic, McEwan. You're closer to the culprit right now than you know. When you find your traitor, I'd appreciate a call."

The uniformed sergeant was waiting at the door and Stone stepped into the buggy to ride back to the NARC aircraft. The man was forty, craggy, wearing a mustache, a half-shaven head and a lot of old unit tattoos on his bare scalp. "You were in the barracks last night?"

"Yes, sir." The sergeant wore an expression of ironic amusement.

"And your alarms were silent? Not tampered with?"

"Checked them myself, Cap, soon as the balloon went up this morning. It's all in perfect working order ... except it didn't work worth diddly last night, and now the big-wheels are lookin' for somebody to hang out to dry for it. It's scapegoat time. It always is when they're peein' themselves in shock up on the executive level."

The observation was shrewd. Stone took the sergeant's salute and watched the buggy arc away about the limousines before he lifted himself into the cockpit. Two minutes later the plane was off, the nose turning back toward the coordinates of Paddington, from which he had rerouted. As he opened the throttles wide for a quick flight over, he called the carrier and relayed what he had heard to Petrov.

The Russian groaned audibly. "Morello was hacked, an underground job? Christ, you're shitting me. You thinking what I'm thinking?"

"Death's Head," Stone agreed. "I'd put money on it, Mischa. We'll know soon enough. Has Chell Tactical asked for any specific NARC action or just routine surveillance procedures?"

"Observe and record only," Petrov told him. "But Red and Gold are on standby. We could *make* Death's Head fight. Flush them out of the woodwork. It's that, or let 'em draw first blood, then nail 'em to the floor."

The question was never easy to answer, and at some point in an assignment it was almost always asked. NARC was a paramilitary unit operating under a legal banner, and it went to war within exacting constraints. To slip NARC off the leash Stone needed absolutely conclusive evidence. Jarrat had sent back a wealth of data and eight Death's Head affiliates, plus Deek Vazell himself. Vazell had traded massive volumes of data in exchange for his life and a cloned limb, if not his liberty. NARC had all the proof it needed. Legally, even morally, they could draw first blood themselves without recrimination. But again, the city of Chell would be a battlefield and Stone would have preferred not to enter into any engagement where suburban streets became the firezone and civilian casualties were utterly unavoidable.

"Let them stew a while longer," he decided at length as he lowered the helmet's thin gold visor. The shuttle banked about into the sun on its final approach to Paddington Field. "Stand to, but hold till Tac yells. If Mavvik starts it, we'll finish it off for him, but I don't want to push him as yet. I'm on my way back to Paddington."

"Copy that," Petrov sighed. There was a long pause and then he said, "Stoney, you know as well as I do, Jarrat's dead. He's gone. All you're doing is tearing the guts out of yourself for nothing."

Anger tightened in Stone's chest. "You're clairvoyant, are you? Just mind the shop, Mischa. Do what they pay you for. Raven 7.1 *out*." The Russian was a good lad in his own way, but he could get under Stone's fingernails and he never knew when to keep his mouth shut.

Paddington came up fast. Stone cut speed and called ahead to the field for clearance to put the shuttle down in the space between a Military Airlift transport and a civilian skybus. On the side of the gorgeous gull-gray hull was the NARC decal, the steel-gloved hand in which nestled the white dove. As he cast off his helmet and sent up the canopy the crew of the transport, two teenagers in brown uniform fatigues, looked down enviously at the aircraft. He caught part of the old joke but pretended not to hear. "Narc, Narc, who's there —"

Five minutes later he was in the programmer's office, watching a short, stout man with a gleaming bald head and Military Airlift tattoos, run through the data retrieval request. Here, he received courteous silence, and he thought of Candice Kwan. Often, silence had a lot to recommend it.

The ATC programmer was quick and efficient. He punched up the files and pinpointed the area in which the Skyvan had landed in moments. "There you are, Captain Stone. Four 'vans of that model are registered in that area. Not a one was tracked ex-Paddy on that day, however."

"Go back to the day before," Stone suggested.

Keys pattered again. "Two. Ex-Paddy, southbound." He looked up from the screen. "Chell is north. I'm sorry."

"You didn't invent the geography," Stone sighed. "I suppose you could keep on going back till the middle of last month, but it makes more sense to talk to all the owners. Four, right? Let me have the personal details." He peered at the screen with tired eyes as the data came up, and then frowned curiously. A nerve in his belly tightened. "This one is registered to the Taylor-Mason Clinic. Is that a general medical center?"

"Yes, Captain. And a very good one. Their ambulance is a Marshall, the same model as your Skyvan — but it didn't go out. It services this region but we get very few calls, this is just a small town."

"Hang the 'van," Stone muttered. He was listening to the pulse racing in his ears. "It's the clinic I'm talking about. A yellow Marshall departs Chell, comes straight to Paddy and lands near a good medical center!"

The ATC man blinked up at him. "So what? I don't follow."

Stone ran both bare palms over his hair, pressing it tight to his skull. The gesture betrayed a terrible mix of excitement and ice-cold dread. "The 'van I'm looking for had an injured man aboard. He'd been beaten half to death, left for dead. A credit gets you a castle, the lady who scraped him off the ground in Chell made a beeline for the clinic to get help." He was moving on the instant, snatching up his helmet as he went. "Thanks for your time, Pop. I think I just hit the jackpot."

If Jarrat had made it to the clinic alive. In a wimpy civilian bus, it was a half-hour flight from Chell. Did Kevin have a half-hour left in him? Over and over, Stone's memory replayed the sounds he had heard from the R/T in those terrible seconds after Jarrat himself stopped transmitting. Adrenaline flooded through him and he used it, sprinting for the shuttle, riding a tide of nervous energy. It woke him up fast, where minutes before a lethal torpor had begun to drag at him.

He sealed the canopy and lifted the aircraft up over the rooftops of Paddington. It was just a ten-kilometer hop to the Taylor-Mason Clinic, down the clearway which connected the local airfield with the city center. He set the shuttle down on the lawn outside a wide, white building with satellite dishes on the roof, and broad windows which vibrated to the roar of his jet noise. He thumbed the remote to lock the NARC aircraft. It would have been safer to leave the machine on the roof, but few civilian buildings were designed to take so much weight in one solid piece.

The inpatients and half of the staff had gathered at every north-facing window and door to watch the plane land. They were waiting for him, and they recognized a military aircraft when they saw one. The steel-glove-and-dove NARC decal was enough to silence them, but Stone knew the staffers were angry. He had disturbed the patients and the repulsion heat of his gravity resist would certainly kill off a large swathe of the lawn.

The receptionist looked up as he approached the front desk. Stone pinned on a sham smile. Behind it, his heart beat like a drum. "An injured man was brought in here the night before last, by a lady flying a Marshall 'van," he said smoothly, as if he knew it as a fact.

The young man did not even have to check. "That's right ... sir," he affirmed cautiously. Few crash cases came into a small-town clinic. 'Paddy' was just a rural community, and a case like John Citizen #34 was a gossip topic all over the building.

"He was alive on arrival?" Stone asked, and held his breath.

"Yes, sir. Doctor Bolt treated him in the Emergency surgery."

"Then, the patient is in the clinic now?"

"Oh, I'm sorry, sir, he was released, signed out."

"Bloody hell." Stone closed his eyes as frustration squeezed his chest. He drew his hands across his face and leveled his voice with an effort of will. "Signed out by whom, exactly?"

"By Doctor Bolt," the young clerk told him. "We found no ID on the patient, not even a tattoo, so there were no legalities —"

"Is Bolt in the building right now?"

The clerk consulted the duty roster. "Yes, sir. Would you like me to page him for you?"

"Please." Stone drummed his fingers on the desk as he waited.

Long moments passed before the intercom said, "Bolt."

The young man behind the hooded computer leaned over to the mic and spoke in a discreet undertone. "Doctor, we have an, um, a NARC officer wanting to speak to you. He's at Reception."

A pause, and then: "There's a *what* —?" Bolt stopped and began again. "Okay, I'll be right there."

The receptionist smiled up at Stone. "He's on his way down, sir."

Bolt must have taken the scenic route. Stone was simmering when the elevator opened and Bolt appeared at last. Stone followed him into a small private lounge, out of earshot of public and staffers alike, and looked the man over. Bolt was pale, nervy, as if a visit from NARC was enough to put the fear of God into him. Perhaps it was.

"My name is Stone," he offered, thrusting out his hand. "You treated a Chell city bottom assault victim the night before last, didn't you?"

"So I did." Bolt shook Stone's hand briefly. His palm was sweating and his voice was brittle with tension.

"Would you describe the victim, please?"

"He was about your height, perhaps a hand's breadth less. Maybe seventy kilos, well built, longish brown hair, wavy here and there. Gray eyes, clean shaven, three scars, two of which —"

"Were gunshot wounds, the other was a quilldart, recent, almost healed," Stone finished. He had heard more than enough. Relief was like a bucket of ice-water thrown in his face. "What did you do with the man?"

Bolt sat down on the edge of the plush leather couch, hands clasped between his knees. "Well, I fixed him up as well as I could on short notice. He was very, very badly injured. Massive internal injuries, broken bones, blood loss, what have you. He'd been beaten and raped. Do you want the details, a copy of the file?"

The ice was in Stone's veins now. "Thanks," he whispered. The file would be grim reading but the carrier's surgeon would need it when Kevin arrived in their own Infirmary. Kip Reardon was the best Stone knew.

"Then I signed him out," Bolt added.

Stone forced his mind back into gear. "In whose company? I mean, he didn't just walk through the doors on his own, did he?"

"Hardly," Bolt said quickly. "A medic I am, God I am not. He went with — with a woman from the outdistricts."

"In a yellow Skyvan. I know." Stone groaned. "You have her details?"

"Well, her name, perhaps," Bolt muttered. "I assumed he was family. We don't bother with paperwork when the patient has no ID. You see, technically we're not supposed to treat anyone without ID of some kind."

Stone made a sardonic face. "I suppose you just let them bleed to death in the carpark."

Bolt was on his feet at that, angry. "No, goddamn it!" Real fury colored his face. "And that's a bloody shitty thing to say. You're a damned cynic. Of course we treat them, but we overlook the paperwork, or the government dickheads in Chell would hang our asses from a lampstand!"

"Fair enough," Stone conceded. "I'll take her name, then."

"Wait here," Bolt said crustily. "I'll see if I can find it, and bring you a copy of his treatment sheet. *That*, we file in the event of legal comebacks."

He left the staff lounge with a stiff gait suggesting anger, and Stone re-evaluated the man. He had scruples, a rare commodity. The file search must have given him trouble, since the doctor did not return until Stone was on the boil again. Bolt came back at a jog with a sheepish, apologetic expression. "We don't seem to have the name, I'm sorry. But here's the treatment sheet."

"Christ almighty." Stone snatched the clipped papers out of Bolt's hand. "Here I go again — and *you're* sorry!" He gave the medic a sour look. "You fixed him up and the woman took him away. What shape was he in?"

"Fair to middling," Bolt said nervously. "He needs a neuro job but the lady said she was going to make arrangements. Poor bugger had been mauled. It's all in the papers there."

"But he was off the critical list?"

"If I signed him out, he was stable," Bolt said indignantly.

Stone sighed and turned back toward the foyer. "All right, Doctor. The fact is, I owe you, big time, and I shouldn't be chewing on you."

"Don't mention it," Bolt muttered. He began to breathe again as the dark young officer from Narcotics And Riot Control strode away. He looked at the ceiling, squeezed his eyes shut and shook his head. "Eve Lang, the things I do for you. Lying to a NARC, for chrissakes! I need my brains examined!" But Evelyn could live happily without NARC knowing her name and number.

On the lawn outside, Stone let himself fall back into the forward acceleration couch, pulled on sunglasses and the headset and called Paddington Air Traffic. The medical sheet lay open on his knee. He scanned a few lines as he waited for the Controller. It was a catalogue of obscenity, viciousness and sexual abuse. His bone marrow seemed to freeze over. "It's Stone again," he said when the Controller answered his page. "Send me a comprehensive of all Skyvans tracked ex-Paddy out of the clinic area between, say, midnight and noon, yesterday." His smoldering blue eyes were glued to the screen before him and he held his breath.

There it was. Just one had left, and Paddington ATC had tracked it two thousand kilometers into the southeast, at which point it would have entered the network directed from the city of Mawson. Given the overlap between the two networks, Mawson would be able to cross-reference and tell him where it had gone. From here on it could get easier.

He pulled on the bone-white helmet and fired the jets. It was going to work. He updated the nav deck, passed the plane into the care of the auto-fly and returned to Bolt's hardcopy. The injuries were typical of physical violence. Any city bottom crash surgeon could have repaired them. Stone was less concerned than he might have been until he came to the bottom line and saw Bolt's evaluation of the damage he could not repair. The retina and knee were fine work, demanding a specialist: Kip Reardon would manage those on the carrier. But as he read the description of the traumas to the patient's brain Stone's heart squeezed again.

Dry mouthed, he signaled the ship and asked for Reardon. When the surgeon answered he said, "I've got some data for you, Kip. Take a look at this, tell me what it means. It's gibberish to me. Not my field." He slapped it on the scanplate and waited a few interminable seconds. "You got it?"

"Got it," Reardon's voice said. Then silence, as he read, and at last a protracted sigh. "You know bloody well what this means, don't you, Stoney? Don't play dumb with me."

"I ... can guess," Stone whispered. "Fixable?"

"I don't know," Reardon said with brutal honesty.

"But you're the best microsurgeon in the service. Surely you can do for him what you've done for troops brought in, mangled in a battle!"

"I can try," Reardon said quietly. "No promises, Stoney, but I'll try."

Stone's teeth closed on his lip and drew blood. "There's always risks in this kind of surgery, aren't there?"

"You asking what his chances are?" Reardon sounded sad and tired.

"Yes." Stone closed his eyes. "Not good, I imagine."

Reardon hesitated. "Let's say, only fair. Look, bring him in first, if you can track him down. I'll know better when I've scanned him, head to foot. Ask me about his chances then."

"I will," Stone said tersely. He watched the ranging data on the navigation deck with a bitter expression. Now, he was fairly sure he would find Jarrat. But what had once been his goal seemed only the beginning. The note in Kip Reardon's voice rang alarms in his head. Given the tale of woe on Bolt's paper, Kevin's chances were very bad. Stone took solace only in the fact that he was alive. Battered, broken, but alive.

CHAPTER ΠiΠE

Mawson sent Stone on southeast. The Skyvan had flown through their air-space, no stops, and Stone himself paused in the blistering heat just long enough to gather data, put the pieces together and get a meal. The Marshall 'van cruised at a leisurely five hundred kilometers per hour, but it had ridden a tail wind most of the way. It passed through the Mawson regional network between 10:00 and 15:00 hours, holding a steady course.

Stone punched up the charts to project that course on, out over the ocean. Mawson stood on the shore of Johansen Sound. Beyond it was the open sea, punctuated only by island chains, the caps of extinct volcanoes. He swore as he saw the map. The islands were too numerous to be counted, most of them uninhabited, and more than a thousand flyspecks lay on the van's heading. Air Traffic in the region was tracked from the largest, an outpost in the ocean, called Outbound.

The shuttle arced up fast and he nudged the throttles open. Three hundred K's out, he called Mischa Petrov aboard the carrier for an update on the situation in Chell, and held his breath, waiting for the explosion. Petrov was furious, holding onto his temper with a supreme effort of will.

"What's coming down? *Nothing,* Stoney. Zip. Let them stew in their own juice, you said, — it's Tac that's stewing! Colonel Stacy has Mavvik's palace under surveillance. They're all in there, looking back, like they're waiting. Waiting for us to start the shooting? We've got the evidence we need to put them in a hole in the ground, so why don't we just do it?"

"Civilians," Stone retorted. "They get caught in the crossfire, they get killed. We're here to protect them, not frag them!"

"Fuck the civilians," Petrov hissed. "One half of them are too stoned to know what day it is, the other half are working for Mavvik, greasing the guys who try to stand up and fight. So we kill a few more, who gives a —"

"I do," Stone broke in, raising his voice. "And save the crap for an encrypted channel, *Lieutenant.* Open that big, fat mouth of yours wide enough, and some newsjockey is likely to stuff it with a rolled-up copy of next week's Sunday supplement. So long as Mavvik is in his fortress and Tac are outside, he's no more than a prisoner under house arrest, and the Angel stays on the shelf. That's what we want isn't it? To keep the garbage out of city bottom?" He paused. The anger thrummed in his chest. In fact he wanted nothing more than to let Petrov have his wish, turn NARC on Death's Head and wreak some measure of revenge in Jarrat's name. "I want Hal Mavvik's bloody scalp hanging on my belt as much as you do. He gave them the order to pulp Kevin, and I want him. But we have to do it *right,* Mischa. No cock-ups, no comebacks. Got it?"

"I hear you talking," Petrov agreed reluctantly. "So where's Kevin?"

"I'm working on it," Stone said evasively. "I've got some fresh steers. Has Colonel Stacy put Tactical on full alert yet?"

"Hours ago, but they're just running buggy-patrol. Long range ears and eyeballs, telemetry up the kazoo. This could go on for days. Stacy's own informants came home gift wrapped on the mincemeat express. He's been shitting bricks about it on the GlobalNet vidcasts. The killing's started, but so long as it's crimmos totaling crimmos, the law looks the other way. Now it's Tac blood on the pavement, and they're singing a different tune."

Stone made cynical noises. "Give it a chance. The pot'll boil over in its own time, no need for us to monkey with the gas. The more we flex our muscles in public, the more they hate our guts ... I'm coming up on Outbound. I'll talk to you later, Mischa. Raven 7.1 out."

The island was an extinct volcanic cone, the tip of a seamount enclosing a crescent-shaped lagoon. Groundscan showed him the submerged depth. Had it been above sea level, it would have been taller than Everest. The water was green; coral reefs lay scattered beneath the surface like the whitened bones of dead dinosaurs. He gave the vistas a longing glance as he banked through a turn, coming up fast on the ATC radar signals.

This far out he had the air to himself. It was eight in the morning in this timezone but he did not bother to reset his chrono. He was only passing through. The shuttle cruised at Mach 5; he was only ever passing through any timezone and had learned to attach no importance to local time. Outbound ATC gave him landing instructions and he nosed up to the building, into its patch of long, morning shade, with the canopy up. He could smell the sea on the fresh wind as his jets whined down.

He lifted off his helmet and climbed out onto the bleached concrete. Startled by the jet noise, gulls were still wheeling overhead, their harsh voices punctuating the quiet. Warm air danced on the shoulders of jungle-clad mountains. He could hear the crash of the surf. With Jarrat's incredible luck, he would have been repaired by a local neurosurgeon who was as near magician as medic, and be working on his tan while three virginal beauties had a fist-fight over who was going to be first in the sack with him. If Jarrat did not command such luck, he would have died in the alley in Chell's notorious city bottom — or he would never have made it out of the hell-pit of Sheckley in the first place. A good neuro man would mend him. Stone told himself this over and over. Even if Kevin had to be shipped right back to Earth itself, a good microsurgeon, aided and abetted by bio-cyber systems, could do the job. He clung to the belief. It was the last surviving particle of his optimism.

Outbound ATC was just a pebble-dash-and-glass building with one floor and a battery of receiving gear on the roof. The flight director was a woman of sixty with red hair and bare feet, clad in shorts and a halter displaying good muscle tone and an almost-black tan.

"Stone," he said tersely by way of greeting, and offered his hand. "I need to access some data."

It was simpler than he might have expected. This far out, few 'vans flew *into* the airsearch network. Most belonged around Outbound and were island-hoppers, lifting and landing well within range of the big radars up on the shoulder of the mountain. Stone scanned the data and grunted when he saw that his quarry had landed.

"It put down somewhere in the Kingsway area," the flight told him. She froze the multicolored display and illuminated one line. "At the eastern tip of the island, a hundred-fifty klicks from here. They're criminals, I suppose." She was looking out through the window at the NARC jet which stood by the door. Heat haze shimmered about its superhot engines.

He did not explain. "And it took off when?"

She released the display, let the screen cycle, and stopped it again. "It left about an hour later, headed northeast, for South Atlantis. Air Traffic is tracked out of Eldorado, but you'll be wading in 'vans up to your armpits soon as you cross the coastline. Eighty, ninety million people live along that seaboard from north to south, which adds up to a lot of 'vans."

Resignation drew Stone's mouth tight. "You're not wrong. Anyway, I'll buzz down to Kingsway. Maybe, just maybe, someone there got a look at the damned 'van and remembers the reggo. Or knows the owner. If Outbound is a regular stop on the way to Atlantis the lady might have stopped here before."

"Everything stops here," the flight told him emphatically. "It's your last chance to get a coffee, stretch your legs and take a piss before you get into the outdistricts, and that's way over yonder." A vague wave into the east. "Good hunting, Captain."

He left the airconditioned cool of the building and was sweating lightly as he lifted himself back into the shuttle. He threw the aircraft up over the spinal mountain range in a parabolic right arc over the tracking arrays — straight up, straight down — and soon saw Kingsway, a hundred and fifty K's and three minutes from the Outbound ATC. His screaming jets echoed back off the hills as he thundered in over the lagoon, and he scanned the town from altitude as he hovered on a storm of repulsion.

Kingsway was an agricultural and fishing town. He saw sugarcane, orchards, a cannery, a fishing fleet bobbing at anchor in the bay. A few dozen houses clustered above the beach along with a tavern, a tumbledown church, a service garage attached to the shopping arcade. Stone licked his lips. The promise of a beer was seductive.

The shuttle touched down in the parking lot outside the mall. It was deserted. Only a few children and an old man saw him land, but he locked the aircraft and pocketed the infrabeam key before heading toward the tavern. The sun was a weight on his shoulders, no matter the early hour.

The public house was empty but for a lad behind the bar who opened up and gaped at Stone as he pushed in through the glass doors. He ambled up to the bar and set down a few credits. "Give me a cold one." The bottle came from the cold locker; the label was local, a microbrewery. Stone poured the amber liquid into a schooner glass and sipped appreciatively. He topped up the glass before he cast a glance around and said dryly, "You could get knocked out by the crowd around here."

The lad had a deep voice and an odd accent. "Gets busy later, in the evening. You from Starfleet? That your plane?"

Stone shook his head. "No, to both questions."

"Army, then?"

"NARC," Stone told him, and watched him take a step backward. "I'm not here to bust anyone, son, just asking a few questions. You didn't see a yellow Marshall fly in recently, I suppose?"

"Sure, did ... sir. They *all* come here on the way t'anyplace. We's got the best damn' garage on the island. Next stop's Eldorado, so folks come in to fix things 'fore headin' on, use the outhouse, buy a few sodas."

"The service garage." Stone drained the schooner glass. "I'll give it a shot. Thanks for the beer. Keep the change."

The town's only service station lay a kilometer closer to the beach. Stone adjusted the shades on his nose and, like other visitors to Outbound, enjoyed the opportunity to stretch his legs. Once he left behind the shuttle he would not draw attention on the street, since he was in plain clothes, like any officer. Blue shirt, white slacks and the Tactical uniform boots to which he had grown accustomed during the years he served with them. He had worn these clothes under the armor when he left the carrier. He had begun to long for a shower and change.

The trail would surely be short from here on if someone at the garage knew the 'van or its owner. Stone — and Jarrat — could be back on the carrier so soon. And then Kip Reardon could make his own diagnosis of Kevin's condition. *And mend him*, Stone thought. He had seen Reardon perform miracles with men brought out of combat situations with horrifying injuries. Reardon had a magic touch which made him the best surgeon NARC had. Stone placed his faith in his CMO and clung to optimism by his fingernails.

The town was near-silent. The sound of the ocean came up from the headland and he gazed at the glittering lagoon as he turned into the wide asphalt forecourt of the garage. The roller doors were up on the workshop and powertools screamed from within. He strolled up to the shop and paused to glance at the special offers in the baskets outside. Beachballs, swimfins, insect repellents. Passing by, he pushed open the door.

A bell tinkled overhead. He took off his glasses and found himself looking at a young man. He was tall and slim, bronzed by the sun, his yellow hair roped into a think braid on his left shoulder. He wore blue shorts, cut off and frayed just under buttock level. Huge brown eyes looked up at Stone out of a lean face with high cheekbones and a square jaw. Feature by feature, the boy was not beautiful, but the overall effect was stunning. Stone could not help but smile.

The lad smiled back. "Anything I can do for you, chief?" A light voice with the same odd accent as the bartender at the pub up the road.

"My friends call me Stoney," he said silkily.

The boy's smile widened. "What can I do for you, Stoney?"

He glanced from the lad's face to his slim hips and back again. "Well, for a *start*, I'm looking for information." The expression about his mouth had nothing to do with what he was saying. The kid tilted his pelvis expressively and Stone was amazed to discover his glands still in working order. He chuckled. "We'll get to *that* information in a moment. Did anyone work on the yellow Marshall that stopped here a couple of days ago?"

"There were three 'vans. Two local jobs and a stranger."

"Tell me about the stranger," Stone prompted hopefully.

But the boy shrugged. "We didn't really do any work, but we sold the lady a bunch of spares, machine parts, you know. She said the 'van was going okay."

"You get the name or the reggo on the chit?"

"Sorry, man, she did cash. We don't bother with details for a cash sale." The lad saw Stone's expression turn to disappointment. "Hey, what d'I say? Can I do something for you? You look blue."

Stone lowered both forearms onto the cool, glass-topped counter. In the display case beneath it were fishing knives, chocolate, cameras. "I am blue. I've been tracking that damned 'van from Chell. Now it'll be lost in the traffic around Eldorado. I don't know the owner's name or the registration code — I'm right back where I started. Shit!"

"Well ..." The boy seemed to reconsider what he had been about to say and then cast caution to the winds. He scraped a stool up to the other side of the counter and leaned closer. "I'd know it if I ever saw it again. A lot of 'vans have the flame scallops, they're speedy fashion, real trendy, and a lot of 'vans are yellow. But that one, I can pick out of the crowd."

"How?" Stone's strung-out nerves came alive again. He looked across the counter, liking what he saw. Brown, frank eyes looked at him with a lively mischief. How old was he? Twenty? No older, surely.

The boy grinned impishly. "I hit it with the back of my groundie when I was on my way out. I backed straight into it. The lady didn't notice so I didn't say anything, but I put a dent in it, somewhere on the left side. I *must've*, 'cause I've got her yellow paint scraped off on my rear bars."

"You little devil," Stone chuckled. "What's your name, kiddo?"

"Riki." A lean brown hand was thrust out. "Riki Mitchell. Hello."

79

"Hello." Stone took the offered hand for a moment, found it smooth and warm. "You do know you're in violation of standard traffic regulations, don't you? You should have reported the collision." The old Tactical training still came to the surface occasionally.

Riki groaned. "You're from Tac. You're gonna bust me."

Stone shook his head. "I'm a NARC. I don't give a toss about traffic offenses, your secret's safe with me, love." He began to think hard. "Look, Eldorado will have tracked the vehicle, but they'll load me with a hundred of the bloody things to chase up. If I had an eyewitness along it'd take the hard work right out of it. Are you game?"

"You — you're a NARC?" Riki said hesitantly.

"Unless you're a crimmo, what's it matter?"

He looked away, both hands rubbing boyishly slender arms, an expression of anxiety. "I dunno."

"I'm not going to twist your arm ... but I do need your help." Stone softened his tone. "I'm a NARC. So what? Somebody told me not long ago, underneath the riot armor, surprise — we're human after all."

Riki shot a glance at him. "I'm not a crimmo. But you'd make trouble for me. I just know you would. You'd have to, wouldn't you?"

Stone's brow lowered. "Now, why in hell should I do that?"

The brown eyes averted and the words came out as a breathy rush. "I ... I'm a user. Angel. Not much, not that often, but I use it, I like it. I kind of have to have it. Sometimes I just *need* it, and it's bad if I can't get it." He would not look up now. "There. Bust me if you want to."

But Stone was silent, his face a mask of cynical regret. His heart weighed like a brick. He knew he should not even be surprised. In any age group one would find thousands like Riki. More. "How long?" He asked quietly. "How long since you started using it?"

"Two months. My Dad doesn't know yet."

"He will soon." Stone sighed. "When you start needing it every day, thieving to buy it. When you're bombed out of your skull all day, every day, you won't have to tell him. He'll take one look at you and know."

"You think I don't know that?" Riki looked up, and the brown eyes flooded. "You think I'm proud of it?"

Stone exhaled through his teeth. "Don't blame me for the facts, sweetie. I only read the news, I don't write it. You think it'll never happen to you, but it will. It's always the same. Jesus, *why* did you take the crap?"

The tears welled up and spilled. Riki cupped his chin in his palms, elbows on the counter. "I was so miserable, I wanted to die. Or get drunk or something. There was a man —"

"There usually is," Stone said. How often had he heard the same approximate story? It must have been a thousand times, first with Tac, later with NARC. "Let me guess. He loved you and left you."

The boy nodded. "So I took it. Angel. It was ... fantastic, like having an orgasm for hours, and you're floating, and the world changes shape. You can fly, you can hear the trees singing, you can swim in ice. Better than fucking with that asshole. Better than getting hurt, then getting dumped. So I used it again. It was better than anything I ever knew."

"If he such a sonofabitch," Stone asked quietly, "why did you get so miserable when he wandered off that you took Angel?"

Riki shrugged. "Maybe I was just plain stupid."

"Maybe you were. And you take it how often?"

"Couple times a week, maybe three times if I'm blue."

He had eighteen months to live. In a year, Riki would look forty. By the time his heart gave out he would be an old, old man. Stone's eyes strayed across the brown young skin and he shook his head at the tragedy of it. "How old are you, Riki?"

"Nineteen, I'll be twenty in two months," he whispered, and the tears spilled again. "I know what you're thinking. I know what they say about Angel. I should have known better. I'm going to die, aren't I?"

Stone ached to lie to him, but Riki already knew the truth. Anything he might say to the contrary would be pitifully transparent. The kid had no hope of rehab. In all the years of research, the chemists and therapists had found no way to wean an addict off the drug. At nineteen, Riki Mitchell was already dead, and he knew it. He could use Angel and die of the effects or he could try to kick it and die in withdrawal. Either way he was just as dead. He might as well go out happy.

And worse, he was alone here. There was no one, Stone realized, in the small island community, to whom Riki could turn, lean on, because as yet his family had not noticed anything was wrong. And when they did find out, in this isolated rural community Riki's predicament would be called a 'disgrace.' He might be ostracized rather than helped. In all probability Stone was the only person who knew, other than the supplier, who was less than likely to be supportive when the end grew near.

As Riki began to cry quietly Stone walked around the counter and took the boy in his arms. Riki buried his face against Stone's chest and the NARC man sighed heavily. "Look, there's work going on all the time in a hundred labs between here and Earth," he reasoned. "Someone has to be the first to beat it — why not you? It's not as if you're going to drop dead this afternoon. Who knows what'll be happening in a year or two? You've got that long, kiddo."

He lifted his blond head and his eyes were pink. "Thanks. But you're lying. I'll be dead in two years, won't I? No, don't answer that." He drew his palms across his face. "I should have cut the balls off that bastard and fed them to the seagulls, shouldn't I?"

Stone shrugged. "You could have thumbed your nose at him and gone out and got yourself another man. There's hundreds of them out there, all shapes and sizes and colors to choose from, and all just waiting to be seduced. It'd be like shooting canaries in a cage for a beauty like you."

He drew away, hugging himself. "Thanks. Yeah, I was a fool, who's denying it. But what's done's done." He looked around at the shop full of machine parts and tools and fishing tackle. "Do you know, this place is all I've ever known. I started work here right from school, I've never been anywhere. If I'm going to cock my toes, I want to see someplace else before it happens. You offered me a trip to Eldorado. You still offering?"

"Still." Stone lifted a brow at the kid. "It won't be a long trip, though. I'm in a military jet."

"Any trip's a trip," Riki said, angry with himself now. "I'm game, Stoney. I want to go with you. When are you shoving off?"

Stone stepped back from the counter. "Whenever you're ready. I'll be in the plane. I'd better call home, my ship, before they get itchy."

Riki began to move. "I'll tell my dad. He won't want me to go, but it's got zip to do with him. I'll pack a few bits and pieces and change."

"Don't change on my account," Stone said huskily, looking down at the delightful backside in its cutoffs.

At the door leading into the rear premises, Riki paused to look back at him. "You sound like a randy beast, Stoney. Am I safe with you? I hope not, or this is going to be a real wasted trip!"

With that he was gone and Stone watched the door swing closed with a rueful expression. At the very least this was going to be interesting. If it had been a vacation he would have been glad to kick back, give his glands their heads, and enjoy. But Jarrat haunted him. Waiting for Riki, he stood in the shade of the spaceplane, headset on, glaring impatiently at the brazen blue sky, the dusty trees and white-walled houses of Outbound.

Mischa Petrov's voice in his ear was not a welcome distraction.

He was sitting on the bench in the summerhouse, under the palm fronds, with Harry's second-eldest son, Malcolm. Malcolm, with the brown eyes and fair hair and hands born to play the mandolin. Music wafted out across the courtyard as Evelyn approached the cane-and-trellis structure, lilting melody echoed by laughter, and as she came to the arched doorway she watched Mal set his mouth over lush, smiling lips and kiss John fondly.

A pace behind Evelyn, Tansy chuckled. "See? He's made friends, he's not frightened any longer, and Mal thinks he's the sweetest kid he's ever seen." Malcolm was seventeen. John was much older ... yet much younger. Evelyn sighed and Tansy caught her shoulder to hold her back. "Harry and I talked. John can stay with us. No institutions. And he won't get in Simon's way. God knows, this place is big enough for another kid."

Stay here? Evelyn was in the same moment astonished, resentful and relieved. She had braced herself for a pitched battle with Simon, never imagining Harry's enormous family would open ranks and adopt one more. John was Harry's eighth adoption. She had spent the last day growing resigned to domestic upheaval. Losing John so abruptly was absurdly painful.

In the summerhouse, Malcolm had both arms about him and was whispering into his ear. John smiled tiredly and Evelyn admitted to herself, he was happy here. Malcolm's kisses would soon become lovemaking, which was exactly what John needed now. He needed more time, attention and TLC than he could possible get in the busy, stressful, business atmosphere of the Lang household.

Just then Malcolm looked toward the door and tugged John to his feet. "Hey, babe, look who's here. It's your friend! Show her how you can walk. Come on, Johnny, you were doing fine before. It's gone stiff again?"

"A bit," John murmured as if he were shy. He held both of Malcolm's hands and took several steps. He was limping but he was up and walking. "It feels funny."

"Of course it feels funny," Malcolm retorted. "It was only just fixed this morning. Come on, walk a bit more. Show her."

"Okay." John waved, and Malcolm let go of him. He stepped carefully toward Evelyn and caught her hands instead. Both gray eyes were open; the repaired one was just a little bloodshot. He was freshly shaven, boyish, smooth. "I can walk! Mal says I can stay here with him. It's good here. They've got horses and dogs. Can I really stay?" He slurred the words but his voice was a little stronger.

Pain lanced through Evelyn's chest. She forced a smile. "Of course you can, sweetheart, as long as you like. How do you feel now? Aching?"

"They gave me some stuff," John said vaguely. "I had an awful head-ache afterwards, but they gave me this stuff and I'm just dizzy now. Harry says I'll get better real quick."

Tansy caught Evelyn's hand and tugged her away, back to the house. "Come and have a coffee. Leave the kids to amuse themselves and have a look at his scans."

Silent, troubled, Evelyn followed her, sat on the banana lounge on the terrace and tried to make sense of what Tan was saying. Harry was work-ing in the biolab through the open double-doors. He waved, test tubes in each hand. Fungus, Evelyn guessed. She sipped the strong black coffee, which had the distinctive, bitter flavor of the locally-grown bean, and tried to follow Tansy's explanations of what she and Harry had done. The pros-thetic work had not presented any problem. The hospital plates were cleaned, packed, ready to be shipped back to 'Paddy' with the life-support machine. John's new teeth were superb.

It was the work Harry had done on John's brain that had made the kid's head ache till he cried. "We gave him a little more tetraphine," Tan said softly as she looked out toward the summerhouse. Malcolm had his new friend flat in the grass by the door, tickling. "Harry tried everything he could with a probe, Eve. And Harry's the best in the business. Believe me."

"I do," Evelyn said quickly. "Nothing?"

Tansy shook her head. "The damage is like raveled-up yarn. The more you try to untangle it, the worse it gets. A Gordian knot. I don't think you could take him to any cutter in the city and get the job done. He's lucky to be alive, love. Be grateful, eh?" She leaned over and kissed Evelyn's cheek. "I know how disappointed you must be. I called Chell Tactical this morn-ing, when Harry had done his best and come up dry."

"You called Chell Tac? About what?" Evelyn poured a second coffee.

"I was wondering if they'd lost anyone answering his description. I thought he might have been wearing a Tac uniform a few days ago! Any-way, they said they don't have any MIAs that sound like him, so unfortun-ately you can be sure of one thing. He ain't on the legal side of things."

Evelyn digested this. "Meaning he's civvy, and he sassed them, like I said before. He went up against Death's Head like an idiot. You just don't do that, Tan. Not if you know what's good for you."

"Tell me about it." Tansy watched Malcolm stretch out along John's supple body and kiss his neck. "Anyway, that's all by the by. Those days are over. Look at him. He'll be happy here, and Malcolm's ... enchanted."

Evelyn found a faint, sad smile. "So I see. But John's a retard. Don't let Malcolm forget about that."

"He's a *man*," Tansy corrected. "You think busting his brain up is go-ing to disconnect his gonads?" She shook her head. "He's got all the same physical needs he had a week ago." She winked at Evelyn and chuckled. "You let old Ma Nature take her course — she usually knows best."

And Evelyn could hardly argue. She looked over the scans and read-outs littering the table about the ceramic coffee pot, able to make sense of only a small fraction of what she saw. What was going on out in the sum-merhouse made more sense. John and Malcolm were curled about each other, kissing deeply while the wind stirred the palms overhead and multi-colored parrots squabbled raucously in the canopy of eucalypts, red gums, trees from Earth itself. John was almost as nearly mended as he would ever be. If he did not find his home here, where on Rethan would he go?

"Hey." Tan leaned across the table and took Evelyn's hand. "You can come over any time you get away from business. I know you care for him."

"This is ridiculous," Evelyn muttered as her eyes prickled. "I've only known him a few days."

Tansy wrinkled her nose. "I knew I loved Harry in a few hours. I asked him to marry me the same evening. The bugger turned me down flat. It took me three weeks to wine, dine and screw him, and another three to make him sign the piece of paper with me!" Evelyn laughed. "You're welcome here, any time, Eve, you always were."

"Thanks." With a sigh Evelyn got to her feet and leaned on the balcony, looking over the garden to the forested hills. "John'll be safe here."

"Better, he'll *learn* here," Tansy added. "Some of his memory might eventually come back. Harry told me he's sure it's all in there, intact, but the kid can't get access to it. Almost as if he has some kind of traumatic amnesia *as well* as the damage caused by the hemorrhage. It'd be fairly predictable, since he was so badly beat-up. I don't know if I'd want to remember that myself! The mind has its ways and means of protecting us." She paused, hesitated, and went on very softly. "There's still the one alternative, you know. Harry has other skills. He can do a lot more than any simple cutter." When Evelyn did not answer she sighed. "You don't hold to the theory that says the T/87 gene makes folks like Harry perverted!"

"You know I don't," Evelyn said quickly, "but it's not my skull he'd be in, Tan, it's John's. John might bust my nose when he found out I'd let a ... a 'deviant' healer into him."

"You make it sound like rape," Tansy said quietly.

"Well, isn't it, of a kind?" Evelyn lifted a brow at her; Tan only shrugged and looked away. "Worse than rape," Evelyn went on, "or so they say. Rape of the mind. Christ, Tan, I don't know. I just know I don't have the right to make another person's decisions for him. Let John grow. Let him learn, you said he has the capacity." Tansy nodded. "Try to explain it to him, let him understand what Harry is and does."

Tansy's brows arched. "Let him make his own decision? You're passing the buck, aren't you? He's about eight years old between the ears. You want someone who's technically a juvenile to consent to an act you called rape a moment ago?" Evelyn opened her mouth to protest, thought for a moment and closed it again. "Nice little problem you got there," Tansy observed cheerfully. "No hard feelings, Eve. I heard every vicious story they tell about healers when I took up with Harry. I heard all the snide cracks, the dirty jokes about what he does to me in bed. There isn't one smut joke I haven't heard and been the butt of. If you've got second thoughts about asking Harry to get into John, so be it."

"No hard feelings?" Evelyn asked with a faint, rueful smile. "I'm not trying to insult Harry and what he does."

"I know you too well to think so." Tansy poured the last of the coffee. "Come look at the fungus. We've bred up a new hybrid, it produces some of the effects of Angel without the addictive properties."

Following her along the balcony toward the glasshouses, Evelyn heard John's quiet voice and looked back toward the palm-shaded lawns. Malcolm had the clothes half off him, his head was down over John's chest as he sucked his nipples. John must still be impotent after the trauma and drugs, but he held Malcolm's dark head to his breast and arched his back sensuously. When he was well and strong — oh yes, he was a man, with all the same physical needs he ever had.

For just a moment Evelyn wondered about the lover John must have left behind in Chell, the partner who was right now going through the hell of grief, never able to imagine John was alive, healing, relearning. Evelyn sighed heavily, and followed Tansy into the aromatic humidity of Harry's vast, hangar-sized glasshouses.

CHAPTER TEN

It was the first time Riki Mitchell had been off Outbound, the first time he had been aloft in a military jet, far from home, whisked away by a man who was essentially a stranger. Stone caught some of his thrill and indulged him. He took the shuttle through a series of loops for the fun of it on the crossing to South Atlantis. Like riding a rollercar, Riki said, like the corkscrews at the carnival ground.

He had let his hair loose. A blond cape hung thickly about his shoulders. He wore sheer lycra from neck to ankles, bronze, skin-toned, and from just a short distance away he looked naked. Stone watched the kid attract no few wide-eyed glances. It was tragic. If Riki had got off Outbound a year or two earlier he might have found a lover who was good to him, not a bastard who would screw him one minute and disappear the next, leaving him to find his solace in a nose full of Angel.

Stone slipped his arm about the young man's waist as they walked into the crowded Eldorado ATC complex. The building boasted a decent restaurant, where he bought them an expensive meal before he hired a jet roadster and let Riki have the wheel.

"Just don't run through any Tactical radar traps with your foot on the floor, will you?" he asked with wry humor as Riki queued with the slow, prosaic traffic to leave Eldorado Field. It was late in the afternoon here and the commuter crush had already begun. "Remember, this car is out on a NARC hire slip, and it's my balls that'll be in plaster!"

"You could say you were in pursuit," Riki suggested. "Chasing bad guys." The brown eyes danced. One hand on the wheel, he reached over to mold his palm about Stone's muscular thigh. "You're too good to me."

"You think?" Stone laced his fingers into the kid's brown ones. "You just have a high time and enjoy it." They had a lot of work to do, and Stone sighed as he watched the Eldorado cityscape flash by. He had left the shuttle in the 'port's security compound and carried the R/T in his pocket. As Riki negotiated slow traffic and put his foot down again, Stone brought out the powerful transceiver.

"Raven 7.1 to *Athena*."

The carrier answered a moment later with Petrov's voice. "Still chasing your tail down there, Stoney?"

Stone cast a glance at Riki's legs. "Well, chasing someone's," he said with a fleeting, fragile humor. "Status, Mischa. I didn't call home to chat."

"Tac are on alert but no one's shooting yet," Petrov reported. "The Chell underground is like a crypt. Nothing doing. I want to stir them up a little, see what kind of scum rises to the surface."

"Stir them up?" Stone echoed. "By doing what?"

"We received the full inventory of missing hardware from Vincent Morello. They've lost everything short of a nuclear warhead and our guys are getting twitchy, Stoney, very twitchy. Morello's making excuses, but they backtracked through the network and they can pinpoint the computer that was used to hack their own. It's got to be the Black Mountain Engineers' mainframe. Fundamentally, it's an AI database, but it's the only system equipped to do the business. Morello's system is biocyber, and *very* good. I had Chell Tac run a probe on BME. You want to make a guess at who's a major shareholder, with coded access to their computer facilities?"

"Hal Mavvik," Stone said bleakly.

"Give the man a cigar," Petrov quipped. "Which gives us all the excuse we need to send a squad right into Mavvik's parlor and put the bugger in the hot seat. Shake him down, see what falls out his pockets."

Stone considered this for a moment. "You stand to lose the squad, Mischa. Okay, you'd have stirred them up, got them to initiate the firefight, but our squad, or some poor bastards from Tac, would be the first casualties. I don't like it."

"Yeah, it stinks," Petrov agreed. "We can do it by vidphone, then. See if I can needle Mavvik till he jumps."

"Do it." Stone watched Riki's hands on the wheel. "Give me a call when you're done with him. Raven 7.1 out."

As he pushed away the R/T Riki glanced sidelong at him. "What's that all about?"

"NARC business, honey," Stone said evasively. "Nothing to worry your head about ... and I think you want the next right exit."

They were headed for three of the sixty possible leads given to Stone an hour earlier by the Eldorado tracking network. The air over the congested seaboard was so filled with civilian traffic, it became impossible to track single vehicles under a ceiling of a thousand meters. But a grab-bag of sixty possibles was better than the hundreds of radar traces that flew through the network every hour. They had a lot of work to do, a lot of ground to cover, but Stone was sure it was just a matter of time now.

The Skyvans were parked in yards, in gardens, their owners uniformly disappointing. Stone sighed, systematically crossing them off the list as dusk began to fall. Jarrat was almost certainly in this city or close to it, but Stone knew he was running out of time. Petrov was anxious to settle accounts with the Chell syndicate. Too anxious? Stone was uncomfortably aware, the only available command rank officer should be on the carrier at a time like this. He was pushing his luck, and wondered how much further he could push it.

A forest of neon lit up as night fell, dazzling, garish. The smoggy overcast reflected the light right back, making the whole sky glow orange-red. Stone was tired. He had been on the run for days, sleeping in snatches, surviving on beer, junk food, peps and his nerves. Too many peps were not wise, but like any NARC he had done it before. He was sticky, he wanted a shower and fresh clothes, a decent meal and sleep.

They could do nothing till morning, since Eldorado, like any city, came alive at night. Most of the 'van owners would be on the street, wined, dined and bedded. Stone leaned back to watch Riki drive. Long legs in sheer lycra reminded him of Jarrat. Kevin wore his jeans tight as a second skin. They hugged his ass and cupped his groin, making indifference difficult. Stone closed his eyes.

Having Kevin so close, knowing he was in safe hands, no matter the neural work he needed, was the best feeling he had known in days. But the notes given him by Jeff Bolt remained troubling. Stone had read and re-read the treatment sheet. The notes made better sense to Kip Reardon, but Kip would not commit himself until he had performed his own series of scans. Either he would do the crucial work, or it would be done by the best man NARC could find in the homeworlds. Stone had faith. Jarrat would make it. He must. And then ...

And then at last, two weary years late, Stone would screw up his courage and find the guts to tell him the truth. *Transfer out if you have to Kev, but you better know. I want you. Want to be lovers with you. Want to love you.* Jarrat would have fits. It was discouraged by the NARC hierarchy and the grunts at the boot end of the service alike: officers just did not get involved, even close friendships were frowned on. Loyalty must be to the service, not to comrades. Involvement was too costly.

Stone remembered the words of the psyche testers, when he signed on. 'Have all the affairs you want. Sex is good for you. When a bum wriggles your way or a cock gives you the come-on, take it! But don't get involved. Never *ever* get involved. Involvement will kill you when the other guy buys the ranch.'

Wise words. When Stone told Jarrat the truth, Kevin would first laugh and then run. They had already bent every regulation in the book. They felt kinship for each other, deeper than the bond between most brothers. But Stone wanted so much more, and had wanted it for so long. The pretense had often been painful and he knew, now, it could go no further.

He was almost certain Jarrat was straight. No few crewgirls would swear it was so. An invitation to bed would flatter Kevin, Stone knew, and had they been civilians Kevin would have probably have accepted, straight or not, for the sheer fun of it. A man did not have to be gay or bi to have a fine time between the sheets with his best friend. But it was Pandora's box for NARC people: best left closed. Jarrat would be flattered, would be kind enough to let Stone down lightly.

And then he would file a transfer application, citing 'irreconcilable differences of opinion' as his reason for quitting his partnership with Stone, and the sting of lust unrequited would be over at last. It was a bitter forecast but Stone accepted it. The scene would play out as it must, and with a new partner he could settle into the kind of purely professional working relationship NARC wanted from its people.

The Volvo sports roadster braked down at a junction beneath a blaze of overhead neon and Stone returned to the present. "Make a left," he told Riki. It took them onto the up-ramp of a skypark. The jets howled at low power as Riki cruised, looking for a vacant slot. Only minutes later they were out, on foot, threading through the early evening market crowd.

Prices were inflated in Eldorado but he had three credit cards and a NARC ID, and the option of quoting his purchases on his expense chit. He bought black slacks, several shirts and outrageous underwear of Riki's choice. A scarlet posing-pouch with the word 'suck!' printed on the front. The underwear would go straight into the bin later, but Riki was having too high a time for him to spoil it.

The NARC identification got him a room with a view of the city from ten floors over the street. It had a hot tub, an unspeakable luxury to Stone, who was accustomed to the somewhat spartan conditions aboard the carrier. He locked the door as the boy went to look down on the city lights, and dumped his bags on the foot of the enormous bed. Riki looked at him over one shoulder and through a blond mist.

"One room, one tub, one bed. You're a randy beast after all."

"You can sleep on the couch if you like," he offered. "But I get the tub first if you're making out a roster." He pulled off his shirt and threw it away. "I've forgotten the last time I saw a tub."

A rich chuckle answered him. "The couch? Are you joking?" The brown eyes roamed over Stone, from his black hair to his Tac-issue boots. The way Riki looked at him brought Stone's tired body back to life. He felt himself growing hard as his blood began to pump. The feel and smell of men in his arms made him think of Jarrat, and sex had become a bittersweet pleasure. He opened his arms, eager to feel the press of a male body, and Riki stepped into his embrace.

The lycra was like warm, silky skin, but he wanted real, human skin. A rasp of velcro at the neck, and it split down the side. Riki shed it like a snakeskin and stood up, bare and beautiful and aroused. He was well endowed. Stone saw a lovely, rosy cock stand up to attention as Riki pinched his own nipples and tossed back his long yellow hair. Stone held him at arm's length to look at him, then bent to cover his mouth.

Soft lips opened readily to the kiss and Riki wanted his tongue. He thrust deep into the hungry young mouth, hands roaming restlessly over the hard, sinewy back and soft round buttocks. He felt between them, found the clenching muscle and pressed his fingertips to it. He lifted his mouth away to ask huskily, "What do you want, kiddo? You'd better tell me before this goes any further."

"This," Riki told him. He closed his hand about Stone's groin and squeezed the erect shaft trapped there. "In my mouth. In the other end of me. Every time you can get it up, it's mine. Okay?"

"Demanding little sod." Stone kissed him again and Riki mewled like a kitten, rubbed himself against the friction of the NARC man's clothes. Then nimble hands stripped Stone. Caressed him. Riki suckled him, bit his nipples hard enough to make him yelp. The slacks fell to his feet and he kicked them away. "Slow down!"

"Why?" Riki was panting, tugging him toward the bed. "I've waited all my life for someone like you. Gorgeous. God, Stoney, I don't believe this!"

Stone had a spacer's tan, even and uniform, gathered under a sunlamp during off-duty hours on the carrier. The hair on his chest was as black as that on his head, but not dense. His cock rose, a nine inch cudgel nested in raven curls. Riki's fingers traced it as he lay down, and Stone stretched like a cat, waiting.

The blond hair veiled the boy's face as he put his head down and began to suck. *And he calls me a randy beast,* Stone thought. He let Riki do it all, sucking him to a climax that was explosive. Then he rolled the kid over onto his back and spread the long, blond legs to lie between them and return the favors. He tucked his fingers between the lush buttocks and stroked there as he sucked. Riki was moaning, wanting. He thrust one finger in, and the kid came with a shout.

"Damn," Riki panted. "Damn! I wanted you to fuck me."

"Give me a chance," Stone said with a rueful chuckle. He leaned over to kiss across the smooth, brown chest and lick at little brown nipples.

"Where's your rush? We've got all night, and I want a bath first."

They shared the tub, drank wine and indulged in a languid foreplay that had Stone's balls aching before they pulled the plug and dried off. A bottle of skin oil stood on the side of the bath, compliments of the hotel. As Stone watched, Riki used it to prepare himself and went to stretch out across the bed. He lifted his knees up into his chest and waited.

He was young, and he was tight. Stone was surprised to find Riki deep enough to sheath him to the hilt, but the kid writhed and twisted until he had it all and then gasped out his fierce pleasure as Stone began to ride him. Before Stone's hazy eyes was Jarrat's face, taunting him as he pushed them on toward climax. Riki's fingers raked across his back, bruised him, and then he felt a spurt of wet heat as the boy cried out and came powerfully.

Limp, lax, he lay panting under Stone. "Oh, that was good." He rolled his muscles about the big cock still throbbing deep inside of him. "Go on. What are you waiting for? Nail me. Fuck me. Shag me till I can't walk."

"That what you want?" Stone stroked Riki's spent cock.

"That's what I want," Riki purred. "Feeling you in me, moving in me, having you there ... do it to me."

And Stone was happy to oblige. The second time he had control, he knew he could last as long as he desired. Like Riki, he wanted it to go on for hours. He lost all track of time, stopped to rest, rolled them from one position to another ... and came at last, much later, emptying himself into Riki's insides in long, hot gushes that destroyed him.

For the moment he had forgotten the beautiful kid was addicted to Angel. It was only later, when they shared the tub again, sent down for a meal and brandy and lazed the night away in each other's arms, when he remembered. Then Stone could have wept for him. Riki lay sleeping on his chest. He was so young, still just nineteen, and Stone perceived an unlikely fragility about him as he slept.

And Riki would never get the chance to be a man. Whatever life had to give him, he had to have *now*, before it all went sour and then came to an abrupt, cruel end. Stone cradled Riki against him in gentle arms and, in the small hours of the morning when he woke and stirred to lust again, made love to him the way he wanted it.

Jarrat could so easily have been like this. Sheckley was a bad place to grow up. Stone had never been there, but he had seen it on numerous vidcasts. The halfway station was essentially one big 'gas station' for the heavy freighters which made their way out among the colonies and returned, loaded, to the homeworlds. The 'rink' was where the action happened, a two-klick-wide 'tocamac' originally designed to dock ten colony ships at a time, back in the days of the sleeper ships. Now the rink serviced orehaulers and a few starclippers. Sheckley's zenith was long past and the old colony was declining, impoverished. It was dying, and festering with Angel. Jarrat's stories of Sheckley were about the growl of heavy machinery, the chill and dimness of an inhospitable world: a ball of rock, hollowed out, sleeved with metal and plastex, warmed by nuclear generators. Humans lived and worked there until they could figure out a way to escape. Not a good place to be a foundling kid, abandoned to the hospice, with the Angelpack running wild right outside.

In the hour before dawn Stone was awake, frowning at Riki's face and thinking bleakly, many times Kevin Jarrat must have come close to ending like this: youth and beauty masked Angel's terrible secret. Death was as yet no more than a shadow in Riki's eyes; time made the shadow lengthen and darken. Kevin, Stone realized, had been just lucky to get away from Sheckley before he, like his friends, went down before the succubus.

Stone's eyes prickled sharply. He turned over and pulled up the sheet, determined to grab another hour's sleep if he could get it.

Rain misted the mountain foothills and sheet lightning flickered from the cone of the grumbling volcano to the sea, which lay like a leaden ribbon, low on the western horizon. Evelyn Lang swore as she labored through the ankle-deep mud and struggled with the tow coupler. The tropical storm had come up out of nowhere, making her work much harder. A flatbed ground truck had lost its repulsion power and gone off the road under the slopes of Mount Sequoia. Its driver caught a ride into Gresham's and called for help from there. The nearest commercial towing operator was Roadrunner Charter And Salvage, out of Ballyntyre. Evelyn read her trading name, a decal on the side of the heavy towtruck, and not for the first time wished she had stayed with Military Airlift.

The tow coupler was greasy, rain-slick. It connected under the weight of a kick and she thumbed the infrabeam to cue the winch to take up the slack. The ground truck had bottomed out on a slight slope in the rank underbrush and was up to its doors in mud as the storm filled the washaways to overflowing.

As the winch brought up the tension on the tow cable she keyed the autodrive to back up her vehicle. The stranded truck came unstuck with an obscene sucking sound, and the autodrive pulled it back onto the road with a grinding of metal on bitumen. She had its keys in her pocket, and popped the service hatch to look at the repulsion system. It was fused. The insulation had been allowed to burn right off the wiring until the whole harness had melted down into a puddle of indeterminate scrap metal.

She sighed and wiped rain off her face. The sky was growing lighter in the south, so the storm would pass over soon. She wore oilskins but was still drenched, and inside them sweated in the tropical heat and humidity. From the back of her vehicle she wrestled down the jack and crammed it under the flatbed. It whined under the load as it picked the woebegone truck up off the bitumen, far enough for her to get a powerful repulsion sled underneath. As she retrieved the jack and returned it to its clamps the shortwave issued a burst of white noise and her name.

"Roadrunner Base to Mobile Three. You there, Eve?" It was Simon, excited and impatient. She paused to heel off boots that had thickened with mud, and before she could lean in to the cab and answer Simon was on the air again, bawling at her.

"Yeah, I'm here, for chrissakes, Simon," she replied, cutting him off. "I've got it riding repulsion. Tell Art he can head for home, no need to come this way, it's under control. What's your trouble, kid?"

"My trouble? Not mine," Simon retorted. "Tac's out here."

"At our place?" Evelyn was trying to peel off the oilskins. "What the hell do they want with us?"

"Not here, but in Ballyntyre. A squad flyer landed an hour ago. There's been trouble."

"Trouble? What kind of trouble?" The last time Tac had shown up in Bally was the day of the earthquake, three years before. Bally was too small for them to even be aware it existed, save as a flyspeck on the map.

"Someone called for Eldorado Tac," Simon told her. "The way I heard it, there's been a murder. A dead body at the hotel. Yeah, two days dead and gone green! Better come home, Eve. They're turning this whole place inside out."

Over a murder in a little country town? That did not sound like Tactical, Evelyn thought as she shut down the radio and stepped up into the cab. She twisted the key and the jets ignited. The towtruck rocked on its tractors as she shunted up toward the flatbed and nudged into the tow coupler. It was riding the gravity-resist sled now, and easy to maneuver, but her steering became ponderous as the autodrive's sensors registered the aft-harnessed mass. She swung in a wide arc on the empty road and opened the throttle as she entered the clearway.

Tactical rarely took any interest in a murder. Bodies were so common on the streets of any city that an investigation was a ten minute affair. If computer forensic analysis did not turn up a suspect the case was filed under 'pending' and that was that. Only rare killings involved Tac, so this one must be something special. In Bally? Evelyn could scarcely believe it. Nothing ever happened in Ballyntyre.

She left the flatbed at Gresham's timber mill, took payment on a credit card and turned back onto the road for home. Before she ran into the town she saw the Tactical squad vehicle, parked on its stout hydraulic landing gear at the juncture with the clearway. The road was closed. Armed, flakjacketed troopers had put up a red roadblock, and waved her down as she approached.

The window rolled down and she leaned out. "You want my ID?" She indicated the trading name on the side of the cab. "Run that as well. Here." A young man in black fatigues took her ID wallet, removed the card and swiped it right there on the roadside. Evelyn waited a few moments and then took it back. "What's the circus about, officer?"

He was bored and irritable. "Dead body."

"That wouldn't bring Tac out this far," Evelyn observed tartly. "Someone special, was he? No one local, surely."

"Courier from Chell," the young man said as if it was of no interest.

"Syndicate courier?" Her brows rose. "An Angel runner?"

"That's what they told me, lady." He jerked a thumb at the road. "Mine not to reason why, you know? I'm thinking about fainting in all the excitement."

She ran up the jets. An Angel courier from Chell, out this far? Now, *that* just might get Tac off its ass. But Bally was nowhere, a backwater that made Paddington seem like a burgeoning metropolis. She smiled mechanically at the young officer and took the towtruck on into the town. But rather than heading home she pulled up, nose to the wall, beside the single hotel. The Havelock was as much a tavern as a hotel, and Maurice Havelock was not the kind to allow Angel dealing under his roof, where Bally's kids congregated to play and screw for want of somewhere better to go.

Small, rotund, unprepossessing, Havelock was chain-smoking in the publican's yard. He looked up nervously as Evelyn appeared and offered her a cigarette. She lit it and took a drag before leaning on the wall beside the crate where Havelock sat.

"You been getting the third degree, Morry?"

"Tac bastards," Havelock muttered. "Jesus, it's like they think I shot the guy myself!"

"If you did, and there's one less Angel runner in this world, you'll collect a reward," she said dryly. "Stop worrying. Shot, you said? What with?"

He stubbed out a spent butt and lit another smoke. "Steyr .44, they said. They dug a round out of the body." Havelock was green to the lips. "Sent a microscan back for analysis. They're looking for matches to some cannon that killed a big-noise in Chell a month ago ... f'chrissakes, Evelyn, a Steyr .44? That's a *pro* gun! Who'd have a cannon like that, in this mudhole? We've got a syndicate shooter in Bally. What would bring him here?"

"He must have followed the courier here," Evelyn guessed. "That was his contract, kill the bastard and get out."

But Havelock shook his head and looked up with a worried expression. "They arrived together. I've already had the thumbscrews from Tac about this, given them a description of the shooter. They know him. It's a cityside contract boy, and he came in *with* the dead guy. They booked the same room, fucked their brains out the first night and then — boom. I didn't hear a friggin' sound out of the room, and the shooter vanished into thin air. I thought they must've both gone, shot through without paying the bill. A lot of buggers do. So I opened up the room." He gulped and dragged on the cigarette again. "He'd been dead two days. Had a hole in him the size of your fist. Shot with the shooter's own cannon."

"And Tac knows the pair of them," Evelyn mused. "One night they're bonking their brains out, the next minute the mule's stone cold and the shooter's vanished?" Havelock nodded miserably. "Doesn't make sense."

"It would if someone else killed the mule with the Steyr when the shooter was out." Havelock rolled his eyes to heaven. "I didn't hear the shot. I was stoned myself that night. I do a trip now and then, it's harmless, nothing illegal. Bloody Eldorado Tac wants me to do piss-tests!"

Evelyn dismissed Havelock's concerns. Most drugs had been harmless and legal since antitoxin research produced neutralizing agents, blockers, which acted in moments and curtailed a trip at will without withdrawal. Addiction was virtually unknown. Angel was not the same. For Angel, there was no antitoxin, nothing to neutralize its effects or impede runaway addiction. And users swore no other trip was like an Angel trip. After Angel nothing else would do.

"Vigilante?" Evelyn asked shrewdly as she ground out the cigarette. "I mean, we've got a lot of old farts in this town who would quite literally kill to keep Angel out of Bally. And to be candid with you, I can't really grieve over one dead mule."

"Ask Tac," Havelock said, pained. "They must be just about finished by now. They set up their lab in my wine store."

In fact, the forensic crew from Eldorado Tactical Response were packing up as Evelyn knocked on the storeroom's open door. A sergeant, tall, sparely built with thick yellow hair and a darker mustache, looked up at her from the case he was locking. Evelyn recoiled in surprise and then laughed. "My God, it's Troy Bowden! Where did you come from? The last time I saw you, you had both arms in splints after that squad from Aerodyne shelled you into a ditch!" On Sheal, in the corporate bloodbath, so many years before. Troy Bowden had changed. He was a man now, where she had known him as a gangly youth in uniform. The difference between the boy and the man was striking. "Look at you! You grew up nice, Corporal."

He chuckled and pointed at the three stripes on the sleeve of the black Tactical uniform. "Onward and upward, Eve. God, you look good. Don't tell me you're still living in this nowhere place."

"I like it." She shrugged and gave Troy her hand in greeting. "It's quiet. I had enough of the rat-circus out there to last me a lifetime." She cast a glance at the equipment he had been working with. A girl in the familiar black fatigues was dictating notes to a handset. "Looks like the rat-circus followed me here. Any answers, Troy?" Evelyn thrust her hands into her pockets. "I mean, this is the biggest show we've seen in Bally since the 'quake. You're not going to keep us in suspense, are you?"

He chuckled. "Hardly. No need, ma'am. We're not going to make sense of this in a hurry." He nodded at the heavy bodybag in the corner of the room. "One deader, one .44 round out of a Steyr that was loose in the Chell underground last month. Two guys come to this nothing town, fuck like long-lost lovers, then wham. One's dead, one's missing." He knocked on the case he had just repacked. "Half a kilo of Angel. Too much for a place like Bally — it'd kill the whole population in a week!"

"So was the mule just passing through?" Evelyn wondered aloud. "Was the shooter his minder?"

Troy Bowden made negative noises. "From the kid's description and the gun ID'd by ballistics, it has to be Joel Assante, upmarket talent from Chell. Very young, very good ... very deadly. The courier was an Eldorado face, name of Weaver. You're not going to find Assante taking hack work like minding for a smalltime runner like Hank Weaver."

"But the two of them turn up in Bally at the same time," Evelyn added. "By accident?"

"Or intent." Troy winked at her. "Long-lost lovers? It's possible. Weaver was a good looking sonofabitch, young, twenty-two years old, yupping as hard as he knew how ... and from the file images, Assante is a beauty."

"Or was," Evelyn said thoughtfully. "You don't know he's still alive. If he didn't kill Weaver, who did? If a local vigilante — and we have 'em, Troy! — wasted Hank Weaver, he might have done Assante too. You just haven't found the body yet. Morry Havelock was stoned when it happened, so he told me, and the kids play the steelrock so loud, you wouldn't hear a pitched battle over it. If I were you I'd be out looking for a body."

"Maybe," Troy mused as his assistant packed up and began to carry out cases of equipment, the computers and highband transmitters. "But it's stretching credulity, Eve. I can accept your small town vigilante fragging Weaver. The man was a courier, nothing special in the physical stakes. Assante? No, The kid lives on his toes. It'd be a different ballgame." He leaned over, kissed her ear. "God, it's good seeing you again. Why don't you call me? I'm available any time I don't draw duty, and all yours, sugar." Then he winked, and as his assistant called his name, hurried away.

She stood in the empty storeroom, brow creased in thought as she watched a couple of Tac troopers carry out the bodybag. So a mule was just passing through Ballyntyre on his way to Eldorado, perhaps taking the back way in, which was safer than running the Tac gauntlet at the spaceport. A young king shooter from Chell city bottom was in Bally at the same time, his business nothing to do with the Eldorado Angel trade. They roomed, had sex ... and then some local town father took vengeance into his own hands. Weaver was dead.

And Joel Assante? What would bring a top-line cityside shooter to what was, as Troy said, a nothing town? Her mouth dried. She heard the Tactical flyer's big engines ram up to takeoff thrust and caught a glimpse of it, lumbering away over the rooftops as it lifted and headed north toward the city, almost eight hundred kilometers away. Only a contract job would attract talent like Assante. She closed her eyes and groaned.

They tracked me home? They must have! Does John have a biocyber implant, a transmitter? Oh Christ.

"John, who the hell are you, what are you?" She was muttering but Morry Havelock looked up at her, wondering if she had spoken to him. She shook her head and fended him off. "Just talking to myself. Old age, Morry. Got things to do, man. Ciao."

Knots of townspeople stood in the street, chattering excitedly about the show. Evelyn gave them a sour look and ignored them all. She slid into the cab of the towtruck and had fired the jets when the shortwave crackled for attention. But instead of Simon's voice she heard Tansy Del, and her belly churned. "Tan? What is it?"

Tansy hesitated. "It's your boy, John. You'd better get over here, love, fast as you can. It looks bad. I'm so sorry."

"Bad?" Evelyn reversed out from the wall and headed fast for home, where the Skyvan was parked. "What kind of bad?"

"He just collapsed. Some of Medic Bolt's cerebral work broke down. It's not Bolt's fault. This can happen, it's why we keep them under observation. But you'd better get over here ... and Evie, don't be long."

Dry mouthed, Evelyn put her foot down hard.

CHAPTER ELEVEN

The cryogen tank was a relic, sold at auction when the fittings of an old rimrunner, a long-duration freighter, were broken down for disposal by a junk dealer. Since the development of the hyperdrive there was no necessity for the suspension of biological functions to make deep space travel feasible. Harry Del bought the tank for medical purposes and had used it perhaps a dozen times in twice as many years. It was in use again today.

John Citizen was a delicate shade of pale blue. He looked dead, but in fact he was in perfect suspension, preserved for as long as a trickle of power was delivered to the tank. Evelyn stood in the infirmary, frowning at his face through the tough plastex casket.

"It was the best thing to do at short notice," Harry said softly. He sat at a nearby bench, fingers scurrying over a keypad. "He just fell on his face. Malcolm screamed blue murder, and he and Allen carried him straight here. Tan had sense enough to turn on the tank and shove him into it, or it could have been much worse."

"Worse?" Evelyn glanced sidelong at the man she knew was a genetic deviant. "What could be worse than this?" He turned off his slave terminal and joined her beside the tank, arms folded, frowning at his patient. "One or two of Bolt's tissue welds, in the frontal lobes of his brain, gave under increased blood pressure. Malcolm said they were fooling around and John became excited. That put tension on the cerebral welds and they gave."

"They were fucking?" Evelyn demanded. "The idiots!"

"No, no," Harry argued. "See it this way, love. If the welds were going to break down, better they do it now than later, when he's within shouting distance of the only cryotank between here and Eldorado. That boy is one of the luckiest kids alive."

"Alive?" Evelyn put her flat palm on the plastex. It was cold enough to burn. "You call this alive?"

He smiled patiently. "Very much so. Many years ago, when the robot terraformers shipped out and the first colonists arrived on this planet, everyone came out from the homeworlds in this condition. We don't do it now, we don't need to, but the mechanics are very simple and almost foolproof. It takes less juice to run the tank than to power a flashlight. And if you want him out of there you hit the red switch marked *retrieve*. Oh, yes, he's alive. But it's all academic, isn't it?"

She sat on the edge of the littered computer desk and rubbed her face. "What are you telling me? You can't mend the welds that broke down?"

"Not with a laser probe," Del said thoughtfully. "I could try, but you must understand, this new damage is radical. The hemorrhage was severe. He's lost his motor complex and the Broca's tissue." He tapped the left side of his forehead. "Which means he won't walk and talk ... now, I might get in there with a probe and make a bigger mess! Take him to a cutter in Eldorado if you like: if he's honest, he'll tell you the same. If he's not, he'll do the work, bugger the kid's head up for good, then pass you a monster bill with one hand and a mental vegetable with the other."

"So Jeff told me." Evelyn bit her lip. "But you could mend it ... the other way. Couldn't you?"

A sigh whispered from Harry Del's lips. "Even genetic mutations have their uses every now and then, don't they?"

"I'm sorry, Harry," Evelyn said tiredly. "I know I put you off before. I gave Tan some shitty reasons for telling you to stay out of his head."

But Del was unperturbed. "They were good reasons, actually, at the time. But you've reached the last-ditch scenario, Eve. Understand this. He can stay in the tank for the next millennium, outlive us all. Or you can take him out and bury him tomorrow morning. Or I can do what I do. And I have to tell you, love, it's been taken out of your hands. Malcolm already made your decision for you. I'm going to do the work for Mal, he's agreed to take responsibility, and if John blacks anyone's eye, it'll be Malcolm's. My son is infatuated. We had to sedate him after the shock of watching his precious Johnny collapse at his feet. This is why Tan gave you a buzz, told you to come over here."

"So you could tell me I've been usurped?" Evelyn gave an odd-sounding chuckle. It was as if a great weight had been lifted off her shoulders. Someone else had taken station in the 'responsibility seat.'

"Yes. Still, There are one or two legalities to be tied up." Harry looked at the young man's pale blue face. It was as if he were simply asleep behind a mauve veil. "Mind you, I'm not promising either you or Malcolm any miracles. When I wade around in Johnny's mind I'll leave footprints, it's unavoidable. I'll traumatize him, and he'll fight me as if I'm raping him. When I'm done, he may not remember these last two days. Traumatic amnesia works this way. Many patients suffer it after the kind of experience I'll put him through." He spoke softly, regretfully. "If he doesn't remember what's happened to him since you brought him here, he will of course have forgotten Malcolm." He sighed heavily. "Mal is willing to take the risk. For Johnny's sake. He's a sweet, beautiful kid who must have been quite a man. The odds are with him, Eve. He could be quite a man again."

Evelyn smiled at the healer. "You're special yourself, you know?"

"I'm just a garden variety 'devo,'" Harry quipped, eyes sparkling. "Tan wanted you to know the state of affairs before I do my stuff. Technically, you will have to sign a release form, absolving me of culpability in the event something goes wrong. You salvaged the patient and brought him in, you see. Legally he's still your responsibility."

"In the event that *what* goes wrong?" Evelyn demanded. "You want to shoot that by me again?"

"The paper is just a standard release," Harry said offhandly. "They make you sign one before they'll drill a tooth for you, in case you faint at the sight of the drill and break your face on the floor as you fall. This is a registered clinic, I'm qualified in orthodox quackery, you know. I've got to keep my paperwork straight, but nothing will go wrong, I promise you."

How could he make such promises, Evelyn wondered, when even he did not know what he did, what his 'magic' was. She nodded and held out her hand for the form, the regular pink slip, bulk printed by the Surgeons' Guild. "When will you do it?"

"Soon." Harry drew her to the tank's control panel. "See here? He's in deep coma, not brain dead. Not yet." She studied the instruments, then the patient. "I swear, I did everything I could with a probe the other day. Gave him a crusher of a headache. Tan had to give him a little shot of tetraphine, it was that bad. It's not a cutter the boy needs now, it's a bloody miracle."

She looked up over the inert body. "The kind of miracle a healer can work. You did it for the miserable old bitch who got swiped by the speedy car. Do it for him. Look at him! He's got most of his life in front of him, you can't let him finish this way."

The healer smiled benignly. "Right. I've already 'busted my buns' as you delicately put it, to sort him out this far. You think I'm going to let him go now? If I did, you could take his body out and shove it through a trash compactor. He's beautiful, but he's just that much —" a snap of his fingers "— less than dead meat. The cryotank was the last resort." He chuckled quietly. "Isn't it just good luck I'm a queer?"

"You're special," she argued.

He smiled at the patient's colorless face. "*Empathy.* You know that's what they call it? Empathic healing. Some kind of 'laying on of hands,' as if I say 'hocus pocus,' and the rest is touchy-feely, feel-good magic. Jesus!"

"The cross you bear?" She asked ruefully, making him laugh.

"Maybe. Look, I'm going to grab a few hours' sleep, get a meal and a shower, and then I'll do it. I promised Malcolm. You can stay if you like. You can even come watch, but it's not much of a show. No bangs and sparklers. The doom-sayers will tell you it's more intimate than if I rolled him over and fucked his little fanny, more perverse than rape. In some ways I suppose it is. But it's a lot less physical. There's nothing to see."

"Because you'll be in his mind," Evelyn finished.

"Yes. And it *is* queer. Damned queer. So am I, same as all empaths. Some of us have the power to heal, some don't, but none of us is what you'd call 'normal,' and none of us denies it." Harry stirred and rubbed the back of his neck. "So, are you staying or leaving? You can hold Malcolm's hand. He's scared and taking it hard. He knows the chances. John probably won't know him when he loses his most recent mnemonic impressions, which is a damned shame, because they were starting to get close."

"I'll stay." Evelyn stretched muscles grown stiff with tension. "Hold Malcolm's hand, maybe. I know what he's feeling. Intimately." She looked down at the man she knew only as John Citizen. "And what about his deep memory, his whole life. Will he remember any of that?"

Del was fiddling with the keypad again. "It's all in there, if he can find a way to get access. No major brain structures were destroyed, and old memories are stored redundantly in lots of places, all over the brain. The trick is finding them. But it isn't important. He can make a new life, start again, well away from the men who beat crap out of him."

"Maybe," she said doubtfully. "Things just got a tad more complicated, Harry." He looked up sharply and she nodded. "A Tac squad was working over in Bally not two hours ago. Seems we have a syndicate shooter loose around here, and an Angel courier who turned up shot dead. Now, you tell me what would bring an expensive contract shooter to a backwater like Bally." She arched a brow at Del. "Did you scan John for implants?"

"You mean, a biocyber device, transceiver?" He shook his head. "It never occurred to me to scan him. You're thinking they might have tracked him here and sent a shooter to finish the job they bungled in Chell? My God, Eve, we could all be dead," he whispered. He rummaged in the desk drawer and fetched out a small probe. "This will do the trick. I'm scanning for the cyber part of the device, I've set for silicone, platinum, gold, in minute quantities ..."

The probe played over John's whole body and back again. Nothing registered, and they both began to breathe a little easier.

"It's nothing biocyber, or I'd have found it. So even if there's a shooter in Ballyntyre, he's got to figure his way here before he can make trouble for us, if he's looking for us at all ... and there's no way to be sure." Harry snapped off the probe. "Damn." He wore a thoughtful frown.

Evelyn rubbed her palms together. "It's almost vital John regains his memory. I just don't know what to make of him. I've been wondering, lately, if we're harboring a wanted criminal out of the Chell underground."

"Rival syndicates have an argument, their operatives get burned, some are left for dead in city bottom," Harry mused.

It was far from impossible. "We could get into some deep shit," Evelyn said quietly, "on the wrong side of the law. We could get five years behind a security fence in Eldorado. And if he's just an innocent bystander who saw something he wasn't supposed to, and took the fall, we could get shot in the crossfire as Death's Head tries to finish the job." She shook her head over the body in the cryotank. He looked simply asleep, like a masculine version of the sleeping beauty, peaceful, very beautiful, guileless. Helpless. "Who the hell is he? Where is he from?"

"Ask him later," Harry suggested with a certain wry humor.

She stirred. "I hope to God you know what you're doing."

The healer winked, ushered her from the lab and turned out the lights. "Give the deviant his chance. He may yet surprise you."

If Del had not been confident he would never have spent hours working on John's ravaged body. Evelyn had faith enough to be an unconcerned observer. She drank coffee with Tansy and sat with Malcolm for an hour, but Mal was flying on something, too strung out at the prospect of

97

losing someone he loved to face reality. He murmured John's name and held Evelyn's hand tightly before plunging into sleep. She closed his door and joined Tansy on the verandah as dusk settled over the rainforest.

Two hours later, Harry returned to the infirmary to do the empath's strange work. He had changed into shorts and a gaudy shirt and looked more like a beachcomber, or one of the students, but he moved with professional alacrity, total certainty in what he was doing. Evelyn stood aside with Tansy to watch.

The cryotank was parked in the middle of the infirmary. As Harry drew up a chair Tansy threw the switch to start the retrieval mode. Red lights peppered the control panel, and the plastex case popped open. A waft of freezing air gushed out. Harry moved closer and took the patient's cranium in both large hands. He murmured as he encountered supercold skin, but the tank's systems were already beginning to warm John. The work had to begin before his life processes resumed and he began to die again. The healer's fingers gripped lightly among the sun-streaked brown hair, a curiously tender touch. He closed his eyes, bowed his head, and neither spoke nor moved for over an hour.

There was nothing to see, nothing to hear. Whatever he was doing was beyond Evelyn. Jeff Bolt said it was like the gang-banging of a quadriplegic, but since Jeff had never experienced it personally Evelyn was disinclined to put much faith in the analysis. Jeff was a combat medic, one of the best who ever worked with Military Airlift. But he had been taught by his peer group to fear what he did not understand, and Harry *was* a queer, a genetic quirk of nature on this specific planet out of the scores of colonies. A healer. Moreover, he was an *empath*. Harry could never knowingly hurt anyone, Evelyn was certain: he understood pain all too well.

After a while she and Tansy left the infirmary and sat on the back verandah to drink tea in the cool of the evening. Laborers in the glasshouses were playing music and it was distracting. Tansy was about to ask them to turn it off when Harry appeared at the back door. He was pale, drawn, white about the lips with fatigue. But he was smiling.

He tapped his temple with one long index finger. "The man's a certified, card-carrying genius, no?"

Evelyn leapt out of her chair. "He'll be all right?"

"He damned well ought to be after that marathon," Del said ruefully. "He fought me every bit of the way — he's a tenacious sod, I'll say that for him. Wherever he comes from, they either breed them mean or train them hard." He leaned on the balcony rail and rubbed his temples. "As a rule, when I get inside someone's head I end up knowing them better than their best friends do. Peccadilloes, foibles, kinks, the lot."

"Hence, they call you queer," Tansy said, mocking very gently.

"Yes." Harry looked at Evelyn. "I usually get the works, whether I want them or not. But not this time, Eve. Not with this kid." He watched a rainbow parrot swoop from the roof to the trees in the humid expanse of the garden. "I don't even know his name, let alone who he is, where he comes from. He beat me off a dozen times. I had to jump all over him to get it done. It's as if ..." He gave Evelyn an odd look. "I'm certain of it. He's been conditioned. You're ex-military. You know about that crap."

Evelyn sat down in the wicker chair, elbows on her knees, intent on Del's face. "I was only with Airlift, Harry. Conditioned? In what way?"

"Deliberately. Do you remember, during the corporate war on Sheal, Aerodyne Techtronics and CyberWorld used to condition people to reject mind probing, that sort of thing. Interrogation techniques. Agents, spies, Intelligence runners. I think John might not be as innocent as we thought."

"Damn." Evelyn shifted in the yielding wicker basket. "You're sure?"

The healer shrugged. "As sure as you could be. He might have natural capacities, a strong mind, a tenacious will to survive." He rubbed his forehead. "But it can't all be natural. It's systematized, practiced. He's given me a skull-cracker. It feels as if I've gone ten rounds with a streetfighter. I'll have to pop something and lie down — thanks a whole bunch, Eve. That was a fun way to spend the evening."

"I'm sorry, Harry," she said honesty. "How the hell could I know? But it makes you think. If he's had this training he could be undercover from Tactical, or even Starfleet Intelligence."

"Which would explain the contract shooter showing up in Bally, out of the blue," Tansy added. She got to her feet, arms folded on her blue kaftan. "We might not be safe, Harry. I had the whole story from Eve while you were working. If this shooter, Joel Assante, came here looking for John, we're in the crossfire."

"Yes." Harry sighed. "As soon as he wakes, you'd better get him out of here, Eve. You realize that." Evelyn nodded. "There's some consolation in this, though. The bullshit brigade, Death's Head, probably wouldn't go in for this kind of deep-level conditioning. I'll give you ten to one on, he's not a crim. That's something. The bullet scars could mean he was shot in line of duty. And he'll wake before long."

"When?" Evelyn pressed. "How long does it usually take?"

Harry's lips pursed. "Depends on the individual. The old woman was two days, but this boy's tough as nails. He ought to come around by morning. Someone ought to stay with him, he shouldn't be alone when he does wake since it'll be traumatic. He's going to be disoriented as all hell."

"I'll stay with him, if you like," Evelyn offered. "Malcolm's high as a kite, poor kid. I'm so sorry about putting him through this. If I hadn't brought John here —"

"Hey." Harry leaned over and kissed her forehead. "That's life, love. Now, let me get something for this headache."

As Harry and Tansy returned to the house Evelyn went through into the cool quiet of the infirmary. It was a genuine pleasure to look at John and know, now he was merely asleep. As she watched him, he confirmed this as the truth. He drew up one knee and turned onto his right side, already hovering nearer to consciousness.

Malcolm woke long after midnight and sat with him. He had come down, taken something to cancel the euphoric he had used after John collapsed, and was painfully sober as he sat by the bed in the infirmary. Evelyn wished she knew what to say, but Malcolm had faced facts. The odds were against him. The trauma of the work Harry did would probably erase John's recent memories. As much as this would hurt Malcolm, it was the least of Evelyn's concerns. The specter of a contract killer in Ballyntyre haunted her and she waited impatiently for John to stir at last.

Dawn was an hour old when he began to move. The gray eyes blinked open. He focused with an effort and coughed. Harry slopped water into a beaker, supported his head and held it to his lips. "Quietly, son. You're fine but you're going to be woozy for a while." Malcolm stood by the door, pale, drawn after the long, hard nightwatch.

The water was gone in three gulps and the healer pulled the pillows under the patient's shoulders as he struggled to sit up.

John drew his hands across his face, squinted in the fragile daylight of very early morning. His vision came into focus at last and he found a hoarse voice. "Where am I?"

"In my infirmary," Del told him quietly. "And you're going to be fine."

For a moment he stared at the bed linen. "Why am I here?"

"You were hurt." Del frowned at him. "It's not unusual for the kind of trauma you suffered to cause memory blockage. What do you remember?"

The patient leaned back into the pillows and regarded the high ceiling, first blankly and then with an increasingly perplexed expression.

"The people who did you over?" Del prompted, but the man he knew as John Citizen shook his head slowly. "What about your name?"

Then he saw the panic start. John's gray eyes widened. "I don't know. I — I don't remember! Not anything. Not even my own name."

"There's no need for concern," Harry said soothingly. "It'll come back in time. You were badly hurt. Almost killed, in fact. Do you know me?"

The gray eyes peered at him, closed to slits as John tried to focus. "No. Should I?"

Harry sighed and looked at his son, who stood in the doorway. Malcolm's face set into anguished lines, and he fled. "No, perhaps not." Harry offered his hand. "My name is Harry Del. I'm a microsurgeon. I did most of the delicate work on your repairs. How's your vision?"

"Okay," John whispered. "But my knee feels stiff as hell."

"It's a reconstruction," Del told him. "In a day or two it'll settle down, when the inflammation has completely subsided. The new joint is stronger than the old one, John."

"John?" he asked hoarsely. "Is that my name?"

Harry smiled. "It might have been. 'John Citizen #34' was printed on your sheet back at the clinic in Paddington. I know you don't remember any of it, but it will come back. Your memories are quite intact, as is your neural circuitry." The smile widened. "That is, your brain is mended. *Healed.*" He waited for comprehension and outrage, but John did not react. "I shan't lie to you. I'm a healer. That's how I did the work."

Still John did not react, as if he did not even know what an empathic healer was. He was sucking his teeth. "My mouth feels weird."

"Your teeth are reconstructions too. Your own were too badly broken to be repaired. They broke your jaw and your nose too, but ... I have a mirror here somewhere. Ah, there it is." Harry held it up to show him his reflection. "Good as new."

John took the mirror from him. It was like looking at a stranger. He saw a smooth face, gray eyes brooding beneath unruly brown hair. "They did me over? Why? What did I do — and to whom?"

In answer, Del could only shrug. "We were hoping you could tell us." He pulled up a chair and keyed the intercom in the bedhead. "Evelyn, your friend is awake. He's doing fine but he's a little short on memory. You know more than I do. Come and fill him in."

The disorientation was frightening. John fought it, grateful that his head was clear. They had not pumped drugs into him, so he was not hung-over. His skull felt tight, even bruised, but he knew he was healed. He had his balance, vision and hearing. He guessed they must have let him sleep to facilitate healing, let the operation sites stabilize. He had no sense of time, nothing to base his perceptions on. He watched a blonde woman come into the quiet, clinical room. She smiled at him, delighted, but she was a stranger. Del had to make her introductions. John watched her face fall, then she hid her disappointment and sat, cross-legged, on the end of his bed. She and Del shared some worried frowns, but at last the surgeon only shrugged and the woman he had called Evelyn Lang began to speak.

John listened for twenty minutes as she told him everything she knew, clearly trying to stir his memory, but he remembered no more when she finished. She spoke at length about an organization called 'Death's Head,' and hatred almost choked her. "Death's Head is some kind of syndicate?" he asked when she paused to brood on something left unspoken.

"A bastion of private enterprise," Evelyn said bitterly. "An enclave of killers. Stand in their way and they'll chop you down, dance to their tune and you're dead anyway. Their merchandise is the drug called Angel. If you don't remember that, you're better off, kiddo."

"I don't remember much," he said, troubled. "Just fragments. The smell of coffee. Sound of birds. Nothing important. You'll have to tell me."

She made a face. "Potted pigshit. Snort it, smoke it, shoot it. The trip of your life, joy beyond endurance, prolonged until you can't live without it, then it kills you." She locked her arms about her knees. "Death's Head bashed you, no doubt about it. Problem is, we need to know why."

But he shrugged. "I don't even know who I am. Call me John, if you like. Why did you do this for me, Miss Lang?"

She sighed. "For chrissakes call me Evelyn or Eve. Why did I do it? I've been looking out for you for days. I might be a stranger to you, but you're no stranger, not to me. The longer you were my responsibility the easier it got to look out for you. But, no, it goes back before that. Ten years ago Death's Head killed my brother, Stevie. Beat his head against the ground till he didn't have a face left, cut off his hands so he couldn't be ID'd, or so they thought." She closed her eyes. Ten years later, the memory still made her ill. She shuddered visibly. "I looked at thirty dead kids before I recognized Stevie from an old scar. When I saw you were alive I was damn' sure Death's Head was going to get cheated of *one*. I did it for Stevie, really. You came later, when you turned into a person, not a greasy puddle." She frowned at him. "Now you're okay. What will you do?"

John blinked at her. "I don't know. I don't remember the way back. I don't know if I'm trained to do anything, I don't own anything, not even clothes, as far as I know. If you asked me to pay the bill, I'm not sure I could even start to cover it."

"I told you, this one's for Stevie," Evelyn said. "If you don't remember the past, start over. You're young. Come to Ballyntyre with me. That's my home, I've a business there. You're welcome to work with me, if you like."

"Doing what?"

"Driving. I run a commercial towing service. A lot of loons come up out of the city in suburban crap-bangers, and end up in bits in the mountains. We pull them out and shunt them back into Eldorado, for a fee. That's the city, a long way from here. It's good money."

His gray eyes misted. "I think I could do that. Drive for you."

"Give it a shot," she invited. Then she took a breath, let it out slowly.

101

"I've got to warn you, though. There's a contract shooter in Ballyntyre." He looked searchingly at her. "He might have come here after you. We're not certain, but ... after what happened to you in Chell, where I found you, and the bullet scars on you, and the conditioning of your mind —"

"What are you talking about?" John demanded as he swung his legs off the bed and stood. He put a hand to his head. "Oh, that aches."

"I imagine it does." She lent him her arm. He was naked, warm, beguiling. "Conditioning of your mind, probably to resist interrogation."

"How the hell do you know that?" John frowned at her.

"Harry's a healer. It's how the work was done," Evelyn explained, and then stopped. "You know what a healer is, don't you?" John shook his head. "Do you know what an apple is? A car? A vidphone?" He gave her a withering look. "Then your basic memory is intact. But you've never heard of a healer." He was waiting. "Well, your accent's a bit strange."

John's mouth compressed. "I could say the same of yours."

She smiled faintly. "I think you're offworld."

"Lady, I don't even know what planet this is," John retorted. "What the hell is a healer? I'd be lying if I said I understood a word of this."

"Harry's an empath," Evelyn said quietly. "John, I'm sorry. It was the only chance you had."

"An empath," he echoed, and shrugged unconcernedly.

Either he did not understand, or he understood and did not care that someone had rummaged in his mind, dredged it from cellar to attic and, but for his conditioning, would have learned his most lurid juvenile masturbatory fantasy, his darkest desire for masochistic submission, his most violent passion, the deepest secret and greatest shame of his life. No one was without such secrets, ancient embarrassments, failures, foibles. No one would willingly give another access to them. Evelyn passed the moment over with a dizzying relief.

If he did not understand what Harry had done to him, he could not be furious. An offworlder might not be aware of the quirks of genetic deviance that had created empathic healers on this planet out of all the colonies. The slight oddity of his accent impressed her again as he spoke.

"Can I get some clothes, or do you want me to walk around stark naked all day?"

Evelyn chuckled. "Well, if it were my choice, honey, I'd tell you to stay just the way you are, but I'll respect your modesty. Wait here, I'll see what Harry's got that would fit. And I meant what I said. There's a shooter out there somewhere, and it's even money he's looking for you."

"Looking to kill me," John whispered. "If I stay with you, that makes you a target too."

She shrugged. "Wouldn't be the first time I've been shot at, and I've got my old service cannon. I was with Military Airlift on Sheal. Medevac, pulling out survivors. Somehow I survived too." He seemed impressed. "But I don't think you should stay here," Evelyn added. "Harry and Tansy don't know one end of a gun from the other. There's not a damned thing they could do in their own defense if the man came here looking for you." He nodded soberly. "Let me get you those clothes."

Twenty minutes later John was dressed in baggy slacks and shirt. Harry Del was much larger, with a broader frame, but the looseness of the clothes was good, since no pressure was placed on the recent repairs. For an hour Evelyn spoke quietly to him while Malcolm hovered, watching from a distance, anguished and bruised. Then John grew tired and Evelyn left him to doze on one of the treatment beds. Disappointment had become intense frustration. She paced about the verandah and met Harry and Tansy in the glasshouses where they were tending potted herbs.

"He seems to be okay," Evelyn said slowly, "except for the memory. He's blank. Damn! This could get dangerous. I'll take him away with me. You'll be safer with him out of here. How long before he can leave?"

Harry straightened from his work and rubbed his back. "I wanted to keep him under observation till this afternoon. He's drug-free and full of antibiotics, but remember, he's very sore and very disoriented. Make sure he sleeps a lot, and don't give him anything strenuous to do till the tissue welds are sound. But otherwise he's as strong as he's ever going to be. I expect you have to get back to your business."

"Before we go broke," Evelyn admitted. "Simon's a useless little sod. It's not safe to leave him alone for long."

"Well, you can take John as soon as he's on his feet," Harry said thoughtfully. "You know, you're lucky. A hundred years ago the boy would have been flat on his back for weeks and pumped so full of tetraphine he'd still be talking to fairies a week from now."

"The miracles of modern surgical technology," Tan said dryly. "No incisions, no complications. What really pisses me off is that the guys who do the bashing use methods any caveman would have used, and they can undo our work in five minutes. Less. See if you can keep him out of sight, Eve. If the shooter finds him, he's dead *again*, and you could be stone cold too. Our John could give Death's Head to Tactical on a silver plate — or hand them to NARC, for that matter. NARC would be glad to bust Death's Head ... and Death's Head doesn't know John's memory is up the spout."

Keep him out of sight? Evelyn wondered. Ballyntyre was a very small town and it would be difficult, if Joel Assante, the contract shooter, was still there, watching. So John would take his chances, along with the rest of them. Bally lay in a fold in the mountains, far from Eldorado and about as far from Chell as it was possible to get. With luck, Assante would grow exasperated with the job of eyeballing a rural town from a hide in a steamy, wet forest, and leave with the job undone. It was not the kind of work a king shooter expected to do. It was, she admitted, very possible Assante had pulled out already and would tell his bosses in Chell there was no sign of the man they had tried to kill that night.

Since John did not know who he was, he should be content to stay in Ballyntyre until his memory began to return. She watched him get onto his feet early in the afternoon. He walked with a limp that diminished as he got the circulation going around the regenerated nerves, the new ligaments and tendons. Harry had drained the bruising about the knee. All he had to show for the implant work was a slight redness and the silver lines of the welds. He complained of his ribs and right wrist, but Harry assured him the mends were secure and merely settling in. The limp had eased with exercise by mid-afternoon. Malcolm withdrew to the summerhouse and Evelyn heard the sound of the mandolin as she stood with John on the back verandah. He had his hands in the pockets of Del's baggy slacks and was gazing at the rainforest behind the house.

He concentrated every erg of energy he possessed on memory, but nothing would come back. Frustration was wearying. He leaned on the balcony at the edge of the hardwood decking, and a pace behind him, Evelyn swore softly, sharing his frustration. "It's time to go," she said, studying his somber profile. "If you're coming with me, that is."

"To Ballyntyre," he whispered. "To start over."

"You have to do something. And you can't stay here and draw a contract shooter to these people."

"So I'll draw him to you instead," John said acidly. He straightened and frowned at his hands. "I must be a pragmatist. I get the packing knocked out of me, God only knows what for, and I start over as if nothing's happened."

She perched on the balcony rail. "So sit in a chair and feel sour about the world for a week. It won't help, lovie, I promise you. Look at yourself! You're built like an athlete, a dancer, you're fit enough for an assault course. What have you got to gripe about?"

John's mouth compressed, then he allowed a smile, displaying the glistening new teeth. "I just want to know where I'm from, who I am. Or *what* I am," he added darkly.

"Search me," Evelyn sighed. "Though I could make a few guesses."

"So guess." He thrust his hands back into his pockets.

"Well, you used to run a lot. The muscles in your legs say so. And you liked to pump iron. And if I'm not mistaken, you moonlighted as a stud of some repute."

He laughed shortly. "I expect you read tea leaves."

"No." Evelyn looked him up and down shrewdly. "I read people, and I'm pretty good at it. I saw you slide out of bed, buff-naked ... honey child, no one with a bod like yours sleeps alone." She held out her hand. "Now, are you coming to Ballyntyre? No law says you have to, and unless the shooter's packed up, gone back to Chell, he's out there, probably looking for you. You can't stay here, but I can give you a ride, anywhere you want to go. I've got to get moving, John."

He studied her silently. She was very blonde, with striking, angular facial bones. Cornflower blue eyes looked back levelly. The green coveralls she wore could have been paramilitary fatigues. She had snatched his life back out of hell and given it to him as a gift. And he owed her. A lot. With a sigh, John Citizen took her hand. "Okay. I owe you."

"That's the shittiest reason for coming," she said almost angrily. "Come because you want to, because you're interested in what I do, because you want to live again, because you fancy me. I'm not looking for gratitude, man. What I did was for a poor kid who got his head busted in and his hands cut off!"

Surprise made him recoil. "Fair enough, lady. I'll come anyway. I want to live. And I don't want some bloody contract shooter *itemizing* you on account of me."

She nodded briskly. "Good enough. You'll see Bally in twenty minutes if we get airborne right now."

She marched away from him, and it was the green paramilitary fatigues that tripped some tiny fragment of his memory. He clawed for it, desperate to grasp it, but achieved only the most nebulous impression. Uniforms; cold and dark ... blue neon shining on mirror-polished surfaces, the red wink of a spinner, the blare of sirens counterpointing a thunder of jets ... and a man. Big, muscular, dark, handsome. A man smiling at him with blue eyes, not like the woman's, but crackling, electric. *Male.*

Then the thread of memory was gone as suddenly as it had assaulted him. Unexpectedly, a throb of lust arrowed through his groin, taking him unawares. His brows rose and he smiled, mocked himself as he realized at least one truth about himself. He turned on to men. And there was someone special back there, in the cavern of his memory. The man with crackling blue eyes. Lang had style, real class, but the lure of maleness called to him, enticing, taunting. He closed his eyes, tried to concentrate on the face he had half-seen, memories lasting only an instant. The lust remained but the memory eluded him utterly and he swore in disgust.

The yellow Marshall Skyvan was parked on the raked gravel at the side door. Harry and Tansy Del gathered with four of the youngest to wave as it lifted off. Evelyn saw Malcolm's face at a window. He had been crying and her heart bled for the kid. John knew nothing about it, the pain was not his fault. As Harry often said, life could be a bugger. The eldest son, Alex, was missing. "Out screwing, I shouldn't wonder," Evelyn guessed as John gazed down at the house.

The 'van climbed steeply away. The sensations of flight were a familiar thrill. As she leveled out, Evelyn saw his expression. "I've certainly ... flown before," he said quietly. *Jet noise, spinners, sirens, blue neon.*

"Passenger or pilot?" She asked as they headed away from Del's property toward Ballyntyre, thirty kilometers in the southeast.

"I ... can't be sure." His voice was taut with stress.

"Try it. Find out." With several hundred meters under the aircraft she let go the controls. "It's all yours. Course is 238°, there's a crosswind from the northeast and a mountain right in front of you at five thousand meters. Don't worry, you can't hang it up, the autofly won't let you. These things come from the factory idiot-proof."

But she need not have offered the information. He read the instruments like an old pro, his hands feathery on the controls, and Evelyn just sat back for the ride. Flying the 'van felt very good, but wrong. John was annoyed by the ponderous speed, the sluggishness of the control surfaces and delayed responses of the machine, but he could not guess why. He said nothing, held the vehicle on course and climbed over the mountain with its microwave relays and enormous groundstation antennae.

Then he was dropping down toward a cleft in the lushly-forested slopes which Evelyn described as Ballyntyre. A small town stood below, slumbering in the heat of the afternoon. She took the 'van back from him and he watched her home emerge from the clutter of the rural settlement. A white-plastered building with wide yards at front and rear, in which stood two heavy trucks equipped with tow couplers. A tall radio mast was tethered by four steel cables in the back, a satellite dish stood at the bottom of the cabbage-patch garden, and a four-meter cyclone fence surrounded the property. The name of 'Roadrunner Charter & Salvage' was painted up above the garage's roller doors.

"It may not look like much, but it's all mine," Evelyn told him. "I have one driver, I drive myself, and my brother Simon looks after the radio."

"And what do you want me to do?" John asked quietly.

"At first, stay out of sight. If you don't show your face no one can shoot it off! Rest, get well. Later, you can help us out. I can use another pair of hands, if you're game to get them dirty. The turbo biscuit boxes get themselves screwed up in the worst possible places, it can be hell getting set up for a tow."

"Why not?" John shrugged. "How do I know I didn't do this kind of work before — in between pumping iron and getting laid a lot."

Evelyn shot a glance at him and laughed. "Glad to hear you haven't lost your sense of humor."

"Who's joking?" He demanded, and then relented and smiled, though the expression was filled with irony. "Jesus God, who am I? Harry says it'll come back. Maybe it needs a trigger. I don't know. I don't remember anything, Eve. Not my name, not my mother's face. Nothing."

The 'van settled on its stout hydraulic gear. Evelyn killed the flight systems and lifted the gullwings. "Don't fret, sugar. Come and meet the folks. Eat, sleep, let it come back on its own. And then tell *me*, before I bust a seal! I'd trade six months of my life to know why they took you apart."

"So would I," he said darkly. "If you knew the truth, you might not like it. I might not like it myself." He lifted himself out of the 'van and stretched carefully. The repairs felt better every hour.

"Anyone who gets a greasing from Death's Head has got to be on our side," Evelyn argued. "There's only three sides. Us, them, and the apathetic bastards who don't give a shit. Simon belongs to the latter. He's an irritating little bugger, but he's the last family I have. Don't let him get up your nose, John. I keep thinking, maybe he'll grow out of it."

As she spoke she led him toward the house. One end had been converted into a garage but the roller doors were locked down. Insect screens clattered at the door as they went inside. It was dim, and John blinked at the lounge's cane furniture, polished parquet floors and powerful comm set. At the radio sat a boy with yellow hair and an angular face, who had to be Evelyn's brother. He wore only faded denims and had a can of beer in his hand.

One look at the survivor's face, and Simon knew. He whistled through his teeth. "You let that devo into his skull."

"First chance, last chance," Evelyn muttered. "John's fixed. I don't see that anything else matters." She gave her brother a glare, a signal to drop the subject, fast. The radio was on but he had tuned it to the Tactical Response frequency. As she heard it Evelyn's mouth compressed. "A bloody lot of good it's going to do us if you're listening to Eldorado Tac! You've got a job to do, for chrissakes, Simon. Do it!"

The boy's face grew sullen. "Tac's gone on full alert. Something's happening out there — they're starting to use scramblers. They're firing signals to Chell."

"So they're using scramblers, who cares?" Evelyn snapped.

"There's signals about Death's Head," Simon insisted. "And NARC."

It was the first time John Citizen had heard the word and it rang about in his head for minutes. Impressions echoed, out on the far periphery of his mind where conscious thought misted into memory. He clawed after them — and the face he had half-seen —

A man's face, dark hair, smoldering blue eyes, a quirk of humor, dark sensuality, irresistibly appealing. A voice calling to him, deceptively soft, even silky, before a winking amber light turned red and all at once the voice was barking as if in command. *Neon-blue reflecting in a polished black surface, cold and dark, the thunder of jet noise, a falling sensation —*

"You look like you just saw a ghost." Evelyn was looking curiously at him, and the half-formed memory dissipated.

Ice-cold sweat prickled John's skin, head to foot, and he took a quick breath, ragged in his throat as his pulse sped. The adrenaline rush was uncomfortable here, in Evelyn's house, but the racing pulse and the heady feeling of excitement were also too familiar, and they belonged with ... with ... John groaned as he lost it. "Ghosts," he muttered. "Maybe I did see a ghost. I saw something ... familiar."

"Death's Head," Simon grunted. "They'd be damn' familiar, wouldn't they? They did everything from bust your head to punch your ass, and they must have done it for something. Maybe you were a dealer, a bag man."

"Shut it, Simon, or I swear to God I'm going to bust *your* ass!" Evelyn hissed.

The boy slammed his can of beer down beside the radio. The contents frothed through the top. "I've had it up to *here* with your fucking bleeding heart, Eve! Stevie's been dead since I was six years old —"

"And you're behaving like you're still six," she said tartly. "Grow up, Simon. I don't mean your foul little mouth and the bimbo from Gresham's. I mean open your eyes and learn, see, understand."

Simon made a mocking face. "Understand what? People get bashed into chopped liver every day on the street in city bottom? Stevie got his head knocked in? That they fucked him like *he* was a bimbo before they finished him? I do understand, Eve, I understand all that. I also know Stevie, your precious fucking Stevie, had a nose so rotten with Angel it would have fallen off his face in another six months!"

The blow was closed-fisted and knocked Simon off his feet. His lip split and blood spattered his bare chest. Evelyn flexed her fingers and turned her back on him. She paused only to adjust the comm back to the citizens' band before going in search of plastiskin for her split knuckles.

John stood at the bathroom door, watching as she sprayed the white fibrous mist over the cuts, and she muttered over her shoulder, "Don't let Simon annoy you, kiddo. He's family but he gets so far up my nose sometimes I could paralyze him myself."

John cleared his throat uncomfortably. "They uh, did my butt, Eve? That true? You heard it at the clinic?"

She replaced the pocket-size aerosol and closed the cabinet. "Yes. But the medic who fixed you up in Paddy saw to that. Don't fret about it, you're okay now. Check yourself out if you're worried, but a good mate of mine mended you."

He colored beneath his tan and looked away. "You realize Simon could be right. I could have been a dealer. It's far from impossible."

"You?" Evelyn frowned at him, studied him intently. "No, you're not the kind. You're a nice kid, not a pervo. Your memory's gone but you can't lose your personality, it's the one thing they can't steal. Come on, I'll show you your room. The other guy who works here is Art Pedley. I guess he's out on a job. Thank Christ someone's working."

The room was small, overlooking the yard at the back. It was already hot, and Evelyn threw open the window for air. She left John for a moment, and returned with an armful of Simon's clothes. Her brother was almost as tall as the stranger, and the same approximate weight. John tried on the faded denims and they fit well, but the shirts were tight through the chest and shoulders: Simon was still built like a youth.

But the mirror told John he was a man, broader, muscular, though not too much heavier than the kid. How old was he? He did not even know his own name, let alone his age, but a young man was framed in the mirror, his hair sun-streaked, his eyes some shade of gray, his brow creased in a frown of concern. John glared at himself for some time but no answers came. At last he gave his reflection an obscene salute, changed out of Harry Del's loose garments and rolled them up.

Fatigue drained him to the bone marrow. Even the struggle to remember was wearying. He ached from head to foot and settled to rest. He fell asleep quickly and it was dark when he woke. The last vague tendrils of his dreams haunted him: a smell he did not recognize, some chemical reek, he thought it might have been smog ... engine noise, voices shouting. An amber spinner reflecting in the curved surface of the weird black helmet which was cradled in the crook of a man's elbow.

The man turned toward John, but he was outlined against a harsh glare of floodlights ... he laughed, and all at once a voice spoke in John's ears. A man's voice, with an accent so familiar to John, yet very different from Evelyn Lang's or Harry Del's, or anyone else John had met since he woke and his life began, just hours ago. The accent was a world apart. *A world apart.* He knew the man's voice as well as he knew his own, yet it swam in his ears, out on the far edge of perception. On the level of animal instinct he knew it belonged with the face — the dark, blue-eyed man in whom seduction smoldered, the man who sent a throb of lust aching through John's whole body.

He fought to nail down the memories, grasp them, hold on, but in the seconds after he woke the dream dissolved, leaving him more frustrated than ever. He sat up, for a moment disoriented in the unfamiliar surroundings. The angle of the sun had shifted; the room was hot. He heard a water cannon firing arcs of irrigation into the garden out behind the house, and the chirp of cicadas, the squawk of parrots, a rustle of wind in trees.

Muted voices issued from the lounge, and the background chatter of the radio. John smelt some unfamiliar food cooking, and realized only then, he was ravenous. He pulled his fingers roughly through his hair to straighten it before padding, barefoot, in search of a meal. It was the first time he could remember feeling hungry.

Art Pedley was big, bluff, fifty. His face was weatherbeaten, seamed, his hands square and leathery. He shook John's hand with a smile showing teeth stained by tobacco. He was doing the cooking, grilling thick pork steaks. Someone had shot a wild pig in the forest. The big 'razorbacks' were dangerous, so Pedley said, and had to be culled regularly.

Wary, watchful, John took his place across the table from Pedley and Simon. The boy's lip was swollen and black. Pedley and Evelyn were ignoring him, talking between themselves and to the newcomer as if Simon were invisible. During the meal, John learned the commercial towing operation had belonged to Evelyn's parents, who were both dead. Pedley was an ex-Army man who had worked for Brad and Kaye Lang for years, and stayed on with Evelyn when she left the military. She had flown with Military Airlift in many conflicts, including 'the big one' on Sheal.

Pedley was pleased at the prospect of having help on the job and welcomed John to the Roadrunner fold at once, but Simon was overtly resentful. He nursed a sullen silence until Evelyn had left and Pedley went out to patrol the yards and lock up for the night. Then Simon fixed the stranger with a sour look. John wore a deliberately neutral expression and waited.

"She's a bleeding heart," the boy said, "a bloody fool. Collects stray cats as well."

"As well as stray people," John said quietly. "Luckily for me."

108

"Oh, sure," Simon said acidly. "Though in this case I suppose she comes out of it way ahead, doesn't she?"

"Meaning what?" John prompted. He knew he would like the answer about as much as he liked Simon. Not much.

The kid laughed. "Take a look in the mirror, sweet thing, and make a shrewd guess. Life's been a walkover for you, hasn't it?"

"I wouldn't know," John said honestly. The observation was disquieting. A large part of him suspected it might be true.

"Oh, sure it has. You just wiggle your bum in the right direction and doors fly open. Doesn't matter. You'll know soon enough. You'll get to the payoff, and when she's got a fistful of your cock you'll know it's time to pay the bill." Simon scraped back his chair and left, pausing only to grin at the newcomer. "G'night, pretty thing, sleep tight," he said mock-sweetly.

The suggestion stung. John felt cynicism tighten his face. So he was a cynic as well as a pragmatist, was he? He shut the door on his room and lay down, head pillowed on both forearms. The aches stabbed at him again, ribs, jaw, knee, wrist. But he knew all the welds were settling fast. Weariness swept over him again and he slept soundly.

His last coherent thought was the longing for the dream ... the big man with the black hair and smoldering blue eyes who smiled at him, and set aside the mirror-polished helmet so as to extend his hand in welcome.

CHAPTER TWELVE

"Raven 7.1 to Raven Leader," Stone called by R/T as he watched Riki Mitchell talking to his father on the hooded vidphone at the end of the buffet bar in the Eldorado first class terminal. Mischa Petrov was on duty in the carrier's ops room, reveling in his role as acting captain. Stone did not begrudge him the temporary rank. It was good practical experience and Petrov had done a decent job. Without his services, Stone would have had to abandon the 'wild goose chase' at least a day before. The owners of the scores of Skyvans Eldorado tracking had routed him to were scattered far and wide through the enormous city, and it had taken time. Stone was tired, impatient, but the long list of contacts had been whittled down to just the outdistrict owners. He had only four more chances of finding Jarrat before even he had to admit, the game was up.

"*Athena,*" Petrov responded. "Where in God's name are you, Stoney? I'm wading in it up to the goddamned gonads, and you're *joyriding!*"

Joy riding? Stone damped down on his temper with an effort. "I'm nearly through, *Lieutenant*. And no, I haven't found Kevin. Yet." *But I will.* Hope hung on even now. "Chell status?"

"We're on standby, pending the opportunity to deploy. We could have gone any time in the last two days and only the press would have squealed. Death's Head is in its hole, but I had a gunship overfly the palace and scan them. We're not reading much, and that doesn't make sense. They're armed like a corporate security force, we should be scanning everything up to depleted uranium ammunition."

Memory stirred and Stone said, "Kevin told me they've got some old nuke bunkers under the house. Chances are they're using them for an arsenal. If they're rad-shielded, which they will be, you wouldn't get data."

Petrov grunted eloquently. "I'll buy that. I've had a pushy bastard called Gene McEwan on the blower, looking for you and trying to winkle info out of me. Wants to know who used the Black Mountain Engineers mainframe to hack his biocyber AI, and emptied out his toybox."

"And you told him what?" Stone asked as Riki broke the vidphone connection with his father on Outbound and sauntered down the buffet table, collecting an enormous meal as he went.

"I told him zip, which seemed to annoy the man," Petrov said acidly.

"I'll just bet it did. And Hal Mavvik? You leaned on him by vid?"

"You must be joking. I got secretaries, PR officers, I even got the director of one of his subsidiary, legit companies. The bugger is 'indisposed,' whatever the hell that means. Seems he's 'unavailable for medical reasons,' and he'll produce a certificate to prove he's two gasps short of dying if I push for it!"

Stone chuckled. "So you got the diplomatic handout from the hirelings. What's coming down on the street?"

Now Petrov sounded puzzled. "We're getting Tactical updates every hour, and it's weird, Cap. The Chell underground seems to be fragmenting, breaking up. Okay, our data is secondhand, but ... a lot of the informants Tac have relied on for years are turning up dead. Mavvik's command corps seems to have jumped into the bunker like they mean business. But according to Tac, a lot of the top contract men are leaving, bugging out by the droves, or trying to. Tactical caught Konrad and Yashimoto at the 'port, and these are bastards they've wanted for almost a year, since they blew that congressman into confetti, you heard about that?"

"It was in the dossier," Stone said thoughtfully. "So the rats are deserting, like they expect the ship to sink."

"That's the way it looks." Petrov swore. "Tac picked up Strauss in Clune, heading out on a private charter. A lot of the shooters are running, Stoney. Romero, Assante, McGrath, Kujo, they're *gone*, like you said. Rats getting off the ship before it drives up on the rocks."

As his tired mind began to work, Stone draped an arm about Riki's shoulders and kissed his cheek. Riki popped a slice of chicken into his mouth. Chewing methodically, Stone said, "Sounds to me like Mavvik is determined to make a circus of it. He's going to try his hand against us, against NARC. Some of his shooters, the top men who don't need the money and don't have to take his orders, don't fancy the odds. Have Tactical traced the runaways?"

"As nearly as they can, through known associates," Petrov told him. "In fact there's one in your area, one of the best. Over forty confirmed kills to his credit. He was terrorist-trained as a mercenary, like a lot of the top shooters, then auctioned his skills on civvy street. Joel Assante. You might know the name. He's a city bottom celebrity, for all the wrong reasons."

"I've heard of him." Stone helped himself to sliced mushrooms from the side of Riki's plate. "Nothing good. Where is he?"

"Colonel Stacey guesses he caught a ride to Sunshine, down the coast from Eldorado, to bypass the Tactical security cordon at the 'port in El. He hitched up with his old mate, Hank Weaver, who was the Angel pipeline into El until he took a bullet, three days ago. Christ knows where Assante's gone, but with Weaver's body left behind him like a signpost he'll be out and running if he's got a shred of sense left."

110

"Interesting, but Assante is Tac business, not NARC," Stone said indifferently. "How long have the Ravens been on standby?"

"Too long," Petrov said bitterly. "I keep rotating the squads on call. Pete Stacy has Mavvik's palace staked out but he's getting flak from high places ... Chell Congress doesn't want a war fought out in the city."

"Understandable," Stone admitted. "But it's Stacy's decision, not theirs." He broke off as Riki leaned against him, head on his shoulder. "Look, Mischa, I've only got a few calls left to make down here and the show's over. I've gone as far as I can."

A brief pause, and then Petrov said, "And you haven't found Kevin." Stone did not reply, and the Russian sighed. "It was worth a try, Stoney. You're a good mate. If ever I land in the shit, I'd want you on my team. I'll give you a buzz when there's more to tell. *Athena* out."

Riki popped a slice of ham into Stone's mouth as he put away the R/T. Around them, first class passengers milled about the buffet table. Stone gave Riki a hug and released him. The boy had been eating steadily for an hour. Sex made him hungry, and also, as Stone well knew, a full belly offset the first stages of the craving for Angel. Riki was starting to need it. Soon, he would have to have it, and he recognized what has happening to him. The brown eyes were troubled, and he did the only thing he could. He ate ravenously and he had sex as often as he could get it. Stone said nothing, nor was he about to comment. Riki seemed to be grateful for the compassionate silence.

"Finish up, kiddo, we've got to move," he said as Riki picked up a glass of beer. "Time's starting to run out for me. Just a few more calls to make here, and then if I don't get back to the carrier I'll be in hot water."

"I heard," Riki said with a nod at the pocket into which he had pushed the R/T. "Packwar in city bottom. Which city? Chell, is it?"

"The whole syndicate is up and moving, they're well armed and Hal Mavvik isn't going to budge. But some of his best shooters have bugged out and run, and he'll be madder than all hell." Stone glanced about the first class lounge, idly scanning for faces he might recognize. He would know Joel Assante on sight from file pictures, and if Tac was right, the contract man was not far away. Riki finished his beer, stuffed fudge into his mouth and allowed himself to be shepherded from the buffet. Stone looked down at the bowed blond head and frowned.

"Hey, kid, are you okay?"

Riki wore a brave face, but it was a mask. "I'll manage. Good meal inside me, few drinks, a good fuck. It makes it easier not to ..."

Not to use the garbage for another hour, another day. The longer he could deny the craving, the longer he would live. It was downhill all the way but the slide could be slowed. Stone winked at him. "There's societies to help in Chell. We'll see what we can do. Unless you want to go home."

"Go home to what?" Riki's arm snaked about Stone's waist as they walked out to the cordoned area where the NARC shuttle stood in the blistering noonday sun. "My father's started whining. He always whines when shouting doesn't work. Christ, I'm calling home from half the world away, I tell him I've ... got a problem. I don't say it's Angel, I don't dare! And what's he do? He chews on me, it's my fault, I got nobody to blame but myself!" Riki flushed with anger and looked away. His voice was thick and he cleared his throat. "If I go home it'll be to sleep alone and sit in that goddamned shop all day, same as I have since I was fifteen and got out of school. No way, Stoney. That'd finish me off even sooner. Wouldn't it?"

It would. Stone tipped up the boy's chin and kissed his mouth lightly. "You know what's best for you. I'll find you somewhere in Chell, Rik, you won't have to go back and face the music."

The security guards stood down as he showed his NARC ID. He and Riki climbed the boarding ladder as the infrabeam remote sent up the canopy, and ten minutes later the shuttle was in the air. Flight was the thrill of Riki's life. For these moments he could forget the Angel craving that gnawed into the pit of his belly like ravening hunger.

"Where are we going?" he called over the comm from the rear.

The aircraft was at eight thousand meters and Stone had just swung the nose about toward a flyspeck town called Ballyntyre. "Just a nowhere town in the foothills. But there's a 'van owner and a yellow Marshall down there, and it's about time I got lucky! Hold tight, Rik."

He took the shuttle down fast after a short hop of just a few minutes. Two hundred kilometers south of the city of Eldorado, he pointed over the side. "Look down, that's Ballyntyre. Quick. Blink and you'll miss it!" He cut back to hover and dropped in over the town. The jets screamed as he paused to scan thoroughly. And then, "Son of a gun," he muttered. "You see that? Parked beside the towtrucks there, see the red scallops?"

Riki peered, eyes slitted in the bright sunlight as Stone brought the shuttle down in the open space of the front yard. "This could be the one, Stoney. Soon as I see the left side I'll know for sure. If it's wearing my dent, it's your 'van." He had said the same approximate words many times since they left Outbound.

"Cross fingers," Stone said dryly.

"I hope it isn't," Riki said honestly. "If it is, I lose you. I don't want to lose you. Not yet. This has been too good."

The canopy went up as the hydraulic landing gear rocked into stillness and the superhot jets whined down. For the fifteenth time that day, Stone pulled off his helmet, finger-combed the damp, helmet-mussed hair, pulled on a headset and green lenses. He swung over the side and reached up to help Riki out. As he set the boy on the concrete, Riki clutched at his arm.

"It's the one, Stoney. I can see the dent from here, on the left engine cover, see? My tow coupler did the damage. I just backed into her."

Stone saw it, a deep dent the shape of a ground car's coupler, on the bottom curve of the engine cover, among the flame scallops. He gave the boy a grin. "You're beautiful. I mean that. Come here." He tugged Riki against him for a moment and kissed his mouth hard, till he laughed. "My friend has to be here, he *must* be."

"He's your friend, or is he your lover?" Riki wondered in a hushed, odd little voice, as if he did not want to know the answer.

"Just a friend," Stone said with well-concealed regret. "NARC doesn't allow for more, even though I might wish it. They don't even like their officers getting friendly. Too many of us turn up dead and the survivors get depressive. The old fogeys at Central want a professional working relationship — unquote. It makes sense. It just doesn't make life too easy." He gave Riki a grin and turned away toward the steel roller doors.

A woman stood there, tall, angular and very blond. Jackpot. Stone's belly churned and he pinned on a smile. The details of Jeff Bolt's medical treatment sheet haunted him: a broken body, a ruined mind. But Jarrat was *here*. If the 'van was in this nothing town, so was Kevin. The woman watched him warily. The sight of a military jet touching down in her fore-court was enough to shock her into silence, but still she came out into the bright, hot sunlight. Her eyes were drawn to the emblem on the side of the plane. The steel glove in which was cradled the white dove, and the legend 'NARC-*Athena*.'

"Good day to you," Stone said, his tone pleasant though he was riding a wave of impatience. "You were in Chell a few days ago. I'm looking for the man you found in the alley there." She blinked up at him mutely, but the sealed lips and shuttered eyes could not prevent the color draining from her face. She was hesitating, as if she were on the point of giving him what he wanted only to close her mouth again and say nothing. "The man who was bashed," he elaborated. "I want him."

The remark seemed to galvanize her. She drew a mask over her face, even her eyes shuttering. "I don't know anything about any man."

Stone gave her a disbelieving look. "Lady, I can *prove* it was you."

"I haven't done anything," she said carefully, defensively.

"You've done me a favor," Stone told her brashly. "You took the survivor to a clinic in Paddington, and then brought him here. I followed you via the tracking network. Give me the man and I'll get out of your way."

"I came over from Chell," the woman admitted, "but I don't know what you're talking about. There's no man."

"The injured man," Stone growled. "You were seen putting him in *that* Marshall. The same 'van dropped into the Taylor-Mason Clinic in Paddy where Doctor Jeff Bolt patched him up. You stopped at Outbound in the islands. You swung by the service garage, bought a bunch of machine parts and candy. I know the whole story, blow by blow. Give him to me!" The woman's face whitened another shade. "Oh," Stone went on, "it all rings a few bells now, does it? So where is he? I know he's here somewhere close, he has to be. Which means you're lying to me. Why?"

Her voice shook a little but she had it under control. "All right, he was here. But he's gone now. He was feeling okay and he left — yesterday. I swear, he's not here."

Truth or more lies? Stone stepped up, toe-to-toe with her. He could search the house by force, and the temptation to do so was overwhelming, but if she was telling the truth there would be trouble. 'Dope lawyers' had little affection for NARC and hovered like vultures, waiting for any opportunity to snipe at the paramilitary department. An instance of NARC 'brutality' would be just what they wanted.

"You're lying to me. I'll be back," he said quietly, "and then I'll have the truth one way or the other, with a Tac intrusion permit." His voice was deep, ominous.

Not twenty meters away, behind the half-drawn blind in the lounge, Simon Lang shouldered the HK machine rifle, and squinted along the shrouded barrel. He drew aim in the middle of the NARC man's chest. Sweat glistened on his face. His breathing was deep and erratic. "I could blow him away. I could gut the fucker," he crooned.

John felt a deep, acid distaste. Somehow, at the deep level of gut and marrow, he knew it was not the first time he had seem a person turned on, physically aroused, by the capacity to kill. He knew what it was like, intimately, at firsthand, to hold another person's life in the palm of his hand.

"Put the bloody gun away," he said bitingly. "You'll kill the NARC, will you? They'd bury you so deep you'd forget what daylight looks like."

"The NARC makes a move and I blow him the hell away," Simon repeated, taunting, as was his way. "What do you know? Pretty-ass hustler, don't even know where you come from. Sugar boy."

The name got under John's skin like splinters of broken glass. Anger throbbed in his head. "Well, if you're going to grease the NARC, you better charge the goddamned cannon, hadn't you?" he snarled. He grasped the charging bar in his left hand, wrenched back on it, almost pulling the service rifle out of Simon's grasp. It primed with a serpentine rasp of steel on steel. "And you're holding it wrong. Higher, stupid, into your shoulder, and in your left hand like *this* or the peripheral exhaust'll blow it straight up in the air. Duck your head into the sights, you loon, keep both eyes *open*. Heavy, is it? Tough shit. You got the barrel going round in circles. Where's your target? The way you're going, you'll grease everything but!"

Now he transferred his attention to the target, eyes narrowing against the brightness outside. The anger smoldered in him, fury at Simon, at himself, at his own willfully forgetful mind. The NARC was tall, raven-dark, built like an athlete, dressed in plain clothes, which meant he was an officer, a field agent. This much was common knowledge, but John Citizen knew it without knowing *how* he knew. He focused on the man's face.

And his belly gave a lurch. Too-familiar cold sweat prickled about his ribs as his heart skipped a beat and began to race with the adrenaline rush he was becoming accustomed to. Fireflies of recognition danced about the peripheries of his mind: he *knew,* but could not fasten onto the memory for long enough to make sense of it.

He knew the man — but, as an enemy? A rival? A friend? Had the man pulled him out of danger or locked him in a cell? *This* was the face that belonged with the red spinner, the blue neon, the jet thunder, the cold and dark ... but was he friend of foe? He could easily have tracked a runaway syndicate supplier to this place, and if John showed his face he would be right back in Chell, looking at the wrong side of the bars.

Uncertainty choked him, tied his tongue. Speaking up in this moment could mean salvation or disaster. The NARC could even be here to kill him. So John held his breath and said nothing.

Out in the yard, Evelyn was standing up to the man, talking to him, telling him enough to get rid of him. Behind the NARC stood a young man also in plain clothes, but he was too young, too small, to be any kind of operative. Somehow John knew this too. So the boy was more than likely an informant ... and he watched the NARC officer with a lover's intent.

Nearby was the jet, graceful, gorgeous, heat haze shimmering about its tailpipes. Not just an aircraft, but a spacecraft. Its repulsion had shaken the whole building as it came in. John swallowed, his breathing shortening as his bones recalled the punishment of high-G maneuvering. His hands remembered the lightness, the responsiveness of military control surfaces, the precision of state-of-the-art instruments.

It was an agony to stand at the window, silent as a statue, while Simon waved the battered old service rifle at the NARC, crooning about killing him, as if killing and fucking were the same thing. Then the NARC man turned away. He gave the house and its owner a level, withering look, and John watched him return to the aircraft ... watched the broad back and long legs, the tilt of his head, the way he moved. The gestures and body language were painfully familiar.

114

Recognition was a lance through John's chest. But, friend or foe? He knew the man! The cold and dark shaped themselves into a hangar the size of a cavern, and it was filled with a thunder of jet noise. Engines ... men. Voices he knew, almost-seen faces. Blue neon flowed into overhead strips, shining, glittering on and in those mirror-black surfaces —

Armor. NARC riot armor. A piece of the puzzle nudged into place. But John had no sense of *himself* in the scene. Had he been manacled, had the NARC taken him up to the carrier? Some deep part of his mind, far beneath the levels on which conscious thought took place, knew NARC often took suspects, prisoners and informants up to the carrier. He might be one of them, a suspect who was later released, and then beaten to jelly in Chell's rancid city bottom. Because his associates there assumed he had betrayed them, and was probably fitted with a biocyber implant, a transmitter, before he was released ... and a king shooter, Assante, had already shown up in a flyspeck town like Bally. Tracking him, to finish the job?

Another piece of the puzzle seemed to drop into place and John could barely breathe. His near-death made sense, and so did the flock of signals Simon had been hearing on the Eldorado Tactical band: a sudden outpouring of Chell's underworld 'talent.' A lot of it was heading to South Atlantis, trying to vanish into the outdistricts, since El was locked down tight. If this NARC had taken him to the carrier for interrogation, everything made a hideous sense, and only a weird, corkscrew feeling of *wrongness,* drilling through John's bones, gave him a moment of doubt.

Or was it simply denial, the desperate desire to disbelieve what he knew must be the truth, because — if the puzzle was what it looked like, the syndicate would not rest until he was in a hole in the ground. NARC would slam the cage door. Tactical would be glad to help them do it, and Evelyn would stand back and watch, because John turned out to be everything she had ever despised.

Pain scythed through his skull, stress and dread finding every laserweld, every repair, and testing it without mercy as he watched the scene out in the yard. Evelyn had stepped back into a patch of shade under the old cypress tree. The NARC took the young man in his arms for a moment and they kissed briefly. John's innards lurched painfully. Then both strangers climbed up the hardpoints, into the cockpit. The NARC pulled on a helmet as the canopy whined down, locked. Repulsion howled like a hurricane. The main engines ignited with an earsplitting crescendo of noise, the tailpipes jetted flame, and the aircraft was gone. It looped up into the sky in a backbreaking arc and climbed away into the northwest. Half a minute later even the echoes of its engine thunder had faded to nothing.

"Shit," Simon muttered. "I could have cut his guts out." He ran into the forecourt, still carrying the rifle, and called his sister's name. "So what did the bastard want with us?"

John followed, wary and silent. His muscles trembled in reaction and he held his tongue as the sun dried the sheen of sweat on his skin. Evelyn looked from his face to Simon's and back again. "He wanted John."

"The NARC wanted you," Simon said through his teeth. "I was right! You *are* a crimmo! A dealer? A money man? A mule?" He lifted the rifle to his shoulder. "And I was about to defend you."

"Don't point that thing at me unless you intend to use it," John barked in a tone of voice Evelyn and Simon had never heard before. Normally he spoke softly, but not now. He took the HK out of Simon's hands in one clean swipe. "And if you do, you better be ready to have your ass kicked from here to Eldorado. Besides, these weapons are illegal in civvy hands."

"It isn't illegal, it's mine," Evelyn said loudly. "I'm a veteran still listed with the Airlift Reserve. I've got a license. You know cannons?"

In answer, without thinking, he shouldered it, chose a limb on a tree a hundred meters back from the road and emptied the whole clip, dead on target. The wood splintered away and the limb fell heavily. His whole body remembered the feeling of the big weapon braying and vibrating. He felt the familiarity in his bones, and a voice spoke in the back of his mind, called him by name, and the name danced away again like a firefly.

The concussions rang back off the building. When they were silent once more Simon swore. "A shooter. You were a shooter."

"Is he right?" Evelyn asked very quietly. "Were you, John? Come on, man! I just fed a crock of shit to that NARC, he's coming back with a Tac intrusion permit. You can't stay here much longer, not unless you want to go with him, maybe in manacles, maybe in a bodybag. He came here for *you* and, God help me, I almost handed you over without thinking! Your bullet scars, the conditioning of your mind. You could be Tac or NARC."

"Or you could be syndicate," Simon added. "I've been listening to the Tac band. There's something on, something *huge*, and Death's Head's going to play rough, with real hardware. S'what they're saying, Eve."

She took a breath. "That's not what I'm thinking." She looked searchingly at John. "You probably are, or at least were, from Tactical. But you could be in trouble. Real trouble. On the run, between a rock and a hard place. NARC would bury you and ask questions later. Tan Del called Chell Tac, asking if they had an MIA fitting your description." She shook her head. "Not a one. Which probably means you left Tactical not long ago. We just don't know why."

Fired, resigned? Convicted — justly or wrongfully? On the run from Tac, NARC *and* the syndicate? John handed the weapon to her. "Christ almighty, I don't know. I wish I did. Thanks for getting rid of ... of him." Sweat broke from every pore again as he turned away, left them, retreated to the house and flopped belly-down on the bed.

He took his skull in his hands and rubbed his forehead hard. The face of the NARC haunted him. The blue eyes glittered at him, but whether in mockery or welcome he could not tell. "Remember, goddamn you," he groaned, "you sonofabitch, *remember!*"

The man's face was still there, tormenting him as he exhausted himself and sank into a fretful sleep filled with acid-hot, dislocated dreams.

Mischa Petrov's voice barked urgently into Stone's ears. "Raven Leader to Raven 7.1. Respond right now, Stoney. The code is Black Alpha."

'Black Alpha' meant showtime had arrived. Stone's skin crawled unpleasantly. The shuttle was seven thousand meters over the plain of Eldorado and heading for the city center. His sole objective at that moment was an intrusion permit, which Tactical would supply to a NARC officer without question. In the rear cockpit, Riki had on a helmet. He heard the call but Stone switched up to channel 95 to cut him out of the loop.

"Raven 7.1. What is it, Mischa?"

"Tac want to get the show underway," Petrov told him tersely. "They want Mavvik, the Angel, the arsenal lifted from Vincent Morello. Colonel Stacy has units staking out every syndicate strongpoint he knows, they're going to chop off the arms and legs off then take Death's Head off at its goddamned shoulders. All Ravens are standing by. There's going to be a shooting match, Stoney. Time to come home, *right now*."

Stone swore bitterly beneath his breath. "When is Stacy moving?"

"15:30 shiptime," Petrov informed him. "That's one hour, Cap. Gives you a chance to suit up before NARC deploys."

"I'll be there," Stone said tartly.

"Or your absence makes me acting captain." Petrov chuckled.

"And you'd love it, wouldn't you?"

"I could live with it. An hour, Stoney. And keep your ears on. Mavvik is monitoring the Tac-NARC frequencies, we're encrypting everything but security is no better than usual. Shithouse. He might draw first blood yet, if he thinks he can catch us napping. A lot of their shooters got out, but there's still an army in city bottom. Don't underestimate them."

"I don't intend to. And I'll be there," Stone repeated. "Raven 7.1 out." He switched to the personal band. Riki was talking to him even then.

"— was that all about?"

"NARC business, love. There's going to be a war soon. A real shooting match. It's time to go back."

"But what about your friend? We just found the 'van we've been looking for! You *know* your friend's down there!"

"And the woman's lying through her teeth," Stone added. "I just don't know why. My friend is busted up, remember." Stone's belly churned as he spoke, and he heard Riki take a breath. The kid had read Jeff Bolt's sheet. "Maybe she's trying to keep the nasty big bogeyman away. She could be protecting him. Christ knows. I look like the bogeyman?"

Riki chuckled. "You'll do me, Captain." Then he sobered. "I'm starting to feel bad, Stoney. I'm ... I'm real sorry, man."

"You can expect to," Stone whispered. "You've gone too long without it. Feverish, aching?" Riki said nothing. "Get a few drinks into you, eat some more. A few tranks, then sack out, get some quality sleep."

"Be better if you fucked me," the boy muttered.

"I just haven't time, not anymore," Stone said regretfully. "Hold on, now. We're going."

CHAPTER THIRTEEN

Colonel Pete Stacy took the R/T from the hood of the Tactical Response command vehicle. He was a short man, stout, with a stomach inflated by beer, a ruddy face and silvering hair. The stub of a cigar smoldered between his teeth. He did not remove it as he addressed the R/T.

"Tac 101 to Raven Leader."

"Raven Leader, reading you on channel 95," Petrov responded.

"Where the shit are those troops of yours, Petrov?"

"All four descant units are on launch procedures and will be in the air in fifteen minutes, Colonel," the Russian told him tersely. "They'll be over the dropzone on time, on target. "What's your hurry?"

"What's your hurry?" Stacy mimicked, in a bad Russian accent. "We're looking an army down the throat, Lieutenant. Where's Stone?"

"I'll hail him for you," Petrov offered, not quite solicitously.

Six thousand kilometers in the east the shuttle was bucking a head wind at ten thousand meters and Stone had decided to go up over it when he heard the call.

"Raven Leader to Raven 7.1 on channel 95."

"Raven 7.1, go," Stone responded as he switched up to cut Riki out of the ship-to-ship loop.

"It's *on* Stoney," Petrov barked. "Have you dumped the little cunt?"

"No need. He's coming to Chell for the ride."

"Then get yourself moving, *Captain*. Lovey-dove can hitch a ride home or wherever he's going later. Put your foot on the loud pedal, Stoney. Tactical are getting twitchy and you've got Colonel Stacy yelling for you. Where the hell are you anyway?"

"Heading your way fast," Stone assured him.

"I'm glad to hear it. If you're trying to get yourself strung up by the balls, you're going the right way about it. I'll stall Stacy till you get here. He's just in love with the sound of his own voice. Raven Leader out."

Stone grinned mirthlessly. In the back, Riki was waiting, and at last he said, "Hang on tight, now, I'm going to take us up into space for a quick crossing." The wings and canards swept inward until the aircraft assumed the configuration of a missile. Stone pulled back on the cyclic stick in his right hand and shunted the twin throttles forward to maximum. It was as if the plane were alive. It took off like a startled eagle and crammed them into the acceleration couches under six Gs until Stone labored to breathe.

Before them the sky faded through mauve to black and the stars appeared. He leveled out at Mach 18 on the fringe of space and Rethan rotated beneath them. He watched the ocean go by, saw the red-brown land mass come up, and turned the nose down again. The hull glowed and the shuttle bucked under them.

Exuberant, Riki whooped his excitement and Stone smiled as he remembered how it felt the first time he had done this himself, eight years ago, when he transferred from Tactical to NARC and came out from Earth on assignment for the first time. Gil Cronin transferred over with the same wave of recruits and they trained together. Jarrat's day came much later. Kevin had risen through a different service. The Army was a school of hard knocks, and Jarrat had taken them all.

Kevin, he thought, *where are you?* And he was so sure the blonde woman, Lang, was lying that he radioed Eldorado Tactical with the request for an intrusion permit before Chell airsearch picked him up. He was going back to Ballyntyre the instant this action was over. Jarrat was there somewhere, and he had *not* just walked out, not when a satellite dish stood in the backyard and he could have called the carrier for a pickup. Stone had begun to wonder if Kevin were a prisoner inside Lang's tall cyclone fences. The thought was troubling.

The shuttle thundered in over Chell and he came about, coaxed it down the Tac location beam as he began to hear the Raven descant units crosstalking on the security channel. They were about to jump. "I'm going to land this thing and let you off," he told Riki. "I have to get into the armor, and there's going to be a firefight. This isn't a joyride anymore."

"They're going to be shooting at the plane?"

"It's possible. And I'll be shooting back at them," Stone said. "I've got four rotary cannons, a brace of Phoenix III missiles and a powerful little laser. The skin is armored, don't fret for me."

"So why can't I stay with you?"

"Because I'll be pulling some damned tight maneuvers and you're not fighter-qualified," he told the boy flatly. "You could get sick, and if you throw up in your mask, you suffocate. If you don't wear a mask, and they punch a hole in the hull and we get a chemical fire, you still suffocate. It's dangerous, sweetheart, so out you get. You just sit on your lovely little ass and drink rum coffee with the Tac telemetry people, and I'll find you somewhere to go after the show."

"Somewhere to go?" Riki faltered, as if he realized for the first time, soon he would be on his own in a strange place.

Stone sighed. "A good place with kids your own age, downs and peps and booze to keep the craving away, and all the fucking you want, which helps more than anything, I know. You're feeling bad. Aren't you?"

"Getting that way," Riki whispered. "You'll take me there?"

"Count on it," Stone promised. "And I might be able to find a day or two now and again, so long as we're on assignment here, for some creative tomfoolery. How's that sound, kiddo?"

"Great," Riki said wistfully. "I wish ..."

"Yeah, so do I," Stone agreed, and let it go.

The repulsion came on, battering through the airframe. The shuttle dropped fast toward the mobile HQ set up by Tac just above the smogline. At noon the city looked like a miniature under a plate of smoked glass, but up above the sun was bright and the air relatively clear. The duty flight director turned on an acquisition beam and Stone homed on it to land neatly between the two Tac troop transports and the buggy truck.

The canopy whined up and he helped the boy out. A Tac sergeant jogged toward them and sketched him a salute. He was clad in the characteristic black uniform fatigues, the bulky flakjacket and baseball cap. And he was distressingly young, no more than Riki's age, Stone thought.

"Captain Stone, sir, Colonel Stacy wants to see you yesterday."

"Soon as I get into the hardsuit," Stone agreed. "Then I want this bird off the ground. It's a big, fat target ... here, Sergeant, take care of my friend." He leaned over and kissed Riki's lush mouth softly. "Take him somewhere safe. Have someone fetch him coffee with plenty of the hard."

"There's nowhere safe here," the sergeant protested.

"Are you guys eating? Then you've set up a mess. That'll be safe enough."

"But we're a target, Captain!"

"The whole bloody city's a target, son," Stone said tiredly. "Soon as Stacy's Angel war blows up, there won't be a safe square meter down there." He gave Riki a smile and a pat for his backside. "Kiss for luck?"

Riki reached up and pressed his lips to Stone's. He felt the boy lick across his teeth. "It's been fantastic," Riki whispered. "I guess, if I died tomorrow I wouldn't have a lot to complain about. You're something special, Stoney."

Then he was gone. The last Stone saw of him was the swing of the supple young body and the old anger welled up again. Riki was dead on his feet even now, craving the Angel. Swallowing the grief and anger, Stone climbed into the rear cockpit, lifted out the deck plates and took the riot armor out of storage.

It was in sections and he wormed into most of it in the aircraft, neutralizing the weight segment by segment as he went. He was locking the wrist seals and lifting the helmet out of the underdeck compartment when he heard his name, bawled by a voice he knew.

"*Stone!*"

"Yo." He looked over the side to see Pete Stacy's pear-shaped body, squeezed into the black Tac uniform and made stouter yet by the flakjacket.

"Where the Christ have you been? Is that your bimbo over there?"

"A witness to a crime." Stone lifted his armored body over the side. "NARC business, Stacy, keep your nose out. What do you want?"

The Tactical Response commander regarded the younger man sourly. Stone was taller, stronger, twenty years his junior and outranked him. A NARC captain was automatically in charge no matter where he was or who else was present. They were field agents, Intelligence officers, soldiers, firezone observers, whatever they chose to be or were required to be. And the government would back them to the hilt every time. The underground feared them, the other services resented them, yet needed them.

Stacy spat into the grass. "We've got their cutting lab staked out. That's where we want to start. It's defended, so there's going to be a shooting match. Could be some heavy cannons, Stone."

"And you want NARC armor between your burgeoning beergut and their rockets," Stone observed. Stacy glared at him. "Surprising. Have your stakeout unit activate an acquisition beam, I'll give you a gunship."

"Christ, I don't want it blown off the map!" Stacy shouted. "There's five hundred civilians in the way!"

"Then move the civilians out of there! Get your department into gear!"

"You guys are assholes, the whole shitty lot of you," Stacy said with a depth of feeling Stone would not have anticipated from him.

"But you just can't do without us, you know that, I know that," Stone added. He disliked Stacy intensely, and had for months, since the carrier entered orbit and took station over Chell. "So what's Target Alpha?"

Stacy tugged at his heavy flakjacket. Within its bulk he was sweating profusely. "It fronts as a restaurant —"

"Armand's? Jarrat mentioned it once or twice."

"You got it in one. But it's a lab. They cut half the horseshit for the Chell marketplace there, and the rest comes out of a speed shop north of the spaceport. I want it busted, Stone. No cannons, no laser, no rockets, are you listening to me? Just *bust it*, and have your trigger-happy bastards watch what they're shooting. I want prisoners for Intelligence."

Stone locked down the locust-like helmet and screwed the umbilici down tight. Now the suit was a completely sealed environment. His voice was a little distorted by the public address speakers. "We'll do the best we can for you, Stacy. You want to get out of the way now? I have to get this bird in the air before somebody drops a demolition shell on it."

"Right." Stacy stepped back. "Where do you want your bimbo?"

"His *name* is Mitchell," Stone snapped. "You call him *Mister* and you look after him! Now, shove off, will you, before this thing roasts you."

The Tactical commander raised two fingers at him but did as he was asked. Stone had the shuttle closed up within the minute and was in the air seconds later. He bobbed up to two thousand before taking a sensor sweep and officially assuming command. "Raven 7.1 to carrier. I am over the dropzone and in the hardsuit, Lieutenant Petrov."

"Roger that," the Russian's voice responded. "All Raven units, Raven Leader is in the field. Acknowledge."

Gil Cronin and the three other sergeants in command of the quartet of descant units called in quickly. Stone turned the shuttle's nose for the west of the city. "Blue Raven 6, have you located the Tactical acquisition beam at Target Alpha?"

"It's coming up now," Cronin told him. "Tac are set up in a civvy location, Cap. You want to evac the folks?"

Let the civilians out and alert the enemy. *Nice choice,* Stone thought. "Give them a two minute warning to take cover." He could only opt for a compromise. "Tac wants the target busted, not leveled, which means you guys jump out and mark selective targets."

"Jesus friggin' Christ," Cronin muttered unhappily. "Stacy doesn't give a mother about us, does he?"

"No, he does not," Stone agreed. "It's why we were invited to this party. How long before insertion, Blue Raven 6?"

"I can see the goddamned target," Cronin snarled. "You want we jump, we jump."

Gently, carefully, Stone nudged the shuttle around the Chell Trade Center. The Blue Raven gunship was dead in front of him, eight kilometers downrange of Target Alpha so as not to telegraph its presence with its engine noise. It was a heavy, slab-shaped, ugly but functional craft. Its many projections gave it the aspect of a porcupine, while floodlights blazed about it even in daylight. Down below the smogline the streets were perpetually dim. Stone saw the jump bay, already open to the sky.

"Blue Raven, follow me in," he called. "All the world and his uncle are down there, we'll let them have two minutes."

As he bypassed the gunship, coming up fast on the target, he recognized the location. This was the very area where Jarrat had been beaten within a breath of his very life. He saw the street where Blue Raven found the ruined Rand limousine and Earl Barnaby's dismembered corpse. Hot fury choked him for a moment before he hit the public address. Amplified a hundred times, his voice rolled out across the city.

"Attention, attention. This is a NARC operation. If you can hear this you may be at hazard. You have two minutes to find a place of shelter. Keep your head down until the all-clear sounds. You have two minutes to secure your position. I repeat —"

The courtesy period dragged. The gunship butted up in the shuttle's wake and Stone watched the gunners rotating their weapons in test mode, though they were under orders not to open fire. He said nothing. If it came to a duel between heavy weapons, NARC came first and Stacy could file a complaint later.

Down below, under the rage of engine noise, civilians scattered in all directions. Most headed for the basement garages where they would be quite safe. Many buildings also had nuke bunkers which had been installed after a bad crash at the spaceport very nearly irradiated half the city. Some civilians would certainly be injured as bystanders, when they deliberately remained on the street to watch and shoot video. The cheap thrill of a live show could turn out to be costly indeed, but no one blamed anyone but the foolhardy spectators, who should have been in the nearest bunker.

Stone was not overly concerned about civilians as he watched his chrono count out the last seconds and then transferred his attention to the CRT. Armand's restaurant was framed in it. On either side were factories with shop frontages. To the rear, an alley, to the fore the street where Jarrat had been driving the Rand Solstice the night it had all happened.

"Time's up, Blue Ravens," he said. "Insert now." He keyed to the Tac-NARC security band. "Ravens are in the air, Colonel Stacy."

The twenty-five mirror-black locusts fell out of the gunship's belly as he spoke. They dropped fast, went down like stones and landed hard, and they were under fire before they hit the ground. Shots *whanged* off the armor, semiautomatic, some full automatic, and big-caliber rounds with enough 'knockdown' to tumble two of the Blue Ravens to the ground and sweep them along. But the armor was not so easily breached. When the gunfire stopped the NARC descent troops simply clambered back to their feet, and rotary cannons locked on target.

The cannons mounted on the right forearms cycled fifty 9mm rounds per second, and they were actuated by an eyeblink trigger mechanism. Two of the Ravens stood shoulder-to-shoulder to put hundreds of rounds into the restaurant. Windows exploded inward, smoke belched from an empty frame on the upper floor, a man jumped, impacted sickening with the ground and lay twitching.

At the fore of the Blue Raven unit, Gil Cronin took the locked door of the restaurant in one steel-gloved fist and tore it from its hangings as if he were ripping through a sheet of paper. He raised his left hand. On the armored forearm was a stun cannon that would project a discharge heavy enough to overload the brains of anyone in range not wearing a helmet.

A volley of gunshots slammed down from above, big-caliber, military issue, and Cronin's mouth compressed behind the fullface visor. "These buggers have some real weapons. Watch yourselves. Tighten up for chris-sakes!" He broke off and looked up as sensors registered concussions from above. A few shots punched through the ceiling. One impacted with his shoulder, he felt the blow though the armor turned it aside.

Cronin raised his right arm and the rotary cannon on it sawed a wide hole in the plasterboard. His mics picked up a short scream of anguish, but only a few semi-recognizable fragments fell through. A boot was attached to one of them. The restaurant had only two floors. Downstairs had been a shambles before they entered, with the fire ripped into it from the street. Cronin crunched over a carpet of broken glass on his way to the stairs leading from the public area to the private facility. The cutting lab was up above. The stairs were wide, set back from the doorway. Two bodies lay on them, one hanging together, one wrenched apart. Cronin stepped over them, six Ravens on his heels.

Smoke filled the upper level. The flooring groaned under the combined weight of men and armor. Cronin transferred to thermographic imaging to see through the pall. The heat of the fire complicated the picture but he could make out two men in helmets. They had some large but man-portable weapons system. It took him a few moments to identify it, and then he barked a warning at the men behind him.

"Rockets!" He brought up the rotary cannon on reflex.

A tenth of a second before he could fire, a light anti-armor projectile screamed out of the launcher. It passed so close, he felt it go by. His helmet displays lit up red with proximity alarms, and from behind him came a stunning blast as the missile found its target. Whirling debris hammered on the suit and the shockwave almost knocked the Ravens off their feet. Cronin did not pause to see who was down. He completed the action and put three hundred rounds into the corner of the room. The two men were slammed back into the wall, then the wall itself ripped away. Cronin took a thermoscan. No one else stood between them and the fire. Now, he turned back to the Blue Ravens behind him.

"Who bought it?"

"Warren," responded Blue Raven 7, Joe Ramos, Cronin's second. "He's stone-cold dead, Gil."

"What a surprise," Cronin said sourly. The smoke made it difficult to see the tangle of wreckage that had been Blue Raven 14.

"It took the middle right out of him." Ramos checked his ammo counters. "We've taken enough shit, Gilly. I say we blow the lid off."

"So do I," Cronin agreed. "You listening, Cap Stone?"

Above the building, hovering in company with the gunship like a pilot fish on a whaleshark, Stone cut out the Tac-NARC band. What Stacy did not hear would not hurt them. "You've got the place burning," he said, "but you're not through them, Gil. They're up on the roof, trying to get onto the building next door ... they've got some kind of launcher. I wouldn't trust them not to take a potshot at the gunship." He watched the three helmeted figures scrambling on the parapets above Armand's. They had shouldered their weapons but were struggling with a heavy piece. It was a demolition cannon, devastating against aircraft or vehicles, and the gunship made an inviting, irresistible target, too delicious to ignore, too big to miss. "Oh, what the hell," Stone muttered, and flipped the safety off the trigger on the right side of the cyclic stick.

Gunsights appeared as a green schematic in the head-up display. He nudged the nose cannon over and down a fraction. The three men came apart in a welter of red. Some of Stone's rounds must have found the demolition rocket. It went up and took the corner off the roof. Windows blew in on the next building, exploded under the shockwave.

Then Cronin's voice was on the air bawling at his airborne observer. "What the fuck was *that*?"

"Just me blowing the lid off for you," Stone told him. "I see three on the roof, dead. Is that the lot, Gil?"

"I reckon it might be," Cronin judged, and then bellowed at his men, "Roof's coming in! Watch yourselves!"

Stone was unconcerned. The Ravens were armored in the same skin of kevlex-titanium he wore himself, and a furnace could not damage it. He dropped the shuttle into the street where an open space lay between two abandoned cars and a tumble of masonry. As he watched, Armand's collapsed on itself. A wall of fire gushed in its place, and a moment later the twenty-four surviving Blue Ravens stepped through the billows of flame, scorched but undamaged.

He keyed to the Tac channel. "Target Alpha is busted, Colonel."

"Prisoners?" Pete Stacy demanded.

"I'm not aware of any," Stone reported dryly. "I've got one man dead and a little fire to extinguish. Have the bucket boys stand by but we'll smother it for you ... Raven Leader to Blue Raven gunship, douse the fire before the whole block burns."

The gunship's pilot called across the chaos of chatter. "As soon as our guys extract, Cap."

"You heard that, out you get, Blue Ravens," Stone called over the chaotic loop. He shunted power to his own repulsion as he spoke. The shuttle went up like a feather in the breeze and about it the twenty-four NARC troopers rose back to their gunship. One man was missing.

Gil Cronin was on the personal band. "That was a goddamned waste of time," he said bitterly. "We could have wiped them off the map with one shot from the carrier."

"Them and half the block," Stone mused. "Civilians, remember."

"Screw the bloody civilians!" Cronin was furious. Hurting. Only on very rare occasion did NARC lose descant troops. When a unit was just twenty-five men strong, one death was keenly felt. NARC frowned on friendships between its people but in reality nothing could prevent relationships springing into being. Friendships and love affairs blossomed in the most unfertile soil. Warren, the dead man, had been Cronin's friend, Stone knew, and his sometime bedmate.

"Stone!" Pete Stacy yelled over the com loop. "I wanted prisoners!"

"You don't say," Stone said resignedly. "Pull out your observers. Do you want Target Beta trashed now, or do you want to do a post mortem on Alpha first?"

"Get your ass back here, *Captain*!"

"Negative your request," Stone barked. "A NARC action is conducted under NARC authorization, not Tactical. You don't like the scores, Stacy, file a complaint."

The Tactical commander skipped a beat, took a deep breath and began again. "Request you return to Tac 101 for a briefing session and staff conference, Raven Leader."

It was on the tip of Stone's tongue to tell him to transmit his data and skip the conference, but he bit back the remark. "Will comply. Raven Leader out." Much as Stacy got under his fingernails, he had to work with the man. "Gold Raven, Green Raven, Red Raven, report."

The responses were predictable. The three gunships were running patrol duty. One hung over Mavvik's palace on the mountainside where, for two months, Jarrat had lived and worked as one of Death's Head's elite. One hovered over the speed garage to the north of the spaceport, Target Beta. The third roved between the two, panning a battery of sensors over the city. Stone threw the shuttle up and out of the smog blanket and looped back to the mobile command post.

Tac 101 was a clutter of vehicles and trailers. Anything that could fly was off, since everything was a target. He was reluctant to leave the shuttle long on the ground, and did not waste time getting out of the armor. He had his helmet in his hand as the canopy went up, and three minutes later climbed into the back of the wagon housing Tactical Command. The suspension bellied down under the deadweight of a NARC hardsuit. A scattering of officers and two civilian observers sat inside, in the illumination of twenty or more comm-relay terminals. Printers chattered constantly. Stacy stood behind the littered plot table, teeth clamped on a new cigar. Stone put his helmet down on the table and looked levelly at him.

"What do you want from me?"

"I wanted prisoners!" Stacy erupted.

"When they're shooting back with military hardware? Military cannons and rockets?" Stone demanded. "If you're making a funny, you're doing fine. If you're serious —"

"Fuck with me, son, and I'll show you how far your authority goes," Stacy warned. "You're NARC, not God almighty."

"Damned right," Stone agreed. "If you want to try out your new text-writer, signal NARC Central, be my guest. They'll get the dispatch in three weeks, *if* it gets boosted through the network on priority, and maybe I'll be up on charges six weeks after that. Maybe. More likely they'll read our stats and hand out another bunch of honors." He froze Stacy with an arctic glare. "No civilian casualties, minimal civilian property damage. One Death's Head enterprise shut down permanently. Total elapsed time, fourteen minutes and twenty-seven seconds. Put *that* in your report, Colonel. Our telemetry goes back to Sector Central every minute of every day."

Stacy stood glaring at him. Fury whitened his face. "All right, Captain." His tone moderated. "I read you. NARC *is* God almighty, is what you're telling me, and the rest of us belong on our knees, weeping tears of gratitude." He drew one palm over his sweating forehead, reined back on his temper and forced his brain to work. "Those military weapons match the inventory of the haul from Vincent Morello?"

"A lot of it. Light anti-armor pieces, automatic rifles, rocket launchers, and a demolition cannon that could have made a real mess of the gunship," Stone told him. "They blew away one of my men, armor and all. The rockets are ether Hawks or, if we're really out of luck, Avengers." He paused to let the data sink in and smiled sardonically. "Heat-seeking. An Avenger up the tailpipe will knock down an aircraft, even the shuttle, and it wouldn't do a gunship much good. You want to see one of those go down in the city? Even if the reactors didn't spill, you'd hear the bang from here. Immediate casualties in four figures ... then the reactor spills. Add a zero."

"Jesus." Stacy had sobered fast. "They can do that?"

"Oh, yeah." Stone glared at the reams of hard copies, the flickering CRTs. "And if we give them half a chance, they will. Now, understand me, Colonel. When I see a military target, it gets blitzed. Death's Head has acquired the hardware and used it: they are classified *military*, as of now."

"You'll have civilians in the crossfire."

"And what about the civilians who'll be incinerated or irradiated if a gunship goes in?" Stone snatched up his helmet. "We kill half a dozen or your syndicate blows a gunship out of the air and kills five thousand, take your pick, and — file your opinion. This is a NARC operation, Stacy. We're the ones whose guts are getting torn out, we're the ones who draw the flak. We decide how the job gets done. I've said my piece. I'm going to get the shuttle off the ground before it gets greased. It's been fun chatting."

Stacy still seethed with fury but he had clamped a lid on it. He glared at Stone's departing back, then keyed in his headset. "Tac 101 to Gold Raven unit. Stand by to move on Target Beta."

"Hold up out of the dropzone till I get there," Stone bawled over the confusion of cross-chatter on the scrambled security channel. "Jump fast, jump low, they've got anti-armor pieces. Gold Raven gunship, clear for air-to-surface fire and scan for laser target acquisition. Pull out of the dropzone *immediately* the Gold boys are away. Acknowledge."

The shuttle was thundering down off the mountainside as the acknowledgment came in, then Stone listened as Tac 101 hailed Chell Field to suspend all air traffic over the battle zone. Maverick missiles and NARC aircraft made for hot conditions, Stone thought acidly. He opened the twin ramjets. The power pressed him back into the acceleration couch. The gunship appeared on his instruments, riding on repulsion at two thousand meters, twenty k's downrange of Target Beta. Stone shut back and came up alongside. Below, smog dimmed the city, made it hard to see.

This time the two-minute warning to civilians would have been sheer suicide, and he did not make it. Lives might be lost in the crossfire but the chances of a heat-seeking missile homing on the sun-bright tail of the gunship were too high. Stone's one great dread was of a Death's Head shooter putting an Avenger into a sterntube. In his mind's eye he could see the explosion, when the missile's detonation blew back through three fusion reactors, the drive engines and the heavyweight repulsion sled.

Such a disaster had never yet happened, but sometime, somewhere, it must, and the prospect haunted Stone. "Raven Leader to Gold Raven 9," he called. "Sergeant Hellstrom, take it away."

The gunship fell like a brick into the smog and butted into the dropzone not much above rooftop level. Windows shattered and already the civilians with enough brains must be taking to their heels. The engine noise alone was sufficient warning. Most of them would make it to the underground vehicle parks before the shooting began. The roasting, stinking engine wash and the glare of floodlights heralded the start of the action.

The descant unit was already on the way down. Stone pinpointed the target, framed it in his CRT. It was a speed garage called Turboworld, single-storied, built of concrete blocks with big yards at front and rear filled with a king's ransom in cars and bikes. He saw Chev, Mercedes, Rand, Honda, Lapman, Ferrari, and groaned as the firefight began. The roadsters were parked where they were sure to be casualties.

Flaretails chased upward among Sven Hellstrom's men, and Stone heard them cursing on the air, with good reason. One missile had found its target already, cut a Gold Raven into a snowstorm of spinning shards which scattered away like superhot gravel. Overhead, the gunship pulled out fast, engines screaming back off the canyon of the street. As it departed the zone became dim under the blanket of smog.

Stone watched the ship go and dropped the shuttle into the cover of a tall building. His instruments warned him a laser target designator had picked him up. As he took the plane into cover the missile chased by over the outswept starboard wing. It tore the corner out of the building. Masonry pelted the shuttle and he swore. Hawks or Avengers?

"Come on, Hellstrom," he muttered, "bag me the shooter with the rocket tube!" No one could have heard him. The loop was a din of commands, warnings and bitter cursing. He heard a scream as someone else bought it, then Hellstrom shouting: "Up above you! The sonofabitch on the roof!" Stone bobbed up out of cover in time to see a section of the speed shop's roof explode outward, cut away by multiple rotary cannons.

Rockets detonated in the shoot-hole and the east wall blew out. It collapsed on a gold Ferrari sportsjet, and Stone groaned. It was the model Jarrat had always dreamed of. *One shooter down,* he thought. No more rockets from that direction. He checked the CRT, and when he saw no laser target acquisition warnings, lifted the shuttle to oversee the whole zone. As he went up he heard Pete Stacy, shouting across the confusion.

"Stone! Stone! Tac 101 is taking fire! Cover us, for chrissakes!"

"Gold Raven gunship, Red Raven gunship, respond to Tac 101," he barked. He felt naked without topcover, but Blue and Green were too far downrange now, and since Mavvik's people were working with military hardware, speed counted. He took the shuttle around in a blistering arc. Under his right thumb the triggers were armed. He orbited the target once at three hundred meters and read the heat signatures of fires in the building. Vehicles were blazing. Perhaps civilian customers had been inside, but it was unavoidable. "Gold Raven 9, report," he called. For long moments Sven Hellstrom did not respond, and when he did Stone was suddenly too busy to hear what he said.

Red enunciators winked at him. A laser target designator had picked him up. He pulled the shuttle about, back toward cover, but the missile was already homing. He threw the aircraft into a backbreaker loop. Shock diamonds floated in his field of vision as the soaring Gs squeezed his eyeballs out of shape, but the enunciators still winked. The missile had looped about with him.

An Avenger. Death's Head had taken twenty from Vincent Morello, and the whole city was about to pay the price. The missile was homing on his superhot tail. Stone pulled seven Gs as he stood the shuttle on its tail, hoping to make the heat-seeker chase the sun and go ballistic, but its tiny, design-specific brain was a rudimentary AI, and *smart*. The Avenger out-turned and out-climbed him, and as the Vincent Morello Aerospace advertising promised, it knew every trick.

He felt the stunning impact through the airframe as it hit the port engine. The whole system detonated and took a section of the tail out with it. Electronics shorted, circuit breakers blew out and the aircraft struggled to reroute power to instruments and flight systems. Stone knew the shuttle was streaming coolant. The starboard engine ran hot in seconds and the plane began to shudder, hanging in the air like a brick on repulsion. The control surfaces were leaden and some functions were not operating at all.

With a curse Stone shut down the starboard engine and looked at his coolant pressure. He was venting liquid nitrogen too fast to be able to restart the engine, but for the moment gravity resist was still working. He was going down, but it would not be hard enough to write off the shuttle.

"Raven Leader," he called urgently into the noisy loop. "I'm hit, I've lost an engine. Green Raven gunship, where are you?"

The response was immediate. "Covering for Blue Raven, we're taking fire, Cap. Will be with you when we've doused it."

"I'm going down," Stone shouted into the audio clutter. "Green Raven, mark my position and relay to the carrier!"

"You're marked and we're tracking," the gunship's pilot assured him. "Are you going down hard? Do you require emergency backup?"

"I've got repulsion but no forward engine thrust. I'm drifting ... Raven Leader to carrier. Launch me the retrieval tractor, locate on my signal."

"Stoney?" Mischa Petrov called. "The engineer's transport will launch in five. Your signal is clear. What the hell happened?"

Breathless as he fought the freezing controls, Stone told him, "I took an Avenger up the tailpipe, port engine. Those bastards are armed as well as we are, and *we* don't dare shoot back because of the goddamned civvies. Tell Tac to disengage, pull their casualties out ... shit, here I go!"

The shuttle had drifted miles out of the dropzone. Repulsion was still on but power was minimal. Red lights peppered the boards and as the liquid nitrogen coolant hosed away from ruptured tanks Stone had no option but to shut everything down. Now he was searching for an open area in which he could land safely. He saw nothing but rooftops, yards, factories, loading bays, until he had begun to prepare for a hard, ugly impact. With seconds to spare he saw trees, a swathe of dusty green under the brown sky, a pond, statues, a fountain, a baseball diamond.

The recreation area was filled with people, but they knew what was happening. He tripped his spinners and sirens, and while most people ran a few stood like idiots to watch the crippled plane limp over the line of the factory roof across the street. A number of the spectators were actually shooting video, and only at the last instant did it occur to them to flee.

Stone overran the repulsion as long as he dared, dropped the gear at the last moment and coaxed power out of a system which was clinically dead. The shuttle flopped hard, belly-down onto the grass. The impact jarred every bone in his body, rattled the teeth in his head. He shut down the electricals and purged the engine systems in seconds, but the enunciators still signaled a real possibility of fire or explosion. The starboard engine was so hot, it was overheating the underbelly grav-resist generators.

"Out you get, Stoney," he muttered to himself. He had done all he could to protect civilian lives and property. If she went up now, there was nothing he could do to prevent it. He released the harness and sent up the canopy, vaulted over the side and landed hard in the riot armor. The suit cushioned him and he rolled to his feet to hurry away from the crippled plane. Heat shimmered about it; the grass under the belly was starting to smoke. She would touch off a spot-fire very soon, and Tac Fire Control would surely beat the NARC engineer's tractor to this location.

Only as he got clear did Stone realize his armor was not primed with canons and projectors. The weapons were in storage, and he had no time to retrieve them. He jogged out to a safe distance and turned back to look at the shuttle. It sat bathed in its heat haze but had not ignited yet, and he had begun to hope its systems could dissipate heat fast enough to escape self-destruction. The sodium veins in the engine —

The blow knocked him clean off his feet. The next shoved him along the grass. He was collecting big-caliber rounds squarely in the back. His first thought was for the powerpack mounted between his shoulders. The armor casing could take around fifty 9mm rounds in the same spot, but fifty-five might be the end of it. It was the armor's single Achilles' heel. And whoever was shooting at him was aware of it.

He rolled over, let the shots slam into his breastplate instead. His eyes raked the near distance in search of the shooter. The man stood in the shrubbery with a gun in both hands. He came forward as he realized the NARC was unarmed. Repeated impacts bowled Stone over again and again — the shooter knew exactly what he was doing. He aimed tightly for the same place on the powerpack with every round, and his weapon was cycling ten per second.

"Raven Leader to any Raven unit," Stone panted. The loop was alive with confused signals. He was not even certain he had been heard. "Raven Leader to any —"

And then the instrument lights inside his helmet winked out. A moment later the air began to grow warm and stale, and the repulsion went off. The suit weighed two hundred kilos. Without repulsion it was like being pinned to the ground by a force of three gravities, and he would soon suffocate. Stone labored just to lift his arm as he groped for the chin contour and unscrewed one umbilicus to let in fresh air.

As it opened he looked up. Three men had jogged out of the bushes, the shooter in the lead. He still had the weapon in both hands. Stone glanced once at it and swallowed. It was a Colt .60, identical to Jarrat's. Or was it the same gun? As far as NARC was aware, Jarrat's was the only 'wild' AP-60 in the city. "Kevin," he murmured. "Kevin's gun. Oh, Christ."

The Colt was in the hands of a tall, leggy, darkly-tanned man with a shaven head and diamond earrings. He went down on one knee to shove the hot barrel into the port where Stone had unscrewed the left umbilicus. He could not hear what the man was saying since the helmet mics were out, but he could guess what he wanted. He was pleased to break the neck seal and lift the helmet off. The air inside was soon toxic with the weapon's choking exhaust gasses.

He dragged in a breath as he got it off and squinted up at the shooter who still held the machine pistol on him. The man was not looking at his face but at the armor's left breastplate. "Captain R.J. Stone," he read in a thick Chell accent. "Well, holy shit, we caught ourselves the headman!" He bent down, grinning into Stone's sweated face. "I'm going to grease a NARC, Jase. A *captain*! Mavvik's going to bust out in smiles when he hears what got the top of its skull shot off!"

The man called Jase was tall, fair, panting in the cloying humidity. He peered at Stone without expression and Stone's blood turned to ice-water. He was sure they would do it. His eyes fixed on the Colt, Jarrat's own weapon, and he held his breath. But then Jase nudged the shooter with one thin elbow.

"Hal could smile a whole lot wider if you gave him the NARC with its skull intact," he suggested.

The two men straightened, and as the shooter seemed to agree Stone began to breathe. "Market value, yes? Cash or trade, m'I right? You thinking what I'm thinking? Like, one of theirs for maybe twenty-three of ours?"

Stone found his voice, pushed his luck. "Twenty-three to one sounds about right," he said hoarsely. He watched the shooter stoop toward him and clenched his teeth as a fist closed on a handful of his hair and jerked.

"I can always give them a corpse," the bald man offered. "Don't make it any worse for yourself than it already is, R.J."

He was wondering how it was possible to make matters worse when the barrel of Jarrat's gun hit the back of his head. He felt a moment of nausea perforated by pain, then darkness. He knew nothing as they lifted his enormous weight. Cursing and straining, they manhandled him away from the roasting aircraft, and collected even the discarded helmet.

When the engineer's transport arrived even from the carrier only minutes later to lift the shuttle out, there was no sign of him. A Fire Control flyer was in attendance and the shuttle stood in a lake of foamy white chemical liquid, abandoned, forlorn, still shimmering with heat, but the spot fires which had sprung up about it were drowned.

Combat Engineer Karl Budweisser brought the R/T to his lips as he stood frowning at the crippled plane. "Raven Leader, where are you?" He called Stone's name a dozen times before he abandoned the attempt and called home instead. "Engineer to carrier." The air was still so cluttered with electronic noise, competing signals and the spaceport radars, it took five calls to reach the carrier. "Raven Leader's put the crate down in one piece and taken a hike on his own," he said then. "You got him on instruments? I can't raise him."

"No sign of him," Petrov answered. "We've been trying to raise him for the last ten minutes, but he's not answering."

"You want we should look for him, maybe?" Bud asked doubtfully.

"Negative that suggestion," the Russian said emphatically. "Pick up the shuttle and get your crew the hell out. Stone's a big boy. If he wants to play cowboys, it's his ass. Kicked or kissed, it's his business."

"Will do," Budweisser agreed with a fat grin. He was a short, muscular, middle-aged Canadian with a Toronto accent. After thirty years with NARC he had seen a hundred hotshot young officers come and go. With the rank of captain they were in charge, they took the risks, gave the orders and were killed with monotonous regularity. Jarrat and Stone had lasted two years, which was longer than many. It was a short-lived profession and the engineer had no doubt he would see a hundred more like them come and go before he retired with his service pension.

Stone was thinking similar thoughts. He came to without so much as a muscle twitch, not about to betray himself or attract attention. The weight of the riot armor still dragged at him. He lay on his face and could not move his hands. He suspected they were chained together. His head was splitting but he could hear. He was listening to the shooter's silky voice, and as the man paused he recognized Mavvik's American voice over the R/T, distorted by the effects of powerful, military signal encryption.

"Stone?" Mavvik echoed. "Now, there's a name I know. We hacked the Tactical computers after Jarrat turned up NARC, and there they were. Jarrat and Stone. Now, Jarrat's dead, and if we've got Stone we're holding their other ranker. Providence, Viotto. Providence. Bargaining power."

"So you want him alive," Viotto — the shooter with the bald head and diamond earplugs — concluded.

"You grease him, you start running," Mavvik said genially, "because I'll be in back of you with an ax. You're at the warehouse?"

"On Windrigger, under the junked mass driver," Viotto confirmed.

"Then get out of there, it's not safe. Jarrat got the location out of that asshole, Vazell. Take the NARC to the stadium, that'd be as secure as anyplace. Don't take any shit, but don't bust him up too bad. He's valuable."

"He'll make trouble, Hal," Viotto said doubtfully. "God only knows how to get the armor off him. Jase reckons he's given himself a hernia already, carrying this heap. It weighs a tonne. If Stone gets up on his feet he'll chop us into dogmeat. He has gloves like a pair of steel hammers."

Mavvik did not answer for a moment. "Then he won't have to get up on his feet, will he? If he's bombed out of his head, sky high, how much trouble can he give you?"

The shooter hesitated. "You want to skull him?"

"Comprehensively. What *resources* do you and Jason have on you?"

"Only a few smacks of Angel," Viotto said thoughtfully as he studied the captive. "I thought you wanted to trade this Stone off for our guys."

The Death's Head mogul laughed delightedly. "So they'll get him back second hand, damaged goods. I like the sound of it. Listen, Viotto, you *fix* him. You and Jason give the bastard the *de luxe* treatment. Soak him in it till it's coming out of his ears. He goes back as an object lesson, right? Fuck with Death's Head and you book yourself a first-class ticket to hell."

On the floor, Stone snapped open his eyes. Real fear tightened his insides and his mouth was dry as sandpaper. His wrists were chained together behind him. He strained uselessly at the steel links. Viotto looked down at him as the heard the metallic tinkle.

"Our boy's awake," he told Mavvik. "We tied him down but that god-damned armor's going to be a ballbreaker. We might have to cut him out."

"Stuff his nose with Angel," Mavvik retorted. "When he's high enough he'll tell you how to get it off. The seals are on a coded system, so they tell me. Get moving, Viotto. If they've got a buggy truck anywhere near Wind-rigger they'll be getting every word you say, and a computer unscrambles these signals pretty damned fast. They could be on top of you. Call home from the safeplace."

"On our way, Hal," Viotto agreed. "Close down."

Stone's breathing was shallow and fast. His pulse rate doubled as, cursing and panting, they hauled him up to his knees and let the weight of the armor hold him captive. He looked up at Viotto but said nothing. Viotto brought a small plastex bubble of golden powder from his inside pocket. Stone knew Angel when he saw it. "Jase?" Viotto prompted darkly.

Behind Stone, Jason grabbed him by both his ears and chuckled his delight, telling the prisoner how a man could be chronically addicted in a single day. Sent flying, kept flying, until the drug dependence was as advanced as a year's normal progression from 'virgin' to terminal case. Stone did not need to be told the details. He had seen it too often, like anyone of his generation, on any world.

His heart thundered against his ribs. He wrenched his head in Jase's grasp until his ears began to split away and blood trickled wetly down his neck, though he felt no pain. His focus was elsewhere as he heard the plastex bubble break open with a *popping* sound. The weight of the armor was his enemy now. It fought him as hard as Jase and Viotto, as the shoot-er emptied the bitter golden dust into a little plastic scoop and grabbed a fistful of Stone's hair. The scoop rammed under his nose and Viotto cup-ped his hand over it, as if he fully expected Stone to blow — which he did. But the dust was trapped in Viotto's closed hand, there was no escape.

The captain from NARC held his breath until his lungs began to burn, his ears were ringing and the old warehouse dimmed. He was on the point of blackout when his chest spasmed against his will and he dragged in a deep breath. His sinuses blocked at once, stinging and reeking of the acid bitterness. A moment later his balance went out, the whole world reeled, but at the same time colors sharpened, sounds reverberated.

His body felt light, his nerves were on fire. Stone felt wonderful, as if he had never been even half-alive before. He felt more than human, as if his muscles were made of steel. His cock was achingly erect, his balls throbbed, and no cell in his brain remembered, arousal was one of the pri-mary effects of the drug.

Then the hallucinations began, and as Riki Mitchell had promised they were beyond comprehension. He swam in a blue-green sky, higher and higher, tumbling through the air with the wind cool on his bare skin, no hull or engines or armor separating him from the elements. He spun around, as if in midwater, buoyant, the sun warm on his face, and dove to-ward a white mountainscape of clouds. Stone had known nothing like it since his student days, when he flew ultralites, sail planes and even kites, for the sheer thrill of silent, powerless flight.

Jarrat was with him then, not with the ruined mind and broken body which had haunted Stone's private thoughts, but healthy, laughing. Stone reached out to him, joyous, reveling in his presence. He had to touch him, hold him as they swam in a blue-green sky. It might have been a lagoon

131

between coral reefs.

In his hands, against his body, Jarrat was warm, not like a wraith at all. Hard, sinewy masculinity pressed against him as Kevin found his mouth with a bruising kiss. Stone opened wide to him, breathless as he was ushered into a world that was unreal, euphoric. Every fantasy he had ever harbored was taking shape about him at once ... and somewhere in the depths of his brain, some molecule whispered a word. *Angel.*

His body was charged with the energy of sex, driving and demanding. Angel? A drug? Dimly he remembered, as if in a dream, some kind of golden dust smarting in his sinuses, but the memory was fading, lost in the welter of perception. He was drunk on reverberating color and luminous sound and sun-bright feeling, as Kevin writhed against him. Teeth closed on his neck, branding him there with the sharp pleasure-pain of a bite, and he felt the heat of Jarrat's cock against his hip.

He did not care to grasp after memory any longer, not while Kevin was doing things to him, maddening things which dragged a scream of delight from the bottom of Stone's lungs. Long fingers slid inside him, probing between his buttocks, two, three of them, finding the place deep inside, from which pleasure erupted. The fingers brought a bright, hot corona of fierce pleasure while Jarrat issued a wicked chuckle and went down on him. Kevin sucked him in deep, impossibly deep, as if demanding Stone surrender himself utterly in the luscious mouth.

He screamed again, felt his body tear itself to shreds as he came with a heaving and straining and fell back into Jarrat's arms. "Kevin?" He fought open his eyes and focused on the face resting against his shoulder. How long had Stone thought it the most beautiful face he had ever seen? He had no knowledge, now, that none of this was real, and if a part of his mind had whispered it to him, he would have denied it. *This* was Stone's reality now, this world into which he had been seduced.

Colors faded as he caught his breath, until the air was thick and dim. They lay together in a haze of heat and joss smoke while the seductive rhythms of steelrock beat out of a noisebox not far away. It was a den, a sex shop Stone had visited years before in Venice, way back on Darwin's World. He had not seen the inside of it since his first furlough after NARC retraining, before he was assigned to a carrier, but he remembered it well: the expensive, uptown Companions with long, blond legs, the satin sheets and ice-cold champagne, and any pleasure the colonies knew. Any vice money would buy, any dream a man could conceive.

"Kevin?" He peered into Jarrat's pagan, painted face. Big gold earrings, nipple rings, cockrings, gleamed in the warm lamplight. He was decked out for a night on the tiles and Stone laughed. "Oh, Christ, Kevin, that was ..." He dealt Jarrat's long, elegant cock a lingering caress.

"It was good," Jarrat said sensuously. "It was *bloody* good. Want to do the same to me?"

"Yeah. God help me, I do," Stone confessed. "I want to do everything to you." He fingered the rings, bracelets, the chains about Kevin's neck, hips, ankles. He breathed deeply of the clean, male scent and cedar cologne rising from Jarrat's heated skin, and felt every pulse in his body begin to throb again. "You're dressed up for a wild night. Where's the party? Am I invited, or shall I just gatecrash?"

"No party. It's for you," Kevin told him.

He would never know it, but Angel colored and molded the phantasm.

132

Jarrat turned sultry eyes to him. The lids were gold, the gray irises a darker shade, silver within gold. Kevin's tongue flicked out, moistened his lips, and a pulse beat like a drum in Stone's head.

"Oh, I know what you want," Kevin growled. "Want to fuck me, don't you? Good and hard. Screw me through the floor. You want to shove this beautiful big cock of yours in me ... deep inside me."

Stone groaned, aroused and aching as he listened to the rich, coarse speculations. "You know I do." His fingertips brushed the fine gold chains shimmering on Jarrat's velvet skin, all he wore.

"Go on then." Jarrat stretched his sinuous body, displaying a still unappeased erection. "Do it to me. Just the way you want to. Like this, do me deep and hard." He turned over on the cushions. Joss smoke writhed about him, dizzying, as he lifted his hips and spread himself wide. Oil glistened between his buttocks. He was more than ready. Stone touched him there, found the heart of him open with needing.

He was beautiful, every part of him, beautiful, Stone thought as he stroked, kneaded, made Jarrat squirm and gasp. He learned the feel of the soft, hot silk of Kevin's skin, the steel of his cock, the tang of his musk. The *taste* of him. Jarrat growled and grew wild as he was tormented and denied, and Stone laughed, delighting in his own abilities to drive a beautiful man to distraction.

Then he was mounting Jarrat, every erg of him concentrated on the straining shaft between his legs. He plunged into the body he knew he loved more than any he had merely toyed with. Jarrat opened, stretched to sheath him, tight, hot and moist, heaving under him in encouragement. The steelrock thundered through his head, the joss smoke sang in his ears.

"Go on," Jarrat purred. "Do it, give it to me hard."

And Stone obeyed, shaking sweat from his eyes as he took what was offered so freely. No part of him remembered, now, this was only an Angel dream. It *was* Kevin Jarrat beneath him, Jarrat in gold rings and chains and paint, as if he were headed for a wild night, running the dizzying caverns and labyrinths of city bottom from twilight to dawn, finding places and people Stone had never even imagined. It was Jarrat opening for him, needing to be fucked not by anyone, but by *him*.

He wanted to hear Kevin scream his pleasure as he came, and Jarrat did. A hoarse, dry yell of mingled anguish and rapture. He wanted to hear Jarrat tell him, this was real, it was special, and it was forever. "Ah, God help me, I love you," Jarrat whispered as he crawled into Stone's arms and began to lick his chest. He suckled Stone's nipples, drew them up and bit into them, just short of hurting. Arrows of rekindled lust speared into Stone's groin and Jarrat chuckled. "I love you so damned much. Always did. If you were less of a jerk you'd have seen it before. I've always wanted you, Stoney, always had fantasies." He spoke against Stone's throat, a husky murmur, infinitely seductive. "Fantasies of seducing you ... tumbling you on gold satin sheets."

Stone's mind had begun to spin. He rolled Kevin over and pinned him to the cushions. Gold chains tinkled. He teased the nipple rings with his tongue and kissed Kevin's mouth hungrily. "Always?"

"You heard me." Jarrat's legs scissored around him to hold him close. "You're so bloody gorgeous. You have no idea, have you?" He bucked under Stone, his cock big and hard again, as if he could find no rest. "You're going to be fucking me all the time, now. Promise me."

It was exactly what Stone had dreamed of hearing and he whooped, pulled Jarrat up into his arms, rolled them both over and pinioned him again to ravage the soft heat of his mouth. "I love you. Jesus, listen to the sound of that. I love you."

"It has a nice sound." Jarrat purred like a tiger cub. He hugged both long legs about Stone's hips. "I'll make you hard again. I can do it. I know you better than you know yourself, and you don't realize what you're capable of here, in this place, with me. You can do *anything*, Stoney. Now? A little kiss here, a little nip there, and that big cock will be mine again."

"Big?" Stone was teasing. "You think so?"

"Oh, he's big," Jarrat decided. He used his fingers to measure Stone, root to crown. "And he's beautiful. He looks like he belongs on a stud like you." He squirmed against Stone's body, gasped and arched his back. "And he's mine. Along with the rest of you. Yes?"

"Yours." Stone had both knees between the smooth, slender legs. He felt Jarrat's knees lifting, close to his chest. He took them over both shoulders and closed his eyes. "God, have I gone mad?" Jarrat laughed softly and kissed him. "Are you mad, then?"

"We're both mad," Kevin growled. "Fuck me again."

"Mad," Stone whispered, and smothered him with a ravenous, consuming kiss. "The pair of us. Gloriously insane." And he could not imagine wanting to be any other way.

Jarrat was wriggling deliciously under him, wild and wanton. "So we deserve each other," he said breathlessly as Stone slid into him once more.

The second time was more joyous than the first and Stone was certain he felt the foundations of his sanity beginning to slip, slither, as if they were not quite anchored securely. He buried his face in Jarrat's hair as he came, listened to Kevin's cries as he spent himself, and it was a long time before he opened his eyes.

The sex shop was gone. Before Stone's astonished eyes, now, was a landscape of fall, a forest of gold-clad trees, aspen, birch, cottonwood, and a line of mountains where the peaks wore early snow while down here on the lakeshore the sun was still warm, the grass still soft. He rolled off Jarrat's body and blinked down into his face as Kevin yawned and stretched-ed luxuriously beneath him. "How did you do that?"

"Do ...?" Jarrat glanced at his groin and licked his lips salaciously.

"Not that. This." Stone knelt, and nodded at the landscape. "You must have brought us here."

But Jarrat's tousled head shook. "You did. This is what you wanted. The sex shop in Venice was too loud, too dark, too hot." He gave the mountains an appreciative look. "I like this. Where are we?"

In fact Stone recognized the place. "I think ... no. I *know*, this is the Hudson River, Darwin's World. I spent a few weeks here after I shipped out from Earth for the first time. I was thinking about it when we ..."

"When you were fucking me?" Jarrat laughed. "You were thinking about a fishing trip while you were plowing me?"

"No! Well, yes," Stone protested, "but only because something reminded me of ..." He felt ridiculously vulnerable as his secrets were stripped bare before Jarrat.

"Of?" Jarrat just seemed to *know*, as if he could read Stone's very mind, or perhaps his heart. He sat up and his arms went around Stone, fetched him close. "Humping me reminded you of what?"

134

"Of the only other time in my entire life when somebody said those three goddamned stupid little words to me." Stone was mocking himself now, with a lopsided grin.

"'I love you,' those words?" Jarrat guessed. He was not taunting.

"It was right here." Stone's eyes skimmed the beauty of the Hudson River. The Kernaghan Range was like the pavilions of an army of the gods on the horizon. It was so familiar, he caught his breath as he returned to Jarrat's face. Wide gray eyes were watching him. Jarrat was waiting. "I'd transferred over from Tactical," he said slowly. "I was ready to be assigned to carrier duties, when ... his name was Sean. He probably still works at Sector Central. We got close that summer, and he asked me to apply for duties on Darwin's. 'Stay the hell off the carriers,' he said. 'Carrier duty'll just get you killed.' But I'd come out from Earth wanting carrier assignment, Kevin. Needing it." He hesitated. "I suppose I might have been on a crusade in those days. You know the way you start in this game. The dumb-ass idealism gets kicked out of you along with the crap before long, but while it lasts you *burn*, you're inspired. If I'd wanted to take some groundside assignment, I could have stayed back on Earth. God knows, I could have stayed with Tac! I'd have been a colonel by now, if I'd wanted the rank, the power-games, the politics. If I'd survived," he added darkly.

"You told Sean you couldn't do it," Jarrat said in soft tones. He stroked one hand the length of Stone's body, from nape to ankles.

Stone nodded. "He told me he loved me."

"Those three goddamned stupid little words," Jarrat whispered.

"Stupid?" Stone took a breath and looked into the somber eyes beside him. "They sound stupid to you?"

"Not to me." Jarrat shuffled closer and kissed him, his neck and cheek, his mouth. The kiss deepened, but Stone was not quite ready yet. Jarrat flowed back into caresses, offering unashamed comfort instead. "I've always been in love with you," he added. "Since the moment I first saw you. I walked onto the *Athena*, and there you were. Big and beautiful."

"And scared silly," Stone added.

"Of me?" Jarrat chuckled.

"I'd seen the file pictures. I knew your record. I had a feeling, an intuition, I was going to fall in lust like a tonne of bricks." Stone looked Jarrat up and down and nodded. "I was right. Loving you happened later."

"Same here." Jarrat smiled, eyes narrowed against the sun, and got to his feet. "Hey, you want to take a swim?"

"The water's way too cold." Stone gestured at the mountains. "Four hours ago it was on the Kernaghan Glacier, it's just above freezing."

"So make it warm," Jarrat challenged. His brows arched. "For a guy who can swim in the air and teleport us here just by thinking about a day on the Hudson River, nothing's impossible." He reached down, caught Stone's hands and pulled him to his feet. "You have no idea what you're capable of, Stoney. But you're going to find out." He reached up with both hands, as if he might capture the afternoon sun in his fingers; the gold of bracelets and chains shimmered, dazzling Stone.

Then he was gone, jogging down to the boulders by the water's edge, and Stone shouted a warning. Too late, he was diving — he broke the surface like a fish and was under in one smooth movement. Stone held his breath, waiting for him to come up again, but Jarrat stayed under. He stayed under a long time. The sudden shock of cold could stop a man's heart, Stone knew this for a fact, and he took a half-step toward the river.

The water had to be warm. It *must* be. A man could be injured by the sudden cold, and if he stayed in too long he could be maimed. A fierce power rose up in Stone's inside, burning hot and bright, like need or hunger. He sucked in a breath and —

— And Jarrat resurfaced with a whoop and beckoned. "You took your sweet time! Come on in, Stoney, the water's wonderful now. Told you."

"Damn," Stone murmured as he walked to the bank, took a step into the water, and found it warm as a tidal pool by a coral reef. "How?"

Arms wound around him. Jarrat pressed against him. "I told you, you have no idea what you're capable of, not here, not with me."

"But I'm going to find out." Stone's eyes squeezed shut. He *wanted* ... and when he opened them again the trees were not aspen and birch but palms, and the Hudson was gone. He knew this location too.

The island of Outbound was as sun-baked as the day he had visited on his way over from Chell. Jarrat was dark-tanned, buff-naked save for a pair of amber aviator's glasses perched on the bridge of his nose. The sounds of the ocean beckoned them along a street toward a white beach of coral sands. Green parrots squabbled in the jacarandas overhead.

Stone swallowed hard. "I ... can do this."

"You always could. I'll show you how," Jarrat purred. "You're going to be happy with me. You can have anything. Everything you ever dreamed of, and a lot you haven't dreamed of yet, but you will. Now."

"With you," Stone whispered.

"That's the deal, Stoney." Jarrat held out his hand. "Come with me."

CHAPTER FOURTEEN

Voices called his name but he could not quite hear it. He knew the voices well, and one of them in particular. The one that was sharp with concern. He struggled to get up out of the darkness, but something was very wrong with his leg. It as wet. He touched it and his finger came away red. He had to have help. He fought for his voice, found it and struggled to remember the names, the name of the one who was so frightened for him.

Frustration, then white-hot terror clawed at him. He could not remember. He choked on the fear, fighting for his life. The darkness was thick as honey, suffocating. If he did not get out he would drown.

"Help me!" He was shouting out aloud. "Help me — *Stoney*!"

The name came back like a blue-steel blade through his chest. As he opened his eyes the curtain of darkness lifted and he focused on the face he had longed to see. Handsome features, crackling blue eyes, black hair. *Stone.* The big man came into the darkness, waded into it as if it were a pit of tar and dispelled it. "Kevin? Kevin, you're here! Thank God ... You frightened the crap out of me, Jarrat!"

A bearhug crushed the breath out of him. Lips feathered moistly across his cheek towards his mouth, stubble rasped on stubble. He turned toward the promised kiss, hungry for it, and then memory returned like an electric shock. He cried out as he wrenched himself awake.

The room was stifling in the full heat of afternoon. No breeze stirred the blind at the window. The knife wound in his thigh was just a few weeks less than two years old. The scar marked the first time he had been injured in service aboard the *Athena*, and Stone had fussed. He had made too much of the wound, and Jarrat reveled shamelessly in the fussing. *Jarrat.* The name consumed him. *His* name. It came to him like a gift. People never understood the value their own names. He clung to it as he clung to the image of the black-haired, blue-eyed man, and another name. *Stone.*

Kevin Jarrat rolled off the bed, shoved the window open wide and stood there, hands splayed on the frame, to drag hot, humid air into his lungs. He felt weak in the legs and his heart was hammering. About him milled joy, horror, bewilderment, a storm that made him physically ill. Nausea churned in his gut and he slumped down onto the bedside, head in his hands, a faint breeze from the window in his face.

Behind him, the door opened and Evelyn appeared. "Are you okay, sugar? You yelled out." She came into the room to look at him. "Jesus, you're white as a sheet. What's the matter?"

He turned toward the woman as he fought his raw nerves steady. His voice was hoarse. "My name is Jarrat." It was like wine on his tongue. "Kevin Jarrat. I'm an officer, a captain with Narcotics And Riot Control. My carrier is the *Athena,* my operative number is Raven 9.4, and the man who came here this morning is my partner. My best mate, Captain R.J. Stone, Raven 7.1."

Evelyn gaped at him. "You're one of them? You're a NARC?"

"A field agent. A runner." He took a deep breath. The sickness had begun to settle. "I've been with NARC since I transferred out of the Army, seven years ago. For the past two years I've been assigned to this particular carrier, before that I was on the *Avenger.*"

"Then what in the name of God were you doing on the ground in Chell?" she exploded in exasperation.

Jarrat *knew.* "I'd been under cover for weeks. Deep cover, working the Chell underground, sending Death's Head people up to Stoney. I was on their payroll, working as a shooter, a 'corporate gun' ... they jumped me. I made a mistake. One's all it takes. I ran, they caught me, and they thought they'd killed me. Then you happened along." He smiled faintly. "I'm glad you did, or I *would* have been dead."

"A NARC." Evelyn sat down on the foot of the bed. "You don't look like one of them. I mean ... you're human, you look like a kid."

His smile widened. "Clean living. I'm thirty-one. And we *are* human." He watched her try to assimilate what he had said. "You hate NARC so much? Why?"

"I don't hate NARC at all," she said defensively. "If you're against Death's Head, honey, you're on my side. Or I'm on yours. Whichever." She met his slate gray eyes levelly. "But I'm afraid I lied to your friend, and as I understand the law, lying to NARC is a felony."

"You thought you were protecting me." He shrugged. "I'm just thankful Simon didn't put a bullet in him. Not that it'd bother Stoney, he's as strong as a horse. They've put a half-dozen in him before now."

"And in you."

"Goes with the job. I'm still in one piece, more or less. I know when to duck, right?"

"The way you ducked in Chell that night?" Evelyn asked acerbically.

"Point," Jarrat admitted. "It's all part of the job, Eve." He drew his hands over his smooth face. "What was it he told you? Somebody saw you putting me in the 'van, he tracked you to a clinic in Paddington, and then here ... the boy who came out with him ID'd your 'van by a dent?"

"Nothing wrong with your memory now," she said ruefully, then sighed. "Which means you'll be pushing off out of here, doesn't it? Damn."

He nodded slowly. "I've still got half a job to do. I want the guy who gave the order to grease me ... I want the guy who abused my butt, and I can't do it from here."

"You know who it was?"

"Oh, yeah. A charming character by the name of Grenville. There were any number of hardcases and headcases at the palace above Chell, Grenville was just one of the most vicious." He gave Evelyn a dark look. "Another was Ballyntyre's traveling celebrity, the young shooter who blew through here and left the mess at the hotel. Joel Assante. He was at the palace for a week or so. Mavvik seemed to be recruiting. Assante gave me a hard time ... I was the competition, you understand."

"Shit." She hissed the expletive through clenched teeth. "I wondered if the bastard had come here looking for you."

But Jarrat shook his head. "They were satisfied they'd killed me. Mavvik was specific. His goons were supposed to grease me, permanently, and they believed they had. He wouldn't send Assante to clean up after them."

"But Assante's here," she added. "He vanished after the scene at the Havelock, and Tactical have had the roads and 'ports under surveillance. He can't have gone far."

"Tactical won't take him down," Jarrat said bitterly. "He's way out of their league. I don't know what brought him here, but he didn't show up in Bally on my account. Trust me." He paused, brow creasing. "I owe you, I'm not denying it. NARC will pay up in cash."

"I'm not asking to get paid off," she said quickly.

"I know you're not," Jarrat said with a genuine smile. "But I want you to take the money. Stick it in the bank, and the next time you find a kid with his head busted in, do for him what you did for me. Deal?"

Evelyn shook her head over him. "You're nothing at all like your public image."

"Thunder and lightning, death and destruction?" Jarrat only shrugged again. "The stories they tell about us are often true. If I'm shot at, I can get annoyed ... it's like being a soldier in a private army that's at war. You're a vet yourself. You know what I mean. I'm going to go back there and do it all again. With extreme prejudice, as they used to say."

"I'm not trying to play judge and jury," she said quietly. "It's just that I hadn't expected you to be leaving so soon." She watched his expression darken. "What did I say?"

"It's not what *you* said," Jarrat muttered. "It's just something Simon suggested. He doesn't seem to think as much of you as you do of him. He told me to beware of you, said I'd 'get the bill,' repayable in the oldest tender in the world." He patted the bed behind him. "He's got a tough opinion of you." He said no more and waited for her to react.

Her cheeks brightened with anger or embarrassment. "One of these days I'm going to jam that kid's head in the vice and squeeze the bullshit out through his ears!" She got to her feet as she realized they had been sitting close together. "Look, that was never part of any deal, John — Kevin, is it? All right, I'd need my eyes fixed not to find you bloody attractive, but

138

it's incidental. I wouldn't ask it of a hustler I'd done a favor!"

"I'm glad to hear you say it." Jarrat smiled and followed her up. "I'm not one of those people who can whore for their supper." He thought of Lee and smiled. "Maybe I'd be rich by now if I were! I didn't say much, but I was somewhat pissed by Simon's little suggestions ... I'm not a hustler."

"Simon!" Evelyn exploded. "That kid has got to be the case for contraception!"

Jarrat laughed. "Isn't he a little old for that?"

"And I watched him grow through every one of his sixteen godawful years." She swallowed the anger with a visible effort and thrust out her hand. "Well, hello and goodbye, Kevin Jarrat, It's been nice daydreaming about you."

He took her hand and held it. "It's been nice knowing you."

"Really?" Evelyn Lang smiled, seeing the perverse humor in it.

He took her face between his hands. "I meant that."

"Friends, then? In spite of Simon and his big mouth?"

"Oh, kids are all the same," Jarrat said easily. "They think with their balls. Let him grow out of it. You might have made things too cushy for him since your brother was killed. Everything Stevie should have had, Simon's been handed on a plate."

She drew away from him and perched on the window ledge. "Maybe. I've tried to shelter him, keep him out of the cities. Eldorado is as soaked in Angel as Chell. Tell me someplace that isn't. Simon's good looking."

"It runs in the family," Jarrat said generously. The remark earned him a smile. A little honest flattery often scored a lot of useful points.

"They'd eat him alive in the city. Give him six months — oh, he'd be thinking with his balls. The hustlers are the only kids in work these days." Evelyn shook her head. "Bad company. The dens are full of Angel. I've heard horror stories. One time, a fraternity stag night turned into a nightmare after a stupid prank. Some shithead cut the coke with Angel. Thirty of the buggers bought it in all innocence. You can blunder straight into hell, never know you've done it till it's too late. Ah, damn."

She was still grieving for her brother. Jarrat touched her shoulder and she looked up at him. He saw the glitter of unshed tears. She would grieve forever. "Listen, love. I've got to call home. They're probably getting a civil pink slip right now to come back here and turn this place inside out looking for me, and if Tac shows up, they could wreck the place. You wouldn't put Stoney off with a fistful of lies. I'll have to use your highband."

"You're welcome to, but you won't reach your carrier or anything else in orbit for an hour or two." Evelyn gestured vaguely at the yard behind the house. "Art's still working on the groundstation. It's been on the fritz for weeks. Now there's a reason to fix it ... some big ballgame in Chell, you understand. Vitally important." She rolled her eyes. "He won't see a single play till the groundstation's back online, so it gets fixed at last."

"Damn." Jarrat pulled both hands over his face, which wore a thin sheen of sweat in the hot, close room. "An hour?"

"Or two." Evelyn stood. "Look, let's get out of here, John ... Kevin. Let me buy you a beer. There's a halfway decent roadhouse between Bally and Glenshannon. They brew their own beer in the basement, it's the best you can get in this neck of the woods."

Frustration redoubled. For an instant Jarrat was about to say he would go out and help Pedley, but the man knew his job and a second pair of hands was worse than a waste: it was an insult. The offer of a beer was not unwelcome and he stood aside, motioned Evelyn ahead of him.

Simon was absent. The whine of power tools issued from the yard. Pedley would be monitoring the shortwave via a handset, and Evelyn did not hesitate to swing up into one of the two towtrucks. The repulsion came on with a howl, and Jarrat climbed up out of the hot bluster. The cab was battered, dusty, the footwells muddy, the seats patched up with tape, the windscreen liberally spattered with dead bugs, but it was chill with a/c which started up with the repulsion. So much like numerous trucks he had driven during his Army years, Jarrat might have smiled. In the rack above the driver's seat were two big rifles and a handgun, and all three were wearing red and yellow Army warning tags: they were loaded.

"You get some weird types up here," Evelyn told him as she noticed his interest in the guns. "They come up from Eldorado to hunt, and they're not too bothered about *what* they hunt, if you follow me."

The big Rand truck hung a left out of the front yards, headed away from Ballyntyre. "Is it far?" Jarrat wondered, conscious of the time.

"Ten minutes. Enjoy the scenery."

The hillsides were thickly forested, but everywhere he saw the signs of clear-cutting, and was unsurprised when they passed a timber mill where an area of the river flats had been turned over to a freight-loading dock. A wasp-yellow heavy lifter with thick blue chevrons, a company logo Jarrat recognized, was on its way out as Evelyn drove by. The din of big engines reverberated off the mountains, and Jarrat watched it angle away toward the city of Eldorado. Soon it was lost in the dense overcast.

Five kilometers beyond the mill, the Rand swung off the road into a gravel lot in front of a long low, timber building. The signs on the roof read 'Skinny Dick's Sushi Tavern and Microbrew.' Evelyn parked the truck to the right of the door and killed the motor. The a/c whispered into silence.

Jarrat stepped out into the sultry heat of an afternoon which seemed to be promising a storm. A thunderhead was building off the side of the tallest peak above Bally. Evelyn saw the line of his eyes and gestured at it with the truck's keys. "Mount Madison, highest point in the Rosenfeld Range, higher than Sequoia, though not by much. Big enough to divert the local weather, throw the shit at us instead of at El. You're right, it gets stormy here a couple times a week, and when the big ones come boiling over the mountains, the fireworks can be quite a show."

He was still watching the brooding face of the gathering storm when she held open the tavern's door and waited for him. Soft music and the smell of beer wafted out. "You like living out here," he observed.

"I like it one hell of a lot better than the city." Evelyn let the door close behind them. "I tried living in El after I got home." She gestured over one shoulder with her thumb. "I was with Military Airlift. You?"

"Army," he told her as memory scorched him with visions he thought he had forgotten. "I served with one Air Mobile unit after another, this carrier, that carrier. Unlike a lot of kids, I had a knack for surviving. I scored a promotion here and there, a few commendations for distinguished service ... one day NARC noticed me, and they made me an offer."

He blinked the memories away, forced himself to concentrate on the dim cavern with the bar on his left, a few tables on the right and a dance floor dead ahead. Daylight made its way through long windows in the west wall, but the tavern was dim enough for the patrons to be shadowy, indistinct. Three figures were in the back, on the other side of the dance floor, where a few booths hugged the wall. A tall, rail-thin man with sparse silver hair was leaning on the bar.

"The proprietor, no doubt," Jarrat guessed. "Dick himself."

"In the flesh." Evelyn hoisted herself onto a stool and nodded at the taverner. "We'll take a couple cold ones, Dick. How's life treating you?"

The man spoke with the odd local accent, to which Jarrat was starting to become accustomed. "I could stand here and complain till hell freezes over, but no bugger'd listen." He offered his hand to the stranger. "I'm Richard Lambert Reznik. Folks around here call me Dick."

"Or Skinny, for short," Evelyn added helpfully.

"Jarrat." He shook the offered hand.

"You're new in Bally." Reznik was busy with the beer, which was on tap. "Or are you from Glenshannon? Jesus, you haven't come down from El, have you?"

"I'm from ... a little further afield." Jarrat took the beer, enjoying the chill of the glass in his palm.

"Staying on?" Reznik's eyes flicked from him to Evelyn and back. One brow rose. "I been tellin' you, Eve. Get yourself a goddamn' partner, so's you can unload that little shit, Simon. Pack him off to college."

"Be a waste of money, Skin, and you know it," Evelyn argued. "He wouldn't last a semester before he dropped out, vanished into city bottom, and the next thing you'd know he'd be running with the dopeheads."

"And good riddance," Reznik snorted. He thrust a glass into her hand but spoke to Jarrat. "So? You staying on?"

But Jarrat made negative gestures. "I'm just waiting for a ride. I've ... got people waiting for me."

A shape had detached from the shadowed booths across the dance floor. As Jarrat lifted the glass to his lips he saw the movement out of the tail of his eye. Reflexes that had been trained before he was ten years old, in the dockside maze of Sheckley, made him turn quickly toward the figure, but the light was confused. The man was outlined against the long windows, his face shadowed. Only the body lines alerted Jarrat.

The beer was forgotten as his hackles rose. Reznik was talking, but Jarrat heard nothing. The figure had frozen on the edge of the dance floor, face turned toward Jarrat. The hands were held well out from his sides, a deliberate posture. The gesture was clear enough. The shooter was not about to make his move here, in bad light and confused surroundings.

Tactical had kept the roads and 'ports under surveillance since the killing at the Havelock Hotel. Getting out of the area was not as easy as getting in. So he was here, in one of the very few social centers outside Ballyntyre itself, which was under Tactical surveillance. Jarrat was not even surprised.

"Kevin?" Evelyn had noticed. She held up a hand to stall Reznik, who was still talking. "Hold it a second, Skin. Kevin, what's wrong?"

"Outside," he said very quietly. He was not talking to her.

"Kevin! For godsakes, what —"

"Get down!" Very carefully, Jarrat eased off the stool.

He kept his face to the other man. Kept his own hands well out from his sides, a mirror of the same deliberate posture. It was a dangerous bluff, but he only had one card to play: Joel Assante did not know he was unarmed. Assante might still know him as the king shooter on Hal Mavvik's payroll, and the Kevin Jarrat he remembered from the palace above the Chell smogline would never be unarmed, even in a dead sleep. Jarrat's sole advantage was that Assante had learned to respect him too well to try a cheap shot, or he might already be dead.

Crabbing sideways, he moved slowly, deliberately toward the door. Just one thought was on his mind: the gun rack in the towtruck's cab. Two big rifles and a handgun, all wearing Army tags. He did not take his eyes off Assante for an instant as he held out his left hand to Evelyn. "Keys."

She slapped them into his palm. No questions were asked now: she could see the scene taking shape. "You want me to call Eldorado Tac?"

"Not unless they can get here in the next ninety seconds." Jarrat could see Assante's face clearly now, as the shooter also crabbed sideways, moving into better light. High cheekbones, wide, light eyes, Eurasian looks, pale Celtic complexion. There was no mistaking him. Jarrat took a careful breath and said to Evelyn, "Stay inside."

"But, Kevin —"

"*Stay inside!* And get down," Jarrat barked. And then, to the shooter, "What brings you this far out, Joel?"

Assante was six years younger than Jarrat, a hand's span shorter, with the leanness of a runner and the feral eyes of a hunter. "I knew it was you, Jarrat. Goddamn. They told me you were dead."

"They were wrong." Jarrat was at the door now. Behind the bar, Reznik was looking on, mouth gaping open. Very deliberately, slowly, not alarming the shooter, Evelyn joined him there and just as deliberately dragged Reznik down into cover.

"They told me," Assante added, "you're a NARC."

"They were right." Jarrat shifted the keys into his right hand and reached for the door with his fingertips.

"You got more lives than a fucking tomcat," Assante observed. "When Hal finds out you're alive —"

"You think you're going to live long enough to tell him?" Jarrat's teeth bared in a thin smile. The truck was six meters away. Locked. And Assante was armed. Six meters was a long way. Beside the door was a shelf carrying tourist crap, and Jarrat marked its position in his peripheral vision.

The shooter looked him up and down with a familiar sneer. "Hal's boys are getting soft. They were supposed to beat holy shit out of you, make it so NARC just scraped a smear off the pavement. He's going to pay big money for your head, pretty boy. I can retire on this."

"Really?" Only Jarrat would know how good a job Mavvik's men had done, but he was not about to inform Assante. "So what are you doing here, Joel? You didn't come to Bally for the nightlife or the climate."

"My business, Jarrat."

"I heard about Hank Weaver." Jarrat was poised on the balls of his feet, waiting for the right moment.

The pale blue eyes set oddly in the Eurasian face narrowed. "What in hell are *you* doing here?"

"NARC business," Jarrat purred, and in that moment it was no less than true. The moment a Death's Head associate appeared, Jarrat was back at work. He gestured at the ceiling. "I'm just waiting for a ride. They can pick you up at the same time. You'll be a guest of NARC, on the carrier, in twenty minutes."

For an instant Assante froze, and then his left hand was reaching toward the right side of his chest. A pulse hammered in Jarrat's temple as he scooped the tourist paraphernalia off the shelf by the door and flung the whole display box at Assante. The shooter ducked reflexively, and before his weapon was clear, Jarrat was through the door and diving under the towtruck's heavy-duty repulsion sled.

The Rand was built like a tank. Jarrat rolled under its belly, feeling the last heat from the motors on his cheek and neck. Then he was up, aiming the infrabeam key at the driver's door. It popped and he scrambled in. Through the windscreen, he saw the tavern's door swing wide open, but it took him a moment to pinpoint Assante.

Then — there he was, bolting like a jackrabbit toward the nearest corner of the building, the only cover he was likely to find, since the parking lot was otherwise deserted and the treeline lay almost a hundred meters away. Jarrat swore as he took the handgun and the heavy rifle from the rack, and a moment later he slithered out of the truck.

The humid heat was oppressive. Sweat stung his eyes as he tore off the red 'loaded' tags and charged both weapons. "Assante!"

His answer was in the form of twenty rounds which punched into the side of the truck. Assante might not be able to reach Jarrat, but he knew where to shoot to cause a very satisfying explosion in the Rand's drive systems. Only the truck's armor, necessary for the job it did in harsh terrain, had protected it so far. On his next volley, Assante would be through.

Swearing fluently in several languages, Jarrat shouldered the rifle and bobbed up out of cover. A dozen big-caliber rounds took the corner clean out of Skinny Dick's Sushi Tavern. A dozen more sent rubble scampering across the gravel lot in which it stood. Jarrat's eardrums protested the concussions, and as the shots echoed into silence he listened for muffled sounds of pain.

What he heard was footsteps, fast retreating: Assante was bolting again, using the roadhouse for cover, and Jarrat took off after him fast. He felt jabs of pain in many places as his body began to work hard, but the knee was well mended, and whatever Harry Del had done inside his head was much better than any tissue weld. Kip Readron could have done no better. He pushed himself harder, skated around the blown-out corner in time to catch a glimpse of Joel Assante's departing back, but the shooter was smart enough to know when he was outclassed, outgunned, and had lost the advantage. He was headed into the treeline, thirty meters behind the tavern, and before Jarrat could make a decent shot he was gone.

If he had known Jarrat was unarmed, he would have taken one shot, across the dance floor. Sweat prickled Jarrat's skin and he dragged a forearm across his eyes. He was the luckiest man on this godforsaken planet, and he had the good sense to know it. The knowledge aroused a white-hot burst of some reaction between anger and fear. The day a man began to fall back on luck to survive was the day he should get the hell out. Jarrat choked off both the anger and fear and searched the treeline visually, though he did not leave the cover of the roadhouse.

Going into the forest after Assante would be terminally stupid. With the benefit of cover, Mavvik's man was back on the advantage. He could choose his shoot-hole at leisure and pick off anyone who came near. Jarrat flicked the safety onto the rifle and shifted it into his left hand, but he kept the pistol in his right. It was an Austin, of local manufacture; and if he knew Evelyn Lang, it was in good order as well as loaded.

His eyes narrowed on the whole area around the roadhouse, but nothing was moving. Evelyn's impression was that the shooter had known only one person in Ballyntyre — and Hank Weaver was dead. So Joel Assante was alone here, cooling his heels, lying low, waiting for his chance to get out, as soon as Tactical looked the other way.

Adrenaline sped Jarrat's pulse like a performance drug as he visually swept the road, the treeline, the few other vehicles in Reznik's lot. Nothing. The pulse in his temple slowed, and as he heard the clatter of the door he turned to see Evelyn coming out. Reznik was a pace behind her, wailing at the top of his lungs.

"Jesus God! Will you look at ... Jesus, Mary and Joseph, I just don't believe ..." He kicked at a bundle of rubble and delivered a tirade of profanity which impressed even Jarrat, who had learned the full repertoire on a troop transport, two days out from Sheckley.

"Ignore him, he's well insured," Evelyn said acidly.

"I hope he is." Jarrat handed her the rifle but held onto the Austin pistol. "I may have a problem."

"I was listening." Evelyn nodded in Assante's wake. "He heard the story from this Hal Mavvik character, he knows you're a NARC. He also thought you were dead ... and if he gets out of here, he'll make a call."

"Mavvik will pick up the contract," Jarrat said bitterly.

"The contract?"

"Me." Jarrat stirred. "Evelyn, I have to get out before I endanger your household and Harry's family. I just turned into one massive liability."

"Yeah." Evelyn's face was taut, her tone filled with regret. "I think you did." She held out her hand. "Keys." Moments later they were in the truck. The repulsion was roaring when she added, "I'll take the back road, over Kinnon Hill. This vehicle's easy to recognize. There's no sense being predictable, making it easy for them. He could follow us ... *me* home."

"He could be there waiting for us," Jarrat added.

She dropped the truck into reverse and backed out fast. "Then you'll do your thing and we'll call Tactical to collect the body." She spoke cynically, but they were out of options and they both knew it.

"It might be easier if Assante did try it," Jarrat mused. He turned the Austin .50 caliber over in his palms. "This is a nice weapon. And I can take the little bastard."

Evelyn angled a hard look at him. "You're goddamned sure."

He returned the look. "I'd better be."

"NARC," she muttered, and tramped her right foot to the firewall.

His memories of Joel Assante were of an arrogant, self-centered sonofabitch to whom the Companions in the palace were live toys. As a hustler in Chell, Lee had seen and done it all, yet he hated Assante and refused to share his bed even when Mavvik threatened to fire him. But the shooter was very good at his trade. Dangerous. Jarrat did not underestimate him.

The Kinnon Hill road was a series of switchbacks climbing up above the timber mill at Gresham's and circuiting the crown of the hill to service the clear-cutting operation. From that vantage point Jarrat could see the rooftops of Glenshannon in one direction — down and to the south — and the communications relays in the other — north, and up, on the shoulder of Mount Madison itself, which reared over the Rosenfeld Range. Three dish antennae and a forest of pylons, aerials and masts, each surmounted by surreal lightning conductors.

Jarrat frowned at the storm front brooding in the south. Rain was already falling over Glenshannon and Evelyn picked up the pace as the truck came down around the logging camp. The road was better now, and Kinnon Hill had flattened out. The slopes were denuded; vast scars traced the paths of torrential mudslides. Evelyn sped by the concrete wilderness of a civil airfield. A handful of planes, assorted trucks and several orbital shuttles were parked beside the skeleton of a gantry and a ramshackle fueling complex. Then the towtruck was heading down again, losing altitude fast enough to pop Jarrat's ears. A sign at the junction at the bottom read 'Ballyntyre 20.' The truck turned right onto the main road and the jets roared.

For fifteen minutes they held back on the road, watching the house and garages, but of Joel Assante there was no sign. Which did not mean he wasn't there, Jarrat thought bleakly as Evelyn moved on. "If Pedley got your groundstation working I can be gone in a half hour," he said quietly, "and Assante has no interest in you. Soon as I'm out, you're safe."

"I know." Evelyn glared at the Roadrunner establishment. "I have some friends in Tactical. Old Airlift buddies. I can get backup." She gestured at the gun rack. "And Airlift taught me how to look after myself."

There was no sign of Art Pedley in the yards as Jarrat stepped down out of the truck, and the other towtruck was also absent. A job had come in, then, and the groundstation was either online, or it had been abandoned till later. Jarrat was abruptly out of time, and gave Evelyn a look of mute apology. She knew what was on his mind.

"Give it a shot, be my guest." She held open the screen door, led him into the dim, cool lounge.

The powerful comm set was tuned to the citizens' band but a red sticky-note on the panel said Simon had gone out on a towing assignment with Pedley. They expected to be home soon. Jarrat switched up to the Tactical band on which Simon loved to eavesdrop, then hooked in the satellite dish, shifted up again, and wished he knew how to pray as he called, "Raven 9.4 to *Athena*. Raven 9.4 to carrier."

Static white noise blanketed the whole channel. He was about to call again when the thick Russian voice of Mikhail Petrov said, "Jarrat? *Jarrat?* Is that you?"

"Unless somebody's moonlighting as 9.4," Jarrat observed. Relief was like a pail of cold water in his face. "It's a long, long story, Mischa. I need a pickup. I've got no wings, no wheels, no ID. If I call Eldorado Tac they'll probably lock me up for impersonating a NARC, after they get over the hysterics."

"Nothing doing, Cap," Petrov said. "Everything I've got is still in the air over Chell. Gunships, the lot. Even the Engineer's tractor. Can't give you a pickup till we get the mess sorted out. Death's Head is giving us a run for our money, but we've busted several targets. Tactical's screaming blue murder. Tac 101 was rocketed, totally wiped out. Stoney gave them a couple of gunships to cram a lid on it, but they gave us a standup fight. There's a lot of casualties, civvy and Tac, and we took a few ourselves."

"Patch me through to Stoney, will you?" Jarrat asked hopefully. A vast warmth spread through his insides at the prospect of hearing his partner's voice. That lick of pure lust returned, uncomfortably demanding at the wrong moment. If you could call being yanked back from the edge of death a kind of rebirth, Jarrat was reborn. And given the chance at a new life, he

145

was disinclined to make the same old mistakes over again.

"Nothing doing there either, Cap. The shuttle took a heat-seeker in one engine and bottomed out on repulsion. Stone took off on his own, groundside in the city, downrange of the dropzone. We can't raise him but it's no big deal. There's one hundred percent ECM over Chell, plus the 'port radars, plus our own radio clutter. Chances are, unboosted suit broadcast wouldn't punch through. He could be talking, we just can't hear. He'll hike it back to the dropzone for a ride when things cool down."

Jarrat recoiled. Stone had been shot down? It would not be the first time for either of them. "Stoney's a big boy," he said cautiously, aware of the hot churn of his belly, the curious, cold prickling in his extremities. "What shape is the shuttle in?"

"Budweisser picked her up. She'll fix, but it won't be a quick job. Engine and repulsion systems are halfway melted down. Curt Gable's in the standby, covering for Stoney." Petrov paused and then said quickly, "Look, Cap, it's great talking to you but I'm hellaciously busy. I've got your position — Eldorado, is it? A couple of grids south of there. I'll send you a ride as soon as I can get something to you."

"Which will be when?" Jarrat pressed.

"An hour or two. Let me get the fires doused, Tac smoothed over and our boys extracted. You've missed quite a party, Kevin. Watch the videos later, right? Raven Leader out."

He was using the callsign 'Raven Leader,' Jarrat thought sourly, because Stone was missing in action. As the frequency went dead he tuned back to the public band, cut out the groundstation and tuned in the gibberish of the civilian traffic. He gave Evelyn a lopsided smile. "You heard the man. A couple of hours. I owe you, lady. A lot. Don't think I'm trying to run out on you because I don't realize it."

But she rejected this emphatically. "You don't owe me a thing." She was by the front windows with the rifle, as if standing guard there.

"Assante won't make a move on us now," Jarrat told her. "We've got cover, we're well armed, there's two of us. He's not a fool."

"All right." She relaxed a little. "Coffee?" He nodded. "Talk to me. Tell me who the hell you are."

He smiled faintly as he watched her rummage for mugs and pour two strong coffees, topped off with brandy. "Who am I? Just a brat out of a hospice. No home, no family. I was dumped, so they tell me. With the rest of the garbage."

"Don't say that." She thrust a mug into his hand. "Which hospice? Not one on this planet, surely. Your accent isn't local."

"No. Out yonder." He waved vaguely into the ether. "One backstreet is very much like another. You ever hear of a place called Sheckley? It doesn't matter." He sipped the scalding coffee appreciatively. "When I got out of there the Army seemed a good idea. Christ, what an education!"

"Tell me about it. I had three stripes up when I finished my second tour and quit. I'm still listed with the Airlift Reserve. You made officer. You must have, since you're a NARC now."

"You have to be clever at bowing and scraping," he said glibly, and winked. "You know the drill: you get medals if you salute fast enough."

Evelyn chuckled richly. "Sounds like you hated the Army crap damned near as much as I did. So you rotated into NARC. You were seduced by the high life, Kevin? Or did you have a mission to fulfill?"

146

"A bit of both," Jarrat admitted. "Old scores to settle." His face darkened. "I watched a lot of friends go down the drain on Angel. I saw a lot of decent kids, my own age, in Tac uniforms, getting greased by civvies with heavy cannons. NARC is all that stands between the dopers and Tac, unless you want to send in the Army and start a massacre. NARC exists to *stop* trouble, not start it. People get a scare out of the riot armor, but the truth is, it's for their protection as much as the NARC man's." He leaned forward in the basket chair, elbows on his knees. "Let's say a Tac man in a regular kevlex flakjacket gets jumped by some doper, or a Death's Head shooter with heavy weapons. The Tac man doesn't stand a chance. If he wants to live, he blows the civilian away. Now, a NARC man in riot armor can take the fire, walk right up to him, take the gun out of his hands and march the doper away to the squad wagon. You get an arrest not a 'legit kill,' as the Tac jargon goes. In a riot the same applies. Tac *must* shoot if the dopers come in armed with real weapons — and they always do. It's a matter of survival, Tactical or the Angelpack. So they cut down the civvy mob and the press labels them murderers."

He shrugged. "Easier to call for NARC. We can walk through the same mob, they can shoot what they like at us and we can stroll in and make a clean arrest. They know that, the dopers with the big cannons. It's what riot armor was designed for, not to scare crap out of little old ladies!"

"So they hear a gunship on approach," Evelyn mused, "see the lights and spinners, and they scatter."

"Sometimes," Jarrat said quietly. He glanced pointedly at the big comm set. "And sometimes they don't. Death's Head has been giving us a hard time. Which means they have military hardware. Damn."

They spoke in undertones in the quiet heat of the afternoon. Jarrat acknowledged the burden of debt but could not find the words to tell the woman what he felt. She seemed to know. She had served two full tours as a Medevac pilot in a corporate bloodbath that had run away into such chaos, in the end the Army was drafted in to put a stop to it. Jarrat had also been on Sheal, two continents away and six months later than Evelyn. Swapping war stories with her was an odd way to spend a hot afternoon.

He was waiting to hear the engine noise of a shuttle from the carrier when Simon and Art Pedley pulled into the forecourt and parked the towtruck up by the house. Simon was first through the door, and cracked a can of beer before he spared anyone a glance.

"We towed the crap-banger into Gresham's," he told Evelyn as he handed her a thick wad of notes, the local currency, blue-and-red colonial dollars. "Sash Connally's bragging his ass off to his mates."

Connally was a local character who drove a dozer, cutting back the forest and clearing the way for the robot logging machines that fed the sawmill. Pedley often played poker with him.

"Bragging his ass off about what?" Evelyn asked indifferently, pouring another coffee.

"He reckons he shot the Angel courier at Havelock's." Simon drained half the beer and plopped into the swivel chair by the radio. Evelyn looked at him dubiously over the rim of the mug. Simon nodded. "It's all over town. He says that little thief, Iris Chow, found the Angel and the gun belonging to the contract boy, the shooter, Assante. She was looking for something to steal, going through bags and pockets. The guys were in the bathroom, fucking their brains out under the shower, when she came creeping in. It's what she does, Morry Havelock hasn't woken up to her yet. She found the Angel and the gun. Then she ran like a scared rabbit, straight to Sash Connally ... she used to hang out with his daughter."

"The daughter Sash buried after an eighteen month flirtation with Angel, five years ago," Evelyn mused. "I never saw Sash as a vigilante."

"He *says*," Simon went on, "he snuck into the room when the contract boy went down to the bar. According to Sash, he just picked up the Steyr .44 and blew a hole through the courier the size of your mug, and it wasn't even hard. The Angel-man was totally shit-faced."

"Complacent," Evelyn guessed. "They thought, Bally's on the edge of the world, what can happen here?" She looked at Jarrat, one brow arched. "Then Sash sneaks away, and when Assante returns to the room ... shock, horror. His lover's been gutted." She paused. "If I were Assante, I'd stay put till I found the killer, and I'd waste him. Slowly."

"Call Connally. Tell him to get his butt the hell out of Bally while he has the chance." Jarrat nodded hello to Art Pedley as he came in and banged the screen door closed. "Connally should learn to keep his mouth shut. Even if Assante and Weaver hadn't been in bed together, Joel would never let your man get away with killing a courier. As soon as word gets back to him, he'll take Connally without even working up a sweat."

"You said you knew Assante quite well," Evelyn mused.

"I ran into him several times at Mavvik's palace. He does special contract work for Death's Head ... he's an arrogant pain in the ass."

"You knew the shooter?" Simon began, outraged.

"Put a lid on it, kid," Jarrat snapped. "Watch your mouth. It's not what you seem to hope it is. I'm a NARC. Got it? Same as the guy you were trying to kill!" Simon paled by several shades and shut up fast.

"Assante could have just headed out here to an old fashioned lover's tryst," Evelyn suggested. "Apparently he and the courier booked the room and hit the sack. Neither of them seemed interested in anything in Bally."

"All the more reason for Connally to keep his mouth shut," Jarrat said acidly. "I know Assante as a vengeful young bastard. If the courier was his lover, he'll have Connally's balls for breakfast."

Evelyn leaned back in the chair, one knee hooked over its arm. "At one point we were worried Assante had traced you here, but Harry scanned you ... no implants. Biocyber devices."

"NARC wouldn't use them," Jarrat told her. "We do a lot of work in deep cover and they'd be a dead giveaway to anyone monitoring their frequency. The only way I could have been followed is exactly the way Stoney did it. But Assante believed I was dead. He left Chell about the same time you did ... he came here to meet his lover, like you said, the two of them staying the hell out of the city till Mavvik's war's over. They ran into a small-town vigilante on a personal crusade. And Connally's going to die for it. Assante won't forget or forgive."

"A war?" Simon asked eagerly. "A real shooting war?"

Jarrat gave him a cynical look. "The real thing. You'll probably see it on tonight's newsvids. They'll roast NARC. Again." Simon wanted to know more, but before he could speak Jarrat had heard a whining howl of approaching jets, echoing back off the mountains.

Evelyn was at the window, holding the blind aside. "Here's your ride."

And as those jets came closer, if Joel Assante had this building under observation, he would once again take off like a rabbit. Jarrat had no doubt the shooter would be twenty K's away before the NARC aircraft landed. He leaned on the sun-hot wall to watch the standby shuttle drop in out of the northwest. It was identical to the plane Stone had been flying when he was shot down, and he hoped his partner would be in this one. If he had joined up with a descant unit and extracted with them, Stoney would have made the flight back here with a smile. Jarrat jogged out to the craft as the jets shut down. It was roasting, aromatic. Waves of heat washed over him, stinging his sinuses.

The canopy went up and he was disappointed. Curt Gable had just pulled off the helmet, and waved down at him. He was a new transfer from Starfleet, a career pilot with a good record, an athlete's physique and a lot of ambition: his sights were set on carrier command. He was a good looking kid too, Jarrat thought as Gable waved at him over the side. "Hey, Kevin, you son of a gun! What you been up to?"

"Bit of this, bit of that." Jarrat's smile covered his disappointment. "The party's over?"

"All except the bellyaching," the pilot confirmed. "Stoney's still on the loose, God knows where. Petrov's really pissed about it. He's taking flak from Tactical that Stoney ought to be fielding. I mean, Jesus, I wish that partner of yours would call home once in a while!"

"If he can," Jarrat said softly. "Has Petrov told Tac we've got an MIA? If Stacy's sitting on his duff, he's not going to have a duff left to sit on much longer!"

"You're going to chew it off?" Gable laughed.

"With my bare teeth," Jarrat promised.

"Hey, Kevin, hang on to your temper. I know you and Stone are like fingers in the same mit, so does Petrov. He got hold of Stacy when Blue Raven extracted — Cronin's crew pulled out last — and asked for a Tac exercise. Location-sweep, looking for Stoney. Colonel Stacy's had it up to his nuts with us, you know, but he's got a squad out looking. Jeez, what can happen to a guy in riot armor anyway?"

He made a good point. Jarrat reined back on his temper. "Give me a minute, Curt. I've got to make a heartfelt farewell and then you can take me away from all this."

"Take your time," Gable sang. "You've got plenty of it."

Jarrat returned to the house, sun-blind in the sudden dimness. At the window, Simon was gaping speechlessly at the aircraft. Art Pedley winked at Kevin, silently celebrating his return to the land of the living. Evelyn stood at the door, admiring the sleek, savage configuration of the military warplane. On its flank was the NARC decal, the steel glove, the white dove. Jarrat took her hands as she turned toward him.

"I have to leave. I'll transfer the credit to your bank to cover the work that was done on me. Next time you find a pulp in the gutter, pick him up. Cheat them out of another one, on me." He took her head between gentle hands.

"I'll see you again?"

"Of course you will." He smiled. "Busting Death's Head won't stop the Angel Trade. We'll be here for some time, and we'll be rotated back later. This whole colony is notorious, you know. Big population. I'd stick around if I could, love, I really would. But, you remember that friend of mine who was here this morning looking for me? He just got himself shot down in the battle over Chell. Christ knows where he is, and I owe him one. In fact, I owe him a whole bunch. He followed me half way 'round this planet to find me here. Now I have to find him."

She forced a smile. "I hear you talking, Captain. Damn. I just gassed the afternoon away with a NARC. The job comes second?"

"First," he corrected, "second and last." Then he sighed, an admission of the truth. "Right after Stoney."

Evelyn frowned. "Your lover?" It was a shrewd guess.

"No," Jarrat said quietly. "Well, not yet. It might happen. I hope it does. We'll be breaking every rule in the book, but what the hell? We're not supposed to get involved, they just don't like it when their boys get friendly. Too many of us get greased, like I almost did." He touched her cheek. "I'll call you. And I want you to call those friends of yours in El-dorado Tac, right now. Better safe than sorry. If they stall you, or if there's trouble they can't handle, call the carrier. The callsign is NARC-*Athena*."

"There's trouble, and you'll be here?"

"I owe you," Jarrat said honestly. "The only way I wouldn't be here is if something else is blowing up in our faces someplace else, in which case I'll ..." He smiled faintly. "I'll send you a gunship."

"No joke?" Evelyn sounded skeptical.

"No joke," Jarrat insisted. "But I'd rather be here myself, pay my own debts. If I can't make it personally when the trouble shows, you get your gunship to fix it fast, and I'll be along later." He gave her and Pedley a grin. "I'll be in touch."

She watched him lope out to the shuttle, tall and lithe, and shook her head over him. "No, you won't. You'll find your Stoney, who busted his buns to find you, and you'll forget. Why the hell should you remember?"

It was Art Pedley who said quietly, at her shoulder, "He'll remember because he owes you everything he has. His *life*. And you heard him. He pays his debts."

"I wonder," Evelyn whispered, eyes narrowed on the retreating figure.

The twin ramjets ignited and spat sheets of flame. The repulsion downwash hammered on the concrete, then the acceleration shoved Jarrat back into the angled couch as Curt Gable sent the space-to-surface aircraft spearing upward with its wings and canards inswept. In the back, Jarrat enjoyed the ride as a passenger.

It was two months since he had seen the carrier. The ship hung over Chell in a high geosynchronous orbit, sensor-shielded, invisible to civilian systems, even the spaceport radars, its radio traffic encrypted to the point where the general public in the city might not even know it was there. Coded radio location was used to mark its position for the safety of incoming traffic, but it could ride in orbit with the security of the invisible. Hal Mavvik had not known it was there for six of the seven weeks Jarrat had spent in deep cover, in the palace. Below the kilometer-long slab-shape of the ship, Chell sprawled about the equatorial launch facilities.

Chell was the nucleus of it all. If it happened, it happened in the fetid, smog-toxic warren of the spaceport. On the fringe of space, as the sky ran through mauve to black and the stars appeared, Jarrat keyed in his head-set. Gable was about to turn the spaceplane for home when he said, "I want to take a look at the battle zone."

"But Petrov wants you aboard PDQ, and Kip Reardon is waiting with the whole medlab standing by. He's not sure what shape you're in. I gave him a buzz while you were talking to the lady, said you looked fine to me, but like he said, Cap, I'm a pilot, what the hell do I know?"

"Forget Petrov and Reardon for an hour, they can wait," Jarrat said tartly. "Chell airsearch is tracking us. Come on, Curt, move your ass."

"I've got orders," Gable argued. "The Russian will flay me alive."

"Then release the controls and I'll hijack you."

The Starfleet pilot laughed. "All yours, Cap."

It felt good to fly again. Jarrat derived a certain joy from the sheer power. He had been flying since he was in his teens, even before he signed an Army recruitment form. It was in his blood, as it was in Stone's.

As the hull began to superheat and the wings began to glow a dull cherry-red, he keyed to the Tac-NARC band. "Raven 9.4 to Tac 101. Give me Colonel Stacy." He waited only a moment, then Stacy was on the air.

"Who the hell is this?"

"It's Jarrat. I'm coming up on Chell."

"Jarrat? They told me you were dead!"

"Sounds like they were wrong, doesn't it?" Jarrat said with wry humor. "What's your situation, Stacy?"

"Somewhere between shitty and totally fucked," Stacy said tersely. "We were rocketed from a position on Mount Ararat, about four, five hundred meters above Tac Mobile HQ. They blew the guts out of us, Jarrat, same time as Stone was ditching. Jesus Christ, the mess is like a blow up in the butcher shop. Eighty civilians dead that we know about, including the dolly boy Stone brought over for the joyride. He was drinking tea, they dropped a demolition shell on him."

Pain arrowed through Jarrat's belly. He remembered the tall, blond youth with brown skin, kissing Stone briefly before they climbed back into the shuttle for the flight out of Eldorado airspace. "You've found the kid's body?" He had the city on the CRT and cut back to Mach 2.

"We pulled him out of the rubble. Medevac put the pieces together so there's something to send back to his folks ... Stone's going to be thrilled. I need someone to ID what's left. Stone's the only one qualified."

"I'd recognize him," Jarrat said quietly. "You found Stoney yet?"

"Oh sure, I waved a magic wand, and there he was," Stacy snarled. "No, we haven't found him — and how you could miss a guy legging it around the city in a fucking NARC hardsuit beats hell out of me."

"You couldn't," Jarrat agreed. "Which means he isn't legging it. You want to try using the gray matter once in a while, Stacy. It helps."

"Oh, thanks a whole bunch, Jarrat," Stacy said sourly. "You've got your location signal. You reading it?"

The locator beam had refined to a blue arc in the frame of the comm-relay terminal. "Sliding on down. Did you get Mavvik? I didn't read any traces of a fight at the palace."

"Because there wasn't one. You lost five Ravens, I lost forty-three of my kids. We totaled the labs, Armand's and Turboworld, that speedy garage, then Tac 101 bought the fire and we shut down to clean up. Sort out the crap, get the fires doused, ship out the wounded, demolish the wrecked buildings, send out for backup. I've got five units coming over from South Atlantis, and it's not going to be enough. We've won the battle, Jarrat. We'll win the *war* later, when we've made sense out of this crud."

Civilians came first, Jarrat thought as he homed on the location beam. Below him was the Chell Tactical Command building, tall, plate glass, chrome-and-ferroconcrete, rearing above the cityscape with a landing bay on the roof. The structure was stressed to take the shuttle's weight. He brought the aircraft down like a feather between the troop transports and satellite arrays. Curt Gable shuffled about in the forward seat to watch him take off the helmet and lift the canopy.

The air stank of smog and the exhausts of the big rimrunners. It was humid, like a greenhouse, and he was grateful to get inside. Armorglass doors held out the toxic, damp air. Stacy was waiting for him and directed him first to the morgue.

He stood outside a decontamination screen to look down into the face of a boy ... nineteen years old, not a line in his skin yet. Long blond hair was combed about his shoulders, and he seemed merely asleep. Medevac had done a good job. He had been Stone's lover, for so brief a time. Jarrat sighed heavily. Stoney had really taken to the kid. This was going to hurt him bitterly.

Stacy was waiting. "Well? That him?"

"Yes, it's the boy who was with Stoney. I never knew his name, but I saw him one time. You found his papers?"

"His ID just turned up in the rubble ... name of Riki Mitchell, he's from Outbound, from the service garage. I'll notify the family."

"No," Jarrat said quietly. "I think NARC should do that." Stoney would want to do it personally, he was sure.

"Suit yourself," Stacy said indifferently, and snapped off the morgue's lights. Jarrat was already through the door.

Stacy's office was like an icebox. The a/c unit was on high, fluttering the paper still churning out of the printers by the ream into the baskets beneath several computers. They were processing the data collected during the battle. Jarrat stopped in the doorway as Stacy produced a couple of beers. One was tossed into Jarrat's hands as he perched on the corner of the cluttered desk.

"You want to show me the pictures?"

The Colonel thumbed the remote and the Tac observers' telemetry came up on the big monitor behind the desk. Jarrat watched an edit of both actions and the assault on Tac 101. "Nice, neat, quick," he said, "and against military weapons. Where were Mavvik's shooters before it started?"

"My crystal ball is at the cleaners." Stacy crushed the empty can and lobbed it into the waste bin.

"It's your job to know! Find your weak links and weld them. And while you're at it, find Stone!"

"The city's like a pig market," Stacy protested, "You think I've got resources to waste looking for one man? Even if he *is* a NARC? You pay your money, you take your chance, like the rest of us, Jarrat. You did. If that's all you came for, bugger off out of here and let me get on with it!"

Jarrat got his feet under him. Anger shortened his stride as he stalked back out to the shuttle, but he said nothing. Stacy was right in his own way. NARC looked after its own. No one else was going to look out for them. He pulled on the helmet and locked down the canopy. Gable had stayed in the plane, reading something lurid.

"You want to head for home, Kevin?"

"No. I want to sniff around the site where Stoney ditched."

"The engineers picked up the shuttle," the pilot said doubtfully. "Stoney was far enough away even then for them to miss him."

Jarrat felt a familiar sinking feeling. He knew before he went through the motions that he was wasting his time, but he performed a full sensor sweep of the recreation park from low altitude and called Stone's name repeatedly on the NARC frequency. No signal answered and he kicked in the public address. Amplified a hundred times, his voice boomed out over the park and streets, calling Stone's name. Again, no response.

At the bottom of him, Jarrat had expected none. Stacy had it right: how could a man get lost in a city, when he was wearing NARC armor? He could not. Which boded very ill for Stone. Something had happened. Jarrat only wished he knew what.

He pulled up the nose and shoved the twin throttles forward. The shuttle bounded up for space, arced through the Chell radar net and closed with the carrier. In the belly of the big ship, hangars opened. He nosed into the blinding glare of the floodlights and saw the shuttle Stone had ditched in, under repairs. Its dismembered pieces had been temporarily abandoned as the hangar decompressed to allow him to land.

Five minutes later Jarrat was standing in the ops room, looking at Stone's own telemetry. Anything displayed on a screen aboard a gunship or shuttle was repeated here, on several CRTs, in realtime. One wall of the ops room was a flickering silver-blue gallery of screens; in the middle was a plot table displaying a micro-detailed threedee map of Chell.

Stone's telemetry told Jarrat nothing new. He rubbed his face hard. Mischa Petrov sat at the radio boy's right. He was a thickset man with cropped fair hair and a taut body which was the product of many hours of effort. If he stopped, he ran to fat, and the next physicals would be his undoing. NARC could not afford to carry passengers.

"We tried to raise him for an hour," the Russian said almost apologetically. "Either his suit radio is out, or he's discarded the suit, or he just doesn't want to talk to us. None of it makes any sense, unless he's picked up a hustler for a bit of R&R, and that's just plain absurd at a time like this. What harm can you come to in a hardsuit?"

"Depends what they're shooting at you with," Jarrat mused. "Portable anti-armor pieces will punch through a hardsuit. Big caliber automatic fire, something like the AP-60 I use, would cut through it like a jackhammer if — mind you, *if* you could stay on target long enough."

"And these assholes had all sorts of cannons," Petrov said unhappily. "If they cut him down, someone will report the body. Tac will notify us."

Jarrat's insides lurched painfully. He passed a hand before his eyes. "God almighty, how did we get into this?"

"I don't know," Petrov agreed. "Look, Reardon's waiting for you. Stone sent him a treatment sheet from a clinic that worked on you in Paddington, and he's been climbing the walls for days. We all saw it. A bunch of the Blue Ravens held a wake, they were so sure you were dead." He accorded Jarrat a wry, crooked smile. "Reardon would have filed the KIA report, but Stoney wouldn't countersign it! You were supposed to report to Infirmary instead of coming here. Humor the man, Kevin."

"I suppose I'd better." Jarrat touched Petrov's shoulder. "Stand down, Mischa. Get some sleep. You look like you've been to an all-night orgy."

"I feel hung over," Petrov admitted. "Starting to think about popping peps to keep going." He smiled tiredly. "What can I tell you, Jarrat? I thought you were dead. I'm pleased to be wrong."

"Not half as pleased as I am," Jarrat said ruefully, and headed aft to Kip Reardon's medical labs.

CHAPTER FIFTEEN

The haze was like a shroud over Stone's mind but he was conscious again. He had no sense of time or place and lay still for minutes, content just to breathe. His sinuses were blocked and he smelt the bitter, acid reek of the drug. It was easier to be high, and be oblivious to the truth. With consciousness came the cutting pain of realization. He was a user. A dopehead. Stone fought his eyes open with difficulty.

He was in a bedroom. The drapes were closed over and it was dark outside, though a distant neon billboard flashed gold and purple at intervals. The door was closed, he was alone, and he could hear music from another room. He was not tied, as if they were sure he was useless, and would be useless for hours yet. But even now Stone had the fitness and strength of an athlete to draw on. Consciousness had returned early.

He was naked, and the bed was a tangle of sheets that smelt strong. He moved carefully, feeling out his arms and legs. He should have expected the slight numbness. Angel deadened the nerves for hours after the trip. His fingers were clumsy as he examined himself and swore. His buttocks were greasy. Someone had been using his body while he flew, while in his mind he lay in Jarrat's arms and was in love.

He came to his feet and stood with arms and legs splayed, unsteady and fighting for balance. His bare soles could not even feel the carpet. When his middle ears righted he moved to the window, lifted the drapes apart and looked out into a yard. This room was on the second floor of some building, and it was the third place he had been confined.

First, the warehouse, where he had taken his virgin lungful of Angel. Then the stadium. He remembered a warren of locker rooms, the underground labyrinth beneath the football pitch, echoing sounds ... chemical smells, and a blue-tiled room where they had keyed the release mechanisms and taken the armor off him. He had no memory of giving them the codes, but he must have.

Then, a trip that kept him flying high as a kite until this moment. How much Angel had he ingested? Stone did not know, didn't want to know, but he suspected he had been close to overdose several times. He felt weak, sick. Only the athlete's reserves of strength had kept him alive. Mavvik's people had committed the sin of underestimating him. They were about to pay the price for complacency: Hal Mavvik would flay them when they reported the NARC captive missing.

He coughed quietly and took a breath to steady his belly before trying the window. It slid smoothly aside and a bug-screen lifted right off. In the next room the heavy beat of the steelrock stopped and he froze, heart pounding, but moments later the music resumed as another track began. Stone sat on the ledge, felt the night wind, cool on his bare skin as he peered in the gloom, searching for some way out, either up or down.

The best he could do was claw his way down the conduit which carried power cables up to the roof-mounted satellite dish. He leaned over and took his weight on his hands on the thick, rigid back plastex pipe. He knew he was tearing the skin from his fingers but he was too numb to feel it. The world reeled as he swung out from the ledge, and down.

He might have been suspended in freefall. His balance went out again and he concentrated only on his grip, going down, hand over hand. He felt weightless as he hit the ground, unable to sense anything as his bare feet encountered coarse asphalt. Reeling, he cast about for the gate out of the yard. It squealed as he opened it a crack, but the din of the steelrock from the apartment carried out into the street, and no one heard.

He stood swaying in the wash of halogen illumination from the overhead lamps. A Chevy sports stood at the curb, but he was too drunk to handle it, though he might have bypassed the ignition, hotwired it. The world spun, and Stone knew he could trust neither senses nor reflexes.

Which way? He peered past the halogen wash and saw apartment blocks to left and right. Lights shone in windows and he almost moved toward them. All he needed was access to a phone. A few minutes, and he could call Tactical. But who would trust a naked dopehead, reeling in the aftermath of a brain-buster of a trip? Doors would slam in his face. It had to be a public vidphone, and the emergency code which overrode the phone's presets and called home directly: NARC-*Athena*.

Stone took off on instinct, hurrying away from the gate. His eyes wandered into and out of focus. Lights blurred into haloes. It was difficult to tell if he were looking at small things up close, or large objects in the distance, and more than once he fell heavily, rolled, scrambled back up.

He did not even know if he was still in Chell. He could be anywhere on the planet. Moments after they took the armor off him, his nose was crammed with the bitter golden dust again, and he was sky-high. They might have doped him again after that, and again. The dreams he remembered were vast, encompassing the world, the whole cosmos. Most of all he remembered Jarrat, and love. The warmth of homecoming. Safety and welcome. Reality was a bitter pill to swallow.

He stumbled past a clutter of rhododendrons and frangipani that somehow managed to survive in the omnipresent smog, and saw the blue-and-white shape of a vidphone booth up ahead. Whooping for air, he dove toward it. Mirage-like, it danced in his vision, and he grabbed for it, leaned against the side of the hooded booth for balance.

The world spun like a child's gyro toy and sweat coursed from him. He reeled into the booth and propped himself against the transparent wall. The phone was working but every surface was covered in fluorescent graffiti. The vidscreen was shattered. He did not need picture to make the call, and settled for voice-only. With difficulty he read the local emergency code, 9900, printed in several languages beside the keypad.

Clumsy, numb, he punched the numbers and a synthetic voice responded. He ignored it, and without pause keyed in the override, eight digits which gave him command of the phone. The computer was several seconds processing the input. Double-checking with home base, he guessed, before the synthetic voice was back.

"NARC-*Athena*," he panted into the mic, and then could only wait.

A pause, extended, abyssal. At last a human dispatcher answered. "This is Chell Tactical. You have accessed a restricted channel. What is your emergency?"

So he was still in the city. "This is Stone," he wheezed. "NARC Raven 7.1. Give me NARC-*Athena*, and make it fast."

"Say again," the dispatcher requested. "I am not reading you clearly."

He realized he must be slurring, and raised his voice, forced his tongue around the words. "Stone, Captain Stone, NARC Raven 7.1! Give me NARC-*Athena*. Put a trace on this call and get hold of Colonel Stacy!"

Was he speaking clearly? His tongue defied him. It seemed furred and glued to his palate. "Trace this, for godsake!"

"Your call is being recorded, sir," the dispatcher assured him. "Please hold this line as long as you are able. I am raising the carrier for you."

"Get Stacy too," Stone rasped. "Pete Stacy. Tell him it's Stone. Tell him to call Petrov on the carrier. He'll know. I need —"

The muzzle of a gun tucked in under his ear, cold and hard.

Stone groaned and sagged back against the wall of the vidphone cubicle. A hand reached in past him and closed down the connection with Chell Tac. He peered up into Viotto's half-seen face, with its shaven skull and the flash of diamond earplugs. The shooter was impassive as he played the muzzle of the little Edson pistol about the contours of Stone's cheek. He would never pull the trigger, Stone knew, but there were other measures, very real threats. Sweat broke from every pore as he waited.

"I told Roon you ought to be doped again," Tate Viotto said blandly. "You're a big boy, heavy. You need more of the shit than the average user. Rooney's a fool, always was. What do you want, boy? You want to be tied to the bed? I do that, R.J., dead-easy."

Stone took a deep breath. "Who's been using me?"

A smile crooked one corner of Viotto's mouth. "You didn't complain at the time. Roon said your ass was sweet as honey but you were just so much whore to me. Who's Kevin?"

"What?" Hearing Jarrat's name from Viotto's lips was unpleasant.

"You were talking to some guy, name of Kevin. Every time I plow your ass, you're groaning to this Kevin."

Fury was a flashfire blazing in Stone's chest and his hands leapt out and up. He did not quite touch Viotto's throat, and he knew he was moving in a weird slow-motion. Viotto had ample time to step back. His face hardened and the flat of one hand smacked hard across Stone's cheek. But Stone was so full of Angel, he barely felt the blow.

"You should have kept running, R.J.," Viotto told him. "Open window, open gate, nearest vidphone booth. Not much of a paperchase to follow. Then again, your brain's packing up on you, isn't it?"

It was the truth. His mind was barely functioning at all. How he had got this far clearly astonished his captors. Stone reeled like a drunkard as Viotto took his arm, manhandled him out of the cubicle and into the waiting Chev. Roon was at the wheel, watching out for Tac squads.

Stone glimpsed his thundery face as he was shoved into the back of the car. The butt of the Edson pistol jammed into his ear. He did not move a muscle as Roon took the car about in a wide arc, back the way Stone had run. He had come to hate Brett Rooney with a passion. Several times, Jarrat had spoken of him, and always with derision

"The NARC made a call?" Roon's voice, taut with anger.

"The line was open but he was on hold." Viotto's fist thrust between Stone's legs and grasped his testicles, tight. "Who did you call, boy?"

Stone winced and swore. Lying would be pointless and painful. "Tac, who else would I call?" No need to tell Viotto he had accessed a priority channel and was waiting for a connection to the carrier.

"They might have had time to trace it," Viotto mused. "We'd better move him again. The apartment might not be safe. Keep going, Brett."

"Keep going, where?" Roon demanded as he put his foot down hard, heading fast toward a merge lane on one side of the Chell Spaceport Clearway. In the distance the massive arclights of the 'port lit up the night like battlefield searchlights. "You want to go to the fleapit?"

"Why not?" Viotto squeezed Stone's protesting genitals once more, for sheer spite, or to wrench a gasp out of him, and released them. "It's as secure as anywhere in this shitty place. Move it, Roon!"

The car merged into the traffic and Stone's head was forced down. The world became a dazzle of lights, some passing, some being passed. The Edson never left his ear and he took the opportunity to lay his cheek against the cool leather and rest. The fleapit, he saw long minutes later, was a holotheatre, and rather than being old, derelict, abandoned, it was open for business and noisy with the late evening crowd. The car pulled around into the loading bays in the back. The gullwings went up and a security door growled open.

He was manhandled upstairs by the rear access used by technicians and caterers, well away from the crowded foyer. Stone gritted his teeth as he was dumped onto a day bed in the manager's office. The door locked and Viotto perched on the edge of the desk, held the gun on him while Roon took precautions he should probably have taken hours before.

Cuffed by one ankle to the frame of the cot, Stone was unlikely to make it away again, and he choked off a groan as Viotto produced another capsule of Angel. He cradled it in his palm as he put away the pistol. Stone's eyes were drawn to it with a dreadful fascination, and a cold sweat broke over him as he realized a horrible truth.

The bitter, acid dust was a kind of escape, the means to get away from the living nightmare which had descended like a funeral shroud. Viotto was leering at him. He didn't need to breathe the Angel, he was already flying on the power-trip of holding a NARC captain under his heel. Stone blinked drunkenly at Viotto's groin and saw the big erection outlined under thin denim. The leer intensified as Viotto unzipped the jeans and Stone closed his eyes. He was too numb even to feel the wet warmth of fresh blood on his ankle as he pulled at the cuffs.

Resistance was a futile exercise. Part of him, a much larger part than he would ever have admitted, embraced the bitter dust, welcomed it as his only refuge from the truth. When the dust came, Stone froze in paralyzing horror for a moment, and then took a long breath. Five minutes later, he was far, far out of his mind and oblivious as Viotto jammed into him and began to thrust vengefully.

The restaurant was dim and quiet, with burgundy-red drapes and cloths on the tiny tables, the soft, nostalgic sound of centuries-old Italian music, the aroma of French food from the kitchens and the lingering aftertaste of a good Ouzo on the back of his tongue. Across the table, Jarrat lifted his glass in toast. He was drinking a local Chardonnay from a winery in the hills above Venice. Darwin's World was very 'wine-friendly,' with a climate fine-tuned by terraformers decades before humans arrived.

Stone lifted his own glass and the rims chinked together. "The toast?"

"You're going home." Jarrat drank. "That should be the toast."

"We," Stone corrected. "*We* are going home."

But Jarrat shook his head. "I've never been to Earth. You can't go

157

home to a place you've never been."

"You can," Stone argued. "The thing is, you don't realize it *is* your home for a few years. Then you wouldn't be anywhere else."

"Your point." Jarrat drained the glass, sat back and looked at Stone, mellow with the good food, good wine. He was in the brown leather jacket Stone liked, the black jeans, a blue shirt cut low across the chest. Venice chic this year, if Stone remembered correctly. Gold jewelry glimmered in the soft light and Kevin's skin was brown as coffee-cream. The light was in his eyes, which danced with mischief and shameless lust. "You want to get out of here?"

"Get out of here, and ...?" Stone prompted.

Jarrat gestured at the restaurant's wide windows, which fronted onto the Spaceport Clearway. Their car stood at the curb. He saw its outline through the windows as a heavy lifter blasted out of the 'port, sternflares bright among the clouds. They were in the jet roadster tonight, the Chevvy Phaeton. "Maybe," Jarrat suggested, "go up and park on the shoulder of Mount Albany? Maybe ... get friendly in the back seat?"

The back seat was vast. A grown man could stretch out under the curve of the gullwings. "Get laid under the stars," Stone added, "with the city down below like a carnival from horizon to horizon." He finished the Ouzo and pushed back his chair. "You're on."

The PET scanner hummed and whirred as Jarrat rolled through it for the sixth time. Bored, he lay on the sliding examination table, hands at his sides as his body, which had been poked, prodded and probed with every instrument Kip Reardon knew, was passed through the positron emission machine for the last time. Reardon was still making notes, shaking his head as he took readings, measurements.

"I just don't believe it," he muttered again. "I've never seen anything like this, Kevin. Not in thirty years of practice in two services."

"My ribs still hurt, and the knee," Jarrat told him. "My eye is sore."

"Oh yes, yes," the surgeon said dismissively, "you can expect all that. You don't get pulped and have no tale to tell! Turn over again."

With a resigned sigh, Jarrat rolled over onto his belly. He was naked, enduring the surgeon's hands under protest. Reardon had checked him from retina to anus, taken him apart a bone at a time, and Jarrat knew the tests on his body and brain alike had only just begun. He closed his eyes, tired, exasperated, and let Reardon do his job.

At last the surgeon stepped back and turned off his equipment. "Well, that's nothing short of amazing," he murmured as he scribbled notes. "When I read Medic Bolt's records I would have said you were a writeoff, Kevin. Bolt probably overestimated the damage, otherwise you'd never have made such a recovery."

Jarrat dressed quickly in the clothes he had arrived in, Simon Lang's jeans, shirt, boots, and pulled his fingers through his hair. "Wrong, Kip. The damage on Bolt's sheet was only the start of it. According to Evelyn Lang, some of the welds broke down, I fell on my face and they shoved me headfirst into cryogen before I could check out permanently."

"That can't be," Reardon argued. "Look here." He tapped a rhythm on the sensitive screen and an enhanced graphic of Jarrat's brain appeared. "That, my boy, is a normal, healthy brain. If the damage you're talking about had occurred, you'd have junk where your brain ought to be."

"Have it your way, Kip," Jarrat said mildly. "But Harry Del showed me his data after I rejoined the living. I was busted. I saw the scans. Before you say anything, I know the work was impossible, surgically. Del is an empathic healer, which is not the same thing at all."

"Phew." Reardon whistled through his teeth. "You really had a *healer* inside your head with you? Rather you than me, boy! I did some research into local ailments and facilities when we drew this assignment. Turns out, the terraformers missed a few 'bugs' in the ground or the water. In the first two generations after colonization a number of genetic mutations showed up ... not all of which were bad." His brows rose. "The empathic healers, with their uncanny abilities. The 'laying on of hands,' as it was once called." He shook his head thoughtfully. "I don't think I'd like to let one of those people loose in my skull, eavesdropping on secrets *I've* forgotten!"

But Jarrat was unconcerned. "What's it matter? It's Harry who'd have suffered, eavesdropping on my sordid past. If Sheckley's city bottom, Army troop transports and the battlefields of Sheal are too much for his virginal sensibilities, that's his problem."

Reardon laughed out loud. "I researched the healers after we got here. I admit, genetic mutation which breeds true interests me. Call it a hobby. Groundside on this planet they'd like to burn healers, you know?" Jarrat's brows rose, and Reardon nodded. "Bloody minded prejudice."

"I didn't know that." Abruptly Jarrat recalled Evelyn's apologetic explanations, and laughed tersely. "My God, she was scared I was going to give her a crack in the teeth! A few things make sense now." He stretched and worked cramped neck muscles. "Do you want more tests? I could use a shower and a meal."

"Go," Reardon told him. "I'll give you a buzz when I want you. Let me collate this data-collect first. You realize, I'm going to have one hell of a time explaining this to the boffins at Central, so I better be thorough. They could suspend you, Kevin." He paused. "In fact, you probably ought to be suspended from duty until you've been through the official test-set."

The younger man turned back, his face set in lines like granite. "Not while Stoney's MIA. Don't do it to me, Kip." A note of warning hardened his voice, but in fact Reardon could suspend him at the stroke of a pen.

"Rest," the surgeon said thoughtfully. "That's an order, *Captain*. Sit out the next few rounds. Let me run some further tests, on-the-fly, and ... we'll see. The telemetry I transmit today won't reach Central for three weeks. Gives you a little grace." He winked one brown eye at Jarrat. "Go on, wash up, eat, sleep. You may not know it but you're bushed."

In fact Jarrat was intimately aware of his body's weary protests. His cabin was aft of the ops room. It adjoined Stone's, with a common door between the two. He peeled off Simon's ill-fitting clothes and bundled them up to be returned before he keyed the intercom for service.

He called for a quick meal of junk food to be sent in, then stood in the shower stall with the water set to scalding. He was strung out, trying to adjust to shiptime, which was a little before midnight. It was somewhere near midnight in Chell too.

The burden of Stone's disappearance weighed heavily on him. He had won back his memory just in time to blunder into a hornet's nest. Hours before, he had been reborn out of uterine darkness and was looking forward to going home. Now 'home' was an empty place overburdened with a terrible intuition. Stone must be an unlisted casualty in Stacy's war.

When the call came in his heart pounded against his ribs and half the food went untouched. "Tactical for you, Cap," the radio boy said sharply. Petrov had gone off duty after a round-the-clock watch. "And you'll want to hear this. It's, uh, about Cap Stone."

It was Pete Stacy himself on the screen a moment later, looking weary and annoyed. "Something for you, Jarrat, not that I'm sure what it means. This came in on the public phone line. Are you recording?"

Jarrat touched a switch. "I am now. Play it."

The voice was Stone's, no doubt about it, but he was panting, hoarse, as if he had run a great distance: "NARC-*Athena*." Then a dispatcher, curious and curt: "This is Chell Tactical. You have accessed a restricted channel. What is your emergency?" Stone again, his speech slurred, blurred: "This is Stone. NARC Raven 7.1. Give me NARC-*Athena*, and make it fast." The Tactical dispatcher was taking the call seriously now: "Say again, I am not reading you clearly." And Stone spoke slowly, clearly: "Stone, Captain Stone, NARC Raven 7.1! Give me NARC-*Athena*. Put a trace on this call and get hold of Colonel Stacy! Trace this, for godsake!" A sharp edge in the dispatcher's voice: "Your call is being recorded, sir. Please hold this line as long as you are able. I am raising the carrier for you." Stone was panting with fatigue or fear, or both: "Get Stacy too. Pete Stacy. Tell him it's Stone. Tell him to call Petrov on the carrier. He'll know. I need —"

Then the line went dead so abruptly, Jarrat knew the connection had been deliberately cut. Swallowing hard, listening to the fast, hard rhythm of his heart, he rubbed his face. "You traced it?"

"It's a public vidphone on Gramercy Mall. We assume he was on the run because he was out of breath, and he couldn't have run more than a few klicks. All we can do is search the whole area, but it's a long shot, Jarrat. Understand. He cut off so fast, it's a safe bet he was caught."

"And he's a prisoner," Jarrat whispered. "Death's Head picked him up. Jesus Christ."

"It looks that way," Stacy said bluffly. He was never pleasant, but real concern gentled his tone. "Hey, Jarrat. I never worked well with Stone, you know. We rubbed each other the wrong way, big time, from day one. But I'm not cheerful to watch this happen. I just don't see what I can do about it. I got nothing to work with but a trace on a vidphone —"

"And if he was caught, which he surely was, they'll have moved him, fast and far," Jarrat finished. "They're not fools. They'll know who he called, they'll know NARC will be right behind them. Damn." He paused and took a deep breath. "Okay, Stacy. Thanks for the call. It's my ballgame now. NARC looks out for its own."

Without a word, Stacy cut the line and the screen darkened. Jarrat sat looking at it for some time, his mind a tired confusion. Then he punched a number he had long before memorized. He had often used it, when he was calling 'home base.' The palace. He selected voice-only, deliberately encrypted the transmission so his voice would be distorted, and waited for a full five minutes before he conceded that as far as Mavvik was concerned, the phone was turned off.

Exhausted, Jarrat slumped down across his bunk and pressed his face into the pillow. He did not expect to sleep but in fact was jerked awake

160

when the comm shrilled for attention once more. He rubbed his eyes, and a glance at the chrono showed that he had slept like the dead for almost an hour. He touched the toggle.

"Yeah, Jarrat. What?"

"Colonel Stacy again, Cap. And it's urgent."

His belly knotted, and Jarrat hoisted himself up off the bunk. "Put him on ... Stacy, what is it this time?"

"You wanted action, Jarrat? You got it," the Tactical Commander said by way of greeting. "This came in five minutes ago on the public band. Listen to these words."

The recorder started a moment before the message came through. "Record this, it will be said once only." A man's voice, speaking without inflection, one of the upmarket Chell accents, Ironside or Trieste. It could have been anyone. "We have the man from NARC, Captain Stone. He is alive and, at this time, unhurt. We are willing to arrange a trade, his life for the liberty of the twenty-three Death's Head men and women who are confined in your prisons. A simple exchange of prisoners. We want a spacecraft, fueled, provisioned for a long-duration flight. Have it and the twenty-three prisoners on the open field at Chell Spaceport, 22:00 Central Time, tomorrow. Stone will be brought there, alive. The terms are not negotiable. Confirm acceptance of this agreement on the civilian band. We will not respond but we are monitoring for your signal."

Jarrat stared sightlessly at the black plastex face of the comm panel. "Jesus God."

"Gives us twenty hours." Stacy hesitated. "Maybe we can find them."

"I suppose you've got resources to waste on one man now," Jarrat said acidly, "and a NARC at that. Did you trace the incoming message?"

"No chance to even start, Jarrat. It came in as a squirt, compressed, total transmission time was .032 of a second."

"They're not fools," Jarrat observed for the second time in an hour. "Look, Stacy, forget it. Tac has enough on without a full-scale manhunt."

A short, uncomfortable pause, then Stacy said, "So what do you want to do, Jarrat?"

"What do I want? We do as they say. *Exactly* as they say."

"And calmly hand over twenty-three life-sentence crimmos?"

"If they're lifers they're worthless to you," Jarrat reasoned. "You can only sentence a man and lock him up once. We're lucky you've got prisoners they're eager to trade for. Any other planet in this sector, and your crims would have been executed long ago. Stone's worth the damned lot of them, twice over."

"Jarrat," Stacy interrupted, "I am *not* having the likes of them released onto the open street! They belong right where they are, in the cage. If this colony had the death sentence I'd have shot the hoons personally, and been delighted to dig the hole to bury them in!"

"You want them executed, Stacy?" Jarrat asked. "I can make it happen. They give us Stone. We give them their ship. Then a gunship pulls the plug on it before it gets out of orbit if they refuse surrender orders."

The Tactical commander hesitated. "I, er, I don't have the authority to sanction it. Not the shootdown, the release of the prisoners, the requisition of a ship to be destroyed, not the, uh, the field execution. I'd have to go to Congress for special sanction. It'd take two weeks to get the license."

Jarrat's teeth bared in a wolfish, humorless smile. "Good thing I have

161

the authority, isn't it? I'll clear the release of their people. You'll get the documents. Lay on a security truck — and lock the bastards down in it. As for the ship, buy a junker, bill NARC. And leave the rest to us, Stacy. Anyplace outside of Rethan, these 'hoons' of yours would have been executed. So they might just get executed a few years late. Where the hell is the difference? They'll get the chance to surrender — or not. It's up to them."

"You're a hard man, Jarrat," Stacy observed.

"I'm a NARC," Jarrat said tiredly. "Get on the air, tell them we will comply. Tell them ... NARC is a spiteful, vengeful pack of sonsofbitches. If anything happens to Stone, anything at all, Kevin Jarrat is going to get very bloody annoyed. Use my name. Stress it. The shock they'll get should make them think twice about trying to double-cross us."

"They'll try anyway," Stacy said tartly. "You know they will. You buy it, Jarrat? You believe they'll hand Stone over?"

"Not unless they're made to," Jarrat said sourly. "And, oh yes, they'll try to double-cross. Mavvik knows NARC expects it of him." Jarrat tapped his temple. "Triple-think, Stacy. Get busy. We don't have much time."

"Fair enough," Stacy acknowledged. "So long as it's a NARC operation it's out of my hands — and well out. So long as it's not my ass that ends up in a splint, who gives a fuck?"

He cut the line and Jarrat sank onto the side of his bunk and glared at his reflection in the long mirror on the bulkhead opposite. He was still naked, tousled, beard-shadowed. He thought he looked tired, thin and older. But his nerves had returned to life. Stone was in one piece, and an exchange of prisoners was a stock solution to the classic hostage situation. If Jarrat could think his way around Mavvik's triple-think.

Nothing Hal Mavvik did was ever as it seemed, no word he said was ever what it sounded like. Jarrat knew full well, an offered exchange of prisoners was just the bait. The lethal barbs were hidden inside.

He turned on his razor and started work on the day's stubble.

CHAPTER SIXTEEN

A thermite-phosphor grenade made a mess of a vehicle. The Tac mobile surveillance truck was reduced to marshmallow, a heap of white-hot scrap belching black, greasy smoke. It stood on the long, low curve of the Spaceport Clearway, two kilometers from the access road to the palace, and Hal Mavvik watched it burn with a deep sense of satisfaction. Brett Rooney was a trigger-happy bastard but so long as he was supervised he could be trusted to do the job.

The Lapman convertible had raced up the clearway, passed the Tactical vehicle and braked hard. Before it had stopped rocking on its repulsion cushion, Roon had dragged the rocket tube out of the back, writhed around in the seat to get it over his shoulder, and put a single grenade through the truck's armorglass windscreen. Mavvik watched the whole game through powerful binoculars, and indulged in a thin smile. Tac had kept the palace under observation for months, even before Jarrat arrived. Now, both Tac and NARC were in full retreat. Death's Head was on top.

Alarms bleeped from the gate, but the guards were waiting for the

Lapman. They had heard the explosion as the Tac vehicle erupted. On the security vidscreen, Mavvik watched Roon grinning and waving his arms as he bragged to the guards, then the car pulled on into the garages. Mavvik switched the whole security system onto automatic and helped himself to another brandy as he waited for Roon and Viotto to come on up.

They carried the NARC man between them. Captain R.J. Stone was barely conscious, oblivious to his company and surroundings as he was dumped onto the carpet at Mavvik's feet. The Death's Head mogul looked down at him, ignoring Roon's crowing as he described the destruction of another Tactical squad.

So this was Stone, *Captain* Stone from the NARC carrier *Athena* which was in a geosynchronous orbit, high above the city of Chell. Mavvik saw smooth, muscular limbs, supple with youth, black hair, a handsome face, its cheeks flushed with the effects of the drug, jaw heavily shadowed. He saw powerful genitals, swollen, the man's cock half erect, while grease or oil glistened on his ass cheeks. Knowing Rooney and Viotto, he would have been well used. They were not the kind to pass up the opportunity of fucking a NARC captain. Mavvik felt a similar vengeful impulse, and had he been one degree less than straight as a ruler he would have had Stone then and there. But it would have been an empty gesture: the man was so far out of his skull, he would know nothing about it.

The chrono on the wall above the security screens showed 15:00 and Viotto was obviously jittery, with good reason. He was a pilot, qualified to fly 'heavies,' but he had not flown in years, since he quit the Cygnus Logistics cargo run, just weeks before Tactical and NARC busted the Angel smuggling buried deep inside the company's infrastructure. Tate Viotto had been turning the official blind eye for more than three years, and he knew when to get out and run. He kept the pilot's certification current, but that was a matter of paperwork and fees. The truth was, since he quit Cygnus he had not flown anything bigger than the spaceplanes and raceplanes in Mavvik's stable.

Tonight, Viotto could not afford to make mistakes: he was the only 'commercial heavy' pilot available for the flight out of the colony. Mavvik lifted a brow at him as Stone turned over with a deep groan, belly down, and began to hump the carpet, so lost in some delicious erotic fantasy, he did not know where he was or what he was doing.

It was disgusting, and Mavvik's lip curled. "What is it, Viotto?"

"The prisoners, Hal. They shifted them yet?"

Since Tac's mainframes, buried in the basements under Rimini Plaza in the central business district, had been hacked after the night Jarrat blew away Earl Barnaby, Mavvik was privy to any item of Tac business he wanted to know. In a few days Tactical would rotate their codes, but they would be hacked once more. It was tedious but not especially complicated.

"Their AIs have been talking to NARC. The prisoners are on the way from Easy Street by air. They'll be here. Stop worrying, you'll go gray."

It was a witticism, and Viotto grinned nervously as he drew one palm across his smooth, bald head. He had a lover among the prisoners, Mavvik knew. A shooter whose luck had expired, the same way Jarrat's luck was supposed to have quit. Even the thought of Jarrat was sufficient to arouse Mavvik to fury. He knelt beside Stone and turned him over. One eyelid pried up to reveal a dark, dilated pupil. "How much shit has he had?"

Roon chuckled fatly. "As much as he could take without turning up his

163

toes. He's a big boy. A *lot*, Hal. It's coming out of his ears. Can give him another dose before the hand-over."

"The hand-over?" Mavvik's brows arched at Roon. "What gives you the impression he's going back to NARC tonight?" Rooney recoiled. "Use your brain," Mavvik told him harshly. "He's the only trump card you have, yes? So, as soon as you hand the boy over, Jarrat is certainly going to frag you. Oh, they'll get him back, later rather than sooner, as an object lesson. But not tonight. Not till our people are away and safe. Then they can have him, pick him up in a life capsule, maybe."

"You mean take him aboard, jettison a pod before we cut in the drive?" Viotto wondered, and nodded. "They can scoop him out of space when we're gone. They won't shoot us out of the sky with him on board."

But Mavvik was less complacent. "One man against a shipload of escaping crimmos? They might. You forget, Jarrat's one real sonofabitch."

"But —" Viotto took a breath. "I'll be on that ship, Hal, for chrissakes! If you're even thinking about setting me up —"

"Then you'd be dead and hardly in any position to do fuck about it," Mavvik said tartly. "Calm down, Viotto. Get yourself a drink, pop something. They're not getting Stone tonight, and they're not shooting the ship out from under you. This much I promise you, Tate. Trust me." He looked down at Stone, critical of what he saw. Stone was panting and moaning, caught in the grip of some orgasmic fantasy. "Dump this garbage somewhere else, Rooney, before the carpets need cleaning."

With a dirty chuckle Roon hoisted Stone up by the shoulders and Viotto took his feet. Mavvik watched them carry the NARC toward the wine cellar where he could be locked away until showtime. Before the men had returned the R/T on the polished mahogany table gave a discreet chirp. Mavvik picked it up.

"Problems, Curry?"

The pilot's voice was thinned and distorted by the tiny speaker, the weak signal boosted by the big receiving gear on the roof. Curry was half the world away. "No probs, Hal. We got it and it's in good shape. I'll hide it, run a full systems check, see to the modifications, but it's looking good."

"Casualties?" Mavvik asked. Death's Head could not afford to lose men now. Too many of the young punk shooters had taken fright and scattered before it started. The best had stayed. Or most of them, anyway, Mavvik thought grimly. Joel Assante was on his mind, and a knot of anger clenched in his gut. Assante had real talent, but he had shown himself for a wimp. He argued against an all-out war, and when he didn't get his own way he bugged out before it could start. Mavvik forced his mind back to the call, and Curry's thin, nasal voice.

"None of us were hit but there's security goons flat on their faces back at the service dock. This baby's been overhauled, right down to the reactor housings. She's not new, probably needed the work, which is why they brought her groundside. But she'll do the job." He paused. "Hal, Tac must be reading this transmission. I know we're encrypted, but —"

"So shut down. Go silent, go dark till it comes together. Then be there, Curry. You just fucking *be there*." The words were sharp with overt threat. If Curry botched it, he would be top of the shit-list, and he knew it.

The pilot closed down and Mavvik turned off the R/T as Roon and Viotto returned. Viotto poured three brandies and sprawled on the couch under the window. "We're going to do it, Hal. Tactical are running about like hens with their heads cut off. And NARC's just disappeared off the street. They responded to a riot alert in Eldorado, it was in the newsvids. But they took a beating they won't forget in Chell."

"And they've never been beaten before." Mavvik smiled as he savored the priceless, century-old brandy. "There is a first time for everything. We'll finish the job here and then pull out. I want Tactical crippled — another object lesson. This whole colony belongs to *us*. But we're a target here, and I never liked getting shot at. When the war begins, a large part of it will happen right here." He gave the elegant lounge, and the landscaped gardens beyond, a regretful look. "Set up again in Eldorado, maybe. And if Tac knows what's good for them they'll stay well out of our way."

As Tactical usually did. Colonel Stacy was a fool, Mavvik thought. Only a fool started a fight he could not win, but Stacy had tried to use Narcotics And Riot Control to fight his war for him. NARC frequently entered into such conflagrations, but never before had they been whipped into submission. Mavvik poured himself another brandy and looked at the time.

By midnight the Death's Head prisoners would be out of the Rethan system. Stacy would know his game was up. The concept was infinitely gratifying. Mavvik savored it and the brandy both, until the R/T chirped for attention once more. He was wondering what calamity had overtaken Curry in the last ten minutes when he heard another voice. One he knew. One he had not expected to ever hear again.

"Where are you, Joel?" He heard the ice in his own voice.

"Like I'm going to tell you, on the air?" Assante mocked.

Punk, Mavvik thought acidly. He said baldly, "What do you want?"

"You might like to know," Assante said in the same mocking tone, "your boy's alive. I saw him. He's not even bruised, Hal."

Mavvik took a deep breath for patience. "That's not news to me. Jarrat's back on the carrier. We're … doing business right now."

"I saw him fly out." Assante skipped a beat. He had played his ace and come up dry. He backed off and started over. "You know what happened to Hank?"

"It was on the newsvids. That was too bad. Weaver was a guy you could trust and I knew his father, way back when." In fact, Hank Weaver had been a promising kid, whose only weakness was 'exotics' like Assante. Young men with honey-brown skin, blue slanted eyes and racehorse legs. Mavvik glared at Roon and Viotto, who were listening with guarded faces.

"I just found out who blew Hank away, and how." Assante paused. "You interested? Jarrat left, but I'm still in the zone."

"And for hire," Mavvik sneered. "You're a whore."

"Oldest profession on any world," Assante said indifferently. "Do you want the old man who greased Hank or not?"

"I want him." Mavvik set aside his personal dislike of Joel Assante. Hank Weaver deserved vengeance.

"The hit'll be reported on GlobalNet," Assante promised. "The fee?"

"Same as usual, paid as usual." Mavvik frowned at Viotto and Roon. "Did you take a shot at Jarrat?"

"No." Assante's tone was surly. "No opportunity. He might be back, though. You want I should hang out here a while?"

Mavvik was surprised. "What would bring him back?"

"Friends. A woman."

Now Mavvik choked off a snort. "Jarrat doesn't go for women. You

165

know it was Lee in bed with him, every night he was here."

"He might swing both ways now and then, when something tasty enough comes along," Assante argued. "She's big, hard, still with Military Airlift Reserve. And a looker. I know where she works, who she drinks with, where she hangs out. I saw them together, Hal. Her and Jarrat."

For a moment Mavvik hesitated. Assante could have stumbled onto gold: even wimps could get lucky. "I doubt very much you're going to get the contract, Joel, because when my war comes to fruit, I am personally going to fillet Kevin Jarrat like a fish. But in the unlikely event he makes it out of Chell alive and returns to your ... *zone*, by all means take him."

A satisfied breath whispered over the R/T. "The fee?"

"For this one you can name your own price," Mavvik said darkly.

"And if you buy the ranch when this dumb-ass war of yours starts?" Assante barked. "I won't get diddly-squat."

Mavvik's mouth thinned to a razor-sharp line. "You know better that that, chickenshit. The roots of Death's Head are buried deep in lots of places, some of them right out of this system. They can put me in a hole in the ground, and you'll still get your money." His pulse rate kicked up. "I want Jarrat. I want to take the bastard down with my own hands, but if they do put me in a hole, Assante, I want to draw my last breath knowing Kevin Jarrat is going to be on the down elevator right behind me."

"You can count on it," Assante said quietly.

"You're sure about the woman and her friends?" Mavvik pressed.

"Sure as you can be. You want Jarrat, there's your bait. The woman, her kid brother, a guy who works for her. There's also a big house in the mountains where she hangs out. A local crank-medic, name of Del. I've done my research. Long-range audio. I tailed her, she was there not four hours ago, telling the witchdoctor about your boy. Turns out, this Del did a lot of work on Jarrat. Got him back up on his feet."

An ice-cold thrill prickled through Mavvik's nerve endings. "So Jarrat owes him, big time. You *sure*, Joel? You heard all this, it's not guesses?"

"I recorded every word," Assante said curtly. "They had dinner on the back porch, they never knew I was within fifty K's. I got every syllable, they made it easy. Civilians." He spat the word contemptuously.

Like or loathe him, Assante was so good, you couldn't do without him. Mavvik nodded thoughtfully. "You have your contract, Joel. Whether I make it through the war alive or not."

"Deal," Assante rasped. "See to it."

The R/T issued a blast of white-noise and Mavvik shut it down. For some time he stood glaring at it, weighing the high cost of vengeance. And then his eyes returned to the chrono. Every second now, part of his brain was counting down.

The junker was just barely spaceworthy. Jarrat went aboard and ran the preflight check himself to make sure there would be no complications. Stacy's agent had paid only a small fee, since it came from a local breaker who asked just the salvage value. It limped into the spaceport in the late afternoon and would limp into space one final time, an old starship's lighter, big enough to ferry fifty passengers and a load of cargo between the surface and a ship not designed to land. It would do, Jarrat decided, and scrawled his name on the bottom of the purchase authorization.

The wrecker went away happy, Stacy's lieutenant returned to Tac Command bewildered, and Jarrat watched the digits on his chrono count away the time. Sunset over Chell Field was bloody, spectacular. The G3 star was bloated, distorted by the smog, the air was a too-familiar chemical soup, and the temperature did not drop much as night fell.

Jarrat arrived groundside two hours before 'showtime.' He took a car from the motor pool and cruised the security setup. It was adequate but he was far from satisfied, and called the carrier for a squad of Green Ravens in plain clothes. They were down by 18:00, armed but inconspicuous, to monitor the whole area. Jarrat himself sat on the hood of the Chev Equinox, drinking fruit juice in the lee of the battered old spacecraft and watching the sternflares of departing ships. The R/T was open, on the Tactical band. The Green Ravens made smalltalk and he let them chatter. It was not strict radio procedure but it did no harm. His own belly was taut as piano wires and he envied them the levity.

Around the spaceport perimeter were the men from Green Raven unit; Gil Cronin and Blue Raven were on standby to cover the upper atmosphere; Curt Gable was in the shuttle, ready to overfly Chell Field and provide topcover for the squad from Gold Raven who had come down in riot armor an hour before. They were well out of sight, concealed in the cargo holding area. Jarrat had to assume Mavvik had eyes and ears everywhere, and if he saw just one NARC hardsuit, Stone's life would surely be forfeit. The whole area was well covered and under surveillance from the carrier, and he could do no more.

Spaceport Security came on the air as he finished the juice. He slid off the hood of the car and tossed the empty cup in the general direction of a trash-picker drone.

"Cap Jarrat, a big armored groundie just pulled in through checkpoint 9. We let it straight through as per instructions. Your man's in the back. He looks in decent shape."

So far so good. Jarrat brought the R/T to his lips. "Copy that. Tactical, bring out the truck, they're on their way in."

The same signal was being received by the Raven squads, and it was a safe bet Mavvik was listening in.

A deep rumble of engines and a flood of headlighting announced an armored troop transport, designed for packriot patrol. It was driven by a young Tac sergeant in a flakjacket and helmet. He brought it to a halt beside Jarrat's car and got out, leaving the big engines idling. Jarrat slid in under the wheel.

In the back were the twenty-three men and women who had been sentenced to life imprisonment by the Rethan colony's judiciary — and who might soon be as dead as they would have been long before, had they been tried in some other troubled colony. They were on borrowed time, but they expected to be out and running soon and they were ecstatic. Jarrat listened to their excited chatter as he waited for the car carrying Stone.

Quadruple driving lights lanced up out of the night. Jarrat's heart gave a squeeze as he saw the limousine. It braked down, riding a storm of repulsion, two hundred meters from the old spacecraft. He pulled the truck slowly toward it and left the engines running as he stepped down from the cab of the transport. He held his hands well clear of his sides. Visible in his left fingers was an infrabeam key.

Three men got out of the blood-scarlet Chev limousine. Two of them were armed. Jarrat recognized them at once. Roon would never be anything more than a toady but Tate Viotto had become a shooter, a good one, since he quit Cygnus Logistics, fleeing ahead of the Black Unicorn bust. Tall, elegant, with his shaven skull and diamond earrings, Viotto held the car's third occupant in a choke-hold, one forearm across his throat.

The prisoner was dressed in white slacks, black shirt, bound, hands behind his back, and he was comprehensively blindfolded. He stumbled as they brought him around to the front of the car, and Jarrat's heart was in his mouth. "Stoney?" He called just loudly enough to be heard as he looked his partner over from head to foot. Stone was in one piece and up on his feet. At this point Jarrat could ask no more. "Stoney, you all right?"

"Kevin?" Stone was muffled inside the blindfold. He sounded groggy. "Kevin, s'at you? Wha's happenin'?"

"Just stand still, mate, it won't be long now. You're not hurt, are you?" Stone's thumbs were wired together behind him and he was blindfolded with a red scarf tied into a kind of hood. His shoulders were stooped but he seemed uninjured.

"He's all right, goddamn it," Roon barked. "You must be a cat, Jarrat. Got about three lives left now, have you?" He stepped forward. "Give me the keys to the truck, fuckface."

Jarrat held them up in full view but hung onto them. "You give me Stone first."

"And let you stick me with an empty truck?" Roon laughed shortly. "I know you, Jarrat. You're a fucker of the first water, *Captain*. The biggest sonofawhore I ever worked with."

"All right, I'll open it, then you give me Stone, then you get the keys," Jarrat amended. "You'll need them. Your maggots are manacled in there and the disengager is in my hand." He turned and aimed the infrabeam key at the truck's rear door. It rumbled open to reveal a motley assortment of men and women. They sat shackled together, blinking in the sudden wash of the limousine's powerful driving lights.

Roon was satisfied. "Give me the keys," he snarled, and shoved Stone forward a pace. "You throw me the keys and you get your boy. Come on, Jarrat! Or it's no deal. We turn around and leave, and you get him back in a box tomorrow." He held Stone by a handful of his hair. "Move it, Jarrat! Or will I waste him right here and now?"

Jarrat threw the keys to the ground at Viotto's feet. As the shooter stooped to retrieve them, Kevin slipped the tiny palm gun from the hip pocket of his jeans. It was useless over more than a hundred meters, but Roon and Viotto were close enough for the sneak weapon to afford good accuracy. "Let him go, Roon, or it's over. *Don't even think it, Viotto!*" The shooter had half-straightened and his own gun, a neat Edson pistol Jarrat recognized, was coming into line. "Drop it!" But Viotto froze, keys in one hand, pistol in the other. Neither he nor Rooney moved a muscle, as if they were waiting for something. Jarrat clasped the palm gun in both hands and barked at the R/T in his breast pocket.

"Green Ravens, where are you?"

"You bugger, you tried to trick us!" Roon growled, filled with rage and hate. "I ought to grease him right now. I've got a gun in his back, fuckface. What kind of fool do you think I am?"

"Stoney?" Jarrat hissed.

"Can feel it ... the gun." Stone gasped as Roon's hand clutched into his hair and wrenched back his head. "He'll do it, Kevin."

"'He'll do it, Kevin,'" Roon mimicked in a whimpering, mocking tone.

"Then we all die here," Jarrat said bitterly. "You thought I'd let you double-cross me, Brett? This whole place is crawling with NARC security. Any tricks and we all buy it. There's a dozen cannons aimed at you right now. Give him to me!"

The squad from the carrier was calling in on the Tactical band. Jarrat dug the R/T from his pocket and turned up the volume so Roon and Viotto could hear every callsign. They were showing the whites of their eyes now. Viotto straightened but kept the pistol down, and Jarrat's palm gun never wavered from the middle of his chest as he took a step forward. He was prepared to physically wrench Stone out of Roon's hands if he had to.

And then a blaze of halogen floodlighting probed across the wasteland of the spaceport's outfields, accompanied by a thunder of engine noise, and Jarrat felt the stormy downwash of repulsion. He brought the R/T to his mouth and bellowed over the din.

"What the hell is that? Gable, are you there? Gable! *Curt!*"

The pilot responded a moment later. "I can't make it out for the flood-lights — got it on instruments. Chell airsearch have been tracking it. It's on a legit flightplan, south-bound approach ... it reads as a commercial heavy. That sucker is *big.*"

"It's on top of us!" Jarrat roared as the searing hurricane of repulsion tore at him, scorched his face, parched his eyeballs. "Get rid of it, Curt!"

Gable hailed the aircraft on the open channel. "Commercial south-bound over Chell Field, move along. Move along, you are obstructing a security exercise." And then, less bantering than angry, "Hey, turkey, get that crate out of the way!" The shuttle dropped in out of the night, its running lights and exhausts bright against the overcast. "Commercial south-bound, if you do not move along I will take you in tractors."

It was not a threat Gable could deliver on — the shuttle had only a fraction of the big ship's mass and power — but perhaps the commercial pilot would not know it. The air was so full of ECM and interference, sensor images were confused. Naked-eye scanning was almost preferable. Jarrat's own eyes stung as the downwash of the repulsion flung dust and sand into his face. He got an impression of immense bulk behind the corona of the floodlights. Viotto glanced up at it, unsurprised at the sudden intrusion, and Jarrat's mouth dried.

"Curt! Curt! Fire on it, get it out of here!" He shouted over the noise, but a blaze of tracer from overhead drowned out his voice. Someone was shooting out of an open hatch in the heavy craft, big-caliber rounds interspersed with tracer, like bolts of argon laser in the darkness.

On the fringe of the storm, Jarrat saw the Ravens coming in. Those wearing riot armor had neutralized their weight and bounded effortlessly across the stained concrete. Rotary cannons loosed streamers of armor-piercing incendiaries into the craft, but they might as well have thrown pebbles.

Roon was screaming at Viotto, and of a sudden, as the armored Ravens approached, Mavvik's men split up. Viotto leaped forward, his gun tugging up into line. Jarrat saw it in the instant before he dove at the concrete, and a round passed so close by his shoulder he felt it nick the fabric of his shirt. He rolled and emptied the palm gun's small magazine after

Viotto, but the rounds smacked harmlessly into the side of the Tactical transport. Viotto was in the cab and the jets whined up as he backed it quickly toward the old spacecraft's lowered loading ramp.

"We're losing it," Jarrat muttered feverishly as he got to his knees. "Jesus, we're losing it!" A hail of fire still pelted down from above but the Gold Ravens were drawing it. Jarrat's eyes remained on Stone. As Viotto made his run for the transport, Roon propelled Stone's seemingly unprotesting body back toward the limousine and pushed him headlong into it. "Stoney!" Jarrat shouted. "Stoney, you can make a break!"

But, blind and deafened by the roar from the massive craft above, Stone only sprawled into the Rand and lay still as Roon ran up the jets. Jarrat swore bitterly as he sprinted back toward the big groundcar he had taken from the spaceport's motor pool. "Curt!" Was Gable reading him? "Raven Leader to shuttle! Curt!"

"Right here, Cap," Gable's distorted voice responded at last. "The ship's a heavy lifter, looks like some kind of cargo tug. That thing's eight hundred tonnes of steel and engines, three onboard reactors. I can't punch a hole through that hull, boss, not with anything I've got on this bucket — and I wouldn't *dare*. You want a reactor spill all over the 'port? Where in Christ's name did it come from?"

The Rand was already powering away from the old spacecraft, and Jarrat opened the throttles of his own Chev Equinox, grateful that his taste for powerful cars had spurred him impulsively to take the best in the garage. The Equinox was not armored, as was the car Rooney was driving, but it was faster. He juggled the R/T against the wheel as he swung wide about the field in Roon's wake.

"I don't give a shit where it came from. Don't let it get out of here!"

Up ahead, Roon was racing toward the lowered boom of checkpoint 9, on the outer perimeter. He was not going to stop. A security man jumped out in front of him with a heavy rifle, but Rooney barreled straight through, barely missing the man. The lowered boom exploded into fragments and the Rand was out. Two Green Ravens fired several volleys after it as Jarrat speared through the wreckage, and impacts thudded into the rear of the limousine. But Roon was accelerating away from the spaceport with everything the jets had to give.

Gable shouted Jarrat's name. "I'm not going to be able to stop it, Cap. This thing's built like a battleship! It's an ore-tug, there's no way I'm going to even put a dent in it."

"Gold Raven gunship is on standby," Jarrat bawled over the chaos of the loop.

"But they can't shoot it down over the city," Gable protested. "Oh, holy shit. NARC Forward Observer to Gold Raven gunship, get down here and cover me!" A pause, and then, "Jarrat, they just closed up the junker. They're on takeoff procedures. Running lights are on … the lift engines just ignited on preheat sequence."

"Put a shot in it," Jarrat called. "Don't let it get off." He wanted Viotto. He wanted the pleasure of handing the whole party to Stacy, intact.

Two hundred meters ahead, Roon was weaving through slow traffic, taking stupid risks and twice shunting smaller vehicles aside. Jarrat's heart was in his mouth as he put his foot to the floor. The Chev Equinox bolted through a narrow gap between heavy vehicles and made up fifty meters.

"No can do," Gable told him bitterly. "The tug is in between me and the scrapheap. Cannot get a clear shot. They're not going to let us jump them ... what now?"

"Go with original plan." Jarrat braked sharply, wove out around a family 'van and crammed his foot down again. In seconds he was riding Roon's tail and the slow traffic had fallen away behind. Ahead, the Chell Spaceport Clearway opened up like a rainbow of multicolored light, twelve lanes wide and sixty K's long. Rooney tramped hard on the accelerator, and Jarrat was right behind him. "Raven Leader to Blue Raven gunship. Talk to me, Gil. Where are you?"

Cronin: "Holding station in low orbit. I'll be tracking them as soon as they're off, Cap. They won't get out of here."

If they did, Jarrat would be facing a tribunal on Earth. Not that it would be the first time, he thought grimly, but this time he could not expect to double-talk his way out. A man's luck stretched only so far, and his own was already vastly over-stretched. "Catch or kill," he told Cronin. "Let the buggers get away, and my ass is in a sling!"

Then Gable: "... they're off! You hear me, Leader? I said the scrapheap is off and running. The ore-tug is flying topcover and I cannot get a clear shot. Hang on!" White noise sheeted out the whole band. "Jesus Christ, what are they shooting at me with? Gil, watch yourself, it's armed!"

"Scan it," Cronin shouted. "Armed with what? Come on, man!"

"Trying to scan ... launch tube of some kind, mounted in the nacelle where the geocannon should be. Missiles. Woah! Flaretails. They're going to frag me if I don't bug out. I've got nothing heavy enough to hurt them."

Jarrat lifted the R/T to his mouth. "This is Raven Leader. Retreat to safe distance, let the gunships handle it. You hear that, Blue Raven, Gold Raven?"

"I hear you," Cronin called. "I'm tracking them now, two marks coming up fast, running in close company. If I take out the ore-hauler the blast is going to total the junker, Cap. Can't be choosy now."

"Then total them both," Jarrat muttered as Roon braked sharply and changed lanes to get around a knot of slower vehicles, and suddenly the Clearway was wide and empty. They had already left behind the exits feeding traffic to the residential sectors and the Interstate. From here the Clearway ran into the southern industrial complexes, and at this hour everything was on automatics. Human staff had gone off-shift long ago.

"Copy *that*," Cronin said vengefully. "Carrier, you monitoring me?"

Petrov: "You're on tracking and scanning. I'm watching your CRT, Gil. Telemetry is on realtime broadcast to Central. And I'm seeing two targets outbound, coming up fast on your position."

The gunship would take them, Jarrat thought feverishly as he put the wheel over and swung wide about a stalled trailer. Roon grazed the side of it and the limousine rocked on its gravity resist cushion. Jarrat closed his ears to the intership radio traffic, tossed the R/T onto the dash and concentrated on driving. Roon was too fast, too wild. He was heading for disaster. Jarrat would not have cared, save that Stone was in the Rand, and if Roon hung it up, it had all been for nothing. Jarrat swore as his quarry clipped a parked wagon and skittered dangerously across the road.

Playing a hunch, he groped for the R/T and switched down from the Tac-NARC band to the wide range of frequencies Mavvik had used in the months Jarrat had worked for him. He grunted as he heard Roon's voice, furious, near panic.

"I've got him! I said, I've got Stone."

And then Mavvik's voice's answered. It was the first time Jarrat had heard it since the evening he had been given his orders to fetch Leo Dressler to Armand's. "I heard. Where are you?"

"On Tyberg, south of the 'port. Bloody Jarrat's right behind me. I can't shake him ... I'm going to write the car off, Hal." He was pleading, whining, a second away from panic. The Rand swung too wide about a right-hander and again Jarrat's heart was in his throat as it barely missed an oncoming car.

"Head for the fleapit," Mavvik barked. "If Jarrat's right behind you when you get there we can finish what we started. Do you hear me, Roon? The fleapit! I'll tell them you're coming."

Fleapit? A holotheatre? Jarrat flicked the band selector back to Tactical. "Raven Leader to Stacy." Pete Stacy had been monitoring the whole show, as if he hoped to see NARC knocked down several pegs. "*Stacy!*"

"Yo," Stacy responded. "Your targets have almost made orbit, Jarrat."

"Never mind them. I'm southbound on Tyberg, about thirty kilometers from the 'port, in pursuit of a runaway. He's making a left onto Bray. What holotheaters have I got up ahead?"

"You going to a movie, Jarrat?" Stacy bellowed.

"Come on, Stacy! Holotheaters. Fleapits."

"That would have to be The Plaza," Stacy guessed. "Renovated now, but it was half derelict."

"You tracking me?" Jarrat snapped. "Locate on my signal."

"Got you, and the runaway" Stacy said, puzzled. "What you doing, Jarrat? Your crims are two hundred klicks out with a gunship on their ass."

"I've got one down here," Jarrat muttered, "on the clearway, turning left by the bottling plant. Am I headed for the fleapit?"

"It's about five klicks in front of you."

"Get me some backup," Jarrat shouted. "Anything. I'm running into rough company, Stacy. They've got Stone in that car, and Mavvik knows I'm coming. He'll have his goons waiting for me at the theater."

"You armed?" Stacy paused to find and route a squad. "Jarrat, I said, are you *armed?*"

"Yes, goddamn it!" Jarrat closed up until he was riding the tail of Roon's car again, the heat of the Rand's jets taking paint off the nose of the Chev. "I can see the theater up ahead. Where's your squad?"

"Be with you in two minutes," Stacy warned. "Watch yourself, Jarrat."

Sound advice, Jarrat thought feverishly as he braked down hard, still glued to the tail of the Rand. Two hundred meters short of the holotheater, close enough for Jarrat to see the neon-bright, animated signage, the two vehicles rocked together, slewed sideways across the road, and the Rand plowed hard into a parked truck belonging to a Volvo dealership.

It tipped onto its side and, as the repulsion became ineffective, slammed into the ground. The autodrive shut off the repulsion, and the Rand became three tonnes of dead mass. Jarrat felt the shocks of multiple impacts down the side of the borrowed Chev, but was still upright when the Rand groaned to rest. He let the Chev's jets stall out and scrambled for the Colt AP-60 he had checked out of the carrier's armory hours before.

The Rand's uppermost gullwing squealed open a crack, and Roon's face appeared. He looked ill, white with shock. Jarrat lifted the gullwing on the lee side of the Chev and slid out into the cover of the car's heavy body.

172

Roon coughed and swore in an odd, asthmatic voice. Were his ribs cracked? Jarrat bobbed up out of concealment and saw him waving to three men in the alley beside the theater, across the wide, empty road. All three were armed.

"Help me!" Roon shouted weakly. "I've busted everything. Help me, I can't get out. I've got the man, the NARC man!"

So his ribs were broken, or an limb, a collarbone. Jarrat transferred his eyes to the alley mouth beside the bright theater entrance and, as the men stepped cautiously out, ripped a dozen rounds into the wall behind them. His voice barked over the hum of distant traffic and the spill of music from the theater. "Stay where you are! Put a foot out, and you're dead!"

They dove back into cover and Jarrat clawed the R/T from his pocket. "Stacy, where's that squad? I've got them pinned down but they must be sending for the cavalry. Stacy!"

"It's coming, Jarrat, it's coming," Stacy told him. "You got Stone?"

"He's in the other car, but the driver's rolled it. It wasn't too bad a smash." Jarrat took a breath as he saw a face appear at the alley mouth. A volley of full-automatic fire spattered into the side of the already abused Chev, and as the shooter ducked back into cover Jarrat answered with a dozen armor-piercers from the Colt. If he craned his neck he could see in through the rear window of the Rand. Stone lay against the seat, flat on his back, and he was moving. The impact had thrown him, but he had not been twisted as Roon had, nor had he taken a steering wheel in the ribcage. Jarrat swore softly as he loosed another volley into the alley, but he had already heard the approaching whine of engines. He looked up to watch the Tactical squad rise over the rooftops behind him.

Searchlights speared down. A deafening public address boomed over the street: "Drop your weapons! Drop your weapons or we will open fire!"

Very carefully, Jarrat set the Colt AP-60 onto the ground and lifted his hands level with his head. The Tac squad was coming in blind and from the air would not be able to tell him from the Death's Head people. He waited, seething, as the flyer touched down in the middle of the street.

Approaching traffic braked down and queued to wait, but as a young sergeant stepped down from the aircraft Jarrat produced his NARC ID and waved the kid away to make the right arrest. Tac's one golden rule was, 'You see a gun? *You* shoot first.' No one with a shred of sense tempted fate. Jarrat retrieved the Colt and slid it back into its holster.

Roon had scrambled out and, green to the gills, he collapsed facedown on the asphalt as the Tac squad left their flyer. The Rand's gullwing opened under protest. Jarrat climbed onto the side of the car, just forward of the roasting engines, and kicked the molded plastex until it lifted, little by little. With space to wriggle through, he let himself down into the back.

"Stoney? Stoney, you hurt?" A groan answered him, but he saw no blood. He fumbled with the hood, released the red silk scarf and looked down into Stone's drawn, stubbled face in the gloom. Slitted eyes looked back. "Can you roll over? I'll cut you loose."

He was groggy, and Jarrat guessed he had shaken himself up, perhaps hit his head, but he struggled to turn over, and Jarrat untwisted the wire from his thumbs. "Can you stand? We'll ride back with the Tac squad. There's hell to pay at Chell Field. And I want a medic to have a look at you. This thing really rolled." He forced up the gullwing, hoisted himself onto the side of the wreck and took Stone's hands to pull him up and out.

Stone was so much dead weight, and Jarrat swore as he lifted him onto the road. "You banged about?" Jarrat panted. "Stoney!"

The other man stood breathing deeply, blinking stupidly at the Tactical aircraft's blue spinners. Jarrat took him by the arms. "I think a medic had better have a look at you, PDQ." He cupped a hand to his mouth. "Sergeant! Can you give us a ride back to the 'port?"

The three shooters who had been waiting for Roon were manacled in the rear of the squad flyer. Roon was on his face on the deck, out cold. In the nose, the pilot and copilot were talking to base. Jarrat settled Stone in one of the forward seats as the sergeant slammed the side hatch and the aircraft lifted. Below them, they left two damaged vehicles and a knot of sightseers who had ambled down from the holotheater to see the free show. A salvage contractor would come out for the wreckage. Jarrat gave a thought to Evelyn Lang as he brought out the R/T.

"Raven Leader to Blue Raven 6. Gil!"

"Right here, Cap," Cronin responded. "Tracking the buggers. They just made orbit. The ore-tug is flying topcover for the junker. I'm going to have the gunship loop around, see if I can get a shot from the other side."

"Do that. Keep me posted." Jarrat cast a glance at the city lights, stretched out below the aircraft, and then turned back to Stone. His heart had just begun to decelerate and he was uncomfortably aware of sweat-damp clothes. Stone was leaning back into the deep padding of the seat, eyes closed, shuddering slightly with the vibration from the big engines. Jarrat bit his lip, wondering if he should call ahead for a medic, but if they extracted with the Ravens, Stone could be on the carrier in minutes, and Jarrat trusted Kip Reardon ahead of any local medic. He leaned closer. "You're hurt, mate, aren't you?"

Stone did not move at first, and when he did it was slowly, awkwardly. He seemed to be fighting for focus, but then he discovered Jarrat's face and smiled tiredly. "'Tis you. Thought I must be dreaming again."

"Oh, it's me," Jarrat said, breathing a little easier as he saw his partner smile. "It's ... a long story. Sit tight now. You're on your way home."

Even then, the Tactical pilot was dropping in toward the wilderness of the spaceport outfield. Jarrat watched as he maneuvered the flyer into the recess between the radars and the rear of the domestic terminal building. He looked over his shoulder as it touched down. "This do you, Cap?"

"Yeah, thanks." Jarrat touched his shoulder and went back to collect Stone. He slipped one arm about him to fetch him to his feet, and half lifted him down out of the aircraft. The last he saw of Roon, the toady was clutching at his ribs and breathing windedly against the deck plates.

The flyer took off, headed back toward Tac Command. Stacy would have a field day with Roon, as soon as a medic welded the broken ribs and certified him fit for questioning. Jarrat could find no pity. He cast about, saw a buggy runabout parked against the rear wall of the terminal, and appropriated it. Stone stood swaying, as if he could not move another step under his own steam, and Jarrat manhandled him into the vehicle.

The Green Raven transport stood a half kilometer away across the windy concrete expanse, its exhausts still shimmering. The NARC troops were already aboard, they were waiting only for him. Jarrat brought the buggy up to the side ramp and helped Stone out. He hit the autodrive, and the runabout trundled back to the terminal as he slipped one arm about Stone and urged him up the ramp.

174

In the muted hatch lighting Stone blinked at him with a faint, weary smile. "Kevin. It's so great to see you." The words were slightly slurred and he sounded as if he had a cold.

"And you." Jarrat winked at him. As Stone reached out he hugged the man hard. "What you been drinking? You sound dozy."

Stone's whole body stiffened. "Haven't been drinking." He drew away from Jarrat and scrubbed his face with both hands. "Can't think straight. Can't stay awake."

"Hey, you're doped," Jarrat observed. "Come on home, sleep it off. Tell me the stories later." A young sergeant he knew shouldered by to secure the hatch. Jarrat stood aside, let the girl do her job. He felt only a marrow-deep sense of relief. He had Stone back in one piece, and the game was very nearly played out. He brought out the R/T as the hatch locked and the green 'pressurized' light come on. "Raven Leader to Blue Raven 6. Status?"

"Targets are outbound, running in tight formation," Cronin told him. "I think the junker has engine trouble. They've tried to ignite the main drive three times but she keeps shutting down. Did you bugger-up their ignition, Cap? That's what it'll look like to the jetjock flying that thing."

"I preflighted it myself, it read okay on the ground," Jarrat mused. "Have you taken a shot at it yet?"

"Negative. They're floundering around just above the atmosphere. If I total them at this altitude it's going to be raining irradiated shrapnel over half of this hemisphere. And they haven't shot at me yet — Curt swore they were showing him missiles."

"Means their supplies of ordnance are limited," Jarrat guessed. "Keep in touch, Gil." He took Stone's arm across his shoulders. "Come on, son. Got to strap down."

Stone had followed half the radio exchange. His senses were distorted, hearing and vision only partially accurate. He was coming down now. All he wanted for the moment was to sleep. He was exhausted, physically and emotionally, after the trip. But he would not sleep it *off*, as Jarrat had said. When he woke it would be worse. He knew the trap of Angel, and knew he was caught in it.

He searched vainly for some way to say it and was mute instead. He slumped into a seat in the officers' compartment and let the weariness engulf him, content just to watch Jarrat. Beautiful. The man was beautiful. Dream images haunted him still ... Jarrat in warpaint, gold rings, gold chains, headed for a wild night's fucking. He closed his eyes tightly.

Jarrat gave him a fond look. They had probably been wise to pump him full of sedatives. Stone was built like a professional streetfighter. He would have pulped Rooney and Viotto if he were wide awake. If it came to a choice between downers and concussion, the mortal drowsiness of the dope was the lesser evil. Stone was asleep in moments, while the pilot ran through launch procedures. The engines rammed up for takeoff as Jarrat strapped himself down in the seat beside his sleeping partner.

The sudden vibration of engine thrust woke Stone again. In the bright cabin lights he looked flushed. His face was waxen with sweat, his jaw heavily stubbled. His eyes were very dark with whatever they had shot into him, the whites bloodshot. Jarrat frowned at him. "What's wrong? You shake yourself up when that idiot rolled the car? What hurts? Come on Stoney, let's have it."

175

The other man shook his head groggily and rubbed his eyes. "It's ... I can't ..." Stone clenched his teeth. *Say it, goddamn it!* His stomach knotted up. He was coming down hard now. Body temperature soaring, pulse racing. His sinuses were so clogged it was impossible to breathe. How could he say it? *Kevin, I'm a user.* He shook his head savagely. In fact, he had hardly been aware of the crash, and like the drunk who did not hurt himself taking a fall downstairs, he knew he had suffered only bruises.

He was ill, Jarrat could see it now. A bad reaction to the downers? The ship bucked through atmospheric turbulence. He watched Stone's head loll in sleep and keyed the R/T again. "Blue Raven 6."

Cronin responded at once. "The main drive just lit. They're going to do a runner." He had a master gunner's ticket, was a specialist with heavy cannons, their unit champion. "We're standing by with tractors on the ore-tug. It's going to give us a run for our money, Cap. That mother is *big*. They've got so much engine power, they're moving the gunship around by our own tractors! Hailing them now. I don't reckon they're going to pull up. You want them totaled?"

"Give them a chance," Jarrat said levelly. "Give them two chances. But don't let them get out of orbit."

"Will do," Cronin responded.

In low orbit, the Blue Raven Gunship idled along to match speed with the junker and its companion heavy lifter. The commercial ore-tug was built to ferry enormous loads of asteroid rubble from the mines to the smelter. It was armored as heavily as any warship, since it would sustain countless impacts as it negotiated the accretion of debris trapped in the gravity well of an asteroid being systematically pulverized. What it was doing groundside in the hands of the syndicate, Cronin had no idea, but his instruments told him someone had modified it. He was reading warheads — nothing nuclear, but heavy-duty military hardware, the kind taken from Vincent Morello Aerospace just days before. A heat-seeking warhead could hurt a gunship badly, and Cronin was far from complacent.

He sat in the starboard gunbay with one thick index finger on the sensitive trigger and a headset feeding him communications from the flight deck. The pilot was on the air, repeating the same message, over and over, giving the runaways every chance to surrender. Cronin wondered who was flying the junker. Who would take responsibility if it went bad.

"We are a NARC gunship. Pull up. You are under tractors. Pull up, or we will fire," Tanya Reynolds, the Starfleet pilot, warned for the fifth time. No response. Cronin had not expected any. His wide mouth compressed. The pilot hailed them one last time before she gave Cronin the word he had been waiting to hear. "They've made the altitude we need, Gilly. The bastards are all yours. Gold Raven gunship is coming up astern. Tractors are on, but we can't hold the tug alone ... Look out! That scrapheap is going to make a run!"

"It's going to *try*," Cronin corrected. The old ship was lit blindingly in a cruel wash of sunglare. Cronin flipped down his helmet's gold visor. He knocked the safeties off the triggers and armed the cannons. The pilot of the old lighter would be calculating a flight plan to take the ship out of orbit. Cronin glanced down at the CRT. They had space to themselves, nothing was within the target area.

The Gold Raven gunship nudged up alongside, cutting out the sunglare, and Cronin looked at the ponderous, ugly shape of the heavy tug. It was still maneuvering, despite the gunships' tractors. Huge engines and enormous mass were a match for the NARC ships. It swung around again, as it had before, putting its armor between Cronin and the junker.

"Shit," Cronin swore. "Get that fucker out of here. Gold Raven 5, can you get a shot at that thing?"

"I can put a Phoenix up its ass," Gold Raven 5, Buck Dumas, called. "I'm looking right at the sterntubes. But I'll blow its reactors if I do, and we're way too close to ride the blast. Safe distancing?"

The Blue Raven pilot was listening. "I heard that," she called into the loop. "Stand by for safe distancing. All personnel, get into your hardsuits, imminent radiation hazard. One minute, Gilly ... blast screens are locked ... fifty seconds. Mark your target, Buck."

"Marked," Dumas responded. Then, "Oh, Christ, no. They're coming around again! They know what we're up to, Gil."

"Forty seconds," the pilot read off. "Minimum safe distance in thirty ... twenty-five —"

"Missiles!" Buck Dumas shouted. "Gil, I'm counting three flaretails!"

Cronin swore and ran his straps up tighter. Before him, the blast screen slammed down and he transferred to instruments. A vid display showed him the same view, and the CRT at his elbow relayed Dumas' tracking data. The Blue Raven pilot's voice called out a moment before the missiles hit: "Stern section, lock everything down! Grab something!"

And then the whole airframe shuddered as the warheads slammed in, one after the other, impacting with the same hull section. Cronin read the data on his CRT and thumbed a switch. Behind him, the gunbay door slammed and locked, and his compartment pressurized.

Reynolds was bawling on the air: "Stern section seven is hit, the hull is breached! Is everyone in armor?"

Damage reports came in fast. An airlock had ruptured when three warheads hammered into it, one on top of another. The shooter knew exactly where to hit the gunship to hurt. The explosive decompression was still ripping through the unsecured compartments, and he was not surprised to hear several of the Blue Ravens calling in. Joe Ramos, his own unit second in command, was one of them: "Jesus! Lost my handhold. I'm out, floating free. Have you got my locator signal?"

"Got it," the pilot told him. "I'm going to take you in tractors. Gil, hold your fire till I call it! We've got three blown out. If you total the junker while our guys out there, you'll fry them."

"I'm holding." Cronin watched the heavy lifter come about, shielding the battered old lighter once again. He counted minutes as the retrieval crew caught the armored Ravens and reeled them in like fish on a line. No further missiles leapt at the gunship, but the ore-tug was ponderously maneuvering, and he made a guess. "Gold Raven 5, they're coming about to take a crack at us with the launchers on the starboard side. I'm going to try for a shot as they swing stern-on. They're masking the junker, I can't see it on instruments. Can you pick it up?"

"It's tucked in like a bedbug," Dumas told him. "Blow the tug and you'll take the old lighter with it. You'll get one shot, Gil. Make it good. They'll have another brace of warheads for us, and those fellas *smart.*"

It was a matter of timing. Cronin set up his gunsights and waited. "Flight deck, am I cleared to fire?"

"Ten seconds, Gil." The pilot's voice was taut. She was handling the tractors with the delicacy of a surgeon. "Blue Raven 7 is still out there ... five seconds. Okay, son, go for it."

With a scant second to spare he dropped his thumb on the trigger and felt a little shudder through the airframe as twenty heat-seeking Phoenix III missiles launched from the tubes five meters below.

Every missile plowed into the superheated sterntubes, and the reactors detonated with a blast that bathed the gunship in brilliance and hard radiation. "Kiss my ass and wave bye-bye," Cronin muttered. "Cap Jarrat, you can tell Tac they got one pack of dopers less to worry about groundside. We gave them every chance they were getting to pull out with their lives. Like Stoney says, no cock-ups, no comebacks. But we got damage, Cap. A little hull breach. Returning to the carrier to put a patch on it."

"Copy that," Jarrat acknowledged. "Tac are listening in. Paint yourself up another killflag, Gil." He shut down the R/T and turned to Stone. "There's your revenge, mate."

Stone lifted his head wearily. "Sweet. Viotto. Blown away." He leaned forward, doubled up about his crawling, cramping belly. "Viotto's the ... the shooter," he added.

Jarrat heard the bitter hatred in his voice. "I know Tate Viotto well," he said quietly. "I knew him at the palace. He was supposed to be a pretty good pilot in his day. He flew for Cygnus before the Black Unicorn bust. I'll give you short odds, he was flying the lighter." He put a hand on Stone's back and felt tension, fever-heat. "You want to tell me about it?"

But Stone shook his head, eyes squeezed shut. He was aching to say it but knew he never could. Not to Jarrat. He sniffed on his blocked sinuses. Every nerve ending felt burned now. Chronic withdrawal.

Jarrat studied him with an icy shrewdness stretched taut over panic. High temperature, profuse sweating, drunkenness, cramps, dilated pupils, cemented sinuses. He swallowed hard. "Stoney, what did they give you?" The other man said nothing. His face twisted. The expression spoke truths he was too stubborn to ever put into words. "Stoney?" Jarrat repeated. His fingers dug into Stone's muscular arms. "Angel? Christ, was it Angel? Did they —? Oh, Stoney." His own vision blurred as scalding tears stung his eyes. He pulled Stone into his arms and held on tight.

Stone felt a vast relief as it was said, and relaxed against Jarrat's lean body with gratitude. "Mavvik said I'd come back as an object lesson." His arms went about Jarrat. He pushed his burning face into the curve of Jarrat's neck, eager for the coolness there.

Heart in his throat, choking him, Jarrat said nothing for a long time. Nothing he could say would make it easier and Stone would not thank him for lies, platitudes. "How much?" he asked softly against the tousled black hair. "How much did they give you, how often?" Stone was feverish, trembling. Massive shudders racked him. Jarrat held on.

"I don't know. A lot. Every time I started to come down they crammed it into me again. I was flying, Kevin ... you don't know what it's like." He lifted his head from Jarrat's shoulder. "I dreamed you." He shivered, as if the memory were painful. "What am I going to do? It's over for me, isn't it? Hospital, licensed supply, the icehouse." The glitter in his eyes spilled onto his cheeks. "Jesus, Kevin, you have to help me."

And do what? Jarrat wondered bleakly. He had never felt so helpless, not even in the alley that night. He took a shallow breath and leveled his voice with an effort. "I'll get you something for the pain for a start. You need food and sleep. Kip Reardon must have something to help you rest," he said quietly. "Won't be long. We're coming up on the carrier now."

Stone barely heard him as he doubled up about his cramping belly and clutched tight to Jarrat's hand.

CHAPTER SEVENTEEN

Stone walked from the hangar deck to the Infirmary and passed out cold. Surgeon Captain Kip Reardon had been waiting for him to come in. Jarrat liked the man. He was not good looking, with his receding hairline and crooked, broken nose, but he was the consummate professional, and a good friend, always ready with a smile. But Reardon was grim as he played a sensor probe over Stone's inert body. Jarrat stood back and let him work. He did not volunteer the information. Let the surgeon do his job, discover the truth for himself.

"You do know it's Angel, don't you?" Reardon asked quietly, though he did not look up from the buzzbox probe.

"Yeah, I know." Jarrat's voice was a mere whisper.

"Christ almighty, he's pickled in it. Temperature's five degrees high, pulse is 125, BP is through the roof. He's dehydrated, he's sweated himself dry. Short of body salts and minerals, of course. He'll have been coming as fast as he could get it up. You know what Angel's like. He's had a knock on the head, too. Bruises here and here, he's taken a couple of falls. Probably got thrown when the car rolled. Nothing's broken or ruptured, which is something to be thankful for." He turned off the probe and rubbed his eyes. "What do you want me to tell you, Kevin?"

"Just do something for him," Jarrat said quietly.

"I'll get an IV into him, cycle his blood a couple of times, see if we can flush out some of the muck. Vitamins, minerals, glucose and body salts. Get his ATP level back to something like normal. He won't stomach food just yet but when he can, he ought to eat as much as he can. Uppers, booze. Some good sex." He lifted a brow at Jarrat. "That's something else you ought to know. Someone's been using him."

"You mean raping him?" Jarrat took a shallow breath.

"Not quite rape. He's still greasy and there's no injury. He's just been banged, repeatedly. I read traces of genetic material in him, could be two DNA prints. I might be able to get an ident. I'll scan for clap and get some broad-spectrum antibiotics into him before I do anything."

"Oh, God." Jarrat sat down tiredly in the swivel chair behind the workstation. "I should have expected it."

"They had a go at you," Reardon said cynically. "He hasn't been abused the way you were, Kevin. Be grateful for small mercies."

"I am. And if the maggot who stuffed the Angel into him — a small-time shooter called Tate Viotto — is the same guy who nailed him, the culprit's already dead. Viotto was the kind who'd take any liberties he could get away with, and he always liked his boys doped. And he'd have been flying the old lighter. Viotto used to brag about his skills, said he could fly anything." Jarrat stirred with an effort. "What can you do for him, Kip? There must be something!"

Reardon leaned both palms on the exam table where Stone lay. "Well, I can break this fever and slow his pulse. But what do you want from me? If I can get ten percent of this shit out of him I'll buy him a month. A *month*. He's got five or six months left, if he's bloody lucky, and a bodybag at the end of it. There just isn't much I can do. I can pump in the mineral salts he's losing, get some dope into him to reduce the craving, but he's coming down hard. He's going to need more before long."

"Angeldeath, or die in withdrawal," Jarrat murmured. He rubbed his face, fingernails raking through the evening's stubble. "Great choice."

The surgeon nodded sadly. "Nature set us up for it. The human brain has chemical receivers to match the Angel molecule. If it hadn't, we wouldn't get such a bang out of it. What happens is, the Angel screws up the neural wiring. Tangles it, glues it together, like a mess of bailing twine. It encourages the production of more chemical receivers so, the more you use the more you *can* use, and the more you have to have. The endocrine system goes askew. Hence, the pain, the fever. Then, endocrine disorders, immune system failure. Death due to infection, if not through a plain, old-fashioned heart attack." He drew a swab over Stone's waxen forehead, swept back his hair. "Also, when you get into advanced addiction ... like this ... you need bigger doses more often. In the end you're flirting with overdose all the time." He regarded Stone with a sigh. "His brain is already in one hell of a state. I'll do a PET scan."

The machine whirred obediently and Stone rolled through its central tube. On the screen at Jarrat's elbow appeared a schematic of his friend's brain. The autodiagnostics highlighted the troubled areas. The majority of Stone's neural pathways were already a shambles; some seemed to be gone altogether.

"Can any of this be fixed?" Jarrat asked quietly.

"With a laser probe?" Reardon turned off the positron emission tomography machine and looked up with a cynical twist of his mouth. "Oh, it's been tried. The most we do is buy them a few more months, if we're lucky. It just drags the agony out, Kevin. You want to do the kind thing for him? Help him to die right now, before it starts to rip him up. You want to watch him get old, raddled, dilapidated?"

Jarrat closed his eyes. "But even then, they dream, don't they? They fly, they feel, they can live in the dreams. Laugh, love. Can't they?"

"I suppose so." Reardon looked down at Stone. "Well, it's his decision, not yours, not mine. I'll get him sobered up, then you can tell him."

"Tell him?" Jarrat echoed. "He doesn't need me to bloody tell him! He asked me to *help* him. Help him die, maybe. What else can I do for him?" He leaned on the computer's hooded monitor. "I helped a kid out once before. A mate of mine, at the hospice where I grew up. He was strung out, I got him booze, tetraphine, screwed him until I was exhausted. It helped for a while, and then one day it stopped helping and..."

"And he overdosed on the tetraphine?" Reardon guessed.

"On Angel," Jarrat whispered. "Isn't there anything new, anything experimental? What the Christ are all those bio research labs doing? They guzzle public money and give back nothing!"

"Well, there's a cocktail," Reardon mused. "It's dopehead lore, but it's not a bad remedy, all things considered. I've got the makings here, it'll take an hour or so in the lab. Dextromoramide, barbituric acid, psilocin, ibonetic acid. Psychoactives plus downers and analgesics, delivered as a suppository, Save his veins, spare his nose." He looked levelly at Jarrat. "They call it a Zombie. And that's what he's going to be, using this kind of rubbish. The idea is, it'll curb the withdrawal pain, keep them calm and cause some kind of hallucinogenic reaction similar to the Angel trip."

"That cocktail is a one-way ticket to the morgue, sooner or later," Jarrat protested, appalled at the ingedients Kip had just listed.

"I didn't say it was a cure," Reardon said sharply. Jarrat shut up. "Kevin, understand. There's *nothing* I can do for him. You could take him to a neurosurgeon on Earth and there's still nothing to be done. I'm sorry."

"So am I." Jarrat looked at the hard copy of the PET scan of Stone's chaotic brain tissues. "You'd have to get into his head, unravel the mess one cell at a time, and ... Jesus." He caught his breath. "Get into his brain. Jesus, that's it. That has to be it! There's a man I know. The healer."

"What, the empath, the 87/T genetic deviant?"

Jarrat tapped his temple. "The man who put humpty dumpty back together again."

"Groundside, they call them queer," Reardon mused doubtfully.

"I know what they say. He's a *healer*," Jarrat snapped. "The man's all right, Kip. I know what they say, but I didn't get shagged when he was into my skull, and I did get my brains fixed."

"Your problem was simple crash damage," Reardon argued. "It just isn't the same as Stone's problem."

"Then I'll be taking Stoney there for nothing." Jarrat sighed heavily. "I have to try. Do what you can for him. How bad is he?"

"Pretty damned bad," Reardon said brutally. "Look, scram, Kevin. I'll give you a buzz when he comes to. And incidentally, before you plan on gallivanting all over this colony, remember you're due in here, in the buff, flat on your back for a whole series of tests. I'm not a hundred percent sure about you either, and Central would pull my license if I let you get away without a proper program."

"I'll be here," Jarrat said bitterly. "You're going to whip together one of these cocktails, are you?"

"For what it's worth," Reardon said, and sighed. "Go get some sleep. I'll call you when there's any point hanging around here."

"Thanks." Jarrat stood looking at Stone for a long time as Reardon ducked into the lab and began to measure tiny amounts of this and that chemical. Stone was dead to the world, limp, wrung out. His features, normally lean, fine and humorous, were pinched and white. "Harry," Jarrat whispered. "Harry Del, he's your man, Stoney. He's got to know what to do." But he sounded a good deal more confident than he felt. An icy knot of dread tightened under his heart, choking the breath out of him.

For two years he and Stone had broken every rule in the NARC book. They were nearer brothers than friends. They were involved in all ways but one. They had never shared the same bed. A kind of kinship blossomed among warriors in any age, closer than family blood ties. They lived with death, courted it, cheated it, as if it were a beautiful, fickle and capricious lover. It was like a ritual dance, a mating rite, and it welded them together.

Each of them had known since the beginning, the game could end at any moment. A bullet, a knife, a hard landing. But not like this. Not Angel. Jarrat scrubbed at his eyes as Reardon worked on the narcotic cocktail that would buy Stone time and peace enough to be lucid. He stood by the door, mute, watchful, as the surgeon cut away the fever-soaked clothes and swabbed Stone's burning skin. Jarrat looked away as IV and transfusion needles hooked in. Reardon knew what he was doing.

On the wall behind the workstation were the certificates, the awards and commendations of a lifetime career: Kipling Francis Reardon was actually born on Mars, but went to medschool in London — the same city where Stone spent most of his first nineteen years. Kip qualified as a surgeon aboard the Army carrier *Musashi*. Little was outside his experience.

To the right of the array of certificates and awards was a framed snapshot which meant infinitely more to Jarrat than any commendation. It was a holo of Kip Reardon with his Medecav unit, from the *Musashi*. Twenty-two men and women in surgical greens, spattered with blood and mud, pale with weariness ... in the background, veiled by rain and mist, was the smashed city skyline of Bangor. *Sheal*. Jarrat's eyes closed, his belly turned over as memories assaulted him, real enough to raise a cold sweat.

He turned his back on the picture and frowned down at the still sleeping Stone. While he was asleep, he was at least out of pain. Machines were his companions, while his blood was cycled again and again, stripping out some fraction of the poison. Jarrat's eyes prickled with useless, helpless emotion, a crippling melange of rage and grief.

At this moment he could do nothing for Stone. With an effort he roused himself and returned to the ops room. The computers were working, still collating data from the prisoner exchange. Telemetry had been broadcast in realtime, but Jarrat would also edit an official package for transmission on the subspace band — the official version, for which he would take ultimate responsibility. Three weeks to boost the signal as far as Darwin's World, and specifically to NARC Sector Central. The compound outside the equatorial city of Venice.

Jarrat stared blindly at the data. Only one word echoed and reechoed in his head. *Angel*. He forced his brain to work and reviewed the telemetry package in minute detail. With his signature, the compressed data was squirted to the nearest deep space network relay. Only then did Jarrat subside into the empty navigator's seat. Petrov had retired, the descant units had stood down, Chell Tactical would be cleaning up for another week. Jarrat himself felt like jumping into a deep, dark hole.

And Mavvik? Hal Mavvik would be laughing right now. The fury burned Jarrat's insides like acid. He felt physically sick. Stone's face haunted him. Once warm, alive with amusement, affection, now twisted, ill. The name of Mavvik became a knife between the ribs. Jarrat looked up at the chrono, consciously marking time, waiting for Reardon to buzz him. As a field agent he did not stand fixed duty watches. That was the business of the carrier's Starfleet crew. Now the action was over he was technically off-duty, but he could not rest. Half the job was left undone. Mavvik.

It was an hour before Kip Reardon spoke over the comm. "Kevin? He's awake."

"I'll be right there." Jarrat got stiffly to his feet, hurried aft and down two decks. The Infirmary was softly lit. Stone was the only occupant. Reardon waved through the OR's observation window as Jarrat appeared. He was gowned-up, about to take the shrapnel out of a Gold Raven whose riot armor had imploded before a brace of fragmentation grenades. Jarrat returned the wave and swallowed as he tuned toward Stone.

He was looking better. The days' heavy beard stubble had been shaved away and his hair combed. B-negative blood hung up beside the bed. The

IV was taped into the back of his hand and purple shot bruises marked his neck, but he was sitting up, awake and much more lucid. And he was clean, Jarrat saw, dry. He was barechested, a sheet drawn up loosely about his middle as he sat against the sterile white pillows. The fever had broken. The flush had left his face, his eyes were clearer, but he was still much nearer ill than well. Jarrat forced a smile and sat down on the bedside.

"So how's life?"

Stone took a deep breath. "I've been better. I'm hurting a bit, but Kip gave me something. Whacked it right up my ass, better than a needle, and my nose has had enough!" He sniffed pointedly. "He reckons he'll be able to flush a lot of it out of me with transfusions." A vague gesture at the blood bag. "He's got me drinking so much, I never want to see a glass of water again." He paused to clear his throat. "I'm not going to use it again, Kevin. I just won't take it again."

"Withdrawal will kill you," Jarrat said quietly.

"Angel will kill me!" Stone's bruised eyes looked at him, first angry then soft, limpid with their dilated pupils. Reardon had given him just enough of the dope to bring him down gently and level him off. "You don't know what it's like," Stone whispered. "Angel is like ... Christ. Being in a warm, soft bed with the most beautiful lover you ever knew, and there's caresses all over you, and if you do what comes naturally, you're dead." He closed his eyes. "It isn't going to be easy."

"It's that good?" Jarrat asked with reluctant curiosity. Like anyone who had never used the stuff, he was curious.

"That good." Stone looked up into the other man's slate gray eyes and remembered the dreams the Angel had inspired. It was impossible to look at Jarrat and not remember. The soft lighting of the Infirmary made Kevin look like a kid again, incongruously gentle and very beautiful. Stone looked away as the needing began to hurt keenly.

"What is it?" Jarrat touched his shoulder.

"Nothing. Fantasies. Hallucinations. You imagine a lot of things."

"White rabbits with pocket watches, tea parties and shrinking houses?" Jarrat arched a brow at him.

Stone looked haunted. The eyes were the windows of the soul, so went the old saying; Stone's betrayed the pain inside him. "I'm not a kid, Kevin. Your mind does funny things to you. I don't have kids' fantasies, do I? I was skulled out." He was wistfully studying Jarrat's tense hands.

Jarrat knew. A flash of intuition, and he knew. Stone's face was soft with wanting, his mouth lush with some terrible yearning. A great warmth wound through Jarrat's belly. "Hey ... it doesn't matter, Stoney. See?"

And he leaned over to press a kiss to Stone's lips. Surprise first paralyzed Stone, then his mouth became pliant under Jarrat's. Their tongues touched for the first time, twisted and thrust. Jarrat took him in a punishing embrace, mindful of the tubes in his arms, half-afraid for his ribs, but Stone wanted it hard, needed to be crushed against his friend while they had this privacy. They broke apart, breathless, and from somewhere Jarrat found a faint, rueful smile.

"Why, you old son of a gun. You've been holding out on me, haven't you? You idiot. I'd have jumped your bones two years ago if I thought I had half a chance."

"Break the rules?" Stone blinked at him. "Noninvolvement."

"Bugger the rules," Jarrat said aridly. "I never read the book anyway."

183

"Oh, Kevin. Come here." Stone sank back into his pillows and pulled Jarrat with him. "I dreamed ... you'd better not know what I dreamed."

"Angel dreams, with me as the star attraction?" Jarrat asked with a certain wry humor as Stone's touch thrilled him. "I think I can imagine."

"But you're straight," Stone whispered against Jarrat's soft hair.

"What gave you that idea?" Jarrat kissed his neck. His newly-shaven skin was as smooth as a boy's.

"Well, I just assumed. You enjoyed the crewgirls," Stone said lamely.

"Maybe I did." Jarrat said with a self-indulgent smile. "Girls are kind of cute. I also enjoyed the boys, but you didn't bother to notice. I like anything short of pain. Me? I'm just your old-fashioned, natural-born hedonist. I thought you knew."

Stone blinked his vision clear. "Warpaint and gold?"

"Come again?" Jarrat laced his fingers into the other man's, surprised to find them trembling a little. The drugs, or emotion?

"Oh, a dream I had," Stone confessed. "You, with warpaint on your face. Pagan. And rings — earrings, rings in your nipples, cockrings. Fine gold chains, worth a mint, everywhere you could drape them. Dressed up for a night on the town. Only it was for me."

Jarrat smiled at Stone's vivid imagination. "Would you like that?"

"I dreamed it," Stone whispered.

"If you'd like it, you've got it," Kevin offered.

Stone turned his face away. "Hearty breakfast for the condemned man, is it, before you zip the bodybag shut?"

"Stoney!" Jarrat withdrew his hand from Stone's and stroked the broad, smooth chest with its uniform spacer's tan. "Before you launch into this self-destruction kick, stop and listen to me. I know a man who can help you beat this. I'm sure of it." *Half-sure. Hoping. Praying, if I only knew how to pray and believed in something to pray to!*

"Don't make it worse, Kevin," Stone whispered. He hunted for Jarrat's hand and clung tightly to it. "I've thought it out. My best shot is cryogen. I know it costs a fortune, but I ought to have a service pension. That would cover it. I thought you might ... see to it for me."

Cryogen? Jarrat recoiled. "You mean, put yourself into cold storage?"

Stone nodded. "Pending research. They've been saying for decades, they'll find a cure for it one day."

Jarrat had not considered this as an option. "It could take years, Stoney, and there are no long-term facilities out this far. You'd have to rotate back to Central. At least as far as Darwin's."

"I thought I'd go home," Stone breathed. "London. Earth." He looked up into Jarrat's troubled face.

"And leave me behind?" Jarrat whispered, caught in the vice-grip of a terrible grief. "It could take a long, long time for the research to show results." Jarrat spoke slowly, carefully. "That's too long, Stoney."

"In a cryogen tank I wouldn't age a minute," Stone reminded him.

"I know. But what about me?" Jarrat's brows arched.

"You?" Stone swallowed.

"What do I do for thirty or forty years, you bastard!" Jarrat demanded. "I just muddle along and get old, do I? I can certainly see you sweating and panting in a fever of lust for a seventy-year old — and that's how old I could be when they retrieve you! Christ, listen to me. Selfish? You ought to give me a good kick where it hurts most." Stone was looking up at him, puzzled, and Jarrat forced his brain back on track. "I've always wanted you. I guess you always want what you can't have." He looked away, not proud of his entirely selfish reactions. "It's okay, mate, and you're right, I'll see to it for you. If the tank's what you want."

"Hey." Stone lifted one leaden hand to stroke Jarrat's cheek, and solicited a kiss. "Have I got any choice? I don't have to go into cryogen right away. I've got a month or two before it gets really ugly, so Kip said."

A month or two? Jarrat flinched. He wanted a lifetime. He saw now, with a dazzling clarity, what he had not allowed himself to see for two long years. A month or two seemed a bitter exchange.

Stone saw him flinch and sighed. "Kevin, I just don't have a choice. It's cryogen, or you bury me. You want to bury me?"

"I know a man," Jarrat said thickly. "He could help you."

"Don't make this worse," Stone begged.

"I'm not. For chrissakes, I'm trying to fix it!" Jarrat took Stone's shoulders, his grip tightening when Stone tried to turn away. "Let me tell you about it. Let me tell you what happened to me *after* they scraped me off the street in Chell."

The dark blue eyes clouded. It was as if Stone were remembering that episode for the first time. "I talked to a medic at a clinic somewhere ... Paddington? Bolt. He said you were..." He swallowed convulsively. "He said your brain was screwed up."

"Same as yours is," Jarrat said softly. "I'm healed, Stoney. I know a man, an empathic healer. He mended me."

The story took ten minutes to tell. Stone listened reluctantly at first, then with growing interest, and finally with a glimmer of real hope. It warmed Jarrat's wayward heart to watch the life rekindle in him.

"An empath," he finished. "They're a local phenomenon. Something about the environment here, something the terraformers missed. A lot of people in this colony don't like them, I know, as if the healers are some kind of freaks because they carry the 87/T gene. But will you trust me?"

"Trust you?" Stone echoed quietly. "Trust *you?* You have to ask?" He absorbed Kevin feature by feature and searched for a smile. "Kip'll be running blood into me for a day or so. I wish I could leave right now."

"You're not up to it. Let Kip do his stuff. He'll give Harry a head start," Jarrat decided. "Get some strength back into you." He glanced over Stone's bare torso. "Not that you look delicate. You look a lot like you used to. Like a bloody brick wall."

"You're looking tired," Stone observed. "But the teeth are great. Better than your own were. Whiter."

Jarrat blinked in surprise. "I've begun to forget about them. You read the medical reports, did you?"

"Jeff Bolt's sheet, yeah." Stone reached for Jarrat's hand. "I know what they did to you. I'm sorry."

A flush warmed Jarrat's cheeks. "They pounded my ass, you knew that?" Stone just nodded. "Bolt fixed me up. I'm fine, really."

"Yes. Same here." Stone's hand slid up Jarrat's arm and the fingers cupped at his nape, massaging there. "Forget it. It's all past tense."

"Yeah." Jarrat closed his eyes, loving the fingers at his nape. "You want to rest? I'll push off and leave you in peace if you want."

But Stone shook his head. "I'm frightened, Kev. I've looked death in the face a hundred times. A thousand. But never like this. I don't want to be shoved headfirst into a cryotank." He caressed Jarrat's face tenderly. "I don't want to miss all your youth, your best years. And maybe miss your death, when I should have been there for you, and wasn't."

Jarrat's eyes misted. He rubbed them hard. "Stoney —"

"I'm craving that muck, Kevin. That shit. In *here*." He rubbed his chest, his belly. "I want it. God only knows how much I want it." He bit his lip till his teeth drew blood. "And the more I use, the quicker you'll be locking me in that goddamned tank or zipping the bodybag on me."

"You're hurting," Jarrat observed. "I'll get the medic."

"And cram my ass full of dope?" Stone shook his head. "No more." From some hidden reserve he produced a rueful smile, a mere twist of his mouth. "I know something that's as good as Angel dreams. Come here."

He wanted Jarrat's mouth again, and got it.

But before his second blood transfusion was complete he was in real pain. Withdrawal was brutal. Jarrat and Reardon stood in the doorway of the surgeon's inner office to watch him thresh, delirious, retching, as if he were being tortured. Mavvik's name was on Jarrat's lips. He cursed the Death's Head controller bitterly but it was futile, impotent rage.

"For chrissakes, do something for him, Kip!"

"He's had all the dope he can tolerate," Reardon said quietly. "He's on the way to tetraphine addiction as well as the Angel need. What do you want me to do, sedate him till it's over? Or has he decided to terminate?"

Jarrat shot a hard look at him. "He's talking about cryogen."

"Then he needs to be on the next clipper back to Darwin's, or Earth. It's a hell of a long ride home, Kevin. If he can get a ticket out of here in this next month he'll make it. Just."

"He's that bad?" Jarrat asked hoarsely.

"He's dying," Reardon said very gently. "I'm so sorry, Kevin."

"Then it's Angel or nothing," Jarrat concluded with a surreal calm. "If he fixes he'll last a while longer, won't he?" Reardon nodded. "So give it to him," Jarrat said between clenched teeth.

The surgeon rolled his eyes to the gods. "I don't have it to give. Our labs don't do therapy research, we don't get a licensed supply — and I don't moonlight as a dealer on the side!"

Of course. Jarrat took a deep breath. "How much blood have you got into him?"

"About one full transfusion. His veins are collapsing, he's not taking it as quickly as I'd hoped."

"It'll have flushed a lot of it out of him," Jarrat reasoned, "which is why he's coming down so hard so fast."

"Right. I'd like to cycle it through, transfuse him again —"

"Where's the point?" Jarrat demanded. "He's going to die if he doesn't get more of that crap *now*. Why bother putting him through the meat grinder when the bottom line's the same? He's going to put it all right back, first chance he gets, or he'll cock his toes, if not tonight then tomorrow, the next day. Look, thanks for your trouble, Kip, and I know I hassled you to do what you could for him, but ... it's just no good. Face it, he's had it. They've cut the insides out of him. Get the needles out."

Reardon stirred. "You're going to take him to the healer?"

"The empath," Jarrat corrected bleakly. "Right after I get the poor sod enough Angel to buy him a couple more days."

"Angel?" Reardon was pulling needles. "Are you serious?"

186

"I'm going to go out and buy it," Jarrat muttered. "Get a gurney in here. Get some clothes on him, pump him full of all the vitamins and salts you can get into him, anything to buffer the narcotic shock. But no more dope. Angel reacts with that crap, and he's weak enough as it is. Then stay out of my way, Kip. I'm going to bend the law so far, it'll be a bloody miracle if it doesn't snap. If I take a fall, there's no point you going down with me ... and I could land very hard indeed."

Reardon sighed. "Well, my lips are sealed, but cover your ass, Kevin. A fall of a thousand meters begins with one little trip. NARC could hang, draw and quarter you." He had the needles out of Stone's bruised veins and was turning away to call for the duty orderly as he spoke.

"Kevin?" Stone groaned as he felt the last of the needles withdraw. He reached out blindly. Jarrat took his hands. "Kevin, what's happening?"

"It's okay, Stoney. I'll see to it. Make or break. I'll get you out of this, one way or the other." Jarrat watched Stone slide back into the delirium and bit his lip until he tasted the warm, iron tang of his own blood.

The gurney rattled over the hangar decking. Two orderlies lifted Stone's dead weight into the rear cockpit of the spaceplane and Jarrat got a helmet onto him. He wore denims but was barechested and unshod. Bloodshot eyes searched Jarrat's face, then Stone doubled up in agony once more. *How long? How long before some organ packs up on him?* Jarrat wondered. Kidneys, liver, heart, brain, everything was overstressed. And this time Reardon would not even pick up a laser probe to work on him. Not now.

Without a word he closed up the shuttle. Two minutes later the hangar had reduced to partial vacuum and he nosed out into the dark well of space. He turned the nose down and headed fast for the bright lights of Chell, where city bottom reverberated with the savage rhythms of steelrock and the Angelpack ran wild, dusk to dawn.

He identified himself simply as 'NARC Airborne,' and was granted landing space in the security compound on the perimeter of Dock Row. The shuttle dropped into Bay 6, and Stone jerked awake as the hydraulics settled with a soft shushing sound. The canopy was already going up.

"Sit tight," Jarrat told him. "I know where to find a man on the street. I'll be back in ten minutes, no longer, Stoney, I swear it." He locked the shuttle up behind him. Then he ran.

Dawn was not far away and the sky had just begun to lighten in the east over the sectors of Arezzo and Pamplona. A rimrunner was firing up its engines in a docking bay not far enough away, and crowds had already gathered for the early holoshows. Jarrat skirted them, dodging gyrobikes and plush roadsters. He knew exactly where he was going, and headed fast through the portside warren, toward a dance shop called Phantasm.

He pressed in through the congested doorway and began to shoulder through the crowd. Purple, green and scarlet neon blinked at him. No matter the early hour, the thunder and screams of steelrock battered the ears. Naked bodies writhed in their sexual dance rhythms, sweating in the intense humidity. Dreamsmoke buzzed his head as he fought through toward the small office at the rear of the shop.

The man called Charbonneau was skeletally thin with blued, glued hair. He lay flat on his back under a plump girl with pneumatic appendages which made Jarrat blink. He closed his left fist to hammer on the half-open door. The girl levered herself to her feet and clawed on a short black robe, which did not begin to cover the situation. Charbonneau sat up with a tirade of invective, his cock drooping, woebegone, as Jarrat watched. "What the fuck are you doing here, Jarrat? Whaddaya want f'chrissakes?" The girl glared at Jarrat, mouthed some blistering curse, and stepped past him into the crush of the dancers. Charbonneau pulled on a scarlet kaftan and shot a murderous look in Jarrat's direction.

"Angel," he said shortly as he pulled a wad of notes from his pocket. "I said I want Angel, four smacks, right now, the best shit out of Armand's, none of you gutter-cut crap. You gone deaf, Charbonneau?" He threw the gaudy colonial dollars at the man.

They were snatched up, rapidly counted, and a case of the little plas-tex bubbles was unceremoniously tossed at him. Each bubble was filled with the dust-fine, golden-brown powder. Jarrat pushed the case into his pocket and gave the dealer a hard look. The temptation to bust him was overwhelming.

Charbonneau still knew him as a king shooter. The news had not leak-ed this far down the pipeline, that Jarrat was a NARC, and a *dead* NARC at that. Time and Stone consumed him, and he turned his back on the dealer to force his way out through the dancers. He hit the street and took to his heels like a thief. Charbonneau's time would come soon enough.

He mounted the side of the shuttle, hardpoint to hardpoint, as the canopy whined up. Stone had taken off the helmet and sat curled in a fetal ball, gasping. The acceleration couches were molded to accommodate the bulk and shape of the hardsuit, and Stone looked very small, fragile, deathly ill. It was an agony for Jarrat to watch him. He perched the side of the cockpit and took a capsule of Angel from the case in his pocket.

"Stoney. Come on, Stoney, sit up. Use this."

Stone lifted his head with an effort. Bloodshot eyes fixed on the plast-ex bubble. Jarrat saw the moment of raw hunger, then pure horror sup-planted it. He shook his head. "No more, Kevin. I won't."

"You're going to die," Jarrat said hoarsely.

"So?" Stone gasped. "Do it for me, Kevin. Kill me, for godsakes. Do it now, before —"

"Stoney," Jarrat pleaded. "Give me a chance. I'm going to take you to Harry Del, but you'll be dead before you get there. Please, Stoney, take the stuff, just once. Just this time. Give yourself a chance!"

The bloodshot eyes blinked groggily and Stone forced in a breath. He hovered on the brink of delirium, Jarrat knew. He could hardly tell what was real anymore. He reached up with one hand to touch Jarrat's cheek gently, traced his lips, his jaw.

"Trust you? All right, Kevin. God, it hurts." Fingers trembling a little, Jarrat broke open the capsule. He emptied the golden brown powder into his left palm. Stone took his hand and bent over it. It was strange and terrible to see him inhale the precious, lethal dust, choke, retch, and then slowly relax. Jarrat brushed away the remaining powder and Stone slump-ed heavily backward.

He might have been taking the poison for a year. More. He was a ter-minal case, and Jarrat's heart squeezed painfully as he watched. The with-drawal trauma eased away. Stone smiled up at him, happy, laughing, out of his skull and loving it.

"Oh, Stoney," he whispered. "What the hell did they do to you?"

"Viotto," Stone slurred happily. "Dead."

"But Mavvik," Jarrat added. "Alive." He let himself down into the forward cockpit, pulled on his helmet and closed up. "Next stop, Eldorado. Harry'll sort you out." *Keep telling yourself* he thought acidly. *You might even start to believe it.*

As he brought up the repulsion Stone was laughing at some dream only he could see. Jarrat longed to shake him out of it, or to hold him tightly while he healed himself. But it was ridiculously impossible. There was no way back from Angel.

Unless Harry Del knew a way.

Jarrat lifted the gear and gunned the shuttle fast into the east as dawn rose over Chell.

CHAPTER EIGHTEEN

"You realize he's soaked in the shit." The microsurgeon who was also an empathic healer looked up over Stone's sleeping body. He lay in a bed in a private room in the clinic. Outside, tropical birds caroled in the rainforest.

"I know." Jarrat watched the medscanner ply back and forth over his friend, reading glands, organs. "My CMO told me most of the damage is knotted nerve fibers in his brain. Chemical receptors, something like that. It's not my field by a long shot, Doc."

"I'm reading barbituric acid, psilocin, and something synthetic. Dextromoramide, is it? Who's been giving him what?"

"Downers and hallucinogens," Jarrat told him. "My CMO said they'd help to cushion the comedown."

Del sighed. "Yes, but that's all they do. Delay the reaction. And this," he added, lifting Stone's bare arm to survey the puncture bruises, "this cycling of his blood was not a good idea, if only because it hastens the very reaction the rest of the dope is trying to delay!"

"Yeah." Jarrat drew both his hands back through his hair, massaging his scalp to ease the tension there. "So I brought him here. I thought, if there was even a chance you could do for him what you did for me —"

"I'm not a magician," Harry said sharply, exasperated. "Crash damage is one thing, chronic Angel addiction is not the same!"

Jarrat nodded miserably. "My CMO told me that as well." He looked down into Stone's pale, waxen face. "So tell me. How long has he got before the best thing for him is to put him in a cryogen tank and file him away? Two months? Three?"

"Less, I should say," Del said sadly. "I'm sorry, Kevin, really."

"Not half as sorry as I am." Jarrat sank into a chair and put his head back against the wall. "Will you keep him here, Harry? Feed him what he needs. I can get you a legal, licensed supply. You have a tank. It's the only one in civvy hands I know of in this region. If you can suspend him, I can have a new one shuttled out from Central and transfer him for transportation. Save him a long flight home that'd probably see him off."

"I can do that," Harry said levelly, "but think of the time factor, Kevin. It could be *decades* before a breakthrough is made in biochemical therapy research, if ever. I'm doing better work here in my own lab than they're doing in the big, government-funded institutions ... because I'm not getting stinking rich on a research grant that quits when my program ends!"

"You're onto something?" Jarrat pounced.

"Not a cure," Del said gently. "Just a cushion, the same sort of thing your surgeon tried to do for him. To be honest, I don't believe there *is* a cure for Angel, because of the nature and extent of the damage it causes. Unless you count a rehabilitated mental vegetable as a cure! I don't. But suppose we consider a substance that replaces the Angel, without adding to the neural damage, and suspends the user's degeneration indefinitely. This would give the new user the chance to back out. If he stayed 'clean' afterward, there'd be no further degeneration. That's where my research takes me." He indicated the glasshouses with a thumb over his shoulder. "Tropical tree fungi."

"Results?" Jarrat pressed.

Harry looked searchingly at him. "Promising. It's purely experimental. I've never given it a practical test, but in theory it looks good. You're not seriously suggesting I try it on Stone?"

Jarrat sighed. "Perhaps not. So it's a licensed supply and the cryotank. Maybe for decades." He closed his eyes. "And if you're right, if there's no cure, if the so-called research is just a grant-getter, we might as well just let him dream himself to death. What's the point in tanking him for thirty years and then burying him at the end of it?" Del said nothing and Jarrat's insides twisted. His vision blurred with scalding, painful tears. "Do it for me, Harry. Help him die while he still has some dignity left." His throat constricted as he looked down into Stone's quiescent face. Stoney was unreachable, locked into another world. The bitter bereavement had begun already.

"I've never believed in euthanasia," Del said levelly.

Jarrat gave him an angry glare. "And you do believe in watching a human being turn into wreckage? Look at him! He's young, he was an athlete! Soon he's going to be on old dreamhead. You know how they die? Do you? Humping something or someone who isn't there once too often!"

"Heart attack, brain hemorrhage, renal failure, drug toxicity. I know." Del sighed. "I didn't say I wouldn't *try*, Jarrat. All I'm saying is, don't start gambling on the outcome. It isn't the same as what I did for you."

"But you'll try?" Jarrat leapt at the offer. "Do it soon. Do it now, before he wakes." He touched Stone's hot cheek. His face was peaceful, even serene. He was still riding the Angel high. Under the sheet his cock was up again. "When he's coming down he's drunk and hurting," Jarrat whispered. Why am I telling you? You're the doctor."

"And you're a NARC," Del said with curious gentleness. "You've seen more of this city bottom nightmare than I ever have, or ever will. I'm a surgeon, not a drug therapist." He smiled faintly at Jarrat. "You two are close, aren't you?"

"For two years," Jarrat told him. "Since I transferred aboard. He was on the *Athena* for a couple of years before I arrived. He made me welcome, like I belonged, right from the start."

"You're lovers?" Del swabbed Stone's sweating face with a wet cloth.

"No, not yet. It'll happen soon though ... if you can mend him. We're closer than most brothers. Family. We broke every rule in the manual. NARC people are not supposed to get involved, but we did. Ah, bugger the rules, it's Stoney that counts." He looked up at Del's attentive face.

"Which is why I'm here. And why I'm asking you to help him die if it doesn't work. String him along until it gets too bad. If you don't want to help him out —" He swallowed hard, as if he were trying to swallow his heart. "I will. I've seen them die. They don't scream, they shout with joy while they're fucking themselves to death, and it's ugly. It's not going to happen to him."

Del nodded soberly. "I respect your love, Jarrat."

Love? The word sent Jarrat's brows up, hit him hard in the chest. But it was the right word. The time had arrived for truth. He watched Del pull up a chair at the head of the bed. Long, brown, talented fingers threaded into Stone's black hair. Jarrat held his breath as the healer — the queer, as his kind had long been called in this colony — closed his eyes and began the work. Harry lowered his head, his breathing became shallow and for a long time there was nothing to see.

What Harry was doing, Jarrat had no idea. He had looked through a few pages of Kip Reardon's research into the 'Rethan mutation 87/T,' as it was prosaically listed in government survey records. All the Rethan mutations showed up in the first generation after colonization, and were largely ignored, because it was assumed the next generation would not be troubled by telepathy, empathy, telekinetic and precognitive abilities. The assumptions were wrong. Rethan 87/T 'bred true.' The first 'healers' were working their miracles right across this colony long before the big cities grew old, raddled, and opened their arms to Angel.

For a long time Del worked in silence and Jarrat had almost begun to doze, testimony to the weariness he refused to acknowledge. Then Stoney began to thresh and shout. His shoulders hunched as if he were trying to throw off an aggressor. His long legs twitched, his voice rose to a pleading wail. Jarrat leaned his weight on his partner to hold him down, but the spasms grew stronger.

Stone was a powerful man, his physique the product of NARC training and good genes. The muscles corded in his neck and arms. His mind was powerful also. He and Jarrat had undergone psyche training, as did all field agents. Men like Mavvik often used devices and drugs to turn a man's mind inside out. A NARC field runner learned early how to fool his interrogators. Jarrat's memories of the training simulations were searing, and he knew Stone had become aware of Del's presence, and started to fight.

With a sharp cry Harry wrenched away. He let go Stone's head, and Stone slowly subsided. Jarrat stood back to watch the older man rubbing sore temples. "He beat me off," Del gasped. "He's fighting like a demon. You did the same, but you were a crash job, not a bloody basket case."

"We had training," Jarrat said apologetically. "Psyche routines, simulation, that sort of thing. Interrogation is one of the hazards of the job. I guess he's falling back on the old conditioned reflexes. We all do."

"Yes, but there's more. The Angel is making him paranoic, psychotic. He's strong as all hell, but he's unstable. I'm going to drive him right over the edge, Jarrat. Right *now*, he may be a terminal Angelhead, but he's still as sane as you or me. He won't be if I go on much longer."

For some time Jarrat studied Del's darkly-tanned face. "But if you could go on, you could do the work? What did you see in there?"

"I ... don't quite know yet," Harry admitted. "I think it may be possible. I'm the eternal optimist! But he just won't let me even try."

Soberly, Jarrat digested this. "What about more drugs? Downers?"

191

But Del was emphatic. "Not right now. He's close to his overdose threshold already, what with the Angel he inhaled a couple of hours ago and the dope your CMO pumped into him. He'll have to come down, or we'll finish him off. And electrosleep won't calm his subconscious mind." He clasped his hands together until the knuckles were white. "I don't want to give him barbiturates or tetraphine. He's close to dependency already." He looked up soberly at Jarrat. "There's not much left to try."

"Except an experimental drug," Jarrat added. "Tropical tree fungus."

"Yes." Del studied his clenched hands. "The trouble is, I'm not sure of it. I've run computer models, but you never know how a new substance will react in humans." He hesitated. "It could kill him as easily as cure."

"Even money?" Jarrat asked very quietly.

"If he was fighting fit and drug-free, I'd have said his chances were much better," Del mused. "But he's toxic, stressed way out, and his mental condition is ... precarious. Even money. It's either this or tetraphine, which will just knock him out and keep him out."

"Until he sleeps himself away." Jarrat took a deep breath. "Tetraphine or the cryotank ... or I arrange the licensed supply today, and that's the end for him," he said sourly. "Some choice, Harry."

"Even money's not bad odds. A gambler would take them. You play poker?" Del got to his feet. "Look, Kevin, the decision has to be yours. He's in no condition to make critical judgments about any aspect of his life. Let him come down. When it starts to hurt too bad, you tell me what you want to do. More dope's just a ticket to hell, literally. We're trying to get the shit out of him, not cram more in!" When Jarrat said nothing, he sighed. "We'll move him to a more comfortable room. Stay with him. He ought to come around by evening, and we'll see what shape he's in." He put a hand on Jarrat's shoulder. "I know you love him. When all's said and done I'm an empath, remember. And you're both my patients, not just Stoney. I'm trying to do what's right for both of you, and trying not to play favorites just because I healed you first. Trust me, eh?"

"I do," Jarrat whispered. "And thanks, Harry. Really."

They transferred Stone to a bedroom on the east side of the big plant-ation house. In the late afternoon, with the blinds drawn, it was dim. Thick granite walls kept the whole house cool. Jarrat sat against the carved wood headboard, dragging listlessly on a cigarette. It burned his lungs. Kipgrass and jasmine usually soothed, but not today. He stubbed it out half-finished and went to the window to breathe fresh air.

He could see along the balconied verandah in one direction as far as the glasshouses where Harry cultured his odd fungi, and the summerhouse in the other. And he heard the sound of a mandolin. He knew the instru-ment must be in the hands of Harry's second-eldest son, Malcolm.

Strange, tangled memories had begun to swim on the periphery of his mind. He half-recalled dappled sun, music, birds, gentle hands on him, lips on his own ... and pain, groggy senses, blurred vision, a limping gait. Mal-colm Del was a large part of those memories, but Jarrat could not properly get hold of them. For some time, while Stone slept, he struggled after them, but they wriggled away like live eels, and in the end he let them go.

Tansy was out. Harry said she and Evelyn had gone up to Eldorado for a show and dinner, but Harry expected them back soon, unless they de-cided to visit friends in the city. The whole property was quiet, balm on Jarrat's raw nerves. He watched the sun set from Stone's window, drank a little wine, and listened to the acid banter of his thoughts.

It was twilight when Stone began to stir. Jarrat returned to the bed, quickly stripped and slid into the warm linen. He tugged Stone into his arms before his eyes had opened, and Stone seemed to move from some Angel dream into the reality of a lover's embrace without noticing the transition. His tongue tasted bitter, telltale of the drug, but Jarrat kissed him deeply and held him tight.

Holding him was the oddest sensation. Stone was bigger than Kevin, hard with muscle, smooth, hot. Frighteningly vulnerable. Electric thrills coursed through Jarrat's willful body, making him shiver as his hands traveled his friend's skin, discovering him at last in one long caress.

Stone woke with a moan, both arms about Kevin's smaller body. "I've died," he slurred. "This mus' be heaven."

"We're at Harry's," Jarrat said against his ear. "You're okay here. Harry thinks he can do the work, but you've beaten him off once already. Must have given him a migraine. Do you remember any of that?"

"Bad dreams," Stone whispered as he nuzzled along Jarrat's shoulder. "It was ice-cold, dark ... and some gorilla was raping holy shit out of me."

No such nightmare was ever part of an ecstatic Angel fantasy, Jarrat knew. He held Stone closer. What had Harry said? He was paranoid, psychotic. Del's mere presence in his mind was enough to make Stone conjure a scene of violation. He rubbed his cheek over Stone's, whiskers rasping on whiskers. "Why won't you let Harry do the work?"

"I love you," Stone said suddenly, as if he had not heard a word.

Kevin caught his breath. He stroked Stone's muscular back, soothing. "Do you, now? Well, that's good to hear, since I was about to say the same to you. How do you feel?"

"Tired. Sore. Rubbery." His voice was low, his words indistinct. He rolled over onto his back and urged Jarrat to lie against him. Both his big hands cupped Jarrat's face gently. "You look like hell, Kevin."

"Thanks a bunch," Kevin said dryly. "Stoney, if you don't let Harry work on you, you're heading for a tank." *And if Harry's right, and there's no possibility of a cure? I can't tell him that!* "Let him try."

"Why not?" Stone's eyes were dark, dilated, but they were sane, and sad. "Did I mention, I love you?"

"You did." Jarrat leaned over, kissed him, his forehead, his mouth. "Could you eat?" Stone shook his head. "What about a drink? Irish coffee. Get some booze and caffeine into you. It helps."

"Fucking helps too," Stone slurred huskily.

"Later. You've had more than enough in the last couple of days." Jarrat slid his hand down across Stone's flat belly and found his groin lax and moist. He curved his palm about the velvet bulk of cock and testicles, and smiled as Stone's own larger hand closed over his and held it there. "Stay in bed," Jarrat whispered. "I'll get that coffee."

He pulled on his jeans and padded barefoot into the kitchen where Harry and Malcolm had just stacked the dishwasher. Malcolm took one long, wide-eyed look at Jarrat, flushed scarlet and hurried off. Harry glanced after him with a fond, regretful expression, but when Jarrat was about to make an awkward apology he said, "Malcolm isn't part of your problem, Kevin. Rule One is, shit happens. Frequently. Rule Two is, Rule One cannot be changed." He dropped a hand on Jarrat's shoulder. "Stoney ...?"

"He's awake," Jarrat told him. "What about coffee with a drop of the hard? I don't think he could eat yet. Do you want to examine him?"

He brimmed three mugs and took a tray to the bedroom. Harry shook Stone's hand with absurd, belated formalities and busied himself with scans. He covered Stone from head to foot and back again before turning off the probe. "You're lucky to be alive, Captain Stone."

"Half-alive," Stone corrected drowsily. "Kevin said I hurt you when you tried to help me. I didn't intend to."

"No, no," Harry said quickly. "It wasn't deliberate! I understand you've had various ... training methods that make it virtually impossible for me to do what I must."

Or was it the psychoses of a mind broken by Angel? Jarrat wondered. He sat on the bedside, drinking coffee, stroking Stone's chest. Stone caught his hand and held it.

Harry looked Jarrat in the eye for a moment, one brow up. "Captain Stone, you ought to know the drug I need to administer is an experimental substance, developed on these premises. It hasn't been tested in live subjects. I never perform animal testing ... ethics aside, animals and humans simply don't react the same way. Animal drug-testing is worthless. But my new compound has been amply tested *in vitro*, in human tissue."

"No more drugs," Stone murmured. "Had enough."

"But you'll be coming down soon," Jarrat remonstrated. "You're in freefall right now, but it's going to start hurting. You won't take more Angel, will you?" Stone shook his head minutely. "And you're halfway to tetraphine addiction! Don't blame Kip, it was all he could do for you. He doesn't have Harry's resources." Jarrat shook Stone's shoulder to keep him awake as the alcohol hit his blood and began to soothe. "Stoney, you've got to do something! Let Harry do the work, damnit!"

But he was asleep again, and Del said softly, "I don't think he understands. I told you before, the decision is yours ... and the responsibility."

"Christ." Jarrat stretched out on the bed. "You must have antitoxins, in the event he reacts badly to the new drug."

"Yes, but you realize they also are in experimental stages."

Jarrat mulled over his options. "How far from practical testing do you reckon you are with this drug? Live subjects."

"A month. Two. I was about to apply for a permit to begin. Even in this blighted colony, Kevin, research is strictly controlled." Del toyed with a scanner. "It's the best I've been able to develop in five years of research."

"Then use it." Jarrat closed his eyes. "We don't have a choice, Harry, do we? We give your new magic potion a shot, or we bury him."

"Sad to say, that's about the size of it," Del said with deep regret. "I'll do my level best, Jarrat, but I've told you before, I'm not a magician." He withdrew from the room, leaving the NARC men alone.

Jarrat lay watching Stone sleep for almost an hour, then padded out of the house and across the long, sloping lawns to the gravel area where the shuttle stood. The last glimmer of daylight was mauve in the west as he lifted the canopy; stars glittered, mocking him, as he climbed into the fore cockpit and pulled on a headset. "Raven 9.4 to *Athena*." What time was it in Chell and on the carrier? It must be midnight.

"Carrier." Petrov's voice, dull with fatigue.

"You're not on-shift, Mischa," Jarrat observed. "What's doing to keep you out of the sack?"

"Packriot in Chell, nothing much ... nothing worth bothering you about," Petrov reported. "Red Raven are down. Blue Raven gunship is still being patched up. The usual routine crapola." He paused. "But there's some trouble simmering in the Chell underground. Stacy's got informants in city bottom. Supply is low and the dopers are starting to get panicky."

"No Angel coming into Chell lately, no labs to cut it, money men on the run?" Jarrat chuckled. "I guess we gave Mavvik a headache or two after all. Anything happening at the palace?"

"They're fragging anything that looks even vaguely like a Tac vehicle on the road up the mountain, or in the air over it. Stacy's ordered all patrols pulled. He's got surveillance on the palace from orbit, through a synthetic aperture contractor, but he's taking too much flak from above to challenge Mavvik a second time. Congress is going apeshit, the private sector insurance companies are screaming about the property damage and as you may be aware, the press we're getting stinks."

"What else is new?" Jarrat said acidly.

"Sure," Petrov agreed. "Except this time GlobalNet went on the air saying the syndicate busted NARC flat on its ass. It's in the newsvids: all we're good for is terrifying civilians, and the first time we're given a solid fight we get whipped."

"Nice." Jarrat looked across the lawns to the house. Lamplight shone yellowly from half-drawn blinds. "How long to get the Blue Raven gunship back in the air? I'm not going into any fight without a full compliment."

"Engineer says three days, but in a pinch you could call it two. You know Budweisser. Stacy called a while ago. Tac think they've intercepted some Death's Head transmissions. Seems they're going to pull out of Chell, but we don't know where. They could even leave the colony."

"Offplanet," Jarrat mused. "Damn. If we let it fizzle, Stacy's war was for nothing." Also Stone's predicament, he thought, but he didn't say it.

"And the next time we try to lean on a syndicate we'll be wading in shit up to our eyeballs," Petrov added. "Give the buggers any reason to believe they can actually win a standup fight, and every city will be a warzone. We can't afford to let it fizzle. When are you coming home? If Mavvik starts to bug out, things could heat up quick."

"Soon," Jarrat whispered. "This can't take long, one way or another."

Petrov hesitated. "I was talking to Kip ... I'm sorry about Stoney. That was bloody rough. If there's anything I can do, name it."

"Just cover for me," Jarrat said quietly. "Buy me time, Mischa. Like I said, I don't want to get into a scrap without all four gunships operational, but if Death's Head is going to bug right out of the colony, and if Tac's muzzled ... we might not have a choice. I'll check in later. 9.4 out."

He closed up the shuttle and jogged back up to the house. Overhead the stars were brilliant, the night moonless. Muted voices issued from the lounge. Several of Harry's kids were playing blackjack. The eldest, Alex, was making love on the verandah, in the swing seat. Jarrat wondered who his partner was. He smiled at the boys as he passed by, and returned to the room to find Stone awake and a little less hung over.

He was suspended, now, in the dopehead's only lucid time. The narrow margin before the craving set in and pain began. But for the moment his eyes were clear, he was awake, aware of his surroundings. With sobriety came pain of another kind. Dread, self-disgust, shame. Stone's eyes were dark with those. Jarrat's heart went out to him.

"Are you hungry yet?" he asked as he closed the door quietly. But

195

Stone shook his head and held out his hands. All he wanted was to kiss, to roll over on the bed in a tangle of limbs and hold Jarrat pinned beneath him. If that was what he wanted, Kevin saw no reason to deny him. His struggle to survive would begin soon enough.

They lay in the dim room, silent for a long time before Stone said with surprising clarity, "You trust the healer."

"He mended me. I was done for, Stoney, but here I am. Harry's a ... well, Kip knows them as 'Rethan mutation 87/T.' It bothers you?"

"No. I mean, they didn't come out of a genetic design lab. The terra-formers finished with this planet, gave it the seal of approval and shipped humans in. Nature took over as bloody usual, and made Del's people what they are. Like mind parasites, they probably can't even live without other people to leech, but they didn't *beg* to be born deviant." Stone paused to think it over. "And they're useful now and then." He sounded resigned.

Kevin propped himself on one elbow to look down at him. For the first time since the prisoner exchange Stone was fully in command of his faculties. His eyes were filled with some mix of fear and shame, but he was painfully lucid. The moment had come for the truth to be told. Jarrat had dreaded the words, and cleared his throat.

"I won't lie to you. You can't take more dope without getting cross-addictions. Added to the Angel they'd screw the lid down on you. If you won't have more Angel, you'll be in the tank before noon tomorrow." Stone's half-seen face twisted. "You've got the one chance. Let Harry try."

"An experimental drug," Stone whispered.

"It's been extensively tested in human tissue cultures," Jarrat added. "It's Harry's job, and he's damned good at it. Oh yes, I trust him. I *learned* to trust him."

Stone's fingers combed through Jarrat's hair, tousling it. "You want me to risk the dope, this ... what did you call it? Tropical tree fungus."

"I want you to consider it," Jarrat said soberly. "Or this is the farewell scene. You haven't got long, Stoney." His voice caught, though his face was a careful mask, as always. A kid growing up alone in city bottom learn-ed fast how to keep his thoughts and feelings private.

A quiet sigh passed Stone's lips. "I know how long I've got better than you do, Kevin. It's already starting again. Down inside. The craving."

"Already?" Jarrat was appalled. He pulled Stone against him. "Jesus, how much of the crap did they cram into you?" He hunted for Stone's mouth with an almost savage kiss. "I'd better get Harry."

"No." Stone's arms tightened, holding him captive. "Give me an hour. Let me have you, just for an hour before it all goes sour."

"It won't go sour," Jarrat said huskily into Stone's mouth. "Harry can do it. If he made sense of my brain —"

"Blind faith?" Stone was gently mocking. "They used to call them 'faith healers,' didn't they? Don't lie to me. I have one chance in ten."

"Even money, according to Harry," Jarrat said very quietly. "He told me a while a ago, asked if I play poker. I've won big, on worse odds."

From somewhere Stone produced a smile. "So have I." He pulled Jar-rat against his chest and his hands explored the contours of bare back and warm denim. Jarrat lay still while Stone stripped him, but Stone was too dizzy, too disoriented, to go beyond intimate embraces and weary kisses.

Jarrat knew the moment the real pain began. Stone's skin streamed with sweat and he pulled his knees into his belly. Now, he must have more

196

Angel, or a tetraphine knockout dose. Or cryogen. Jarrat reached for his jeans. "Showtime, kid. Let me get Harry. It has to be *now.*"

Now Stone did not even murmur to argue, much less try to stop him, and in fact Del was waiting for Jarrat in the little biolab. Grim-faced but entirely professional, he showed Kevin a hypo preloaded with a pale orange-red liquid. The dose was already calculated for Stone's body weight.

"It's derivative of the Devil's Club fungus. Toxic in large quantities, but in regulated amounts it's psychoactive and analgesic. What makes this risky is, I don't really know the dosage I ought to be using. I thought I'd give him a little, then a little more, and so on. He's very strong, physically. Mentally ... well, at least this time he's not riding an Angel high." He ushered Jarrat to the lab's open door, and there he stopped. "How are *you?*"

"Me?" Jarrat was surprised.

"Making the gamble, wagering the life of a loved one, taking ultimate responsibility for this whole production ..." Harry's brows arched. "Older and wiser heads than yours have gone gray under the load."

Without effort, Del had seen right through Jarrat's careful façade. Kevin was about to protest, but thought better of it. Harry was an empath, of course he knew the truth. Jarrat ducked his head. "I'll survive."

"Yes," Harry said thoughtfully. "I believe you will." He stood aside to clear the doorway. "Shall we?"

Palms sweating, Jarrat held Stone's shoulders as the needle picked up an artery and Del injected just enough to begin. Stone's dark lashes fluttered, his lids dropped, and Del set aside the hypo.

"He's out," Jarrat murmured.

"I gave him enough to put his conscious mind into neutral. I don't think it'll have much effect on his subconscious, but I'll try. I won't push him. He's balanced on a knife edge, Kevin. If you hadn't been here when he woke, God knows, he might have been in a padded room by now."

He pulled up a chair and Jarrat watched the lean, brown fingers thread into Stone's tousled hair. Harry's face twisted with effort, sweat sprang out, his teeth clenched as he gave every atom of himself to the work. Stone's mouth opened, first to pant, then to moan. In minutes Harry withdrew from the empathic contact.

Jarrat was exhausted merely from watching. "No good?"

"He thinks I'm hunting him down to strangle him, or rape him," Harry said hoarsely as he drank from a water bottle. "You see? *This* is where we get the name of pervo, devo. If we wanted to, we could be incubus, succubus, vampire, rolled into one, leaving trails of broken minds behind us."

"Has it ever ...? Jarrat could not form the question.

"Has someone like me ever been pushed so far, persecuted, till he or she jumped the tracks, turned into a monster?" Harry checked the hypo and picked up the artery in Stone's arm again. A series of fresh shot bruises was taking shape. Jarrat looked away. "I honestly don't know if an 87/T has ever gone rogue, but I'll be honest with you, Kevin. It's far from impossible ... which is something people conveniently forget when they're hounding my *kind* ... there. Done." He swabbed Stone's arm.

"How much more is safe?" Jarrat asked hoarsely.

"One, maybe two more. If they don't work I'll poison him before we get the effect we want," Del said flatly. "I've already given him enough to kill a squirrel monkey, which has a body mass of around ten kilos. I'll administer an antitoxin when I'm finished — if he ever lets me start!" He pulled the chair back up. "Round two."

Standing back against the wall, hands in hip pockets, Jarrat was conscious of a sense of blistering impotence. A minute assumed the proportions of an hour, until Del cried out again and wrenched himself away.

Jarrat swore. "No joy, Harry?"

"Worse than before." Del knuckled his eyes and drank again. "Jesus Christ, Kevin, what kind of goddamned training do you NARCs get?"

"It … hurts," Jarrat admitted. "I was sick for days after I did the course. Some of us don't stay the distance, but if you don't, you can't work in the field. Add that kind of training to the psychoses of the Angel —"

"He's borderline," Del said softly as he checked the hypo again, "dancing on the edge of an abyss. This is the last I can give him, and even this is risky. There's already enough in him to drop a horse in its tracks and his subconscious is still in gear. He could go comatose or hemorrhage, and if he does — it's over. He won't let me get in to do for him what I did for you. It's the NARC bullshit, fueled by the Angel fantasies." The needle slid in. "I'm running out of options fast, Kevin." He looked up grimly at Jarrat for a moment before returning to the work without a word.

Minutes stretched to a seeming infinity, but according to Jarrat's chrono Del withdrew from the contact much sooner than before. He was pale, weakening. On the bed, Stone was deeply drugged, his face ashen, waxy, gray under a sheen of sweat. Harry drew in a deep breath and got shakily to his feet. At the basin in the corner of the room he washed his face and drank. He leaned on the enameled unit for long moments, head down, as if he were seriously considering throwing up. Jarrat could only wait until Harry recovered enough to speak. Then the healer turned toward him and surveyed him with a frown.

His question startled Kevin. "How badly to you want to pull him back? What's the boy worth to you?"

Jarrat's tongue tip moistened parchment-dry lips. "What do you mean? You want me to put a price, a cash value, on Stoney's life?"

"You could say. And on your own."

"You've got something dangerous in mind?" Jarrat's pulse kicked up.

"Not dangerous in any physical sense, but …" Harry took a deep breath, massaged his temples and took a moment to marshal his thoughts. "What Stone needs is a cushion against me. Something to buffer my presence, calm him, keep him stable while I get in there and do my stuff. That's got to be you, Kevin. You're the only one he's going to trust."

"So what do I do?" Jarrat demanded without preamble.

"It's not so simple," Del said patiently. "I wish it were! Let me explain before you jump in at the deep end. Neither of you is an adept."

"What the hell is an adept?" Jarrat sat on the side of the bed.

"A … queer. Someone like me, the good old 87/T model." Del smiled tiredly. "Now, I can link you together securely, so you share the empathy. Deeply, fully. I can do this, and make it work, so Stone *knows* it's you, turns to you, even takes shelter in you … certainly listens to you when you tell him to quit freaking every time I try to work on him." He spread his hands and shrugged. "The trouble is, what Del hath joined together it'd take half the gods in Valhalla, pulling in harness, to split asunder."

Jarrat's brow creased. "Back up and start over."

"I can't unlink you," Del said baldly. "You follow? That's something the adept has to do for himself. It's like trying to *unlearn* something. Nearly impossible. I can link you, I can't unlink you." He looked intently at Jarrat. "Do you understand what I'm saying? I've seen it happen before. It's one of the reasons they call us parasites. Once you're linked you'll stay linked, Jarrat. For life. Empaths. What one feels the other will feel. Everything — pain, joy, anger, sorrow." He paused. "Love." Jarrat saw his discomfiture. "Your relationship has been very close, you said. Like brothers, was it?"

"For two years," Jarrat said softly.

Del took a breath. "You'll be closer yet if you're linked. More than brothers, more even than lovers. His feelings will be yours, and yours his. In fact, what you feel could be very beautiful, if you allowed it to be."

The frown deepened as Jarrat looked down at Stone. His heart quickened. "What are you telling me? I already love him. I've admitted that, to myself as well as to you. I'll feel — what, more? How can it be more?"

"Sometimes it'll be as if you're the same person, sharing the same skin, the same body," Del said slowly. "I know it sounds kinky, not to say perverse, but I don't think it ever did anyone any real harm."

"Yet," Jarrat said dryly. "You don't know what he's like. I could tell you about the time five Starfleet replacement staffers drew up a petition to get him fixed. And I'm going to feel everything he does?"

The healer chuckled, appreciating any fleeting attempt at humor. "I'm afraid so. If the link is strong enough, and if you're close enough to begin with, which you are, the outcome will be like ... a Siamese twinning through the nervous system. I suppose it's why they call us deviants, isn't it? You fuck him, it'll be like fucking yourself at the same time. As I said, it could be very beautiful. If you let it be." Then he sighed. "You must make up your own mind. I can't help you. Do you love him? Do you love him *enough*? What's he worth to you? He lives, he dies ... it's in your hands."

With that Harry fell silent. Jarrat drew a hand across his eyes, weary to the bone. Lust had always crackled between him and Stone though they had almost verbally denied it, to keep NARC's rules intact. If Stoney had a foible, Jarrat had known and laughed about it, and the reverse was true. Stone was going to have to make the best of Jarrat's wayward nature.

"I think I've loved him a long time," he admitted to Del. "We never let it get physical but it's always been there. We had bigger things to think about — the job, the department. Higher commitments. Bigger things in life than sex. Damn."

"Look." Del leaned toward him. "Understand. When you touch him, if you're linked empathically, you'll be incapable of keeping away from him. It'll be like touching yourself. You're going to feel another man's lust in your own nerves, Kevin. You'll turn on. If he jerks himself off, he'll jerk you off at the same time, every little touch will transmit like radio. Pretty soon you'll decide it's less bothersome if you do it together. There'll only be a problem if you make one. Oh, good gods, you're not one of those stupid old prudes, are you? Screw your brains out so long as you have the privacy of your own feelings, but spend the rest of your life in the closet if you have to share what it *feels* like *inside* to suck cock and get sucked! Some damned macho ego trip!"

A bubble of irrational laughter rose in Jarrat's chest. "No, I'm not an old prude. If you must know, I've sucked enough dick in my time to have rationalized my machismo. Not that it's any of your goddamned business, but an Army troop transport is an education, and at the Academy you get confined to barracks a lot. You can quietly go cuckoo in a corner if you don't take care of yourself and your buddies. I've just ... never done the honors for Stoney, nor him for me. But I have no problem with sharing the feelings. Good enough?"

"All right." Del smiled. "Just be sure you know what you're getting yourself into. The time for schoolboy sex games is over, Jarrat. You can't 'fuck and forget,' screw like ferrets on heat and take a hike in the morning. Do you *love* him? Because if you don't, you'll find yourself hating him a week from now. And the only way you'll get rid of this particular albatross is to shoot him dead." He folded his arms, brows arched, baldly challenging. "Are you willing to accept the consequences, pay the price for his life? Last chance to back out, Kevin. Once we start, it's too late."

Back out? *And where does all this leave me? Us?* Jarrat's thoughts spun in dark, furious circles. The future was not as simple as Del believed. They had NARC to consider, and regulations. Since NARC officers were not permitted to get friendly in any profound sense of the word, this would be the end of their careers. Civvy street was probably waiting for them. Would that be so bad? The end of two careers, Jarrat thought, or the end of Stone's life. In fact there was no decision to be made.

He gave Del a hard look. "Empathy, for chrissakes! How do we function as a NARC unit after this?"

"Perhaps you don't. Search me, kid," Del said indifferently. "What you do to earn an honest, or dishonest, crust is no concern of your doctor's. Keeping his patients alive so they can go on making messes of their bloody silly lives is all we do. We tend to do it rather well." He stirred restlessly. "Are you waiting for an engagement ring?"

"A lot of sympathy I'm getting." Jarrat's voice carried no sting. He was looking down at Stone through newly-opened eyes. Trying to picture him beyond the regimentation of NARC routine. A lover, a beachcomber, sharing a civilian life that was at best uncertain. He had seen Stone naked countless times, and had held him for hours, kissed him, here in this bed. He wondered how Stone might taste as he came, how his musk would sting the sinuses, close up, when he was ready for it and feverish with lust. How would it feel to lie straining against him, fuck him deep, and be fucked? Giddiness swamped him and he swallowed again. "You're sticking me with a tomcat on heat who's just coming down off Angel," he whispered.

"Which is why I asked what it's worth to you," Del said soberly. "You could come to hate him in a month as much as you think you love him now. If you're going to put a price on his life, it better be a high one, because it's going to cost you. You'll pay up in spades. Look, I'm sorry, Jarrat. I know what it sounds like. I'm asking you to be his whipping boy, take the backlash of his Angel tripping, be his whore. If you want to let him go, I'll do as you asked. He has a place here as long as you can get me the legit supply. I can't get on the wrong side of the law. I already have a hard time with locals who call me 'the mutant from the old Petrocelli place.'"

He gestured at the house. "You know, I was born in this house. My parents were laborers on the plantation. When I got out of medschool I came back here like a pigeon. It was always home to me. I had the opportunity to buy the property sixteen years ago, when the plantation closed down, but the community never *really* let me in. So you'll understand if I draw the line at going out and buying the shit on the street."

"The legit supply is no problem, but ..." Jarrat shook his head. "Let me have a decent grumble, will you? I thought you were a 'queer adept.' You ought to know what I'm feeling. It never crossed my mind to back out. Jesus, I've put my career on the line already. Who do you think went out and bought the garbage for him on the way here? If my bosses get wind of it they'll have me on a spit at New Year with an apple in my mouth." He bit his lip. "All right, Harry. Do it. I'll try and keep my sordid adolescent fantasies to myself when you start rummaging in my skull."

"I don't eavesdrop," Del said mildly as he collected an extra chair. His eyes sparkled. "I've been in your skull before. I caught one or two vague impressions. When you were twelve or fourteen you thought you would rather like to be tied to the bed and paddled before being laid." Jarrat's cheeks warmed. Harry winked at him. "Did it ever happen?"

"I grew out of that particular fantasy." Jarrat was furious with himself for being flustered. "If anyone had actually tried it when I got to sixteen I'd have *laid* him out — cold." He sat down at the bedhead, opposite the empath. "What do you want me to do?"

Harry pulled up his own chair. "Thank Christ for tender mercies. I thought you were going to get up on your rocking horse, read me a purity lecture, march out of here with your snoot in the air and let the poor bastard cock his toes." He smiled. "I know it's a damned tough decision."

Jarrat allowed himself a fond if apprehensive smile as he looked at Stone. "No. It's the only decision I could make. He'd do the same for me. He chased me 'round this planet when the rest of them had closed the book on me. With a mate like Stoney I've never wanted for family. He can get under your fingernails sometimes but I trust him. With my life. In fact I *have*, so many times I've lost count, and I'm still here. I'm going to love him? Want his cute little body all for my own?" He mocked himself with a soundless chuckle. "If I'm going to make an idiot of myself over someone, I can't think of anyone better than him."

"Sit closer then," Harry said. "Take my right hand in your left. Put your right on his shoulder, firmly. Press down with your palm. Now, I'll put my hand on your head, like so ... try to relax, Kevin. You're strung up like a cable car. Breathe deeply. Shut your eyes. Let yourself float. Get weightless ... freefall. *Relax*, I said! Let me do the work. Let yourself open up ..."

The healer's voice grew indistinct in Jarrat's ears. The world outside his closed eyelids drifted away. He knew only a kind of warm darkness. At first it was suffocating, he felt himself choke and fought for air, then he realized Stone was with him and he forgot the suffocation as he felt Stone's surprise and delight. The darkness grew lighter. He might have been looking at the sky through closed eyelids when Stone's voice said,

"Kevin! Where d'you come from? I hoped you'd come again."

"Again?"

"Like before. No, that was the Angel, I suppose."

Deep sadness reverberated through the thought. The comment triggered cascades of memories. They rolled through Jarrat like waves hitting a beach. Sights, sounds, smells, sensations. And Del was right, he felt everything. He was caught in a vice-like embrace that knocked the breath from his lungs. He was full of Stone, as if he were being wrenched hip from hip, but he felt his own cock alternately sheathed in Stone's tight ass and sucked by that talented, generous mouth.

He felt madness reel about the periphery of his senses as the confusion of his perceptions deepened. His mouth was invaded, plundered by thrusting heat. He gasped at the bewildering intensity of the *dreamsense*. Angel dreams. Little wonder they called it flying —

He and Stone were tumbling through the sky, an electric-blue vortex with a pad of fleecy clouds far below. The whole sky opened up as they reveled in the incomparable thrill of living flight. No aircraft between them and the wind. It was beyond anything he had ever imagined and he whooped for the sheer joy of it. Stone laughed.

"That's my dream. Glad you're enjoying it."

Flight had always been Stoney's other passion. Even as a kid he had flown anything he could get his hands on, from ultralites as a student to front-line fighters with the Starfleet training squadron when he came over from Tactical to NARC. But Stone had begun to play now, and Jarrat felt a strangeness at his back. He twisted his head about and saw wings, pumping hard to keep him aloft. He saw the oily sheen on blue-green feathers, rode the upthrust on every downbeat, and discovered a childlike thrill as he angled the feathers at the tips of his wings, trimmed his flight.

He laughed aloud. "Stoney, stop, for godsakes!"

And Stone's voice, thrumming in his ear, vibrating in his chest: "Why? It's my fantasy. You don't like it? Dream your own."

The clouds cushioned them as they settled, like a mattress. Jarrat spread the wings wide, wanting to see their tips. Jewel green and gold plumage spread about him and he flexed the wings. Sensuous feelings doubled, intensified, as he felt Stone stroking his back. He felt the caresses even in the wings, deeply erotic.

He caught his breath, needing, wanting. He lifted his wings. The feathers brushed Stone's sides as Jarrat was mounted, his legs spread wide, his body probed first by fingers that asked, then a cock that demanded. His nerve endings ripped into liquid fire as Stone took possession of him. The big, hard shaft seemed to lay claim to him and his body began to heave. The wings fluttered to lift their doubled weight. He humped back, drove Stone in deep, and Stone laughed.

"Oh yeah, you like that, always did." Whispers against his neck. Warm breath tickling his ears." The words did not mock, but celebrated love.

"Do it to me," Jarrat gasped. The wings Stone had given him beat the air, buoyed them up as Stone clung tight to ride him. He reached back, turned his head to find Stone's mouth. It should have been impossible to kiss, but here nothing was impossible. His mouth was full of Stone's tongue as the deep thrusts seemed to reach his heart.

They tumbled through an ocean of blue. Climax tore Jarrat apart and he cried out. Stone was still riding, tireless, plundering and at the same time cherishing. Jarrat heard his own whimpers as, much later, Stone came deep inside him. Every sensation was magnified by the Angel.

"Oh, Christ, yes," he whispered hoarsely, dragging air into his protesting lungs. "We should have done this years ago."

"Would have, but we played by their rules," Stone panted. "Two years ... too chicken to break NARC regulations, come out and say it, take what we wanted." He slipped away, crawled under Jarrat's arch-backed body and pulled him into an embrace. The wings dissolved into nothing as the game of flight ended and another began.

They lay, pressed tight together. Joss smoke coiled about them as they writhed on silk cushions and the thundering bass of steelrock reverberated through their very bones. Dreamsmoke buzzed Jarrat's ears. He rolled over onto his back, wondering what Stone had done to him now. Lamplight gleamed on the gold he wore. It was *all* he wore. The nipple rings taunted him as Stone twisted them in his flesh, pulled them gently.

He laughed. "Oh, so this is the party dress you wanted?" Cockrings felt good about his throbbing genitals, as gold as the rings in his ears and the fine, filamentary chains about his neck, hips, wrists and ankles.

"Beautiful," Stone whispered. He smothered Jarrat with his weight, breathed the breath from his mouth. "I always ... always wanted ..."

They could not be still, but writhed and twisted, filled with vital energy, as if they had not spent themselves only moments before. Neither of them noticed Harry Del going quietly about the business of performing the complex, delicate work of the healer. Even Del could not properly explain how his work was done. It *was* nearer faith than science.

Jarrat no longer cared to wonder. The empathy between himself and Stone was already strong. They would not separate, would never want to. Jarrat gasped and arched as Stone mouthed him, nibbled the tender scrotal skin, licked him from root to crown. "Careful! You think I'm edible?"

"I know what you are," Stone retorted. "And you're getting a bigger bang out of my dreams than I did. Lucky thing Riki isn't here or you'd have him too. You're a satyr. You always were."

Intense regret broadcast clearly from Jarrat. Stone felt it as keenly as his own emotions and the sensual teasing stopped. "He's dead, Stoney. Tac 101 was rocketed not long after you left. Riki was right where you left him, in Stacy's camp, where he should have been safe. A lot of Stacy's people bought it in the same assault. I went to the morgue, ID'd the body."

"Dead?" First Jarrat felt Stone's stubborn disbelief, but the empathy was already so strong, Stone received Kevin's emotions powerfully. Belief chased on the heels of denial. Pain blossomed inside him, deep and racking, hurting Jarrat as if Stone had punched him. He turned into Kevin's arms, pressed his face into the curve of a warm, hard shoulder, and wept.

The empathy redoubled as Jarrat began to kiss him. If either of them had been an adept they would have known they had passed the point of no return. They shared the pleasure, the annoyance, the grief of the past week, roved through each other's most bitter memories without questioning what they experienced. Jarrat felt Stone's sorrow for Riki with painful clarity and soothed him. He felt the white-hot terror as Stone inhaled the first lungful of Angel, and offered his arms, his mouth, whatever it took to divert Stone from the web of recollection.

Stone gasped, choked off a scream, as he blundered into Jarrat's own memories. An alley in Chell, the suffocating reek of smog, the thunder of monstrous engines as the heavy lifters pounded their way to orbit ... dread and agony, and then the dark, abyssal peace of oblivion.

"Kevin, I knew what happened to you, but I couldn't —"

be there share it find you kill them hunt down destroy

The words were unformed in Stone's mind, seething, acid-hot with rage. The tide of fury hit Jarrat broadside and he recoiled with a gasp.

"Let it be, Stoney."

"Let it be? What they did to you —"

"What they did to *you*." Jarrat caught him, held him. "We'll settle with them. Let it be now. I love you."

Love had a hue all its own. A blue-gold shimmer haloed them and Stone seemed to breathe it in. He tipped back his head, let the fantasy sweep him up again, and Jarrat relaxed one bone at a time, unaware ...

...Harry Del was a shade in the background, rummaging, fiddling...

Stone no longer noticed. The Angel had taken him again, and for once Jarrat was content to let it. Angel dreams were distressingly real. Jarrat knew he was physically erect again, it was not a phantasm, as Stone began to love him. He tried to draw away but could not. They were in a plushly expensive hotel room now, and he knew the city was Eldorado. He knew the room for the one Stone had shared with Riki Mitchell. He lay pressed into the bed, felt the silkiness of the quilt against his back as he hooked both his legs about Stone's neck. His body was besieged utterly. Stone arched over him, sliding in deep, one long thrust that seemed to touch Jarrat's heart. He shook his head clear as his senses overloaded.

"Stoney, for godsakes. If you're not interested in me, think of yourself. You've screwed your damned brains out already — how much more of this do you think you can take?"

But it was too late. He was caught up in the frenzy of the wild joy, threshed with Stone, hunted for release in a fever of white-hot lust he could scarcely believe. This was Angel. This was 'the ride,' as the Angel-pack called it. The ride from which there was no return.

In fact, Stone was using him now, as Harry Del had warned. He was still full of Angel, needing to rut, he had no choice. Left to himself he would fantasize it all, but Jarrat had blundered into the middle of the fantasy and could only comply. In fact it was not difficult to play his games. They were not physical, he would pay no price later for the indulgence. He was fucked, and fucked again, as if Stone could not stop. As if Jarrat was all he had ever wanted. Yet, one cell at a time, Stone's mind had begun to work again. Grief for Riki bruised him; fury for what had befallen Jarrat himself made Stone wild with rage and grief.

For a horrified moment Jarrat thought the anger was directed at himself, then realized it was for the shooter, Tate Viotto. The one who had popped the capsule of Angel and forced Stone to inhale the golden dust. Now Jarrat felt every part of it keenly ... the suffocation, the desperate fight not to breathe. The abject surrender to what he knew would be his death. Pain hammered through his chest, too much like the pounding in the alley. He cried out, gasped for breath and pulled away out of Stone's arms before the dream could ensnare him. He felt Stone's concern at once, and the punishment diminished, faded to nothing before blossoming into affection.

"I'm sorry, Kevin. I didn't mean to ... you feel *everything* I do?"

"God help me," Jarrat gasped. "Harry warned me. I suppose I knew what I was getting myself into. I love you, you stupid sonofabitch. That's what I'm doing here. Stop fighting me, will you? I'm only here to help you. You want to jump off the deep end, don't take me with you — somebody has to be there to break your fall!"

"Kevin?" Stone reached for him, held him locked between steel-strong arms and legs. "You love me? I didn't dream that part?"

"I'm embarrassed to admit, I do," Jarrat said ruefully, amused and annoyed with himself in equal measure, but no longer able to deny what he felt. Not wanting to. Instead he basked in Stone's unashamed affection.

"So do I." Stone's discomfiture rolled through both of them and became nervous humor. "Love you, I mean."

"I know what you mean." Jarrat took his mouth, hard and deep.

"You've humped me enough to prove it." He squirmed as Stone's fingers found the moist, tender center of him.

"Want it again?"

"You need it," Jarrat said levelly. "You're rutting, you know that, I know that. It's the Angel. You'll rut till it wears off, you have to mount and mate. I understand. But I'd sooner do you now, I really would. Right inside you." He was stroking his own cock as he spoke, bringing himself erect with the touches he liked best. He knew Stone could feel every caress through his own nerves like an echo. "I can wait if you need to have me. But I want it."

"So do I." Stone wore a sheepish expression. "I had such dreams. I couldn't tell dreams from reality for a long time. I didn't want to." Shame rushed through him, hot and painful. "It was the only way to escape from ..." He shook himself deliberately, setting the bleak memories aside. "You had me a lot. Go on." The long, sturdy legs spread invitingly and he took Jarrat down on his chest. "You're so bloody beautiful. Remind me to keep telling you that. Every bit of you."

"Every centimeter?" Jarrat teased. His cock slipped between sweat-slick buttocks, the skin so smooth and moist that he was inside Stone's eager body before he fully realized he had begun. His head tipped back and he closed his eyes. His voice was a rasp. "Jesus. The feel of you."

"Deeper," Stone panted, and locked his legs about Jarrat's narrow waist to pull him down. "Oh yes ... like that. Go on now."

They were inseparable as Siamese twins sharing a single heart, single brain. The empathy was complete. And they were infinitely aware that there was no way out, no way back. Each mutual remembrance welded them more firmly together until the empathy was almost tangible. It was impossible to tell who was in whom, who was kissing or kissed, who was holding or held. Or where the Angel dreams ended and reality began.

Not quite three hours later, Harry Del broke out of the web he had spun about them. Jarrat and Stone did not withdraw with him. It would be dangerous to break them apart, like waking a sleepwalker, but he tried, gently shaking Jarrat's shoulder. The gray eyes snapped open. Jarrat moaned, twisted sharply around, but his gaze was blind. He looked clean through the healer. His throat made a string of incoherent sounds and Del was unsurprised when his eyes rolled up and he passed out, collapsing over Stone's legs. The sheet tangled about them, the bedding was drenched in sweat. The room smelt of sex. Harry stood back from them with a deep frown. He was weary to the bone, his head splitting, his hands shaking. He wanted painkillers, a cool shower, fluids, sleep.

At the open door, Malcolm looked in, concerned by the odd sounds he had heard. "Harry?" He spoke very quietly, assuming Jarrat and Stone were merely asleep. "What have you been doing? You look terrible."

"A healing, three-way," Harry told him hoarsely. "I don't dare touch them now. Jarrat's deeply traumatized. They can find their own way out, just leave them alone, as long as it takes. They ought to come around by morning." He walked stiffly from the room.

For some time Malcolm stood at the door, looking wistfully at the men in the wide bed. With a sound of regret he set the lock and keyed the access code. "They'll yell when they want out. We don't need the kids blundering in. Johnny's going to be okay, isn't he?"

"Yes." Harry slid one arm about the boy's waist to hug him for a moment. "And his name is Kevin. *Captain* Kevin Jarrat. Evelyn was right all along. Your Johnny was someone special. But he's gone now."

The boy's eyes brimmed. "What about the other ... his lover? John ... Jarrat's partner. You said he was soaked in Angel."

The healer rubbed his aching head but gave his son a smile of deep satisfaction. "Mal, it worked. I did it. My brain feels like a squashed tomato, but it worked. Stone's brain *can't* respond the Angel molecule. I did something with his chemical receptors, twisted them into a different pattern."

"You mean, his brain just can't 'see' Angel anymore?" Malcolm asked, taken aback. "He could snort a nose full of that crap —"

"And it might make him puke but he wouldn't trip." Harry pushed away from the wall where he had literally propped himself up. "Damn! When Jarrat came in here with a bunch of crazy notions I thought he was just plain mad. If you'd asked me last night if it'd work, I'd have told you to start ordering firewood for the funeral. I never thought it was possible."

"And what about them?" Malcolm glanced pointedly at the locked door. "What are *they* going to make of it?"

Harry's smile faded. "That," he said guardedly, "is up to them, isn't it? I must shoot Stone with the antitoxin. I gave him enough Devil's Club to drop a horse." He touched his son's face gently. "Your Johnny is safe and whole again, and he's been in love with Stone for longer than he knows. Much more than a year, though even he doesn't realize it. He was never yours, Malcolm. Don't punish yourself."

The young man's eyes brimmed again and he returned to bed without a word. Harry sighed and went to the biolab to prepare a hypo. Time for Stone to come down for the last time, very, very gently.

CHAPTER NINETEEN

Before Jarrat woke it was comfortable. He was aware of the wonderful sensation of not being alone, of being with someone to whom he was so close, he could drop the mask he showed the world and be himself. He was as aware of Stone's feelings as of his own, and knew Stone was dreaming good dreams: Jarrat's own feet felt the chill of something like a mountain stream, his eyes contracted to a brightness, like a cloud-swept sky, and his bare back felt the heat of a bigger, whiter sun than anything Kevin knew at firsthand. A cool wind stroked him. All he need do was let his body translate the sensations, and he could piece together a whole environment.

The sensations of delight may have come from outside but he felt them as keenly as Del promised, and in the half-doze his imagination was quick to supply images, building the reality. Jarrat had no complaints. To share Stone's feelings was a pleasure.

When he woke it was disturbing. He floated toward consciousness and memory jolted back like a punch. He was curled on the foot of he bed, Harry had not moved him. He lay on Stone's legs, but Stone had not yet stirred. Nor did he wake as Jarrat sat up.

In the early morning sunlight streaming under the half-open blind, Stone looked peaceful, younger. The blue shadows around his eyes had faded, his face was not clenched and his skin was cool and dry. The fevers were gone, and so was the pain. From the look of Stone's face and body, Jarrat could tell at a glance, Stoney was neither flying nor craving, merely exhausted now. Relief washed over him in a prickling cold torrent.

It was moments before the rest of it hit him like a physical blow. As he moved he realized his jeans were still damp. He had come several times, his body reacting to the intense stimulation of the Angel dreams. Stone's feelings continued to hover around the periphery of his mind. The gist of the current dream was beyond him — he did not 'hear' thoughts; they shared an empathy, not telepathy — but emotions were keen-edged. Stone was happy, laughing. Again, Jarrat felt the warmth of some sun on his back, the wind in his hair, and the soles of his feet prickled ... dry grass?

It was a weird sensation, and his conscious mind reeled for an instant. He reached out to shake Stone awake but drew his hand back, suddenly afraid to touch. It would be like touching himself. And when Stoney woke, how would the world feel, through someone else's nerves? A moment of panic gripped him as Stone began to come to, woken by Jarrat's anxiety.

Jarrat got to his feet, self-conscious about the damp patch at his crotch but unable to deny the telltale stain. He hugged his arms about his chest and forced a smile he knew must be transparent. There could be no secrets now. No masking of what he felt. Stone's blue eyes opened, very soft, dilated. Very beautiful, Jarrat thought. And they were sober.

Jarrat cleared his throat. "Well? Stoney? Stoney!"

Stone took a deep, careful breath and let it out slowly as his eyes came into focus on Jarrat's face. "Hello, Kevin," he said levelly, lucidly. His voice was stronger, the words clear.

"He did it? By God, he did it?" Even now, despite his desperate hopes, Jarrat could barely believe it. "How do you feel?"

"Light headed, tired, sore. Weak as a kitten, and I've got a little headache," Stone said slowly. "Then again, you know all that. Don't you? It doesn't hurt anymore. I'm not drunk, not craving garbage." He blinked up at Jarrat, seeing him for the first time without the haze of narcotic stupor. Kevin needed to shave and was smudged about the eyes with fatigue. Stone's fingernails raked through his own stubble and he saw Jarrat's jaw twitch. "Oh. So it's true, then."

Two sets of perceptions ran parallel through his nerves, one a mirror image of the other. Jarrat knew intimately what he was feeling, right down to the surprise. It was a warm sensation of sharing, as if they were joined physically, almost the same person, yet two separate bodies. It was wonderful, it was terrifying. The jolt of Stone's perceptions made Jarrat gasp.

"Calm down, Stoney. It's strange, I'll grant you, but Harry says it's never killed anyone."

"Yet," Stone added. He wrapped his arms about his chest, unconsciously mirroring the way Jarrat was standing, because he could feel through the other man's nerves so clearly. "You mean I'm going to go through life yelling every time you burn your fingers? Laughing every time you think of a funny?"

"And jerking off every time I get a hardon," Jarrat said pointedly.

Stone made an aghast face. "Even that's true, then."

"Especially that." Jarrat sat on the bedside. "You remember everything?" Stone nodded. He looked so mortified, Jarrat felt the onset of irrational laughter and choked it back. "Don't get into a guilt trip. It wasn't a punishment. I went to the slaughter willingly."

"But —" Stone dragged in a breath. "Jesus, the things I did to you."

"Angel dreams are like that," Jarrat said very softly, almost amused by Stone's discomfiture. Stone felt his amusement and looked up out of dark, dilated eyes. "You said you loved me." Stone steeled himself, expecting a rebuke now. Jarrat felt him tense. Then Stone felt the flare of warm emotion from Jarrat and relaxed, little by little. "It's true, then."

"It's true." Jarrat focused on Stone to explore the stirrings of his mirror feelings. "Tell me the truth."

"I've wanted you for years, all the time, one way or another," Stone confessed. "Since the day you came aboard, I guess. Oh, it was lust at first, and that's healthy. Loving you came later. I just never took it into my head to roll you over on your belly and cram my cock into you. Sorry."

"For the crudity, or for never having nailed me to the deck?" Jarrat demanded ruefully.

"Both." Stone chanced a glance at Jarrat's flushed face. "It's a hell of a nice little bum and I was sadly crude about it."

"Then again, crudity comes naturally to the likes of you." Jarrat was trying to lighten up as his nerves strummed like harp strings. "All right, this predicament is no laughing matter but we ought to be celebrating. You're not hurting, are you?"

And Stone shook his head. "Not at all. I don't want the stuff. The hunger's *gone*. Harry's a magician. And you're making me anxious."

"Sorry," Jarrat said curtly. "I *am* anxious. Trying to figure out how I'm going to go about living with you under my skin for the rest of my life. I expect we'll get used to it."

Stone held out his hands. "Come on. We better see what it feels like. Can't go through life terrified to touch, when we're sharing the pillow."

Their hands slid into a loose clasp. It was odd but not unpleasant. A simple touch of hands was like kissing, as sensitive and rewarding as the more intimate act. The sudden pleasure made Jarrat hungry for Stone's mouth and he moved gratefully into Stone's waiting arms. To kiss was to drown in pure sensuality. Whiskers rasped as their mouths sealed. What making love would offer they could not imagine, but thrills of lust persisted even while they were spent, for the moment incapable. Jarrat felt Stone's hand go to his groin and discover the damp patch.

"You came," he said huskily, busy nibbling Jarrat's ear.

"Of course I did," Jarrat retorted. "What did you expect? Physical manifestations of the Angel, it's how users burn themselves out. What worries me is, we'll turn each other on with every unguarded feeling. We'll finish each other off if we're not careful, and we won't need Angel to do it."

"Yes." Stone withdrew his hand and kissed Jarrat's mouth thoughtfully. "It'll take some getting used to. I wonder if Harry knows any tricks."

"I'll ask him." Jarrat rubbed his tingling palms together. We're in big trouble, Stoney. NARC is going to decommission us, no doubt about it. We're through, at command rank. They'll never give us a carrier."

"I know." Stone looked away. Jarrat felt a sudden rush of guilt from him. "You put your career in the crusher. I didn't want that."

"I did." Jarrat spoke only the truth. Stone shot a hard look at him but he could not suspect the old fashioned diplomatic lie. Empaths knew better. "I sat right here in this room and weighed it up," Jarrat told him, "shrewd as a corporate accountant. My career against your life. Hell,

Stoney, I'm on borrowed time. I've survived longer at command rank than fifty percent of NARCs live, same as you. I came *this* close a few days ago. Next time I'll be dead. It might be time we got out anyway, both of us, before they send us home in bodybags."

"Not that you've got a home to go back to," Stone said softly. "I know all about Sheckley. A rat-hole, three weeks from Earth. No parents. The Academy, the Army, then NARC, are all the family you ever had."

"You've been there?" Jarrat was surprised. "What the hell would take you to Sheckley? It's twenty-five cubic kilometers of girders and conduit."

"I saw it in the newsvids," Stone corrected, and his cheeks colored with the hint of a faint, attractive blush.

Far clearer was the rush of his chagrin. Jarrat felt it at once. "What?"

Stone sighed. "In one of the dreams I took you home. Earth."

"Well ..." Jarrat's brows rose. "It's an option. I've never been there, but I've —" He chuckled. "Seen it on the newsvids. I might get to like it."

"Depends where you land," Stone said thoughtfully. "City bottom in London and Paris and Chicago is the same as city bottom anywhere. I grew up in London, went to school in Paris. That's in France. Went to the Tac Special Ops school in Chicago, in the States. You heard of them?"

"I can find them on a map," Jarrat said aridly. "I don't want to land in city bottom, Stoney, not in any colony. We wouldn't go right back to Earth just to find a sewer and climb in."

Curious blue eyes studied Jarrat with a surreal calm, so different from the recent frenzy of Angel fevers. "That's what I meant," Stone said softly. "You know me, I always loved to fly. There was a place I used to fly ultralites when I was a young kid, before my parents gave me the royal ultimatum. The mountains of northern Spain. You might like it."

"Royal ultimatum?" Jarrat echoed, then memory clicked back into place. "The day they told you, if you signed with Tactical, don't bother coming home, because they were so 'bitterly disappointed to lose you.'"

"You got it." Stone stretched, head to foot. Jarrat heard the pop and crackle of his joints and sinews. "I was supposed to attend some mausoleum of a science institute in the States, take a brilliant doctorate at the age of twenty-five, stand the academic community on its ear and make the old folks famous." From a hidden reserve he produced a wry chuckle. "It was never going to happen, but they didn't want to see the truth, face the facts. The whole scene was my fault."

"Angel?" Jarrat hazarded.

"Angel." Stone sighed. "It tore our generation apart on Earth. People back on the 'old world' were so ... so *surprised* when Angel arrived on Earth. As if it couldn't get into their cities, like it was strictly a colonial disease. Colonial 'trash' might use Angel, but Earth-born folks were too good for it. You know how arrogant Earth-borns often are."

"Hal Mavvik." Jarrat's brows arched. "He waves it like a flag, has one of the American accents. I couldn't tell which."

"West Coast. I've heard him on audio." Stone flexed his back.

"But you don't share their arrogance," Jarrat added.

Stone shrugged. "I've got nothing to be arrogant about. I bummed around, flying anything I could get my hands on, and buried my friends and lovers when they went down to Angel. I could have been one of them, same as you. It's the same story all over, Kevin. So I joined the crusade, signed with London Tac." His brow creased. "NARC was away in the colonies, beating crap out of this syndicate, that syndicate. At nineteen, I didn't have any ambitions. I just wanted do *something*, hopefully on the right side of the law, and I knew a few people in Tac. Enlistment was easy." He yawned, knuckled his eyes. "Now it's over. I can hear my dad's voice, saying 'I told you so.' But, damn him, we're getting out *alive*."

Silence reigned between them for some time before Jarrat stirred. "You look — feel — done in, mate. Why don't you sleep?"

"I've been sleeping for days," Stone argued, though his eyelids were heavy and his speech slurred.

"You've been balling your brains out for days," Jarrat corrected sharply. "There's a difference. Jesus, what a way to go."

"Screwing you to the point of destruction," Stone said with another powerful surge of guilt. "I'm sorry, Kevin."

"I know you are." Jarrat smiled. "It's flattering. Being wanted, being loved. And I can feel that from you, no need for you to say it."

"Right." Stone closed his eyes. "Riki ... was a user. Did you know?"

Jarrat recoiled. "No, I didn't. He didn't look too far into it."

"Couple of smacks a week." Stone shrugged. "He wouldn't have made twenty-one. If it was a choice between going out the way he did and dying in a gutter with a head full of Angel, there's a lot to be said for going out clean, with a little dignity left intact."

He was bitter about it. Jarrat felt the pain of grief, sour in his gut. But they had both seen too much of it, the senseless, needless deaths of innocent bystanders, for them to question that it should happen. The reality was, it happened every day, in every city back as far as Earth, no matter the arrogance of 'old worlders' who often considered colonials to be trash.

A shudder coursed through Jarrat as he realized, what he felt was entirely alien but no less moving. He was grieving for a boy he had never met in life. Stone hurt for Riki, and Kevin felt it in every cell. He wanted to help, and Stone would know that too. They looked at each other with startling sobriety, and Jarrat offered his arms, his mouth, for a moment's celebration of life. "Welcome back, Stoney," he said when his lips were released.

At last Stone smiled. "Glad to be back, Kev."

Soon enough, physical debility overtook him and Jarrat watched him pass out cold, worn ragged. He tossed a rug over him and wandered into the adjacent bathroom. A careworn face peered out of the mirror, and he took a few minutes to wash up. A green silk kimono embroidered with white dragons hung on the back of the door. He shrugged into it and dropped the spaceplane's infrabeam key into its pocket. His jeans, he left with Stone's denims in a laundry basket by the door, which was locked.

Stone was deeply asleep as Jarrat hailed Harry on the intercom. The microsurgeon hurried to let him out. He studied Stone quietly for a few moments, and spoke in an undertone. "How is he this morning?"

"He's clear," Jarrat whispered. "Exhausted, weak, but the craving isn't there and he's not coming down."

"Ah." Satisfied, Harry surveyed the patient, who lay sprawled across the bed, naked, face-down, in the sun. "He needs rest," he warned.

"And he knows it. We don't have to run away immediately." Jarrat gave the laundry basket a discreet kick with one bare foot.

"I'll send someone. Let him sleep now." Harry beckoned Jarrat away, and they strolled onto the balcony overlooking the gardens and rainforest.

The morning was cool but humid. In minutes the silk was clinging to Jarrat's back. He saw a yellow Marshall 'van parked in the courtyard and smiled. Tansy and Evelyn must have arrived back before he woke.

"He'll be weak for a while," Harry was saying, "but he will recover, I promise you. Remember, he's still full of Angel, but the chemical flushes out in sweat and urine. He's not strong enough to work out, but when he is, in a few days, the gym and sauna will be the best medicine a physician could advise. His brain doesn't register the chemical anymore, so although he's still full of it he's only physically under par with the toxic hangover. He's as strong as a horse, Jarrat. Don't worry on that account."

"Thanks." Jarrat looked sidelong at Del. "What is it you do? You share the deepest quirks and kinks of a patient's sexuality, so they call you a pervo. You have the trick of empathy, you're born with it, so they call you a genetic deviant, a queer. But what do you *do*, Harry?"

Del puffed out his cheeks. "What do you know about telekinesis?"

"The ability to move objects by projection of alpha-wave energy? Not a lot." Jarrat leaned back against the column that held up the pergola and turned his face to the sun. "I know a lot of lab work was done twenty years ago. Even NARC looked into it. The human brain generates many kinds of waves, alpha, beta, so on. It works on electricity, you can measure the voltage. The human body is really an electrical generator, and the power the brain develops can be tapped to run a model railway. I saw it done. I saw a woman roll cigarettes around a table by just looking at them. They measured her output. It was enormous. She was exhausted in five minutes."

The doctor nodded. "You're getting close. Nobody knows how it's done, but it *is* done. Something similar to the fable of 'broadcast power,' save that the psychic achieves what science has only recently been able to duplicate. A very, very small minority of adepts have the trick of moving quite large objects. A table, say. Now, what I do is nothing so spectacular. I screw around on the molecular level."

The remark made Jarrat laugh. "You what?"

"I rearrange molecules. You see, the receptors in your brain that accept this and that chemical are in the pattern of a lock. The incoming 'agents' — hormone, drug, virus — are in the pattern of a key fitting the lock. Two molecules line up exactly, they couple and you get a bang out of it. Or you get dead," he added darkly. "Say, aspirin works for you but not for someone else, or that man over there is an alcoholic and this man over here can put the booze away by the bucket and not get tanked. Some people report having used narcotics such as heroin and noticing no effect whatever." He shrugged. "No receptor cells in the brain."

"So what you do," Jarrat concluded thoughtfully, "is change the molecules of the receptors so the garbage doesn't mesh."

"That's what I did for Stoney," Harry affirmed. "It was purely experimental. I've never done it before. More complex than lifting a table or rolling cigarettes around on broadcast alpha-waves! And I'd like your Chief Medical Officer to thoroughly examine Stone, make very sure I haven't made any mistakes. I could have unwittingly made him susceptible to some other harmless substance. Take a drag on a cigarette and fall down drunk, for example. I was as careful as I knew how to be, but all the same ask for tests, and ask your surgeon to be very thorough."

"I will," Jarrat promised. "What did you do to my brain?" He wondered if the empath felt his chilling disquiet.

"Oh, the work was similar to what I did for Stone, but it was mainly your neural synapses that needed attention. Your brain was congested with a lot of old blood, some neural tissues ruptured. As I said, I screw around on the molecular level. Don't ask me to explain what I do. I can't. But I get a *feeling* for what's busted up, and I get a *feeling* when it's fixed. I'm a queer. An 87/T. Bloody damned queer. Good enough?"

"Not by a long shot." Jarrat put a hand on his shoulder. "I'd like to see your gifts properly researched."

Harry shook his head. "A college in Eldorado researched me when I was young. They hurt me. A lot. I walked out of the lab and kept walking." He looked away and waved. Out across the lawns, Tansy and Evelyn were feeding the peacocks. "I do what I do, Kevin. I started out mending broken bones when I was a boy. I picked up a little bird, mangled after a storm. I just ... mended it. My father saw me do it and realized what I was. I had good teachers, other queers like myself. I mended a dog's broken leg when I was ten, and I took a tumor out of a stud stallion when I was fourteen. I've felt my way along since then, till now I can meddle in a man's head. You *can* trust me, Jarrat. Your friend will be fine."

"I do trust you." Jarrat smiled faintly as he remembered what he had shared with Stone. "I'm just glad you warned me about the ticklish aspect."

"Your virtue was assaulted?" Del asked quietly.

"Along with the rest of me," Jarrat confessed. "I've been fucked every way you can imagine and a few you probably can't. It doesn't matter. I liked it. But it burns me up. It's like feeling every sensation with twice the intensity, till I'm exhausted. You must know what I mean."

"Yes." Del folded his arms as he sat on the guard rail beside Jarrat. "If it helped him heal, what else is there?"

"He's dreaming," Jarrat said abstractly. "I think he's running. I feel it in my legs. It feels good."

"It's going to be difficult for you to work together now, isn't it?" Harry asked shrewdly.

Jarrat snapped back to reality. "I don't know. We don't actually work together. NARC ships run with two captains because of the nature of the work we do, and the dangers. The chances of one of us getting hurt or killed, or into the kind of hostage situation we just came through, are very high. There must be a command rank officer available at all times, on the ship and groundside, in the field. If he's on the carrier, I'm in the field, and vice versa. Working, usually we're only in contact by audio or comm-relay. It's riot armor and cannons, or deep cover for weeks, even months at a stretch." His face twisted. "Jesus Christ, he's dreaming about me."

"You'll learn to control it," Harry said quickly. "It's a lot like learning to swim. You sink a lot at first but you get better as you go. If you had time I could show you a few tricks."

"Time is one thing I don't have right now," Jarrat said ruefully. "But NARC is going to junk us off the payroll, you can bet on it, so we'll be back. But I want the Death's Head episode closed before it happens. File the paperwork, and then ... find a new life somewhere. Here, maybe. I like it here, and these people need all the help they can get. Angel is a disease around Chell and Eldorado." He stirred and sought a smile. He wondered if Harry could tell it was a mask. "Stoney is what matters. The rest is something we'll learn to live with."

"NARC won't junk you because your relationship is sexual?" Del asked. "I'm not prying, Kevin, just interested! I never was sure how their rule book is worded."

"Oh, no. They're not interested in who or what we sleep with," Jarrat told him. "A man, a woman, a biomech, a monkey, take your pick. What bothers them is when people get close, form attachments. Pretty soon the job goes down the chute because one partner decides to save his friend, his lover, at the expense of a month's worth of surveillance and field work. It can cost a king's ransom. We run a support crew behind us of more than two hundred on the carrier, every one a professional on top salary. The NARC budget reads like the GNP of a small colony. Against that you have two guys getting friendly, and one has his back up against the wall —"

"And the other pulls the plug on a ten-billion credit operation, to yank him out of whatever deep shit," Del finished.

"Right. All NARC cares about it that the job gets done properly. It's the empathy, not the fact we're sleeping together, that'll have them running around screaming at Central. We might get the chance to prove ourselves capable of doing the damned job. Go through basics and psyche all over again." He shook his head resignedly. "I doubt they'll give us the chance, and in any case I'm not sure I'd want to. You live and learn, Harry. And like I just said to Stoney, I'm on borrowed time." He stirred and checked his chrono. "I have to call home before they send Tactical out looking for me."

The microsurgeon watched him walk out to the aircraft. "I need a few minutes of your time, Kevin. Paperwork. I'm a legit organization, and I get audited too often, being queer. Tie off the loose ends before you leave."

"I'll be right there," Jarrat called over his shoulder.

He was limber now, looking good in the green silk, but the educated eye could still pick up a very slight favoring of the reconstructed knee. Harry studied him with a professional eye. In a another week Kevin would forget the work had ever been done. Jarrat waved to the two women, stopped to talk for a moment, far out of Harry's earshot, and then dug through the kimono's pocket for an infrabeam. It lifted the plane's cockpit canopy and he climbed up the hardpoints, pulled on a headset. His voice did not carry. Del smiled after him, congratulating himself: *I do good work.*

"Raven 9.4 to *Athena*," Jarrat was saying, and when the radio boy answered he went on, "give me Doc Reardon."

A moment's pause, and then Kip Reardon's voice said, "Infirmary."

"It's Jarrat. Ice up a cold pack, Kip."

"It worked?" Reardon demanded. "No bullshit, Kevin?"

"Damned right," Jarrat told him. "He's weak, he's dizzy, but Harry says his brain doesn't register the Angel molecule any longer —"

"No comedown, no craving," Reardon said. "Damn. He's a lucky bugger. You know he's the first one to beat Angel! I don't know what this queer healer of yours does, but he ought to get a license and bottle it."

"No arguments from me," Jarrat agreed. "Harry might allow some research, some data sharing, so long as you don't try to put him under the microscope. He's been there, done that, and all they did was hurt him."

"Lead me to it," Reardon breathed. "You coming home?"

"Soon. I want you to set up for a full series of tests on Stoney. Every test in the book, specially chemical analysis of his brain. What is he receptive to, what not. That sort of thing. Harry wants to be sure he didn't make any accidental alterations to his basic brain chemistry."

"I'll set up the lab," Reardon promised. "And incidentally, you're long overdue for your own tests, Kevin. I have to run everything in the manual from olfactory memory trigger to sperm count. So get your butt in here."

"Soon," Jarrat said resignedly. "Give me the ops room, Kip. Business first. I'll talk to you later." When the duty officer — a NARC woman, Petrov's relief — answered, he said, "Have you had an update from Tactical?"

Then he listened to a tale of woe. A hundred and eight civilians died in Stacy's war. Property damage ran into tens of millions. Tactical had shut down, suspending aggression, licking its wounds and burying its dead. They were hurt. Jarrat swore as he listened. The Chell Congress, local colonial government, was howling for blood and the press was vicious.

Worse was the news out of the underground. With the Angel supply growing short smalltime entrepreneurs were making fortunes, and Tac was spread too thinly to stop them. The 'dope lawyers' and the vigilantes met head to head in the media and on the street. Four riots erupted in the night just past; seven Tactical men died and NARC's only option was to come down hard on the Angelpack. Meanwhile, encrypted signals had been intercepted between Death's Head and its affiliates.

Hal Mavvik counted it a major victory. The local press, even Global-Net, which was supposed to have scruples, was screaming that Death's Head had taken on NARC and won. In a week those headlines would be blazing across the newsvids in other colonies. The bad press was not merely insulting, it was dangerous. Syndicates scattered through the Cygnus Colonies were watching. They would soon be receiving a clear message: NARC had its vulnerabilities. NARC could be hurt, could be whipped.

Anger seethed in Jarrat's gut as he closed the ship-to-ground loop and turned back toward the house. Stone's feelings coursed through him distractingly and he struggled to differentiate between them and his own perceptions. It was not easy, but he found fractional differences that made it just barely possible. It was as if Stone's feelings were a different 'color,' blue against his own green. He shuddered, thought he felt the icy cold of water on his skin. Stone was dreaming he was swimming, Jarrat was sure. And what happened when he dreamed he was making love? Jarrat gritted his teeth and urged his mind onto other subjects.

He was so preoccupied, Tansy had spoken to him for the second time before he heard her. "I said, it's good to see you, Captain! Memory intact and everything working. Smile, show me the teeth."

He laughed. "I'd forgotten about them. Stoney says they're better than my own were. They're very comfortable."

"And the knee?" Tansy wanted to know. "I watched you walk in from the plane. You're still favoring it."

"It aches," Jarrat said indifferently. "But it's strong, I can tell you that. My Medical Officer stress-tested it. You do good work, ma'am." He winked at her. "I owe you."

Evelyn chuckled delightedly. "You fixed up pretty, Kevin. Simon hasn't shut up about you yet. He's told the story all over Ballyntyre, like he was your bosom buddy instead of a bastard."

"Damn." Jarrat's lips compressed.

"Something wrong?" Tansy asked.

"Maybe." Jarrat gestured vaguely in the direction of Ballyntyre. "You know you still have a king shooter in the area? The less Joel Assante knows, the better. With Simon mouthing off this way, Assante's almost certainly connected me, and NARC, with this household and Harry."

The observation sobered both women. "It's to late now to gag him," Evelyn said. "I called an old friend of mine, at Eldorado Tac. They put on two extra squads in Bally."

"Surveillance?" Jarrat shook his head. "Don't get complacent."

"Backup," Evelyn corrected. "I don't want anybody to do my fighting for me, Kevin. But I wouldn't turn down the offer of backup." She paused, looking Jarrat up and down appreciatively. "You fixed up nice. Harry told me about your friend. It was on the newsvids, actually. A NARC aircraft had been shot down in the battle. They had pictures. They didn't mention Stone had been taken prisoner."

"Classified info," Jarrat said tersely. "And Harry must also have told you, Stoney's going to be okay."

"He did." Evelyn thrust her hands into the pockets of her pale green coveralls with the big yellow chevrons on the legs, the paramilitary fatigues that had been the first subtle trigger to Jarrat's willful memory. "Speaking of our king shooter, Assante must have blown through Bally again, not that anyone saw him ... Sash Connally turned up dead this morning."

"The price," Tansy said acidly, "for having a mouth that big. Christ. He shoots the dope runner then brags about it! I'm surprised he lived so long. And I'm delighted the shooter didn't come looking for you, Kevin."

"He may not have come to Bally looking for me, but he knows I was here, and I'm *connected* here. Which ... bothers me." Jarrat watched a flock of rainbow parrots wheel about the plantation house. "Assante was one of the shooters who ran out on Mavvik before the show started. Not all of them believed the war was winnable, and they'll turn out to be right. Still, Hal Mavvik will scalp Assante if he gets the chance."

"But Death's Head won that round," Tansy observed. "The news we got here said NARC took a pasting and Chell Tac was crippled."

Jarrat smiled humorlessly. "That's partially true. Tac was hurt badly. NARC withdrew to patch up and collate data. A city becomes a battleground, and you're wading in confusion. Crimmos hide behind innocent bystanders, and if you don't want a bloodbath you back off and regroup. Evelyn knows what I'm talking about." The blonde woman nodded. "But as for Mavvik winning that round, forget it. Next time we fight, NARC picks the field, NARC makes the running. Last time we fought to Stacy's specifications and it was a circus."

He stirred, uncomfortably aware of Stone's feelings. Was he dreaming he was eating? Jarrat's tongue *tasted* something sweet. In fact it was past time Stone actually did eat. "Any chance of breakfast before we leave?" Kevin wondered. "Stoney ought to be able to stomach food by now."

"I'll whip something together," Tansy promised. "Coffee, Eve?"

The two women ambled toward the west end of the house and Jarrat stepped onto the verandah. Harry was in the lab, preparing drugs for batch testing. He looked up with a smile as Jarrat appeared, then frowned. "You're angry."

"With Death's Head. They paste Tactical, then we paste them, but Stacy pulls the plug too soon, which makes it seem on the surface that Hal Mavvik won. Well, not for much longer." He drew one index finger across his gullet. "They go down. Soon. Can you pump something into Stoney to get him on his feet fast? I need him in something like working order."

"Half his problem is, he hasn't eaten in three or four days," Del said as put the drugs into the refrigerator. "And if he was the only hustler in a twenty-four hour sex shop he couldn't have worked his body any harder."

"And I didn't help," Jarrat said uncomfortably. He remembered the scenes they had shared, the way he and Stone had savaged one another. Angel dreams, quickly becoming reality. It was fortunate they were merely empathic. If they had found access to each other's actual memories there would have been real trouble. He wondered how telepathic, or how simply polite Harry was. How much he was aware of. Stone had a lot of staying power and Jarrat's own reputation had been earned the hard way. At that thought he choked off a chuckle. English was an odd language.

The microsurgeon grinned impishly at him. "Yes, it will be a little ... ticklish, as you said, until it settles down. It will, my word on it. I'll prepare a shot for him. Ginseng, glucose, proteins, minerals. He ought to be able to eat a little bland food by now."

Stone woke naturally as Jarrat clattered a meal down on the table at the bedside. A hypo lay on the tray. He left Stone's veins alone and popped the shot slowly just under the skin of one muscular thigh. Still, Stone made a face. "I'm going to have more bruises than a prizefighter."

"You'll live," Jarrat said tersely. His jaw clenched as he felt the sharp smart of the shot in his own leg. "I'm pleased to say." He sat down on the mattress and groaned as Stone's emotions rolled powerfully into him. "You're on the mend by the feel of it, my lad." He felt a caress at his knee and looked into the other man's anxious face. "It's all right, really. I won't change my mind. Just tell me what you want of me. All I ask is honesty."

"What I want?" Stone pulled himself up against the pillows and studied Jarrat with heavy eyes, from his tousled hair to his stubbled jaw. "To be with you somewhere quiet till we get used to this. To love you, physically and every other way. Make you happy. I guess I want all the things we ever had. Trust, companionship, friendship. But now I want the sex as well."

Jarrat smiled at him. "Nothing much has changed. I think I can live with this. Come here." Stone's mouth opened against his and Jarrat tasted the berry juice he had sipped moments before. His tongue explored so easily now, ventured between Jarrat's teeth almost demandingly. They were breathless when they parted. Jarrat pushed the food at him. "Eat. Your stomach must think your throat was cut."

He gave Stone the Tactical update while he picked over the assorted cereals and fruit. Stone's anger punched into him, redoubling his own outrage. "Tac go up against military hardware and get cut to shreds. This is out of Stacy's league," Stone said at last. "It's our game now." He looked up into Jarrat's set, immobile face. The empathy between them rang like a bell. "You're chewing me up, Kevin. Calm down."

"Sorry." Jarrat swept a caress about Stone's face and stood. Stone's anger was like splinters of ice under his skin, distracting, troubling. It was easier to wallow in mutual lust. "There'll be an arsenal, stuffed to busting with military hardware, the haul from Vincent Morello Aerospace, and I don't want to send troops into a firefight any more than Stacy does."

"So deploy a couple of gunships," Stone said brashly. "Air to ground bombardment. Shell the palace right off the mountain. We've got the NARC sanction to do it with ... until they suspend us, but that won't be for weeks yet because of the telemetry time lag."

"Kip Reardon could suspend us," Jarrat said quietly.

"But he won't." Stone clattered his dish back onto the tray.

216

"Technically he should," Jarrat mused. "But we can call in a few favors. All I want is to close the file on Death's Head. Then they can suspend us if they want to. The Blue Raven gunship is just about fixed. We'll be ready to deploy tomorrow."

"This is why I transferred out of Tac in the first place, you know," Stone said, yawning deeply as he stretched his joints one by one. "I got pissed, knowing who the crimmos are, where they are, what they're doing, and never being able to lay a finger on them. Either that, or you pick them up one minute and a bunch of flash lawyers have 'em back in the open air the next, before you've even got the report filed. Tac has some good boys, but a flakjacket and a service machine pistol are not going to do you much good when you're up against the likes of Hal Mavvik. And they are."

Which was the whole reason NARC, as a department, had been formed, some few years before Jarrat and Stone were born. Jarrat smiled at him, watching the spirit return to the blue eyes a little at a time. It felt good, a kind of pride in his lover. Lover? The term remained an exaggeration, unless Angel dreams counted for anything. Before it was true they would have shared a bed and the real-life replay. He shivered.

Stone lifted a curious brow at him. "That felt interesting. What's going through that tousled skull of yours, Kevin?"

"Just thinking about us," Jarrat admitted. "Forget it. I don't think either of us is capable at the moment. You feel ready to get on your feet, and the lab is set up." Stone moaned expressively. "Tests, kid. Orders. Mine."

"Pulling rank?"

"Why not? I don't see why I should suffer alone," Jarrat said dryly. "Kip's going to put me through the shredder! I want you to take it easy for the next week. You'll know when you're ready to get back into harness. Right now you're not as fit as you think you are." He picked up the littered breakfast tray. "Harry told me he knows ways to control the empathy."

"Thank Christ," Stone murmured. "Pamphlets are on sale in the foyer as you leave the operating theater. I hope."

"Not quite." Jarrat appreciated the humor. "But when we get done with Mavvik we've got leave coming up even if we're not on suspension. I thought we might come back and see what Harry can do for us — before I start kicking you so hard you can't sit down!" Stone was stripping him with his eyes, idly sensual. Jarrat fidgeted, getting the backlash from the Angel dreams. It was only natural but to Jarrat it was an exquisite form of torture.

Stone colored a little. "Sorry. If you weren't so irresistible it might be easier. I'll try thinking of something else. Mathematics." He pushed off the bed, found his feet and staggered a step or two. "Dizzy. Oh, I wish I hadn't eaten." He straightened and pinned on a smile. "I'll manage. Let's get out of here. Right now, I want to see Mavvik go up in the kind of demolition show they've never heard in Chell."

"You're mending," Jarrat observed. "You want to try to get back into gear? Wait till you can stand up straight! Lean on me before you fall over." A hot, wet mouth fastened, leech-like on his neck as Stone leaned on him. Every nerve was filled with the double load of Stone's feelings and his own. It was maddening. He caught his breath, teeth closed on his lip. "We're not going to get Mavvik from here by remote. Look, take a shower, get your bearings. Harry needs to file some forms. I'll see to it, and preflight the shuttle." At the door he paused. "You know what makes me furious? Mavvik is broadcasting all over this sector that he took on NARC and whipped us. It's not just Chell, it's every city in subspace broadcast range. We owe it to the department to finish what we started."

"Whip NARC?" Stone echoed, framed in the bathroom door. "If that's what he's crowing about he's going to buy a big — *nasty* surprise."

"Great minds think alike." Jarrat, always the pragmatist, set the anger aside for the moment. "Take your time, Stoney. I'll see what Harry needs."

It was a pair of standard treatment forms, identical to the one Medic Jeff Bolt had issued. Jarrat filled them both in. He knew Stone's details as well as his own. Name: Stone, Richard Jeremy. Age: 32. Born: London, England, Earth. Educated: Floyd Webber Polytechnic. Employment history: London Tactical, and NARC. Current assignment: NARC-*Athena*. Marital status? After some thought, Jarrat checked the 'single' box, but in fact it was far from true.

Harry looked over the forms before filing them, and questioned only one point. "You're listed as 'Jarrat, Kevin J.' What's the 'J' stand for?"

"Nothing," Jarrat told him with a wry smile. "The computer barfs if you don't have an initial. The fact is, I'm lucky to *have* a name! When I was maybe three years old the authorities picked me up on the rink. That's the freighter docks ... Sheckley. I knew my name was Kevin, but that's all I knew. I have the faintest memories of a man. I assume he was my father, but he could just as easily have been an officer off the ship that left me. He was tall, maybe thirty-five, red-haired. Probably a vet, with some old battle damage: he had a biosynthetic left arm. He was a guy you'd remember. Folks on the rink recalled seeing me with him before the *Lombard Explorer* shipped out. A few had drunk with him, knew his name. Keith Jarrat."

"They didn't try to contact him?" Harry looked disturbed. "He might not have realized you weren't aboard when the ship left."

"They tried." Jarrat only shrugged. "The *Lombard* was headed out to open up a new mining colony, way past the frontier. Life there wouldn't have been much more pleasant than on Sheckley, even if she'd made it ... which she didn't." He knew only the bare details, and as Stoney had often told him, the incredible 'Jarrat luck' had begun almost before he could walk. "The *Lombard* suffered drive ignition failure. Implosion. There wasn't enough left for the investigators to figure out what went wrong."

"And here you are," Harry said quietly. "While I was in your head I caught glimpses of a place ... dark, cold, heavy machinery, blue steel."

"Sheckley." Jarrat physically pushed the memories away. "Harry, if you're done, we have to get moving."

"Done and done." Harry turned his back on the terminal. "Let me take a look at Stoney, now he's up and moving. Professional ethics."

In fact, balance and coordination were returning fast. By the time Stone was showered, dry, clad in fresh denims, and had walked about the house's wide verandahs, he was standing straight and a little strength had returned to his thighs. Harry made no comment but wore a smug, tired smile. Stone wished he knew words to thank the man but the healer only waved him away when the tried.

"Nothing to thank me for, old man," Harry said offhandly. "You were a guinea pig though you didn't know it! The next time some woman brings her kid up here, soaked in that crap, maybe I can do something to help. Pull them out of the mire one at a time. It may not sound like much —"

"It sounds," Stone said aridly, "like a miracle. Do it, Harry." He took the healer's hand tightly. "If you need help, funds, facilities, whatever, my

218

bosses will supply. If the department argues, contact a surgeon called Rear-don, Surgeon Captain Kip Reardon, CMO NARC-*Athena*."

"Who wants to use *me* as a guinea pig, I believe!" Del laughed. "Still, this time around I'm not a kid. I don't mind a few lab sessions, so long as I'm the one in charge." He gripped Stone's hand and released it. "So how do you feel? It should just be a kind of chronic fatigue now. The Angel is still in you, buckets of it, but your body isn't reacting to it. It *can't*."

Stone closed his eyes, focusing not on the view of the rainforest but on the sensations from without, as Jarrat jogged to the shuttle to run through the preflight checklist for the hop into space. "I'm tired, a little sore. After the last few days I'm not physically capable but I'm trying to turn on. I can feel him. I ... want him."

"There were enough nutrients and proteins in that shot to stand a reg-iment on end," Del told him. "You'll get on your feet, fast. You have to, or you'll start losing muscle tone, and then it's a long haul back to health and fitness." He touched Stone's muscular shoulder. "Just rest and eat, sleep all you can. And if you turn on, grab him and improvise! You weren't injured or ill, just doped. Angel is extremely toxic, but simple food poisoning will do much more harm in the short term. How long were you on that garbage? A few days? Now, imagine spending *two years* soaked in it!"

The proposition made Stone shudder, and he knew Jarrat would reg-ister the sudden rush of revulsion. "I ought to be on my knees thanking you. What do I say, Doctor?"

"Nothing," Harry smiled warmly at him. "You were a guinea pig, and I've left you and Jarrat up the proverbial, I know."

"In love," Stone amended almost sheepishly. Del chuckled. "I feel good, Harry. Just weak in the knees, short of breath. Even the dizziness is getting better." He took a deep breath of the humid tropical air and watch-ed Jarrat out on the lawns, making his farewells to two women. They kissed cheeks, parted, and Jarrat climbed up into the shuttle and pulled on his helmet. "I've got to go, he's waiting for me. But we'll be back. You can teach us how to make sense of all this. I hope." He stretched out his shoulders. "Oh, that feels good."

"You're alive," Harry Del said fiercely. "Get out of here, Stoney. Go do what they pay you for. Shut down Death's Head once and for all, eh?"

Out beyond the lawns, as Jarrat hit the igniters the shuttle came to life with the whining howl of big military ramjets. The sound was familiar, wel-come. Stone gave the healer a grin and got his legs into gear. His body moved with an unaccustomed slowness and his extremities tingled, not quite numb. He could only guess how much poison was still in his system, and he climbed the side of the shuttle with a touch of awkwardness, which was unusual. Jarrat had already strapped down, and handed him a helmet. With a grunt, Stone settled in the rear seat and ran up the straps.

"You okay, Stoney?" Jarrat's voice was intimately close over the head-set. "Walking out here, climbing up ... you felt weird in my muscles."

"I felt weird in *my* muscles," Stone retorted. "Forget it. I just need to hit the gym, work like a dog, then get in the sauna and sweat like the pro-verbial pig." He paused. "And eat," he added plaintively. "I'm hungry."

"I know," Jarrat informed him. And then, "Stoney, jack into the local highband. What do you make of this?"

The canopy was whining down as Stone began to listen to local area communications. "Something encrypted. A lot of power behind it ... the sender's bouncing it off a satellite ... so the receiver could be on the other side of the planet. Hmm." He frowned at the data framed in the CRT at his elbow. "That's not Tactical, and it's off the civvy band. Military?"

"Nope. Those I know." Jarrat kicked in the repulsion and the shuttle lifted off, straight up above the white-walled house with its red-shingle roof and sprawling gardens. Parrots of every color fled in noisy cartwheels, diving into the cover of the forest as the twin tailpipes spat flame.

"And the encryption matrix is unlisted," Stone mused. "Syndicate."

"Has to be. Can you pinpoint it?"

For almost a minute Stone toyed with the groundscan, and at last made negative noises. Jarrat felt the prickle of his annoyance as he said, "It's moving. It'd swear it's moving, and ... it just shut down."

"Let it go," Jarrat said quietly. "I have a feeling I know who it is."

"Assante?" Stone guessed. "It would make sense ... he's still here."

"There's a couple of Tac squads in Ballyntyre. I'll call it in, soon as we get home. Hold on, now." At three hundred meters Jarrat swept in the wings, pulled back on the cyclic and pushed the throttles to the redline, headed for space.

"You're sure it was a NARC aircraft?" Hal Mavvik demanded. His voice was muffled, he sounded as if he were talking out the bottom of a well. Highband scramblers were not known for improving audio quality.

"I'm telling you, the plane was at Del's place," Joel Assante said loudly, and for the third time. "I popped up my videodrone, my camera. Took a look from a hundred meters up. I saw the plane, saw the NARC decal on the side, and I saw that asshole, Jarrat."

"And you didn't take a shot," Mavvik observed.

Assante was speechless. "With a fucking *warplane* parked right outside the house, and an open line right to the carrier? Jesus Christ, get real."

The R/T whined and sputtered with the weight of the encryption. Assante could only wait for it to clear. He was sitting in the cab of a Marshall groundie, a big, battered pickup truck riding a repulsion sled which had seen better days. Beggars, he thought sourly, couldn't be choosers. Even if any of the local shit-hole towns had even *had* a rental agency or a dealership, he could not have hired a car without announcing his presence to Tac. And Tac were buzzing around Ballyntyre like the owned the place. A stolen car would draw them like flies to dead meat. Assante had one option: he hitched a lift into Glenshannon, bought a lot of beer for a lot of local yokels, and paid cash for a junker. The Marshall may be a piece of crap, its repulsion may be intermittent, but it was anonymous, cheap.

It was parked, idling, on a hillside halfway around Barometer Mountain, the five thousand meter peak between the Del property outside the town of Chandler and the Lang house outside Ballyntyre. Assante was sitting in the best place to run surveillance on both establishments, but the wind seemed to scream across the hillside twenty-seven hours a day, and it seemed to rain there even when 'Bally' and Chandler were dry. Assante was in a foul mood. Only the fee for the Jarrat contract kept him there.

The highband cleared for a moment. Mavvik was talking. "So Jarrat's been and gone. You missed your chance." His voice was disdainful.

"I'll get him next time." Assante took a breath and courted patience.

The pickup chose than moment to stall out, leaving only the silence of the tropical hillside. He cursed as he twisted the key in the ignition.

"There won't be a next time." Mavvik sounded infuriatingly sure. "Joel, quit wasting my time. If I hear your voice again, you better be saying Jarrat and/or Stone are dead. Any other *syllable* from you, and you'll join them right on the top of my shit-list. Do you understand?"

The R/T blared static at Assante as Mavvik closed out, and with a growl he threw it into the passenger's footwell. The pickup restarted with an asthmatic wheezing and Assante headed fast down a powerline trail, putting distance between him and the transmission point. "There'll be another chance, asshole," he said to the dead R/T. "You can count on it."

CHAPTER TWENTY

The carrier was still on standby pending the resolution of the Chell action, and Tactical's final data analysis had not yet come in. The Blue Raven gunship was under test in its bay as Jarrat landed the shuttle. Over the comm loop he heard Combat Engineer Budweisser and his crew, working in hardsuits as they took the whole hangar deck down to partial pressure and checked the gunship's aft hull compartments for insecure seals.

NARC could do little until Stacy's data came in, and Jarrat deferred the whole question for the moment. First things came first. Kip Reardon wanted Stone in the Infirmary the moment the shuttle touched down, but Stone took a half-hour to grab a snack, get into fresh clothes, try to relax, run the recent data, catch up.

Moments after Jarrat had called Eldorado Tac about the unidentifiable highband transmissions they had picked up out of the Ballyntyre area, he was summoned to the ops room to review the night shift's telemetry package. The reprieve was welcome, but he did not expect to escape Reardon's attentions for long. As he dispatched the data the surgeon buzzed him, and the tone in his voice said Reardon would brook no further delays.

For two hours they let the surgeon go over them with every probe in the kit. Naked, bored, growing annoyed, Stone lay on the diagnostic table as Reardon examined him with his hands, since he seemed to mistrust his instruments. The computer was even then processing the results of the chemical analysis of his brain. Reardon shook his head over the data. A lot of Angel remained in Stone's bloodstream. The machines registered it and issued urgent toxicity alarms. But Stone's brain did not respond to the molecular structure of the drug, and in thirty years' service, most of that time spent with NARC, Reardon had never seen anything like it.

"Can I get up now?" Stone demanded at last. He reached for his clothes, irrespective of what Reardon might want. Jarrat sat before a monitor, methodically punching keys as prompts were fired at him, each calculated to test some facet of his memory, reflexes, even his IQ. He was tight-lipped with annoyance and merely enduring since he knew he was close to the end of the interminable, complex routine. Stone faced it next.

"Patience is a virtue," Reardon said sharply. "Nothing's doing groundside, I know our status as well as you do. Tac's just licking its wounds and Death's Head has gone to earth. So you settle yourselves to the tests. Central would string me up by the balls if I let you duck them."

Groaning, Stone took Jarrat's place behind the computer. He sent for coffee laced with sugar and ran the program as Jarrat stripped and let Reardon do his job. PET scans, MRI, ultrasound, chemical analysis, blood, urine, skin and hair, eye moisture and semen samples were taken and processed. At last, Reardon turned off his machines and sat down with coffee and a danish.

"Physically, you two are not much under par. You could both use a week's R&R but that's the worst of it. I just don't believe what I'm seeing. Not to put too fine a point on it, you should both be dead."

Jarrat pulled on his pants and sat down at the monitor beside Stone's. The psyche program had just finished and the evaluation was running out of the printer. Reardon tore it off and read the bottom line. "Are we cleared for duty?" Jarrat asked quietly. He was pushing his luck.

The surgeon arched one brow at him over the printout. "I'll release you on probation while I draft a preliminary report for Central, the first of several files I'll have to make up." He paused. "You can expect questions."

But the response would be weeks coming back due to the incredible distances involved. Even boosted subspace broadcast could only fire a signal so fast. Then, Jarrat thought bleakly, the shit would hit the fan with a vengeance.

"Look, take five," Reardon told Stone. "That's the *preliminary* medical out of the way, but I'm just starting. They'll want a proper psyche evaluation, not that computer quiz. This generic test crap just gives me somewhere to start. It estimates your capacity for logic."

"And what will you be testing?" Stone asked cynically.

"Your emotional profile," Reardon said thoughtfully. "And before you take umbrage, I'll be as delicate as is possible. It's only the routine evaluation. You went through it when you signed into NARC."

"Jesus." Stone thrust his shirt into his pants and buckled up. "You're going to make us jump through the hoops like goddamned raw recruits."

"Right back to basics," Reardon affirmed. "By the book — or you two are out on your ears! If you want to rate any chance at all of retaining your commissions in some capacity, you accept NARC routine."

"And we're probably out anyway," Jarrat observed. Reardon sighed. "Then, Kip, why bother with the testing? Why don't we just resign and save ourselves the aggravation? The veterans at Central are going to have kittens. Don't get involved, don't get friendly, they tell us. They wouldn't care if we were just sacking out together —"

"Which you are," Reardon guessed.

"It'll happen," Stone said with spurious blandness. "Soon enough. You want to make something of it, Kip?" Reardon shook his head, but penciled a note on the psyche result printout.

Jarrat raked all ten fingers across his scalp, hard, as Stone's anger clutched at his insides like a fist. "But it's more than sex. Empathy. And that goes beyond just being in love. Being family. Don't ask me to explain, Kip, I can't. It's ... like being two limbs on the same body."

"Rather you than me," Reardon said tartly as he began to tap keys. "You have the option of resignation, as you said yourself a moment ago. If you don't want to hang onto your commissions by your fingernails, simply tell Central to close the file on you." He looked up curiously at Jarrat. "But you won't do that. Will you?"

The two younger men studied each other searchingly, and Stone shook his head. "We've got a lot of time and energy invested in NARC. But even that's not the real argument. We both signed on to do a job that can't be done otherwise. It's a job we still want to do. Kevin?"

"That just about crams it into the nutshell," Jarrat agreed thoughtfully. "Otherwise we'd tell you where to shove your scanners, Kip."

"I imagine you would," Reardon said disdainfully. "Look, get out of here for now. I'll promise you this: I'll do the flat, bare minimum of testing, I'll work as fast as I can and still maintain accuracy, and I'll treat everything you tell me in confidence. I'll give the boffins at Central only what I think they should know. Good enough?" Jarrat and Stone looked at each other. "Any other tests they want, they can do later, after they've passed sentence on you loons. Junked you out of the department, or whatever."

"Or whatever?" Stone demanded. "What's going through your mind?" Reardon had been with NARC more than twenty years. Stone was not above picking his brains if the opportunity arose.

The surgeon frowned. "I don't know. At this stage I'm only guessing, but there might be more to this than you expect, Stoney. Why don't you go and eat? You could use a meal."

"I'll force-feed him," Jarrat offered. He left the Infirmary with a wink at Reardon, who gave him a salute of the obscene variety. Then they were alone in the passageway, and Stone leaned both palms on the bulkhead.

"Tired?" Jarrat asked quietly.

"Shaky on my legs, as if I've had 'flu," Stone admitted.

"So lie down before you fall on your face."

"If you'll lie down with me," Stone said glibly. "You're not on duty till Stacy's intel comes in, and then you'll be on 'round the clock. And you'll be hip-deep in flak when you lead the Ravens." He looked Jarrat in the eye very soberly. "There's a real chance you won't come back, like they always tell us. Follow me? Don't go out and get chopped to shrapnel before we've made it real, even just once, is what I'm trying to say."

"I hear you." Jarrat felt the warmth of Stone's affection as they went forward, to the cabins. "You're a sentimental sonofabitch, aren't you?"

"Makes two of us," Stone accused. He stifled a yawn. "Then I'll sleep. Scout's honor, and such gibberish."

"I don't need promises," Jarrat said, amused. "I can pull rank. Maybe you've forgotten, but since you're on the sick-list I'm in the hot seat." They were at the adjoining doors of their cabins and he gave Stone a push toward his own. With privacy at their command they were at liberty to relax. "I can pull rank on you all over the place till you're cleared for duty. Or till we're right out of the department. I can hand out all kinds of directives."

"Oh?" Stone perched on the edge of the reading desk. "Like?"

"Like, 'get those fatigues off and get in that bed, *soldier*,'" Jarrat barked in a drill sergeant tone, a legacy of his Army days, not so long in the past as they sometimes seemed. The service had molded Jarrat in so many ways. Some of them, he would never quite outgrow.

Stone's brows rose as he considered the proposition. He had never been Army — had never nursed much regard for that service before he met Jarrat. The Army worked the real colonial rim, out beyond the long-settled worlds, where the frontier grew wild, and syndicates, privateers and the immense terraforming corporations were at liberty to write their own law. As a service the Army was autocratic, and had to be, because a battle group often worked in complete isolation, cut off from its command structure. Fiefdoms generated themselves, on both sides of the law, and the next natural development was a corporate war, a violent blowout. Sheal.

"Well, soldier?" Jarrat prompted, in an amused tone now.

"Sounds like a decent idea." Stone stood, undressed clumsily, heeled off his boots and slid in between the cool synthetic sheets on Jarrat's bunk. Jarrat's eyes were hot on him, eating him alive. "Orders, Captain?"

Jarrat laughed. "Christ, forget it." He sat on the side of the bunk and leaned down to enjoy Stone's soft, open mouth. "You sure you feel up to this?" He was uncomfortably aware of the tremors in Stone's muscles, which he perceived as a strange, phantom weakness in his own.

"I feel okay," Stone told him. "Just a bit woozy, nothing much. Harry pumped so much stuff into me, I can feel myself mending. He gave me about a week's dose of every mineral and amino acid, proteins, glucose, ginseng, in one shot. Got to get on my feet before I lose muscle tone, apparently ... I'm getting frustrated though. Can't you tell?"

In fact, Jarrat could actually *feel* Stone's cock filling with every beat of his heart, feel the throb and pulse of a big erection. He put his hand on the sheet, pressed his palm over it and felt the steady pressure at his own groin. "God. What happens when I screw you? It's going to feel like you're screwing me." He paused. "Or I'm screwing myself."

"Interesting," Stone agreed. "There's no space for half-assed domination games even if we felt inclined to play them." He sighed, exasperated. "Kevin, will you just get in this bed, now, and stop worrying about it?"

"Worrying?" Jarrat pulled up short. Yes, he was apprehensive. "I'm not worried about having sex with you," he said tartly. "Just about being able to work with you, function as a unit. They're right, Stoney. They didn't write the rules for the fun of it or the convenience of grunts." He stood, stripped and let Stone's eyes devour him.

"So maybe we can't work together," Stone said quietly, watching as Jarrat gathered his clothes, which he had dropped in an untidy heap. "Maybe we go our separate ways after this. Different ships, different assignments. Take R&R together when we can fiddle the duty schedules."

Jarrat threw his jeans at the nearest chair. "You want that?"

"I want you." Stone was intent on his partner's groin. Jarrat was big, hard. His body was like whipcord, his skin like brown velvet, his cock blindly seeking its pleasure.

"You like what you're getting?" Jarrat asked huskily.

The emotional kickback from Stone was dizzying. They had never actually touched before in a state of arousal. One large, strong hand extended to take Jarrat's cock in a firm grip, and tugged him closer until the throbbing crown lay against Stone's waiting lips. Jarrat held his breath, aching for it. As the sucking began he felt it in his own nerves, felt its echo through Stone's. Weakening, he sagged onto the bunk.

"That good?" Stone whispered as he maneuvered Kevin into the bed. Jarrat squirmed in on top of him.

"You kidding?" Jarrat was on him, shoulder to shoulder, hip to hip. Bone and muscle rode together. "I'm going to fuck you till you think you've never been done before," he promised. "But not now. When you're strong enough for it, when we haven't got a half-finished war waiting for us. For now..." He began to hump against Stone's hard body. Stone kicked the sheet away. His long legs clenched about Jarrat's waist and hips.

Their mouths sealed hungrily. It was better than the Angel dream, Stone decided at once. It was real, not some figment of his frustrated imagination. It was Kevin Jarrat writhing and twisting in his arms. Beautiful, willful Kevin Jarrat, ravenous for him, biting his shoulders while that perfect ass undulated and the fine, hot shaft of him stroked the length of Stone's own erection. Maddening.

The empathy was overwhelming, driving them on. Stone was sweating heavily, his body slick against Jarrat's coolness. He felt feverish, knew he was still suffering the aftereffects of the drug. Jarrat was desperate now, cursing, his fingers like talons. Suddenly Stone wanted more.

"Kevin, wait. Kevin!" He knotted his hands into Jarrat's hair to stop him. "Do it to me. Come on, damn it, you know what I want. Put it where it's supposed to go. Do it right now." Jarrat's eyes were clearing but uncertain. "You want it spelled out? Fuck me, goddamn it!"

"You're not as strong as you think you are," Jarrat panted.

"Let me worry about that. Have you got anything to use?" Jarrat sat up and reached into the top drawer by the bunk. He rummaged among an odd collection of personal effects, and produced a tube. "This'll do. And before you say anything, yes, I'm a naughty boy, I don't deny it."

"Partial to indoor amusements?" Stone teased. "You haven't still got the ivory toy? The one those crewboys gave you as a gag-present?"

"No," Jarrat protested. "I gave it as a double-gag to Petrakis. You remember him, the pocket-size Starfleet courier pilot who was mooning after Gil Cronin and scored Joe Ramos instead, which must have been the 'David and Goliath' match of the decade." He gave Stone a rueful smile. "No, if I'm going to have something inside me, it's going to be part of you ... I always wanted this. Funny the way things have of working out." He uncapped the tube. "Okay, spread 'em." He daubed the lube into his palm and stroked it deep into Stone's body. Then he laughed shakily. "You're not exactly a shrinking virgin, Stoney."

"You wanted me to be?" Stone arched his head back into the pillow, eyes closed as Jarrat prepared him. His voice was a deep, bass purr. "Even if I had been before they caught me ... which I wasn't ... the shooter, Viotto, and some little punk called Roon would have changed all that."

Jarrat's fingers stilled, knuckle-deep. "Mavvik's toady, Brett Rooney?"

"Mm." Stone twisted on the fingers in him. "You know him?"

"I know him." Jarrat could barely breathe. The dual sensations were almost the end of him. His own anus quivered with Stone's pleasure. "You may like to know, Stacy'll be *interrogating* Roon about now."

"Good enough." Stone looked up into Jarrat's troubled face. "Kevin, we're neither of us factory-fresh. Does it matter so much?"

"It doesn't matter at all." Jarrat leaned down and kissed him. "Oh, God, you realize what this is going to feel like?"

"Do it." Stone's head tossed on the pillow. Kevin withdrew his fingers, moved up to cover him and lifted his legs. Jarrat knew he would feel everything, pleasure and pain alike, through the empathic link. Stone knew he would get every tremor from Jarrat in addition to his own physical sensations. He held his breath. When it came the sudden possession was like a shaft of lightning, unbearable, dizzying. Stone flew high as a kite as Jarrat moved in him. Steady, solid thrusts filled him. Heat and hardness seemed to force them both wide open. A moment's pain lanced back and forth as muscles protested and hearts raced. Then discomfort was a memory and

225

Stone's body broadcast its pleasure in vast waves, making Jarrat cry out. A long, languid slide of his cock into Stone's fierce grip, and he was no longer sure who was gasping, who was shouting.

Dizzy, they lay spent when it was over. Jarrat felt leaden. Against him, Stone was lax, limp. The comm chose that exact moment to buzz. Jarrat groped for it, selected voice-only and said windedly, "Yeah, Jarrat, what?"

It was Petrov. "Tac's data just came in, better late than never. I've called a briefing in a half-hour. Are you and Stoney cleared for duty?"

In fact, Jarrat was not sure. "Well, Reardon didn't *not* clear me," he told Petrov evasively. "I'll be there." With a herculean effort he slid out of the bunk and stepped into the shower stall.

He looked back at Stone as the water began to scald the skin off him. "You're not hurt. I don't have to ask. I can feel … everything. You're tired out, though."

"Tired, sore, weak," Stone yawned. "And lucky. I'm damned lucky to be alive, and I know it, kiddo. Good enough?"

"For the moment." Jarrat soaped his chest. "Just sweat the Angel out of you. Leave the rest of it to me. I owe Mavvik, for both of us. I —" He paused as the comm buzzed again. "Get that, will you?"

Voice-only was selected again. "Stone."

Reardon was on the line. "Just the man I wanted to see. You'll have to come down to the Infirmary again, soon as you can."

"What for?" Stone grumbled. "We only got out of there less than an hour ago."

"I need a set of readings to transmit with the telemetry," Reardon explained. "My fault. I should've taken them last time. I was so preoccupied with Del's work, I forgot a few details. Come on down, Stoney, what's the hardship? Drink coffee, share your gossip. It won't take long."

"You want Kevin too? Petrov's called a briefing in half an hour. One of us had better be there."

"No, it's part of your chemical analysis. I didn't need to run those tests on Kevin."

"Give me ten minutes." Stone killed the line and levered himself off the bunk. As he stood his back gave a twinge and he grunted cynically. "Damn. Reardon's going to know what you just did to me."

"If he sticks a scanner probe up there, he will." Jarrat shut off the water. He toweled dry and dropped a kiss Stone's mouth in passing before selecting fresh clothes. "Don't let Kip get malicious. There's no need. Central's not interested in your butt, just your bloodstream and your brain. If I remember anything about anatomy, that *ought* to be in the other end."

Stone caught the warm, dewily-naked body against him for a moment, then gave Jarrat a push. "Go. I'll humor Kip, and then get some sleep."

"Do that." Jarrat pulled on slacks and a shirt and slipped out of his cabin as Stone set the water.

Tactical's datafeed played on the big vidscreen in the ops room for the briefing. It was an edit of the observers' telemetry, forensic work and file searches. The weapons with which Death's Head had crippled Tactical were listed in redundant detail, down to the serial numbers, on an inventory supplied by Vincent Morello Aerospace. A similar but year-old manifest of goods stolen from Welland Dynamics provided the missing pieces. Gil Cronin was present with his second, Joe Ramos, and Curt Gable who would fly the Blue Raven gunship. All three men were muttering under their breath as they reviewed the details.

"These shit-kicking bloody private armies," Cronin said bitterly. "Security's a joke. "

And a sour joke at that, Jarrat agreed soundlessly. He sat at the head of the table with his hand on the remote, freezing and replaying segments. It would, he was sure, be the last such NARC operation he would oversee. When Central received Reardon's files, he and Stone must lose the carrier. He put the future from his mind to concentrate on the Tactical data.

The list of stolen weapons produced a general groan. Curt Gable was taking notes. Cronin and Ramos, who would lead in their descant unit as usual, merely swore, frequently and fluently. Petrov's face was like a thundercloud. He was in no physical danger, since he would monitor the run from the carrier's ops room, but often it was more rewarding to be in the field with the catharsis of action. Petrov had not said it, but he was looking forward to the chance to move up to the temporary rank of acting captain, partnering Scott Auel from the *Avenger*, while Jarrat and Stone drew an overdue furlough. Petrov and Auel might, Jarrat mused darkly, simply inherit the *Athena*. Both were good officers, in line for a command. But still, the thought stung. For some time he had come to think of the *Athena* as his own and Stone's. It was a complacent mistake.

As he plowed through the briefing, Jarrat was certain he had assumed the mantel of Raven Leader for the final time, and the session felt odd, off-center. Or perhaps the oddness was the result of trying to concentrate on statistics and strategy while he was painfully aware of Stoney, under his skin. Stone was in no condition to deploy, no matter what he claimed. Jarrat gritted his teeth as he felt Kip Reardon's examining hands on his partner's body. He felt Stone's irritation at being put through the whole NARC physical months ahead of the due date, and focused on the screen in an attempt to shut Stone out. There must be ways and means.

Morello and Welland were rich, powerful companies. Both maintained massive private armies for security purposes, to counter the private armies of their industrial competitors. When they fought it was hard, dirty, costly. Evelyn Lang's bleak memories of the bitter, bloody conflict on Sheal were the mirror of Jarrat's own. The two development companies were missing real hardware. Hawk, Avenger and Phoenix III missiles, automatic weapons, two rotary cannons, a man-portable charged-particle projector.

"Forget the energy weapon," Jarrat said shrewdly as he scanned the list. "I know the power system in the palace. Mavvik's on the Chell grid, no in-house generators. We can pull the plug on them before we deploy. They'd blackout half of Chell anyway if they tried to use that projector. Mischa, clear it through Power and General. I want them in the dark before we go in."

"You got it, Cap." Petrov also was making notes.

Cronin leaned forward across the table toward Jarrat. The lines and planes of his face could have been carved in stone "We'll still be jumping into hell. Hawks'll make dogmeat of us, let alone Avengers. And Phoenix IIIs could knock the gunship down. If we jump high to give the gunners a chance to get the missiles before they hit the ship, the Ravens are going to be confetti. If we jump low to let them bottom out fast, the gunners won't have time to get the missiles. The ship's a big, fat target."

"What else is new?" Jarrat asked cynically. "The Kronos system will scramble their missile guidance, which buys us back the odds."

"And they're still pretty damned long," Petrov added. "Decoys?"

"Right." Jarrat drummed his fingers on the table as he considered his options. He had served five years in the Army of Earth itself, not some corporate defense force, before transferring to NARC, and the wealth of experience stood him in good stead. "We've got twenty-five Blue Ravens, we'll deploy a couple of hundred decoys, nice and hot. If the heat-seekers go for anything, it'll be the rubber ducks. I figure two, maybe three casualties on the drop. A high drop, cannons cleared for anti-missile function. We can level the building prior to insertion, but I wouldn't count on bagging the shooters. If they lifted this gear from Morello and Welland, you can take it as read that they have enough surveillance hardware to see us coming from a couple of hundred klicks out. Added to which, the palace has several strongpoints, so they can get under cover — some old nuke bunkers and the vaults, down deep. If they were really smart they'd get out of there altogether and into vantage points higher on the mountain."

"How well are they trained?" Cronin asked shrewdly. He was looking at Jarrat for answers. Jarrat had spent two months as one of them.

"Not one among them is ex-military, though a lot were terrorist-trained. Mavvik's people might know one end of a rocket launcher from the other," Jarrat mused, "but you've got a lot of individuals with big mouths and competing egos, and vacuum between the ears. They're not a team. They'll mark targets, panic when they don't cut us into scrap with the first volley, and then they'll scatter."

"Catch or kill?" Ramos asked pointedly.

Jarrat shrugged. "Give them the choice. If they throw the guns down and start waving at you, Tac will be thrilled to take them in for intelligence work. But if they open fire on you, drop them fast. All of them." He paused. "So long as I get Hal Mavvik himself, you can have the rest."

"Revenge, Kevin?" Petrov asked quietly.

"Call it what you like." Jarrat sounded indifferent. He was too preoccupied with the sensations feeding through his body from Stone's. Stone was on his belly, something tickling his back. Jarrat had no idea what Reardon was doing but it felt peculiar. Would Kip read the telltale signs of recent sex? And if he did, what of it? The sex was not NARC's concern. Only the empathy worried Jarrat.

If he and Stone could convince the specialists it was controllable, that they could perform as efficiently as before, they had a chance. NARC might find a niche for them. It would not be the same niche they filled now, the risks were surely too high, but there could be other options. They had six weeks to make sense of their position before Central processed the current telemetry and a ship came out with an investigating officer.

Setting aside Stone's disturbing feelings with an effort, Jarrat gave Petrov a hard look. The Russian was making noises of concern at the suggestion of vengeance hunting. "I see your side of it, Kevin. I'd like to see shit kicked out of Death's Head as much as you would. Just don't let it get personal. It gets personal, it gets dangerous."

"It already is," Jarrat said bitterly. "If it's going to be my swansong, Mischa, I'm going to make it good."

Petrov sat back. "What time do you want this show to roll?"

"Have we got an Engineer's report on the Blue Raven gunship?" Jarrat asked. Down the table, Cronin produced a hardcopy, which Jarrat read through quickly. "Twelve hours. That suits us fine. I want darkness ... Call it 22:00, Chell time. Let Tactical have the details. Stacy is going to want prisoners. Tell him we'll do what we can. Okay, people, questions."

"Why don't we just throw a Pulson warhead at them from here?" Cronin muttered. "Save ourselves the aggravation."

"Civilians," Jarrat said glibly. "And I know — screw the civilians, you've said so before. But there must still be some innocent folks down there somewhere, and it's Death's Head we want, not them. The blast from a Pulson will take everyone out, they're not selective. Anyone else?"

"Who's Raven Leader?" Petrov asked quietly. Jarrat stiffened. The Russian exhaled through his teeth. "Has Reardon cleared you for duty? Jesus, Kevin, I saw your sheet from the clinic in Paddington. You were creamed!"

"And I was fixed," Jarrat said sharply.

"So has Reardon cleared you?" Petrov pressed.

"What is it, Mischa? You want to gaff this show yourself, is that it?" Jarrat gave the lieutenant a hard look. "What's on your mind? Say it!"

Petrov ran one hand over his close-cropped hair. "I don't want to get into deep shit with a squad leader who's likely to come unstuck. The Ravens will second me on that. Gil?"

"Sorry, Cap," Cronin said reluctantly. "If Doc Reardon signs you to duty, I guess I'll bite my tongue."

"I see." Jarrat swiveled his chair out from the table and stood. "Then I'd better go talk to Reardon. You're all on pre-op standby as of this time. Let's make it quick, hard and so damned loud, the dealers and bagmen down in Chell jump back in their holes and stay put till the middle of next year! If you need me, I expect I'll be in the Infirmary."

Jarrat stalked out of the briefing room and the meeting broke up behind him. He could feel Stone's anxiety. Reardon had finished with him now. He would be waiting for the same kind of verdict as Jarrat himself wanted. Fit to return to duty, even light duties? Jarrat left Petrov to dispatch the datafeed to Central and went directly to the Infirmary. The Tactical intel report accompanied the update. Soon enough the veterans in Venice, on Darwin's World, and right back in the NARC offices in Chicago, London and Tokyo, would be nursing their ulcers tenderly. The image made Jarrat almost smile. Technically, he and Stone should simply surrender command. Jarrat bit his lip, very much aware of the trouble that could descend from high places.

But if the Chell operation ran like clockwork he and Stone would be halfway to personal exoneration. Their commissions would be suspended, not simply terminated. Though they must be recalled and were sure to lose the carrier, they might remain with NARC in some active capacity ... if, Jarrat thought, they cared to make the commitment to Central's exhaustive evaluation and retraining requirements.

He was feeling his own aches as well as Stone's as he walked toward the Infirmary. If NARC work was not a man's vocation, it was a thankless occupation, high stress and high risk. He weighed the rewards of NARC service against those of an early retirement on a service pension. He and Stone would be out of the firing line and living well on superannuity. No more risks. *And no more kicks,* he thought, wary of his own admission of thrill-addiction. It could be as lethal as Angel.

Stone gave a grunt as another shot punctured his skin. Jarrat felt the sharp, stinging pain. As he entered the Infirmary Reardon was still scribbling notes. "Just a booster load of vitamins and mineral salts," he explained as Stone rubbed his arm. "To bring you right back up to par." He looked up as Jarrat appeared. "Oh, and here's the guilty party."

"Guilty of what?" Jarrat demanded, a little slow on the uptake or he might have expected what was imminent.

"For banging his little fanny an hour or two ago," Reardon said cheerfully. "Well, so long as you enjoyed yourselves."

"As a matter of fact, we did." Stone glared at the surgeon.

"Not my scene," Reardon said indifferently. He was thirty-five years married, with two daughters almost as old as Jarrat and Stone. "But it's whatever gets the old glands going for you." He angled a curious glance at Jarrat. "And you?"

"Me?" Jarrat felt a blush warm his cheeks. His own blush, or Stone's? It was difficult to tell, and he gave his partner, his lover, a sidelong glance.

"Did you enjoy him," Reardon asked succinctly. "It's for the psyche report. I have to ask, Kevin." He was waiting to note Jarrat's reaction, and even the obvious reluctance to speak would be recorded.

"Yes, I did. I always enjoy sex, and being in love makes it even better. What's it to you, Kip?"

He scribbled a line into the psyche profile and chuckled. "None of my business, kiddies, but the fellows at Central like to know every last detail. Anyway," he went on, speaking to Stone now, "you've had enough to dose an elephant in the last couple of days, proteins, enzymes, the works. You'll live." He surveyed the shot bruises along Stone's arms without comment.

"I get clean bill?" Stone watched Jarrat go quickly over the medical data for transmission. Kevin had sprawled on an unoccupied bed.

"I didn't say that." Reardon set aside his papers at last. "There's too much still floating around in you. You don't know how toxic you are."

"But I'm functional," Stone argued.

Reardon chuckled. "Up to a point." He gave Jarrat a rueful, mocking glance, then sobered. "But you're going to tire fast, get dizzy and fall on your face if you're not careful. What you need is a week in the sun, R&R, then a gentle warm-up program to ease you back into harness."

"Vacation?" Jarrat looked up from the file. "We've got leave coming up. Scott Auel will be transferring aboard to relieve us, leading Petrov."

"Petrov as acting captain," Reardon muttered. "That guy's wires are strung so tight, you could play a tune on his colon. Still, it's as well. Neither of you should be clear for duty, by the book." He looked pointedly at Jarrat. "The empathy ought to suspend you both, and you know it."

"We do. And I don't disagree with the system." Jarrat sat up and studied his palms. "But don't suspend us till after the op, Kip. Not till Mavvik is past tense."

The surgeon hesitated. "The decision remains mine."

Jarrat's gray eyes glittered like those of an angry cat. "Kip, don't do this to me. I can cut it."

"You think you can." Reardon thrust his hands into his pockets. "But can you cut it in a combat situation?"

"We'll never know till we try," Stone said quietly.

"If you can't, you're dead." Reardon looked probingly at them. "I don't want your deaths on my conscience."

"Damnit, Kip!" Jarrat rubbed his face hard. "If we screw up, we screw up. That's the way the game goes. Look, we owe Hal Mavvik big time. There's a score to settle. After the dust clears we'll play by your rules. In the meantime we're in charge till Scott Auel transfers over, and then you'll have Petrov, tight wires and all. There's a lot of pressure under his cork but he'll simmer down. Give him time." He stood, and his fists clenched. "Don't do this to me ... to *us*, Kip."

For a long, electric moment he and Reardon glared at one another, each trying the other's mettle, and then the surgeon shook his head in exasperation. "You're insane."

"Very possibly. Sign me to duty," Jarrat said brashly.

"And *I'm* insane," Reardon added. "I should lock you two up till further notice!" Instead, he punched keys, and Jarrat's name would appear on the duty roster moments later.

Jarrat relaxed muscle by muscle. "Thanks, and trust me. I can do this." Reardon looked doubtfully at him but forewent comment, as if he would merely wait for time to tell. Pick up the pieces later. Jarrat rubbed his flat belly distractedly. "You want dinner, Stoney? You're making me hungry."

"The empathy's that clear?" Reardon asked.

"I told him the lot," Stone said almost apologetically. "It has to figure in the evaluation, and Central have a right to know what they're getting for their money."

"I suppose they do. And yes, it's that clear, Kip. But we can manage." He accorded the doctor a challenging look. "Stand back and watch us.

Stone got his feet under him and stretched. "Empathy? You want me to tell you about Kevin's new knee? It's aching fit to cripple him but he's keeping his mouth shut." He gritted his teeth as he tried to shut out the feedback. Sometimes it could be more distressing than pleasant.

"Still bothering you?" Reardon selected a scanner probe.

"A bit." Jarrat watched the delicate instrument examine his leg. "Not surprising. Harry rebuilt the whole thing almost from scratch. It twinges a great deal bit it's stronger than the old joint. Synthetic ligaments, regenerated nerves. Harry's wife is the bio-engineer, she made the replacements. I was impressed. So, you're letting Stoney out of here?"

"Free to go." Reardon turned off the probe. "So long as he rests." He gave Stone a hard look. "I realize this is like asking the nine-year-old to put the new bike back in the shed and dig into his homework, but do yourself a favor, Stoney. Rest. Stay off each other's backs for a few days, will you?"

"I'll make you a deal," Stone offered. Reardon waited with a pained expression. "You take care of your business, I'll take care of mine." Stone graced the older man with a smile and left the Infirmary on Jarrat's heels.

The officers' mess was empty at that hour. It was a long time since Jarrat had felt genuinely hungry, but Stone's growling innards were a sharp discomfort. He chewed mechanically as he watched the other man eat, and relayed the battle plans set down at the briefing. Stone looked up at him over the meal, met Jarrat's eyes and colored with a faint, attractive blush. Everything was different between them now. Jarrat had known it must be. Did Stone welcome the changes, or resent them? Jarrat searched his own feelings.

"Kevin?" Stone prompted, well aware of Jarrat's apprehensions.

"Hm? Oh, it's the future that bothers me, not the Death's Head bust. Look, don't let me hassle you. Shut me out. Think of something else ... Schedules and strategies." He trusted the empathy to convey his resolve to make sense of their predicament.

Stone went over the battle data mentally and approved Jarrat's decisions. He looked at the chrono as he began on dessert and drained his coffee almost to the dregs. "Twelve hours and we go."

"We?" Jarrat echoed. "What's this about *we?*"

"We as in, you and me," Stone retorted. "There's a man down there I'd like to meet face to face for three full seconds before he pulls a cannon on me ... and I close his file. Permanently."

"Hero's prerogative, old son." Jarrat tapped his own chest. "You'll be up here on your duff, monitoring carrier communications. You heard Kip."

"Kip told me to take it easy and not fuck too much," Stone argued. "So I'll take it easy. Riot armor takes the hard work out of standing up. I can adjust my weight to thirty kilos. Forget it, Kevin. I'm going with you."

"You're not duty cleared!"

"So you clear me." Stone clattered down the empty mug and met his partner's furious eyes. Their pupils dilated as emotions from outside rushed into Jarrat. Stone sighed. "Don't look at me like that, Kevin. I know what you're feeling. If we're not careful everyone else will too. It doesn't matter much, they can take it or leave it, but ... you know Gilly Cronin's going to rib the life out of us." The attempt at levity was flat. Stone sobered. "Kevin, I want Mavvik. I want him for what he did to you."

"He ordered you crammed full of Angel," Jarrat retorted.

"He ordered you done the hard way," Stone said quietly. "And they took turns to mangle you every way they could think of. I heard it all on radio. Mavvik's *mine.*"

Jarrat looked away. "I was debating how much to tell Kip. I wound up just giving him Jeff Bolt's data. He ought to have the details. I know I'm mended, give or take a few aches and pains, but you — I'm not so sure. You're still soaked in Angel. You'll be lucky if the evaluators don't pump you for dream realities."

"The horny details?" Stone said dubiously. "Psyche testing?"

"Angel dreams would tell the examiner a lot about a guy's subconscious," Jarrat said flatly. "Be prepared for them to ask. They will. That's a hell of an imagination you've got, Stoney."

"When I was a kid, I had a teacher who said I should be a novelist." Then Stone reached over the table and took Jarrat's wrist in a vice-grip. "Sign me to duty."

But Jarrat shook his head. "You could hardly stand up yesterday."

"That was yesterday." Stone took a deep breath. "Give me a chance at Mavvik, Kevin. I'm only going to get one crack at this and it's just a piece of paper getting in the way."

The fury punched into Jarrat so hard he caught his breath. He looked at Stone's fingers which circled his wrist like a manacle and sighed. "All right. It's your neck if you want to break it. But do as Kip says till showtime. The action should be short and sweet. Christ, how much energy can you burn off, sitting on your bum in riot armor in the shuttle?" He swore eloquently. "But I'm telling you right now. If I see Mavvik first, he's mine. Don't get in my way. Fair enough?"

"Fair enough." Stone returned to his meal, picking over the dessert. He was no longer hungry, Jarrat knew. The empathic feedback crackled, blue-white, like an energy field. Stone exhaled through his teeth. "This is not going to be easy. I get angry, you get angry, and the two of us angry together is exhausting."

"So hit the sack," Jarrat told him tersely. "*Alone.*" He clamped down on the distressing wave of Stone's turbulent emotions. "I've got a million things to do and you need the rest."

He left Stone sleeping and entered his name into the duty roster with reluctance. Reardon would take a dim view of his decision if he happened to check the crew rotation schedules, but the final responsibility lay with Jarrat. Make or break. Stone could make a show of it, but Jarrat was uncomfortably aware of what was going on inside him. As he left the cabin and took the elevator down to the hangar bays, Stone began to dream. Jarrat felt vibration and vertigo. Was he dreaming of flying? Something powerful enough to compress the chest, shake the spine and fill him with a kind of wild joy.

The red spinners were on in the Blue Raven launch bay. Jarrat stood in the inner airlock, watching Cronin and Budweisser climb over the black metal hull with a battery of scanners. They were suited up in riot armor and the bay was open to space. At last, satisfied with this phase of the work, Budweisser signaled the hangar controller. The hatch rumbled shut in the carrier's belly, vibrating the deck beneath Jarrat's feet, and cycling machines blasted hot air into the bay. Still, the air was cold as the wind off a glacier when the lights turned to green, the airlock released and he stepped out onto the ringing metal deck.

Helmet under his arm, Cronin waved as he saw him coming. "Hey, Cap ... Kevin, no hard feelings. Petrov's got a big mouth. I was just sweating for my boys. It could get vicious down there."

Without a word Jarrat strode to the nearest terminal and punched up the roster. His name appeared at the head of it. "Satisfied, Gil?"

Cronin puffed out his cheeks. "I'm glad to have you with us." He dropped his voice. "Most of my lads are screaming for blood. We lost five in the last fracas, dead before they made it back to the carrier. Two were from our own unit. Petrov can say what he likes, but you know the truth: it's not justice we want, it's *revenge.* I know how you feel, Kevin."

"Do you?" Jarrat smiled faintly at the much bigger Cronin. The huge figure in mirror-black armor shadowed him as they left the freezing launch bay. In two years he had come to know Cronin well and call him a friend. "You want to get one back for Stoney?"

"And for you. And for the Blue Ravens who bought it." As they entered the Ravens' ready room Cronin drew off his gloves, preparatory to desuiting. "I heard the scuttlebutt. Mavvik's shooting his mouth off on the subspace band. It'll be all over this sector soon, how the NARC-*Athena* Ravens let a craphead whip them, and let both field rank officers get pulped." He broke the seals and lifted off the breastplate. "We're not proud."

"Bruised honor?" Jarrat took the armor section from him and placed it into storage in Cronin's locker. "Honor comes at a price, Gilly."

"And we're ready to pay up," Cronin said flatly. "We owe you. If Colonel Stacy hadn't screwed up his operation you'd have had better cover. That night you were beat up, Red Raven were mopping up Tactical's mess, or they'd have been with you before you got caught. And when Stoney was shot down half of us were flying topcover for Tac 101 because Stacy didn't evac his whole shitty command post when his observers tracked a brace of incoming missiles. We figure we owe you and Stoney."

Surprised, pleased, Jarrat allowed a smile. "I never knew you cared."

"You kidding?" Cronin clambered out of the lower armor. "We all know you'll be shipping out after this go 'round. Chell's going to be the last ballgame they let us play together." He offered his hand and Jarrat took it. "We've had a good run, Kevin. But it's time you and Stoney shove off before it happens for real. You've worn out your luck. That's what me and the boys reckon."

Jarrat's brows arched. "You and the boys could be right." He stirred restlessly, uncomfortably aware of the time. "I'd better check out my gear. I'll catch you later, Gil."

He busied himself, checking every piece of armor, every weapon, a pre-battle ritual as old as the warrior tradition. It could be the last time. Reardon would have his way and Petrov would get the temporary promotion he hungered for, monitoring the carrier's operations at field rank, with Scott Auel from the *Avenger*. Auel was a good guy, a year or so younger than Jarrat. He had been aboard the *Avenger* for six months before Jarrat transferred over to the *Athena*, and Kevin remembered him well. Scott's record was good, he got results, and he knew how to look after his people.

For the first time, Jarrat felt the reins of command physically slipping through his fingers, and was unsure if he should snatch them back. First, he and Stone drew scheduled leave. Then a clipper would arrive from Earth, on its way through the colonies, stopping at Rethan for a matter of hours before heading on across the rim. And the sword of Damocles would fall from a great height.

Deliberately, Jarrat put the future from his mind. If his career was finished, it was the price of Stone's life. And it was a cheap price to pay. A new hardsuit with the words 'Capt. R.J. Stone' stenciled on it stood with his own in the officers' suiting room, adjacent to the shuttle hangar.

He drew rotary cannons, stun projectors and snappers from armory. They went into storage in the shuttle's underdeck lockers. He lifted himself into the fore cockpit and preflighted the aircraft's systems. A mechanic would have done the work, but Jarrat continued the old pilot's superstition and did the job himself.

As he finished an armory tractor growled toward him, loaded with Phoenix III missies. He stood back to watch the shuttle primed with everything it could carry. As the tractor rumbled away again he looked at the time. Eight hours, and they would be in the air.

He returned to the cabin to find Stone dead asleep, and his own body, so recently repaired, was aching, tired. Rather than disturb Stone's rest he slid into the bunk in the adjoining cabin, and set the computer for a wake-up call with two hours' grace before the Blue Ravens went to prelaunch standby. Tired though he was, sleep was hard to find.

CHAPTER TWENTY-ONE

The Blue Raven hangar rang with activity. The mechanics were tinkering with the gunship's engines even now, though the big ship was on launch alert. Jarrat watched them through the suiting room's open doors as he got into the armor. He had a headset on, and as he locked up the kevlex-titanium sections he called, "Jarrat, looking for Petrov."

The Russian was in the ops room already, setting up the comm-relay terminals to monitor every NARC aircraft. "Petrov," he responded tersely.

"Are we cleared with Tac and Power and General?"

"Tac will monitor our audio, and Stacy had the presence of mind to buy time with their usual synthetic aperture provider," Petrov reported. "Chell P&G are standing by to blackout on our signal."

"Buzz Blue Raven," Jarrat said quietly. "Time to launch the show." The gunship's engines roared for a moment. A wave of heat blasted across the hangar deck and he turned his back on the acrid draught. He was waiting for Stone. If Stoney slept through the Blue Ravens' call, so much the better. He would be furious later, but Jarrat would endure. And then Kevin felt the subtle stirring of Stone's emotions as he woke, the pleasant rush of affection as he thought of his lover ... the jolt of anxiety and annoyance as he noticed the time and began to hurry. Jarrat was waiting for him when he appeared from the heavy armory elevators. Helmet under his arm, he waved one gloved hand and Stone gave him a slightly obscene salute.

"You're a bastard, Kevin. You'd have let me sleep."

"Damned right," Jarrat said mildly as he stood back to watch Stone rush through the task of suiting up. They shared the same tensions and apprehensions. It was unnerving, and they could only make the best of it. Deliberately, Stone lifted on the armor, and each piece locked into the next with a dull, mallet-sound. The suit flexed at the joints and as each segment locked down it was completely sealed against pressure, radiation, temperature. Its repulsion came up gradually on automatic to neutralize a load which would otherwise put a man on the deck. As Stone sealed the gloves and set his apparent mass at thirty kilos a red spinner began to blink across the hanger, the warning that the whole bay would depressurize in five minutes.

Jarrat put a hand on his partner's arm. "Last chance to back out," he offered quietly. "Be very sure, Stoney. It's going to be rough."

"I'm sure." Stone settled the helmet on his head and screwed the umbilici into place. He was pacing out toward the shuttle as Jarrat closed the lockers.

The digitals of the helmet displays, ten centimeters from Jarrat's nose, showed both shiptime and Chell time. It was three hours after sundown in the equatorial city. Hal Mavvik would be selecting a woman from his stable of expensive imports ... Lee would be painting his beautiful body for the evening. Tiger stripes, warpaint, jewelry, and he would be ready to combine business with pleasure as only the professional Companion knew how. Jarrat hoped to God the kid knew where the palace's hardpoints were, and ducked for cover at the first shot. For Lee to be killed the way Riki Mitchell had died would be too much. Lee would certainly be in the palace, but unless he was with one the shooters or a guest, he would be on his own time. Sometimes he danced in the games room. Down below that room was a deep vault, an old nuke bunker they used as a wine cellar. *Dive in, kiddo,* Jarrat prayed as he followed Stone.

The moment's fretting transmitted clearly to Stone. He looked back over his shoulder, one hand on the steel rung of the boarding ladder. "What's the matter, Kevin?"

"There was someone at the palace. A Companion called Lee. A gorgeous kid. He's going to be a casualty unless he has the luck of the devil."

"Like Riki." Stone mirrored all Jarrat's wayward emotions. "You're really fond of him."

"I was. I shared a bed with him for two months," Jarrat admitted. "He's an uptown hustler, and a real beauty. I don't want to be in the morgue, IDing him the way I did Riki Mitchell."

"Same story all over," Stone said regretfully. "Poor little Riki. Jesus, if he'd lived long enough, just another week, Harry might have been able to do for him what he did for me."

Pain from Stone threaded like hot needles through Jarrat's nerves. "Don't punish yourself," he said quietly before they keyed their helmet comm system to the Blue Ravens' busy loop. "It happens, Stoney. Fate."

"Pragmatist," Stone accused.

"Cynic," Jarrat corrected as he climbed the side of the boarding platform and let himself down into the fore cockpit. "I watched you fight Angel. Riki didn't have to go through the ugliness. I can see a lot to be thankful for."

In fact, he was right. Stone mounted the side of the ringing, yellow metal stepway after him and lowered the bulk of the suit into the rear cockpit. Anger churned to the surface and his fingers itched to feel Mavvik's throat. "I owe his family an explanation," he said as Jarrat rode out the wave of his fury. "They'll say I got Riki killed, you know. I don't want to tell them the truth. That Rik was already as good as dead. A user."

"They don't need to know," Jarrat agreed quietly as he keyed into the loop. "Raven Leader to Blue Raven Hangar Central. Ready to roll."

"Hangar Central. You are cleared to proceed, Raven Leader."

The voice belonged to a Starfleet staffer Jarrat knew. Her name was Krystal Jones; her uncle was a bigshot general, high-up in one of the Starfleet R&D divisions. Strings had been pulled to get her into NARC fast, when her husband became an Angel statistic. Jones was still riding the idealistic crusade which brought many people to NARC, and Jarrat spared a moment to wonder where his own idealism had gone. Any long-term veteran knew it for a costly self-indulgence, while cynicism came cheaply. But at the moment he almost envied Jones the passion.

"Thank you, darling. On our way." He checked the onboard deck and both CRTs, which even then were relaying data directly to Petrov, rotated his guns in test mode and scanned the boards for red enunciators. All flight systems were clear. "All Raven units, launch procedures."

The hangar crew ran for cover as sirens wailed. The breathing mix was pumped out of the sealed compartment by powerful extractors, reducing the whole bay to a few bars above vacuum before the hangar's hatches in the belly of the carrier opened to space. Across the black decking, the gunship's repulsion was running up, neutralizing its mass, but the shuttle nosed out before it lifted. Jarrat was flying from the fore cockpit, his hands feather-light on the delicate controls. The plane responded like an uptown hustler, sensitive to the slightest caress. Both he and Stone had qualified in fighters only after transferring to NARC. Flying was a joy they had always shared, and Jarrat felt Stone's thrill as the plane dropped out into space.

As they looped up from the belly of the carrier they spared it a glance. The *Athena* was a big ship, almost a kilometer from her blunt bow to her massive sterntubes. She looked like a silver-gray whale, idling through the navy-black ocean of space. The four gunships launched as Jarrat watched, Green and Gold Ravens looping in around the carrier's spine. Five NARC craft assumed a loose formation, five pilots turned their attention to the glaring crescent of the planet below and the comm loop was busy with coded signals.

Rethan was velvet black beyond the terminator, blue and white on the sunward side, with the dense haze of the oxygen-nitrogen atmosphere which had made the planet so attractive to terraformers. Near-Earthlike environments were rare and precious. Many colony worlds were a challenge to technology and humans alike, and the humans who opened up those worlds were becoming subtly *different*. Jarrat was thinking soberly about Harry Del as he frowned down at the crescent of Rethan. From orbit it looked serene. The truth was another matter. Chell lay on the dark side, just past the west-creeping line where night met day.

The shuttle's wings heated, glowed, as it bucked through reentry. Jarrat was on channel 95, the security band, to clear their flight path with the spaceport. Tactical had already given notification of the coming action. The NARC aircraft received clearance to proceed without question. Civil air traffic was on hold, rerouted, until the all-clear was broadcast. Chell Field was oddly quiet, and the airlanes over the city were reduced to domestic traffic which would disperse, spontaneously disappear, when the action began. Stacy himself had elected to ground his flyers and instead put every road squad he possessed into the zone, to minimize airborne confusion.

"Raven Leader to Blue Raven 6." Jarrat cast a glance at his CRT for a fix on the gunships. They were riding his tail, strung out two and three klicks behind the shuttle. "Coming up on target. Standby with decoys and full-spread ECM, and jump *fast*. Remember, they'll surely see us coming."

"Shit," Cronin muttered, just in the audible range. "You have to keep saying it?"

The smog blanket obscured the city lights. Above the smogline, rich people's dream houses shone like beacons, parklands were floodlit green oases, landscaped pools shone with submerged lights. Hal Mavvik's palace was bright, but almost in the instant Stone saw it on the observer's CRT it went dark. "Right on cue," he whispered. "Blackout."

The ship-to-ship loop was alive with crosstalk. The gunners were on target acquisition mode as the gunships dropped in over the palace. On the Blue Raven flight deck Curt Gable said, "Kronos jamming is on. Hello ... you're right, Cap Jarrat, they've got the gear: they see us. I'm tracking a big groundie. Speedy limousine by the looks of it, leaving in an ass-burning hurry on Clearway 7, from the rear of the palace ... whoever it is has better sense than to try a getaway by air! You want to bet it's Mavvik?"

"I'd bet next year's pay," Jarrat said acidly. "Can you get a shot at it, Curt?" Not that he wanted Mavvik accounted for so easily, so impersonally, but they could not afford risks.

"I can *paste* it," Gable said glibly, "if you don't mind writing off a few dozen civvy buses. He's about to run into crosstown traffic, which was his plan from the start: he can use the street for cover."

"Track him as long as you can," Jarrat advised. "Get Tactical on it. We don't want to lose the bugger on round one!"

Then Cronin was on the air: "Over the dropzone. Stand by to insert."

Gable again: "Rubber ducks ready to go — woah! Missiles away below. I'm reading twenty flaretails, could be any variety."

The shuttle responded like a startled greyhound under Jarrat's sensitive hands. He sent it looping into the Blue Raven gunship's cover, putting the big ship's armor between it and the missiles as the other three gunships came in to cover for them. Tracer and laser blazed out of four port gunbays as the NARC shooters marked their targets and loosed enough fire into the air to intercept the warheads. Sunbursts glared briefly as they detonated, and the air was filled with windmilling shards of twisted steel enveloped in incandescent gasses. Shrapnel tore into the gunship's armored flanks but the missiles had blown before they hit.

The volley was followed by a period of quiet. In it, Cronin yelled, "Blue Ravens away! Red Ravens, follow us in." Jarrat and Stone watched the strange, exoskeletal shapes drop fast out of the bellies of the gunships, their numbers swelled by a vast flock of hot, radio-noisy decoys.

"Dummies are away," Gable reported. "Heads up — incoming missiles. I'm counting sixteen."

Flaretails chased up out of the blackness below. Multiple detonations rolled one on top of another as they homed on the radiant, chattering decoys, and anything getting through was picked off by the gunners. Whoops of celebration cut across the comm loop before the gunners turned their attention to Target Alpha. The palace itself.

As the descant units went down fast, surrounded by decoys, the NARC shooters switched to standard Hawk warheads, air-to-ground demolition rockets, locked on target by laser acquisition. Forty Hawks slammed into the building, and in moments the palace was a memory. In its place was a vast eruption belching smoke, as if the mountain had become a volcano. Art collections, priceless cars, expensive whores and all, it was gone. And Lee? Jarrat prayed silently that the kid was in the old nuke shelter under the games room, or in the deeper vaults. Lee deserved better than to pay for Mavvik's crimes. He felt a spreading, consuming satisfaction as they watched the palace erupt.

Stone chuckled with brief, rueful humor. "You enjoyed that."

"What's not to enjoy?" Jarrat jinked the aircraft around to get a clear camera angle on the Blue Ravens. "But it's just a building. Unless they were all dumb enough to run inside and hide when they saw us coming, they're out here waiting to snipe at us. Raven Leader to Blue Raven 6, anything doing, Gil?"

Gil Cronin was watching 9mm semiautomatic fire ricochet off his armor. He brought up the rotary cannon and put a hundred rounds into the gazebo where the shooter lay poorly concealed. His armor-piercers cut through the construction like a chainsaw. Inside it, the man came apart in a welter of red. "They're ambitious," he told Jarrat. "With any luck they'll have thrown all their missiles at the gunship. It could get shitty if they've kept any back, but we must have knocked down fifty."

Curt Gable was listening to them. "We tracked fifty-three hits, Gil."

"Two million's worth of hardware," Stone said dryly. "Not bad for under a minute's work. What did Morello and Welland list as stolen?"

"Fifty-*five*," Jarrat read of his CRT. "So unless there were two duds, they could have a couple tucked away in reserve somewhere, and they'll punch through riot armor like eggshells. Watch yourself, Gil."

"Same occurred to me," Cronin muttered. His voice was drowned out as another explosion ripped through the night. All at once thousands of rounds seemed to be in the air and he yelled, "Cover! *Cover!*"

"The arsenal," Jarrat guessed. "Christ, listen to what's cooking off. They must have had enough stockpiled to flatten half the city."

"They've been arming for some time ... after the Black Unicorn bust, it's not so surprising," Stone mused. "And they didn't let you see the arsenal when you were here," he concluded as he clearly felt Jarrat's surprise at the enormity of the explosion.

"It wasn't here then. They must have decided to tool-up for a doomsday run when I blew it that night, let the gorilla jump me." Jarrat whistled through his teeth. "No wonder the bastards fancied their chances."

Clouds of toxic smoke belched from the building Jarrat had known as a garage. Ammunition and explosives were still going up sporadically when Cronin barked at the Blue and Red Ravens to spread out and cover the perimeter. Above them, as they got to their feet and began to fan out, the Gold and Green Ravens deployed as backup and topcover. Tracer leapt up like bolts of laser in the darkness. NARC rotary cannons howled in answer as blazing phosphor grenades burst among the descant units.

"Now, that's nasty," Stone observed as Jarrat panned the cameras over the scene below. Save for the armor, phosphor weapons would turn a man into bubbling marshmallow.

On the vidscreens they watched Joe Ramos uncoil the snapper and charge it. The uninsulated cable sang out like a whip and flung a man to the ground where he lay twitching, reverberating with the stunning electrical discharge. It was a mob dispersal measure but equally effective on the battlefield.

The Red Raven gunship dropped in low over the palace ruins as cries went up for a Medevac squad. Jarrat watched the armored medics lift three men out fast. They went up, weightless on gravity resist. Shots punched into them as they rose swiftly into the aft hatches, and Jarrat knocked the safeties off his triggers. Down below, a shooter had taken cover behind the fountains. A sculpture of Ganymede, seated on a flying swan, shattered into a million fragments as he tripped the massive rotary cannons.

The shooter was gone when he released the triggers, and Jarrat swore. "Damn. I liked that fountain."

Before Stone could make any glib remark Curt Gable shouted over the confusion of the Ravens' audio: "I've lost the ground car, Jarrat. It tucked into the jumble of the traffic. I can't pinpoint it any longer. Tac sent out a groundie patrol but they didn't connect. Too much traffic trying to get out of the zone at one time, the roads are a nightmare."

"Shit," Stone hissed. "That's just great. What's the last position you had on him, Curt?"

"Take a look for yourself. I don't know Chell, but Jarrat might make sense of the map." Gable's data was on Stone's CRT a moment later.

Both Jarrat and Stone were intent on the screens. They saw the car, heading south into the urban clutter of the city, depicted as a red blip on a blue grid-sectioned map. The signal grew less distinct as it went, until tracking was unable to pick a single vehicle from the fleeing mob. Jarrat watched the display bitterly. He was about to call Tactical for a report when intuition hit him like a physical blow.

The icy fingers of his hunch found their way into Stone's nerves too. "What is it, Kevin? What are you thinking?"

"I know where the sonofabitch is going. There, just ahead of the point where Curt lost him. That's the old Drummond Park. The arena, the old stadium. It's scheduled for demolition but they haven't started work yet, and I know for a fact Death's Head uses it. The place is — Jesus, Stoney, what's wrong? You feel —"

Stone's insides had given a painful lurch, his heart was pounding, making Jarrat's pulse race. "Mavvik keeps a safeplace there. They took me to the stadium after they crammed the Angel into me. I was high but I came to a couple of times. I remember the place, big and empty, with a warren underground. They took the armor off me down there. He'll already be inside, Kevin. He's got a stash, guns, ammo, supplies, the lot. I caught a few glimpses. Blue Raven 6, what is your situation?"

Cronin replied at once. "Resistance is weakening. These bozos are too keen to wake up in the morning to stand up and fight. They're starting to scatter. I'll see if we can round them up for Stacy to play with, but I couldn't give a fuck about Tac Intel, Cap. It stinks at the best of times."

"Blue Raven gunship," Jarrat called, "Red Raven gunship, stand by the descant units. Gold and Green, pull out and fly topcover. Report to the carrier. Raven Leader is going to pursue the runaway. Lieutenant Gable, take over data gathering."

"Will do," Gable called. He was already preoccupied with incoming signals. "Good hunting, Cap. Buy yourself another killflag."

"Thanks," Jarrat said grimly, and then to Stone, "It's Mavvik. You can bet your pension on it."

The shuttle arced tight about the mountain and Jarrat turned the nose down into the smog. He was flying blind on instruments now, literally navigating by the streets. The crowns of massive buildings adorned with aerials, lightning conductors, a/c plants, loomed up out of the gloom and the ramjets thundered back off the city walls. He imagined the panic down below and the outcry in the media, but ignored the problem.

Shouting always erupted after any NARC action. People did not want any kind of conflict fought out on their streets. But they also screamed for blood when one in ten kids in college was using Angel and would not live to get his degree. Parents lusting for vengeance became cruel vigilantes. Hapless dopeheads died as often as dealers and bagmen. Jarrat thought fleetingly of the vigilante killing in Ballyntyre, and Joel Assante, who had run out on Mavvik at the first sign of this war. Right about now, many other shooters on the Death's Head payroll would have begun to wish they had gone with him.

There was only one way to stop the disease of Angel, in any city: shut down the syndicate that ran the local trade, permanently. In a matter of minutes a city could throw off its bondage, but toes were always going to be trodden in the action and in the morning the newsvids were going to be poisonous. When the underworld lawyers began to whine Jarrat reread the official NARC sanction and closed his ears. It was enough that the Angel-pack was muzzled for a time.

Drummond Park had been closed for years. A bigger, better stadium had been built thirty kilometers away. The old ballpark dated from almost a century before, when the city itself was new, and was now rated structurally unsound. Jarrat had never been inside. He had heard mention of it in the palace several times, and knew Mavvik kept an emergency facility in the bowels of the place. He had often driven by on his way to play the part of the tough, ruthless young contract shooter.

How much did Mavvik have here? Missiles? Hawks and Avengers could hurt the shuttle badly. The aircraft was the same in every detail as the plane in which Stone had been shot down. Anxiety fed into Stone and rebounded back into Jarrat. "Cool down, Kevin," Stone whispered. "Keep low. He's going to hear the jets but the noise is bouncing around, chances are he won't know which direction we're coming from."

Jarrat's teeth closed on his lip as he dropped the spaceplane to roof-top level and rode the contours of the cityscape. He kept the Kyral Industries plant between the plane and the stadium until he was almost over the perimeter fence, and then the rearing walls of the grandstand were before him. At zero feet he nudged the shuttle forward over the vast, deserted parking lot.

"He won't take a shot at us if we're inside," he mused, largely for the benefit of the helmet recorders. The specialists at Central liked to pry into a man's head, know what was going through his mind as he worked. "If he tried to take out the shuttle that way he'd blow the whole stadium and go up with it. Hold tight." He lifted the plane fifty meters on its blustering repulsion and then dropped it in fast. It set down on the stout hydraulics in the middle of the soccer pitch. Jarrat flipped on the groundsearch to take a complete reading of the stadium, and swore.

"Heat traces," Stone read off. "They're here. That's the car. Other side of the grandstand, in the parking bay. I'm not reading much. Jesus, this place is a maze."

"Where did they take you?" Jarrat asked as he completed the sensor sweep and released the canopy. He lifted out the deck plates at his feet and groped for his weapons.

"Down below. There's a tunnel, left of the centerline, I don't remember too much after that." Stone paused then, looking at the CRT. "Over by the goal, Kevin, what is that? A heat signature? It's very faint."

"Feral cats," Jarrat guessed. "These old places are infested with them. Vermin of all kinds." He reached down into the underdeck compartment. "You stay in the plane, cover for me."

"Not on your life," Stone hissed. "Unless Mavvik's up in the grand-stands somewhere — and if he was we'd have him on sensors — you're going to be in the tunnels. As soon as you get out of sight I can't cover for you worth a damn." He was pulling out the deck plates as he spoke.

Jarrat swore. "All right, Stoney. You win. I just hope you know what you're doing. It looks like we're going hunting in the dark."

"It's just as dark for Mavvik," Stone reminded him wryly. "Darker, maybe, if he doesn't have imaging gear."

The riot armor had thermographic, infrared and vision intensification equipment. All were commercially available, though exorbitantly expensive when they appeared in the civilian market. Jarrat did not count them a luxury. If Mavvik had them — and he must have — imaging systems were a necessity. He locked the rotary cannon into its clamps on the right forearm plate, locked the stun projector into its fixture and clipped the coiled snapper into place on the left thigh panel.

"You got your gear on, Stoney?"

"And ready to mark a target," Stone said grimly. "If he's up here."

"He'll be in the tunnels. The man is devious. I know him, remember." Jarrat gasped as Stone's emotions rolled powerfully into him. Anger, resentment, naked hatred.

The empathic feedback might have been distressing, but since both of them were generating very similar impulses and both were focused on the same specific objective, Jarrat found the intruding emotions less troublesome. But he was keenly aware of a disquieting sense of being hounded, driven. He and Stone were goaded by each other's tensions. They shared the same hunger to have the job done. Petrov might have called it a lust for vengeance. Jarrat could live with that.

The canopy whined up and they dropped lightly to a battered carpet of artificial turf, long ago threadbare. Jarrat closed up the aircraft. Against anything short of missiles, a hull designed to withstand reentry and fly at Mach 15 in atmosphere would be imperious. Even the canopy was a lexan compound, closer to armor plate than plastex.

They went onto vision intensification and scanned the whole stadium. It was dark as the pit under the blanket of smog, and the Drummond and Lambeth sectors were industrial, just fields of robot factories, barely half-lit at the best of times. Power was still on in the factories, which were independent, but the illumination was poor and Jarrat saw nothing. Tension crackled between him and Stone like a Kirlian field. The stadium was depicted in the helmet displays, outlined in lime green, grotesque, forbidding, but nothing moved.

Jarrat had begun to turn toward the tunnel mouth when a bright streamer of automatic fire, lit up by tracer rounds, leapt out of the side of the grandstand. The shooter was wide of his target but held the trigger down, correcting as he went. The rounds caught Jarrat in the chest and shoved him backward toward the shuttle's heat-shimmering hull. He kept to his feet with an effort.

Two rotary cannons howled in unison. Concrete and plastex exploded in the grandstand and the shooter was silent. Stone had registered the impacts of the shots as surely as Jarrat had felt them. His heart pounded and sweat prickled his ribs. He turned up his suit's repulsion and set his apparent weight down to forty kilos.

"You okay?" Jarrat asked quietly.

"You can feel —?" Stone said no more, since every word was being recorded.

"Of course I can bloody feel it!" Jarrat's own heart echoed Stone's uncomfortably. "Stay with the plane."

But at forty kilos Stone felt light, and jogged easily toward the grandstand to look for a heat signature. He found several faint ones. The shooter was scattered in so many pieces among the first class ticket-holders' seats. "One down," he said tersely. "No more up here."

"They'll have ducked below when they heard us coming," Jarrat muttered. "Do you —"

And then a blast of static cut him off in mid-sentence and Stone swore. Full-spectrum jamming. He switched up to the higher bands but found no way to get over it. He keyed to channel 95. "Raven 7.1 to *Athena*." No response. "Raven 7.1 to Blue Raven gunship!" Still nothing. He took a breath and cast about for Jarrat. The lime green environment of vision intensification was alien, hostile. He turned on his public address. "Kevin. Kevin!" But the flood of powerful ECM had even overridden the helmet mics as well as some of his sensor systems. He was hearing nothing from the outside. The only sounds in his ears were his own breathing and the quiet blips from his helmet instruments. He was totally deaf-mute, and it was a bad feeling.

It was moments later when he realized, he knew exactly where Jarrat was without looking for him. He could not get a signal through, but he was intimately aware of what Kevin *felt*: his pulse rate was fast with annoyance and anxiety, the reconstructed knee ached and he was sweating lightly despite the suit's cooling system. He stood behind Stone, ten meters closer to the shuttle, and was intent on the upper decks of the grandstands.

Then Stone felt Jarrat's jolt of surprise, as he too realized he could use the empathic feedback as a locator. He spun about, beckoning. They traded hand signals, a crude exchange of ideas, enough to confirm that they shared the same intention, to get down into the decaying underworld beneath the stadium. Jarrat patted his helmet and indicated the neck seals. He shook a finger in warning, and his meaning was clear. At all costs they must keep the helmets on, jamming or no. One sharpshooter up in the stands, and they could be decapitated. The danger of grenades and nerve gas was also very real. Morello Aerospace stocked every conceivable weapon, and Mavvik's people had hijacked a wide selection.

They strode shoulder-to-shoulder toward the centerline tunnel. Jarrat could not hear Stone's voice and did not need to. "No audio at all," he said quietly to the recorder. "Mics are not working in this ECM. I don't even know if I'm recording this. Some of my instruments are out, but I've still got some imaging and repulsion, and that's all I need." He felt the jump of Stone's pulse, like an alarm ringing through him, as they both picked up a heat signature. His reactions were not a tenth of a second behind Stone's.

The tunnel mouth spat tracer in both directions for a moment, then the heavy rotary cannons whined in answer. Big caliber rounds punched into Stone's armor and spun him around, but he was back on target fast. Splinters of concrete and a haze of dust filled the air. Then, silence.

"Two down," Jarrat said to the recorder. He glanced at Stone's armored shape, aware of the other man's grim determination to get into the basement warren. Mavvik must be there somewhere. Jarrat had speculated that the Death's Head mogul might have been the man shooting out of the tunnel mouth, but knew he was wrong as he saw the body. Not much was left, but he saw the back of a dark head. Mavvik was gray.

The darkness was absolute, uterine, suffocating. On impulse, Jarrat brought up the stun projector and put a blistering discharge into the tunnel. It bounced back off the walls, thundering in the confines. He felt the vibrations through his own armor, and through Stone's body.

"Kevin?" Stone called quietly as the stun field dissipated. He wondered if the jamming might be any less pervasive inside the basement, but Jarrat still did not answer. Instruments indicated the electronic interference grew even stronger as they prowled deeper into the complex. Stone adjusted his breathing mix for a shot of oxygen to clear his head as he and Jarrat drew level with intersecting passages.

It was a perfect ambush point. To one side were dilapidated, paint-peeling dressing rooms, to the other, the medical station. A wall had been cut out to salvage equipment when the building was condemned. In hand signs they each selected a passage, matched their timing and stepped out.

To Jarrat it seemed the world turned into one vast fireball. His imaging system registered only the gasoline-yellow billows of flame and the pall of greasy black smoke hugging the ceiling. Thermographic and infrared shut down and he saw by the illumination of the fire itself that drums of flammable liquids were scattered on the ground before him.

As he brought up the cannon a single incendiary round from one of the branching passages found another drum. It exploded like a bomb, flinging shrapnel and blazing liquid at him. A chemical compound, it clung to his armor like gel and burned fiercely. The suit temperature soared but he ignored it. It was just uncomfortable. The kevlex-titanium alloy could withstand much higher temperatures. The rotary cannon flung a hundred rounds into the curtain of smoke and flame. He felt the vibration of Stone's own cannon through his shoulders as Stone, back to back with him now, filled the passage opposite with a hail of armor-piercing rounds.

The fire burned out the oxygen in moments and doused itself back to a smoldering chemical mess. The ground was slick, treacherous. They trod with grim caution, stepping over and about rolling drums. Two bodies lay sprawled in the passage where Jarrat had dropped them. Both were burned black, bones thrusting sharply among charred flesh. He and Stone gave them more attention than they deserved. Was one of them Mavvik?

They felt each other's intuition clearly and passed on, deeper into the complex. As they left the smoldering wreckage behind thermographic and infrared came back on to augment the grotesque, hostile image of vision intensification.

"Stoney?" Jarrat called. No answer. "Still nothing on audio," he told the recorder. "If I can trust my instruments, I'm reading some kind of nerve gas. Someone's popped a grenade." Up ahead were two more passages, branching off to left and right. Jarrat fed power to his comm system, trying to get over the jamming by sheer force. "Stoney, can you hear me?" But the computer still registered heavy interference and if Stone had heard, it would have been a mere fluke.

He touched Stone's shoulder plate and gestured into the passage to his left. Stone took the passage on the right and they split up cautiously. The maze of tunnels was a confusing environment but they had already covered a respectable distance.

Few booby traps would remain in a complex so rudimentary and ancient. Soon they would be coming up on the ramps leading to the carparks beyond the grandstand. Stone took a scan of the way ahead and swore. His nerves prickled constantly with Jarrat's feedback. He saw dark, forbidding shapes in every corner. Twice he laid fire into unclear recesses, carved through lockers and benches. He was beginning to wonder if he had not passed by the quarry when a splintering concussion tore through the roofing above his head. Crossbeams sagged, ancient prefabricated slabs glanced off his back armor and a veil of dust filled his field of vision.

The shooter who had brought down the roofing could see through the pall no better than he could himself. Thermographic showed nothing hot enough to register, but a pelting shower of incoming fire pounded him, big caliber rounds, cycling fast. He pulled up the rotary to aim a response into the dust, but the shooter paused only briefly. Stone swore fluently. He was sure he must have been dead on target at least a dozen times. At such close quarters it was not possible to miss with every round.

Again, heavy shells punched into him. Tracer was like bolts of laser in the womb-dark, stinking passage. The shooter must be wearing a respirator, Stone guessed, as the air was too toxic to be breathed. "Jarrat!" He shouted, but the jamming was at battlefield intensity, he might as well have whispered.

A hundred meters away, Jarrat did not hear, but he felt the physical shocks of rounds landing hard, and the jolt of Stone's soaring pulse. He did not need to hear the words. If he concentrated he could feel the muscles in Stone's legs working, pushing him up against the wall, out of the line of direct fire, and the slap of brickwork in the back. Jarrat keyed his weight down to fifty kilos and turned toward the firefight at a dead run.

The dust rolled over him. Masonry was scattered like landmines underfoot and he slowed. He knew almost exactly where Stone was, and homed on his partner's anxiety with startling accuracy. Shots still punched out of the pall of dust, big caliber, *whanging* off the armor. He saw Stone hugging the wall, ripping off a hundred rounds at a time, aimed loosely into the murk. But impossibly, the shooter was still replying.

Jarrat slithered to a halt against the wall beside him to add his own fire. In the helmet display, a counter read off the weight of ammunition left in the rotary's drum magazine. He was beginning to run low, and Stone must be almost out. They triggered in short bursts, working a grid pattern.

The dust was settling little by little, swirling about half-seen, halfrecognizable shapes. A water cooler, an uptipped locker. So many of his instruments were out, and Jarrat caught the movement beyond the dwindling pall visually, seconds before any of the electronics registered it. He peered at the hulking shape and swore bitterly. It was a figure in armor. NARC riot armor. Jarrat swallowed on his dry throat.

So *this* was how the bugger was still on his feet after the hundreds of rounds he must have absorbed. Stone made a wager with himself.

Few automatic weapons used .60 caliber and cycled a regular ten per second. Heavier rifles cycled at half the speed and smaller machine pistols cycled ridiculously fast. Only the Colt AP-60 fit the description, and they were rare in civilian hands. But Stone knew of one, 'wild' in this city. Jarrat's Colt, lost in the street in Chell, in the midst of a nightmare. It had to be the weapon that had them pinned down. And if it *was* —

"He's about out of ammo," he muttered to himself. "He has got to reload soon. Kevin? Kevin!" But Jarrat was intent on the hulking figure shrouded by fine gray dust, and he knew exactly what he was looking at.

Only one NARC hardsuit was unaccounted for on this whole planet. Stone's. So Mavvik had ordered the powerpack repaired and recharged, and kept it stored at his bolthole. In the armor, he was as nearly invulnerable as any trooper from a descant unit. "Christ," Jarrat growled, "no wonder we can't drop him."

They had cornered him, but the 9mm laid down by the rotaries would not easily cut through kevlex-titanium. And the Colt? Stone was the living proof of what the Colt could do, in the right hands. For just a moment Jarrat's mind returned to a scene on the palace's gun range, when Mavvik had displayed his talents with the antique weapon Jarrat had restored and refurbished. The man knew guns, and Jarrat's blood iced.

He took a step forward and brought up the rotary. In his helmet, the ammo counter read 150. He triggered sparingly, aiming in the middle of the dust-shrouded figure. The counter dropped to 90, and the figure that could only be Mavvik dove into concealment, a room or passage to his right. Was he reloading? If they gave him a chance, the Colt would live up to its astute nickname. Its aficionados called it the 'buzz saw.'

Stone could attest to the accuracy of the name. He and Jarrat strode cautiously through the settling dust. Thermographic imaging was useless, since riot armor was completely ambient with the environment. Down in these tunnels, which were dank and chill as a freezer, the armor was too cold to register. Vision intensification showed only the dust itself, and infrared was intermittent, overloading with the electronic jamming.

Jarrat flicked on his helmet lights, and the passage ahead flooded with blinding halogen illumination. The ground sloped up on a shallow angle now — they had already begun to climb the exit ramps. Beyond the sealed gates at the top was the concrete wilderness of the vast parking lots. The gates were jammed shut. There was no power on to operate them, and after years of disuse they were probably seized with corrosion.

The only way out of the labyrinth was back the way they had come. Stone took a breath and added his own floodlights to Jarrat's as they came up on the corner around which Mavvik had disappeared. As an ambush point, it could not be bettered, and as they had expected .60 caliber tore out of the old ticket office. Jarrat dove left, Stone dove right, going down hard and rolling against the walls on either side of the doorway.

Jarrat swore lividly. "This is just great," he panted to the helmet recorder, and hoped it was working. "We've got him cornered but we can't touch him. Can't get a signal through for backup. Christ, what do we do, sit here till he's out of battery power and the jamming shuts off?" Stone's fury burned him, magnifying his own.

As the Colt silenced for a moment Jarrat dared edge into Mavvik's line of fire. Another burst answered him, the rounds slamming into his breastplate and tossing him back into the wall. The impact brought all his aches alive again. His mended body was protesting its harsh treatment, and save for the interference Kip Reardon would be reading his soaring pulse and temperature as telemetry.

He lay back against the wall, winded, panting and furious. Sporadic rounds scattered from the ticket office. Mavvik seemed to have ammo to waste, but when Jarrat looked at his own counter he saw 48. He pushed up to his feet and drew in a deep breath. The welded ribs twinged sharply as he bent to uncoil the snapper and charge it. While the current ran up he keyed up his weight, adjusting it until a force of over a hundred kilos held him to the ground. The more he weighed, the harder if would be for impacts from the Colt to knock him off his feet.

Stone felt Jarrat's pains so keenly, for a moment he thought he had fallen badly and hurt himself. He was lightheaded, breathless, but with his weight set at forty kilos he was not laboring. He watched Jarrat uncoil the snapper and adjust his repulsion setting. "What the hell is he doing?" he muttered to the recorders. "He's going to get himself trashed."

He pushed to his feet and put a hand on Jarrat's arm. The full-face, featureless visor turned toward him, and he shook his head, trying to caution Jarrat. He felt a rush of resentment and anger from his partner, and Kevin thrust him aside as he shook out the snapper.

The steel cable scattered magnesium-bright sparks across the concrete. He plied it like a whip and it snaked about his feet, flexing sinuously as he slithered along the peeling plaster toward the door of the ticket office. As his shoulder plate appeared in Mavvik's line of sight a dozen rounds spat at him. He ducked and flicked the snapper into the room at hip height.

The charge earthed through Mavvik's armor in great blue arcs that shriveled the irises. Jarrat's visor darkened to compensate. But the armor absorbed the enormous voltage, and Jarrat knew he would lose the advantage of surprise in another moment. Mavvik could never have been faced with a snapper before, but he would only freeze for a second. He had the Colt in one mesh-gloved fist and a replacement magazine in the other.

As he saw this, Jarrat's heart quickened. Sheer luck had brought him to the door just as Mavvik's ammunition counter must have been reading close to zero. The snapper crackled and spat at Mavvik's feet as Jarrat lashed it back, lifted it and swung it hard before the man could react.

Like a stockwhip, it snaked about Mavvik's legs, twisted, and Jarrat jerked it back. He snatched the man off his feet with astonishing ease, and realized Mavvik's suit's repulsion must be on high, cutting his weight to no more than that of a child. Mavvik toppled backward, went down hard and rolled. The Colt and its recharge magazine skittered away.

"That's got you, you bugger," Jarrat gasped. He flung aside the snapper and dove.

Two hardsuits collided, tumbled, smashed back into the wall. Plaster dust rained down as Jarrat's steel-gloved hands closed about Mavvik's umbilici, but before he could wrench them out Mavvik's fist slammed up under the chin contour of the helmet, where Jarrat's power couplers connected. The instrument lights flickered ominously. The armored fist drew back to aim another blow, and Jarrat twisted away as he closed both his hands about Mavvik's wrist seals.

Panting and heaving, they rolled and swore. Jarrat caught a glimpse of Stone, sweeping up both the snapper and the discarded Colt, but he did not dare take his attention from Mavvik. The man knew too much. He knew the armor's weaknesses as well as its strengths. Umbilici and power conduits were always the weak points of any sealed-environment system. Without power and air, the suit was a coffin.

The weight of the armor, which he had set so heavy to counter impacts, dragged at him. The knee, the wrist, the ribs, knifed through him while Mavvik was lighter, quicker. Jarrat had not the breath to curse, and merely concentrated on keeping Mavvik's grasping fists away from his helmet. "Come on, Stoney. Stoney! *Load the fucking Colt!*" He gasped as Mavvik rolled them under the ticket counter and began to kick.

A blow slammed the armored joint over his knee into the ground and the breath rushed from his lungs. As his vision dimmed he felt Mavvik wrench out of his grasp, and a moment later the man had struggled up to his feet. Jarrat lay gasping. Sweat stung his eyes as he watched Stone pull the Colt down into line on Mavvik's retreating figure. He had waited only for a clear shot.

Both the NARC men had expected Mavvik to bolt for the door, shoulder Stone aside and run, but instead he flung himself at the wall behind the cashier's window. The thin plasterboard gave way before the mass of the armor. It burst outward, and Mavvik was through into the next room, which had been a souvenir kiosk. Stone stepped forward with the Colt in both hands. Jarrat felt the rush of his fury like fire in the belly, and keyed his weight back to forty kilos before he got his feet under him. Stone was trying for the kill shot. His bloodhunger, savage, primitive, seared Jarrat as he fell into step a pace behind his partner. He brought up the rotary, but with only 48 rounds left in the magazine it was a token gesture.

The bulk of Stone's armor blocked Jarrat's line-of-sight through the rupture in the wall, and the shock of Stone's reflexes hit him hard. Stone dove at the ground, taking Jarrat with him before Jarrat had even glimpsed the danger. The first Kevin knew of it was the sudden blaze of superhot exhaust gasses as a rocket launched from the tube over Mavvik's shoulder.

Light anti-armor, Stone thought feverishly as he fell, half on top of

Jarrat. One of the items missing from Vincent Morello. And Mavvik had more — five red-and-white cylinders lay stacked at his feet. The next would cut them to scrap. The first had raced over them so close, the helmet instruments lit up with proximity alerts. It tore out the sealed gates, leaving a gaping rent twice the height of a man beyond which Stone saw the wide, empty lot.

He rolled over and dragged Jarrat with him. "Move it!" He shouted, knowing Kevin could hear nothing. "Get out before he reloads!"

It took an expert fifteen seconds to reload and shoulder the launcher for a second shot. Jarrat keyed his weight so low, he bounced to his feet like a rubber ball. Then he and Stone ran. Mavvik was no expert with the rocket launcher. Stone counted twenty seconds before the next rocket chased them. Cover was the only option. Instinct was to make a break for the open, but they would have presented Mavvik with clear targets. A lifetime's training sent them diving into the warren under the stadium.

The detonation tumbled the walls and part of the roofing caved in. Masonry, crossbeams, girders, pelted their armor, and Stone gasped as a construction member clipped his shoulders and knocked him off his feet. His head spun, his heart hammered at his ribs. Vaguely, he recalled Kip Reardon's warnings. Dizziness swam about his senses, thoughts seemed to echo, as if he were on the fringe of a faint.

Jarrat knew. For himself, anger sharpened his senses and pain had begun to clear his head. He wrenched the girder off Stone's prone form and took the hardsuit by its left arm to tug him out of Mavvik's line-of-sight. How many rockets did he have left? Morello packed them in cartons on six. *Two down.* He doused his helmet lights and Stone followed his thinking. The lights only made them targets in the darkness.

The third rocket whistled over Jarrat's head and erupted under the grandstand. He felt the thunder, like an earth tremor, as the whole structure began to fold on itself like a house of cards. The way back through the tunnels was blocked. The only way out now was up the ramps and into the open, where Mavvik's first rocket had torn out the gates. Jarrat pressed against the wall and leaned out to chance a glance up the ramp. At his feet, Stone was getting his breath back, the dizziness and nausea beginning to ease again as he rested.

Rubble filled the corridor, which both blocked their way and cut off Mavvik's sight. "He doesn't know which way to shoot," Jarrat whispered. "Blindfire. He's just shooting in the dark. Christ, here comes another one!" He flung himself at the ground as the rocket howled out of its launch tube and screamed into the tangled wreckage behind them.

Again, rumbles, vibrations through the stadium's century-old foundations. Stone took a breath and shoved himself upright. "This place is coming down. It's not going to take another one. Kevin? Kevin!"

Jarrat held out a hand for the Colt, and Stone gave it to him. His head was too light for him to be much use with it, while Jarrat seemed to have disregarded the nagging old wounds. The machine pistol looked like a toy in the big steel gauntlets. Nothing could have been further from the truth.

The magazine was full and the machine pistol's propellant gas pressure was good. Jarrat charged it, took a breath and stepped out into Mavvik's line of fire. Tremors rumbled through the floor and the roofing beams sagged over his head. The fifth rocket was halfway into the launcher when Jarrat's finger tightened on the trigger.

The rounds hit Mavvik in the breastplate, over the heart, knocking him onto his back and sweeping him along, up the concrete ramp. The barrel ran hot but Jarrat held the trigger down as he climbed the rubble. Not until the Colt's overheat warning flashed red did he free the trigger, and by then Mavvik was out of reach of the rocket launcher, which lay two meters closer to Jarrat.

A pace behind Kevin, Stone scaled the fallen beams and stooped to collect the rocket. It was standard demolition ordnance, high explosive, unguided. Behind and above them, the old stadium was shuddering, testimony to the lethal potential of five kilos of Demolite.

And before them, Hal Mavvik had rolled to his feet while Jarrat paused to let the Colt's overheated barrel cool. Mavvik was up and running, sprinting for the open air, and Jarrat swore. Stone was on his heels as he pounded after the Death's Head mogul.

With his weight cut almost to zero, Mavvik bounded lightly through the smashed doors, and out. He was heading for the limousine Curt Gable had tracked out of the palace, but with the bulk of the armor he would never fit into it. So he was racing to *get* something. Stone felt the kick of Jarrat's reaction in the same instant.

Mavvik had no more than thirty meters on them. The hood in front of the car's ride capsule was going up already, opened by remote. They watched him claw clumsily for a heavy weapon, wrestle it out of the locker and ram the barrel with a warhead.

"Grenade!" Jarrat yelled, but the jamming cut him out. Stone did not need to be told.

They dove on repulsion as the grenade spat out of the short, fat barrel. It smacked into the concrete in a welter of chemical fire and shrapnel pelted them like hail. Jarrat landed badly. The welded bones stabbed at him like kicks in a dozen places. Stone registered the sudden pain with a grunt but did not dare take his eyes from Mavvik. He knew he had only eighty rounds left in the rotary, and Jarrat could have few more than that, plus forty in the Colt, fifty if he was lucky. He brought up his right forearm as Mavvik clawed for another grenade and rammed the barrel.

As the rotary began to fire Jarrat triggered the Colt in short bursts that conserved what he had left. 9mm and .60 caliber pounded Mavvik's armor, spun him around and threw him into the body of the car, but as they paused he only picked himself up and scrambled for the grenade. Jarrat made it to his feet just in time to dive again. Mavvik was hunched over the locker, trying to reload as they fired again.

Shots still ricocheted off Mavvik's armor, but now Jarrat was not shooting at him. He was down to five in the magazine when a round found its random target in the locker. One grenade detonated ten others and the car ripped itself to cartwheeling shreds. One of the jets scythed by Stone, clipped his shoulder plate and slammed him into the ground. Jarrat gasped as the shock hit him hard.

Close by the blast, Mavvik was physically picked up and tossed away. As he went down, Jarrat ran. Stone was just winded by the fall, he knew. The Death's Head commander had struggled to his knees when Jarrat collided with him. He keyed the repulsion down until he weighed two hundred kilos to pin Mavvik to the concrete. Then he screwed out the umbilici, broke the neck seal and wrenched off the man's helmet.

Terror made Hal Mavvik look much older. He batted at the NARC on top of him with both gauntleted fists until Jarrat cuffed him lightly. Dazed, he lay still, glassy-eyed and panting. The jammer was mounted on the right forearm in the clamps intended for the rotary. Jarrat's steel fingers closed about it and squeezed, reducing it to a shower of magnesium-bright sparks.

At once the air cleared. "Stoney?" he called quietly.

"Here, Kevin." Stone paced up behind him.

"Come and look at what fixed you up." The suit's instruments showed no hazard, and Jarrat took off the helmet.

Stone went down on one knee, the better to see the man he had come to hate. Hal Mavvik did not move. Stone lifted off his own helmet and looked down without expression. Mavvik blinked owlishly, trying to see his face in the light of the blazing limousine.

"Who ... who the hell ..." he wheezed. "Is that ... Stone? Is it?"

"How perceptive," Stone said brashly.

"Then you're dogmeat," Mavvik told him. Satisfaction snarled richly in his voice. "You're as thoroughly fucked as I am."

"You might like to think so," Stone whispered. "And as if happens, you'd be wrong. *Dead* wrong."

Ice-cold fury rolled into Jarrat like a squall, magnifying his own bitter resentment. "Tactical will take you apart limb from limb," he said, teeth clenched. "Every day you live will make dying look like a walk in the park."

"No shit?" Mavvik muttered. But it was bravado, his eyes were white-rimmed, his voice shook. "You bring me in today, I can still take you."

Jarrat turned toward Stone, one brow arched in speculation, but Stone only shrugged. "He lost me. You spent way too much time in the bastard's company, you know what he's talking about?"

"No," Jarrat mused. He leaned down over Mavvik, close to his face. "You can die right here, right now. Tell me what you mean by that, Mavvik, or is it just more of your bullshit?"

"Bullshit?" Mavvik's tongue darted about his dry lips. "You'll find out soon enough, Jarrat. Kill me if you're going to — right here and right now. And I can still take you."

Anger surged through Jarrat, the urge to strike out blindly, and he choked it back with an effort as he heard Stone groan in reaction. Straightening, he took a breath of the acrid night air, ignored Mavvik deliberately and said to Stone, "I don't know which is more poetic, if he'd died in the battle or ends his days in Stacy's tender care. Stacy'll be delighted to flay this bastard alive. Which suits me just fine. You?"

"I can live with it," Stone agreed tersely. "If he survives long enough I might do duty as a Tactical interrogation observer. I did the training course, you know. Nasty, even by our standards." His teeth bared in a wolfish, humorless smile. "It might be amusing."

"Really?" Jarrat shivered as the power of Stone's fury coiled in his belly. Stone had the greater reason for fury: if it came to a choice between being beaten or filled with Angel, Jarrat chose the beating. Satisfied, he tuned in the ground-to-air loop. "Raven Leader to Blue Raven —"

"Kevin!" Stone barked. "He's going to run!"

The repulsion cut Mavvik's weight so low, he was up before either of them could get a hand to him, and bolting toward the south boundary fence. The same impulse shot through both of them like quicksilver. Two rotary cannons locked on target, tripped by the wrist-trigger mechanisms. 9mm leapt out of the barrels until the magazines were empty.

The riot armor remained impervious but was spattered with blood that looked black in the light of the blazing wreck. About the open neck seal, not much was left. They stood looking at the armor in silence for some time while numbing reaction washed through them.

Without a word, Jarrat bent to retrieve his helmet. He and Stone turned back toward the stadium where the shuttle stood on the centerline of the old soccer pitch. The grandstand on the near side of the ground had begun to collapse. Its roof had fallen in and odd, tortured sounds of over-stressed metal issued from the wreckage.

Sirens whooped on the road as a Tactical ground squad approached. Jarrat watched the blue spinner draw closer as he listened to the NARC radio band. "Raven Leader to Blue Raven gunship."

Curt Gable was on the air at once. "Thank Christ! There's been ECM out your way, Jarrat. Heavy-duty jamming. What the hell goes on?"

"Mawik's dead," Jarrat told him tiredly. "There's a collection of bodies, and a fire at Drummond Park. Extensive damage to the old stadium. A Tac squad is just arriving, they can send for the bucket boys and an ice wagon when we pull out."

"You're safe? Both of you?" Gable called sharply.

"A few knocks and scrapes," Jarrat allowed. "Is the party over?"

"Sure is," Gable said laconically. "We've picked up three prisoners for Stacy, more or less intact. Tactical's standing by with a transport. We can extract as soon as we douse the fires and ship out the vermin."

"Casualties?" Stone asked with a certain grim resignation.

"I was afraid you'd ask. Four. Two Ravens are dead. They walked into a flak curtain on the south boundary, it cut them to scrap. The other two will fix. Doc Reardon's prepping the OR now ... and here comes the Tactical transport. You want to come shoot some video for Central? I've got a lot but remember, my view angle is very limited, and their shooters took out so many of our camera drones, we need to put in a requisition."

"Copy that. Stay on station there a while longer, Curt. We're on our way in," Stone told him as he watched the Tac squad come across the lot toward the wreckage of the stadium.

The blue and white squad pulled up by the limousine, which continued to belch chemical fire, and a middle-aged sergeant got out. At the sight of NARC armor he did not ask questions, but took a brief damage report from Jarrat while Stone was still talking to Gable.

"I'll send you a specialist to get the body out of the armor," Jarrat told him. "The seals are coded, and he changed the access. I just checked."

"Nice of you to offer," the sergeant said, nose wrinkling as he survey-ed the mess leaking out of the hardsuit's neck ring. "For a minute I thought it was one of you guys that'd got chopped. We've been listening to your radio, Annie and me, on the road. Officer Annie Ross." His partner was a tiny blonde woman, the same age as himself. She stood leaning on the side of the squad, and nodded hello as her name was mentioned. "You took some rare kind of shit up on the mountain, Captain."

"But it's over," Jarrat said wearily.

"So who's the deader in the hardsuit?" Officer Ross asked as Stone collected the helmet Jarrat had gingerly taken from the runaway's head.

It was his own helmet, and fingers of ice scampered the length of Stone's spine. Jarrat felt them and frowned at him, but Stone said nothing. Jarrat turned his back on the body. "Mawik. It was Hal Mawik. Come on,

251

Stoney, we need battlefield vids before the Ravens extract."

They left the Tactical squad standing open-mouthed beside the wreck and ambled to the stadium's high, wide wire-mesh loading gates, three meters tall and locked. On high repulsion they went over the top like feathers in the breeze and landed lightly inside. They strode through the tomb-like stadium, listening to the groans and impacts of falling girders. Beneath the smogline the night was almost entirely dark, but a few lights had begun to show on the skyline toward the Kansai and Trieste sectors. Chell Power and General was back online. The order could only have come from Petrov, which meant the action was officially over.

A Tactical flyer and the ambulance howled in on whistling jets to back-up the ground squad, and a cutting blare of radio noise announced an incoming flyer from Fire Control. Stone watched their lights against the dense orange-red overcast, still trying to grasp the fact that the action was *done*. It was over, and they were alive.

At the shuttle's flank they paused, and Jarrat gave his shadowy form a rueful look. "Kip is going to be mad enough to spit when he hears where you've been."

"Worth the chewing out," Stone said tiredly. He pulled on the insect-oidal helmet and locked it down. Umbilici screwed into place. Radio modulated his voice. "And besides," he added brashly, "if anyone's going to be strung up by the gonads, it's you, not me. You signed me to duty."

Jarrat was painfully aware of Stone's trembling muscles and faintness. "You're a silly bugger," he told Stone flatly. "You could have got yourself totaled. You're still so full of that crap it's leaking out of your ears, even if you can't get high on it. You deliberately trying to fall on your face?"

"You're going to chew me out as well?" Stone demanded. "Chew as hard as you want, Kevin. I got what I wanted, and it's cheap at the price. I'd have liked to give you Mavvik's head on a plate."

"But he doesn't have much of a head left," Jarrat said tartly as he aimed the infrabeam at the shuttle to lift the canopy. He and Stone climbed up by the hardpoints and in moments were strapped in.

The old stadium thundered to the screaming voices of military jets as the shuttle rammed for takeoff thrust and fell up into the smog-thickened night sky. The Spaceport Clearway was illuminated now, and as the shuttle rose the lights came on in Skagway and Tyne. Power and General were powering-up the city, and Chell seemed to breathe a sigh of relief. Once more, she looked like the carnival strung out under the low cloud ceiling. Jarrat spared the old, raddled city a glance as he looped the aircraft back up onto the mountainside.

On the CRT, the scene of destruction was awesome, comprehensive. Mavvik's palace was gone as if it had never existed. A clean-up squad was at work, twenty engineers in NARC fatigues, laying out bodybags in orderly ranks as 'deaders' were brought out of the rubble. Others were working with a little dozer, digging out survivors who had been in the bunkers and escaped the chaos. Jarrat hung over the mountain at two hundred meters to run a full spectrum scan on sensors and cameras, then took the shuttle in and set down beside the transport that had come for Stacy's prisoners.

Stacy was on the air, jubilant at the promise of interrogation subjects. For once he and Jarrat were in agreement. Mavvik's operation was only the front. The roots of Death's Head went deep, back to the lab where Angel was made and packaged for shipment. And ultimately, back to the lab where the drug had been designed, close to fifty years before. But enough would be learned here, tonight, for Tactical to locate the local lab, and if they moved fast enough they would seize it, shut it down, no matter if it were as far away as Eldorado. Tactical was back on top. Tonight's data would put Stacy on the right track, and there was an edge in his voice, he was eager to get the tiger by the tail.

When it got away from Tactical again, when the action became too hot for them to handle, this colony's authorities would call for NARC. But next time, Jarrat and Stone would be long gone. Jarrat mourned as he lifted the spaceplane's canopy and let himself down over the side. He stood in the lee of the aircraft, taking off the riot armor piece by piece with a sense of finality and handing the segments to a NARC boy who jogged over to assist. The headset relayed voices — Gable, Cronin, Ramos — crosstalking on the loop. They were more than satisfied. Honor was restored. Jarrat had the armor off when the man operating the little dozer began to shout.

"Come on, son! Reach up to me ... a bit more. *Move it, boy!* Get out of there before it caves in!"

Jarrat turned toward the commotion and saw the scene played out in the glare of the portafloods. The dozer had cleared a mountain of wreckage, exposing a hole in the ground. Bare arms reached up through it, hands grasping, and as he watched the crewman caught the survivor and hauled him out. The sergeant in charge yelled over his shoulder, "Tell the Tac transport to hold up. Got another one for Stacy!"

"No," Jarrat called to the dozer crew and the lieutenant from Tactical. "That's not a Death's Head runner. That's just the hired entertainment ... Aren't you, kiddo?"

Lee was in one piece. Choking on the dust, knees and elbows scrubbed raw, but otherwise simply stunned. He spun toward the voice he knew. He was naked, but for his tiger stripes and jewelry, and his hair hung over his shoulders like a cape, raven-black. The portafloods gleamed on his rings, chains, bracelets. Sandal-shod feet slipped in the rubble as he scrambled toward Jarrat.

"Kevin! It's true, then. They told me —" He flung himself at Jarrat, and Jarrat caught him, hugged him. "You're a NARC."

"I'm a NARC," Jarrat echoed. "Or, I was." Now it was all up to the command oligarchy, and the future was far from certain.

"They said you were dead," Lee added.

"Looks like they were wrong." Jarrat smacked the kid's beautiful mouth with a wet kiss. "That feel like a dead man?"

"They said they *greased* you." Lee held on tight. "I cried like a kid over you, sugar. You were the only decent thing in this place."

"You should have got out weeks ago." Jarrat stroked his back. He was looking over the hustler's tousled head at Stone, who watched them with a bemused expression. "In fact, you should never have been here at all. You want a lift somewhere, Lee? You can't hike it down the mountain dressed like this. You'll be gang-banged in the first five minutes!" He patted both alluring buttocks. "You're still gorgeous. But have you got somewhere to go, sweetheart?"

"I've got a brother down in the city," Lee said. "And I'll make a few calls tomorrow ... you known an old sod called Lou Epstein?"

"The banker?" Stone guessed as he stepped closer. Lee looked over his shoulder, sized Stone up in three glances and smiled invitingly. "Well, hello. I haven't had the pleasure of you. Yet."

Stone laughed. "Stone. Jarrat's other half. What about Epstein?"

"It's a living, breathing pity," Lee said wistfully, looking from Jarrat to Stone and back again. "I could have done wonders for you. Both of you, in fact ... Epstein made me an offer just the other day."

"Epstein was here at the palace?" Jarrat demanded. "With Mavvik?"

"No! I went out, dancing. He was in the dance shop, wanted a quickie in the back seat of his Ferrari. I got these out of it." He arched his back to display the emerald rings in his nipples. "Nice, huh? Expensive. He wanted me to live in. He's got a penthouse on top of the Kline building. I told him I'd think about it."

"Take it," Jarrat said sternly. "Epstein's made of money, and if he can afford this kind of giftware —" He tweaked one of the emerald rings. "Grab it while you can, kiddo. You deserve it."

Lee smiled up at him. "I know. And I will, as soon as I've cleaned up and got some rags. My brother'll let me crash there for the night."

Stone brushed dust and ash from the boy's smooth shoulder. "You don't look very shocked at the circus there's been here."

"Shocked?" Lee echoed fatuously. "You have *got* to be joking! This place has been like Boot Camp for a week. You couldn't get in here for the guns and rockets. We all got the lecture, where the shelters were. Man, I dived in as soon as I heard the alarms trip. They were tracking you as soon as you dropped in over Chell. I was in mid-fuck. I never got *un*-fucked so fast in my entire life. I was in the old nuke shelter, drinking brandy and listening to the fireworks. I was just worried you wouldn't dig me out, but there was a radio in there. No one was listening to me!"

"Poor baby." Jarrat kissed him. "You sure you're okay, Lee? You look okay. In fact, you still look gorgeous. It's your business to be."

"And I'm *good* at it," Lee purred. He looked up at Stone. "You're his better half? Envy, sugar, envy. This one's a sweet lay, a real sweet lay. Of course, you know that." He hugged tight to Jarrat and then let go. "Where's my ride?"

Finger to his lips, Jarrat whistled for the Tactical lieutenant who was loitering with the transport. "You can ride back with the truck, they'll drop you wherever you want." He touched Lee's nose with one fingertip, "I'll check up on you, kiddo. I want to know you're safe. If you'll be with Epstein on top of the Kline building, I'll know where to find you."

"Find me, find me," Lee begged self-mockingly. He gave Stone a wink and was about to turn away when his brow creased in a frown. "I don't know if it means anything, Kevin, but I heard your name a lot in the last few days. Mavvik took some calls, and I know he was talking about you."

"Who was calling?" Stone asked.

"I ... can't be sure," Lee warned. "The line was pure crap."

"Military grade signal encryption," Stone guessed. "Kev?"

Jarrat nodded. "Did you hear a name, Lee? The caller."

Lee shrugged. "Joe somebody. They were setting up a deal, and it was something about you, which is the only reason I listened. Eavesdropping could get a guy killed!" He paused to wave at the Tactical man who was waiting for him. "I should have known you weren't dead when I heard them making a deal! I just didn't connect it." He fluttered his eyelashes, once again mocking himself. "Hey, if I had brains, I'd be designing raceplanes like my brother. You do what you can, right? My ride's leaving. I have to go, if I don't want to hike. I'll catch you later, Kevin. Promise me?"

"I'll call you," Jarrat told him, and watched as the Companion jogged away to the Tactical vehicle.

Stone watched the kid go, lithe, naked, physically perfect. "Joe somebody," he mused, and took a breath as he felt Jarrat's tensions ball up.

"Not 'Joe,'" Jarrat corrected. "Joel. As in *Assante*. So that's what Mavvik was talking about. There's a contract out on me, and it won't stop because he's dead. Death's Head has affiliates in lots of places, and offworld. In fact, since Mavvik's dead they'll triple the contract fee on me."

"Us." Stone waved as the transport pulled out with a growl of big engines a bluster of repulsion. It swung wide around the NARC contingent and threaded into the organized chaos on the mountain road, headed toward the smogline. "*Us*, Kevin. You think Assante, or Mavvik's beneficiaries, will stop at one NARC command rank officer when they can have two? And where you go, I go. No arguments."

"Well ... shit," Jarrat said succinctly and with feeling. He knuckled his eyes. "Eldorado Tactical's known for a week, Assante is in their region. They're stuffing up the job, Stoney, and we don't have the time or resources to get in there and do it for them. Send a gunship, and we'll never even *see* Assante. This one's about stealth, not main-force."

Stone dropped a hand on his shoulder, gave him a companionable squeeze there. "Let it rest for the moment. Assante will be doing the same as everyone else tomorrow: watching newsvids, wondering who lived and who died. They'll be calling it 'the Battle of Chell.' With Mavvik reported dead, Assante will have to connect with whatever remains of Death Head in South Atlantis and confirm the contract."

"They could be in the next colony by now," Jarrat said tersely. "Two clippers have swung by Rethan since the night ... it started." The night he was mauled, and Mavvik announced his war, and a good number of the more intelligent shooters promptly bugged out in every direction.

"We have a couple of days to pull it all together," Stone speculated. "We'll kick the Assante question right back to Eldorado Tac, it's their business anyway. If they haven't accounted for the bastard by the time we stand down, we'll deal with it ourselves. Good enough?"

"Good enough," Jarrat decided, and gave Stone a sidelong, rueful smile. "Last loose ends to tie off before we get the hell out?"

"Probably." Stone gestured after the departing transport, which was waiting to go through the portaflood-lit roadblock, two hundred meters below. "So that's the Companion who shared your bed for two months."

"The only spark of life in the palace," Jarrat said ruefully.

"He's ... a tough act to follow, Kevin," Stone observed.

The remark was philosophical. Jarrat studied his partner in the harsh glare of a dozen blue-white portafloods and blinking red spinners. "I'm not complaining. I got what I've wanted for years."

"And fritzed your career," Stone added.

"That too." Jarrat looked up at the slab-shaped hull of the Blue Raven gunship, two hundred meters over the wreckage of the palace. "It's all so much spilled milk, old son. What's done is done. I weighed it up on a set of balances. Your life over my bloody stupid career. I ... still hurt, Stoney."

"I know you do. I feel it. I feel everything you do. And the next time, for either of us ..." Stone would say no more. He did not need to.

Jarrat's eyes were silver in the floodlights as he looked searchingly at Stone. "They broke every bone in my body, and some hoon shoved his fist up for good measure. It could happen again, any day. Oh, yes?" He added as he felt Stone's deep shudder. "I can't say I enjoyed getting nailed in a back alley and left for dead, and I can sure as hell live without that, Stoney. Question is, could I live without you?"

They were silent for a moment, then Stone said, "You're an idiot. For wanting a half-assed bugger like me. You should have stuck to Lee and made sense out of your life. NARC is going to junk us, Kevin."

"Probably," Jarrat admitted reluctantly. "But we still have a few options." The clean-up squad was preparing to extract and the Blue Ravens were on standby, pending Cronin's order to go. Red, Green and Gold had already returned to their respective gunships, which had in turn pulled out back to the carrier.

"Options?" Stone prompted as he watched the transport make its way through the roadblock and on, down the wreck-strewn road which wound around the mountainside. How many squads had come to grief there?

"We can RTU. That's Tac for you, Army for me. Or I could transfer to Tactical with you."

"And get carved up like Stacy's people?" Stone shook his head emphatically. "The competition's too hot. It's the reason I got out of Tac when I did. I was pleased to transfer to NARC ... better odds."

"You could transfer into the Army with me," Jarrat suggested as he climbed the side of the shuttle. "We'd go in at a good rank after NARC."

"And get carved up in the kind of shindigs that make this last hour look like a chimp's teaparty?" Stone retorted.

Like Sheal, Jarrat thought. His war, and Evelyn Lang's. "There's always Starfleet. With NARC credentials we would transfer straight in at a decent rank, no problems. Better pay, too."

"And end up as milk-run pilots flying redeye expresses," Stone said acidly. "You could die of the excitement. Not for me, Kevin."

"Then, think about NARC support," Jarrat finished. "They're going to ground us. We'll never fly again at command rank. It would take a miracle to pull that off, and miracles don't happen. But there's Intelligence, Cyber, Cipher, R&D. We could get a promotion instead of being busted all the way back to civilian."

This interested Stone. "All right. Put it to them when an investigating officer gets out here. That's not bad, Kevin. Not bad. I could accept that."

The repulsion began to thrum in the belly of the shuttle. Jarrat was weary, aching, sore. For a moment he wondered if it was Stone's tiredness, and then satisfied himself, it was his own. Stone's perceptions were just that shade different in his nerves, like the difference between blue and green. It was not much, but a place to start.

"First, some R&R," he mused as he ran through a quick preflight check of the shuttle's systems. "I'm thinking, a couple of days in the sun, learning how this ... the empathy ... works. Maybe Eldorado, Ballyntyre. Harry Del's place." He lifted the shuttle, folded the gear and pulled back on the cyclic stick. The space-to-surface interceptor stood on its tail, both ramjets wide open, pressing them back into the couches as Jarrat headed them for space, and the carrier.

Down below, the Blue Ravens lifted back to the gunship. It was over.

CHAPTER TWENTY-TWO

The comm woke Stone out of a tangled dream about data processing. After two days of intensive debriefing and analysis, a man's mind did not just stop in its tracks because the files were closed, the telemetry dispatched. In the instant before he opened his eyes he felt Jarrat wake: a ripple of reaction to the comm ... not annoyance but resignation. Stone pulled the sheet over his head as Jarrat snaked an arm out and selected audio.

His voice was still slurred as he said, "Jarrat. This better be good."

He and Stone had officially stood down and begun the extended period of R&R on which Reardon had insisted. Carrier business went through to Petrov, and Scott Auel had signaled from the *Avenger*: he was waiting for a Starfleet courier, and the flight over from Belgaris was only a two-day journey. Tactical had assumed responsibility for the closure of all arms of the syndicate which could be located on the data gathered from the Death's Head survivors, and NARC involvement had technically been scaled back to observation.

Technically. In reality, the weeks directly following an action like Chell were dangerous. It was common for a syndicate to spring back, drawing on whatever resources, and explode in Tactical's face — especially if the new moguls believed the NARC carrier had gone. The *Athena* was running silent now. Only the deep space tracking network knew her position, and the data was not shared even with Tac. She would remain on station for some time yet, covering Tactical's rear, pending reassignment.

Kip Reardon's voice on the comm surprised Stone. "I woke you?"

"Of course you woke me," Jarrat retorted.

"Us," Stone muffled. "Like he said, this better be good."

"It's ... a little odd." Reardon hesitated. "The call's for you, but it came in on my private line."

At that Stone tugged down the sheet and frowned up at Jarrat. "Who is it, Kip?"

"It's Harry. You know Del and I have been sharing data, comparing notes, since Jarrat made it back here. We've been using my private line for the sake of simplicity. I've just never known him call the *carrier* on it."

"If Harry's calling the carrier," Stone said with a deep yawn, "it's Petrov he wants to talk to, not us."

But Reardon was emphatic. "He asked for Kevin or you, specifically. I offered to get him Carrier Operations or Petrov, but wants you."

"Put him through." Jarrat sat up, pulled both hands over his face and looked down at Stone. "I have the proverbial bad feeling."

So did Stone, though he was unable to tell if the misgivings were his own, or Jarrat's raw feelings blooming in his still-drowsing muscles. He sat up behind Kevin, stretched his shoulders, and began to crave coffee.

A moment later Harry Del's voice said from the comm, "Jarrat?" Two syllables were enough to convey the steel-hard note spelling *trouble*.

"Stoney's here too. What's going on, Harry?" Every nerve in Jarrat's body came alive at once, and the adrenaline rush pumped through Stone.

"I need to see you," Harry said baldly. "Either or both of you. ASAP. You know a place called *Los Amigos* in Chandler?"

In fact Stone had never heard of it, but Jarrat was saying, "We'll find it. Harry, what do you need, and how fast?"

The healer skipped a beat. "I'll tell you when I see you. When, Kevin?"

Jarrat looked at the chrono and then at Stone. "Two hours?" Stone nodded. "That would make it after midnight in your neck of the woods, Harry. Good enough? You can be here on the carrier a hell of a lot faster."

Again, Harry hesitated. Then, "No, I'll be at *Los Amigos* at midnight."

And the call terminated abruptly. "What the hell," Stone growled, "was that about?"

"I don't know." Jarrat swung his legs off the bed and stood. "But that bad feeling just got worse." He turned back and offered Stone a hand to pull him to his feet. "You're better today."

He was right, and he never had to ask how Stone felt. The empathy rang like a rack of bell chimes. A light session in the gym and a half hour in the sauna had done a lot to sweat the poison out through the pores. Stone dropped a kiss on Jarrat's neck, dealt him a swift but comprehensive hug, then fended him off. If they were going to make Chandler in two hours they had no time to waste, no matter how much Stone had been looking forward to sleeping late and indulging in sensuality. Jarrat was reaching for jeans and a fresh shirt. With a resigned sigh, Stone punched for coffee and, out of long habit, reviewed the carrier's current data.

Twenty minutes later they were standing in the long, half-lit cavern of the Armory, and Stone was very much aware of the knotted ball of Jarrat's belly as they signed out a full suite of weapons, as much ammunition as they could carry and, not quite on a whim, a case of 'goodies.' Thumb-sized grenades, fist-sized pop-up sensor drones, two Army-issue handsets which combined the full range of scan functions, and a half-dozen R/Ts, no larger than faux cigarette lighter Jarrat had taken into Mavvik's palace.

"You guys going out looking for a fight?" The voice belonged to Gil Cronin. He had stepped into the Armory minutes before, on Blue Raven business, and could hardly fail to notice the haul at Stone's feet as Jarrat signed it out. Imposingly tall, big through the shoulders even when he was out of the armor and clad in dark blue fatigues and soft-soled boots, he leaned on the terminal and tallied up the hardware. "You're supposed to be off-shift, Stoney. Maybe even off-shift permanently. What goes on?"

"Loose ends," Jarrat said acerbically. "One of them is flapping in the wind, and I *think* it just snared a friend of ours."

"You want I should call Petrov?" Cronin offered.

For a moment Stone considered involving Petrov, but he and Jarrat shared the same hesitation about making this a NARC op. "Not yet," he said at last. "We don't even know what the problem is. Harry Del called ... it could be nothing. Domestic stuff. Petrov's busy enough."

The leader of the Blue Raven descant unit regarded him with shrewd, narrowed eyes. "And it might be all hell about to bust loose."

"If it is," Jarrat said quietly, "a full-on NARC circus could be the last thing we want." He lifted a brow at Cronin. "If you follow me."

"You lost me," Cronin admitted.

"Then trust us." Stone stooped for the case of R/Ts and handsets. "Your boys are stood down now. Can we beg a favor, Gil?"

"You know you can." Cronin swept the crate of grenades up in one big hand. "Where d'you want these?"

Jarrat was already moving. "Hangar 9. We're taking the lighter."

"Not the shuttle?" Cronin's voice rose as he followed them out of the Armory and hung a left, aft, to the service elevators.

"It's not NARC business," Stone said reasonably. "Not yet. Like Kevin said, it could be nothing. If it turns into a firefight, we're not too proud to yell ... in fact, that's the favor I was going to call in." He plucked an R/T out of the case and slapped it into Cronin's waiting palm. "Harry's call might have diddly to with NARC, but it feels ... dead wrong."

With a flourish, Cronin pocketed the R/T. "I'll monitor you, no problem. Standard codes?"

The companion R/T slipped into the pocket of the black leather jacket Stone had chosen to cover his sidearm. He was sweating in the leather, but the Austin .44 was a big weapon, too visible under a lighter jacket, and the last thing they wanted tonight was to be obvious on the street.

They stepped into the wide, battered service elevator for the ride down one deck and two hundred meters aft. "Standard codes," Jarrat agreed, "and use level-4 encryption." He gave Stone a dark look. "We don't want every man and his uncle listening in. Thanks, Gil. We appreciate it."

Hangar 9 was the private bay where numerous individuals scattered throughout the crew, from the lowliest ranks among the support staff to the Starfleet crew who piloted the carrier itself, parked their personal transportation. The assortment of sportplanes, corroding junkers, race-specials and build-ups stored in the big, dim, steel-blue cavern often amused Stone. He had never parked a vehicle here — had never needed to. When he left the carrier, it had always been in the shuttle on NARC business, or on a transport, on furlough and headed for a clipper terminal.

The *Athena*'s lighter was a Yamazake Apogee, sleek, powerful and armed, though not as heavily as the shuttle. The Apogee was an executive courier, not a warplane. Still, Stone would have gambled on it in a fight against any other light spaceplane in civvy hands. In a pinch it would seat four, but the rear of the cockpit was cramped, rudimentary.

Without a word, Gil Cronin opened up the weapons pods and tackled the serious business of arming the craft. Rotary cannons and chain guns offered little defense in a battlefield like Chell, but despite Jarrat's misgivings, Stone could not believe they were headed into any such fight.

A code tapped into a keypad, and Cronin commandeered a tractor from Hanger 5, where the Green Raven gunship was undergoing routine service work. In the fifteen minutes while the gold-hulled Apogee was prepped for flight and her engines testfired, Cronin had fully armed it. Stone rotated the guns, ran the test sequence on the sensors, and gave Cronin a 'good to go' signal. The Blue Raven stood back, and as the red-gold canopy whined down and locked he brought the R/T to his mouth.

"Blue Raven 6 to NARC Airborne."

A third R/T was in the pocket of Jarrat's jacket, the frequency open. "Reading you, six-by-six," Kevin told him. "Encryption is good."

"Then you guys have a nice flight," Cronin said with his own brand of bleak amusement. "I'll be listening in."

As he spoke, he was on his way out of the hangar. As soon as Cronin was on the other side of a sealed hatch Jarrat called Hangar Control. He had barely received launch clearance, the sirens had been wailing for only a moment, when Petrov was on the comm: "Jarrat, you're leaving?"

"Personal business, Mischa." Jarrat was watching the red spinners, only waiting to see green, and performing a routine check of the Colt AP-60 before returning it to the holster under the brown leather jacket. His hands seemed to do the work by themselves. "It's just a social call."

"Destination?" Petrov wondered.

A kick of annoyance wound through Stone's belly, but the feeling was Jarrat's. "A restaurant in Chandler, South Atlantis," he informed Petrov.

It told the Russian everything and nothing. Stone chuckled without any real humor. "We'll be in touch. NARC Airborne out."

The spinners had just turned green and the belly doors were open far enough to allow a small plane to drop out. Jarrat kicked on the repulsion and said quietly, "You want to take it, Stoney?"

As if he had to ask. Stone's hands molded to the Apogee's sensitive controls, and as it nosed into the vacuum he picked up groundscan, locating first on Eldorado. The city lay three hours over the terminator, on the dark side of the planet. Dawn was breaking over Chell as the Apogee feathered into the upper atmosphere on a storm of repulsion. The Eldorado 'port radars were a hot-spot in the background civvy clutter. Stone dropped in toward the city, then looped around, south, following the line of the Rosenfeld Range.

Mount Madison had its own locator beacon. From there it was easy to find Chandler, on the other side of 'the Barometer' from Ballyntyre. Jarrat was a reluctantly amused passenger. "I know this place too well. In fact, I was almost a local." Stone shot him a curious look and he added, "If you hadn't tracked me down ... for which, I don't think I ever thanked you, so consider yourself thanked! ... my memory might have been dormant for years. I was going to stay on in Ballyntyre. I got to like it."

"Except a shooter whose name you couldn't even remember would never have let you live long enough to enjoy it," Stone said quietly. He touched his headset. "N-1572 to Chandler Field." He had deliberately not identified as 'NARC Airborne' and Cronin's ears would already be pricking. "N-1572, requesting landing advice."

The field was just a regional 'port, even smaller than Paddington, with space to spare. A yawning traffic officer directed Stone to Bay 12, on the north of a concrete wilderness which shone wetly in the moonlight after a shower. The night air was sweet. The hillsides were thick with tropical forest; the indigenous night-blooming fungi smelt oddly like citrus.

A buggy runabout trundled out to meet them, and they rode in to the cab rank by the terminal. The sky was quiet as they woke the only driver still loitering at his hour, hoping for a fare. When Jarrat mentioned 'Los Amigos' the old man merely grunted and headed out by the south gate.

Chandler was so small, the cab drove right across it in four minutes. The restaurant stood on the corner of a tiny mall, and at midnight was thinly patronized. Century-old music crooned out of the sound system; a local hustler was trying to make a pickup at the bar, where two drunks had begun to squabble, and the town constable was one of them. The aroma of nachos, pizza and sushi rice invited the visitor to tables in the back, where the lights were low and the shadows thicker than the kipgrass smoke around the bar. And in the very back, Stone saw Harry Del's face.

A waitress drifted toward the table as Stone pulled out a chair. Del gestured with the schooner glass and lifted a brow at the younger men. "The local brew's not bad." And at Stone's nod, "Three more, love," he told the waitress. She was gone before he spoke again. "Thanks for getting here so fast. I appreciate it."

"We told you, Harry, if there was trouble, yell." Jarrat sat, both hands clasped on the table before him, and glanced at Stone. "You're freaked."

"It shows?" Del rubbed his face hard. He was in his usual baggy slacks and garish, oversized shirt, but nothing else about him was relaxed. "Some bastards torched my place last night. They got the glasshouses, the sheds, the garage, three of the cars. We managed to keep it out of the main part of the house till Fire Control showed, so we didn't lose everything. I still have my data and the last harvest in cold store. But the new crop's gone, and the glasshouses themselves. I *think* we can save the house."

"Jesus." Jarrat rubbed his eyes with thumb and forefingers. He was silent as the waitress arrived, and when she left he asked, "Anything like this ever happened to you before, Harry? You know what I mean."

"You mean, has the local community ever taken the piss at the queer in their midst and tried to burn him out?" Harry sighed. "It's been a long time since I was a target, and it never went this far. Broken windows, crank calls, my kids getting hell at school because they might have inherited the 87/T gene. Never anything like this. Up in El maybe, but not here."

"So," Stone mused, "you can be pretty sure it's not a local hitting on you. You've been here too long to draw this kind of flak." He tried the beer, found it light, and sweet. "You filed a report with Tac?"

Harry's eyes shifted to the bar and rested on the constable, who was thoroughly snockered, and not a pleasant drunk. "'Big Al' Kano is our Tactical representative. Sure, I called him. For what it was worth."

"You've had a couple extra Tac squads in the Bally area," Jarrat said in an undertone, "since the scene at Skinny Dick's. Evelyn has an ex-Airlift friend in the department, she told me she'd made a few calls."

"There's one hell of a bust-up going on in Eldorado right now," Del reminded him. "Chell Tactical got access to a lot of data ... you took prisoners, I assume. We saw the battle, the newsvids played like a movie. Anyway, there's a shortage of manpower in El, so one of our extra squads was pulled to help out." He paused and took half his beer down in one swallow. "The other squad disappeared this morning."

"Disappeared?" Stone echoed. His spine tingled uncomfortably and he leaned closer. "A Tactical squad doesn't just disappear!"

"This one did." Harry gazed into the bottom of his schooner glass. "I heard they responded to an emergency call somewhere off Kinnon Hill Road. Out by the timber mill, Gresham's, you know it, Kevin?"

"One switchback after another, a big robot clear-cut operation," Jarrat told Stone. His brows arched. "I could make a Tactical squad vanish in that area. Easy, Stoney. And it'd take you a month to find it."

"The squad could have had an accident," Stone speculated. "Harry?"

"They could have," Del agreed. "Somebody grazed Evelyn's arm with a bullet this afternoon. She was on the road, at work. Pedley did the right thing, brought her straight to me — they hadn't heard about the fire ... shock, horror." He made a face. "Took me an hour to calm them down."

Small wonder Del was so jittery, Stone thought. The Tac squad had been surgically removed, and the whole group which had been connected with Jarrat and himself had already been targeted. Not *hit*, but targeted.

"How badly was she hurt?" Jarrat was asking.

"Just a nick through the flesh," Harry said quickly, "enough to let you know you could have been dead ... and maybe next time, you will be." He leaned over the table. "I've sent Tansy and the younger kids to stay with her folks in Eldorado. Tan's pretty shook up, as you'd expect. I'd have shipped Evelyn out with them, but you know what she's like. I couldn't budge her. She's talking about a man called Assante. She told me to call you, fast. Apparently, you might know what the *fuck* is going on here."

"I'm sorry to say, I think we do," Stone said quietly. He finished the beer and pushed back the chair. "This isn't the place to talk about it. Kev?"

"Maybe not." Jarrat's teeth worried at his lip for a moment. "It's a safe bet Assante doesn't know we're here yet. He'll have staked out either Harry's place or Evelyn's, or both, and he'll be sitting in his web, waiting."

"He could have followed Harry right here," Stone reasoned, and felt the spike of reaction from Jarrat.

"But he can't tail both Harry and Evelyn," Jarrat mused. "He'd have to pick which to tag, and he'd choose Evelyn. It's the only thing that makes sense after the scene at Skinny Dick's. You know about that, Harry?"

"She told me." Del did not have to feign a shudder.

"There's one other thing." Stone knew the hot surge of his own adrenaline must be burning Jarrat. "Assante may not be working alone now. He's had several days to make a call and scare up some kind of backup."

Harry's eyes closed. "Christ, I didn't even think of that."

"It's not your job to. This crap?" Jarrat drummed his fingers on the table. "It's our line of work, Harry. Backup, Stoney?"

And Stone nodded. To the R/T, which was open in his shirt pocket, he said, "You listening, Gil?"

The Blue Raven was there at once: "Every word, Stoney. Curt Gable's right here. He heard the R/T, wondered what was doing. I told him what I know. We're in the shuttle hangar right now."

"Has Petrov been advised?" Stone asked softly.

"Not yet. The ops room is stood down, the carrier's running silent. Petrov's still analyzing the Chell action. How's it look, groundside?"

Jarrat leaned closer to the R/T. "We're not sure, yet Gil, but it's not good. We could probably use a little backup."

"Gunship?" Cronin wondered.

"No!" Stone spoke sharply. "Give these hoons any advance warning and they'll go to ground so fast, we won't even see their dust. We're looking for *stealth* this time. Advise Petrov, get clearance to launch the shuttle, locate on this signal but do not, repeat *do not* approach closer than twenty kilometers. We're in a rural zone, it's so quiet, you can actually hear yourself think. The sound of military jets will be a dead giveaway."

A moment's pause, and Curt Gable's light voice said tersely over the R/T, "Stoney, Jarrat, we can't reach your location for *at least* forty-five minutes, could be more. What's your security situation?"

A white-hot flare from Jarrat scorched every nerve ending Stone possessed as Kevin said, "There's no way to be sure, and I'd feel safer in the Apogee. Harry, what are you driving?" With that, Jarrat was on his feet and headed away to the bar, where he left a few crumpled notes.

"Just my truck, it's parked right there. If you don't mind me asking, what the hell is an Apogee? Some kind of plane?"

"Get me your keys and ten minutes, we'll show you," Stone said glibly.

In the early hours of the morning the street was almost deserted. *Los Amigos* was the only place open for business. Harry was opening up the big Rand ground truck and the empathy was clear as an open radio. Tension and anger broadcast so stridently, both Jarrat and Stone stifled a groan loud enough for Harry to hear. Stone shook his head, as if to clear it of a weight of cotton wadding. Harry turned back, frowning at them. "Is it the empathy? I know it's hard. It can make your job difficult."

"It could either save our lives or get us killed," Jarrat growled. His temples were pressed between both palms. "Harry, help us here."

"Get in." Del popped the gullwings and was in under the wheel moments later. The truck started with a cough, the repulsion seemed to grunt, then the truck was off. Del arced around in the middle of the empty street and took off fast toward the 'port. "Christ! It takes *weeks* to learn how to do this. You think I can teach you some magic in a few hours? I should separate you, put you in different rooms till you know how to locate on each other, like tuning a comm set."

Stone gritted his teeth against the upwelling of Jarrat's exasperation as well as his own. "We did that already. You saw the fight in Chell? We were right in the middle of it —"

"In the dark, with a sensor blackout and a lunatic armed with a rocket launcher," Jarrat added acidly. "We figured that part out. *Not* feeling what the other guy feels is what we need to learn, before one of us is so distracted by the other, the bloody pair of us are greased!"

"Damn," Harry breathed. The driving lights lanced into the darkness as he left behind the town and headed out as fast as he dared. "When I did the job on you two, I never imagined you'd be trying to work. I thought you'd be dumped by your department, or have enough sense to quit!"

"It'll happen," Stone said bleakly, "but you've forgotten the subspace signal lag. It takes formal orders from Darwin's World to dump us."

"Oh. Right." Harry slid down a window for air. "Well, there are ways and means, but it's not easy. Still, you two are already trained in such weird shit, it's possible my tricks are not so different from the mind games you've already played." He glanced sidelong at them.

"We're listening, Harry," Jarrat prompted.

The healer glared at the road. Up ahead, the lights of Chandler Field had begun to glitter over the treeline. "I'd like to burn dreamsmoke for you, let you wander in a realm of pure imagination, explore each other's feelings, learn the *taste* and *smell* and *color* of the other guy's feelings, till you can tell the difference. Like ... a real musician can tell apart two seemingly identical instruments by their resonance. You follow?"

"Yes." At that moment Stone was breathless at the press of Jarrat's feelings, the racehorse tension of him, the eagerness to strike, the conflicting bloom of concern, that his partner was too close, too unwell. The chaos of his own feelings plus Jarrat's sweated his palms, sped his pulse.

"I've caught a glimpse of color in his feelings," Jarrat was saying tersely. "And in my own."

"What color?" Harry demanded over the sound of wind and engine.

"Does it matter?" Stone gritted his teeth as Jarrat's feelings took a sharp turn and flared hotly. What he was a thinking, Stone could not possibly know, but his emotions were a flashfire.

"Blue," Jarrat said into the wind as the truck stopped at Chandler Field's automatic boomgates for the routine ID check.

Harry had been driving with his foot to the floor, doubling the speed of the cab which brought them out. He showed his face to a camera, laid his palm on a scanner, and the boomgates went up. "You or him?" Harry insisted. "Jarrat, are you blue, or is he?"

"He is." Jarrat pointed. "North side of the private field. Look for a gold-chrome aerodyne with a single tail and canards. You'll see it soon."

Peering across the expanse of stained concrete, Harry spared Jarrat a glance. "There's your key. You've picked it up yourselves. It takes the ordinary person weeks to find it, but from here on out, it's a matter of practice, and *that*, I cannot do for you. It's the mind games you buggers play, the simulations, the counter-interrogation techniques. You people," he added with a rare passion, "aren't human, you know that? Shit, listen to me! I'm the mutant, and I'm calling you inhuman!"

"Harry, calm down." Stone heard the edge in Del's voice, and barked the words in a tone of command. Harry had never served in any branch of the military or Tactical. He was way out of his depth and not too proud to admit it. He also responded to the bark of command, as did most civilians. Stone moderated his tone. "There's the Apogee. Pull in by the nose, and lock the truck behind us. Gil, you there?"

The Blue Raven responded at once, so close, he might have been in the truck with them. "Getting every word, Stoney. Curt's with Petrov right now, and we're prepping the shuttle. Petrov's trying to get an update from Eldorado Tac. We're cleared to deploy, I'm suiting up. Curt's going to fly this one." He paused. "You sure you don't want a gunship? The Blue Ravens are itching to launch."

"No, Gil, no gunship." With a twist of wry amusement, Jarrat stepped out of the truck. "Get back to us with Petrov's info."

The Yamazake Apogee's canopy popped as Stone aimed the infrakey. "In the back, Harry. It's cramped, but it's safe. Strap down tight."

'Safe' was a relative term. The hull of a spaceplane was certainly bulletproof, but if Assante had secured some backup of his own, he could have access to any weapons system looted from an aerospace developer over a span of years. Such thoughts troubled Stone as he slid into the right front seat and brought the flight systems alive. The canopy whined down as Jarrat strapped in. The jets spat twin lizard-tongues of flame and Stone called, "Gil, anything from Eldorado Tactical?"

Cronin: "Shithouse, as usual. This *think* this, they *assume* that. They lost a squad in your zone, Stoney. You better watch your ass."

"No, really?" Stone murmured fatuously as the repulsion began to howl and the Apogee lifted straight up. At an altitude of five hundred meters, with Chandler dwindled to a field of glittering lights below, he began to breathe easier. "I was waiting for him to make his shot before we could get out of there."

"Him?" Harry echoed.

"Assante." Jarrat had a headset on and was monitoring the whole region from Chandler to Barometer Mountain, the five thousand meter highland which rose behind Harry's property. "He's here somewhere. We just have to figure out where ... Stoney, I want to take a look at Harry's place, and Roadrunner."

"Going up," Stone said quietly. "Gil, are you tracking us?"

"Sittin' on my ass in the shuttle, Stoney, waiting for Curt ... I can see you. Petrov just cranked up the ops room. The action's official."

"Jesus, it's turning into a circus," Jarrat muttered. "Mischa?"

"I hear you, Jarrat." Petrov sounded as if he were holding his temper on a tight leash. "Stealth, you said. You're supposed to be stood-down!"

"Were," Stone corrected as the Apogee went up fast. "*Were* supposed to be. Just give us the shuttle, Petrov. Keep it quiet."

Below, Barometer Mountain was the highest point in a ridge line, and from six thousand meters Jarrat could see every town from Chandler to Glenshannon, with Ballyntyre in the center of the screen. At this hour of the morning most properties were quiet, dark, but the robot logging operation never stopped. The feet of Mount Madison were 'noisy' on thermographic and local highband, so many heat sources, so many machines firing signals at each other. A heavy lifter was even then on prelaunch. As the engines flooded the area with heat and interference tracking broke up.

The Apogee rotated, drifting downrange toward Ballyntyre. Jarrat picked Evelyn's place out of the landscape simply by local knowledge. He was reading the heat-blooms of the towtrucks and the Marshall Skyvan in the front yard, and for a moment listened to their audio. Simon was chattering on the shortwave, nothing relevant. Jarrat closed his ears to the adolescent babble and turned his attention to the Del establishment. It was dark, cold, almost deserted. Power sources in the surviving part of the house betrayed an occupant, and he asked Harry, "Who stayed home? I'm seeing someone in the house."

"Mal and Alex stayed to make sure the rest of the place doesn't get trashed." Harry could not see the instruments. "They're okay?"

"The house looks quiet," Stone told him. "Just a lick of power here and there ... lights ... could be video, a boombox. Relax, Harry."

"So where the hell is Assante?" Jarrat murmured. "He's well dug-in, Stoney. He's had some time to set this up. And he's a hoon, not a fool."

Under Stone's sensitive hands the Apogee rotated around, performing a sensor pass almost as thorough as could have been made from the shuttle. "You knew the man," he challenged. "Where would he be?"

"I didn't know him well," Jarrat said sharply, and his voice was taut. "Stoney, take a deep breath, cool down! You're burning me up."

"Use it," Harry said quickly. "You have the color, Kevin, the blue? Throw a red screen over it, like a blanket. Smother it. Stoney, do you feel his green, the resonance, the shade of difference?"

In fact, Stone's teeth were grinding as he tried to concentrate on handling the plane, processing a stream of data and holding down the surge of adrenaline which assaulted him as his body responded to the chaos of emotions. "Green, you said," he muttered, "green, where is it?"

Jarrat's voice was hoarse with effort though he was sitting still. "It might not be green. That's me seeing *myself* ... you have to look for me, Stoney. I don't know what color it'll be. Think resonance."

"Damn," Stone murmured, and forced in a breath. His palms prickled with sweat on the control surfaces. "Give me something to key on, Kevin!" And then he gasped. Jarrat had bypassed logic, reason, and with a flash of intuition simply slipped his hand into his shirt and drew a caress about his own chest. The feeling intensified as he thumbed the nipple, and for a moment Stone was not even breathing. "It's not green, it's gold. Got it!"

"Throw a blanket over it," Harry insisted. "Smother the resonance!"

"Like ..." Stone blinked sweat out of his eyes. "Like tuning an R/T off the beam." He was thinking *red*. And so long as he could maintain the vision of blood, it was as if the volume had been turned down on Jarrat's emotions. He still felt them, but as an undercurrent beneath his own, always there but on a different level. He thought he had glimpsed how to do this, and shifted his grip on the controls. He must think *resonance*, just as sounds were all 'waves in a medium,' yet all were distinctly different.

A red enunciator blipped on the panel before him and Jarrat swore. "I don't think we need to worry about finding Assante ... Harry, are you strapped down good and tight? Stoney, stand on it, for chrissakes!"

The red blip was a missile in the air, and in the night sky the tailpipes of the Apogee were certainly the brightest, hottest objects. Deliberately, Stone turned nose-on to the oncoming missile and Jarrat armed the chain guns. The launch-point coordinates flashed up on the CRT at Stone's elbow, but for the moment he was intent on the warhead. "NARC Airborne, we are under fire! Blue Raven 6, where are you?"

"On launch procedures, Jarrat," Curt Gable shouted over the background mush of signal encryption. "Ops room is relaying data ... am tracking your shooter, groundside. You got a fix on him?"

The chain guns howled and Jarrat knew he was on time, on target. The warhead detonated almost a thousand meters out, and Stone threw the Apogee up over the balloon of blazing gases and shrapnel. "We see him, Curt ... looks like a vehicle ... he's launching again!"

A second flaretail chased up out of the darkness of a hillside, but this time Jarrat pinpointed it the moment it left the launcher. The chain guns cut it to a blizzard of windmilling scrap metal, and at least some of the fragments scythed through the tail of the shooter's vehicle. Stone took the Apogee high and wide, and Jarrat had already made a target-lock. The vehicle was moving as Stone came around to line up the rotary cannons.

The shooter was off the ground but not making altitude. Jarrat's screen showed a modified sportplane, but it was hugging the trees, following the line of the hills south toward Glenshannon. "We did him some damage," he guessed. "His repulsion could be fritzed. I don't think he can make any more height."

As he spoke, Skinny Dick's Sushi Tavern passed by below, and Gil Cronin's voice barked over the comm loop: "NARC 101, in the air."

"Forty minutes till we see them." Stone was intent on the screens as Jarrat triggered both rotaries. He was close enough to scorch the paint, before the sportplane ducked into the depression of a wooded valley and vanished from tracking. Stone swore softly. "He's either local, or he did his homework. If this is his backyard he could lead us right into an ambush."

"Take us up. Give me some altitude, let me find his exhaust signature." Jarrat backed off on the triggers as he saw the glitter of lights in the valley. Houses and farms were tucked away in the woods. One careless shot, and it would be easy to erase them from the map.

The prickle of Jarrat's stress raised Stone's hackles and he threw the red shield over the flare of gold before his pulse began to hammer. The chaos of feelings diminished and he forced in a breath. "You got him?"

"He's on the ground." Jarrat made second scan-pass. "I see the plane, down in the woods between those houses. You know what that means?"

"He only had two missiles, his repulsion's jacking around, he's on the run, so he's probably looking for civvies to hide behind," Stone said in bleak tones. "Sounds like your typical contract shooter. Christ, this could turn into a siege. Do you see the man himself?"

"Hold on." Jarrat kicked on the searchlights. "Get lower."

"If I get any lower, I put us in range," Stone warned. "You don't know what he's got. He could knock us down."

Jarrat rearmed the rotary cannons. "Just get me one clear shot."

The white fangs of his anger had sunk deep into Stone before he could blanket them, and for seconds his head reeled. He could not shut it out, so he ran with it, used it. He turned the Apogee's nose down and lost altitude fast as the searchlights lanced into the woodland. "There!"

The sportplane had made a bad landing. It was canted on one wing, and the rear struts, already damaged, seemed to have collapsed. The canopy was up, the cockpit deserted. Sure enough, a figure was running fast into the trees. Jarrat stroked the triggers once, twice, and the fugitive seemed to wrench apart in several directions at once.

"Get closer, lower," Jarrat said quietly.

Ice-cold fingers had knotted into a fist in Stone's belly. "Kevin, what?"

"I'd swear that's not Assante." Jarrat turned to look at him, wide-eyed in the instrument lights. "Wrong body language, wrong body-lines. Put us on the deck, Stoney, we have to make sure."

"This," Stone warned soberly, "would be the perfect ambush. If he's in the treeline with one more missile —"

"Stoney!" It was Gil Cronin. "Jarrat, you've got trouble!"

The Apogee had not yet begun to descend, and now Stone held off. "What kind of trouble, Gil?" Jarrat's voice was razor-sharp.

"A highband call just went through to the carrier. Some guy, name of Pedley, calling NARC-*Athena*. You've been decoyed. Repeat —"

"We heard you. Shit!" Stone spun the Apogee, pulled up the nose and opened the throttles. "Jesus, I thought it was too easy."

"I bloody *knew* it wasn't Assante," Jarrat breathed. "Blue Raven 6!"

"Still thirty fucking minutes out from your position," Cronin warned. "Don't get into something you can't handle!"

"Relay Pedley's message," Jarrat yelled over the roar of jets as Stone opened the throttles. "Is he still on the air?"

"Talking to Petrov," Cronin told him. "Hold on." Then, to Petrov on the open loop: "NARC 101 to carrier. Ops room, patch the civvy through to me, and make it fast!"

Art Pedley was there almost at once. The shuttle relayed the call to the Apogee with a delay of only a second. "Art? It's Jarrat," he shouted. "What's your situation?"

The older man was ex-military himself, but there was a thin edge of panic in his voice. "John — Jarrat," he corrected, "the bastard's here! He got into the house!"

Clear as a bellchime, Stone felt Jarrat's reaction, and nothing he could do would screen it out. Instead, he focused on it as he sent the spaceplane back toward the Lang house. He accepted Jarrat's fiery emotions and tried to smother his own instead. "Two minutes, Kevin."

"Two minutes, Art," Jarrat relayed.

"We don't have two minutes!" Pedley bellowed. "Simon's down, he could be dead for all I know!"

"Where's Evelyn? Pedley!" Jarrat's voice cracked like a whip.

Then the signal cut out, and Stone said tersely, "They lost their highband antenna. No surprise there. Harry, how're you doing?"

In the back, Del had been silent since the action began. "I'm still hanging on," he said in a shaken tone. "Drop me at Evelyn's place. It sounds like Simon needs help."

"If it's safe." Stone was intent on groundscan. "There's no way we'll put you at risk. You're too valuable, Harry."

"But Simon's been shot!"

"And might already be dead," Jarrat added. "You heard Art. Settle yourself, Harry. If it's not safe outside, you stay put, no arguments."

"Kevin, look at the groundscan." Stone throttled back and brought the Apogee into a hover, a thousand meters south of the Lang house. The hot-spots of fires confused the image, which was a composite, generated by thermo, infrared and vision intensification. "Is the house burning?"

For a moment Kevin could not tell, and his frustration barreled into Stone. Then, "No, it's the garage. It's one of the towtrucks. Blue Raven 6, are you monitoring this?"

Curt Gable: "We got it covered, Jarrat. Gil's calling it in to Tac Fire Control right now. We're twenty-five minutes out. Watch yourselves."

As Stone adjusted the groundscan, the image cleared and he picked up the flares of muzzle flashes. "She's giving him a run for his money."

"They're ... in the yard out back." Intimate local knowledge meant Jarrat could put sense to the otherwise dislocated images. "Stoney, swing us around to the east, come up on the property from the treeline, slow and quiet. Just let me get a jump on him."

If she can keep the bastard busy another minute. Stone did not say it aloud. Jarrat knew the score, and Harry did not need to hear it. The Apogee arced about, drifted toward the foothills, and Stone cut speed. The treetops brushed the lower hull as he came in low, slow, with as little engine noise as he would manage. He was five hundred meters out from the back fence of the Lang property when he felt the lurch of Jarrat's belly and looked sharply at the groundscan.

The yards were quiet. No more muzzle flashes. The fight was over ... which meant someone was down. "Did she take him?" he whispered, hoping Harry was not following the action. "Kevin, how good is she?"

"I don't know," Jarrat said honestly as he fine-tuned the groundscan. "I've got movement ... one figure, up and moving. I can't see ..." And then the white-hot wave of adrenaline hit Stone like a punch in the belly and Jarrat's voice was a whipcrack once more: "Move it! He's up, he's in the Skyvan ... it's not one figure, Stoney, it's two. Shit, he's carrying her!"

"Oh, great," Stone breathed. "He's got a hostage." He throttled forward, and the Apogee came up fast on the rear yards. The garage was blazing now, orange flames illuminating the house, the big satellite dish, and the Marshall Skyvan which Stone had chased from Chell. The sight of it made his own belly churn, and he heard Jarrat grunt in reaction. "NARC 101, where are you?"

The signal was very bad, which told him at once, the shuttle was bucking reentry. "Twenty-two minutes, bare minimum," Cronin shouted over the audio mess. "Hold up and wait for us!"

"Can't," Stone yelled at the mic. "NARC Airborne to carrier!"

To his credit, Petrov was there at once. "What do you need?"

"Get an ambulance out to Roadrunner Charter, Ballyntyre. You have one, maybe two civvies down. We are in pursuit of the shooter, and we're in a hostage situation."

A Russian explative was Petrov's only response for a moment, and then he was back. "We just picked up a single mark, outbound from your position. Fat and slow, looks like a civvy bus. That your runner?"

"Assante is aboard," Jarrat affirmed. "He's taken one hostage, we don't know where he's headed yet." He flicked over the comm and called, air-to-ground, "Pedley! Art Pedley! Simon!" No answer. "Damn. Assante must have taken out all the transmitters." And then, on a whim which Stone felt as a twist of something close to ironic humor, Jarrat switched up and called, "Joel? What the hell do you think you're doing? You want to get out of here alive, you put the 'van on the goddamned ground!"

A blast of white noise pierced the eardrums before Assante's voice said, "Jarrat? If you were a cat, you'd have one life left. And it's mine."

"You took Mavvik's contract, I know." Jarrat leveled his voice as Stone brought the Apogee in behind the Skyvan. "Look over your shoulder, Joel. We can knock you down at whim."

"And I can blow the woman's brains all over this piece of crap 'van," Assante snarled. "You ever think about Earl Barnaby? If you want Lang alive, you keep your distance, fuckface."

Stone spoke too softly for the mic to pick him up. "Kevin, you know the area better than I do. Where's he going?"

Keys pattered, and Jarrat pulled up a chart of the whole region. The Skyvan was a blue blip, tracking slowly across it, headed northeast out of Ballyntyre at zero meters, on the deck. The only reason Assante was making altitude was, the ground itself was steadily rising as the foothills climbed into the Rosenfeld Range. The Marshall was not holding any particular course, but weaving through curves, as if Assante had only half an idea of where he was, and where he was going. What was ahead of him?

"Let me talk to Lang," Jarrat barked. "Assante! You better *make* me believe she's alive, or I'll knock you down right now!"

White noise again, two painful seconds, and then, "Kevin, I'm sorry. It's my own goddamned fault, I let the bugger put one in me."

One ball of tension released in Jarrat's chest, another knotted up, and Stone felt them both. He had not known Evelyn Lang well, but Jarrat had only good things to say of her. And if she had kept Assante busy for ten minutes, she must be good. At that point, Assante was shooting to kill.

"What shape are you in?" Jarrat was asking.

"Not too bad." But her voice was raw. "I've got a bullet in my leg."

Harry's voice yelled out of the back. "Eve, how bad are you bleeding?"

"Jesus, Harry, is that you?" Evelyn Lang was appalled. "Jarrat, get him the hell out of here! It doesn't matter about me!"

A burst of static cut her off, and Assante was back. "I think Jarrat would disagree, lady. I think it matters to him, if you live or die ... and *how* you die. Am I right, pretty boy? I could make it interesting for her."

With a vast effort which Stone clearly felt, Jarrat leveled his voice. "You're dead right, and I'll promise you this: if she comes to any more harm, even if you *do* take me down, you won't live to collect the fee."

"Oh, put a lid on the melodramatics, Jarrat," Assante snapped. "She was a fucking Medevac pilot, she already put a tourniquet on her own leg and gave herself a shot. This is her 'van, remember? She's got *stuff* in it."

A nerve relaxed inside Jarrat and he leaned back. Stone was intent on the Skyvan, trying to keep his speed down low enough to not fly right into its tail. "Where the hell is he going? Does he even know? He's weaving!"

Yet the Skyvan's overall course was tending in one specific direction, and as Jarrat scrolled ahead over the chart he took a sharp breath. He had some local knowledge, enough to have clear memories of Kinnon Hill

Road, the robot logging industries, the pylons, aerials and lightning conductors like a crown of thorns atop Mount Madison — and the civil airfield. He had seen more than one orbital shuttle there, and a gantry, like a skeleton, standing beside a poorly-maintained fueling complex.

"He's covering his ass," Jarrat whispered. One fingertip tapped the screen. "There's lifters, orbital, suborbital. It's civvy crap, but when you're out of options, you take what you can get. Stoney, you thinking what I'm thinking?" Stone only nodded, too intent on the Apogee, the groundscan, the charts, to make conversation. Jarrat twisted in the harness to look back at Harry. "We know were he's going. We're going to loop around, get ahead of him, pick our own ground. We'll put you off, get you out of the line of fire. Just sit tight, keep your head down. And trust us."

"If I didn't trust you lunatics," Harry muttered as the Apogee peeled off and Stone headed out fast, at 90° from the 'van, "I wouldn't be here!"

Assante would be far from happy to see the Apogee vanish into the darkness of ten thousand square kilometers of unbroken forest. The moon was down behind Mound Madison and the overcast had thickened, shutting out even the stars. So long as the Apogee was obediently riding his tail, Assante could keep a gun at Evelyn's head and believe he was in control. Now, all bets were off, and Stone was only waiting.

There it was: "Jarrat!" A blast of static. "Jarrat!"

But Jarrat muted the audio pickup. "She'll be okay, he needs her. She's the only shield he's got." He glared at the dark landscape ahead. The Apogee had out-raced Assante, and now Stone banked around, kicked in the repulsion and braked hard as the skeletal structures of a gantry, a crane, a gibbet-like fueling boom, resolved out of the gloom. "Where do you want to be, Kevin? You saw this place in daylight!"

"I caught a glimpse of it from the road while she drove by like a rocket," Jarrat said acerbically. His eyes squeezed shut as he pulled up the memory. "East perimeter. There's a shack, a kind of site office. If anyplace is safe, it'd be there. Harry, unbuckle. We have to make this fast."

The darkness was so solid, Stone thought he could have carved it. He took the Apogee down on instruments, dropping into a surreal green environment where inanimate objects took on monstrous guise. Depth perception was shot to hell, and detail was obliterated. His view of the airfield was blocked by the gantry and crane, but he saw two orbital vehicles parked by the fueling boom. Several flyers, assorted trucks and two 'vans very like the Marshall stood in a rank, well back from the gantry, on the north side. And Stone wondered if Assante might be looking for one in particular. He squinted at the rank, trying to make out shapes.

As the Apogee touched down beside the site office's north wall, Jarrat tapped his screen. "Second from the right, Stoney. It's a Rand Viper, stashed here ahead of time. He'll make orbit in that if he can outrun us."

And if he was aiming to rendezvous with a big ship, Joel Assante could be out of the system and claiming the contract fee in safety. Stone left the engines idling as the canopy went up. "NARC Airborne to carrier."

"Carrier." Petrov was brusque "The shuttle is twelve minutes from your position, just hold up and wait for backup."

"Negative that suggestion," Stone said smoothly. "We're out of time, out of options." He was watching Harry Del scramble out and down. "We think our runner is trying to connect with a orbital vehicle, he's probably heading for a rendezvous. What are you tracking? It'll be in low orbit, in the civvy lanes, loitering."

"Let me check." Petrov paused only for a moment. "There's too many marks, Stoney, it could be any one of forty civvy crates. We can't pick one out of the swarm."

"That's what I was afraid of," Stone muttered.

Harry was out now, standing back in the darkness. Jarrat shouted over the whine of engines, the bluster of repulsion. "Get under cover, keep your head down. No matter what happens, stay put? Understand?"

They were seriously out of time, and Stone lifted the Apogee while the canopy was still coming down. They could only trust Del to have enough sense of self-preservation to go to ground like a wounded fox. "Where do we want to be?" Stone rotated the plane, scanning the whole zone.

"The north side, cut him off from the Viper. There's space to land behind the fuel tanks, he won't see you there. The 'van doesn't have much in the way of sensors. Jesus, there's forty million credits' worth of hardware in this parking lot! Be careful where you shoot." Jarrat reached into his jacket, drew the Colt, and on automatics his hands ran through the ritual of checking the weapon. Very deliberately, he released the flight harness.

Every hair rose on Stone's nape. "What the hell are you doing?"

"Playing the only ace we have. There's two of us, we can split up and cover the field from two angles, catch him between us." Jarrat was taking long, deep breaths. "Stoney, for chrissakes, you're burning me up!"

"Stay in the plane," Stone growled, but he banked down the odd mix of dread and fury which was scorching a hole in his belly. "You can wait till you have a clear shot, take him with the rotaries."

But Jarrat's head was shaking. "The bastard's going to be using Evelyn as a shield. He won't let me have the shot, you know that."

"I ... know." The Apogee set down, and Stone popped the canopy again. "Kevin." He reached over.

"Yeah, same here." Jarrat took his hand, meshed their fingers tightly for as long as he dared. "But I owe that woman. She's the only reason either of us is here, and she deserves better than she's getting."

"I know that, too." Just for a moment, Stone lifted the blood-red cloak he had thrown over the empathy and let Jarrat's emotions blaze through him. The tide was almost painful, and he clamped down on it fast, like shutting off a high-pressure valve. "I'll be right behind you, Kevin."

"I'm counting on it," Jarrat said under the engine noise, and lifted himself out of the cockpit.

The darkness swallowed him at once, and Stone swore. The canopy locked and the Apogee lifted away to the east, with the bloated mass of the half-buried fuel tanks as cover. He switched the fire controls over, armed everything the Yamazake spaceplane had and cleared his triggers. "Blue Raven 6, can you locate on my signal?"

"No problem, Stoney ... nine minutes," Gable told him. "Where the hell are you?"

Nine minutes could be a lifetime. A man could die in much less time. Stone's throat was dry. He had already seen landing lights approaching out of the night, and if he opened himself to the empathy, reached out, he could feel Jarrat so clearly, it was unnerving. Chill night ... wind in his face, cold metal in his palms ... leg muscles pumping — no, *pushing*. He was climbing, scrambling up the escape ladder of either the gantry or the crane. Stone approved though he choked off a curse. Jarrat was a professional. He knew height gave him an advantage, while Assante would almost certainly be looking out for the Apogee.

The landing lights were over the perimeter fence now. The Skyvan came in fast, rotated once inside its own length for Assante to take a good look around, and then it dropped into the open space between the gantry and the parking rank. Stone locked the rotaries on target and waited. The Apogee was a hundred meters out, running dark, but the noise of its repulsion would betray its position as soon as Assante shut down the Marshall and opened up. The forest was thick below, affording no space to set down. "Kevin," Stone whispered to the comm pickup.

He had caught his breath after the climb. "In position. Hold up where you are, Stoney. I only need one shot."

"Let me draw him," Stone suggested. "He's going to know I'm here soon enough anyway, unless he's deaf."

"Do it." Jarrat paused. "He's down ... but I don't think he's going to shut off the 'van's engines. Trying to cover his ass. Smart kid. He may not hear your engines, Stoney."

Rather than kicking in the floodlights, which would blind Jarrat, Stone turned on the public address, and as the Marshall opened up he cranked the volume. "Let the woman go, Assante. Put down your weapon and release the hostage. You can still walk away from this." Amplified a hundred times, his voice rolled around the airfield. Framed in the Marshall's hatch, Evelyn Lang had both hands over her ears. A moment later she took a stumbling step out of the 'van, but before she could take a second step Assante was behind her, one arm across her throat, a big handgun tucked in behind her ear. From Stone's vantage point he saw little more than the woman and the gun. He had no shot at Assante, but the man's back was toward Jarrat.

Kevin's voice was a whisper over the comm. "I can't take him, Stoney. At this range, a round out of the Colt would go right through him, take her as well. I'm going to climb higher, try for a head shot. Talk to him, don't let him look this way."

"Assante, we've got you nailed," Stone boomed across the airfield. "Don't be a fool. You're heading for the Rand Viper? Think again." The Rand was an easy shot. He ripped a hundred rounds into it, slicing the gullwings open, igniting a swift electrical fire that turned the interior into molten marshmallow. "Throw down the cannon, Assante, let the woman go. You don't have to die here."

The shooter was screaming into the darkness, in the direction of the muzzle flashes, but Stone's audio pickups could not raise a word. Evelyn Lang was as tall as Assante, as broad, and probably stronger. She did heavy manual work, while Assante was a kid whose talent with guns, and whose ruthless disregard for life, had made him rich before he was twenty years old. She was lame with the leg wound, but Stone could see her face now: the Viper was burning brightly, and he zoomed visually on the odd couple. Lang's face was not filled with fear, but with an overwhelming fury, and Stone actually saw the moment when rage erupted through her.

She had been walking in shuffling steps, both hands closed on Assante's forearm, which was crushed mercilessly against her gullet. If she wanted to breathe, she kept up the pressure and stayed still. But at some point the Military Airlift pilot decided breathing was overrated. She let go Assante's arm, threw an elbow back into his gut and twisted like a corkscrew in his grasp to get away from the gun. Stone's heart was in his mouth as she moved — and Assante did trigger a round. It would have taken off her head if she had been a tenth of a second slower.

In the same tenth of a second, a window of opportunity opened. Jarrat might have made a shot, so might Stone, but Evelyn's right leg collapsed under her. She went down in a clumsy tangle, and Stone's thumb froze on the fire controls. He heard a whisper of profanity from Jarrat as the Colt remained silent too, and before the shot was clear for either of them, Assante had flung himself into the cover of the fueling boom.

"Lang, run! *Get up and run!*" Stone bawled over the public address.

The same thought must have been driving her, because Evelyn Lang had somehow got up on her feet. She was lurching toward the parking rank when Assante took a shot at her. He missed by the breadth of a hair, and the shot gave away his position. The Colt brayed, hosing twenty rounds into the fueling boom, and Stone ripped a hundred into its concrete feet as the Apogee dove in closer. Evelyn had made it into the lee of the parked trucks. As the leg collapsed again, Stone held the Apogee on repulsion, its body between her and Assante's last position.

Full-auto fire *whanged* off the gantry and Stone's teeth gritted as he felt Jarrat's ice-cold reaction. Assante was still on his feet, still viable, and he had picked Jarrat out of the darkness by his muzzle flash. "Stoney!" Jarrat yelled over the comm. The R/T in his shirt pocket picked up even the rasp of his breathing. "Stoney, I can't see him. Watch yourself, he's got some heavy-cal, he could blow you right out of the sky!"

"I don't see him either," Stone said tersely, "but I might be able to flush him out. Pick your spot, Kevin ... and make it fast." Because if Assante made the shot first, Jarrat would die an instant before the Apogee's rotary cannons wreaked his revenge. Stone was barely breathing as he nudged the spaceplane around and let Jarrat set it up.

"Between the boom and the crane," Jarrat judged. "He's somewhere off to your right. He might be under the —" A dozen rounds pounded into the gantry, and Jarrat flattened out in what cover he could find. "That was close! I guess it tells you where he is. Take out the truck, Stoney, cut right through it, you'll take him with it."

"No, you're to close," Stone argued hoarsely. "If it goes up, you go up. Make it a clean kill and walk away from there. He's ... making his way around, Kevin. You're going to get your shot." Stone was crooning in a rasping whisper. "He's behind the blue Chev with the spoiler. Make it fast, make it good ... ten seconds ... five."

Jarrat was poised to move, muscles coiled so tightly, Stone was aware of every fiber in him. But still Assante moved first, and he was not firing at the gantry. Flat on his belly under the tail of the priceless modified Chev truck, he hosed a whole magazine into the fueling boom. Stone caught his breath as the near-invisible flames of an alcohol fire wreathed the structure.

The pipelines back to the tanks were perforated, and already the weird pale blue fire was a halo around them. Only in outlying regions like Ballyntyre did one find the old fuels required by old machines. Stone had little experience with them, but he knew the danger of a blow-back through the tank was very real. The danger did not seem to have occurred to Assante. The shooter had one ambition: to force Jarrat into the open. Igniting the boom must have seemed an excellent move. The north wind drove the fire directly at the gantry.

Fuel lines snaked away to the half-buried tanks, but from his place under the Chev, Assante could not see them. Stone could. His eyes were wide as he watched the pipes begin to rupture. Fuel was spilling, phantom-transparent flames wreathed the whole boom. The time for caution was gone. Stone was down to playing percentages.

"Jarrat, *cover!*" He kicked in the public address and bellowed across the whole field, "Lang, Del, *get down, stay down!*"

And then the Apogee's rotary cannons scythed through the priceless, modified Chevrolet Jetstream. Assante was still under it when the power system blew, and less of him would survive than would make a stain on the ground. The explosion Stone had feared lit up the night, painted the gantry in red-gold fire. He felt the heat scorch his skin, parch his eyeballs ... but it was Jarrat's skin, Jarrat's eyes.

"Kevin! *Kevin!*" The public address thundered over the airfield, but Stone heard nothing, saw nothing. The blast flare shriveled his irises, left him half-blind for dangerous moments in which the fuel lines between boom and tanks began to split wide open. Dread flayed Stone, squeezed his heart as he turned the sensors on the gantry, but through the heat and chemical pall of the wreck he made no sense of the images. Adrenaline pounded through him, overloading every sense he possessed.

A double-load of adrenaline, a double-load of dread and healthy fear. Stone whooped for air as he recognized gold hues among the chaos of his own sensations, and a bare second later the comm spat a series of coughs and yelled in a hoarse voice, "Get the hell out before it blows!"

"You're in the middle of it," Stone shouted.

"I'll be all right. Go!" Jarrat's voice cracked on the imperative. "*Go!*"

He was panting heavily, Stone felt the phantom spasms in arms and legs, and though he could not see Jarrat he knew Kevin was working hard. He was still somewhere on the gantry, and Stone had angled the floods, trying to find him, when the tanks ruptured.

The blast eclipsed the eruption from the Chev. The fireball rolled in every direction, the shockwave picked up the Apogee and tossed it, and in the inferno of synthetic fuel any vehicle parked around the fueling complex detonated like a bomb. Stone threw the Yamazake spaceplane up and over in an arc, away from the airfield. As the fireball spent itself, the main blaze shrank in diameter until it was a single tongue of near-invisible blue, jetting under pressure from the remnants of the buried tanks. Stone was not even breathing as he heard Cronin and Gable shouting over the comm.

"NARC Airborne, what the fuck goes on?" Cronin demanded. "Four minutes, we'll be with you, Stoney! I see an explosion, your location!"

"Fuel tanks," Stone gasped as the Apogee stabilized at three hundred meters. "Kevin! Kevin!" He called the name instinctively, but with an overwhelming intuition he knew on another level, just as instinctive, he did not have to. He let go the controls and the autofly took over. His eyes watered after the blast and he squeezed them shut, to concentrate.

Impossibly, the gold aura he recognized as Jarrat flared brightly. Stone flexed his limbs, his fingers, feeling for pain. He was aware of every one of Kevin's welded bones, but nothing was burned. Swallowing his heart, Stone cleared his throat. "Blue Raven 6, this is NARC Airborne. I'm all right. I don't know where the hell Jarrat is, but he's okay." The public address blared again, and the floodlights lanced along the periphery of the airfield, where Evelyn Lang had been. Stone called her name and prayed.

For almost a minute he saw nothing, and then a disheveled figure dragged itself to its feet in the lee-side of a shoulder-high pile of crates. She waved, lifted a hand to shield her eyes against the glare of the floods, and Stone cut their power. He was unsurprised to find his hands shaking as he took the Apogee down toward her and called, "Kevin? Kevin? Jarrat, I bloody know you're alive! Where are you?"

Still, no response issued from the R/T, and Stone reined back on his temper with an effort. One thing at a time. He popped the canopy, took a lungful of the outside air and felt his lungs spasm. It was worse than the toxic smog on Dock Row in Chell's notorious city bottom. He had put the Apogee down just a dozen meters from the woman, and she struggled toward him. He reached out, caught her hands and hauled her into the back.

"Kevin," she began as soon as she could speak. Her eyes were watering. "I saw him on the gantry. He was in the middle of it! Stoney —"

"He's fine," Stone said with a curious blandness. "It's Harry I'm worried about. Brace yourself, now."

"Stoney, he had to be incinerated!" Evelyn was shouting at him.

"He's all right," Stone insisted. "I just ... know." The canopy was still coming down when he lifted the Apogee, skirted the devastated airfield and set down again beside a charred, blackened site office. His dread was not for Jarrat now. He could feel Kevin in every sinew ... the flex of his shoulders, big muscles in his legs working steadily, rhythmically. But of Harry Del there was no sign. Stone killed the engines and lifted himself out of the Apogee. Evelyn called after him but he did not turn back. "Stay put. I'll find Harry." *Or what's left of him.*

The forest was garishly illuminated in the light of eight or ten blazing vehicles, and though the flames jetting from the ruptured tanks were so thin a blue, he could barely see them, he heard their roar. He cupped his hands to his mouth, calling over the noise. "Harry! Harry! If you can hear me, call out! Do you need help?"

"I need," a voice said disgustedly from the darkness between the massive rainforest hardwoods, "my brains examined. I need a double whiskey. And I need a bath." Del stepped out of the dense, solid darkness, and in the light spilling from the burning wrecks he slapped the nearest meter-thick trunk. "You know what this is?"

"A tree," Stone said with deliberate patience.

Del gave him a triumphant look. "*This* is a Tasmanian white pine. One of the few woods on any world which won't burn if you hold a blowtorch to it." He coughed on the bad air and jerked a thumb over his shoulder. "I saw the idiot ignite the boom. I ran, ten trees back in the forest. Thank gods I know a little about trees." He knuckled his eyes. "Jarrat?"

"I don't know exactly where he is," Stone admitted, "but I do know he's safe." His ears had just picked up the thunder of jets, and he looked toward the sound. "The cavalry decided to show up." He gave Harry a rueful grin. "Kevin's okay. I don't know how or why. But I *know*."

"Of course you do. It's part of your gift." Harry dropped a hand on his shoulder. "Let me see what I can do for Evelyn. And I want to use your comm. Fire Control and the ambulance should be out at her place by now. I'm worried about Pedley and Simon."

"Help yourself." Stone dug the R/T out of his pocket and held it to his lips. "Kevin, where are you? The shuttle's on approach. Kevin!"

Military jets thundered off the sides of Mount Madison, and he watched Curt Gable set the big plane down right behind the Apogee. To the R/T he said, "Thanks for coming, guys, but it's over."

The canopy was halfway up when Cronin said amusedly, "Looks like you guys had a blast, literally ... but I don't see Jarrat."

"I do." From the cockpit, Curt Gable could see right across the ruined airfield. Cronin had been looking for Jarrat on the perimeter with Stone, but Gable was watching the fires. He had seen the silver-suited figure walking out of the confusion of burning vehicles.

The firesuit was single-use, throwaway, with smart-joints which molded to fit any occupant, a bubble helmet and ten minutes of air. They were common in industry, labs, any place with a high fire risk. Jarrat lifted off the helmet as he drew closer and tossed it to Stone.

Stone fielded it, bounced it from hand to hand, and looked him up and down. "You're in one piece. You mind telling me how?"

"I was on the gantry," Jarrat said for Cronin's and Gable's benefit. "There was no way I was going to get down before the tanks blew. I thought I was toast, then I looked up." He gave Stone a brash grin. "Every gantry where people have to work around volatiles, fuels, has blast shelters. I just wasn't sure I'd get inside in time. The R/T took a knock, Stoney. I could hear you, but I knew I wasn't transmitting worth a damn."

"Scorched your tail feathers?" Cronin had lifted off the helmet, but remained in the shuttle.

"I was lucky. Again." Jarrat shared a glance with Stone.

"You always are," Cronin observed. "NARC 101 to carrier. Show's over. We'll shoot some videos for the record, but it's a wrap here."

"And the shooter?" Gable was in the midst of a sensor sweep. "I see your hostage, your passenger ... no shooter, Stoney."

Stone managed a harsh laugh. "He's a smear on the ground under what used to be a Chev Jetstream. You *might* find enough to make a DNA ident. Like Gil said, it's a wrap ... not that we don't appreciate the back-up." He was watching Jarrat peel out of the skinthin firesuit as he spoke, and he tossed the helmet down beside the castoff thermofoil. "Kevin?"

The comm loop chattered from the cockpit of the shuttle; Cronin and Gable were busy. Harry was in the Apogee, working on Evelyn with the materials from the first aid case, and Evelyn was shouting at someone on the comm. Stone heard her bellow Simon's name, and he stopped listening as he heard, "You useless little shit, put Art back on the line. Art, what in Christ's name —" Stone took stock of the situation and paused to consider himself one of the luckiest men alive. Jarrat was smudged, his knuckles were raw, the brown leather jacket was badly scuffed, but he was alive, whole, bright-eyed with a kind of wry, reluctant humor.

"I'm okay, Stoney, really." He wound one arm around Stone's waist, dealt him a swift hug and released him.

"I'm not. You scared shit out me," Stone informed him tartly.

"I scared shit out of myself," Jarrat said philosophically. "It goes with the job, doesn't it?"

"Job?" Stone echoed. He slung an arm across Jarrat's shoulders and steered him to the Apogee. "Get in. This air's not fit for breathing." He cocked an ear to Gable, who was organizing a Fire Control squad to take care of the blaze. "What makes you think we still have a job? I'm sure Petrov would like to skin us alive. We're technically on stand-down."

The canopy locked and Jarrat took several deep breaths of clean air.

"This one was personal," he said darkly. Twisting in the seat, he looked into the back. "How're you doing, Evelyn?"

In fact, she was furious. "Oh, I'm just fine. I've been shot twice, my Skyvan is fried, one of my towtrucks is history, my garage was torched, I lost my highband system. I'm just having a ball."

Jarrat cut short the whole argument with two words. "Bill NARC."

She glared at him. "Are you serious?"

"Of course." Stone buckled his flight harness. "NARC already owes you a hell of a lot more than a truck and an aerial. Inventory the damage, send the bill. If you get an argument, you know where to find us."

"I do?" She settled into the cramped back seat as the engines came alive and the Apogee bobbed up, buoyant on repulsion.

"We'll be at Harry's place," Jarrat told her quietly. "Learning. Hey, Curt, you got much left to do here?"

"Not a lot," Gable told him. "We'll hang around till Fire Control gets in, shoot some videos ... you know the Russian wants a chunk of you?"

"He'll have to wait," Stone said flatly. The Apogee was four hundred meters over the airfield, with Ballyntyre in the northeast and Chandler just over Barometer Mountain. "Where are we going? Harry?"

"My place," Del decided unilaterally. "No arguments, Eve. There's not one damned thing you can do at home, and I want to treat this wound properly. Get you back up on your feet. Let Pedley take care of it."

The silver-gray of predawn had begun to brighten as the Apogee touched down on the Del property. Tarpaulins and plastex sheets rattled in the morning wind. A finger of smoke pointed into the east — the house's power was out again, and if anyone wanted breakfast or coffee, it would happen on the grill.

Daylight brought the flocks of parrots and the first humid heat. Jarrat stood on the familiar back porch, trying not to notice the blackened area where the glasshouses had been. Evelyn was leaning on the rail, dressed in something of Tansy's which neither fit properly nor suited her, a cigarette smoldering in her fingers with the scent of kipgrass and lilac. They had been silent a long time, waiting for Stone to return with coffee, or food if he could find it. With the power out and the staff gone, the household was a shambles.

At last Jarrat said, "You're wasted here. You know it as well as I do."

Evelyn did not turn to look at him, but dragged deeply on the smoke. "I was born here. What else would I do?"

"Use the skills you worked hard for," Jarrat suggested.

"Go back to Airlift? I don't think so!" She ground out the cigarette and glanced over her shoulder at him. "Would *you* go back to the Army?"

"No." Jarrat studied her with a frown. "Would you join NARC?"

The proposition was so unexpected, she recoiled. "Would I do what? You have to belong to some branch of the service before you can apply."

"You do. You're with Airlift Reserve." Jarrat thrust hands into pockets and joined her at the rail. "People like you are the bones and sinews of NARC. Here in Bally, what do you do? Pull city cars out of ditches, tow them back into Eldorado. Sure, it's good money, but it's a waste of every-thing you *are*." He lifted a brow at her. "You could be flying a gunship.

277

Take a tour with a Starfleet training squadron, and you could be flying the carrier. Think about it."

"I ... will." She rubbed her arms as if she were suddenly cold, though the morning was already muggy. "If I decide ... who do I call?"

He smiled faintly. "I'll give you some phonecodes. Quote my name, mine and Stoney's. They'll take you a long way, and after that, well, we know the people who know the people, right back to Darwin's. We've been with NARC a long time. We're still well connected."

She looked levelly at him, silent again for some time. "You'll be leaving the department now, won't you?"

"Maybe. We don't know. There's so many variables, I can't call it," Jarrat admitted. "I'd like to stay with NARC, same as Stoney. And if it was yourself, I'd call it another one for Stevie."

The name made her eyes mist, and she looked away, perhaps to hide tears. The years had not begun to soften the memory. "I don't know, Kevin. Let me think about it. You'll be here with Harry?"

"For a while." Jarrat stirred as he felt Stone's approach, and watched Evelyn drift away, back into the house.

He was watching white parrots flocking on the fringe of the forest when Stone came around the corner of the house with a plate in one hand, a pitcher of beer in the other. He set both on the deck at Jarrat's feet and sat on the edge. "Eat. You're starving."

"I am?" Jarrat had not even noticed his own hunger, but as soon as Stone mentioned it, it hit him hard. The plate was laden with meat, eggs and vegetables right off the grill. It was an unlikely breakfast, but if the Army had taught Jarrat one thing, it was to take what was offered. He sat beside Stone, took a steak in his fingers and chewed mechanically. Stone was well aware of the emotions churning through him, and waited for him to speak. After a long time Jarrat said, "The mountains of northern Spain. The place you used to fly ultralites when you were a kid."

Stone's brows rose. "What about it?"

"I might like it," Jarrat mused. "If NARC throws the book at us."

"It's a nice part of the world, and a nice world to go home to." Stone drank right from the pitcher and passed it over to him. "Let it be, Kevin. You can't second-guess it. It'll turn out the way it turns out."

He was right, but still the speculations crowded Jarrat. Intelligence, Cyber, Cipher, R&D. He drank, finding the local beer light and too sweet. He leaned his shoulder into Stone's. If he opened himself to the empathy he felt a calm about Stone. Not a resignation, but a kind of acceptance, a patience Jarrat had often envied.

"Kevin, take one thing at a time." Stone hung an arm about his shoulders. "First, we learn how to control *this*." He knew Jarrat was 'open,' and sent a flare of affection tempered with wry humor. "Then ... we play it by ear."

"Play it by ear," Jarrat echoed, basking in Stone's feelings. He rested his left hand on his partner's knee and reached over for another slab of steak. "No regrets, Stoney, no matter what happens."

"Now, *that*," Stoney decided, "is a sentiment worth drinking to." He lifted the pitcher, drank, and passed it to Jarrat.

CHAPTER TWENTY-THREE

The morning tide was out. The low, slack water exposed the coral heads, and fossickers were clamming along the tidal zone, under a sky so blue, it was difficult to believe the smoggy skies of Chell and Eldorado were to be found on the same planet. The glare off the sea was blinding and Stone slid shades onto his nose as he watched Jarrat's distant figure, clad in brief white shorts, jogging on the hard sand. The knee was giving good service, he no longer suffered the aches: Stone *knew*. Soon, they would both be pronounced fully fit, and he looked forward to jogging with Kevin. In their two years together he had never had the opportunity.

The two years had been spent mostly apart, he allowed as he watched Jarrat wave to the clammers and turn back just short of the cliffs, where a breakwater jutted out from the shore. A fishing boat was tied up there; a man called out to Jarrat. Stone could not hear what he said, but he felt the ripple of Jarrat's amusement, saw him wave, before he headed up into the loose, hot sand. He would give his legs a tough workout before warming-down on the hard, wet tidal sand.

With a curious, not-quite vicarious thrill, Stone closed his eyes and let himself feel it ... muscles pumping, heart beating heavily with the slow rate of the athlete, pulses in throat, temples ... it felt good. Such simple pleasure as this, Stone could enjoy through the conduit of the empathy, while he was still banned from strenuous activity. Not only Reardon's orders, but Harry's too, kept Stone at a stroll while he was sure he was ready to run.

The empathy was also, unexpectedly, a source of support. Memory flayed Stone bare to the bone and he closed his eyes to the sun, the beach, trying vainly not to remember. Riki's father was a difficult man, very much older than his wife. Riki was his only son, born when he was in his fifties. The loss was incalculable. Syd Mitchell had been at once white with grief and rage at his son's death, yet too apprehensive of the NARC officers to risk voicing the fury. Stone could have told him, Riki was dead anyway, but instead said nothing. Some things were better left unspoken.

All the while, Jarrat stood back, held his tongue, and Stone left the service garage on Outbound quiet and subdued. The Mitchells cremated the boy. Stone would have been at the service, but the family specifically instructed NARC to 'stay away.' Still, he visited formally to convey the department's gratitude for young Richard L. Mitchell's help, and their sadness at his death. A bronze urn, almost the same color as Stone remembered Riki's skin, stood beside a photo on his mother's table.

He had been a beauty, Stone thought. Not like Jarrat, who was unique, a living, breathing dream. Not even like Lee, an uptown Companion and proud of it. Riki was special in his own way, and Stone grieved. Jarrat felt his pain keenly. It sent them to bed in each other's arms at Del's house the night after their stopover on Outbound. The night before Harry became the teacher. Jarrat's hands and mouth soothed but Stone ached, as if Riki's death were in some way his fault. Jarrat remonstrated, words Stone needed to hear. In the morning he was ready to accept Harry as teacher.

They worked alongside the construction crew, salvaging what could be saved from the house, bulldozing what could not, clearing much of the property for rebuilding. Stone relished the physical work. It occupied his hands as he set his mind to master a new suite of skills.

Half the house was salvageable; the rest was leveled. The *Athena* sent a new generator and two engineers to install temporary conduit. Kip Reardon's contribution was a portable lab, complete with refrigerators. And he sent a copy of a message which was in transit to Darwin's: a requisition for NARC funding for Del's research, and recognition of his previous work. With Reardon's recommendations, the grant of funding, facilities and academic recognition were in no doubt, and Harry was guardedly excited.

Dozers, hydraulics and repulsion engines were an unlikely background to the empath's teaching, and Stone was aware of a bittersweet vein in the lessons. Tansy and the younger members of the Del tribe had not returned from El, and would not be back until the damage had been fully repaired, and Tactical could be certain beyond all doubt of their safety.

It would take more than a year to mend what had been broken in a single night, which in the Rethan colony, with the different orbital characteristics of this planet, meant sixteen or eighteen months, Earth-time. In the same moment Harry was thrilled at the prospect of working with NARC, but bitterly lamented the loss of his old life. He would get it back, but it would never be quite the same. Stone intimately understood his grief.

A month later, when Stone wanted to share Jarrat's perceptions and emotions he had to open a 'window,' as Harry called it. *Make* it happen. Jarrat was just as adept. Much of the time they chose to close themselves off. It made life easier. But sometimes they reveled in the feedback. Fucking was like nothing they had ever experienced, as if Stone *was* Jarrat, while they were joined. If he closed his eyes, let himself feel it all, he felt one body, not two. He had everything short of Jarrat's thoughts. It was an addictive experience. His heart could race at the promise of having Kevin against him. Then they would shut down the link, as Del had taught them.

It was gradually becoming easier. When they were 'closed' Stone felt a terrible isolation, a shattering loneliness. He would grit his teeth and endure until isolation became bearable, then normal. Sometimes hours, sometimes a day would go by in the torment of the man in solitary confinement. They were beginning to 'habituate' to their condition, Del said. A man would habituate to anything, given time and motivation.

And the motivation was simply self-preservation. Their telemetry had been boosted to Central through priority channels in the deep space network, and they waited every day for the ax to fall. Just that morning, Jarrat had called the carrier, wanting an update from Petrov, and spoke at length to Scott Auel instead, since Petrov was occupied ... the order suspending Jarrat and Stone from active service was official. Auel was angry about it.

The word was, Colonel William Dupre was coming out to review the situation. 'Review the situation?' Jarrat had echoed. 'What in blazes is that supposed to mean?' Auel did not know. Policy was made in more rarefied atmosphere than he breathed. But Dupre was a good man and Stone had learned to trust him years before. He had the sanction to make preliminary decisions. To retire them, or defer their case to the Science division.

Stone was unsure which to hope for. To be tossed out of the department meant a service pension and work affiliated to Tac, probably in the field of therapy. They would sweep human refuse off the streets of cities like Chell, patch it up, organize licensed supply and counseling for the stricken families. They were overqualified, but it was a job that never ended. There were never enough skilled people to do it. To be referred to Research was dubious, but the rewards might be rich. Promotion, rotation to a support tender or even to Central. They could climb the ranks young, with better pay and fewer risks. The work was purely academic. The word Jarrat used was *brainbusting*. Jarrat was not an academic. Neither was Stone, no matter his parents' ambitions on his behalf. But the invitation to stay with NARC, transferring to Intelligence, was attractive.

If it were made. To get that far they must first convince Dupre they had something left to give, then endure the lab program. Physical tests, Psyche tests, boring, repetitive, strenuous and dehumanizing. Necessary, according to the specialists. Jarrat and Stone had systematically and deliberately broken every regulation. They would either be commended and promoted, or they would be on charges. Stone wondered which. The vital preliminary decision was in William Dupre's veteran hands.

"Penny for them." Jarrat's voice jolted Stone from his reverie. Kevin looked very fit, darkly tanned, relaxed.

As Stone leaned over to kiss his nostrils flared at the melange of sweat, sunblock and cologne. "How much time have we got?"

"Our ride'll be looking for us in two hours." Jarrat checked his chrono. "Move it, soldier." He swatted Stone's butt to get him moving.

They were staying at a beachfront hotel. Their bags were already repacked and Jarrat wanted only to shower and dress before they handed in the key. Stone sat on the foot of the wide bed to watch him lather his chest and belly. The water gleamed on his skin. To see him was to want him and a pang of lust coiled through his insides.

"Wicked." Jarrat laughed as he rinsed his hair.

"You're open," Stone observed, referring to Jarrat's empathy.

"I like listening in." Jarrat turned off the water and grabbed a towel. "You're strung up, Stoney. Anxious. What's the trouble?"

"Dupre," Stone said tartly.

"Besides that," Jarrat retorted. "Look, what have we got to lose? Dupre isn't the end of it. We can appeal. NARC will listen. We've done good work in the past and our records are clean. Well, mostly clean."

Stone took him by the hips and dumped him onto the bed. "You're a masochist, Kevin. You actually want a transfer to Research."

"I want to stay with NARC," Jarrat admitted, watching Stone's mouth open and suck languidly on his cock. "We haven't time," he groaned. Stone ignored him. "Start this and we'll miss our pickup." Stone continued to ignore him, and reluctantly Jarrat gave him a push. "Save it for later." He caught Stone's head and kissed his mouth hard before he got to his feet to rummage for white denims and shirt. He pushed his feet into soft, Tac-issue boots and pulled a comb through his hair. It was damp, warm. Stone wanted to touch but kept his hands to himself.

The keys were returned to the service desk and a cab took them into Eldorado. It skimmed the city's rooftops and deposited them in the public sector of the field. As he paid off the cabbie Stone's eye was on the time. Their ride was due in five minutes. Eldorado Field was quiet, nothing like the frenetically busy Chell spaceport. Few spacecraft used this field. The usual traffic was an assortment of civil and commercial craft, suborbital, some remote-piloted. Among the underpowered civilian Skyvans a military craft looked arrogant and threatening.

The public address called their names but they had seen the NARC transport minutes before as it landed inside the security fence. They hurried through, passed by the civilian inspectors, and were out in the windy concrete wilderness in moments. Curt Gable gave them a wave as they dumped their bags and Stone slammed the transport's side hatch.

"Is Dupre in yet?" Jarrat asked as he ran up the harness.

"Nope. The clipper's delayed a few hours. Engine trouble, so they told me. Starfleet never could get its birds to fly straight and level." Gable pulled back on the yoke and stood the little transport on its tail. The power of a military spacecraft was irresistible.

"Time to pack up," Stone said quietly as Eldorado dropped away beneath them. Gable was headed for home fast.

"Regrets, Stoney?" Jarrat watched his partner's face in the muted cabin lights. In the front, Gable was talking to the carrier.

"A few. The *Athena*'s has been my home for years," Stone admitted.

"Then think long and hard," Jarrat told him. "All NARC requires of us is that we split up and stay far apart. One of us ships out on another carrier. I'll transfer, you take Petrov and stay put. He's due the promotion."

Stone darted a hard look at him. "Was that a witticism?"

"No." Jarrat folded his arms. His face was bland. "It's up to you. If you want the *Athena*, take Petrov as your partner and I'll move on."

He was not just bandying words, Stone knew. Kevin was sincere. The hand remained to be played out. They had avoided this final question, yet both expected it to be asked. If they separated they could keep their rank, retain carrier command. The only thing they could not do was work together. Be together. Stone lay awake at night puzzling out their options. "In the first place," he said levelly, "I don't really even *like* Petrov."

"Which suits NARC," Jarrat observed. "You won't get emotionally involved if you don't like the prickly bastard."

"And in the second place I love you."

Jarrat sighed. "And there's the rub. So, you want the carrier?"

"I want you," Stone said tersely. "Stop playing hard to get. It's too late for coy crosstalk, loverboy. You made your decision seven weeks ago."

"So get that hangdog look off your face," Jarrat retorted. "You chose between me and the carrier. You got me. Be satisfied."

"I am." Stone allowed a faint smile. He was thinking of the night's sensual games. Jarrat had been his, utterly. Body and soul. Kevin had given him everything, more than he would ever have asked for, and it had been devastating. Through the empathy he knew Jarrat felt it all, *wanted* to give, and give again. He held out his hand, pleased when his partner took it for a moment. "Leave it to Dupre."

The transport touched down minutes later. Most of the descant troopers were occupied. Packwar raged along Dock Row, groundside in Chell, and Tactical was in trouble. Petrov and Auel had no time to talk, and Jarrat and Stone stood aside to give the ops room a nostalgic look. How many hours had they spent there, how many weeks and months?

Their quarters were locked, just as they had left them when the formal suspension came through. As Stone packed for both of them Jarrat called the flight deck for an update on Dupre's incoming clipper.

"No info, Cap," the radio man said hurriedly. He was monitoring the Ravens' chaotic audio. "Last I heard, the clipper had drive ignition trouble. They're on approach, in-system, but are not maneuvering. Chell Field'll send out a tug. I'll buzz you, soon as it docks, if you'll be in your quarters."

"Thanks." Jarrat leaned over to turn on Stone's terminal. He pulled up an edit of ongoing telemetry and statistics marched through the screen.

Stone watched him work as Jarrat fell into the habits of a lifetime. He leaned on the computer to get Kevin's attention, and Jarrat's eyes lifted from the screen. "It's not your job anymore."

Jarrat put the data on hold. "I like to have my finger on the pulse." He kissed Stone's mouth lightly. "I've been thinking. Five gets you ten, Central speculate you and I have been hitting the same sack for years."

"They haven't complained." Both Stone's hands cupped Jarrat's buttocks. The denim was warm and soft. "Sex isn't the issue. Empathy is ... and I always loved you. Always. Call me an idiot."

"You're an idiot." Jarrat gave him a shove onto the bunk and straddled him, pressed him into the pillows against the backrest. For long moments he opened himself to Stone's emotions and they shared the shiver of sensation. "Always loved you," Jarrat echoed. "God help me."

Stone's voice was no more than a whisper. "You're turning me on, Captain." He stroked Jarrat's hard body with probing, knowing hands. Jarrat's eyes closed, the better to concentrate. "Feel it," Stone murmured. "Feel it." He was stripping Jarrat deftly.

"We haven't time." Jarrat tried to remonstrate once more, slapping Stone's hands away, but it was a half-hearted protest.

"You heard the man. If the clipper can't get a drive ignition they'll need a tug. That's going to take an hour, and they'll signal us when she docks. And you're turning on, no use denying it. You can't lie, not to me."

"Yes." Jarrat looked down at him. The gray eyes were dark now. "No secrets. And no damned privacy! It's going to be hard."

"As a rock." Stone had Jarrat's cock in his hand, squeezing it, and was not referring to the problem of empathy. "Come on, time's wasting."

Jarrat's kiss was nearer bite than kiss. Then he stripped, dumped his clothes and straddled Stone again. Stone regarded him with drowsy, eyes. Jarrat pressed down. The weight of his buttocks was a delicious pressure at Stone's groin, echoing through them both. Efficient hands tugged his slacks to his knees. Stone's breath began to shorten. "You've had a few men, haven't you Kevin?"

The question surprised Jarrat. They had chosen not to pry, nor look too closely into past associations. But Stone was serious, needing to know. "Depends what you call a few." Jarrat settled with a breathy moan. "I had boys in the hospice as a kid. We were family but we weren't brothers, if you take my meaning. Then, the Army was an education. I got one promotion in the field ... but I made captain in a general's bed."

"You what?" Stone was delighted, and outraged. Jarrat could still find ways to astonish him.

"I hustled for it." Jarrat took both cocks in his fist and worked them together. "General Malloy sniffed around me for months. I kept turning him down. He kept upping the ante, offering me stuff I couldn't use. What the hell would I do with a jet roadster on an Army carrier? It got funny after a while. Poor Dirk Malloy, panting after me, and the more I turned him down the more he panted."

"Forbidden fruit," Stone said lucidly.

"Maybe. Anyway, in the end I told him to put up or shut up. Offer me something I had a use for or stop sniffing. A commission was going spare after some officer bought the ranch. Dirk shuffled the papers, got my name rotated to the top of the list. I got the promo two years early."

"And paid for it," Stone added.

"In more ways than one." Jarrat stilled as he recalled scenes played out seven years before. "Dirk had a vacation shack in the mountains. A nice place. It was all right, really. He was full of kinks, but harmless ones."

"Kinks?" Stone's curiosity was aroused. "No secrets. I'm open. You're enjoying the memories, so whatever he wanted tickled your fancy. So?"

"He liked games." Jarrat's hands began to stroke again. "He had quite an imagination. Hustler and trade, doctor and patient, you know. Dress up and pretend. One hell of a way to get promoted! I really paid for it two weeks later. I drew a combat unit on Sheal. My NARC application was already in, I was waiting for evaluation. Malloy's department dumped me in the shit, Stoney. A no-win situation, and it would have been my head that rolled. Malloy swore he knew nothing about it. Scuttlebutt was, the clerk who shuffled papers for him had a big mouth. I screwed for my promotion, so I was going to get busted in disgrace in the real world, right? Anyway, it didn't happen." He stooped to ravage Stone's mouth. "It came to a decision: bring out my men or grease a billion's worth of gear. I was so pissed by then, I totaled the equipment. We mined the transport, let them board it, left everything running, heat signatures that looked like people. I blew it on remote. Screw the Army, I though. Who cared?"

"And...?" Stone had never heard this story. Jarrat only rarely spoke of his checkered past. He shook Kevin by the shoulders, demanding the rest.

"I was on charges for the gratuitous destruction of Army property, if you can believe it. I brought *thirty* men out of Sheal alive, and all they cared about was a troop transport! Men are expendable, not equipment, like the old saying goes. I'd have been busted right back to cadet! But my NARC transfer papers came through, they were waiting for me when I got off Sheal, and the case transferred with me. The first thing I ever did with NARC was stand in front of an inquiry court. I had one ace. Trouble was, it was technically a fistful of smoke. We'd had an Intelligence officer with us, a major from one of the hush-hush departments. He was shot up when we found him and I knew he was probably going to turn up his toes. When I rotated to NARC I was waiting, every day, for a call from his doctors, telling me he'd cashed in. It didn't come. When I faced the tribunal I told them I'd had reason to believe Major Douglas had data worth the destruction of the transport to bring him out alive. It was a bucket of bull. The man never regained consciousness after we pulled him out of the rubble."

"The tribunal believed you?"

"I told them he was delirious, semi-conscious, muttering in his sleep. I'd gotten half an idea of his information and it was vital." Jarrat began to move, hunting for pleasure.

"And did he have Intelligence data?" Stone demanded.

"Search me! I said I *thought* he had. Bare faced lie. The Army might not have bought it, they're dull as ditchwater, brute force and ignorance. NARC appreciated the argument. Intelligence is our stock in trade, it's fifty percent of what we do. They cleared me, approved the transfer and gave me a grade for initiative."

Stone laughed. "You're beautiful, Jarrat."

"Flattery will get you everywhere." Jarrat leaned forward, weight on knees and elbows, his cock pressed hard into Stone's belly. "Now shut up, loverboy. Talk later."

Stone kicked off the tangled slacks and lifted his knees. He spread Jarrat's legs with his own, slid his hands down between their bodies and took them both in a sure grasp. "How's this, Captain, sir?" The masturbation was sure, deft. "Kevin?"

"Mm?" Jarrat's eyes were closed. "Just keep that up."

Tingling with Jarrat's pleasure, Stone watched his partner's face twist as Kevin got close. Every sensation bounced back and forth like echoes between stone walls. When Jarrat's deep contractions began they triggered his own. Climax destroyed him. His hand filled with hot, thick fluid. Jarrat weakened, every muscle lax. Stone brought his palm to his lips to savor the rich, musky, pagan offering. Dark, drowsy eyes watched him. He felt Jarrat shiver at the wanton rite. Stone yawned and stretched as physical contentment dispelled his anxieties as they waited for the clipper.

"What did Kip say?" Stone asked at last, "when he took the last data?"

"You mean, when he finished the whole physical?" Jarrat rolled over and scratched idly at his ribs. "Not a word. Not his place to pass judgment on the accused! But he was damned thorough. Morbidly so. Family history, back six generations, looking for madness or genetic disease. Not that I could fill in those details. Christ knows who my parents were. Sexual preference in order, right down to which position you favor, and if you want it rough or smooth, top or bottom. Part of the psyche profile. Say you've been with men — and God help you if you lie, because they've got files you wouldn't believe, it's part of the test! — and they whizz you up the ass with a scanner to make sure you're wholesome and functional."

Stone chuckled. "What did you tell them when you transferred in?"

"The truth," Jarrat said indifferently. "Why lie?"

"Why indeed?" Stone stroked the wide, bony shoulders. "Want a coffee? The clipper can't be far out now."

"Yeah." Jarrat shrugged into his clothes and ordered cream coffee from the dispenser. He handed Stone a mug and sipped his own as he stood watching the data march through the comm-relay. The descant unit was at flat chat on Dock Row. The Angelpack was out, the riot was a monster. And then the flight deck cut in with a message and Jarrat threw his empty cup into the disposal.

"The clipper?" Stone wondered.

"Just docked ... and this says Gene Cantrell came in with Dupre. That bodes ill, Stoney. Cantrell is good, very good. He'll get the carrier with Petrov. Bet your pension on it."

"Safe bet," Stone said sourly. He tossed his cup after Jarrat's and led the way from the cabin.

Cantrell was a captain looking for a command. His old carrier was the *Virago*, recently decommissioned, her crew split up amongst newer ships. Cantrell himself had been on extended leave and then on battlefield survey, waiting for an option. The *Athena* could be that option.

But if the field agents who commanded carriers in this sector answered to anyone, it was to Colonel William Dupre. Their data was routed through his office, on its way right back to Earth. Dupre was tall, slim, a West Indian with thirty years' service in NARC and ten years in Starfleet before that. He had been one of the first NARC recruits, in the days when the department was fledgeling, feeling its way.

He looked deceptively young. Thirty minutes later, he and Cantrell

285

stood in the lounge just inboard of the *Athena*'s docking port, watching for their baggage as the ferry unloaded. Jarrat and Stone hung back to wait. "Here to hand out honors, maybe?" Stone wondered as he observed Dupre's easy laughter. "He looks too cheerful to be here to bust us."

"Unless he gets his kicks busting people," Jarrat speculated.

Cantrell was a small, thick set man, every year of Dupre's age but looking much older. A silver cigarette lighter flicked repeatedly as he waited for his bags. He wore white slacks and a blue sports shirt, casual plain clothes, the officer's privilege. As he collected his luggage he saw Jarrat and Stone and waved. He had known them for years, socially as well as professionally. "Here they are, the magicians," he said dryly as he and Dupre came over from the baggage chute. A robotrolley trundled behind.

"Magicians?" Stone echoed as he gave Cantrell his hand. "Meaning?"

"Meaning," Colonel Dupre elaborated, "you are the first unit we ever knew to get the brass off its ass. When your telemetry came in there was quite a stir at head office." He shook Jarrat's hand, and Stone's. "You want to go settle in, Gene?"

"Sure." Cantrell gave Jarrat a wink. "Catch you later, boys."

"See you, Gene." Jarrat transferred his attention to Dupre. "You wouldn't like to be more specific, would you, sir? We sent all the telemetry we could. Kip Reardon was very, very thorough."

Dupre nodded. "And Reardon is the best in the business. Why don't we go somewhere a little more private?" He gave the crowd a disapproving look. A dozen Starfleet replacements had come over on the ferry from the clipper terminal and were milling about with friends and rivals, bickering over their luggage.

The officers' lounge was quiet. Dupre led the way, seated himself, ordered a pink gin and regarded the younger men with overt curiosity. "I read the whole report." His soft Barbadian accent was pleasant. "I've come, officially, to tour the battlefield, but there's more. Gene could have surveyed the scene of the action and saved me the trip out."

Jarrat felt Stone's belly tighten. "There's news from Central, sir?"

"Yes." Dupre sipped his gin. "This empathy business. Reardon's report was damned interesting reading. But it was not what aroused scientific curiosity. It was your own report on the action over Chell. Specifically, the exercise at the stadium. Intelligence got hold of one or two points in that section of the document. I want to hear it in your own words."

He settled back, waiting. They took turns to relate the filed action, adding observations and commentaries to their memories. Dupre heard it all without a word, his face attentive but betraying nothing. At last Stone said, "That's all there is. The empathy is like a communications band. We did our homework. We're learning how to turn it on and off like a radio, at will. It shouldn't interfere with our work."

"Do I take that to mean you desire command?" Dupre asked shrewdly.

"It's what we qualified for," Jarrat said very cautiously. "But I know it's almost out of the question." He was probing for a response but Dupre's face was a mask. "As Stoney said, the empathy is controllable. In the early days it controlled *us*, but we've had seven weeks. It's been like learning to speak a foreign language. The more you do it, the more you can."

He was still probing for a response to the question of carrier command, but Dupre would not take the bait. "I understand you've become lovers," he prompted blandly.

"That's correct." Jarrat looked at Stone, and then back at Dupre. "We don't feel it's NARC's concern. Sir."

"Perhaps you don't, but I can tell you, Central will not accept that two men who share this empathy will settle for a quick one, twice a month before sackout! Which means you've begun a relationship. Involvement."

Jarrat looked away. "That's the end of us, then."

"I didn't say that." Dupre finished his gin. "As I told you, there's considerable excitement in the Science division. I can't say I envy you, and I ought to forewarn you. When Intelligence gets its hooks into a project, they invariably get what they want. Their feeling is, they've stumbled onto something of great intrinsic value. In fact, a surveillance tool."

"Surveillance?" Stone sobered, surprise.

"Better than being wired," Jarrat hazarded. "You go into deep cover, wired, you get caught. Signals get intercepted. Soon, they're scraping you off the ground in an alley." He rubbed his palms together. "I ran a lot of risks on the Death's Head project. I was just lucky."

Dupre chuckled. "Lucky! I read Reardon's whole report, Captain ... I should say, 'lucky' is the last word that would spring to mind!"

"I'm still here." Jarrat leaned back into the chair. "I'm not sure I like Intel's proposal, sir. We're not lab rats. And rats are what they want."

"I can appreciate that." Dupre studied his empty glass pointedly. Stone waved for a steward and ordered another. "But our Intel division is waiting for you and the lab wallahs are rubbing their sweaty palms together in glee. You're both rotated home to Darwin's for testing."

"We're not on charges, then?" Stone pressed.

"Charges?" Dupre's amusement made his eyes sparkle.

"We commanded the Chell action, in the field," Stone said softly as the steward returned. "Strictly speaking, we were already on suspension."

"Records say Reardon cleared Jarrat, and Jarrat cleared you, Stone."

"I ... suppose I strong-armed Kip," Jarrat admitted.

Dupre chuckled. "I imagine you did. And your psyche profile predicted, seven years ago, in such a situation you'd do just that. It also predicted, based on Reardon's testing, he would allow himself to be strong-armed." Dupre chuckled again. "Prediction is an art, gentlemen. No, you're not on charges. Things might have been different had the action in Chell gone against you, but as it turned out, you were more than capable of handling it, completely against the odds, which supports the command decisions you made. However, we know you had luck on your side."

"Luck?" Jarrat demanded. He thought of the desperate struggle at Drummond Park and was about to protest.

"You knew the lie of the land," Dupre elaborated. "The car vanished into the Chell traffic but you knew where it would go. Still, when you traced it to the stadium and found yourselves isolated by radio jamming, you were very much on your own devices. This is where the surveillance specialists began to pant. As I told you, you're rotated home for testing."

"And if we refuse?" Stone demanded.

"You don't have the right of refusal," Dupre said mildly. "Orders, Stone. They don't take 'no' for an answer, not even from you."

"I could put it in stronger language," Stone offered.

"I imagine you could." Dupre smiled disarmingly. "Don't look at me, I'm not a scientist. I haven't the slightest idea what they want to do with you. But I don't envy you the empathy. If it was up to me, I'd say it was your business, send you into Cyber or Research, let you do your stuff there. But the fiends think they've found something to exploit. You."

Jarrat sighed. "I'd like to make a statement of displeasure to Central."

"Be my guest," Dupre said easily. "I shouldn't think they'll bother to read it."

"No," Jarrat admitted, "I shouldn't think they would. Ah, damn. Exploit us. Nice of them."

"It isn't their job to be nice," Dupre said glibly, "just efficient."

"We might resign," Stone suggested. "Kevin?"

"Junk our careers for the sake of our dignity?" Jarrat looked up at the concealed lights overhead. "It's a last resort, if push comes to shove." He looked back at Dupre. "When do they want us back?"

Dupre finished his second gin and looked at the chrono. "You're supposed to return on the clipper. Your bookings have been made, you're in the same cabin I shared with Gene. Next stop, the lab." He leaned forward. "Look, see it their way. You could be a tool the like of which we've never had. A whole new field of surveillance technology. Play their game. Let them have it their way for a while. If it works out, you'll keep your commissions and you're out on assignment. It's a ballbreaker, mind. I'm not promising you a walk in any park."

"Assignment?" Stone leaned forward. "Carrier command?"

"I didn't say that," Dupre said evasively. "But it's not beyond the bounds of possibility, given — shall we say, special case considerations."

"The *Athena*," Jarrat added. "We know this ship, this crew. Or have they handed Gene the reins permanently?" He gave Dupre a probing look.

The Colonel laughed. "Well, you could go and run the assignment file. You still have the clearance! But no, Cantrell is temporary, pending the launching of the *Huntress* next year. A whole new crew, right down to the mechanics and dockers. Look, you two have earned yourselves the reputation of relishing a challenge. Are you trying to tell me that rep is wrong?"

Jarrat and Stone frowned at each other for a moment in silence. "Not wrong," Stone said carefully. "Maybe over-enthusiastic. Assignment to Intel is not what we had in mind. Not our scene, especially not as a project!"

"They want you," Dupre said flatly, "and what they want —"

"They get," Jarrat finished. "It could be worse. We've spent the last seven weeks learning how to control it. We'll have the upper hand, instead of just letting the lab boys set us up and burn us out while they take notes." Dupre was studying them with overt curiosity and Jarrat sighed. "Short of resigning, we don't have a choice, sir, do we?"

"No, you don't," Dupre agreed. "But you can always quit — if push comes to shove." He paused. "To feel what another feels so clearly ... I'm not sure if I envy you or not. Siamese twins were never born closer. The sex is very good, I imagine."

The question generated a chuckle, and Jarrat smiled at last. "The sex is like you wouldn't believe. NARC is going to have to live with that. Question is, will they?"

"That's for the Psyche team to look into. You're a special case. If they rate you a combat liability — if the odds of you cocking-up a billion credit operation for the sake of your relationship are too high — you can take it as read, you're grounded. But you still have options. Selective assignment, security, where you're well covered. Leave it to head office, they know what they're doing." He stirred, long legs crossing. "I do know, the Psyche team wants to go into the inevitable side effects. Have you considered, Jarrat, Stone, what will happen if one of you is injured? Or killed."

"Or killed," Stone echoed, looking at Jarrat's somber profile. The feedback between them rang like a bell, so strong they were almost surprised Dupre was unaware of it. "We still have to get around to thinking out that part of it. But what the hell? We've always lived with the risk."

"Not as Siamese twins," Dupre argued, "or lovers. Think about it."

"We will." Jarrat got to his feet as he noticed the time. "If you want us out of here on the clipper, sir, we have to get moving. The ferry shoves off soon. And you'll want to get busy. You have a shindig on right now, a packriot on Dock Row. If you want to take a look, both shuttles are in operational order. The standby pilot ought to be Curt Gable."

Dupre followed them up. "Finger on the beat, Jarrat? I like that." He touched Jarrat's shoulder, then Stone's. "Give Intelligence a chance. You may be surprised. If it works out, well, we'll see."

"We want the *Athena*," Stone said as they parted.

The Colonel turned back for a moment. "See how it works out, then … I'll see what I can do. Strings to pull you know." He was gone with that, his robotrolley rolling obediently behind him.

They were silent as they returned to their quarters. Their bags were packed, dumped on Stone's bunk. Jarrat gave them a sour look. "Christ, Stoney, Intelligence. Damn!"

"Would you have changed your mind?" Stone asked quietly, watching Jarrat's face set into uncharacteristic, bitter lines. "That day at Harry's, if you'd known where it was going to go."

"Changed my mind?" Jarrat shook his head. "I'd have done anything. If he'd said, 'Get on your knees, Jarrat, it'll cure him if he nails your butt to the floor,' I'd have been on my knees so fast you'd have been dizzy."

"And if he'd said, 'Jarrat, you'll end your days as a lab rat with a wire up the ass while a team of Research techs see how high they can make you jump?'"

They were silent for a moment. Jarrat pushed his hands into his hip pockets. "I don't know. I like to think I'd have made the same decision. I like to believe it was the right one. Good enough?"

Stone tousled his hair. "Good enough." He kissed Jarrat's mouth, which tasted of the brandy Kevin had been drinking.

"Orally predisposed animal, aren't you?" Jarrat asked a short time later as he was released and picked up his bags.

"It bothers you?" Stone slung his own bags over his shoulders.

"Not unless I'm expected to pull duty with whisker burns," Jarrat quipped. "Get out of here, Stoney, before we miss the ferry."

At the door, Stone turned back. "Be sure. Resignation's as easy as a signature. NARC could cock it all up. Assign us to different ships."

"They'd have nothing to exploit if they did that," Jarrat said cynically. "And we can handfast legally under anyone's law. It's as binding as marriage, NARC would have to recognize it, and it makes separation our decision, not theirs. If they push too hard we've still got options. If I tell you the truth, Dupre's got me interested. Selective assignment, he said. A carrier. If it works out."

"And you're keen to take a crack at it." Stone's kiss was hard. "If you were a fish they wouldn't have to bait the hook, would they?"

Jarrat was through the door before him.